A LINEAGE of GRACE

A LINEAGE of GRACE

Tamar   Rahab   Ruth   Bathsheba   Mary

Five unlikely women who changed eternity.

FRANCINE RIVERS

TYNDALE HOUSE PUBLISHERS, INC. WHEATON, ILLINOIS

Visit Tyndale's exciting website at www.tyndale.com

Check out the latest about Francine Rivers at www.francinerivers.com

TYNDALE is a registered trademark of Tyndale House Publishers, Inc.

Tyndale's quill logo is a trademark of Tyndale House Publishers, Inc.

A Lineage of Grace

Unveiled and *Unashamed* copyright © 2000 by Francine Rivers. All rights reserved.

Unshaken, *Unspoken*, and *Unafraid* copyright © 2001 by Francine Rivers. All rights reserved.

A Lineage of Grace copyright © 2002 by Francine Rivers. All rights reserved.

"Seek and Find" sections written by Peggy Lynch.

Cover illustrations copyright © Vivienne Flesher. All rights reserved.

Author photo copyright © 1999 by John Teague. All rights reserved.

Designed by Julie Chen

Edited by Kathryn S. Olson

Scripture quotations are taken from the *Holy Bible*, New Living Translation, copyright © 1996, 2004. Used by permission of Tyndale House Publishers, Inc., Wheaton, Illinois 60189. All rights reserved.

ISBN-13: 978-0-8423-7110-0

ISBN 0-8423-7110-9

Printed in China

07 06 05

9   8   7   6   5

Unveiled is dedicated to those who have been abused and used and yearn for justice.

Unashamed is dedicated to women who think a past of mistakes ruins any chance of a joy-filled future. Turn to Jesus and experience the wonders He has waiting for you.

Unshaken is dedicated to my mother-in-law, Edith Rivers, whom I admire and adore.

Unspoken is dedicated to women who feel they've lost their reputation forever. God can make beauty from ashes.

Unafraid is dedicated to Jane Jordan Browne, a woman of faith.

contents

foreword

DEAR READER,

You are about to read five novellas on the women in the lineage of Jesus Christ. These were Eastern women who lived in ancient times, and yet their stories apply to our lives and the difficult issues we face in our world today. They were on the edge. They had courage. They took risks. They did the unexpected. They lived daring lives, and sometimes they made mistakes – big mistakes. These women were not perfect, and yet God in His infinite mercy used them in His perfect plan to bring forth the Christ, the Savior of the world.

We live in desperate, troubled times when millions seek answers. These women point the way. The lessons we can learn from them are as applicable today as when they lived thousands of years ago.

Tamar is a woman of **hope**.

Rahab is a woman of **faith**.

Ruth is a woman of **love**.

Bathsheba is a woman who received **unlimited grace**.

Mary is a woman of **obedience**.

These are historical women who actually lived. Their stories, as I have told them, are based on biblical accounts. Although some of their actions may seem disagreeable to us in our century, we need to consider these women in the context of their own times.

This is a work of historical fiction. The outline of the story is provided by the Bible, and I have started with the facts provided for us there. Building on that foundation, I have created action, dialogue, internal motivations, and in some cases, additional characters that I feel are consistent with the biblical record. I have attempted to remain true to the scriptural message in all points, adding only what is necessary to aid in our understanding of that message.

At the end of each novella, we have included a brief study section. The ultimate authority on people of the Bible is the Bible itself. I encourage you to read it for greater understanding. And I pray that as you read the Bible, you will become aware of the continuity, the consistency, and the confirmation of God's plan for the ages – a plan that includes you.

Francine Rivers

acknowledgments

NO project is ever completed without the help of many people. I want to acknowledge my husband, Rick, who has supported and encouraged me from the beginning of my writing career. Thank you for our prayer time and talks in the morning before the sun comes up. Those times are precious to me and set the tone for the rest of the day. Thank you also for sharing your office, building the fire on cold mornings, brewing the coffee, and pausing in your own hectic business schedule to spend time listening.

Thank you, Ron Beers, for sharing your vision.

Thank you, Jane Jordan Browne, for your constant encouragement and friendship through the years. I've always been able to depend on you.

Special thanks to you, Scott Mendel. I appreciate the historical information, resources, and insights you have shared with me. Thank you for your willingness to respond (quickly!) to so many questions.

Thank you, Kathy Olson, for your fine editing and passion for Scripture and for your willingness to dive in and challenge me. I would like to also extend my thanks to the entire Tyndale staff who have continued to follow Dr. Kenneth Taylor's mission of glorifying the Lord – and who have encouraged me as I strive to do likewise. I have felt blessed over the years to be part of your team.

I'm also grateful to Liz Curtis Higgs and her husband, Bill, for sharing their extensive bibliography, and to Angela Elwell Hunt, my favorite superwoman. When I grow up, I want to be just like you.

I extend special thanks to Jim and Charlotte Henderson for their gracious Washington State-style hospitality and to John and Merritt Atwood for the loan of their beautiful cottage on Whidbey Island for a brainstorming session with my dear friend, Peggy Lynch, who is writing the "Seek and Find" sections for these novellas.

I would also like to thank Peggy for her willingness to be part of this project – and for making me dig deeper and deeper into Scripture to find the jewels waiting there. Peggy, you have been a blessing to me from the day I met you. You have always held up the lamp of God's Word. Your life is a living testimony of faith.

Jeffrey Essmann, thank you for sharing historical information, lists of resources, Web sites, and insights on Mary.

I extend special thanks to Rick Hahn, pastor of Sebastopol Christian Church. I always know whom to call when I can't find the Scripture passage rolling through my head. Thank you to Kitty Briggs for sharing materials about Mary. And special thanks to Gary and Patti LeDonne, who brainstormed with me. Thank you, Peter Kiep of Interfaith Books in Santa Rosa, for pointing the way to valuable resource books and sharing your thoughts on Mary.

The Lord has blessed me through all of you. May those blessings return upon each of you a thousandfold.

Unveiled

setting the scene

GENESIS 37:1-38:6
So Jacob settled again in the land of Canaan, where his father had lived.
This is the history of Jacob's family. When Joseph was seventeen years old, he often tended his father's flocks with his half brothers, the sons of his father's wives Bilhah and Zilpah. But Joseph reported to his father some of the bad things his brothers were doing. Now Jacob loved Joseph more than any of his other children because Joseph had been born to him in his old age. So one day he gave Joseph a special gift – a beautiful robe. But his brothers hated Joseph because of their father's partiality. They couldn't say a kind word to him.

One night Joseph had a dream and promptly reported the details to his brothers, causing them to hate him even more. "Listen to this dream," he announced. "We were out in the field tying up bundles of grain. My bundle stood up, and then your bundles all gathered around and bowed low before it!"

"So you are going to be our king, are you?" his brothers taunted. And they hated him all the more for his dream and what he had said.

Then Joseph had another dream and told his brothers about it. "Listen to this dream," he said. "The sun, moon, and eleven stars bowed low before me!"

This time he told his father as well as his brothers, and his father rebuked him. "What do you mean?" his father asked. "Will your mother, your brothers, and I actually come and bow before you?" But while his brothers were jealous of Joseph, his father gave it some thought and wondered what it all meant.

Soon after this, Joseph's brothers went to pasture their father's flocks at Shechem. When they had been gone for some time, Jacob said to Joseph, "Your brothers are over at Shechem with the flocks. I'm going to send you to them."

"I'm ready to go," Joseph replied.

"Go and see how your brothers and the flocks are getting along," Jacob said. "Then come back and bring me word." So Jacob sent him on his way, and Joseph traveled to Shechem from his home in the valley of Hebron.

When he arrived there, a man noticed him wandering around the countryside.

"What are you looking for?" he asked.

"For my brothers and their flocks," Joseph replied. "Have you seen them?"

"Yes," the man told him, "but they are no longer here. I heard your brothers say they were going to Dothan." So Joseph followed his brothers to Dothan and found them there.

When Joseph's brothers saw him coming, they recognized him in the distance and made plans to kill him. "Here comes that dreamer!" they exclaimed. "Come on, let's kill him and throw him into a deep pit. We can tell our father that a wild animal has eaten him. Then we'll see what becomes of all his dreams!"

But Reuben came to Joseph's rescue. "Let's not kill him," he said. "Why should we shed his blood? Let's just throw him alive into this pit here. That way he will die without our having to touch him." Reuben was secretly planning to help Joseph escape, and then he would bring him back to his father.

So when Joseph arrived, they pulled off his beautiful robe and threw him into the pit. This pit was normally used to store water, but it was empty at the time. Then, just as they were sitting down to eat, they noticed a caravan of camels in the distance coming toward them. It was a group of Ishmaelite traders taking spices, balm, and myrrh from Gilead to Egypt.

Judah said to the others, "What can we gain by killing our brother? That would just give us a guilty conscience. Let's sell Joseph to those Ishmaelite traders. Let's not be responsible for his death; after all, he is our brother!" And his brothers agreed. So when the traders came by, his brothers pulled Joseph out of the pit and sold him for twenty pieces of silver, and the Ishmaelite traders took him along to Egypt.

Some time later, Reuben returned to get Joseph out of the pit. When he discovered that Joseph was missing, he tore his clothes in anguish and frustration. Then he went back to his brothers and lamented, "The boy is gone! What can I do now?"

Then Joseph's brothers killed a goat and dipped the robe in its blood. They took the beautiful robe to their father and asked him to identify it. "We found this in the field," they told him. "It's Joseph's robe, isn't it?"

Their father recognized it at once. "Yes," he said, "it is my son's robe. A wild animal has attacked and eaten him. Surely Joseph has been torn in pieces!" Then Jacob tore his clothes and put on sackcloth. He mourned deeply for his son for many days. His family all tried to comfort him, but it was no use. "I will die in mourning for my son," he would say, and then begin to weep.

Meanwhile, in Egypt, the traders sold Joseph to Potiphar, an officer of Pharaoh, the king of Egypt. Potiphar was captain of the palace guard.

About this time, Judah left home and moved to Adullam, where he visited a man named Hirah. There he met a Canaanite woman, the daughter of Shua, and he married her. She became pregnant and had a son, and Judah named the boy Er. Then Judah's wife had another son, and she named him Onan. And when she had a third son, she named him Shelah. At the time of Shelah's birth, they were living at Kezib.

When his oldest son, Er, grew up, Judah arranged his marriage to a young woman named Tamar ...

one

WHEN Tamar saw Judah leading a donkey burdened with sacks and a fine rug, she took her hoe and ran to the farthest border of her father's land. Sick with dread, she worked with her back to the house, hoping he would pass by and seek some other girl for his son. When her nurse called her, Tamar pretended not to hear and hacked harder at the earth with her hoe. Tears blinded her.

"Tamar!" Acsah puffed as she reached her. "Didn't you see Judah? You must return to the house with me now. Your mother is about to send your brothers after you, and they'll not take kindly to your delay." Acsah grimaced. "Don't look at me like that, child. This isn't of my doing. Would you prefer a marriage with one of those Ishmaelite traders on his way to Egypt?"

"You've heard about Judah's son just as I have."

"I've heard." She held out her hand, and Tamar reluctantly relinquished the hoe.

"Perhaps it will not be as bad as you think." But Tamar saw in her nurse's eyes that Acsah had her own grave doubts.

Tamar's mother met them and grabbed Tamar by the arm. "If I had time, I would beat you for running off!" She pulled Tamar inside the house and into the women's quarters. No sooner was Tamar through the doorway than her sisters laid hands upon her and tugged at her clothing. Tamar gasped in pain as one yanked the cover carelessly from her head, pulling her hair as well. "Stop it!" She raised her hands to ward them off, but her mother stepped in.

"Stand still, Tamar! Since it took Acsah so long to fetch you, we must hurry."

The girls were all talking at once, excited, eager. "Mother, let me go just as I am!"

"Straight from the fields? You will not! You will be presented in the finest we have. Judah has brought gifts with him. And don't you dare shame us with tears, Tamar."

Swallowing convulsively, Tamar fought for self-control. She had no choice but to submit to her mother and sisters' ministrations. They were using the best garments and perfume for her appearance before Judah, the Hebrew. The man had three sons. If she pleased him, it would be the firstborn, Er, who would become her husband. Last harvest, when Judah and his sons had brought their flocks to graze in the harvested fields, her father had commanded her to work nearby. She knew what he hoped to accomplish. Now, it seemed he had.

"Mother, please. I need another year or two before I'm ready to enter a household of my own."

"Your father decides when you're old enough." Her mother wouldn't look her in the eyes. "It's not your right to question his judgment." Tamar's sisters chattered like magpies, making her want to scream. Her mother clapped her hands. "Enough! Help me get Tamar ready!"

Clenching her jaw, Tamar closed her eyes and decided she must resign herself to her fate. She had known that one day she would marry. She had also known her father would choose her husband. Her one solace was the ten-month betrothal period. At least she would have time to prepare her mind and heart for the life looming before her.

Acsah touched her shoulder. "Try to relax." She untied Tamar's hair and began to brush it with long, firm strokes. "Think soothing thoughts, dear one."

She felt like an animal her father was preparing for sale. Ah, wasn't she? Anger and despair filled her. Why did life have to be so cruel and unfair?

"Petra, bring the scented oil and rub her skin with it. She mustn't smell like a field slave!"

"Better if she smelled of sheep and goats," Acsah said. "The Hebrew would like that."

The girls laughed in spite of their mother's reprimand. "You're not making things better, Acsah. Now, hush!"

Tamar grasped her mother's skirt. "Please, Mother. Couldn't you speak to Father for my sake? This boy is ... is evil!" Tears came in a rush before she could stop them. "Please. I don't want to marry Er."

Her mother's mouth jerked, but she did not weaken. She pried Tamar's hand from the folds of her skirt and held it tightly between her own. "You know I can't alter your father's plans, Tamar. What good would come of my saying anything against this match now other than to bring shame upon us all? Judah is *here*."

Tamar drew in a ragged sob, fear flooding her veins.

Her mother gripped her chin and forced her head up. "I've prepared you for this day. You're of no use to us if you don't marry Er. See this for what it is: good fortune for your father's house. You will build a bridge between Zimran and Judah. We will have the assurance of peace."

"There are more of us than there are of them, Mother."

"Numbers don't always matter. You're no longer a child, Tamar. You have more courage than this."

"More courage than Father?"

Her mother's eyes darkened with anger. She released Tamar abruptly. "You will do as you're told or bear the full consequences of your disobedience."

Defeated, Tamar said no more. All she had done was to bring humiliation upon herself. She wanted to scream at her sisters to stop their silly prattling. How could they rejoice over her misfortune? What did it matter if Er was handsome? Hadn't they heard of his cruelty? Didn't they know of his arrogance? Er was said to cause trouble wherever he went!

"More kohl, Acsah. It will make her look older."

Tamar could not calm the wild beating of her heart. The palms of her hands grew damp. If all went as her father hoped, her future would be settled today.

This is a good thing, Tamar told herself, *a good thing.* Her throat was hot and tight with tears.

"Stand, Tamar," her mother said. "Let me have a look at you."

Tamar obeyed. Her mother sighed heavily and tugged at the folds of the red dress, redraping the front. "We must conceal her lack of curves, Acsah, or Zimran will be hard pressed to convince Judah she is old enough to conceive."

"I can show him the cloth, my lady."

"Good. Have it ready in case it's requested."

Tamar felt the heat flood her face. Was nothing private? Did everyone have to discuss the most personal events in her life? Her first show of blood had proclaimed her womanhood and her usefulness as a bargaining tool for her father. She was a commodity to be sold, a tool to forge an alliance between two clans, a sacrifice for an assured peace. She had hoped to be overlooked for another year or two. Fourteen seemed too young to draw a man's interest.

This is a good thing, Tamar told herself again. Even while other thoughts crowded in, tightening her stomach with fear, she repeated the words over and over, trying to convince herself. *This is a good thing.*

Perhaps if she hadn't heard the stories ...

For as long as Tamar could remember, her father had been afraid of Judah and his people. She'd heard the stories about the power of the God of the Hebrews, a god who had turned Sodom and Gomorrah to rubble beneath a storm of fire and brimstone, leaving a wasteland of white sands and a growing salten sea behind. No Canaanite god had ever shown such power!

And there were the stories of what the Hebrews had done to the town of Shechem, stories of mayhem ...

"Why must it be this way, Mother? Have I no choice in what's to become of me?"

"No more choice than any other girl. I know how you're feeling. I was no older than you when I came into your father's house. It is the way of things, Tamar. Haven't I prepared you for this day from the time you were a little girl? I have told you what you were born to do. Struggling against your fate is like wrestling the wind." She gripped Tamar's shoulders. "Be a good daughter and obey without quibbling. Be a good wife and bear many sons. Do these things, and you'll bring honor upon yourself. And if you're fortunate, your husband will come to love you. If not, your future will still be secure in the hands of sons. When you're old, they'll take care of you just as your brothers will take care of me. The only satisfaction a woman has in this life is knowing she has built up the household of her husband."

"But this is Judah's son, Mother. Judah's son Er."

Her mother's eyes flickered, but she remained firm. "Find a way to fulfill your duty and bear sons. You must be strong, Tamar. These people are fierce and unpredictable. And they are proud."

Tamar turned her face away. "I don't want to marry Er. I can't marry him – "

Her mother grasped her hair and yanked her head back. "Would you destroy our family by humiliating such a man as this Hebrew? Do you think your father would let you live if you went into that room and begged to be spared marriage to Er? Do you think Judah would take such an insult lightly? I tell you this. I would join your father in stoning you if you dare risk the lives of my sons. Do you hear me? Your father decides whom and when you marry. Not you!" She let go of her roughly and stepped away, trembling. "Do not act like a fool!"

Tamar closed her eyes. The silence in the room was heavy. She felt her sisters and nurse staring at her. "I'm sorry." Her lip quivered. "I'm sorry. I'll do what I must."

"As we all must." Sighing, her mother took her hand and rubbed it with scented oil. "Be wise as a serpent, Tamar. Judah has shown wisdom in considering you. You are strong, stronger than these others. You have quick wits and strength you don't even realize yet. This Hebrew has taken an interest in you. For all our sakes, you must please him. Be a good wife to his son. Build a bridge between our people. Keep the peace between us."

The weight of responsibility being given her made her bow her head. "I will try."

"You will do more than try. You will succeed." Her mother leaned down and kissed her cheek briskly. "Now sit quietly and collect yourself while I send word to your father that you're ready."

Tamar tried to think calmly. Judah was one of the sons of Jacob who had annihilated the town of Shechem over the rape of their sister. Perhaps, had the son of Hamor known more about these men, he would have left the girl alone. When he realized his mistake, he made every attempt to placate Jacob's sons. They wanted blood. The prince and his father had agreed to have every man in Shechem mutilated by the Hebrew rite of circumcision. They were desperate to bring about a marriage alliance and assurance of peace between the two tribes! They had done all the Hebrews required, and still, three days after the Shechemites were circumcised, while they were all sick with fevers, Judah and his brothers took vengeance. They hadn't been content with the blood of the offender; they'd cut down every man by the sword. Not one survived, and the city was plundered.

Hebrews were a stench in Canaanite nostrils. Their presence invoked fear and distrust. Even though Judah had left his father's tent and come to live among Tamar's people, her father had never slept easily with Judah so close. Even Judah's long-time friendship with Hirah the Adullamite didn't reassure her father. Nor did it matter that Judah had taken a Canaanite wife, who had given him three sons and trained them up in Canaanite ways. Judah was Hebrew. Judah was a foreigner. Judah was a thorn in Zimran's side.

Over the years, her father had made contracts with Judah to bring flocks to his harvested fields. The arrangement had proven beneficial to everyone and had brought about a tentative alliance. All through those years, Tamar had known her father sought a better and more lasting way to keep peace between himself and the Hebrews. A marriage between the two households might ensure that, if she succeeded in blessing Judah's household with sons.

Oh, Tamar understood her father's determination to bring about her marriage to Er. She even understood his need for it. She understood her role in all of it. But understanding didn't make it any easier. After all, she was the one being offered like a sacrificial lamb. She had no choice as to whether she married or not. She had no choice as to the man she would marry. Her only choice was in how she faced her fate.

Tamar was ready when her mother returned. Her feelings were hidden as she bowed down to her. When Tamar raised her head, her mother placed both hands upon her and murmured a blessing. Then she tipped Tamar's chin. "Life is difficult, Tamar. I know that better than you do. Every girl dreams of love when she's young, but this is life, not idle dreams. Had you been born first, we would have sent you to the temple of Timnah instead of your sister."

"I would not have been happy there." In fact, she would have preferred death by her own hand to the life her sister led.

"So this is the only life left to you, Tamar. Embrace it."

Resolved to do so, Tamar rose. She tried to still the tremors as she followed her mother from the women's chamber. Judah might still decide she was too young. He might say she was too skinny, too ugly. She might yet be spared from marrying Er. But it would change nothing in the end. The truth was hard to face. She had to marry, for a woman without a husband and sons might as well be dead.

⟨≈⟩⟨≈⟩⟨≈⟩

Judah watched Zimran's daughter closely as she entered the room. She was tall and thin and very young. She was also poised and graceful. He liked the way she moved as she served the meal with her mother. He'd noticed her youthful elegance during his last visit after the harvest. Zimran had put the girl to work in the field next to the pasturage so Judah and his sons could see her. He had been fully aware of Zimran's motives in displaying her this way. Now, on closer inspection, the girl looked too young to be a bride. She couldn't be more than Shelah's age, and Judah said so.

Zimran laughed. "Of course, she is young, but so much the better. A young girl is more moldable than an older one. Is that not so? Your son will be her *baal*. He will be her teacher."

"What of children?"

Zimran laughed again; the sound grated Judah's nerves. "I assure you, Judah my friend, Tamar is old enough to bear sons and has been old enough since last harvest, when Er noticed her. We have proof of it."

The girl's eyes flickered in her father's direction. She was blushing and clearly embarrassed. Judah felt oddly touched by her modesty and studied her openly. "Come closer, girl," he said, beckoning. He wanted to look into her eyes. Perhaps he would glean better understanding of why he'd thought of her at all when the subject of marriage had come to mind.

"Don't be shy, Tamar." Zimran's mouth flattened. "Let Judah see how pretty you are." When she raised her head, Zimran nodded. "That's it. Smile and show Judah what fine teeth you have."

Judah didn't care about her smile or her teeth, though both were good. He cared about her fertility. Of course, there was no way of knowing whether she could produce sons for his clan until she was wed to his son. Life held no guarantees. However, the girl came from good breeding stock. Her mother had produced six sons and five daughters. She must also be strong, for he had watched her in the fields hoeing the hard ground and carrying rocks to the wall. A weak girl would have been kept inside the house, making pottery or weaving.

"Tamar." Her father gestured. "Kneel before Judah. Let him have a closer look."

She obeyed without hesitation. Her eyes were dark but not hard, her skin ruddy and glowing with health. Such a girl might stir his son's hardened heart and make him repent of his wild ways. Judah wondered if she had the courage needed to gain Er's respect. Her father was a coward. Was she? Er had brought nothing but grief since he'd been old enough to walk, and he was likely to bring this girl trouble as well. She would have to be strong and resilient.

Judah knew the blame for Er's waywardness could be laid at his feet. He should never have given his wife a free hand in rearing his sons. He'd thought complete freedom would allow them to grow up happy and strong. Oh, they were happy as long as they got their way, and were strong enough to abuse others if they didn't. They were proud and arrogant for lack of discipline. They would have turned out better had the rod been used more often!

Would this girl soften Er? Or would he harden and break her? When she looked into his eyes, he saw innocence and intelligence. He felt a disquieting despair. Er was his firstborn, the first show of the strength of his loins. He'd felt such pride and joy when the boy was born, such hope. *Ah,* he'd thought, *here is flesh of my flesh, bone of my bone!* How he'd laughed when the young sprout had stood in red-faced fury, refusing to obey his mother. He'd been amused by his son's passionate rebellion, foolishly proud of it. *This boy will be a strong man,* he'd said to himself. No woman would tell Er how to live.

Judah had never expected his son to defy *him* as well.

Onan, his second son, was becoming as difficult as Er. He'd grown up threatened by his older brother's white-hot jealousy and had learned to protect himself by cunning and deception. Judah didn't know which son was worse. Both were treacherous. Neither could be trusted. The third son, Shelah, was following the ways of his brothers. Confronted with a wrong, Judah's sons lied or blamed others. When pressed hard enough to get the truth, they appealed to their mother, who defended them no matter how offensive their crimes. Her pride wouldn't allow her to see their faults. They were her sons, after all, and they were Canaanite through and through.

Something had to be done, or Er would bring Judah's head down to the ground in shame. Judah almost regretted having sons, for they wreaked havoc in his household and his life! There were moments when his rage was so intense, it was all he could do not to pick up a spear and hurl it at one of them.

Judah often thought about his father, Jacob, and the trouble *he'd* endured at the hands of *his* sons. Judah had caused his father as much trouble as the rest of them. Er and Onan reminded Judah of his brothers Simeon and Levi. Thinking of his brothers brought back the black memories of the grievous sin he himself had committed – the sin that haunted him, the sin that had driven him from his father's household because he couldn't bear to see the grief he'd caused or be in the company of the brothers who had shared in what he'd done.

His father, Jacob, didn't even know the full truth of what had happened at Dothan.

Judah tried to console himself. He'd kept Simeon and Levi from murdering their brother Joseph, hadn't he? But he also remembered that he was the one who'd led them into selling the boy to the Ishmaelite traders on their way to Egypt. He'd made a profit from the lad's misery, profits shared by his brothers as well. Only God knew if Joseph had survived the long, hard journey to Egypt. It was more than possible he'd died in the desert. If not, he was now a slave for some Egyptian.

Sometimes in the darkest hour of night, Judah would lie awake upon his pallet, filled with an agony of remorse, thinking about Joseph. How many years would it be before he could put the past behind him and forget what he'd done? How many years before he could close his eyes and not see Joseph's hands shackled, his neck noosed, as he was led forcefully away by the Ishmaelite traders? The boy's screams for help still echoed in Judah's mind.

He had the rest of his life to regret his sins, years to live with them. Sometimes Judah swore he could feel the hand of God squeezing the life from him for plotting the destruction of his own brother.

Zimran cleared his throat. Judah reminded himself where he was and why he'd come to the home of this Canaanite. He mustn't let his mind wander, mustn't allow the past to intrude on what he had to do about the future. His son needed a wife – a young, comely, strong wife who might distract him from his wicked schemes and devices. Judah's mouth tightened as he studied the Canaanite girl kneeling before him. Was he making another mistake? He'd married a Canaanite and lived to regret it. Now he was bringing another one into his household. Yet this Canaanite girl appealed to him. Why?

Judah tipped the girl's chin. He knew she must be afraid, but she hid it well. That would be a useful skill where Er was concerned. She looked so young and guileless. Would his son destroy her innocence and corrupt her as he was so eager to do to others?

Hardening himself, Judah withdrew his hand and leaned back. He had no intention of allowing Er to make the same mistakes he had. Lust had driven him to marry the boy's mother. Beauty was a snare that captured a man, while unrestrained passion burned away reason. A woman's character mattered greatly in a marriage. Judah would have done better to follow custom and allow his father to choose a wife for him. Instead, he'd been stubborn and hasty and now suffered for his folly.

It wasn't enough that a woman stirred a man's passion. She also had to be strong, yet willing to bend. A stubborn woman was a curse upon a man. He'd been laughable in his youthful confidence, so certain he could bend a woman to his ways. Instead, he'd bent to Bathshua's. He'd fooled himself into thinking there was no harm in giving his wife freedom to worship as she wished. Now, he found himself reaping a whirlwind with his idol-worshiping sons!

Tamar was of calmer disposition than Bathshua. Tamar had courage. She appeared intelligent. He knew she was strong, for he'd watched how hard she worked. His wife, Bathshua, would be happy about that. No doubt she would dump her chores upon the girl as soon as possible. The quality that mattered most was her fertility, and only time would tell about that. The qualities he could see were more than enough. Yet there was something more about this girl that Judah couldn't define, something rare and wonderful that made him determined to have her in his family. It was as though a quiet voice was telling him to choose her.

"She pleases me."

Zimran exhaled. "You are a wise man!" He nodded to his daughter. Thus dismissed, Tamar rose. The Canaanite was clearly eager to begin negotiations. Judah watched the girl leave the room with her mother. Zimran clapped his hands; two servants hurried in, one with a tray of pomegranates and grapes, another with roasted lamb. "Eat, my brother, and then we will talk."

Judah would not be so easily manipulated. Before touching the food, he made an offer for the girl. Eyes glowing, Zimran plunged in and began haggling over the bride-price.

Judah decided to be generous. Marriage, though far from bringing happiness to him, had brought some stability and direction. Perhaps Er would be similarly diverted from riotous living. Besides, Judah wanted to spend as little time with Zimran as possible. The man's ingratiating manner irritated him.

Tamar. Her name meant "date palm." It was a name given to one who would become beautiful and graceful. A date palm survives the desert and bears sweet, nourishing fruit, and the girl came from a fertile family. A date palm sways in the desert winds without breaking or being uprooted, and this girl would have to face Er's quick, irascible temper. A date palm could survive a hostile environment, and Judah knew Bathshua would see this young girl as her rival. Judah knew his wife would pit herself against this young bride because Bathshua was vain and jealous of her son's affections.

Tamar.

Judah hoped the girl held all the promise her name implied.

※※※

Tamar waited while her fate was settled. When her mother stood in the doorway, she knew the matter of her future was decided. "Come, Tamar. Judah has gifts for you."

She rose, numb inside. It was a time for rejoicing, not tears. Her father need not fear any longer.

"Ah, Daughter." Her father smiled broadly. Obviously, he'd fetched a high bride-price for her, for he had never before embraced her with so much affection. He even kissed her cheek! She lifted her chin and looked into his eyes, wanting him to know what he'd done to her in giving her to such a man as Er. Perhaps he would feel some shame for using her to protect himself. He didn't. "Greet your father-in-law."

Resigned to her fate, Tamar prostrated herself before Judah. The Hebrew put his hand upon her head and blessed her and bid her rise. As she did so, he took gold earrings and bracelets from a pouch at his waist and placed them upon her. Her father's eyes glowed, but her heart sank.

"Be ready to leave in the morning," Judah told her.

Shocked, she spoke without thinking. "In the morning?" She looked at her father. "What of the betrothal – ?"

Her father's expression warned her to silence. "Judah and I celebrate tonight, my daughter. Acsah will pack your things and go with you tomorrow. Everything is settled. Your husband is eager for you."

Was her father so afraid that he didn't require the customary ten-month betrothal period to prepare for the wedding? She would not even have a week to adjust to her impending marriage!

"You may go, Tamar. Make ready to leave in the morning."

When she entered the women's chamber, she found her mother and sisters already packing for her. Unable to contain her feelings any longer, Tamar burst into tears. Inconsolable, she wept all night, even after her sisters whined and pleaded for her to stop. "You will have your day," she told them angrily. "Someday you will understand!"

Acsah held and rocked her, and Tamar clung to her childhood for one last night.

When the sun rose, she washed her face and donned her bridal veils.

Her mother came to her. "Be content, beloved one. Judah paid dearly for you." Her voice was tear-choked and faintly bitter. "That Hebrew came with a donkey laden with gifts. He returns home with only his seal ring and staff."

"And me," Tamar said softly.

Her mother's eyes filled with tears. "Take good care of her, Acsah."

"I will, my lady."

Her mother took Tamar in her arms and kissed her. "May your husband love you and give you many sons," she whispered against her hair. Tamar clung to her tightly, pressing herself close, soaking in the warmth and softness of her mother one last time. "It's time," her mother said softly, and Tamar drew back. Her mother touched her cheek before turning away.

Tamar went out into the morning sunlight. Acsah walked with her as she headed toward her father and Judah, who were standing some distance away. She had cried herself out last night. She would shed no more childish tears, though it was hard not to do so with Acsah weeping softly behind her.

"Perhaps all we've heard isn't true," Acsah said. "Perhaps Er is not as bad as some say he is."

"What does it matter now?"

"You must try to make him love you, Tamar. A man in love is clay in a woman's hands. May the gods have mercy on us!"

"Have mercy upon me and be quiet!"

When she reached the two men, her father kissed her. "Be fruitful and multiply the household of Judah." He was eager for their departure.

Judah walked ahead, Tamar and Acsah following. He was a tall man with long strides, and Tamar had to walk quickly to keep up with him. Acsah muttered complaints under her breath, but Tamar paid her no attention. Instead, she set her mind on what lay ahead. She would work hard. She would be a good wife. She would do everything within her power to bring honor to her husband. She knew how to plant a garden, tend a herd, cook, weave, and make pottery. She could read and write enough to keep proper lists and records of household goods. She knew how to conserve food and water when times were bad and how to be generous when times were good. She knew how to make soap, baskets, cloth, and tools, as well as how to organize servants. But children would be the greatest blessing she could give her husband, children to build the household.

It was Judah's second son, Onan, who came out to meet them. "Er is gone," he said to his father while staring at her.

Judah slammed the end of his staff into the ground. "Gone where?"

Onan shrugged. "Off with his friends. He was angry when he heard where you'd gone. I stayed out of his way. You know how he gets."

"Bathshua!" Judah strode toward his stone house.

A buxom woman with heavily painted eyes appeared in the doorway. "What are you yelling about this time?"

"Did you tell Er I was bringing his bride home today?"

"I told him." She leaned indolently in the doorway.

"Then where is he?"

She lifted her chin. "I'm his mother, Judah, not his keeper. Er will be along when he's ready and not before. You know how he is."

Judah's face darkened. "Yes, I know how he is." He gripped his staff so tightly his knuckles turned white. "That's why he needs a wife!"

"That may be, Judah, but you said the girl was pretty." She gave Tamar a cursory glance. "Do you really think this skinny girl will turn Er's head?"

"Tamar is more than she seems. Show her to Er's chamber." Judah walked off, leaving Tamar and Acsah standing before the house.

Mouth tight, Bathshua looked Tamar over from head to foot. She shook her head in disgust. "I wonder what Judah was thinking when he chose you?" Turning her back, she went into the house and left Tamar and Acsah to fend for themselves.

≈≈≈

Er returned late in the afternoon, accompanied by several Canaanite friends. They were drunk and laughing loudly. Tamar remained out of sight, knowing what men were like in this condition. Her father and brothers had often imbibed freely and argued violently because of it. She knew the wisdom of staying out of the way until the effects of the wine wore off.

Knowing she would be summoned, Tamar had Acsah array her in wedding finery. While waiting, Tamar willed herself to set aside every terrible thing she'd ever heard about Er. Perhaps those who had spoken against him had hidden motives. She would give him the respect due a husband and adapt herself to his demands. If the god of his father smiled upon her, she would give Er sons, and quickly. If she were so blessed, she would bring them up to be strong and honest. She would teach them to be dependable and loyal. And if Er so wished, she would learn about the God of Judah and bring up her sons to worship him rather than bow down to the gods of her father. Still, her heart trembled and her fears increased with each passing hour.

When Tamar was finally summoned and saw her husband, she felt a flicker of admiration. Er was tall like his father and held the promise of great physical strength. He had his mother's thick curling mass of black hair, which he had drawn back in Canaanite fashion. The brass band he wore around his forehead made him look like a young Canaanite prince. Tamar was awed by her husband's handsome appearance but filled quickly with misgivings when she looked into his eyes. They were cold and dark and devoid of mercy. There was pride in the tilt of his head, cruelty in the curve of his lips, and indifference in his manner. He didn't reach out to take her hand.

"So this is the wife you chose for me, Father."

Tamar shivered at his tone.

Judah put his hand firmly on his son's shoulder. "Take good care of what belongs to you, and may the God of Abraham give you many sons by this girl."

Er stood unblinking, his face an inscrutable mask.

All through the evening, Er's friends made crude jests about marriage. They teased Er unmercifully, and though he laughed, Tamar knew he wasn't amused. Her father-in-law, lost in his own thoughts, drank freely while Bathshua lounged nearby, eating the best tidbits of the wedding feast and ignoring her. Tamar was hurt and confused and embarrassed by such rudeness. What had she done to offend her mother-in-law? It was as though the woman was determined not to show her the least consideration.

As the night wore on, her fear gave way to depression. She felt abandoned and lost in the midst of the gathering. She had married the heir of Judah's household, and yet no one spoke to her, not even the young husband who sat beside her. The hours passed slowly. She was bone weary from lack of sleep the previous night and the long walk to her new home. The tensions of the wedding feast further sapped her. She fought to keep her eyes open. She fought even harder to keep the tears from welling up and spilling over.

Er pinched her. Tamar gasped and jerked away from him. Heat flooded her cheeks as she realized she had unwittingly dozed against his side. His friends were laughing and making jokes about her youth and the impending wedding night. Er laughed with them. "Your nurse has prepared the chamber for us." He took her hand and pulled her up to her feet.

As soon as Acsah closed the door of the bedchamber behind them, Er stepped away from Tamar. Acsah took her place outside the door and began singing and beating her small drum. Tamar's skin prickled. "I'm sorry I fell asleep, my lord."

Er said nothing. She waited, her nerves stretching taut. He was enjoying her tension, plucking her nerve endings with his silence. Folding her hands, she decided to wait him out. He removed his belt sardonically. "I noticed you last year when we brought the sheep to your father's fields. I suppose that's why my father thought you might do as my wife." His gaze moved down over her. "He doesn't know me very well."

She did not fault Er for the hurtful words. She felt he was justified. After all, her heart had not leapt with joy when Judah came and offered a bride-price for her.

"You're afraid of me, aren't you?"

If she said no, it would be a lie. To say yes would be unwise.

His brow rose. "You should be afraid. I'm angry, or can't you tell?"

She could, indeed, and couldn't guess what he would do about it. She remained silent, acquiescent. She'd seen her father in rages often enough to know that it was better to say nothing. Words were like oil on a fiery temper. Her mother had told her long ago that men were unpredictable and given to fits of violence when provoked. She would not provoke Er.

"Cautious little thing, aren't you?" He smiled slowly. "At least you keep your wits about you." He came toward her. "You've heard things about me, I'll bet." He brushed his fingers against her cheek. She tried not to flinch. "Have your brothers carried stories home?"

Her heart beat faster and faster.

"As my father said, you're mine now. My own little mouse to do with as I wish. Remind me to thank him." He tipped her chin. His eyes glittered coldly, reminding her of a jackal in the moonlight. When he leaned down and kissed her mouth, the hair on the back of her neck rose. He drew back, assessing her. "Believe the rumors, every one of them!"

"I will try to please you, my husband." Heat poured into her cheeks at the quaver in her voice.

"Oh, no doubt you will try, my sweet, but you won't succeed. His mouth curved, showing the edge of his teeth. "You can't."

It took only a day of the weeklong wedding celebration for Tamar to understand what he meant.

two

TAMAR tensed as she heard Er shouting inside the house. Bathshua was shouting back at him. Even with the midday sun beating down upon Tamar's back, her sweat turned cold. Judah had summoned his eldest son to assist with the flocks, but it seemed Er had plans of his own. Er's temper was hot enough now that he would seek out some way to vent it, and his wife would be an easy target. After all, no one would interfere.

Keeping her head down, Tamar continued hoeing the rocky patch of soil Bathshua had assigned to her care. She wished she could shrink to the size of an ant and scurry down a hole. Inside the house, the ranting of son and raving of mother continued. Tamar knelt once, fighting against frightened tears as she pried a large rock from the ground. Straightening, she tossed it toward the growing pile nearby. In her mind she built a wall around herself, high and thick, with a clear sky above. She didn't want to think about Er's temper and what he might do to her this time.

"She's losing her hold on him," Acsah said grimly as she worked a few feet away.

"It does no good to worry, Acsah." The words were uttered more to remind herself than Acsah. Tamar kept working. What else could she do? Four months in Judah's house had taught her to avoid her husband whenever possible, especially when he was in a bad temper. She'd also learned to hide her fear. Her heart might race with it, her stomach be tight as a knot, her skin cold and clammy, but she dared not reveal her feelings, for Er relished fear. He fed upon it.

"A pity Judah isn't here." Acsah made a sound of disgust. "Of course, he's never here." She hit the hard ground with her hoe. "Not that he can be blamed."

Tamar said nothing. Her mind worked frantically, searching for an escape and finding none. If only Judah hadn't gone ahead. If only he'd taken Er with him in the first place, rather than send a servant back later to fetch him. When Judah was present, Er could be managed. When he was absent,

Er ran wild. The chaos of this family came from Judah's failure to exercise his authority often enough. Judah preferred the open spaces of hills and fields to the confines of his house. Tamar didn't fault him – sheep and goats were peaceful, complacent company compared to a contentious wife and hot-tempered, quarrelsome sons. Sometimes Er and Onan behaved like wild beasts tied together and thrown into a box!

Judah could run away from unpleasantness. Judah could hide from responsibility. Tamar had to live with danger day after day.

Her body jerked as something large crashed inside the house. Bathshua screamed tearful curses down upon her son. Er retaliated. More crockery hit the wall. A metal cup flew out the doorway and bounced across the ground.

"You must stay away from the house today," Acsah said quietly.

"Bathshua may prevail." Turning away, Tamar gazed toward the distant hills while the battle raged behind her. Her hand trembled as she wiped the perspiration from her face. Closing her eyes, she sighed. Perhaps Judah's command would be enough this time.

"Bathshua always prevails in one way or another," Acsah said bitterly. She scraped angrily at the dry earth. "If screaming fails, she'll sulk until she gets her way."

Tamar ignored Acsah and tried to think of more pleasant things. She thought of her sisters. They had squabbles, but they enjoyed one another's company. She remembered how they had sung together as they worked and told stories to entertain one another. Her father had a temper like any other man, and there had been loud arguments at times between her brothers, but nothing in her experience had prepared her for Judah's household. Each day she tried to arise with new hope, only to have it crushed again.

"If only I had a place here, Acsah, some small corner of influence ... " She spoke without self-pity.

"You will have when you produce a son."

"A son." Tamar's heart ached with longing. She longed for a child more than anyone, even her husband, whose desire for a son was more an extension of his own pride than a desire to prosper his family. For Tamar, a son would secure her position in the household. She would no longer feel such loneliness, with a baby in her arms. She could love a son and hold him close and receive love from him. Perhaps a son would even soften Er's heart toward her, and his hand as well.

She remembered again Bathshua's crushing condemnation: "If you didn't disappoint my son, he wouldn't beat you so often! Do as he wishes, and perhaps he will treat you better!" Tamar blinked back tears, fighting against self-pity. What good would that do? It would only weaken her resolve. She was a member of this family, whether she wanted to be or not. She mustn't allow her emotions to prevail. She knew Bathshua delighted in making hurtful remarks. A day never passed without her mother-in-law's finding some way to stab at her heart.

"Another moon has passed, Tamar, and *still* you haven't conceived! I was with child a week after I wed Judah!"

Tamar could say nothing without rousing Er's temper. What defense had she when nothing she did pleased her mother-in-law or her young husband? She ceased to hope for tenderness or compassion from either of them. Honor and loyalty seemed to be missing as well, for Bathshua had to resort to threats to get Er to obey Judah's summons.

"Enough, I say!" Er shouted in frustration, drawing Tamar's attention back to the altercation between mother and son. *"Enough!* I'll go to Father! Anything to get away from your carping!" He stormed out of the house. *"I hate sheep!* If I had my way, I'd *butcher every one of them!"*

Bathshua appeared in the doorway, arms akimbo, chest heaving. "And then what would you have? Nothing!"

"I'd have the money from their meat and hides. That's what I'd have."

"All of which you'd spend in a week. Then what? Have I raised such a fool?"

Er called her a name and made a rude gesture at her before turning and striding away. Tamar held her breath until she saw he was taking the path away from Kezib. She would have a few days respite from his cruelty.

"It seems Bathshua won this battle," Acsah said. "But there will be another, and another," she added dismally.

Lighter of heart, Tamar smiled and returned to her work. "Each day has trouble enough, Acsah. I'll not burden myself with worrying about tomorrow."

"Tamar!" Bathshua stepped outside. "If you have time enough for idle chatter, you can come clean up this mess!" Swinging around, she marched back into the house.

"She expects you to clear up the destruction she and Er have made of that house," Acsah said with loathing.

"Hush, or you'll bring more trouble upon us."

Bathshua appeared again. "Leave Acsah to finish in the garden. I want you inside this house *now!"* She disappeared inside.

When Tamar entered the house, she treaded carefully so that she wouldn't step on the shards of broken pottery strewn across the earthen floor. Bathshua sat glumly staring at her broken loom. Hunkering down, Tamar began to gather the shards of a jug into the folds of her *tsaiph*.

"I hope Judah is satisfied with the mess he's made," Bathshua said angrily. "He thought a wife would improve Er's disposition!" She glared at Tamar as though she were to blame for everything that had happened. "Er is worse than ever! You've done my son more harm than good!"

Fighting tears, Tamar made no defense.

Muttering imprecations, Bathshua tipped the loom up. Seeing that the arm was broken and the rug she'd made tangled, she covered her face and wept bitterly.

Tamar was embarrassed by the woman's passion. It wasn't the first time she'd seen Bathshua burst into tempestuous tears. The first time, she'd gone to her mother-in-law and tried to comfort her, only to receive a resounding slap across the face and blame for the woman's despair. Tamar kept her distance now and averted her eyes.

Was Bathshua blind to what she caused in this household? She constantly pitted son against father and son against son. She argued with Judah over everything, and in front of her sons, teaching them to rebel and follow their own desires rather than do what was best for the family. It was no wonder her mother-in-law was miserable! And everyone was miserable right along with her.

"Judah wants Er to tend the sheep." Bathshua yanked at the loom, making a worse mess. "You know why? Because my husband can't bear to be away from his *abba* for more than a year! He has to go back and see how that wretched old man is doing. You watch when Judah comes home. He'll brood for days. He won't speak to anyone. He won't eat. Then he'll get drunk and say the same stupid thing he does every time he sees Jacob." She grimaced as she mocked her husband. "The hand of God is upon me!"

Tamar glanced up.

Bathshua rose and paced. "How can the man be such a fool – believing in a god who doesn't even exist?"

"Perhaps he does exist."

Bathshua cast a baleful glance at her. "Then where is he? Has this god a temple in which to live or priests to serve him? He doesn't even have a *tent!*" Her chin tipped in pride. "He's not like the gods of Canaan." She marched to her cabinet and flung it open. "He is not a god like *these.*" She held her hand out toward her teraphim reverently. "He isn't a god you can see." She ran her hand down one statue. "He isn't a god you can touch.

These gods fan our passions into being and make our land and our women fertile." Her eyes glittered coldly. "Perhaps if you were more respectful to them, you wouldn't still have a flat, empty belly!"

Tamar felt the barb, but this time she didn't allow it to sink in deeply. "Didn't the God of Judah destroy Sodom and Gomorrah?"

Bathshua laughed derisively. "So some say, but I don't believe it." She closed the cabinet firmly, as though such words would bring bad luck upon her house. She turned and frowned down upon Tamar. "Would you raise up your sons to bow down to a god who destroys cities?"

"If Judah wills it."

"Judah," Bathshua said and shook her head. "Have you ever seen my husband worship his father's god? I never have. So why should his sons or I worship him? You will train up your sons in the religion of Er's choice. I have never bowed down to an unseen god. Not once have I been unfaithful to the gods of Canaan, and I advise you to be faithful as well. If you know what's good for you ... "

Tamar recognized the threat.

Bathshua sat upon a cushion against the wall and smiled coldly. "Er wouldn't be pleased to hear you were even thinking of worshiping the god of the Hebrews." Her eyes narrowed. "I think you're the cause of our troubles."

Tamar knew what to expect. When Er returned, Bathshua would claim there was spiritual insurrection in the household. The woman relished stirring up trouble. Tamar longed to throw the broken crockery on the earthen floor and tell her mother-in-law it was her own actions that were destroying the family. Instead, she swallowed her anger and collected shards as Bathshua watched.

"The gods have blessed me with three fine sons, and I've brought them up in the *true* religion, as would any *good* mother."

Hot-tempered sons, who do even less work than you do, Tamar wanted to say but held her tongue. She couldn't win a war with her mother-in-law.

Bathshua leaned forward and lifted an overturned tray enough to pluck a bunch of grapes. She dropped the tray again. "Perhaps you should pray to Asherah more often and give better offerings to Baal. Then your womb might be opened."

Tamar lifted her head. "I know of Asherah and Baal. My father and mother gave up my sister to serve as a priestess in the temple of Timnah." She didn't add that she'd never been able to embrace their beliefs or say aloud that she pitied her sister above all women. Once, during a visit to

Timnah during a festival, she'd seen her older sister on an altar platform having sexual intercourse with a priest. The rites were intended to arouse Baal and bring spring back to the land, but Tamar had been filled with disgust and fear at what she saw, sickened even more by the excited crowd witnessing the scene. She'd drawn back, ducked around the corner of a building, and run away. She hadn't stopped running until she was out of Timnah. She'd hidden in the middle of an olive orchard and remained there until evening when her mother found her.

"You are not devout enough," Bathshua said smugly.

No, I am not, Tamar said to herself. She knew she could never be devout when she didn't believe. The gods made no sense to her. All her efforts to worship them filled her with a strange sense of repugnance and shame.

Bathshua rose and returned to her loom. She had calmed enough to begin straightening the tangled threads. "If you were a true believer, you'd be with child by now." She glanced at Tamar, no doubt trying to assess the impact of her mean-spirited words. "It would seem the gods are angry with you, wouldn't it?"

"Perhaps." Tamar conceded with a pang of guilt. Bathshua's teraphim were nothing but clay, stone, and wood statues. She couldn't embrace them as Bathshua did, nor could she adore them as fervently. Oh, Tamar said the prayers expected of her, but the words were empty and held no power. Her heart was untouched, her mind far from convinced.

If the gods of Canaan were so powerful, why hadn't they been able to save or protect the people of Sodom and Gomorrah? Surely a dozen gods were more powerful than one – if they were true gods.

They were nothing but carved stone, chipped wood, and clay molded by human hands!

Perhaps there was no true god.

Her heart rebelled at this thought as well. The world around her, the heavens, the earth, the winds, and the rain said there was something. Perhaps the God of Judah was that *something*. A shield against enemies. A shelter in a storm. Nay, a fortress ... Oh, how she longed to know. Yet she dared not ask.

What right had she to bother Judah with questions, especially when so many other things plagued him?

Someday, perhaps, she would have the time and the opportunity to ask.

In the meantime, she would wait and hope to see some sign of what Judah believed and how he worshiped.

Judah and Er returned five days later. Tamar heard them arguing long before they entered the house. So did Bathshua, for she sighed heavily. "Go and milk one of the goats, Tamar, and tell your nurse to make some bread. Perhaps if the men eat, they will be in better humor."

By the time Tamar returned with a jug of fresh goat's milk, Judah was reclining against some cushions. His eyes were closed, but Tamar knew he wasn't asleep. His face was tense, and Bathshua was sitting close by, glaring at him. She'd probably been vexing him again, and he was doing his best to shut her out.

"Five days, Judah. *Five days*. Did you have to stay that long?"

"You could have come with me."

"And done what? Listen to your brothers' wives? What have I in common with them? And your mother doesn't like me!" She whined and complained like a selfish child.

Tamar offered Er milk. "Wine," he said with a jerk of his chin, clearly in a surly mood. "I want wine!"

"I'll have milk," Judah said, his eyes opening enough to look at her.

Bathshua's head came up. "Here! Give me that. I'll serve my husband while you see to my son." When she had the jug, she sloshed some milk into a cup, thrust it at Judah, and then set the jug within his reach so that he could serve himself next time.

Bathshua was still badgering Judah when Tamar returned with wine for Er.

"What good does it do you to see your father, Judah? Has anything changed? You're always miserable when you come home from his tent. Let Jacob grieve over his second wife and son. Forget about him. Every time you go back to see him, you come home and make my life miserable!"

"I will not forsake my father," Judah said, his jaw clenched.

"Why not? He's forsaken you. A pity the old man doesn't die and spare us all ... "

"Enough!" Judah roared. Tamar saw that it was not anger but pain that made him cry out. Grimacing, he raked his hands back through his hair. "Just once, Bathshua, hold your tongue!" He raised his head and glared at her. "Even better, leave me alone!"

"How can you speak to me so cruelly?" She wept angrily. "I'm the mother of your sons. *Three* sons!"

"Three worthless sons." Judah's eyes narrowed coldly on Er.

Tamar's stomach dropped as she waited for him to say something that would rouse Er's temper. Her husband would control his temper as long as he was in his father's presence, but later she would be the recipient of his frustration. Bathshua kept on until Tamar wanted to scream at her to stop, to leave, to have some particle of common sense. Thankfully, Bathshua stormed out of the room, leaving silence behind her.

Tamar was left alone to serve both men. The tension in the room made her nerves tingle. She replenished Er's cup of wine. He emptied the cup and held it out for more. She glanced at Judah before refilling it. Er looked up at her with a scowl, then at his father. "Onan and Shelah can see to the flocks for the next few days. I'm going to see my friends."

Judah raised his head slowly and looked at his son. "Will you?" His voice was soft, his eyes hard.

Er shifted. He looked into his cup and then drained it. "With your permission, of course."

Judah gazed at Tamar and then looked away. "Go ahead. But stay out of trouble this time."

A muscle jerked in Er's cheek. "I never start trouble."

"Of course not," Judah said drolly.

Er stood and approached Tamar. She drew back instinctively, but he caught hold of her arm and pulled her close. "I'll miss you, my sweet." His expression mocked his words, and his fingers bit into her flesh. He let go of her and pinched her cheek. "Don't pine. I won't be gone long!"

Judah sighed with relief when his son was gone. He scarcely noticed Tamar's presence. Leaning forward, he held his head as though it ached. Tamar hunkered down quietly and waited for him to command her to leave. He didn't. When Acsah came in with bread, Tamar rose and took the small basket from her nurse, nodding for her to take a place on a cushion near the door. Propriety must be maintained.

"Acsah has made bread, my lord." When he said nothing, Tamar broke the loaf and placed a portion before him. She poured a cup of goat's milk, took a small bunch of grapes from a platter, and cut into a pomegranate. She broke the fruit open so that the succulent red beads could be easily removed. "Is your father, Jacob, well?"

"As well as can be expected for a man mourning the loss of a favorite son," Judah said bitterly.

"One of your brothers has died?"

Judah raised his head from his hands and looked at her. "Years ago. Before you were even born."

"And still he grieves?" she said in wonder.

"He'll go to his grave grieving for that boy."

Never had Tamar seen such a look of torment. She pitied Judah and wished she knew some way to draw him from his sorrow. His expression softened slightly. The intensity of his perusal discomforted her, especially when his eyes cooled. "He marked your face!"

She covered her cheek quickly and turned her face away. "It's nothing." She never spoke of Er's abuse to anyone. Even when Acsah asked her questions, she refused to be disloyal to her husband. "Do you also grieve for your brother?"

"I grieve over the way he died."

Curious at his tone, she glanced at him again. "How did he die?"

Judah's face hardened. "He was torn apart by an animal. Nothing was found of him but his coat covered with blood." The words came as though he had said them over and over again and loathed repeating them. When she raised her brow, his expression was one of challenge. "You don't believe me?"

"Why should I not believe you?" She didn't want to anger him. "I would like to know more about my family."

"*Your* family?" His mouth curved ruefully.

Heat filled her cheeks. Did he mean to exclude her too? Anger stirred, along with hurt feelings. It was Judah who had brought her into this household, Judah who had chosen her for his son! Surely he would do right by her. "The family into which you brought me, my lord, a family I want to serve, if only I am allowed."

"If God is willing ... " His mouth curved sadly. He took a piece of bread and began to eat.

"Will you tell me nothing?" she said weakly, her courage dwindling.

"What do you want to know?"

"Everything. Anything. Especially about your god. Where does he dwell? What is his name? How do you worship him? Is he unseen, as my father claims? How do you know he exists?"

Judah drew back. "I thought you wanted to know about my father and my brothers."

"I have heard that the god of your father destroyed the cities that were in the salt flat where the marsh now expands."

"That's true." He looked away. "The Angel of the Lord told Abraham He would destroy them unless ten righteous men could be found among those living there. Abraham saw with his own eyes the fire and brimstone that came down from heaven." Judah looked at her solemnly. "It doesn't matter if you can't see or hear Him. He doesn't live in temples like the gods of your father. He is ... "

"Is ... what?"

"Just ... *is*. Don't pester me with questions. You're a Canaanite. Just go and pick an idol from Bathshua's cabinet and worship it!" His tone was derisive.

Her eyes pricked hot with tears. "You are the head of this household."

Color surged into Judah's face and his mouth tightened. Grimacing, he searched her face. He frowned slightly, then spoke softly. "The God of Jacob turns rock into springs of water. Or can crush a man's life with a thought." His eyes were bleak.

"Where does he dwell?"

"Anywhere He wants. Everywhere." Judah shrugged. "I can't explain what I don't understand." He frowned, his gaze distant. "Sometimes I don't want to know ... "

"How did your people come to know of him?"

"He spoke to Abraham, and He has spoken to my father."

"As you and I are speaking? Why would a god of such power lower himself to speak to a mere man?"

"I don't know. When Abraham first heard Him, He was ... a voice. But the Lord comes anytime and in any way He wishes. He spoke to Abraham face-to-face. My father wrestled a blessing from Him. The Angel of the Lord touched my father's hip and crippled him forever. Sometimes He speaks in ... dreams." The last seemed to trouble him deeply.

"Has he ever spoken to you?"

"No, and I hope He never does."

"Why?"

"I know what He would say." Judah sighed heavily and leaned back, tossing the bread onto the tray.

"Every god demands a sacrifice. What sacrifice does your god require?"

"Obedience." He waved his hand impatiently. "Don't ask me any more questions. Give me peace!"

Blushing, she murmured an apology. She was no better than Bathshua, battering him with her needs, her desires. Ashamed, Tamar withdrew. "Do you wish me to ask Bathshua to serve you?"

"I'd rather be stung by a scorpion. I want to be alone."

Acsah followed her from the room. "What did you say to upset him so?"

"I merely asked a few questions."

"What sort of questions?"

"Just questions, Acsah. Nothing that need concern you." Acsah would not comprehend her quest for understanding the God of Judah's fathers. Acsah worshiped the same gods Bathshua and her sons did, the same gods Tamar's mother and father and sisters and brothers worshiped. Why was she so different? Why did she hunger and thirst for something more?

"Everything you do concerns me," Acsah said, clearly annoyed. "I am your nurse, am I not?"

"I don't need one today." She couldn't tell Acsah that she wanted to know about the God of Judah. While everyone around her worshiped idols of stone, wood, or clay, she merely pretended. The gods of her father and mother had mouths but never spoke. They had eyes, but could they see? They had feet but never walked. Could they think or feel or breathe? And she had seen a truth about them: Those who worshiped them became like them, cold and hard. Like Bathshua. Like Er. Like Onan. Someday, Shelah would be the same.

There was nothing cold about Judah. She felt his brokenness. She saw his anguish. Why didn't the others who were supposed to love him? His wife! His sons! They didn't seem to care about anyone but themselves.

Judah was a Hebrew and strong; yet Tamar saw he was bitterly unhappy and tormented. He never seemed to have a moment's peace, even when left alone and in silence. Everything couldn't be blamed on a selfish, contentious wife and quarrelsome sons. There must be other reasons, deeper and more complex. If Bathshua knew what they were, she never spoke of them to anyone. She didn't even seem to care what her husband suffered. She merely complained that Judah brooded every time he returned from seeing Jacob.

Tamar frowned, wondering.

Perhaps Judah's despair had something to do with his father's grieving. And the brother who had been lost.

⟨≷⟨≷⟨≷⟩

Judah wished he hadn't returned to his house so quickly. Far better had he returned to his flocks and seen to the animals Er too often neglected in his absence. His eldest had handed the full responsibility over to Onan after three short days! Er was a fool and useless as a shepherd. He had no love for the sheep that would one day belong to him. The boy stood by while wolves ripped open the belly of a defenseless ewe, then ran the predators off to become one himself. Er took pleasure in delivering the deathblow to a prized ram. Then he roasted and ate the meat!

Sometimes Judah looked at his boys and saw everything he'd worked to build going bad. He saw Simeon and Levi. He saw himself.

And he saw Joseph being led away in the shimmering heat of the desert sun.

Judah had thought he could run away. He thought he could shrug off the responsibility.

Sometimes he'd think back to the early days with Canaanite companions. His Adullamite friend Hirah had had all the answers. "Eat, my brother; drink; enjoy life to the fullest! Where passion burns, blow on the flames."

And Judah had burned. He'd craved corruption, hoping forgetfulness would come. Drink enough, and the mind clouds. Sleep with brazen temple prostitutes, and your senses melt away your conscience. After giving in to his jealousy and anger against Joseph, why not give in to every other emotion that pulled at him? Why not allow instinct to reign? Why not give lust control? He'd wanted desperately to become hard enough to feel no shame. Maybe then the memory of his young brother would cease to haunt him.

But nothing obliterated or softened the memory. It haunted him still.

Often, when he was out alone, staring up at the heavens, he wondered what had happened to Joseph. Were the boy's bones bleached alongside the road to Egypt, or had he, by some miracle, survived the journey? If so, was he now a slave toiling under the desert sun, without hope or future?

No matter what Judah did, his life had the stench of ashes. He couldn't escape the result of his actions. It was too late to find and rescue his brother. Too late to save him from a life worse than death. Too late to undo the sin that poisoned his own life. He'd committed a sin so heinous, so unforgivable, he would go down to Sheol with it blackening his soul. Every time he saw his father, shame filled him. Regret choked him. He couldn't look into Jacob's eyes because he saw the unspoken question there: *What really happened in Dothan? What did you and your brothers do to my beloved son? Judah, when will you tell me the truth?*

And Judah could feel his brothers' eyes upon him, waiting, breath held in fear that he would confess.

Even now, after all the years that had passed, the old anger rose in him. The jealousy burned. He longed to cry out and shake off the mantle of shame. *If you knew us so well, Father, why did you send the boy? Why did you give him into our hands when you knew we hated him so much? Were you that blind?* And then the pain would return. Joseph hadn't been Jacob's favorite simply because he was the son of his father's favorite wife, Rachel. Joseph had deserved Jacob's love. The boy had always run to do his father's bidding, poured himself out to please him, while the rest always pleased themselves.

As much as Judah wanted to cast away the blame for getting rid of Joseph, it stuck like tar. Sin clung to him, soaked in, sank deep, until he felt his blood ran black with it. He was guilty, *and he knew it!*

And now Er's young wife was asking him about God. Judah didn't want to talk about God. He didn't want to think about Him.

Soon enough, he would face Him.

<hr>

Judah sent word to Onan and Shelah to bring the flocks home. Then he commanded Bathshua to prepare a feast.

"What for? It's not the new moon yet."

"I intend to discuss the future with my sons." He picked up his mantle and walked out into the night. He preferred the darkness and sounds of night creatures to the lamplight and carping sounds of his nagging wife.

Bathshua followed him outside. "They already know what the future holds! They've talked about it many times."

"They haven't talked with me!"

She put her hands on her hips. "What sort of trouble do you intend to bring upon my house now, Judah?"

He gritted his teeth. "Certain things need to be made clear."

"What things?" She was like a dog with a bone. She wouldn't let go.

"You'll know everything when they do."

"They're *my* sons. I know them better than you do! You could at least help me keep peace around here! Tell me what you plan to do. I will try to prepare them."

Judah glared back at her. "That's been the problem from the beginning, Bathshua. I've given you a free hand, and you've ruined *my* sons."

"*I've* ruined them! They're just like you: stubborn, foul tempered, constantly warring with one another! All they can think of is themselves!"

Judah strode away.

<hr>

Tamar had known from the beginning that the feast would end in disaster. Bathshua had spent the entire day burning incense on her private altar and praying to her gods while Tamar, Acsah, and the servants saw to the preparations for the feast Judah ordered. Her mother-in-law was in bad temper, more fractious than usual, tense and looking for trouble. Tamar didn't intend to make matters worse by asking why Bathshua was so distressed over a father gathering his sons to talk about the future.

Er provided a fattened lamb. Tamar overheard one of the servants say he'd probably stolen it, but Bathshua asked no questions. She quickly ordered it slaughtered and spitted for roasting. Fresh bread was made and placed in baskets. Fruit and nuts mounded on trays. Bathshua commanded that all the jugs be filled with wine.

"Water and milk will make for a more amicable evening," Tamar said. Er was given to excess and would undoubtedly drink until he was drunk. Surely Bathshua knew that as well as she did.

Bathshua sneered. "Men prefer wine. So we'll give them wine, and plenty of it."

"But, Bathshua – "

"Mind your own business! This is my house, and I'll do as I please." She moved around the room, kicking cushions into place. "Judah commanded a feast, and a feast he'll get. Whatever happens will be on his head!" Her eyes glittered with tempestuous tears.

Judah's sons began feasting before Judah returned to the house. Tamar thought Judah's temper would erupt when he saw them, but he took his place calmly and ate without saying a word. His sons had already taken the best morsels for themselves. Er was already drunk and in the midst of telling how one of his friends had tripped a blind man walking along the road to Timnah.

"You should have seen him scrambling around like a snake on its belly, trying to find his stick." He laughed and tossed some grapes into his mouth. "'Over there,' I'd say, 'over there,' and the old fool would grovel in the dust. He never even came close to the stick. He's probably still trying to find the road." He threw back his head and laughed, his mother joining in.

Tamar tried not to show her disgust.

Er held out his cup. "More wine, Wife." He made her title sound like an insult. As she poured, he looked at the others. "Wait until I tell you how I got the goat."

Judah tossed his bread back into the basket. "You've said enough. Now I have something to say."

Er grinned. "That's why we're all here, Father. To hear whatever it is you have to say."

"It isn't settled in my mind who will be my heir."

The words were like a lightning strike in the room. There was sudden silence, crackling tension. Tamar looked at the members of the family. Bathshua sat pale and tense, her hands balled into fists. Er's face, already flushed from too much wine, turned dark red. Onan's eyes glowed. Shelah was the least affected, already asleep from too much wine.

"*I'm* your heir," Er said. "I'm the firstborn!"

Judah looked at him calmly, his eyes steady and cool. "It's my decision. If I want to give everything to my servant, I can."

"How can you even suggest such a thing?" Bathshua cried out.

Judah ignored her, his gaze still fixed upon his eldest son. "The sheep don't prosper in your care. Nor does your wife."

Tamar felt the heat flood her face and then drain away as her husband and mother-in-law turned their attention to her. Both spoke at once. Er called her a foul name, while Bathshua came to his swift defense. "She has no right to complain!" Bathshua said, glaring at her.

"Tamar hasn't uttered a word of complaint," Judah said coldly, "but anyone with half a brain and eyes in his head can see the treatment she receives at *your* son's hands."

"If you're wondering about the bruise on her face, Father, she fell against the door a few days ago. Didn't you, Tamar? *Tell him!*"

"Perhaps you tripped her the same way you tripped that blind man along the road."

Er paled, but his eyes were like hot coals. "You're not going to take away what's mine."

"You still don't understand, Er, do you? Nothing belongs to you unless I say it does."

Tamar had never heard Judah speak so quietly or so coldly and with such authority. In this frame of mind, he was a man to be respected and feared. For the first time since she had entered his household, she admired him. She hoped he wouldn't weaken.

"Nothing will be taken from my hand unless I offer it," Judah said, his look encompassing Bathshua and her sons. "I gathered you here tonight to tell you that the one who proves himself the best shepherd will inherit my flocks."

"Is this a test?" Er was contemptuous. "Is that it?" He sneered. "Give the flocks to Onan now, if it pleases you, Father. Do you think it'll matter in the end? Onan is better with sheep, but I am better with a sword!"

"Do you see what you've done?" Bathshua cried out. "You've turned my sons against each other."

"After I'm gone, it's God who will decide what will happen."

"Yes," Er said, lifting his head as well as his cup. "Let the gods decide!" Wine sloshed over his hand as he proposed a toast. "In praise to the gods of Canaan! I vow to give my first daughter to the temple in Timnah and my first son to the fires of Molech!"

Tamar uttered a cry of despair at the same time Judah rose in anger. *"No!"*

She couldn't breathe. Would she conceive and bear children only to see them die in the flames of Topheth or perform intercourse on a public altar?

Er's pride burned white-hot. He rose as well and faced his father defiantly. "Do you think I care what you do? *My brothers will follow me,* Father. They will do as I do, or I will – " He stopped as though the breath had been drawn from him. His face changed; his eyes widened with fear. The cup dropped from his hand, splashing a red stain down the front of his fine tunic. He clutched at his chest.

Bathshua screamed. "Do something, Judah! *Help him!*"

Er tried to speak and couldn't. He clawed at his throat as though trying to pull hands away. Shelah, who had awakened at his mother's screaming, scrambled back, crying, while Onan watched Er drop to his knees. Judah reached out to his son, but Er pitched forward and fell facedown into the platter of roasted meat. He lay still.

"Er!" Bathshua said. "Oh, *Er!*"

Tamar was trembling violently, her heart galloping. She knew she should go to her husband's aid, but she was too afraid to move.

Bathshua pushed at Judah. "Leave my son alone. This is your fault!"

Judah shoved Bathshua back and went down on one knee. He put his hand against his son's neck. When he drew back, Tamar saw her own terror mirrored in his eyes. "He's dead."

"He can't be!" Bathshua said, pushing forward, falling to her knees beside Er. "You're wrong, Judah. He's drunk. He's just ... "

When Bathshua managed to roll him over, she saw his face and screamed.

three

TAMAR wept with Judah's family during the formal mourning period. Judah was convinced God had struck down his firstborn son, and Bathshua, refusing to believe it, was inconsolable. Onan pretended to grieve, but Tamar saw him talking and laughing with some of the young Canaanite men who had called themselves Er's friends.

Tamar was ashamed of her own feelings. She wanted to mourn Er as a wife should, but she found herself weeping more in relief than sorrow, for she'd despised her husband. He'd held her captive in fear, and now she was free! Mingled with her grief was a deep fear of the God of Judah, who clearly possessed the power of life and death. She was more deeply afraid of this God than she had been of any man. When the Lord, the God of Abraham, Isaac, and Jacob, had struck down Judah's eldest and most rebellious son, this God had also delivered her from a life of misery. One moment Er was breathing vows to sacrifice his children and lead his brothers astray, and the next he was dead!

Her emotions were so confused, for the truth of her situation came to roost and feast upon her thoughts. She was not delivered at all, for now she was a widow. Her situation was no better than before. In fact, it was worse! She had no husband, no son, no standing in this household. She couldn't go home. Unless Judah did what custom demanded and gave her Onan as a husband, Tamar knew she would never bear sons or daughters at all. Her life would be useless. She would live without hope.

Only a son could deliver her!

The days passed slowly, and Judah said nothing. Tamar was patient. She hadn't expected him to speak of the matter during the mourning period. He would do what he must, for he was wise enough to know he couldn't leave things as they were and have his household prosper and grow. Judah's clan needed sons and daughters, or his household would diminish and die out.

Her failure to provide children made her a failure as a woman. Judah had chosen her to bear children for his household, and her position was unchanged. She was still the girl Judah had chosen. Judah must give her Onan as a husband. Onan must sleep with her and provide a son to inherit Er's portion. It was the way of both Canaanite and Hebrew. Brother must uphold brother.

Knowing this, Tamar didn't spend her time worrying about when Judah would make the decision. Instead, she spent her time wondering about the God of the Hebrews. Her heart trembled when she considered the power He held. She was filled with questions but had no one to ask. Judah had made it clear he didn't want to talk about the God of his father.

So she rolled the questions over and over in her mind, seeking answers by herself and finding none. If God struck down Er for promising his children to the gods of Canaan, why hadn't He struck down Judah for allowing Bathshua to train up his sons in the worship of Baal? Or was the misery in Judah's life the curse laid upon him for some unknown act of rebellion? Judah had said once that the hand of God was against him. He was convinced; therefore, it must be true. Judah would know, wouldn't he? Fear filled Tamar at such thoughts, for if the hand of God was against Judah, what hope had any member of his family?

How do you soften the heart of a God who is angry with you? How do you placate Him when you don't know what He wants from you? What do you offer as sacrifice? What gift can you give? *Obedience,* Judah had said, but Tamar didn't know the rules to obey.

The fear of the Lord was upon her. Yet, even in her fear, Tamar felt strangely comforted. Er was no longer her master. Her fate was now in the hands of Judah. Not once during the year she'd been in this household had she ever seen her father-in-law offer sacrifices to the gods of Canaan. It was Bathshua who worshiped Baal and Asherah and a dozen others with fervent devotion. She was the one who poured out wine and oil, and cut herself. Judah kept his distance, and Bathshua never opened the cabinet where she kept her teraphim when Judah was within sight of it.

But Tamar had never seen Judah give offerings to his God either.

Did he do so when pasturing his sheep? Did he worship when he was with his father or his brothers? Her father-in-law never said anything one way or the other, and Tamar dared not inquire of Bathshua.

If the God of Judah allowed, she would bear children by Onan, and she would fulfill the hope Judah had to build up his household. Er was dead. She would take comfort in knowing her children would never be placed in the arms of Molech and rolled into the fires of Topheth, nor would they be trained up to perform lewd acts with a priest on a public altar dedicated to Astarte. They would grow up in the ways of Judah's father and not in the ways of her own. They would bow down to Judah's God and not bend to those of Bathshua.

Her heart cried out for this to be true, though nothing was certain. A year in Judah's household had taught Tamar that Bathshua had the upper hand. On the one occasion Judah had exerted his authority, his eldest son had rebelled and died.

She couldn't go to Judah and talk of these things. It was too soon, too painful. When Judah was ready, he would send for her. What else could he do? She was to be the child-bearer.

⨯⨯⨯

Judah pondered the future of his family. He knew what he had to do but still waited seventy days before summoning Tamar. When she stood before him in her black *tsaiph,* slender and dignified, her head up, he realized she had changed. Her face no longer bore the marks of ill treatment. Her skin was smooth and healthy. Yet it was more than that. Poised and calm, she looked at him. She was no longer the trembling child-bride he had brought home to Er.

Judah knew Tamar had never loved Er. She had submitted to Er, showing his son the respect due a husband. Though he knew she'd been beaten, Judah had never seen her cower like a dog. She had accepted her fate and worked hard to become part of his family. She had submitted to every command. She would accept his decision now and abide by it.

"I'm giving Onan to you as your husband so that you can bear a son for Er."

"My lord," she said and bowed down to him.

Judah wanted to say something, anything that might give the poor girl comfort and hope. But what could he say that wouldn't demean Er? No matter how bent upon evil his eldest son had been, Er was still the first fruit of Judah's loins, the first show of his strength as a man. He couldn't speak against Er without speaking against himself.

A blessing would ease his conscience. "May you be fruitful and multiply my house, Tamar." She would not suffer with Onan. As far as Judah knew, his second son took no pleasure in tormenting the helpless.

When Tamar rose to her feet, she lifted her head and looked at him. He was discomfited by the warmth in her eyes. He nodded. "You may go."

She turned away and then turned back again. "May I speak with you, my lord?" Something plagued her deeply.

He raised his brows.

"Since I am to bear children for your household, will you instruct me in the ways of your God?"

He stiffened. "When the time comes, I will speak to Onan about it."

"Surely the time is long past."

He clenched his fists. "Do you dare reprimand me?"

"No, my lord," she said in confusion. She paled. "I beg your pardon. I only meant ... "

He saw the tears well in her eyes but ignored her appeal. "Leave me." Closing his eyes, he jerked his head in command. He heard her quick retreating footsteps.

Why did Tamar always have to ask about God? What could he tell her? God had struck Er for his cruel arrogance and taken vengeance upon Judah as well. An eye for an eye, a life for a life. Er for Joseph.

Judah raked his fingers through his hair, then held his head. Perhaps now the past could be laid to rest.

"This is what he requires: to do what is right, to love mercy, and to walk humbly with your God." His father's words came to him as though Jacob had leaned close and whispered them.

Agitated, Judah rose and left the house.

⊱⊰⊱⊰

Tamar returned to her quarters and told Acsah what had been said. Onan was to sleep with her and give her children for Er.

"Judah spoke with me eight days ago," Acsah said. "He has been counting the days."

Tamar blushed.

Acsah smiled at her. "Onan is a better man than Er. He won't beat you."

Tamar lowered her eyes. Onan was as handsome as Er. He could speak as smoothly. He might also have fists like hammers. She breathed in slowly. She couldn't allow herself to dwell on fear. Fear might prevent conception.

Despite her resolve, her stomach quivered with misgivings. She had no reason to expect tender treatment from Onan. Why should she? He kept company with the same young men Er did.

Acsah took her by the shoulders. "Be joyful, Tamar. Judah's taken your side against Bathshua."

Tamar shrugged her hands away. "Don't be foolish, Acsah. There are no sides to this matter. It is but a thing of necessity."

"A thing of necessity? How you talk! Your mother-in-law has burned Judah's ear for weeks regarding you. She didn't want Onan in the same room with you, let alone the same bed."

"Can you blame her? I would grieve as much if I'd lost a son."

"Or a loving husband." She lowered her voice to a conspiratorial whisper. "We're all well rid of Er."

Tamar turned away, unwilling to agree.

Acsah sighed. "You must be careful, Tamar. Bathshua seeks someone to blame."

Tamar sat on a cushion. "Then she must look to the God of Judah."

"She suspects *you*. She claims you cast a spell."

Tamar glanced up sharply. "What power have I to help or hinder anyone in this household? I am nothing! What did I have to gain by my husband's death? Am I better off now with my husband dead?" She shook her head and looked away. "No one will believe Bathshua. Everyone heard Er reject the God of his father, and everyone saw how he died."

Acsah hunkered down before her. "Do you think that matters?" She took Tamar's hands and held them tightly. "Much of the blame for Er's character can be laid at his mother's feet, but do you think she will ever accept it?"

Tamar pulled her hands from Acsah's and covered her face. "I did nothing to harm Er!" She drew a ragged breath, tears welling despite her efforts to quell them. "What sort of household is this that everyone seeks to destroy each other?"

Acsah pressed her fingertips against Tamar's lips. "I know you did nothing to harm Er. So does Judah. Not once did you ever speak against Er. Everyone knew he beat you, and they all looked the other way."

"Then how can you say ... ?"

"You're too young to understand the ways of people like Bathshua. She's jealous. She's afraid of losing her position. So she lies. A lie told often enough will eventually be accepted as truth."

"I can only be what I am, Acsah!" Tears ran down her cheeks. "I can only live the best way I know how."

Acsah cupped her cheek. "Be at peace, my sweet one. You have prevailed. Judah has given Onan to you. It shows he believes the god of his father took his son's life despite Bathshua's claims that you had a part in it. But be warned: She is as cunning as a serpent. She will be silent now that Judah has made his decision. For a while she will do nothing. But never forget: She is your enemy."

"As she always has been, Acsah."

"More now than ever, but Judah will protect you."

With a sad laugh, Tamar shook her head. "Judah stands neither to the right nor to the left of me. He stands alone, just as he always has. All he's done is take the necessary steps to preserve his family." She turned away, not wanting Acsah to see her hurt and disappointment. Judah had refused to instruct her in the ways of his God, even though this God clearly had the power of life and death. "I am more burdened now than I was the day I came here, Acsah. I want this household to prosper. I want to fulfill my duty."

"You will."

"If I have children."

"When, not if." Acsah smiled. "Onan will give you a child. I've no doubt of that."

Tamar didn't share her confidence. Onan was, after all, Er's brother.

❧❧❧

Acsah was pleased that Judah had finally settled the matter. Her heart ached as she witnessed the indifference in this household. No one in this household deserved Tamar. She was lovely and sweet, hardworking, loyal. Acsah's heart sometimes swelled with pride as she watched the way the girl conducted herself with dignity, especially when faced with Bathshua's slights, insults, and outbursts. There were times when Acsah had had to bite her tongue so she would not speak her mind and cause Tamar more trouble.

Judah had delayed long enough in giving Onan to Tamar. Acsah had begun to fear that Bathshua had succeeded in poisoning him against Tamar. She loved Tamar as dearly as she would have loved any child of her own womb, and it angered her to watch how she was treated.

Acsah had rejoiced when Judah sought her out and asked about Tamar's health. He'd been uncomfortable. She'd understood what he was really asking and spared him further embarrassment. "The best time for conception would be in ten days."

"Ten days. You're certain?"

"Yes, my lord." Acsah hadn't neglected her duty toward Tamar or Judah's household. The girl had no secrets from her. It was Acsah's duty to watch over Tamar's health. She knew the days of her cycle. She counted them from the full moon so that she would know precisely which days offered greatest fertility.

Even though the matter of Onan was settled, Acsah was worried about Tamar's mood. Tamar was pensive and secretive. Before, she had always shared her thoughts and feelings. Acsah knew it was because the girl was becoming a woman, but it hurt to be excluded even in these small ways. She adored the girl and sought only the best for her. How could she lift her spirits when she didn't know what Tamar was thinking? She pressed, but Tamar resisted. She wouldn't say what was wrong. Acsah could only assume it was fear at the prospects of physical intimacy with Onan. And she could easily understand that, considering the heartless treatment her dear girl had suffered at Er's hands. Acsah had been afraid for her and distressed about what to do without causing more trouble for her. A bruise now and then was common enough, but harder blows could cause internal injuries and permanent damage. And then what would become of Tamar?

But Er was dead now. Secretly, Acsah rejoiced. The wretched boy had only gotten what he deserved. He would never lay another hand upon Tamar, and Acsah was thankful to whatever god had struck him down. Countless times she had wished *she* had the power to do it. She had had to plug her ears to keep from going mad when she heard Tamar's muted cries of pain behind closed doors.

Tamar need not fear Onan. Judah's second son was different from the first. Onan was shrewd and ambitious. He tended his father's flocks as though they were already his own. Acsah suspected Onan coveted more than his brother's inheritance. He'd coveted his brother's wife as well. Acsah had noticed the way the boy looked at Tamar. Perhaps the boy's lust would turn to love, and Tamar's life would be easier.

Most assuredly, Onan would be eager to fulfill his duty to her. The first son Tamar bore would be for Er, but others would follow. They would belong to Onan. Acsah could hardly wait for the day to come when she would help Tamar bring a child into the world. Oh, to see her lovely smile bloom again, to hear her laugh, to see her eyes shine with happiness! Tears sprang to Acsah's eyes just thinking about it.

Taking her broom and basket, Acsah entered the room where Tamar and Onan would lie together. She set the basket by the door and worked vigorously. She chanted as she did so, exorcising the divine assembly from the room. Some spirits liked to hinder desire and prevent conception. They must be swept out and prevented from coming back. It was Acsah's duty to see to this. She must protect the young couple and open the way to unfettered lovemaking.

Acsah took great care in her work. She made sure every inch of the walls, ceiling, and floor were swept. Then she mixed mortar and caulked the holes in the stone wall so that evil spirits couldn't enter through them. She brought in rush mats and laid them out neatly over the earthen floor. She filled small lamps with scented oil and placed trays of incense in each of the four corners of the room. The air of the bedchamber would be permeated with a sweet musky fragrance that would stir the senses and stimulate desire. She took a mandrake from her basket and shaved off slivers of the precious root into a cup beside a jug of wine. Mandrake would increase Tamar's fertility. Last, she took out a woven cloth and spread it over the mat where the couple would lie together.

Standing in the doorway, Acsah scrutinized every aspect of the room. She must make certain everything was in place, nothing forgotten. Voices and music came from the main room. The wedding feast had begun. Soon she would lead the couple to this chamber.

As a last precaution, Acsah entered the room again and took fine ground flour from a pouch at her waist. She cast it over the floor from the edge of the walls to the doorway. With every sweep of her arm, she chanted incantations to drive spirits from the room. She wasn't satisfied until a thin layer of flour covered everything. If any spirits returned, she would see footprints in the pale dust and be warned of their presence.

Acsah closed the door firmly. She filled in the crack around the door until the room was sealed.

Finally, satisfied, she sat and rested. She would give Tamar an hour more to celebrate. Perhaps a cup or two of wine would make Tamar relax and enjoy herself. Smiling, Acsah murmured prayers to her gods. Soon she would lead the young couple to the bedchamber. She would make sure no spirits had entered, and then she would close the door behind Onan and Tamar and remain on guard against the spirits who might try to hinder conception. She would sit against the closed door and she would play her small drum, and she would sing a song to drive demons away and make young hearts beat with passion. If the jealous spirits could be kept from the house long enough, Tamar would conceive. And then, finally, this girl Acsah loved and served would be given the respect she was due as a child-bearer.

Tamar soon learned that Onan was different from Er: His evil was more cunning.

Even while Tamar's head swam with wine and her senses with the scents of sweet herbs and sound of Acsah's drum, she knew the exact moment Er's brother denied her the chance of a child. She cried out, but he covered her mouth with his own, silencing her protest. She struggled fiercely and wrenched free, clambering away from him.

"You've dishonored me!" She snatched her garment and covered herself. "And betrayed your own brother!"

Onan sat up, breathing heavily. "I promise, I'll treat you better than Er ever did."

"And this is better?"

"I'll treat you with kindness and ... "

Kindness? Er had abused her. Now Onan was using her. "We're together for one purpose: to conceive a son for Er."

Onan stretched out on his side. "What's wrong with enjoying ourselves?"

Tamar glared at him without response.

Onan's eyes narrowed. "Stop looking at me like I'm an insect you found under a rock."

"You must fulfill your duty to my dead husband, your brother."

"I *must?*" Onan's face darkened. "Who are you to tell me I must?"

"You know who I am and what my position is in this house. Will you do what is right or not?"

"I promise to take care of you. You'll always have a roof over your head and food to eat. I'll give you all you require."

Her face went hot. Did he really think she would allow him to treat her like a prostitute? She could hardly stand to look at him. "There's only one thing I require of you, Onan, and you've spilled that on the ground!" She flung his discarded tunic at him.

Slipping into it, Onan blushed, but his eyes remained calculating. "Er said you were stubborn. You could try to understand my situation."

She wasn't a fool. She knew exactly what he was after. She had known Onan was covetous, but she'd never expected this abominable injustice. "You want Er's double portion as well as your own!" Onan was filled with avarice.

"Why shouldn't I have it all? I've worked for it!"

"You have your portion. You have no right to Er's. It belongs to his son."

He smirked. "What son?"

Her eyes pricked with angry tears. "You will *not* have your way in this, Onan. I am not a harlot to be used."

"Be reasonable, Tamar. Did Er ever care for the flocks as I have? Have I hit you or called you names? Did he ever show kindness toward you? Even once? All my brother ever did was cause you grief!"

"It doesn't matter how he treated me or anyone else! He is your father's eldest son. Er was firstborn. You must fulfill your duty to your brother, or his line will die! Do you think Judah won't grieve over what you've done tonight?"

"Don't tell him."

"I won't join you in this sin. What future have I if you have your way?"

"The future I give you."

"And I should trust a man who denies his brother an heir?"

Onan stood, annoyed. "Er's name should be wiped out! He deserved to die! We're all better off without him!"

Tamar was shocked by his hatred. "You mustn't deny me my rights, Onan. If you do, you cheat your father's entire household."

Jaw tight, Onan made a sound of disdain. "You don't know what I suffered at my brother's hands. Every time my mother looked the other way, Er was using his fists on me. I'm glad he's dead. If you want to know the truth, I rejoiced when Er choked to death. It gave me pleasure to watch him die. I wanted to laugh and dance!" He smiled down at her mockingly. "As I'm sure you did."

"Don't include me in your wickedness. Er's portion doesn't belong to you. It belongs to the son he might have had, the son you *must* give me."

Onan lay down again and propped himself up on one elbow. "And if I won't?"

"You can't really mean to deny me, Onan. Would you have Er's name go down into the dust with him?" It was as though he sought to murder his own brother.

"That's where his name belongs."

What Onan was doing was worse than murder! He was denying existence to all of Er's descendants down through the ages. If he had his way, she would never bear children. What would become of her then?

"Please, Onan. You mustn't do this. Give thought to what you do!"

"I have thought about it. It's *my* name I care about, not his."

"What sort of man are you that you would destroy the household of your own brother?"

"What brother? What household?" He laughed softly. He took the edge of her wrap and rubbed it between his fingers. "I'm a man who intends to hold on to what belongs to him." He grinned. "I can make you happy. Would you like me to show you how?"

Tamar yanked her wrap from him and withdrew even farther. She wanted to scream at Acsah to stop beating the drum and singing. This night was a mockery!

Onan's expression cooled. "Be satisfied with what I'm offering you."

His avarice sickened her. "I won't keep silent."

"What can you do?" He mocked her just as Er had done.

"I can speak to Judah."

Onan laughed. "Go ahead. Father won't do anything. He never does anything. Besides, it will be your word against mine, and who will believe you, Tamar? My mother hates you with every breath she takes. Moreover, she's convinced you cast a spell upon my brother and caused his death." His smile derided her. "All I have to say is I gave my all to fulfill my duty, but the gods have closed your womb."

She blinked back tears. "I will tell your father the truth, and may the God of Judah judge between you and me!" She rose, intending to leave the room.

Onan lunged for her. She tried to dodge him, but he grasped her ankle. When she tried to kick free, he swept her feet out from under her. She came down hard, and he pinned her against the rush mats scattered on the earthen floor Acsah had taken such care in sweeping.

"Be satisfied with what you have, girl, for you will have no more of me than I intend to give! And when my father dies, you won't even have that much unless you make an effort to please me!"

Tamar drew in a sobbing breath and turned her face away. Onan eased his grip on her. "Shhhh ... " He caressed her cheek and kissed her throat. "There now, my sweet little bride. Don't cry." His touch repulsed her. "Everyone's glad Er's dead and gone. You should be too." He cupped her face and made her look at him. "I still want you, Tamar. I've wanted you since the day you came here. And now you're mine." When he tried to kiss her, she jerked her face away. Gritting her teeth, Tamar shut her eyes tightly and didn't move.

"Make up your mind to enjoy things as they are. They won't change."

"I'd rather be dead."

Onan cursed. "Don't tempt me." The rush mats rustled softly as he moved away from her. "Have it your own way. Have *nothing.*" He fell asleep within minutes, his conscience not the least disturbed.

Tamar slept in the corner, her hands over her head, while Acsah went on singing love songs outside the door.

⋙⋘

Tamar spent the night gathering her nerve. She was resolved to fight the injustice done her. It was within her rights, and she must gather the courage to do so. Surely Judah would defend her. Without children, his family would dwindle and die out. The wind would blow away the name of Judah as though it were dust. She must take courage. She must be strong. She would have to speak up for herself because the sons in this wretched household cared only about themselves!

She went to Judah before Onan was even awake. She told her father-in-law exactly what his son had done. She presented the cloth Acsah had placed upon the rush mat to prove her statement. Judah's face turned dark red.

"You've had only one night with Onan! He'll come to his senses. Give him time."

Time? Was that all Judah could say? He should be furious that his son had intended to deceive him. Onan was sinning against the entire household! His actions were clear, his motivation pure greed, and his crime equal to murder. How could Judah overlook this sin against his family? No matter how many times Er had abused her, she couldn't allow her dead husband to be so dishonored. Did she have to scream from the rooftop to make him call Onan to account?

"I will not allow Onan to touch me under these circumstances. I cannot!"

Judah's eyes flashed. "Who are you to tell me what will or will not go on in *my* household?"

"How can I allow this? I'm the wife of your firstborn son! Would you see Er's name die because Onan refused to do his duty?"

"Be silent, girl!"

Anger filled her. "I am a woman, Judah, and shouting at me will not drown out the truth of this humiliation!" She knew Judah didn't want to be pressed by anyone, but it was her right, indeed, her *obligation* to bear children. "Why do you thwart me? It's in all our interests that sons be born!" What would become of Judah's tribe if things were allowed to continue in such an immoral manner as this? "Land cannot be worked without children. Flocks cannot be tended without children."

"I don't need you to tell me that!"

Judah roared like a wounded lion, but Tamar refused to back down.

Judah was not like Er. He wouldn't use his fists upon a woman. And she could take hot wind any day. "It is my right to have children!"

Judah turned his face away, the muscle working in his jaw. "Very well," he said grudgingly. "I'll speak to Onan when I get around to it. In the meantime, let things be as they are." He raised his hand when she started to protest. "Let me finish! Given time, my son may come to love you. Have you thought of that? You might work toward that end instead of causing him trouble. Do whatever you can to make him love you. If Onan loves you, he'll do right by you of his own accord, without my saying a word."

Her cheeks burned. Just as Onan had said, Judah would do nothing. He would go off to tend his sheep and leave it in her hands to woo righteousness from Onan!

"Do you know so little of your own sons, Judah?" Er had been incapable of love, and Onan was eaten up with jealousy and avarice, his only ambition to grasp everything he could now that his older brother was dead and couldn't protect himself. Judah might as well have said it straight out: It was up to her to protect her husband's birthright and portion. It was up to her to find a way to have a child.

"I know my sons," Judah said grimly, glaring at her.

She fought her tears, for she knew Judah would have no respect for her if she shed them. "Why do you refuse to confront the sin that goes on before your eyes? You never called Er to account, and now you look the other way while Onan refuses – "

"Don't tell me how to run my life or my family!"

"I would never assume to usurp Bathshua's place!"

Judah's eyes widened in surprise, and then his face paled in rage. "You've said enough." He spoke with deadly calm.

Tamar saw his anger and didn't care. If he wanted to hit her, let him. She'd been hit before, and in this household she had no doubt she would be hit again. She would not face this lion like one of his sheep!

"When you gave the bride-price to my father, a covenant was made between you." It was all she could do to speak in quiet reason and not scream out her frustration. "I became the wife of your son Er, and as your son's wife, I became *your daughter*. Will you allow me to be treated like a harlot? Surely a man who defended his sister against the prince of Shechem – "

"Those circumstances were entirely different!" he interrupted, his face white.

Tamar realized she had torn open an old wound and tried to make amends.

"I'm part of your family, Judah." Clearly, he didn't embrace her as a daughter, but he still owed her consideration. He couldn't allow her rights to be trodden beneath Onan's feet.

"Be patient, Tamar. I've lost Er. I don't want to battle Onan." He groaned in frustration. "There must be some other way!"

There was, but she loathed mentioning it. He must know as well as she did the only other alternative open to them. She swallowed hard, her cheeks going hot. "If you prefer, you can follow Canaanite custom and perform the duty yourself."

His head came up. Clearly, he thought her suggestion as repugnant as she did. "I'm Hebrew, not Canaanite."

"I meant no offense."

"If you were a woman fully grown, you could make Onan forget himself instead of dumping your problem in my lap!"

Her eyes welled with hurt tears. She was woman enough to conceive. That's all that was required of her. Or had he forgotten? Did she have to become wily and devious in order to fulfill her duty to *his* dead son? Did Judah expect her to behave like a harlot and take from Onan what he should freely give? Perhaps Judah expected her to run to her sister in Timnah and ask for instructions in the erotic arts! Perhaps she should adorn herself in veils and bells so Onan would be so overcome by lust that he would forget his greed and unwittingly fulfill his obligation!

Tamar trembled in anger.

Once again, Judah would turn away from his responsibilities. He wanted her to plot and scheme and entice Onan into doing what was right to save himself trouble.

"I will not play the harlot."

"Why not?" He gave a cynical laugh. "Women have done it for years."

"When will you do what is right?"

"Get out!"

Tamar fled the house in tears. Acsah followed. "What's happened, Tamar? What were you and Judah shouting about?"

Tamar took up her hoe and began beating the ground with it. Tears coursed down her cheeks, and she dashed them away and went on working.

"Tell me, Tamar. Did Onan mistreat you? Is he like Er after all?"

"Leave me alone, Acsah. Just let me work in peace." She would not pile further humiliation upon herself by sharing her shame and Judah's cowardice.

Once again the conjugal room was prepared, for there were still six days remaining in the wedding week. Onan was in even higher spirits, sure that he had won his way. He held his head up like a triumphant warrior and took Tamar's hand as Acsah led them once again to the bedchamber. Tamar went willingly, hoping he would repent and fulfill his duty.

He did not.

While he slept, Tamar sat weeping in the farthest corner of the room, her head covered with her black *tsaiph*. She was bereft, overcome with shame and humiliation. Onan was destroying her hope for an honorable future. If he had his way, she would never bear children for Judah's household. She might as well be dead!

It wasn't until the sun rose that Tamar found death *had* come.

And taken Onan.

four

THE household was in an uproar, and Tamar was in the middle. Those who hadn't believed Bathshua's stories about Tamar being somehow responsible for Er's death were now convinced she was responsible for Onan's. Even Tamar began to wonder if she was somehow to blame. Two husbands dead in a year's time? What ill fortune! How could this be? Her emotions were in tatters. Both Er and Onan had been wicked, but there were many wicked men who were walking and talking and carrying on as usual. Why had her husbands been singled out?

Tamar's throat closed hot; her eyes burned. She was innocent. She'd had nothing to do with these strange deaths, but rumors were rampant. Gossip ripped the household into factions, and Bathshua gossiped most of all. How could her mother-in-law call her a witch? She had never cast a spell or uttered an incantation. She wanted to defend herself, but every time she started to speak, she would see the look on others' faces and know it was no use. They already believed the lies and were afraid.

Tamar was afraid too. From the day she had entered this household, she'd been treated like a despised slave. Everyone knew Er had abused her, and yet no one had uttered a word of compassion or lifted a finger to help her. And now, even though Onan had used her for his selfish pleasure and had denied her right to mother an heir who would claim Er's portion, everyone believed she had wished him dead. It wasn't true! She had come into this household hoping to be a good wife and to bear children. It was the God of Judah's father who had struck these young men down. Hadn't Judah said as much himself the day Er died?

But Judah didn't say that anymore.

Judah didn't say *anything!* He brooded and guzzled wine to forget his troubles while Bathshua filled his ears with lies. Tamar knew it must be easier for her father-in-law to think she was at fault than believe his God was destroying his family. Who would be next? Shelah? Bathshua?

When Judah looked at her, she saw his anger, his suspicion. He sought someone to blame for his wretchedness. And everyone in the household pointed to her. That made it easier for Judah to cast blame as well.

Bathshua's hatred permeated the house. Tamar couldn't get away from it. Even when she was working outside, Tamar sensed Bathshua's malice. "I want her out of this house and away from my family!"

Didn't Bathshua understand that by stoking the fires that already burned, she was destroying her household? Why not plead with the God of Judah for mercy? Why not inquire of Jacob what must be done to turn the winds in their favor? Why did Judah sit and brood in silence and let his family fall apart around him?

Acsah urged Tamar repeatedly, "Try to speak with him, Tamar."

"I cannot. I won't respond to Bathshua's lies, even to defend myself."

"Everyone is against you!"

"If the God of Judah took Er and Onan, what can I do to make things right? It's up to Judah. He's the head of this house."

"Bathshua is the head."

"Judah has allowed it! Whatever happens to me is in his hands. All I can do is wait and see what he will do." Despite what people thought or said about her, custom still required Shelah to give her children. But would Judah follow through now that his second son was dead? Would he entrust Shelah to her with two sons already in the grave?

Tamar wept in secret at the cruel things said about her, but she maintained her composure in the presence of others. Even if she were to grovel and cower and plead before Bathshua, it wouldn't change the woman's blackened heart. Tamar strove to maintain her dignity before her enemies.

The mourning period passed, and the weeks wore on.

Tamar waited. Sooner or later her father-in-law would have to make a decision.

Judah allowed seventy-five days to pass before he summoned Tamar. He had done nothing but think about the girl over the past weeks. She had a right to Shelah and children, but he was afraid his last son would die if he married her. Bathshua insisted Tamar was evil and casting spells, but why would the girl do such things? She needed sons to provide for her. She needed a husband to give her those sons. Why kill her best chances for a secure future? As a childless widow, she had no hope.

Bathshua remained bitter and adamant. "Don't give her my last son! I'll hate you for the rest of my life if you do! She mustn't have Shelah!" When Bathshua wasn't railing and threatening, she was seeking the counsel of her teraphim. The house was stifling with the cloying scent of incense. Every other day some medium was coming to the door, claiming to have messages from the dead.

"Get rid of Tamar." Bathshua was rabid. "Get that evil girl out of my house!"

Judah had never seen Tamar cast a spell or utter a single incantation, but that didn't mean she hadn't. She might not be as open as his wife, who had never made a secret of her passion for Canaanite deities.

Judah knew God had taken Er and that He had taken Onan as well. Perhaps, if he had done as Tamar asked and confronted Onan for his sin ... Judah didn't think long on that possibility. God may have struck down his sons, but the girl was a bad omen. She'd been nothing but trouble since he brought her into his house. If he got rid of her, perhaps he would have some peace.

Shelah was the only son Judah had left. Bathshua was right. The boy must be protected. Tamar was the one constant in the midst of the disasters that had befallen his household. Judah couldn't risk Shelah's life by giving him to her. Besides, Shelah was afraid of Tamar. Bathshua had convinced the boy he would die if he lay with Tamar.

"When will you do what is right, Judah?"

Tamar's words pricked his conscience, but he hardened his heart against them. He was only protecting his family. Why should he give his last son to this dangerous girl? Why take any risk? Why drive a bigger wedge between himself and his wife? Why cause himself more grief?

Besides, Tamar was probably barren anyway. In all the months she'd been with Er, she hadn't conceived. She hadn't been desirable enough to sway Onan. Why should he waste Shelah on this wretched little witch? Shelah was his last surviving son, his only heir, his last hope. He wouldn't do it!

Judah sent for his son. "Go to Hirah and remain in Adullam until I send for you."

Relieved of his duty, Shelah praised his father's decision and obeyed with alacrity. Judah felt a twinge of shame, but it quickly disappeared. He'd protect his son, even at the cost of his own honor.

~~~

Tamar knew something more had gone wrong when Acsah came out to her and worked in disheartened silence. "What is it, Acsah? What's happened?"

"Judah sent Shelah away this morning."

Tamar's heart sank. "He must have sent him to see about the flocks."

"The flocks are not anywhere near Adullam, Tamar. That's where Shelah has gone."

Tamar looked at the ground she was working. "There's nothing I can do but wait, Acsah. And hope."

"Indeed, there is nothing you can do." Acsah wept.

When Judah sent for her, Tamar went eagerly, hoping he would have some explanation. However, the moment she saw her father-in-law, she knew Acsah was right. Shelah was gone, and there was nothing to be done about it.

"I've made a difficult decision," Judah said slowly, unable to look her in the eyes. "Shelah is too young to take on the responsibilities of a husband."

Shelah was two years older than she was, but Tamar didn't quibble. Judah was making excuses. They both knew it. Arguing with him now would only set his heart against her. Let Bathshua browbeat him with lies. The truth would become clear in time. She would be obedient. She would be patient. She would behave with dignity, even if he behaved with cowardice. Time was her ally. Time and necessity. Judah needed her. Er needed a son to carry on the family line. If Judah failed to grant Tamar the right to bear that son, he would be a man who had forsaken all honor. Could such a man ever be trusted?

"When Shelah is older, I will send for you."

Tamar blinked, confused. "Send for me?" What did he mean? She searched his face and saw his eyes grow hard.

"Bathshua is having your things packed as we speak. She will have one of the servants take you and your nurse back to your father's house."

"My father's house? But, my lord, this is – "

"Don't argue!" Judah wouldn't even allow her to open her mouth in her own defense. "This is best. You will remain in your father's house as a widow until I call for you."

"Best?" She was cold with shock. "Am I to be cast out for the sins done against *me?*"

"You're not being expelled. You're going home."

"*This* is my home. As cold and inhospitable as it's always been!"

"Say nothing more against my family. It's for their sakes I make this decision. Your presence has turned my household into a battlefield."

"You are *unjust!*" She began to cry, shaming herself completely.

He looked away. "Resorting to tears won't change my mind," he said coldly.

Anger spurred her. "Do you think my father will welcome me with open arms?" She struggled for control over her unraveling emotions. "A widow twice over? Childless? Rejected and cast out?"

Judah was implacable. "Tell him I want you to remain a widow in his house until Shelah has grown up. When that day comes, I will send for you."

Tamar lifted her head and stared into his eyes. "Will you?"

"I said I would."

She refused to look away. Let him see the faith she had in him now that he had forsaken her.

Judah's face reddened and his eyes shifted. "You don't believe me?"

She gave him no answer, though she wondered. When had she ever seen Judah do what was right?

"I promise you!" he said quickly. "There! Now will you go without more distress?"

Content with that, Tamar did as he commanded.

Bathshua stood just outside the door, triumphant and pitiless. "Your nurse is waiting for you outside." Fighting tears, Tamar stepped past her, but Bathshua wasn't satisfied. She followed Tamar to the door and stood watching. "We're well rid of you!"

Tamar didn't look back. Nor did she look at Acsah, afraid that if she did so, she'd burst into tears and give Bathshua even more satisfaction. "Judah is sending us back to my father."

Acsah's eyes flashed. "I shall lay a curse upon Bathshua and her household." She stepped forward, but Tamar grasped her arm, yanking her back.

"You will not! This is my home, my family. No matter what Judah thinks, this is where I belong."

Acsah's eyes filled with angry tears. "They do not deserve you," she said under her breath.

"Judah chose me, Acsah. I will live in hope of being worthy of his choice. If you must speak, say prayers on his family's behalf."

No servant was given to accompany or protect them. They were given two small barley loaves and a skin of water to share.

When Tamar was well out of sight of the house, she fell to her knees and sobbed. Filling her hands with dust, she covered her head. Unable to console her, Acsah wept as well.

It was only eight miles to Zimran's house. The hot sun was heavy upon them, but not as heavy as their hearts. It was dusk before Tamar arrived at her father's door. He was not pleased to see her.

≈≈≈

Zimran ordered everyone out. Tamar's mother, Acsah, her sisters and brothers all hastened to obey. She wished she could flee her father's wrath as well. She had no choice but to stand silent as he unleashed his fury upon her. Perhaps, in the end, he would show mercy.

"I gave you to Judah's son so that you would bear children for him and keep peace between us! You have failed me! You have failed us all!"

She must keep her wits about her, or she was lost. "Judah gave me his word that he would send for me when Shelah is old enough to fulfill his duty to me."

Zimran turned a scornful eye upon her. "And you believed that Hebrew? You fool! Shelah is only a few years younger than Er. Three or four at the most! And now Judah says Shelah isn't old enough yet to father children? *Ha!* If he's too young, why take him to the sheepshearing? You should have insisted upon your rights!"

She stumbled under the blow of his hand, falling to her knees. "I did all I could, Father."

"Not enough!" Zimran paced, his face red, his hands balled. "You should have remained in his house rather than come back here. What good are you to me? You bring shame upon my house!"

Tamar pressed a hand over her throbbing cheek. Her heart pounded with fear. She must not give in to it. She must *think.* "Judah promised, Father. He *promised."*

"So what? What good are vows with a Hebrew? The Hebrews made an agreement with Shechem, didn't they? Look what happened to them!" He stood over her. "You're no longer my responsibility! If Judah doesn't want you in his house, why should I want you in mine? You'll bring us all ill fortune!"

She must survive. "If you're willing to risk it, Father, ignore Judah's wishes. Cast me out!"

"Judah's wishes? What wishes?"

"To build his household." Was her father still afraid of Judah? She could only hope so. "Will Bathshua bear more sons for Judah, Father? She's dry as dust and cold as stone. Can Judah give Shelah to another woman before he's fulfilled his obligation to me? Judah wants to build his household, and I'm the one he chose to be the child-bearer. Has anything changed?"

Her father's eyes flickered. "If Judah meant to keep his word, he wouldn't have sent you here. He sent you back because he wants to be rid of you. Everyone will know Judah thinks a daughter of my house is the cause of his ill fortune!"

How her father's words stung! Her eyes burned hot with tears.

"Give Judah time to grieve, Father. Give him time to think!"

"Time! All the advantages I gained with your marriage are lost to me! Do you think Judah will bring his flocks to my fields with you here? I'll have to find other shepherds to bring their flocks and herds, or my land will go unnourished." He glowered at her. "You're useless! You're a plague on my house! I have other daughters who need husbands! Will any man offer for the sister of an accursed woman like you? Judah would probably consider it a favor if I killed you!"

The cruel, thoughtless words rained down upon Tamar and hurt her far worse than blows. She quaked inwardly but dared not show weakness. "As you wish, Father. Strike me down. And when Judah sends for me so that his son can have sons, tell him, 'I killed Tamar in a fit of rage!'"

"I'll cast you out the same way he did."

"He sent me home to my father for safekeeping. Will you tell Judah you rejected me? Will you tell this Hebrew warrior that his daughter-in-law was sent away to glean in other men's fields, beg bread, and prostitute herself in order to survive? I'm certain Judah will understand. Hebrews are easily swayed, aren't they? They're given to mercy. They forgive a wrong done to them. My father-in-law will be as merciful to you as you are to me!"

He was listening. Tamar pressed her advantage. "If I'm ruined and made unfit for Shelah, what will happen to Judah's household? I will always be Judah's daughter-in-law. Shelah is Judah's *last* son, Father. Is Judah the sort of man who will let his household die for want of children? He *chose* me!" She paused, giving him a thoughtful look. "Unless you wish to return the bride-price."

Her father paled.

She softened her voice. "Judah has asked a simple thing of you, Father. Give me food, water, and shelter for a time and receive his blessing for it."

"How much time?"

"A few years, perhaps. Whatever time Shelah needs to become man enough to be my husband."

The root of fear had been deeply planted in her father. That fear must be the hedge of protection around her. "You want Judah as an ally, Father, not an enemy. You are not strong enough to stand against him."

He sneered, his eyes cunning. "He is but one man and has but one son now."

A chill washed over her. Had she jeopardized Judah's household by reminding her father of their dwindling numbers? She could see what he was thinking. He had six sons. Her mind raced in Judah's defense. "Judah has many brothers, many fierce brothers. And their father is Jacob, a man who speaks with the unseen, living God who destroyed Sodom and Gomorrah. Don't forget what Jacob's sons did to Shechem. An entire town was destroyed because of the dishonor done one girl. Am I not Judah's daughter now, wife of his firstborn, Er, wife of Onan, promised wife of his last son, Shelah? What will Judah's God do to you if you attempt to destroy his household?"

Zimran paled. He wet his lips nervously. "You will work," he said with bluster. "You won't sit around growing fat and lazy on his promise. You will be a servant in my house until such time as he calls for you."

She bowed her head so that he wouldn't see her relief. "I am your humble servant, Father."

"I had such hope you would build a bridge," he said bitterly. "The stars did not foresee the trouble you would bring me."

Her throat was tight with tears. She swallowed them and spoke with grave respect. "One day Judah will thank you."

Zimran gave a bitter laugh. "I doubt it, but I'll take no risks over a mere girl. You will sleep with the handmaidens. You're unfit company for your sisters."

Tamar knew he sought to hurt her because she'd failed him. She raised her head and looked at him. He frowned slightly and looked away. "You may go."

She rose from the floor with dignity. "May the God of Judah bless you for your kindness toward me."

His eyes narrowed. "Before you go, there's something I want you to think about." His eyes were hard. "You're young. Soon your widow's garb will chafe you. The years will pass, and you'll see your chances of bearing children fade."

"I will be faithful, Father."

"You say that now, but a time will come when you'll long to remove the sackcloth and ashes and your *tsaiph* of black. But I'm warning you: If you ever do, I'll let Judah decide your fate. We both know what that will be."

Her death, no doubt, followed by celebration.

"I will be faithful. Upon my life, I swear. If it's the last thing I do, I will bring honor upon Judah's house!" Despite the tears flooding her eyes, she lifted her chin and looked into his eyes before she left the room.

~~~

Judah would have forgotten all about Tamar if Bathshua hadn't become obsessed with finding some way to take vengeance upon the wretched girl. Even after Tamar was gone, his wife gave him no peace.

"My sons must be avenged! As long as she lives, I'll have no rest!"

And neither would he.

Bathshua ceased running the household, leaving her chores to a few lazy servants while she dedicated her days and nights to beseeching her gods for vengeance. She wanted Tamar dead and disaster to befall Zimran's entire household.

"The girl is gone!" Judah shouted in frustration. "Give me some peace and forget about her."

"As you've done!" Accusation reigned. "I have two sons in the grave because of her. If you were any kind of man, you would have killed her! I will never forget what she's done to me! Never!" She returned to her idols, praying to them for vengeance.

Judah left her alone in her misery. Could stone idols hear? Could wood or clay teraphim change anything? Let her find whatever consolation she could.

Judah thought about taking another wife. Another woman might give him more sons, but the thought of another woman under his roof sickened him. He'd grown up in a household with four wives. He knew the trouble women could bring to a man, even women who believed in the same God he did. His father's life had never been easy. Judah's mother and Rachel, his father's favorite wife, had constantly been at odds in their contest to produce sons. Matters only worsened when they both insisted that Jacob take their handmaidens as concubines, each thereby hoping to win the competition. Their sons had been weaned in bitter rivalry. And nothing had ever turned his father's heart from Rachel. Jacob had loved her from the moment he'd first seen her, and her death in childbirth had nearly destroyed him. In truth, he loved her still. He'd loved Joseph and Benjamin more than all the rest of his sons because they had come from Rachel.

No, Judah wouldn't bring more misery upon himself by taking another wife. One woman was enough trouble for any man. Two wives would be double the trouble. He reminded himself often that he'd loved Bathshua once. She was the wife of his youth, the mother of his sons. He wouldn't set her aside for another, no matter how difficult she became.

Besides, he'd have to build another house for fear of what Bathshua would do to any woman he brought into this one. He'd seen her ill treatment of Tamar.

Judah escaped conflict with Bathshua by staying away from his stone house and tending his flocks. He had a justifiable reason for being away for weeks on end. Yet even out in the fields away from his wife, trouble hounded him.

His calves and lambs were cursed by disease or killed by predators. The sun scorched his pasturage. When he kept his animals protected in the wadies so that marauders wouldn't take them, rains came upon the mountains, sending floodwaters through the wadies. Many animals were swept away by a flash flood, their bloated bodies a feast for vultures. When he returned home, he found blight had killed his grapevines. Beetles had devoured his palm tree. The garden had gone fallow for lack of loyal servants. The sky was bronze, the earth iron!

Even Bathshua sickened as the bitter rot of discontent spread poison through her thinning body. Her face sharpened. Her voice rasped. Her dark eyes became as hard as obsidian. She complained constantly of pain in her neck, her back, her stomach, her bowels. Judah summoned healers, who took his money and left useless potions behind.

Everything Judah had worked twenty years to build was turning to ashes before his eyes. And he knew why.

God is against me!

Lying on the hard ground in the opening of his sheepfold, a stone for a pillow, Judah stared up at the evening sky and remembered the promise God had given his father, Jacob, so many years ago, the same promise God had given to Jacob's father, Abraham. *Land and descendants as numerous as the stars in the heavens!* The Lord had blessed Jacob-Israel with twelve sons.

Judah was haunted by nightmares about the fateful day in Dothan. His own words cursed him. *"What can we gain by killing our brother? Let's sell Joseph to those Ishmaelite traders!"* The dry cistern yawned like a black hole in his dreams, and he could hear the cries of his helpless younger brother.

He knew it was because of what he and his brothers had done to Joseph that his life was now in ruins. There was no way to go back, no way to undo his part in it.

"Help me, brothers! Help me!" Judah remembered the boy struggling against his shackles and sobbing for help from those who should have protected him. *"Help me!"* The boy's sobs still echoed, the same way they had the day he was dragged away to Egypt as his brothers watched.

Judah had shown no mercy to Joseph then.

Judah expected no mercy from God now.

～～～

Though outwardly obedient, inwardly Tamar balked at fate, for it was not her destiny to grow old and die without having children. Four years passed, but Tamar clung tenaciously to hope. She was still young; there was still time.

She worked hard for her father's household. She gave him no opportunity to complain. She made pottery. She wove baskets and cloth. She made tools for her brothers and sisters to use in the fields. Only when the shepherds had taken their flocks away did her father send her out into the fields to work. Though the work was grueling, she preferred the open spaces. Better a burden of rock than the burden of others' contempt.

Her father prospered. The third year Zimran harvested twofold from his fields. "Where is the ill fortune you were sure I would bring you?" she said in challenge.

"Let's wait and see what next year brings."

By the fifth year her father's household prospered so greatly that everyone forgave her presence. Her sisters married, and she was welcomed into the house. Her brother took a wife. Tamar became an object of pity. She would have welcomed their compassion, but she despised their charity. They looked down upon her and upon Judah's household.

She held on to her hope. She clung to it. One day Judah would send for her! One day she would have children! Someday the house of Judah would be strong and held in high honor because of the sons she would give them. She wept, for she ached to take her rightful place as the child-bearer in her husband's clan. What greater dream could a woman have?

Yet sometimes in the night, when Tamar heard the soft mewling sounds of her brother's firstborn son, she wept. Would she ever hold a child of her own?

Surely Judah had not forsaken her. Surely he would send for her. He had given his promise. Perhaps this year. Perhaps next. Oh, let it be soon!

When she was alone in the fields, Tamar lifted up her eyes to the heavens, tears streaking her face. *"How long, oh Lord, how long will I be abandoned? How long before justice is done? Oh, God of Judah, help me. When will this son of yours see that I can give his household the children he needs so that the name of Judah will not die? Change his heart, God. Change his heart."*

Having prayed to Judah's unseen God, Tamar did the only thing left to her.

She waited ...

    and waited ...

        and waited ...

five

ON market day, while her father and brothers sat in the city gate visiting with friends, Tamar remained in the goat-hair booth with her mother and sold cloth made from the flax. Sharp-eyed, sharp-tongued patrons never cowed Tamar, and the booth always showed a good profit when she managed it. Her mother was content to leave it in her hands.

Business had been brisk, and Tamar was kept very busy while her mother sat and stitched the sun, the moon, and the stars on a red gown she'd made for her daughter in Timnah. Every year Tamar's sister received a new gown and veil. Zimran grumbled at the cost of the cloth and colored thread but never refused to allow his wife to purchase whatever she needed. Only the best would do for a temple priestess, and her father coveted the favor of the gods, any and all of them. Tamar's mother spent hours working with her fine threads and tiny beads, trimming the gowns and exquisite veils she made from imported cloth of red and blue. She also made anklets with rows of tiny bells.

Though Tamar wore her mourning garments until they were threadbare, she never asked for more or wished for the finery her sister was given. Tamar was satisfied with her voluminous black *tsaiph* that covered her from head to foot. The garment didn't chafe, but the barren wasteland of her life did. Despair wore upon her resolve.

She'd been born for more than this! She'd been brought up and trained to be a wife and mother of a household! Six years had come and gone, and still no summons from Judah!

Tamar rose and haggled with another customer. It was late in the day, and the man wanted quality textiles for bargain prices. She refused his price and sat down. He offered more. They haggled again. Finally, the man purchased the last of the cloth and left. With a sigh, Tamar sat inside the booth with her mother.

"I'm going to need more blue thread. I thought I had enough to finish this sash, but I still need more. Go and buy more for me, but be quick about it."

Tamar walked past booths displaying baskets of figs and pomegranates, trays of grapes, jars of olive oil and honey, skins of wine, bowls of spices from Eastern caravans. Children played beside mothers hawking merchandise. Tamar saw other widows, all much older than she, sitting content while grown sons or daughters-in-law conducted the business.

Depressed, she purchased the blue thread her mother needed and headed back. She walked down a different aisle of booths displaying wood, clay, and stone teraphim; pottery; baskets; and weaponry. She was restless and dejected, when she noticed two men coming toward her. One looked vaguely familiar. She frowned, wondering if he was a friend of her brothers.

As he came closer, she realized it was *Shelah!* Shocked, she stared, for he was a full-grown man boasting a beard and broad shoulders! His companion was a young Canaanite, and both were armed with curved knives. Each had a wine-skin draped over his shoulders, and they were both drunk! Shelah swaggered down the narrow lane. He bumped into a man, shoved him aside, and cursed him. Tamar couldn't seem to move. She stood gawking at them, her heart racing.

"Well, look at her, Shelah." His friend laughed. "The poor widow can't take her eyes off of you. Perhaps she wants something from you."

Shelah brushed her aside with scarcely a look and snarled, "Get out of my way."

Heat poured into her face, for Judah's son hadn't even recognized her! He was just like Er, arrogant and contemptuous. He bumped into a counter, rattling the clay teraphim displayed there. The proprietor made a grab for his merchandise as Shelah and his friend laughed and strolled on.

"Get out of my way ..."

Tamar fought against the anger and despair filling her. Judah never meant to keep his promise!

What would become of her when her father died? Would she have to beg crumbs from her brothers' tables or go out and glean in a stranger's field? For the rest of her life, she would suffer the shame of abandonment and have to survive on others' pity. All because Judah had forsaken her. *It was not just!* Judah had lied. She was left with nothing. No future! No hope!

Tamar returned to her father's booth and gave the blue thread to her mother. Then she sat in the deepest shadows, her face turned away.

"You were gone a long time. What kept you?"

Hot tears burned Tamar's eyes, but she refused to look at her mother. "The woman was stubborn about the price." She would not expose her shame.

Her mother made no further reprimand, but Tamar felt her watchful eyes. "Is something wrong, Tamar?"

"I'm tired." Tired of this endless waiting. Tired of hoping Judah would keep his promise. Tired of the barrenness of a useless life! She clenched her hands. She needed wise counsel, but whom could she trust? She couldn't speak with her father, for he'd merely tell her he'd been right all along: Judah had cast her out and abandoned her. She couldn't speak with her mother because she was content with things as they were. She was getting older and needed extra hands to help. Her father was wealthy enough now to have servants, but he preferred to sink his profits into a new stone storage house for surplus grain.

The market day ended, and the booths were dismantled. Her father and brothers came in time to load the donkey. It was a long walk home.

Tamar didn't speak of Shelah until she was alone with Acsah.

"Did he speak to you?"

"Oh yes. He told me to get out of his way." Tamar pressed a hand over her mouth, silencing the sob that choked her. She closed her eyes, struggling for control over her emotions. She shook her head.

Acsah embraced her and stroked her back. "I knew this day would come."

"I stood right in front of him, Acsah, and he didn't even know me."

"You were a young girl when you entered Judah's house. Now you're a woman. It's not surprising Shelah didn't recognize you. I doubt even Judah would."

"You don't understand what this means!"

"Yes, I do. You're the one who never understood."

Tamar drew back. "I thought ... "

Acsah shook her head. "You hoped. You were the only one who had faith in that man." She touched her cheek tenderly. "He is the one who has been faithless."

"I must do something, Acsah. I can't leave things as they are."

They talked far into the night but came up with no solutions. Finally, exhausted, Tamar fell into a fitful sleep.

Tamar was milking the goats when her mother came to her. It was clear something was terribly wrong. She rose. "What's happened, Mother?"

"Judah's wife is dead." Tears slid down her mother's wrinkled cheeks, but her eyes were like fire.

Tamar stepped back, her body going cold. "Who sent word?"

"No one sent word! Your father heard about it from a friend who has commerce with the Hebrews. Judah's wife is already buried! You were not even summoned to mourn her." Her eyes were fierce and black. "That my daughter should be so ill-treated by a Hebrew and nothing be done about it will bring me down to my grave!" She wept bitter tears.

Tamar turned her face away and closed her eyes. She wished she could sink into the earth and be spared this final humiliation.

Her mother came closer. "When will you see your situation for what it is? Your brother saw Shelah in the marketplace. He took pity on you and told me rather than your father! Shelah's a grown man! Perhaps he's left his father's household. Perhaps he'll choose his own wife and do whatever he pleases. Judah did!"

Tamar turned away. What she said was true. Judah had never had control over his sons. He'd never been able to rein in Er or Onan. Why should anything be different with Shelah? All the men of Judah's household lived for the pleasure of the moment without thought of tomorrow! Shaking, Tamar paced. She had to do something or scream. She sat down and went back to milking the goats.

"How can you say nothing at such news? This despicable man has abandoned you!"

"Enough!" Tamar glared up at her mother. "I will not speak against Judah or his sons. I will remain loyal to the house of my husband, no matter how they – or you – treat me." She wished she could control her thoughts as easily as her tongue!

"At least we give you bread."

"Grudgingly. I earn every bite I take."

"Your father says you should go to Kezib and shout at the gate for justice!"

So her father knew everything. Her humiliation was complete. Tamar put her forehead against the side of the goat; her anguish was too deep for tears.

"You should have cried out against Judah long ago." Her mother was relentless. "It's your right! Will you sit here for the rest of your life and do nothing? Who will provide for you when you grow old? What will happen to you when you can no longer work? What will happen to you when you're too old to glean?" She knelt beside Tamar and grasped her arm. "Let the elders know how this Hebrew has treated you and brought shame upon us! Let everyone know that Judah breaks his vow!"

Tamar looked at her. "I know the man better than you, Mother. If I shame him before all Kezib and Adullam, he will not bless me for it! If I blacken the name of my father-in-law, will he show me kindness and mercy and give me Shelah?"

Her mother stood in disgust. "So you will go on waiting. You will accept what he's done to you. You'll let the years pass and grow old without children." Tears came hot and heavy. "How many years will it be before your time of child-bearing passes? You won't be young forever! Who will take pity on you when your father dies?"

Tamar covered her face. "Please do not vex me so! I'm searching for a way ... " She wept.

Her mother said nothing for a long moment. She put her hand gently on Tamar's shoulder. "Life is hard for a woman, Tamar. But it's impossible without a man."

Tamar drew a shaky breath and raised her head. "I know that better than anyone." Rubbing the tears away, she looked at her mother. "I will find a way."

Her mother sighed and looked out toward the hills. "The man who spoke with your father said Judah's wife was ill for a long time. Two years, at least. She must have died a slow, cruel death." She hesitated, her brow furrowed. "Judah had only one wife, didn't he?"

"Only Bathshua."

"No concubines?"

"None." Milk splashed into the earthen bowl as Tamar worked. Focusing on her task, she tried to ignore her mother's gentle touch. It would be her undoing, and she'd cried enough to last a lifetime.

"The man said Judah was going to Timnah with his friend from Adullam," her mother said and let the words hang in the air before adding, "The sheepshearing festival will begin soon."

Tamar looked up at her. Her mother smiled faintly, eyes keen. She said nothing more. Brushing Tamar's shoulder lightly with her fingertips, she left her alone to think.

And how her thoughts whirled as she worked. Judah might be unwilling to keep his promise, but she still had rights. According to the customs of her people, if Judah wouldn't allow Shelah to sleep with her and give her a son, then Judah himself owed her one.

So Judah was going to the sheepshearing now that his wife was dead! Righteous indignation filled her. Timnah was a center of commerce and the worship of Astarte. She knew what her father-in-law would do there. There were common harlots by the dozens, who sold their bodies for a scrap of bread and a cup of wine! Such might be her own fate if her father cast her out.

She would no longer sit quietly by, waiting for Judah to honor a promise he'd never intended to keep. If she didn't do something soon, Judah would be led by his lusts and carelessly give up his seed – what rightfully belonged to her – to the first woman in Timnah who tantalized him.

Biting her lip, Tamar considered her options. She could continue her chaste existence and wait upon Judah to do what was right, knowing now that he never would, or she could go after him. She could pretend to be a harlot by the roadside. Shelah hadn't recognized her. Why should Judah?

She carried the earthen vessel into the house, where her mother was putting the last touches on her sister's veil. Tamar set the bowl down and looked at the finery lying across her mother's lap. What if she were to dress in her sister's garments?

"This is the best veil I've ever made." Her mother tied off and bit a thread. "There. It's finished." She held it up.

Tamar took the veil from her mother's hand and ran it carefully through her own. "It's very beautiful."

"Look at the gown." Her mother rose and took up the gown for Tamar to see. "I've made everything your sister needs: headband, veils, gown, sash, anklets, and sandals." She turned toward Tamar. "The veil was the last piece." She stretched out her arm, and Tamar laid the veil carefully over it. Tamar noticed that her mother's hands were trembling as she carefully folded the veil and tucked it into the basket. "Your father plans to send these things to your sister in two days. She must have everything in time for the festival."

Did her mother suspect the plan that was forming in her mind? "I'll work in the fields tomorrow, Mother. I may not return to the house until very late."

Her mother tied the basket closed but didn't rise or look at her. "It's a three-hour walk to the crossroads at Enaim. You will have to start out just before dawn."

Tamar's heart lurched, but she said nothing.

Her mother bowed her head. "If Judah recognizes you, he'll kill you. You know that, don't you?"

"If I die, I die."

"Shelah is a shallow young man. He would be easier to fool."

"Perhaps, Mother. But I don't want another jackal. I'm going after the lion."

The oil lamp was still burning when Tamar rose in the night. Her mother knew exactly how much oil to use so that the light would last through the heaviest darkness. Soon the lamp would flicker and go out, just in time for the first hint of dawn to light the room. Tamar tiptoed across the room and picked up the basket with her sister's clothing. She left the house with it.

The sun was rising, turning the stars into dying sparks in the paling sky. Tamar walked quickly across her father's fields to the hills beyond. The sun was up and the earth warming by the time she reached the crossroads of Enaim. She entered an olive grove, hurrying into its depths where she would be hidden.

Stripping off her widow's garb, Tamar put on the garments and trappings her mother had made for her priestess sister. She loosened her hair, combing her fingers through the thick, black, curling mass until it hung down her back to below her waist. She put on the veil. The tiny bells around her ankles tinkled as she tucked her black *tsaiph* into the basket and hid it behind a tree.

Grim but determined, Tamar walked back and waited at the edge of the grove where passersby wouldn't see her. She kept watch for the rest of the morning. Her heart leaped into her throat every time she saw two men coming down the road, but she stayed hidden. She would show herself to no men but Judah and his Adullamite friend.

It was well past noon when Judah appeared on the rise with Hirah at his side. She stepped out and sat at the edge of the grove. She rose and stepped forward as they came closer. The anklet bells tingled softly and caught Judah's immediate attention. He slowed his pace and looked at her.

Her palms were slick with sweat, her heart hammering wildly. She wanted to run into the orchard and hide herself again, but she vowed not to lose courage now. She must be bold. Deliberately ignoring the men, she leaned down, lifted the hem of the gown, and adjusted the thin straps of one sandal. The two men stopped.

"We're in no hurry," the Adullamite said, his tone amused.

When she straightened, Tamar didn't look his way. She didn't want him to approach her. She fixed her gaze upon Judah – it was he whose attention she sought. Would he recognize her? Her breath caught tensely as he turned aside and came to her. He stopped right in front of her and smiled, his gaze moving downward. Judah didn't recognize her. He had scarcely looked at her veiled face.

"Here, now," he said, "let me sleep with you."

Tamar was shocked at how easily he fell prey to a woman's wiles, even a woman who was completely inexperienced in the art of seduction! Was this the way men bought the services of a harlot? What should she say now?

"She wants you, Judah." Hirah grinned. "See how she trembles."

"Perhaps she's shy." Judah smiled wryly. "Go on ahead, Hirah. I'll catch up later."

Hirah chuckled. "It's been a long time, hasn't it, my friend!" He walked down the road, leaving Tamar alone with Judah. She almost lost her nerve because of the intensity of his eyes. He never looked away.

"So," he said, "we're alone now. What do you say?"

She could tell his need was great, but no greater than her anger. Would her sister have felt pity? Tamar couldn't muster any. Seven years ago she had begged him not to allow his son Onan to treat her like a harlot! Judah had wanted her to entice his son into doing what was right.

Today she would do so with Judah himself.

She took a step away from him, looking back over her shoulder coyly. "How much will you pay me?" She spoke low, in a tone she hoped would beguile him.

"I'll send you a young goat from my flock."

And where was his flock? Her anger heated. How like Judah to promise something he had no intention of giving. First, a son. Now, a goat! She wouldn't accept another promise from his lips. Not on this day, or any other. "What pledge will you give me so I can be sure you will send it?" She lowered her eyes so he would not see the fire that raged within her. Had he sensed it in her voice or mistaken the tremor for unbridled passion?

Judah stepped closer. "Well, what do you want?"

Tamar considered quickly. She wanted something that bore Judah's name. If she became pregnant, she would need something to prove him responsible. "I want your identification seal, your cord, and the walking stick you're carrying." As soon as she uttered the words, her heart stopped. She had asked for too much! No man in his right mind would agree to give up so much, especially to a harlot! Judah would guess now. He would reach out and rip the veils from her face and kill her right there at the crossroads.

She jerked slightly as he reached out. Then she realized he was handing her his staff! Tamar took it, then watched in amazement as Judah removed the cord from around his neck and handed her his seal as well. He hadn't even uttered a word of protest! The man was driven by lust!

A bitter sadness gripped Tamar. It took all her willpower not to wail and weep loudly. All the years she had waited for this man to do what was right, and then to find that he thought nothing at all of handing the keys to his household over to a woman he thought was a prostitute!

The sadness ebbed quickly, replaced by excitement. She had cause to hope. Though she had shed her pride and degraded herself, she had this one opportunity to provide a child for the household of Judah. Acsah had said the time was right. She could only hope so.

"Have you a room in town?" Judah said.

"The day is fair, my lord, and grass far softer than a bed of stone." Judah's staff in her hand, she walked into the olive grove. He followed.

≈≈≈

Judah took his pleasure beneath the shade of an olive tree and fell asleep in the afternoon heat. Tamar rose quietly and left him there. She hurried through the trees, found the basket she'd hidden, and quickly stripped off her sister's garments and put on her own. Looping Judah's cord and seal around her neck, she tucked them beneath her black mourning garment. She folded the red dress, veils, and sash and put them carefully away, tucking the belled anklets deep into the folds, where they would make no sound.

Hope was alive within her. She pressed her hands over her womb as tears ran down her cheeks. Bowing her head, she whispered softly, "I only ask for justice!"

Judah's sons had abused and used her; Bathshua had blamed her for their sins; and Judah had cast her out, broken his promise, and abandoned her. But now, she might yet be grafted into the line of Abraham, Isaac, and Jacob. Without Judah even knowing, he may have given her a child. If his seed had taken, she might yet have her place among the people whom the God of all creation had chosen to be His own. And if the child were a son, he would be her deliverer.

Tamar reverently touched the seal hidden beneath her garment. She picked up the basket and tucked it under her arm. She took Judah's staff from where it rested against an olive tree and headed home.

≈≈≈

A spear of light touched Judah's eyelids and awakened him. The harlot was gone. When he didn't find her standing alongside the road where he'd first seen her, he assumed she'd gone into town. Grim and uneasy, he went on with his journey, spending the rest of the day in regret. He was no better than Esau, who had given away his birthright for a bowl of lentil stew! Why had he agreed to hand over his staff, seal, and cord to a temple prostitute? Having taken his pleasure, he found himself impatient to have his possessions in hand again.

Annoyed, he caught up with Hirah near Timnah. His friend irritated him further with taunts and salacious comments.

"Where's your staff, Judah? Don't tell me ... "

"I'll have it back when I send a goat to the woman."

"And your seal and cord as well?" Hirah laughed and slapped him on the back. "I hope she was worth the price!"

Ashamed, Judah gave no response. He made excuses and went to find Shelah, who had been sent ahead with the flocks. They sheared the sheep together. Judah made contracts with several farmers to bring his sheep after the harvest. Hirah joined them but refrained from further remarks about the harlot by the roadside. "Come, my friend, relax and enjoy yourself," Hirah said, swaying from too much drink. "You have nothing to worry about. Life sorts itself out. Remember how we lived before wives and sons and worries. Timnah has much to offer."

Shelah was eager to try everything. Judah found he couldn't. He kept remembering what an hour of pleasure had already cost him. He missed the feel of his staff in his hand and knew he wouldn't feel right until he had his seal and cord back as well. He was ready to leave long before the festival was over. When it was, he found he couldn't bring himself to follow the same road home again. He made excuses to Hirah.

"I need to take my flocks to better forage. You're going back by way of Enaim, aren't you?"

"As I always do."

"I've done many favors for you, have I not, Hirah? Take this goat back to the harlot by the crossroads of Enaim. Retrieve my staff, seal, and cord from the prostitute and bring them to me at my house. Do that for me, my friend, and I will show my appreciation when next I see you!"

Hirah's eyes gleamed. "Of course."

"One more thing I ask of you."

Hirah lifted his hand. "You needn't say another word, Judah. You're my friend. No one will hear a word of this from my lips." He grinned. "Besides, it will be my pleasure to do your bidding." He headed off down the road, tossing back over his shoulder, "Perhaps I'll pass a few hours in that olive grove myself!"

Judah thought no more about the girl or the cost of his sin until weeks later, when Hirah passed by his house empty-handed. "I made a thorough search for the girl, Judah. I even went into the town, but everyone said there had never been a temple prostitute at the crossroads. They laughed and asked me why I'd think there would be one there when the temple is in Timnah."

Judah had never considered why a temple prostitute would loiter by the road. Now that he thought about it, he wondered why he hadn't! Confused, Judah became angry, convinced he'd been tricked somehow but having no idea of the reason. Why would the harlot lie to him? Of what possible use were his cord, seal, and staff to a prostitute?

A goat could be sold and then the money used for sustenance. Who would buy a seal and staff that bore another man's name, especially a name as well known as his?

"What do you want me to do, Judah?" Hirah sipped his wine. "Shall we both go back and search for her again?"

"Let her keep the pledges! We tried our best to send her the goat. We'd be the laughingstock of the village if we went back again."

When Hirah departed a few days later, Judah went out and cut a straight, strong branch from an almond tree. He whittled the bark and carved his name into the wood. The new staff was a good one, but it didn't have the feel of the one his father had placed in his hands. Nor did the clay seal he made have the same feel of authenticity that his stone seal had had.

But after that, Judah forgot entirely the incident at the crossroads of Enaim.

six

TAMAR said nothing about her successful journey to Enaim, and her mother didn't ask about it. The following morning, Zimran left for Timnah with Tamar's older brother. They took the basket containing the temple garb with them.

When two weeks passed and there was no show of blood, Tamar knew she was pregnant. She was exultant as well as terrified. She kept her secret and went on as always. She rose early and worked all day. No one noticed any change in her, though Acsah was hardest to convince and perplexed by her sudden modesty.

At night, while the others slept, Tamar would spread her hands over her womb. Sometimes her fear would rise, and she would wonder how she had ever dared to trick Judah. What would he do when he found out? She'd been willing to risk everything, even her life, for the chance to bear a child. Now she was afraid for the child she carried. Soon her pregnancy would become apparent, if Acsah hadn't guessed already. If her father learned of it, he might kill her in a fit of rage. If she died, so too would Judah's child – and Judah's line would be lost.

She tried to think clearly and not allow her emotions to run wild. She was still a part of Judah's household, whether he acknowledged her or not. The decision of whether she lived or died must be his, not her father's. Truth was her only protection, but she couldn't reveal it in a way that would bring shame upon Judah. Had she wanted to do that, she would have cried out before the city gates long before this.

She kept her secret, refusing even to confide in Acsah, who plagued her daily with questions. "Where were you that day? Why didn't you awaken me? I searched for you in the fields. Tell me where you went and why."

Finally Acsah challenged her in private. "What have you done, Tamar? Who have you lain with? By the gods, we're both undone!"

"I did what I had to do, Acsah. It's the law of both Judah's people and mine that I have the right to a child by Shelah or by Judah himself. And yet

I've had to risk everything to receive justice at Judah's hands. I have shamed myself and resorted to trickery to beget this child, lest I die in disgrace." She grasped her nurse's hands and held them tightly. "You must trust me."

"You must speak out and tell – "

"No. Nothing can be said. Not yet."

"And when your father finds out? Will he have mercy on you when he thinks you've committed adultery?"

"It will be up to Judah to decide what happens to me."

"Then you'll die, and the child will die with you. Judah thinks you bring ill fortune and are the cause of his sons' deaths. This will give him an excuse to be rid of you!"

"Speak no more of it."

"Your father will kill you when he finds out!" Acsah closed her eyes and covered her face. "You should have waited."

"I would have grown old and died before Judah called for me."

"And so you destroy yourself and a child with you? You've betrayed Judah and brought shame upon this house. Tell me what happened."

"I will tell you nothing." Caution and hope for a brighter future kept her silent.

This was her secret and Judah's, though the man wasn't even aware of it yet. She would guard this knowledge and keep it private, for it was precious. Judah's staff was beneath her pallet, and the cord and seal ring were still around her neck, hidden by her widow's garb. She wouldn't show them to Acsah. She wouldn't wag her tongue and give her nurse or her father cause to laugh at Judah. She wanted to fulfill her duty to his household. She wanted to be embraced by his people. Would Judah thank her if she exposed him to ridicule?

Tamar thought of Judah's pride, his pain, his losses. She wouldn't add humiliation to his sorrow. Judah had forsaken her, but she would not shame the father of her child before any man or woman.

The morning she had walked over her father's fields and stood near the crossroads waiting for Judah, she'd had time to think long and hard about the risk she was taking and what the future might hold. Life or death, Judah would decide. When she had stood over Judah as he slept, she'd trembled with anger. She'd almost kicked him awake and confronted him with his sin. She had longed to shake him and cry out: "See what you've brought me to, Judah! See what you've done!" He had once told her to play the harlot for Onan. Instead, she'd played the part for him.

But she had let her anger go. She didn't want revenge. She wanted justice.

She was gambling everything in the hope of something better, something important, something permanent. A child. A reason to live! A future and a hope! She fanned the tiny flame growing within her, even knowing everything was still in Judah's hands.

"Perhaps you'll be fortunate and miscarry," Acsah said.

"If that happens, may I die with my child."

"You may die before that." Acsah covered her face and wept.

Tamar smiled sadly. What caused her to hope so much in a man who had never done anything right in all the time she'd known him? Had Judah protected her from Er's brutality or seen that Onan fulfilled his duty to his brother? Judah himself had broken his promise to give her Shelah. How could she hope to survive when her life was in the hands of this man?

And yet, she did hope. She chose to hope. She refused to give in to the fears that gripped her, fear for the child she carried – Judah's child, Judah's hope, Judah's future.

But would the man listen when the time came for her to reveal the truth?

⊱⊱⊰⊰

Two more months passed before the day of wrath and judgment fell upon Tamar's head. Acsah shook her awake. Disoriented, Tamar sat up. She realized she'd fallen asleep by the stone wall where she'd been working.

"You're undone," Acsah said, tears streaking her face. "Undone! A servant saw you sleeping and went to your father. He summoned me. I had to tell him. I had to." She gripped Tamar's arms tightly. "Run away, Tamar. You must hide yourself!"

A strange calmness filled Tamar. Her waiting was over. "No," she said quietly and rose. Two brothers were striding across the field toward her. Let them come. When they reached her, they cursed her with foul accusations. She said nothing as they grabbed her arms and headed back. Her father came outside, his face red, hands in fists.

"Are you with child?"

"Yes."

Zimran didn't ask who the father was before he flew at her. The first blow knocked her down. When he kicked at her, she scrambled away and rolled into a ball so that he couldn't harm the baby. "It's not your right to pass judgment on me!" She screamed at him in fury equal to his own.

"Isn't it? You're my daughter!" He kicked her again.

Gasping for breath, she started to rise, but he grabbed her shawl and the braid of hair beneath it, dragging her up and back. She clawed his hands to get free. She had the lion's cub in her womb, and she would fight like a lioness to save it. She stood, feet planted, hands raised. "I belong to Judah's household, not yours! Or have you forgotten?"

"He'll thank me for killing you!"

"Judah must be the one to pass judgment! Not you! Judah and no other!"

Breathing hard, Zimran stared at her. "You've played the harlot beneath my nose! I should kill you!"

Tamar saw the tears of rage and shame in her father's eyes, but she wouldn't weaken. "Why save Judah the trouble, Father? Why have my blood on your hands? He abandoned me six years ago! Let it be on his head what happens to me and my child."

Her father shouted for a servant. "Go and tell Judah: Tamar is pregnant by harlotry! Ask him what he wants done with her!" The servant ran across the field. Zimran glared at her. "As for you, harlot, go and wait."

Tamar obeyed. Alone, she trembled violently. She clenched her hands, her palms damp with sweat. Her heart quaked.

What if Judah didn't come?

≈≈≈

The news of Tamar's harlotry and her pregnancy rocked Judah and enraged him. Though it had been six years since he'd removed her from his house, he expected her to remain chaste for as long as she lived. If he showed Tamar any mercy and allowed her to live, the child, no matter who the father was, would become part of his household. He couldn't let that happen. He wouldn't.

Mingled with his wrath was elation. Tamar had given him an opportunity to get rid of her. She had sinned against his house in the vilest way, and it was his right to judge her. Bathshua would have been exultant. She had been right after all: Tamar was no good. The girl was evil. She had cost him Er and Onan! The wisest thing he'd ever done was withhold Shelah.

Let her suffer. Hadn't he suffered because of her? Stoning was too swift, too easy. Let her feel the pain of her transgressions against him. "Bring her out and burn her! Burn her, I say!" Judah shouted.

Before Zimran's servant was out the door, Judah felt certain his fortune had changed. By tomorrow, the time would be ripe to find a suitable wife for his last son, Shelah. It was time now to build up his household.

Tamar heard the commotion and knew what Judah had decided. Her mother was wailing, her father shouting. She covered her face and prayed. *God of heaven and earth, help me! I know I'm not of Your people. I know I'm unworthy. But if You care about Judah, who is Your son, save me! Save this child I carry!*

Acsah hurried into the room. "Judah said to burn you. Oh, Tamar ... "

Tamar didn't weep or plead. She rose quickly and yanked back the pallet. Removing her shawl, she wrapped Judah's staff in it. She took the cord and seal from around her neck and pressed them into Acsah's hand. "Take these things to Judah. Go quickly, Acsah. Tell him, 'The man who owns this identification seal and walking stick is the father of my child. Do you recognize them?'"

A commotion had started outside. Her mother was pleading hysterically as her father shouted, *"I warned her!* I told her what would happen if she ever took off her widow's garb!"

"No, you can't – "

"Get out of the way, woman! Tamar brought this upon herself!"

Tamar pushed her nurse. "Go, Acsah! Do not fail me! *Run, woman! Run!*"

As soon as she obeyed, Tamar positioned herself in the corner of the room where she could best defend herself. Her brothers entered. "Will you show no mercy to your own sister?"

"After you've shamed us?" They called her names as they grappled with her. She did not make it easy for them. They dragged her away from the wall and dragged her through the doorway. Her father stood outside. "Judah said to burn you, and burn you shall!"

Did they think she would die easily? Did they think she wouldn't fight for the life of her unborn child? Tamar kicked and clawed. She bit and screamed at them. "Then let Judah burn me!" They struck her, and with all her pent-up fury, Tamar hit back. "Let him see his judgment carried out! *Take me to Judah!* Why should my death be upon your heads?" She used her fingernails and feet. "Let him be the one to put the torch to me!"

Judah saw a woman running toward him, a bundle in her hand. Frowning, he shielded his eyes from the sun's glare and recognized Acsah, Tamar's nurse. Gritting his teeth, he swore under his breath. No doubt she had come to plead for mercy for that wretched girl.

Gasping for breath and shaking with exhaustion, Acsah fell to her knees. She dropped the bundle at his feet. "Tamar sent me ... " Unable to say more, she grabbed the edge of a black shawl and yanked it hard. A staff rolled out – his staff. She held out her hand and opened it, showing him a red cord with a stone seal.

Judah snatched it from her. "Where did you get these?"

"Tamar ... "

"Speak up, woman!"

"Tamar! 'Take these things to Judah,' she said. 'The man who owns this identification seal and walking stick is the father of my child. Do you recognize them?'" She bowed her head, fighting for breath.

A sick feeling gripped Judah. He went cold as he picked up his staff. The harlot by the roadside had been Tamar! She'd disguised herself and tricked him into fulfilling her rights to a child. He was awash with shame. Nothing he'd ever done had been unseen. He'd kept nothing secret from the Lord. His skin prickled. His hair raised on end.

"When will you do what is right, Judah?"

The words came like a whisper. Tamar had said these words to him years ago, but it was another voice now, soft and terrifying, that spoke into the recesses of his mind and heart. He gripped his head, trembling inwardly. He shook with fear.

"My lord?" Acsah's eyes were wide.

His heart pumped frantically. He cried out and ran. He had to stop the judgment he'd set in motion. If he didn't reach Zimran in time, two more lives would be upon his head: Tamar's life and the child she carried. *His* child!

"Oh, God, forgive me!" He pushed himself harder, running faster than he'd ever run in his life. "Let the sin be upon my head!" Why hadn't he run like this after the Ishmaelites? Why hadn't he rescued his brother from their hands? It was too late now to undo what he'd done then. *Oh, God, have mercy, God of my father, Israel! Give me strength! Let her life be spared, and the child with her.*

Zimran and his sons were coming to meet him. They were half dragging Tamar, and she was fighting like a mad woman. A brother kicked her as Zimran grabbed her by the hair. Yanking her to her feet, Zimran shoved her toward Judah, cursing her with his every breath.

"Let her go!" Judah shouted. When Zimran hit Tamar again, rage fired Judah's blood. "Strike her again and I'll kill you!"

Zimran was quick to defend himself. "You're the one who told us you wanted her burned! And you've every right. She's betrayed you and played the harlot."

Tamar stood silent now, covered with dust, her face bruised and bleeding. She'd been beaten, dragged, struck, and mocked for *his* sin. Not even her own father and brothers cared enough to show her the least compassion. She stood and said nothing.

Judah's face filled with heat. When had he ever shown this young woman any pity? She'd suffered abuse from Er, and he'd done nothing to stop it. She'd asked for her rights from Onan, and he'd told her to play the harlot. She'd pleaded for justice, and he'd abandoned her. Not once had she cried out before the city gates and embarrassed him. Instead, she'd humbled herself and dressed as a harlot in order to beget a child for his household. And then, rather than expose his sin, she had returned his staff, cord, and seal privately, protecting his reputation.

Tears filled his eyes. His throat closed. She stood before him, battered and bleeding, head bowed, uttering not a word of self-defense, waiting, still waiting, as she'd always waited for him to be the man he should be.

"When will you do what is right, Judah?"

"She is more in the right than I am because I didn't keep my promise to let her marry my son Shelah."

"That may be, but she has no right to play the harlot under my roof!"

Judah looked into the Canaanite's dark eyes and saw a reflection of his own cold heart. Zimran's pride was hurt, and he intended to destroy Tamar for it. Judah's pride broke. Hadn't he blamed Tamar for the sins of others? Without a twinge of conscience, he had rejected and abandoned her. Only a short while ago, he'd felt exultant at the thought of passing judgment upon her and knowing she'd die an agonizing death by fire. He'd sinned against her a hundred times over and in the full sight of God and never once cared about the cost to her. And now that his sins had caught up with him, he had a choice: Go on sinning or repent.

Tamar lifted her head and looked at him. He saw something flash in her eyes. She could expose him right now. She could pour humiliation upon him unendingly. She could tell how she'd tricked him at the crossroads of Enaim, and make him a laughingstock before her father and brothers and everyone else they might tell about it. Judah knew he deserved public ridicule and worse. He saw her anger, her frustration, her grief. And he understood it. But it didn't change his mind.

Judah stepped forward and brought his staff up. He held it in both hands, ready to fight. "Take your hands off her, Zimran. The child is mine." When he took another step forward, Zimran's face went pale. The Canaanite stepped back, his sons with him.

"Take her then. Do with her whatever you want." Zimran strode away with a bemused glance over his shoulder. His sons followed him.

Tamar let out her breath and sank to her knees. Bowing her head, she put her hands on his dirty feet. "Forgive me, my lord." Her shoulders shook and she began to sob.

Judah's eyes filled with tears. He went down on one knee and put his hand gently on her back. "It is I who need your forgiveness, Tamar." The sound of her weeping broke his heart. He helped Tamar to her feet. She was shaking violently. One eye was blackened and swelling. Her lip was bleeding. Her clothes were torn, and scratches showed where she had been dragged across rocky ground.

All those years ago when he'd first seen her in Zimran's field, he'd sensed something about this girl and wanted her for his household. Tamar was a Canaanite, but she was honorable and loyal. She had great courage and strength. Surely it had been God who had led him to choose this girl. She had risked everything to have the child who might preserve his household from complete ruin. He cupped her face. "May the God of my father, Israel, forgive my sins against you!" He kissed her forehead.

Her body relaxed. "And mine against you." She smiled, and her eyes glistened with tears.

Judah felt a deep tenderness toward her. He walked beside her until she stumbled and then swept her up in his arms and carried her the rest of the way home. Acsah ran to meet them, ready to tend Tamar's injuries.

Judah waited outside his stone house, his head in his hands. Pride broken, heart humbled, he prayed as he'd never prayed before, pleading for someone other than himself. It was dusk when Acsah finally came out to him. "How is she?"

"Sleeping, my lord." Acsah smiled. "All seems well."

Tamar hadn't lost his child.

"Praise be to God." He went out among his flock and selected the best he could find – a flawless male lamb. He confessed his sins before the Lord and spilled the blood of the lamb as atonement. Then he prostrated himself before the God of Abraham, Isaac, and Jacob and beseeched Him for forgiveness and restoration.

That night Judah slept without nightmares, for the first time in more years than he could count.

Acsah felt as though she were living on the edge of a cliff and could slip over at any moment. Tamar had changed greatly. She had taken command of the house like a first wife would, and her first order was to have all of Bathshua's teraphim removed and destroyed. Shelah joined in protesting, but Judah was adamant in his support of Tamar. Acsah pleaded with Tamar, but it was no use. So she poured out libations in secret, praying to the gods of Canaan that she had managed to hide in her basket. Daily she did this out of devotion and love for Tamar, but when Tamar discovered her in the midst of the ritual, she erupted.

"If you won't obey me, then keep your idols and go back to my father's house with them!"

"I'm only trying to help you," Acsah pleaded, weeping. "Please heed the ways of the past. It is for you and the child that I make contracts with the divine assembly!"

"Our way was wrong, Acsah. I am done with the old ways. If you insist on keeping them, you must leave!"

When Tamar took the clay idol and smashed it against the wall, Acsah cried out in fear. "Do you want the spirits to come against you?"

"This child belongs to Judah and to the God of his people. No other gods will be invited to assemble in Judah's house ever again. If I find you pouring out libations to Baal, I'll send you away!" Tamar reached out for Acsah, weeping. "Do not make me do it, Acsah. I love you, but we will bow down to the God of Israel and no other!"

Acsah had never seen the girl's eyes so fierce. Convinced that the early stress of Tamar's pregnancy had affected her senses, she went to Judah for help. Surely he would want to make sure all the deities were placated and his child protected! But Judah surprised her.

"There will be no other gods in my house. Do as Tamar says."

Frustrated, Acsah obeyed. She spent the months watching over every aspect of Tamar's physical health. She prepared Tamar's meals and told her when to rest. She massaged Tamar's womb and felt the first kick of the baby. She shared Tamar's joy, for she loved the girl as well as the child she carried. She would sit and watch Tamar stroke her growing belly with an expression of love and amazement on her glowing face. Tamar was at peace, and Acsah found herself praying that the unseen God would show mercy upon Tamar and upon the child Tamar had risked everything to conceive.

As the time grew near for Tamar to give birth, Acsah asked if she could build a birthing hut. "Yes," Tamar said, "but do not go by the old ways. Promise me!"

Acsah promised and kept her word. She built the hut herself. She swept the earthen floor and lined it with rush mats, but she didn't chant or sing to the demons. She didn't caulk every opening to keep the spirits out. Instead, she offered prayers to Judah's God, for this was Judah's child.

God of Judah, protect Tamar. Watch over this birth, and bless this girl who has turned away from everything she ever learned so that she could be among Judah's people. I beseech you out of love for her. Show her mercy. Let this child she carries be a son who will love her and care for her in her old age. Let him be a son who will rise up in strength and honor.

It was a difficult birth. Acsah half expected it to be, after her ministrations to Tamar revealed the wondrous news that Tamar's womb held not one, but two, heirs to Judah's line.

Acsah had acted as midwife many times in the household of Zimran, but never once had she witnessed a birth as hard as this one. She loved Tamar even more fiercely, for though the girl suffered greatly, she did not complain. Hour upon hour, Tamar strained, sweat pouring from her. She bit down upon a leather strap to keep from screaming.

"Cry out, Tamar! It will help!"

"Judah will hear and be distressed."

"He's the cause of your pain! Let him hear! I'm sure Bathshua screamed!"

"I am *not* Bathshua!" Tears came as the cords in her neck stood out. "Sing to the Lord God, Acsah." She groaned as the pains took hold of her again. Blood and water soaked the birthing rock on which Tamar sat.

And Acsah did sing, desperately. "I will proclaim the name of the Lord! I will proclaim His name and ascribe greatness to Judah's God, the God of Jacob, the God of Isaac and Abraham."

"His ways are just." Tamar gasped for air and then groaned again, her hands drawing up her knees as she bore down.

The first child's hand came forth, and Acsah quickly tied a scarlet cord around the baby's wrist. "This one came out first," she announced.

"Oh, God, have mercy!" Tamar cried out then, and the child withdrew its hand. She ground her teeth and bore down again. Acsah prayed feverishly as she laid hands upon Tamar's abdomen and felt the two babies struggling within her. They moved, rolled, pressed. Tamar cried out again, and the first child came forth, pushing down and sliding free into Acsah's waiting hands.

"A son!" Acsah laughed with joy, then gasped in surprise. "What!" It was not the child with the scarlet cord upon his wrist. "How did you break out first? He shall be called Perez," she said, for it meant "breaking out."

Within a few moments, the second child was born, another son who was named for the thread soaked in blood – Zerah, meaning "scarlet" – which proclaimed him firstborn, though he had come second.

Tamar smiled wearily. When the afterbirth came, she lay back on the rush-covered earth and closed her eyes with a sigh. "Sons," she said softly and smiled.

Acsah cut the cords, washed the boys, salted and swaddled them, and placed them in their mother's arms. Tamar smiled as she looked from Zerah to Perez. "Do you see what the Lord has done, Acsah? He has lifted the poor in spirit. He has taken me up from the dust and ash heap and given me sons!" Eyes shining with joy, Tamar laughed.

⋙⋘

Judah couldn't speak when he saw Tamar with two babies in her arms. His emotions were so powerful they choked him. Despite his sins, God had given him a double blessing through this courageous young Canaanite woman. He looked at his two sons and their mother, still pale from her travail, and realized he loved Tamar for the woman she was. He not only loved her, he respected and admired her. When Judah had brought her home to Er, he'd never realized how God would use her to bring him to repentance, to change his heart, to change the direction of his life. Tamar was a woman of excellence, a woman worthy of praise!

She looked at him steadily. "I want my sons to be men of God, Judah. I want you to do to them whatever God requires of you so that they will be counted among His people."

"In eight days I will circumcise my sons, and as soon as you're well enough to travel, we'll leave this place and return to the tents of my father."

Judah watched a trickle of tears seep into the dark hair at her temples. Her eyes were filled with uncertainty, and he guessed why. She had never received tender treatment from Bathshua or his sons. "My father, Jacob, will welcome you, Tamar, and my mother will love you. She'll understand you and what happened between us better than anyone." Tamar was still young, still vulnerable. No woman had ever been more beautiful to him than she was now, precious beyond measure. He would make her way smooth.

She raised her eyes. "How can you be sure your mother will accept me?"

"My mother went to my father in veils."

Her dark eyes flickered in surprise. "Dressed as a harlot?"

"Dressed as a bride, but not the one he wanted." He smiled ruefully. "Still, my father came to love her in his own way. She bore him sons. I'm the fourth of six." Judah saw the pulse beat strongly in Tamar's throat. She looked deeply troubled. It was a moment before he realized why, and the heat rushed into his face. He took her hand and covered it with his own. "Don't misunderstand me, Tamar, or be afraid of our future together. I will show you the respect a man should have for a wife, but you are my daughter now. I won't do as the Canaanites do. I promise." He grimaced, his smile tender and apologetic. "A promise I mean to keep!"

Her dark eyes shone. "I trust you, Judah. You will do what is right."

Bathed in forgiveness, his throat closed. He gently took her hand and kissed her palm.

epilogue

IN the years ahead, Judah was a different man. He renewed his relationship with his father and reasserted himself as leader over his brothers. He led them to Egypt to buy grain so that Jacob's household could survive the famine that had come upon the land. It was then that God brought him face-to-face with the brother he had forsaken: Joseph.

Unrecognized as Zaphenath-paneah, the pharaoh's overseer, Joseph tested them. When he demanded that Rachel's last son, Benjamin, be left as his slave, Judah stepped forward, claimed the disaster upon them was due to their own sins, and offered his life in place of his brother's. Seeing the change in Judah, Joseph wept and revealed his true identity. He'd long since forgiven them, but now he embraced them. Joseph sent Judah and his brothers back to Canaan with instructions to bring Jacob and his entire household back to Egypt, where they would claim the rich land of Goshen.

Tamar returned with Judah, her sons grown with sons of their own.

On his deathbed, Jacob-Israel gathered his sons around him and gave them each a blessing. Judah received the greatest one of all. The scepter would never leave his hands. From him and the sons Tamar had borne to him would come the Promised One, God's anointed – the Messiah!

To his last day upon this earth, Judah kept his promise to Tamar. Though he loved her, he never slept with her again.

Nor any other woman.

seek and find

DEAR READER,

You have just read the story of Tamar as perceived by one author. Is this the whole truth about the story of Tamar and Judah? Jesus said to seek and you will find the answers you need for life. The best way to find the truth is to look for yourself!

This "Seek and Find" section is designed to help you discover the story of Tamar as recorded in the Bible. It consists of six short studies that you can do on your own or with a small discussion group.

You may be surprised to learn that this ancient story will have applications for your life today. No matter where we live or in what century, God's Word is truth. It is as relevant today as it was yesterday. In it we find a future and a hope.

Peggy Lynch

LEADING HOME

SEEK GOD'S WORD FOR TRUTH

Go back and read the Bible passage quoted in "Setting the Scene" on pages 14-16.

✝ What part did Judah play in this sibling rivalry story?

✝ What did he and his brothers tell their father?

✝ Based on this passage, list some possible reasons that Judah chose to leave his family at "about this time."

✝ Have you ever felt ashamed of some careless act you did that affected others? Were you fearful of being found out? What choices did you make?

✝ Judah had choices. What could he have done differently?

Proverbs 28:13 tells us, "People who cover over their sins will not prosper. But if they confess and forsake them, they will receive mercy."

Had Judah confessed to God and to his father, the story would have ended there. However, he did not. Instead, he got married! It would seem that Judah was on a pathway of separation from truth. He chose to run and hide rather than confront the real issues. He chose to handle things for himself rather than let God direct his path.

FIND GOD'S WAYS FOR YOU

✝ What have you learned about Judah so far? Would you consider him confrontational or passive? Why?

✝ In what ways do you identify with Judah?

✝ How do you deal with jealousy? with conflict?

✝ Where do you turn with life's struggles – to yourself? to family and friends? to comfortable patterns? to God?

STOP AND PONDER

People who cover over their sins will not prosper. But if they confess and forsake them, they will receive mercy.

— PROVERBS 28:13 —

Take a moment to ask God to search your heart. Be quiet before Him. Reflect on what He offers here.

FAMILY TIES

SEEK GOD'S WORD FOR TRUTH

Read the following passages:

About this time, Judah left home and moved to Adullam, where he visited a man named Hirah. There he met a Canaanite woman, the daughter of Shua, and he married her. She became pregnant and had a son, and Judah named the boy Er. Then Judah's wife had another son, and she named him Onan. And when she had a third son, she named him Shelah. At the time of Shelah's birth, they were living at Kezib.

When his oldest son, Er, grew up, Judah arranged his marriage to a young woman named Tamar. But Er was a wicked man in the Lord's sight, so the Lord took his life. Then Judah said to Er's brother Onan, "You must marry Tamar, as our law requires of the brother of a man who has died. Her first son from you will be your brother's heir."

But Onan was not willing to have a child who would not be his own heir. So whenever he had intercourse with Tamar, he spilled the semen on the ground to keep her from having a baby who would belong to his brother. But the Lord considered it a wicked thing for Onan to deny a child to his dead brother. So the Lord took Onan's life, too.

Then Judah told Tamar, his daughter-in-law, not to marry again at that time but to return to her parents' home. She was to remain a widow until his youngest son, Shelah, was old enough to marry her. (But Judah didn't really intend to do this because he was afraid Shelah would also die, like his two brothers.) So Tamar went home to her parents.

— GENESIS 38:1-11 —

Shem, Ham, and Japheth, the three sons of Noah, survived the Flood with
their father. (Ham is the ancestor of the Canaanites.) From these three sons
of Noah came all the people now scattered across the earth.

After the Flood, Noah became a farmer and planted a vineyard. One
day he became drunk on some wine he had made and lay naked in his
tent. Ham, the father of Canaan, saw that his father was naked and went
outside and told his brothers. Shem and Japheth took a robe, held it over
their shoulders, walked backward into the tent, and covered their father's
naked body. As they did this, they looked the other way so they wouldn't see
him naked. When Noah woke up from his drunken stupor, he learned
what Ham, his youngest son, had done. Then he cursed the descendants of
Canaan, the son of Ham:

"A curse on the Canaanites! May they be the lowest of servants to the
descendants of Shem and Japheth." Then Noah said, "May Shem be blessed
by the Lord my God; and may Canaan be his servant. May God enlarge
the territory of Japheth, and may he share the prosperity of Shem; and let
Canaan be his servant."

– GENESIS 9:18-27 –

✛ According to the second passage, who was the father of the Canaanites?

Abraham found a wife for his son Isaac from afar – not a Canaanite. Esau
displeased his father, Isaac, by marrying not one, but two, Canaanite women.
Isaac sent his son Jacob far away to get a wife who was not a Canaanite.

✛ How did Jacob's son Judah acquire a wife?

✛ Who helped him? Who were her people?

✛ Their firstborn child was a son. Judah named him Er. Who named Onan
and Shelah?

✛ What kind of son was Er?

✛ According to the following passage, what does God hate?

There are six things the Lord hates – no, seven things he detests: haughty
eyes, a lying tongue, hands that kill the innocent, a heart that plots evil,
feet that race to do wrong, a false witness who pours out lies, a person

who sows discord among brothers.

— PROVERBS 6:16-19 —

We read above that "Er was a wicked man." The Hebrew word here translated as *wicked* is also used in numerous other Bible passages. In Genesis 13, Sodom and Gomorrah were called wicked for their practice of sodomy; in the book of Esther, Haman is called wicked for plotting to exterminate the Jews; in Deuteronomy, anyone leading God's people to worship false gods was called wicked.

✛ What did God do to Er?

✛ What might be the reason for Er's death?

✛ What kind of man does God declare Onan to be?

✛ How did Onan displease God? What did God do to him?

✛ Judah's remaining son, Shelah, should have been given to Tamar, according to marriage customs of the times. What reason did Judah give Tamar for delaying the marriage?

✛ What was the real reason?

FIND GOD'S WAYS FOR YOU

✛ Judah was grieving over the past as well as the present, and he was gripped with fear of the future. What fears grip you?

✛ How do you deal with fear?

Er and Onan did their own thing, and it led to death. As the book of Proverbs tells us, "There is a path before each person that seems right, but it ends in death" (Proverbs 14:12). In contrast, Jesus said, "My purpose is to give life in all its fullness" (John 10:10).

✛ Do you know the One who gives life in all its fullness?

STOP AND PONDER

Jesus said, "I am the way, the truth, and the life. No one can come to the Father except through me"; "Look! Here I stand at the door and knock. If you hear me calling and open the door, I will come in, and we will share a meal as friends."

— JOHN 14:6; REVELATION 3:20 —

✢ Will you accept His invitation?

THE BRIDE

SEEK GOD'S WORD FOR TRUTH

Read the following passage:

But Er was a wicked man in the Lord's sight, so the Lord took his life. Then Judah said to Er's brother Onan, "You must marry Tamar, as our law requires of the brother of a man who has died. Her first son from you will be your brother's heir."

But Onan was not willing to have a child who would not be his own heir. So whenever he had intercourse with Tamar, he spilled the semen on the ground to keep her from having a baby who would belong to his brother. But the Lord considered it a wicked thing for Onan to deny a child to his dead brother. So the Lord took Onan's life, too.

Then Judah told Tamar, his daughter-in-law, not to marry again at that time but to return to her parents' home. She was to remain a widow until his youngest son, Shelah, was old enough to marry her. (But Judah didn't really intend to do this because he was afraid Shelah would also die, like his two brothers.) So Tamar went home to her parents.

In the course of time Judah's wife died. After the time of mourning was over, Judah and his friend Hirah the Adullamite went to Timnah to supervise the shearing of his sheep. Someone told Tamar that her father-in-law had left for the sheepshearing at Timnah. Tamar was aware that Shelah had grown up, but they had not called her to come and marry him. So she changed out of her widow's clothing and covered herself with a veil to disguise herself. Then she sat beside the road at the entrance to the village of Enaim, which is on the way to Timnah. Judah noticed her as he went by and thought she was a prostitute, since her face was veiled. So he stopped and propositioned her to sleep with him, not realizing that she was his own daughter-in-law.

"How much will you pay me?" Tamar asked.

"I'll send you a young goat from my flock," Judah promised.

"What pledge will you give me so I can be sure you will send it?" she asked.

"Well, what do you want?" he inquired.

She replied, "I want your identification seal, your cord, and the walking stick you are carrying." So Judah gave these items to her. She then let him sleep with her, and she became pregnant. Afterward she went home, took off her veil, and put on her widow's clothing as usual.

— GENESIS 38:7-19 —

We learned in our previous lesson that Judah chose to marry a forbidden Canaanite girl. He also chose a Canaanite bride for his son. This young bride's name was Tamar.

Tamar means "date palm." Date palms were highly valued trees, not only for their delicious fruit but also for their stately beauty and ability to thrive in the desert climate. This teenage bride was not named so by coincidence.

✢ What do we learn about Tamar from the preceding passage?

✢ What kind of choices (if any) did Tamar have?

✢ When she went back to her father's house, do you think she expected to ever return to Judah's household? Why or why not?

✢ At what point do you think Tamar realized there would not be another wedding?

Tamar decided to take things into her own hands. She may have thought, *Judah is a widower and free to take another wife. Certainly his own seed would secure his promise to me of offspring.* Or, *I'll take only what is promised to me!*

✢ When Tamar set her plans in motion, she changed out of her widow's clothing. What did she do at the end of the passage? What is significant about this? (If you need a hint, consider the following: Did she stop any other men who were on their way to the sheep-shearing? Did she stay on with Judah? Did she continue to play the harlot? Did she brag about her actions?)

This woman of action now waits. She waits to see if Judah will accept her solution to their dilemma. She waits to see if she will be the one to build Judah's household. She waits to see the God of Judah judge between Judah and herself!

Read the following passage:

> *People may be pure in their own eyes, but the Lord examines their motives.*
> — PROVERBS 16:2 —

✜ What does Proverbs 16:2 say about people's opinion of themselves?

FIND GOD'S WAYS FOR YOU

✜ Up to this point in Tamar's life she had been abused, used, abandoned, and forgotten. Have you ever been treated unfairly? How have you handled broken promises?

✜ In what ways do you identify with Tamar?

✜ Have you ever run ahead of God and tried to fix things yourself? If so, what was the outcome?

STOP AND PONDER

> *Jesus said, "Come to me, all of you who are weary and carry heavy burdens, and I will give you rest. Take my yoke upon you. Let me teach you, because I am humble and gentle, and you will find rest for your souls. For my yoke fits perfectly, and the burden I give you is light."*
> — MATTHEW 11:28-30 —

Pause to consider the burden you are carrying. Will you do as Tamar did and try to handle it yourself? Or will you let Jesus take your grief, disillusionment, unfair treatment, and disappointments? Take on Jesus' "yoke." Allow Him to give you a hope and a future.

EXPOSURE

SEEK GOD'S WORD FOR TRUTH

Read the following passage:

> *About three months later, word reached Judah that Tamar, his daughter-in-law, was pregnant as a result of prostitution. "Bring her out and burn her!" Judah shouted.*
>
> *But as they were taking her out to kill her, she sent this message to her father-in-law: "The man who owns this identification seal and walking stick is the father of my child. Do you recognize them?"*
>
> *Judah admitted that they were his and said, "She is more in the right than I am, because I didn't keep my promise to let her marry my son Shelah." But Judah never slept with Tamar again.*
>
> — GENESIS 38:24-26 —

✛ When Judah heard that Tamar was with child, what was his response? Was this a private proclamation or public one?

✛ Judah may have thought, *This will let me off the hook with my promise to her of Shelah!* He may also have thought, *Who will blame me for getting rid of Tamar?* What was Tamar's response to the death sentence her father-in-law demanded?

✛ Why do you think Tamar asked Judah a question rather than making a proclamation? What does this reveal about her character?

✛ A choice was now laid before Judah. He could once again run and hide, ignoring the truth; or he could, at last, do what was right. According to the passage we just read, what was Judah's response?

✛ What does Judah's response reveal about his character?

Read the following passage:

> *People who cover over their sins will not prosper. But if they confess and forsake them, they will receive mercy.*
>
> — PROVERBS 28:13 —

A heart that has confessed and forsaken sin will be declared righteous by God through Christ Jesus. Both Tamar and Judah found God's forgiveness and saw Him work out His good purposes through their lives. Only God can bring blessing from disaster, deceit, and disillusionment. Only God knows the heart of a person.

Read the following passages:

In due season the time of Tamar's delivery arrived, and she had twin sons. As they were being born, one of them reached out his hand, and the midwife tied a scarlet thread around the wrist of the child who appeared first, saying, "This one came out first." But then he drew back his hand, and the other baby was actually the first to be born. "What!" the midwife exclaimed. "How did you break out first?" And ever after, he was called Perez. Then the baby with the scarlet thread on his wrist was born, and he was named Zerah.

- GENESIS 38:27-30 -

"For I know the plans I have for you," says the Lord. "They are plans for good and not for disaster, to give you a future and a hope."

– JEREMIAH 29:11 –

Judah was the father of Perez and Zerah (their mother was Tamar). Perez was the father of Hezron. Hezron was the father of Ram.

– MATTHEW 1:3 –

✛ Tamar had hoped for a son. What did God do for her?

✛ Judah had hoped for an heir. What did God do for him?

FIND GOD'S WAYS FOR YOU

✛ Have you ever been privately confronted about something you did or said that was wrong? If so, how did it make you feel?

✛ Have you ever been openly rebuked, embarrassed, or corrected? How did you respond?

✛ When Tamar was openly confronted, she presented the truth (as she knew it). When Judah was confronted with the truth, he repented. He had run away from both his family and his faith. God used the consequences of his choices to bring about repentance and restoration. In your experiences of being confronted with something you did wrong, what were the consequences? If you had to do it over again, how might you respond differently?

STOP AND PONDER

Let us go right into the presence of God, with true hearts fully trusting him. For our evil consciences have been sprinkled with Christ's blood to make us clean, and our bodies have been washed with pure water.

— HEBREWS 10:22 —

God saved you by his special favor when you believed. And you can't take credit for this; it is a gift from God. Salvation is not a reward for the good things we have done, so none of us can boast about it.

— EPHESIANS 2:8-9 —

✛ How is God drawing you?

SEASONS FOR CHANGE

SEEK GOD'S WORD FOR TRUTH

From our brief study, we have seen how circumstances offer choices to be made in life. Those choices can lead to destruction and disillusionment or to restoration and a productive life. In review, look back at the Bible passage in "Setting the Scene" on pages 14-16. What kind of man was Judah then?

The following passage is lengthy, but it's important for learning the end of Judah's story. It took place many years after the incident with Tamar, when Judah and his brothers appeared before their long-lost brother Joseph. Joseph had risen to a position of great authority in Egypt. He recognized his evil brothers and decided to put them to a test to see whether they had changed. The brothers did not know that the man wielding the power of life or death over them was, in fact, Joseph.

When his brothers were ready to leave, Joseph gave these instructions to the man in charge of his household: "Fill each of their sacks with as much grain as they can carry, and put each man's money back into his sack. Then put my personal silver cup at the top of the youngest brother's sack, along with his grain money." So the household manager did as he was told.

The brothers were up at dawn and set out on their journey with their loaded donkeys. But when they were barely out of the city, Joseph said to his household manager, "Chase after them and stop them. Ask them, 'Why have you repaid an act of kindness with such evil? What do you mean by stealing my master's personal silver drinking cup, which he uses to predict the future? What a wicked thing you have done!'"

So the man caught up with them and spoke to them in the way he had been instructed. "What are you talking about?" the brothers responded. "What kind of people do you think we are, that you accuse us of such a terrible thing? Didn't we bring back the money we found in our sacks? Why would we steal silver or gold from your master's house? If you find his cup with any one of us, let that one die. And all the rest of us will be your master's slaves forever."

"Fair enough," the man replied, "except that only the one who stole it will be a slave. The rest of you may go free."

They quickly took their sacks from the backs of their donkeys and opened them. Joseph's servant began searching the oldest brother's sack, going on down the line to the youngest. The cup was found in Benjamin's sack! At this, they tore their clothing in despair, loaded the donkeys again, and returned to the city. Joseph was still at home when Judah and his brothers arrived, and they fell to the ground before him.

"What were you trying to do?" Joseph demanded. "Didn't you know that a man such as I would know who stole it?"

And Judah said, "Oh, my lord, what can we say to you? How can we plead? How can we prove our innocence? God is punishing us for our sins. My lord, we have all returned to be your slaves – we and our brother who had your cup in his sack."

"No," Joseph said. "Only the man who stole the cup will be my slave. The rest of you may go home to your father."

Then Judah stepped forward and said, "My lord, let me say just this one word to you. Be patient with me for a moment, for I know you could have me killed in an instant, as though you were Pharaoh himself.

"You asked us, my lord, if we had a father or a brother. We said, 'Yes,

we have a father, an old man, and a child of his old age, his youngest son. His brother is dead, and he alone is left of his mother's children, and his father loves him very much.' And you said to us, 'Bring him here so I can see him.' But we said to you, 'My lord, the boy cannot leave his father, for his father would die.' But you told us, 'You may not see me again unless your youngest brother is with you.' So we returned to our father and told him what you had said. And when he said, 'Go back again and buy us a little food,' we replied, 'We can't unless you let our youngest brother go with us. We won't be allowed to see the man in charge of the grain unless our youngest brother is with us.' Then my father said to us, 'You know that my wife had two sons, and that one of them went away and never returned – doubtless torn to pieces by some wild animal. I have never seen him since. If you take away his brother from me, too, and any harm comes to him, you would bring my gray head down to the grave in deep sorrow.'

"And now, my lord, I cannot go back to my father without the boy. Our father's life is bound up in the boy's life. When he sees that the boy is not with us, our father will die. We will be responsible for bringing his gray head down to the grave in sorrow. My lord, I made a pledge to my father that I would take care of the boy. I told him, 'If I don't bring him back to you, I will bear the blame forever.' Please, my lord, let me stay here as a slave instead of the boy, and let the boy return with his brothers. For how can I return to my father if the boy is not with me? I cannot bear to see what this would do to him."

– Genesis 44:1-34 –

✛ What do we learn about Judah from this account?

✛ In what ways had Judah changed?

Read the following Bible passage, which tells the end of the story:

Joseph could stand it no longer. "Out, all of you!" he cried out to his attendants. He wanted to be alone with his brothers when he told them who he was. Then he broke down and wept aloud. His sobs could be heard throughout the palace, and the news was quickly carried to Pharaoh's palace.

"I am Joseph!" he said to his brothers. "Is my father still alive?" But his brothers were speechless! They were stunned to realize that Joseph was

standing there in front of them. "Come over here," he said. So they came closer. And he said again, "I am Joseph, your brother whom you sold into Egypt. But don't be angry with yourselves that you did this to me, for God did it. He sent me here ahead of you to preserve your lives. These two years of famine will grow to seven, during which there will be neither plowing nor harvest. God has sent me here to keep you and your families alive so that you will become a great nation. Yes, it was God who sent me here, not you! And he has made me a counselor to Pharaoh — manager of his entire household and ruler over all Egypt.

"Hurry, return to my father and tell him, 'This is what your son Joseph says: God has made me master over all the land of Egypt. Come down to me right away! You will live in the land of Goshen so you can be near me with all your children and grandchildren, your flocks and herds, and all that you have. I will take care of you there, for there are still five years of famine ahead of us. Otherwise you and your household will come to utter poverty.'"

Then Joseph said, "You can see for yourselves, and so can my brother Benjamin, that I really am Joseph! Tell my father how I am honored here in Egypt. Tell him about everything you have seen, and bring him to me quickly." Weeping with joy, he embraced Benjamin, and Benjamin also began to weep. Then Joseph kissed each of his brothers and wept over them, and then they began talking freely with him.

— GENESIS 45:1-15 —

✛ Clearly, Joseph was deeply moved by Judah's plea. What was Joseph's response to Judah and the rest of his brothers?

God had made provision for the entire family. He had spared Joseph's life and given him a position of great authority. He had brought restoration to Judah and his brothers.

Reread the following passage about Tamar:

Then Judah told Tamar, his daughter-in-law, not to marry again at that time but to return to her parents' home. She was to remain a widow until his youngest son, Shelah, was old enough to marry her. (But Judah didn't really intend to do this because he was afraid Shelah would also die, like his two brothers.) So Tamar went home to her parents.

— GENESIS 38:11 —

✢ At that point, what kind of future did Tamar have to look forward to? Now read the following Bible passage, written many years later:

And may the Lord give you descendants by this young woman who will be like those of our ancestor Perez, the son of Tamar and Judah.
– RUTH 4:12 –

✢ How was Tamar remembered by her descendants?

Tamar had her hopes and plans, but God had bigger plans. He gave her twin sons, who became the forebears of the tribe of Judah. Ultimately, the Messiah – the promised Savior of the world – came from that tribe.

FIND GOD'S WAYS FOR YOU

✢ Just as God worked in the lives of Judah and Tamar, He works in our lives today. In what ways is God revealing Himself to you?

✢ As you have worked through these lessons, what changes do you sense you may need to make in your life?

✢ Who holds your future? According to Jeremiah 29:11 (see page 110), who is offering you a future?

STOP AND PONDER

For God so loved the world that he gave his only Son, so that everyone who believes in him will not perish but have eternal life. God did not send his Son into the world to condemn it, but to save it.
  There is no judgment awaiting those who trust him. But those who do not trust him have already been judged for not believing in the only Son of God.
– JOHN 3:16-18 –

Are you ready for the future? If you have not given your life to Jesus Christ, you can do so right now. All you need to do is say a simple prayer. Confess that you are a sinner and that you desire to turn around, and invite Jesus Christ to come into your heart as your Lord and Savior. When you belong to Jesus, you can be assured of an eternal future and hope for today.
  Choose life!

BLESSINGS AND SONGS

SEEK GOD'S WORD FOR TRUTH

As we've already seen, the story of Tamar does not end with the birth of her twin sons. We can trace Judah and Tamar throughout the Bible. The following passages are a few examples of the future God had in store for them:

"I am Joseph!" he said to his brothers. "Is my father still alive?" But his brothers were speechless! They were stunned to realize that Joseph was standing there in front of them. "Come over here," he said. So they came closer. And he said again, "I am Joseph, your brother whom you sold into Egypt. But don't be angry with yourselves that you did this to me, for God did it. He sent me here ahead of you to preserve your lives. These two years of famine will grow to seven, during which there will be neither plowing nor harvest. God has sent me here to keep you and your families alive so that you will become a great nation. Yes, it was God who sent me here, not you! And he has made me a counselor to Pharaoh – manager of his entire household and ruler over all Egypt.

"Hurry, return to my father and tell him, 'This is what your son Joseph says: God has made me master over all the land of Egypt. Come down to me right away! You will live in the land of Goshen so you can be near me with all your children and grandchildren, your flocks and herds, and all that you have.'"

– GENESIS 45:3-10 –

✦ How did Joseph feel about Judah?

✦ In the following passage, Judah receives a blessing rom his father, Jacob (also known as Israel). What are the key elements of this blessing?

"Judah, your brothers will praise you. You will defeat your enemies. All your relatives will bow before you. Judah is a young lion that has finished eating its prey. Like a lion he crouches and lies down; like a lioness – who will dare to rouse him? The scepter will not depart from Judah, nor the ruler's staff from his descendants, until the coming of the one to whom it belongs, the one whom all nations will obey. He ties his foal to a grape-vine, the colt of his donkey to a choice vine. He washes his clothes in wine because his harvest is so plentiful. His eyes are darker than wine, and

his teeth are whiter than milk."

— GENESIS 49:8-12 —

✛ Read the following passage. How was Moses' blessing different from Jacob's blessing?

Moses said this about the tribe of Judah: "O Lord, hear the cry of Judah and bring them again to their people. Give them strength to defend their cause; help them against their enemies!"

— DEUTERONOMY 33:7 —

✛ In the following passage, who chooses Judah?

Then the Lord rose up as though waking from sleep, like a mighty man aroused from a drunken stupor. He routed his enemies and sent them to eternal shame. But he rejected Joseph's descendants; he did not choose the tribe of Ephraim. He chose instead the tribe of Judah, Mount Zion, which he loved.

— PSALM 78:65-68 —

Genesis 38 – the story of Tamar and Judah, upon which *Unveiled* is based – can be seen as a celebration of the father and mother of a tribe. Tamar was held in great respect. Her actions were carried out with the sole intention of having a child to carry on the family. God saw her heart and gave her children. God also knew Judah's heart and provided a way for him to be restored to his family, as well as his descendants, to carry on his name. Ultimately, God used the line of Judah to give the world the Messiah. The Messiah is often referred to as the Lion of Judah. Jesus is Messiah!

FIND GOD'S WAYS FOR YOU

✛ Is there someone with whom you need to make amends, as Judah did?

✛ Like Tamar, we all have hopes and dreams for the future. What kinds of things do you hope for?

✛ How do you want to be remembered?

STOP AND PONDER

"My thoughts are completely different from yours," says the Lord. "And my ways are far beyond anything you could imagine. For just as the heavens are higher than the earth, so are my ways higher than your ways and my thoughts higher than your thoughts.

"The rain and snow come down from the heavens and stay on the ground to water the earth. They cause the grain to grow, producing seed for the farmer and bread for the hungry. It is the same with my word. I send it out, and it always produces fruit. It will accomplish all I want it to, and it will prosper everywhere I send it. You will live in joy and peace. The mountains and hills will burst into song, and the trees of the field will clap their hands! Where once there were thorns, cypress trees will grow. Where briers grew, myrtles will sprout up. This miracle will bring great honor to the Lord's name; it will be an everlasting sign of his power and love."

– Isaiah 55:8-13 –

May God's Word always produce the fruit of obedience and accomplish much in you.

Unashamed

setting the scene

THE sons of Israel, the chosen people of God, took their families to Egypt to escape a famine in their homeland. One of the twelve brothers, Joseph, held a high position in the Egyptian government, and as a result, his large extended family were honored as special guests of Pharaoh himself.

But as the years passed and the Hebrews multiplied, they fell out of favor and were eventually enslaved by the Egyptians. It took the leadership of Moses – and a series of breathtaking miracles performed by God Himself – to deliver them. God was taking His people home, back to Canaan, the land He had promised would belong to His people forever.

On the verge of reclaiming their "Promised Land," the Israelites' faith in God failed. Fearing the power of the Canaanites, they refused to obey God's command to advance and take the land. Their disbelief and disobedience resulted in a forty-year delay in the fulfillment of God's promise. During those forty years, the Israelites wandered as nomads in the desert. All of the adults who had left Egypt and rebelled against God died in the wilderness.

Finally a new generation grew up, ready to take its place as God's army and claim the land promised to its ancestors. Of the original multitude that had left Egypt, only Moses and his two assistants, Joshua and Caleb, survived.

As the people of Israel approached the Promised Land for the second time, no one could stand against them. First the king of Arad, then King Sihon of the Amorites, then King Og of Bashan – all were put to the sword, their armies annihilated. In desperation, King Balak of Moab hired a sorcerer, Balaam, to curse the Israelites. To Balak's horror, God used Balaam to instead pronounce blessings upon His chosen people.

Finally, even the five kings of Midian together were unsuccessful in stopping the advancing Israelite army. Kings Evi, Rekem, Zur, Hur, and Reba all died in battle, their armies slaughtered, their towns and villages burned, their wealth seized as plunder.

The time had come. The people of God were ready to claim their inheritance from God – the Promised Land. After designating Joshua as the new leader of Israel, the venerable Moses died, and the people prepared to cross the last remaining barrier between them and Canaan: the Jordan River, swollen with spring floods.

Now, all nations quake in terror at the knowledge that Israel is encamped at Shittim, just a short distance from Jericho. The walled fortress, the gateway to Canaan, awaits.

one

RAHAB studied the distant plain of Jericho from her window in the city wall, her heart stirring with fear and excitement. Out there, just beyond the Jordan River, the Israelites were encamped, only the floodwaters holding them back. Soon they would cross over and come against the king of Jericho with the same ferocity they had shown in battle against Sihon, Og, and the five kings of Midian. And everyone in Jericho would die.

The king had doubled the guard at the gate and posted soldiers on the battlements. But it would do no good. Destruction was on the horizon. The only hope was to surrender and plead for mercy. The king worried about the size of the invading army, but he failed to see the real danger: the God of the Hebrews. All of Pharaoh's warriors hadn't been enough to defeat Him forty years ago. Not even the pantheon of gods and goddesses had saved Egypt. But all the king of Jericho could think about was improving the battlements, stockpiling weapons, and increasing the number of soldiers! Did men never learn?

Jericho was doomed!

And she was imprisoned inside the city, bound by a life she had carved out for herself years ago. What hope had she, a harlot? Her fate had been set in motion years ago, when she was little more than a child, a peasant's daughter summoned by a king.

"You must go!" her father had said. "As long as you live in the palace and please him, I shall prosper. He's arranging marriages for your sisters. And if you refuse, he will have you nonetheless, killing me to remove any obstacles. Think of the honor he bestows upon you. He chooses only the most beautiful girls, Rahab."

An *honor?* "And will he marry me, Father?" Her father couldn't look into her eyes. She knew the answer. The king had several wives, all of whom he had married for political advantages. She had nothing a king needed – merely a body he wanted to use.

Even then, young as she had been, she knew that lust burned hot but eventually turned to ashes. In a week, a month, a year perhaps, the king would tire of her and send her home wearing a beautiful Babylonian robe and a few pieces of gold jewelry her father would confiscate and sell for his own profit.

"When I return, will you allow me to sell dates and pomegranates in the marketplace again, Father, or will I end up like so many others? Selling my body for a loaf of bread?"

He had covered his face and wept. She'd hated him for taking advantage of her ruin, hated him for making excuses, hated him for telling her she would be better off in the king's palace than in the grove hut where he and her mother and brothers and sisters lived. She hated him because he had no power to save her.

She had hated her own helplessness most of all.

Even in her wrath, Rahab had known her father couldn't save her from the king's lust. A king could take what he wanted. Any gifts he gave were meant to dissolve thoughts of revenge. Life was hard and uncertain, but if the right opportunity arose, a beautiful daughter could make a father's way smooth. Tax exemptions. Land use. An elevated position in the court. The king was generous when it served him, but usually his generosity lasted only as long as his lust.

Rahab rested her arms on the window, gazing out. She remembered setting foot in the palace that first day, vowing not to end up as a discarded sandal. She intended to find a way to take advantage of her wretched situation and the man who used her. She'd hidden her fury and revulsion, pretending to enjoy the king's embrace. Every moment in his company, her mind was crouched like a lioness studying its prey, watching, waiting for his weakness to show. And she found it soon enough: the constant arrival of emissaries, spies, and messengers. Without their stream of information, he wouldn't know who his enemies were or what petty jealousies and rebellions were on the rise.

"Give me a house, and I'll gather information for you," she had boldly proposed, once her opportunity became clear to her. How the king had laughed at her sagacity! She'd laughed with him, but continued to entice and solicit for further benefits. She was tenacious in her determination to have something tangible when she left the palace, something with which she could make her own way and sustain herself comfortably for a lifetime. She deserved it after suffering the caresses of that fat, foul-smelling, arrogant old man!

Well, she had gotten what she wanted: a house, a prosperous living, and the illusion of independence. The king had given her this house situated near the eastern gate so she could watch the comings and goings of Jericho. For twelve years she'd looked out this window and picked out men to share her bed, men who might tell her things that would protect the king's throne and increase his treasury. Every transaction she made brought a double payment. The men paid to sleep with her, and the king paid for the grains of information she gleaned. She knew even more about what was happening outside the walls of Jericho than the king did. And when she wanted to know what was going on inside the palace, she beckoned Cabul, the captain of the guard. He could always be counted on to spill out every secret while in her arms.

She owned half a dozen Babylonian robes, boxes inlaid with bone and ivory and filled with jewelry. Her house was furnished with objects of art, her floor covered with multicolored, woven rugs. Her customers slept on the finest colored linen sheets from Egypt perfumed with myrrh, aloe, and cinnamon. She could afford tasty delicacies and rich, heady wines. Everyone in the city knew she was a friend and confidante of the king. They also knew she was a whore.

But no one knew how much she hated her life. No one guessed how helpless she felt in the face of the plans made for her by father and king. Many would wonder why she had cause to complain. On the outside, she had an enviable life. The king respected her, men desired her, and she could choose her clientele. There were even women in Jericho who envied her independence. They didn't know what it felt like to be used, stripped of humanity. Even now, despite a house of her own and plush surroundings, she was helpless to change anything about her life. She was locked into it.

Yet no one knew the fierce heart that beat within her. No one suspected the stored resentment, the gathering fury, the aching hunger to break free and escape. She was in a prison others had made for her, a prison she had succeeded in filling with earthly treasures. But she had other plans, other dreams and hopes.

And they all depended on the God out there, the One she knew had the power to save those He chose. Somehow she had known – even as a young girl hearing the stories for the first time – that He was a true God, the only true One. When He brought His people across the Jordan, He would take this city and crush it as He had crushed all His enemies.

The end of everything she had known was in sight.

We're all going to die! Doesn't anyone else see that? Are they all blind and deaf to what's been happening for the last forty years? People come and go as they always have, thinking everything is going to be all right. They think the walls we've built will protect us, just as I thought the walls of my father's hut could protect me all those years ago. And we're not safe – we're not safe at all!

She was filled with the terror of death, filled even more with a terrible longing to be a part of what would come. She wanted to belong to the God who was coming. She felt like a little girl wanting desperately to be swept up in her father's arms and saved from destruction.

Several months ago, an Egyptian had spent a night telling her stories of the God of the Israelites. "But everyone says those are myths," she had said, wondering whether he believed the tales he repeated.

"Oh, no. My father was a boy when the plagues came ... " He'd talked far into the night about the signs and wonders and about a man named Moses. "He's dead now, but there's another ... Joshua."

She went to the king the next morning, but he was only interested in tactics, weaponry, numbers. "It's the *God* of the Hebrews you need to fear, my king," she said, but he waved her away impatiently.

"You disappoint me, Rahab, talking like a hysterical woman."

She wanted to shout at him. Moses might be a great leader, but no man could break the might of Egypt. Only a true God could do that! And He was out there, preparing His people to take all of Canaan.

But one look into the king's eyes and she knew pride was on the throne. Men listened only to what they wanted to hear.

Now, sitting at her window, she stretched her hands out and waved them. *Oh, how I wish I were one of Your people, for You alone are a true God.* Her eyes were hot and gritty. *I would bow down to You and give You offerings if given the chance!* She put her hands down and turned away. She could wish all she wanted, but she was going to share the same fate as everyone else trapped inside these walls. This fortress would become a slaughterhouse.

Because the king was stubborn and proud. Because the king thought the walls were high enough and thick enough to keep him safe. Because he was too stubborn and stupid to put his pride aside for the sake of his people. The king was afraid of the Israelites, but it was their God he should fear. She had known men all her life, and they were all much the same. But this God, He was different. She could *feel* His presence in some strange way she couldn't define, and she was filled with a sense of awe and urgency. Oh, how fortunate were those who belonged to Him! They had *nothing* to fear.

Although she had told the king everything she learned, he refused to listen. Still, she kept trying.

"I never knew you to be so fainthearted, my sweet. Those Hebrews will tuck tail and flee the same way they did forty years ago when the Amalekites joined forces with us. My father drove them out of the land. If they have such a mighty god on their side, why didn't they prevail against us then? Plagues ... seas opening ... " He sneered. "Myths to frighten us."

"Have you forgotten Sihon?"

He paled, his eyes narrowing coldly at her reminder. "No army can break through our walls."

"Before it's too late, send emissaries of peace with gifts for their God."

"What? Are you mad? Do you think our priests would agree to that? We have gods of our own to appease! They've always protected us in the past. They'll protect us now."

"The same way Egypt's gods protected her? Egypt bows down to insects, and this God sent swarms to destroy their crops. They worship their Nile River, and this God turned it to blood."

"They're just stories, Rahab. Rumors to spread fear among our people. And you add to them! Go back to your house and do what you do best. Watch for foreign spies ... "

"And so she did, but not for his sake.

Cabul talked freely last night, boasting of manpower, weapons, and the continuous sacrifices being made to the gods of Canaan. "We'll be fine. Don't worry your pretty head."

Fools! They were all fools! Surely the God who mocked the gods of Egypt and opened the Red Sea would find it easy to break down these walls! What good would stone and mortar idols do against a God who controlled wind, fire, and water? Rahab was certain that one breath from His lips would blow open the gates of Jericho. A sweep of His hand would make rubble of all the king's defenses!

But no one would listen.

So be it. She had given her last warning. Let it be on the king's head what happened to Jericho. She was going to find a way to align herself with those who would have the victory. If she didn't, she would die.

How could she get out of Jericho without jeopardizing the lives of her family members? If she left, the king would have her followed. She would be captured and executed for treason, and every member of her family would suffer the same fate to prevent the spread of her rebellion. No, she couldn't leave Jericho unless she took her father and mother and brothers and sisters and their families with her. But that would be impossible! Even if she could find a way to leave without arousing suspicion, her family wouldn't come. Her father believed whatever the king said. It wasn't in his nature to think for himself.

Rahab raked her fingers through her hair, pushing the curly dark mass over her shoulder. "Rahab!" someone called from below. She didn't look down. She wasn't interested in a merchant from Jebus or the owner of a caravan taking spices to Egypt or another soldier from a vanquished army. They were all walking dead. They just didn't know it yet. Only those Hebrews out there beyond the river were alive. For their God was no stone idol carved by human hands. He was the God of heaven and earth!

And I am just a rat inside a hole in this wall ...

What a strange and marvelous God He was! He had chosen the Hebrews – nation of slaves – and set them free from Egypt, the most powerful nation on earth. He had taken the lowest of the low and used them to bring down the mighty. She'd heard that He'd even rained bread upon His people. They had nothing to fear, for He was mighty in deeds and yet showed kindness and mercy to them. Who would not love such a God?

Her king. Her people.

I would love Him! Her mouth trembled, and her eyes were hot with tears. *I would serve Him any way He asked. Given the chance, I would bow down before Him and rejoice to be counted among His people!*

Cabul snored loudly from the bed behind her, reminding her of his unwelcome presence. She pressed her palms over her ears and shut her eyes tightly, filled with self-disgust and anger. If she gave in to her feelings, she would shake the man awake and scream at him to get out of her house. He hadn't told her anything new last night. Cabul was a waste of her time.

She watched the road again. She had one small glimmer of hope that had been roused by something her father had told her. Moses had sent spies into the land forty years ago. "We beat them back then." She had wondered about that, mulling over reasons for the Israelites' failure. They had been slaves, freed from mighty Egypt by an even mightier God. But perhaps they had still thought like slaves rather than men under the banner of a true God. Perhaps they had refused to obey. She could only guess why they had failed. But she knew it was not due to any failure of the God who rescued them.

Those who had rebelled all those years ago must surely be dead by now. A new generation had arisen, a generation who had been hardened by desert living, a generation who had been in the presence of Power from their birth. She could only hope that Joshua would do as Moses had done before him and send spies into the land. And she would have to be the first to spot them. With victory assured by their God, the Israelites didn't need to send anyone, but she still hoped the noble leader Joshua would take nothing for granted. Even if it wasn't necessary, it would be prudent to send spies to view the land and evaluate enemy defenses.

Please come. Please, please, please come ... I don't want to die. I don't want my family to die. Send someone ... Open my eyes so that I'll recognize them before the guards do. If they see them first and report to the king, all is lost!

"Rahab!" a man called to her again.

She glanced down impatiently and saw an Ishmaelite merchant waving at her from among the throng gathered at the gate. He was eager to lodge with her, but she spread her hands, shrugging and shaking her head. Let his camels keep him warm. He held up a gold necklace to bribe her. Ha! What good would gold do when the day of destruction came? "Give it to one of your wives!"she called back. Those around him laughed. Another man called up to her, but she ignored the entreaties and flatteries and watched the road.

Let them come to me.

If the spies were ragged from wandering, she would give them beautiful robes from Babylon. If they were thirsty, she would give them fine wine. If they were hungry, she would serve them a feast fit for kings. For they would come as servants of the Most High God. She would show them the honor meant for the One they served. For mighty was their God and worthy of tribute!

Her chest was tight with yearning. She wanted to be safe. As long as she was inside this wall, inside this city, she was condemned. She had to be counted among the Israelites to survive. The gods of the Jerichoans and Amorites and Perizzites and a dozen other tribes who inhabited Canaan wouldn't come to her rescue. They were stone tyrants with corrupt priests who demanded constant sacrifice. She'd seen babies taken from their mothers and placed on an altar, their little bodies boiled until the flesh fell away so the bones could be put into small bags and buried beneath the foundation of a new house or temple. As though murdered children could bring good fortune! She was thankful she had never had a child.

But if I did have one, I would give my baby to the God out there, the unseen One who dwells with His people, who shades them by day and keeps them warm at night, the One who protects those who belong to Him as though they were His children. A God like Him could be trusted ...

"Ah, the light." Cabul groaned. "Close the curtains!"

Rahab clenched her teeth; she kept her back to him. It was time the man was gone from her bed and her house. "The sun is up," she said in a pleasant voice. "Time you were as well."

She heard a muffled curse and the rustle of linen. "You're hard-hearted, Rahab."

She glanced at him over her shoulder and forced a sultry smile. "You didn't say that last night." She looked out the window again, searching, hoping to see someone who looked like an Israelite spy. What would one look like? How would she recognize one if he did come?

Cabul slid his arm around her waist and reached up to lift the curtain from the hook. "Come back to bed, my love." He pressed his lips to the curve of her neck.

She caught his hand before it could move to caress her. "The king will hear you're missing from your post. I wouldn't want to get you into trouble."

He laughed softly, his breath hot in her hair. "I won't be late."

She turned in his arms. "You must go, Cabul." She put her hands against his chest. "Your absence at the gate will be noticed, and I'll not have it said that Rahab caused a friend trouble."

"You are causing me pain right now."

"You're man enough to survive a small discomfort."

He caught her hand as she moved away from him. "Is there a rich merchant below?"

"No."

"I heard someone calling your name."

"And what if you did?" Did he think putting a few coins in her hand meant he owned her? "You know what I do for a living."

He frowned, his eyes darkening.

Stifling her annoyance, she brushed her fingertips down his cheek and softened her tone. "Don't forget I came out of my house to find you." In her business, it was always wise to send a man away feeling he was someone special.

He grinned. "So you love me a little."

"Enough to wish you no harm." She allowed him to kiss her briefly and then disentangled herself. "A crowd is waiting at the gate, Cabul. It's time you opened it. If the merchants are annoyed, the king will hear about it." She crossed the room, leaned down, and swept up his clothes. Opening the door, she tossed them back at him. "You'd better hurry!" She laughed as she watched him dress hastily, then closed the door behind him. Dropping the bar to keep any would-be visitors out, she hurried back to her post at the window.

Solitude was a luxury. She stepped up and sat in the window, one leg dangling out. Ignoring the whistles from below, she watched the plain. Was that a column of smoke in the distance? She couldn't be sure. She had heard that the Israelites' God accompanied them as a column of smoke during the day and a pillar of fire at night.

When the heat became oppressive, she closed the curtains, left the window, and brushed her hair. She ate bread and sipped wine. But every few minutes, she parted the reddyed linen and looked out again, studying every stranger who walked along the road.

≈≈≈

Salmon had waited all his life to set foot in the Promised Land. He could see it from where he was camped. He was eager for the battles ahead, his confidence strengthened by past victories the Lord had given His people. It was the waiting that was difficult. Salmon felt like a horse reined in, prancing, champing at the bit, ready for the race to begin. He laughed, excitement coursing through him as he sparred with his friend Ephraim. It was early, the sun just rising, but every day was an opportunity to train, to prepare for God's work of taking the Promised Land.

Gripping his staff, he made a thrust. Ephraim parried, turned, and struck, but Salmon countered him. *Crack! Crack! Crack!* Ephraim came at him with fierce determination, but Salmon was ready. Turning, he swept the staff in a hard circle and swept Ephraim off his feet. Salmon was too confident, for he didn't expect Ephraim to make another swing at him from the ground, which landed Salmon on his back in the dust. Both lay in the dust, panting and grinning.

As soon as Salmon got his breath back, he laughed. "I'll be less smug next time."

"When do you think we'll attack Jericho?" Ephraim said, rising and dusting himself off.

Salmon sat up and looked toward the rise where Joshua stood each day, praying. "The Lord will tell Joshua when the time is right."

"I hope it's soon! Somehow the waiting is harder than the battle itself."

Salmon stood, his staff gripped in his hand. The desert wind stirred Joshua's robes as he stood on the rise. Since Moses had died, Salmon had turned his full attention to Joshua and Eleazar, the priest, for leadership. Whatever they said was law, for they followed the Lord wholeheartedly and spoke only what God instructed them to say. As a boy at his father's knee, Salmon had heard the story of how Joshua and Caleb had spied out the Promised Land and said it could be taken. They'd believed God's promise to give them the land, but the other eight spies had convinced the people – even the great leader Moses himself – that victory was impossible. The people had lacked faith and lost their opportunity, so the promise was deferred to the next generation. Salmon's generation. Salmon hadn't even been born when the Lord had passed judgment and sent the people back into the desert, but he'd been affected by it. He had grown up in the shadow of his father's shame and regrets.

How many times had he heard his father weeping? *"If only we'd listened. If only we'd believed Joshua and Caleb."*

Over and over again, year after year. If whining could wear down the Lord, his father's surely would have. *"If only we'd listened, we wouldn't be out in this wilderness, wandering like lost sheep."* Salmon grimaced at the memory of his father's complaints and self-pity, for they hinted of the old rebellion and the unchanged attitude of a man's heart.

Lord God of mercy, save me from such thinking, he prayed. *Make me the man You want me to be – a man of courage, a man willing to step out immediately when You say go.*

It was too easy to sneer at the mistakes of others. Such arrogance. Salmon knew he was no better than the man who had fathered him. The danger was in looking too far ahead. He must *wait,* as Joshua was waiting. The Lord would speak when He was ready, and when God did speak, Salmon knew the choice would be presented to him: obey or disobey. He didn't want to hesitate like his father had. Better to fear God than men. No matter how frightened he might be of the battle ahead, he knew it was a more fearful thing to displease the Lord. Therefore, he set his mind on obedience. He wouldn't allow himself to give in to his human weaknesses, his fears. How could one fear men and please God?

Jehovah had promised the land of Canaan to His people. The day would come when He would call them to take hold of that promise. It would be up to Salmon and all those of his generation to obey.

So far, none had weakened, but a few were grumbling at the delay, and a few questioned.

Lord God of heaven and earth, I beg You to give me the confidence of Joshua. Instill in me Your purpose. Do not let me weaken. You are God and there is no other!

"Prepare yourself," Ephraim said.

Turning, Salmon brought his staff up and blocked Ephraim's blow.

When the Lord called him into battle, Salmon intended to be ready.

≈≈≈

"Salmon."

He recognized the deep voice immediately. Jumping to his feet, he pulled back the tent flap and gaped at Joshua.

"I have work for you," the elderly man said calmly.

"Please, enter." Salmon stepped back quickly and bid his commander welcome.

The old warrior ducked his head slightly and entered the tent, looked around briefly, and faced Salmon once more. Salmon shook inwardly with excitement, for what greater honor could there be than to have Joshua seek him out? "Please sit here, sir." He offered him the most comfortable place.

Joshua inclined his head. Setting the bundle he had brought with him to one side, he folded his legs beneath him as easily as a young man. When he looked up at Salmon, his eyes were dark and intent, ablaze with purpose.

Under normal circumstances, the commander would have summoned him rather than come to his tent. "What can I serve you, sir?" Salmon said, curbing his curiosity in order to show respect and hospitality. Joshua would explain when he was ready.

Smiling slightly, Joshua held out his hand. "Nothing. But you can sit."

Salmon did so. Leaning forward, he clasped his hands and said nothing. The old man closed his eyes for a long moment and then raised his head and looked at him. "I need two men to go on a mission of great risk."

"I'll go." Salmon straightened, heart pounding. "Send me."

Joshua tipped his head to one side and considered him in amusement. "It might be prudent to hear what the mission is before you volunteer."

"If you want it done, it needs doing, and that's all I need to know. The Lord speaks through you. To obey you is to obey God. I'll go wherever you want me to go and do whatever you need done."

Joshua's eyes glowed. He leaned forward. "Then here are your instructions. Spy out the land on the other side of the Jordan River, especially around Jericho. See what defenses they have in place. Discern the mood of the people."

Fear caught Salmon unaware, but he set his mind against it. "When do you want me to leave?"

"Within the hour. Caleb is giving instructions to Ephraim." Joshua raised his hand. "I can see you're ready to grab your sword and go now, but hear me out. Other than Caleb and Ephraim, no one knows you're leaving camp. You'll be going in secret. You're young and on fire, my son, but you must be coolheaded and wise as a serpent. Do not stroll into the city like a conqueror. Keep your head down. Seek out an establishment that will know the mind of the people. Blend in. Keep your eyes and ears open. The battlements aren't as important as what the Jerichoans are thinking. Find out everything you can, and then get out of there as quickly as possible. Waste no time. Do you understand?"

"Yes, commander."

Joshua took the bundle he'd set aside and placed it between them. "Amorite clothing and a weapon."

The clothing had undoubtedly been taken from the body of a vanquished foe, for Salmon saw a stain of blood. He knew he would have to be careful when wearing the tunic. It would be difficult for him to blend in naturally among Jerichoans if anyone saw that stain. Anyone looking at it would know the last man who wore the garment had died a violent death. He would have to wear a mantle to cover it.

Joshua rose. Salmon sprang to his feet. Joshua turned before going out, put his hand on Salmon's shoulder, and gripped him strongly. "May the Lord watch over you and keep you safe!"

"Blessed be the name of the Lord."

Releasing him, Joshua swept the tent flap aside, stooped, and went out. Salmon held the flap open long enough to watch Joshua disappear among the other tents of Israel. Letting it drop back into place, he let out his breath sharply and dropped to his knees. Throwing back his head, Salmon closed his eyes and raised his hands, thanking God for this opportunity to serve. Then he prostrated himself and prayed for the wisdom and courage to complete the task.

By moonlight, Salmon and Ephraim girded their loins by drawing up the backs of their tunics and tucking them into their belts. Thus unencumbered, they ran, reaching the eastern bank of the Jordan well before daybreak. Gasping for breath, Salmon dumped his bundle on the ground, grasped his tunic, and hauled it up over his head.

"The river looks swift," Ephraim said, stripping off his clothing and catching the Amorite tunic Salmon tossed him.

Swollen by spring floods, the river rose over its banks. And Ephraim was right – the current was swift.

Salmon shrugged into the Amorite tunic. He nodded toward a sloping bank as he strapped on a leather belt. "We'll go in down there and start swimming."

Ephraim's mouth curved sardonically. "I hate to mention this now, friend, but I don't know how to swim."

Salmon laughed mirthlessly. "And you think I do? The desert hasn't exactly afforded us much opportunity to learn, has it?"

"So what are we going to do?"

"Cross over. Stop worrying. If God wills, we'll make it."

"And if not, we'll drown," Ephraim said flatly.

"Do you think the Lord has brought us this far to let us be defeated?"

Ephraim watched the river. "I'd feel better if I had a tree trunk to hang on to."

"The Lord will uphold us." Salmon spoke with more conviction than he felt. *Give me courage, Lord.* "Fill your lungs with air, keep your arms outstretched, and kick like a frog. The current will carry us."

"All the way to the Salt Sea."

Salmon ignored his friend's grim sense of humor and pointed. "Aim for those willows on the other side." Tying the sheath to his belt, he jammed his dagger into it. "Let's go."

Despite his bravado, fear shot through Salmon as the river's current tugged hard at his legs. Overcoming his fear, he waded into the Jordan until the water was to his waist. Perhaps he could make it this way, one step at a time, using his own physical strength to keep himself on his feet. But the next step proved he couldn't. He slipped on some slick rocks and lost his footing. Panic gripped him as he was sucked into the current. He was pulled under briefly, but he fought his way up long enough to fill his lungs with air. His body rolled and turned, spun back. He hit something hard and almost lost his breath. Salmon fought his fear and the river, as the spring flood carried him along.

Lord, help me!

He saw the trees and kicked hard. Clawing the water, he used the current to steer his body. He kept his neck arched and stiff so that his head was above the water and he could breathe and see where he was going. He heard a shout behind him but didn't have time to turn and see if Ephraim was doing any better than he. Making a lunge for an overhanging branch, he caught hold. Reaching up, he got a better grip and looked back. Ephraim was still standing on the far bank.

"Come on!" Salmon called to him.

Ephraim entered the river with obvious uneasiness. Stretching out his arms, he went in face first. Seeing how fast Ephraim was swept along, Salmon stretched out his body as far as possible so that his friend could reach his ankle. "Grab hold!"

Ephraim succeeded, but the jolt almost yanked Salmon free. His body swung hard around and jerked against the strong pull of the river. Water rippled violently over Ephraim's head. Clinging to the branch with one hand, Salmon reached down and grasped Ephraim and pulled. "Climb!" Ephraim reached up, his fingers biting into Salmon's thigh. Pulling himself higher, his head emerged from the rushing water. He gasped for breath. Salmon grabbed Ephraim's belt and hauled him up farther. Salmon shoved him toward the west bank.

When he made it to shore, Ephraim reached out and gave Salmon a hand and threw himself back as far as he could before the limb broke and toppled into the water. Gaining his footing in the rocky bottom, Salmon slogged his way out of the Jordan and collapsed to his knees. Ephraim was coughing violently.

Chest heaving, Salmon drank in the air. He dug his fingers into the soil and held it up to breathe in the scent of its richness. "The Lord has brought us over, " he said in a voice choked with emotion. They were the first of their generation to set foot in the Promised Land. "The Lord be praised!"

Ephraim was still coughing up murky river water, but he managed to rasp, "May God grant we live long enough to enjoy it."

"Amen." Salmon rose. "It won't be long until daybreak." He was eager for the mission ahead, anxious to be on the move, but it wouldn't be wise to arrive wet and muddy from the river – or too early in the day, making them appear anxious to enter the city. Hunkering down by the Jordan, he washed. "If we hurry, we can make it to the palms before full daylight."

"Just give me a few minutes to rest, will you?"

"We've no time to waste. Rest while we walk!"

As they crossed the arid stretch of land west of the Jordan and gained the road, the sun rose behind them. Even from a distance of several miles, the lush green spring-fed oasis was visible, as were the high, thick walls of the City of Palms that blocked entrance into Canaan. Salmon's heart sank. These walls were so immense, they would be insurmountable by frontal attack. Nor could they be taken from the west, for behind the walled city was a towering backbone of steep, jagged mountains. "The city is well situated."

"And impregnable. How will we ever conquer such a city? Never has there been such a stronghold!"

Speechless, Salmon studied the walls. They were at least six times the height of any man, and there were battlements on both sides of the gate. Guards standing watch would see an army coming from miles away, giving them plenty of time to close the gates and prepare for battle.

Would Joshua have them build ladders to scale these walls? How many would die in setting them up and keeping them in place until enough soldiers could get over the wall? Could those immense gates be smashed or burned? How many would die in the battle for this city? Thousands! Would he be one of them – if he didn't die here today, on this mission?

"May God protect us from such an end," Salmon said under his breath.

"What should we do now?" Ephraim said. "Join the throng waiting for the gates to open?"

"We'll wait until late in the day. Better if we aren't inspected too closely. The guards will be less attentive then."

They found a grassy place not far from a spring-fed stream and slept in the shade of the City of Palms.

two

AT first glance, Rahab dismissed the two men as Amorite soldiers carrying a message to the king. But as they came closer, she noticed their interest in the walls. The men, who carried no packs or parcels, seemed grim as they spoke to one another, watchful of the guard towers. Even more telling was their complete disinterest in her. Soldiers, even those on a serious mission, invariably looked for women of her calling. They were always eager for a comfortable night's lodging, food, drink, and fleshly pleasures whenever they could get them. Amorite soldiers were especially lustful and profane.

Ah, the men had spotted her. "Hello, my fine friends!" she called, smiling and waving. They turned their faces away. Odd. They were young, but not so young they should be embarrassed by a woman's attentions.

Or had that been disgust on their faces? An uncomfortable feeling curled in the pit of her stomach. It had been years since she had felt shame or the desire to cover her face and hide. Not since the first few weeks she had been in the king's company. No matter what her father had said, she knew in her heart that what was being done to her was wrong, and for her to take advantage of it was even worse. It had been a confusing time, a time of degradation and elevation. But no one had dared openly look down upon a young woman chosen by the king. She had been treated with deference during her months in the palace. And with time, she had learned to hide her feelings. She had learned to hold her head up and walk like a queen, even though every prospect of having an honorable future had been stripped from her.

In spite of her discomfort – or perhaps even because of it – her interest in the two men increased. She was certain they were not what they appeared to be. True Amorite soldiers would strut and swagger. They would call out lewd suggestions to her and make offers of money. They would boast of their prowess with women.

Were these the Israelite spies she'd hoped would come?

The desert wind came up, swirling dust around the two. The outer garment on the taller man blew open. He snatched the garment closed. But not before she saw the stain he'd quickly hidden.

Her heart leapt. Rahab drew in her breath sharply and leaned forward. She was determined now to gain their attention. No matter how brazen she had to be, she would make them look up at her. She leaned so far out the window that her black curling hair spilled like a dark waterfall against the stone. "You, there!" she shouted. "You two!"

The taller man glanced up, and his face went red. She waved. "I want to welcome you!"

"We're not interested!"

Clearly, he was displeased with her continued attention. He muttered something to his companion and kept walking.

She wasn't about to give up, no matter how contemptuous he was of her. "I can't remember the last time a man tried so hard to ignore me!"

Irritated, he stopped. "We haven't enough money for your services."

"Have I set a price?"

He gave a dismissive wave, jerked his head at his companion, who was gawking at her, and strode on.

When had she ever had to talk a man into spending time with her? If she leaned out her window any farther, she'd fall at his feet! "I have cool wine, fresh bread, and a comfortable place for you both to sleep." When they still ignored her, she tore off her slipper and threw it at them. "Most Amorites call out my name when they approach the gate!" She'd always been the one to ignore *them*, unless the soldier happened to be a commander and held information of interest to the king. Normally she would not have given these ordinary soldiers a second glance, but they were Israelite spies. She knew it. Clearly, they saw her as nothing more than a common harlot plying her trade.

Fear swept through her for their sake. Did they think the guards posted at the gates were fools and wouldn't see through their disguise? She must get their attention quickly. One look at these wary fellows and the guards would be on top of them, swords drawn. By tomorrow morning, their heads would be lopped off and their bodies tied to the wall!

"Even the king has drunk wine from my cup and eaten bread from my hand!"

The taller one stopped and looked up at her again. "Why do you honor us with your attention?"

His mockery stung, but she swallowed her pride and answered plainly. "Because I have wisdom beyond my years, young man, wisdom I can share with you if you're wise enough to listen." She kept her tone teasingly seductive, for they were close enough to the gate that one of the guards might take note of the conversation. "I know what you want."

"Oh, do you?"

Save her from self-righteous, callow youth! "Every man needs to eat and rest." If he turned away again, she would throw a jug at him. "And a few come for intelligent conversation." She noted the sudden tension in his body. Just to be sure he understood her, she smiled. "The Jordan is high this time of year, isn't it?" She raised her brows and said nothing more.

Perhaps she had gone too far, for never had she seen a fiercer look.

"We are tired and hungry," he conceded.

"You will be glad you tarried with me."

"How do we find you?"

"I'll meet you inside the gate and show you the way." She blew them a kiss for the sake of the guard who had taken a sudden interest. She was shaking with excitement as she stepped down off the stool and yanked the cord holding the curtain back. Raking her fingers through her hair, she braided it quickly before hurrying out.

Rahab raced down the steps and around the corner. It was the hottest time of day. Few people were on the walkway that ran along the inside of the city wall. Many had worked during the morning hours and were now resting. When she entered the gate, she saw that Cabul had noticed the men. Slowing her pace, she sauntered closer, leaning against the cold stone. "Cabul!"

He turned and grinned, then left his post and came to her. "What brings you out so late in the day, my beauty?"

"You, of course." She kept her tone light and teasing.

He laughed. "More likely a wealthy merchant or an emissary from the Philistines."

She raised her brows and gave him a shrewd look. "One never knows."

Chuckling softly, he took her hand. His eyes narrowed. "You're shaking."

"Too much wine last night." She moved closer, toying with the hilt of his sword while looking past him. The two men were entering the gate.

"You weren't drinking with me," Cabul said and tipped her chin. "What do you say I come up after I get off duty and we'll get drunk together?"

"I think I'll forgo wine for a few days."

"Then we could – "

She slapped his arm playfully. No one was challenging the two strangers. Several city elders were arguing among themselves, and the soldier who'd taken Cabul's post seemed more interested in them than in two young Amorites dusty from travel.

"Did you come down here just to tease me?"

"Never." She raised her head again, gazing into Cabul's eyes. "You know I think you're the most handsome fellow in the king's service." And he was arrogant enough to believe her.

Cabul grinned and started to say something when two elders started shouting angrily at one another. Glancing back, he spotted the two strangers. When the taller young man looked her way, Cabul frowned. "Amorite soldiers? I never thought you'd stoop that low."

She shrugged. "Who knows? They may have news that will be of interest to the king."

Troubled, he looked at them again. "These are dangerous times, Rahab. They could be spies."

Her pulse rocked. "Do you think so?"

"Their hair is too short."

"Maybe they've taken some kind of vow." She touched his arm and smiled up at him. "I must say I'm touched you're so concerned for my welfare, but let me conduct my own business. The king wouldn't appreciate your interference in my affairs. If they *are* spies, he'll want to know about it."

"Are you about the king's interests, Rahab?"

She glared at him purposely. "What do you think?"

"Be careful, then. Israelites show no mercy, even to women and children." His dark eyes were filled with fear, but not on her behalf. "I'll tell the king."

"Wait a while. You don't want them to leave before we can find out why they've come." She knew him well enough to sense his tension. He was silent for a moment, undoubtedly calculating what would please the king most. She planted a suggestion. "Give me time with them, Cabul. They'll be easier to take if I fill them with good wine."

"You may be right."

"Of course I'm right." She toyed with his tunic.

"Besides, I know the king better than you." She looked up at him through her lashes. "These men could bring me a fat pouch of gold, and if you allow me more than an hour with them, I'll give a portion to you."

His jaw clenched and unclenched. She knew his greed warred with his sense of duty. Would his desire for money outweigh his fear of failing to report immediately to the king? "I'll give you as much time as I can," he concluded.

When Cabul walked away, she looked at the two men trying so hard to appear inconspicuous among the bustling Jerichoans bargaining in the gate. She motioned to them. Perhaps they hesitated now because they'd seen her speaking with Cabul and thought she was setting a trap.

Cabul was watching them. He glanced at her and jerked his chin. Go on, he was saying. Take advantage of the opportunity. She could imagine what he was thinking. Better she risk her life than he risk his. So be it!

Smiling boldly, she strolled over to the two men. "Welcome to Jericho."

❧❧❧

Salmon followed the woman along the walkway. He'd thought her disturbingly beautiful even from a distance, but close up, she took his breath away. He hadn't expected to face any kind of temptation on this mission, but he was having a hard time keeping his eyes off her hips and his mind on his business. How old was she? Thirty? Thirty-five? Her body didn't show it, but her eyes did.

She opened a door and entered quickly, standing just inside and beckoning them impatiently.

Salmon entered first, Ephraim following.

"Look at this place," Ephraim muttered under his breath as he stood, gaping, in the middle of the room. Salmon glanced around at the carpets, cushions in all colors, and red curtains held back by thick crimson cords. He tried not to look at the bed that dominated the room. The air held the fragrance of incense and cinnamon. He looked around. Evidently her profession paid well.

Closing the door behind them, the woman threw off her shawl. "I've got to hide you!"

"What are you talking about, woman?"

"Don't pretend ignorance. You're Israelite spies. If it wasn't written all over you before, it is now." She went for the ladder against the back wall.

Ephraim looked at Salmon. "What do we do?"

Salmon stared at her. "How did you know?"

She rolled her eyes and shook her head. "You mean aside from the way you studied the walls and battlements?" She dragged the ladder across the room. "There's a bloodstain on your tunic. I imagine the man who wore it before you died in it."

Salmon blocked her way. For one brief instant, he considered killing her so he could complete his mission. She lifted her head and straightened, her brown eyes clear and intelligent. "The soldier you saw speaking to me? He knows who you are."

"You told him?"

"He guessed." She grew impatient. "You came for information, didn't you? It would be better if you lived long enough to get it." She thrust the ladder at him and pointed at the hatch door to the roof. "Hurry! What're you waiting for? The king's executioner?"

Ephraim protested. "The roof is the first place the soldiers will look!"

"They won't have to look if you're still standing in the middle of the room!"

Ephraim looked around. "There must be a better place!"

"Fine." The woman put her hands on her hips. "If you don't like the roof, how about my bed?"

Horrified, Ephraim went up the ladder.

Her expression became pained as she watched Ephraim's hasty retreat. "I thought he'd feel that way." She looked at Salmon. He thought she had the most beautiful dark brown eyes he'd ever seen. No wonder Joshua and Caleb had given so many warnings about foreign women. "Now, how about you?" she said, her mouth tipped ruefully.

Salmon put his foot on the bottom rung, then looked at her again. "What's your name?"

"Rahab, but we haven't time to talk now. *Move!*"

She followed him up the ladder. Pushing him, she gestured to Ephraim. "Lie down over there, and I'll cover you both with the bundles of flax."

Salmon did as she instructed and watched her as she worked with quick efficiency, stacking the bundles carefully over them. Finishing the task, she leaned down and whispered, "I'm sorry I'm unable to make you more comfortable, but please be still until I return." She hurried back to the ladder, pulling the hatch over the opening as she went down.

"We're putting our lives into the hands of a harlot!" Ephraim said in a hoarse whisper.

"Have you got any better ideas?"

"I wish we had our swords!"

"It's a good thing we didn't, or we'd be in the hands of that guard at the gate who spoke with Rahab."

"Rahab? You asked her name?"

"It seemed appropriate under the circumstances."

"What makes her important?" Ephraim said. "You know what she is." His tone dripped with contempt.

"Keep your voice down!"

"Should we huddle under these bundles of flax like cowards? Better if we kill her now and get about our business."

Salmon caught hold of Ephraim before he could throw the bundles off. "Better if we finish what we were sent to do! Or have you forgotten the mission Joshua assigned us: get into the city, get information, get out! He didn't say to shed any blood." He released his friend. "Who better to know the pulse of Jericho than a whore who's broken bread with the king?"

"I'd rather die by the sword than be caught hiding behind a woman's skirts."

"We're not hiding behind her skirts," Salmon said with some amusement. "We're hiding under her bundles of flax."

"How can you laugh? We have only her word about the king. Why should we trust the word of a harlot?"

"Didn't you look at her?"

"Not as closely as you did."

"She's beautiful enough to attract a king's attention."

"Perhaps, but did you see how familiar that guard was with her? She's probably broken bread with every man in the city and hundreds who've come to trade, besides."

"Then she'll know the pulse of the city."

"And probably have every disease known to man."

"Be quiet! We're where God has placed us." Salmon wondered why his friend's words had roused such anger in him. Rahab was probably everything Ephraim said she was. So why this strong desire to defend her? And why was he trusting her with their lives?

He let out his breath, forcing himself to relax. "We'd better rest while we can. I have the feeling, one way or another, we won't be inside these walls for long."

Rahab knew the king's men would come soon. The moment she departed the gate with the two Israelites, Cabul would have run to his commander to give a report on the two strangers who'd entered the city.

She descended the ladder, grasped it, and swung it down.

"Rahab! Open up!"

Pulse jumping, she ran her hands over her face to wipe away any perspiration. Patting her hair and straightening her dress, she went quickly to the door and opened it wide, pretending relief at the sight of the men standing outside. "I wish you'd come sooner, Cabul."

Flushed and tense, Cabul remained where he was standing. Other soldiers were behind him, armed and ready for a fight. She could see the fear in their eyes, a fear that matched her own, though for different reasons. If Cabul conducted himself properly, he would enter her house and make a complete search, including the roof. And if he found the spies, she was a dead woman.

"The king's orders are that you bring out the men who have come into your house. They are spies sent here to discover the best way to attack us." His gaze darted past her. "Produce them."

"The men were here earlier, but I didn't know where they were from. They left the city at dusk, as the city gates were about to close, and I don't know where they went. If you hurry, you can probably catch up with them."

"Where did they go?"

"I don't know," she repeated. Cabul would have more to face now than two spies. He would have to answer to a frightened, angry king for failing to take them into custody. "Quick! Go after them. You still have time to overtake them if you hurry!"

He didn't question her. Why should he suspect her of treason when she had proven herself loyal to the king so many times? Hadn't she made a prosperous living gleaning information from strangers so that she could report to the king and receive a reward? Her word was enough to send him on his way. Turning on his heel, Cabul shouted orders and headed straight for the gate.

Rahab stepped out of her house and watched them depart in the deepening twilight. As soon as they rounded the corner, she went back into her house, closed the door, locked it, and ran to her window. Her palms were sweating, her heart pounding wildly. By now, Cabul and the others were at the gate. She could hear him shouting for the guards on duty to open it so they could pursue the spies. If Cabul paused long enough to speak with the men on duty, he might learn that the men fitting the strangers' description had not left the city.

She breathed easier when she saw Cabul appear outside the wall. The others followed him as they hurried away from the city. They were heading east for the Jordan, running now, spears in their hands, certain they could overtake the spies before they crossed the river. And the gate was closed behind them.

Rahab shut her eyes and smiled. She waited several more minutes to be sure Cabul and the others were far enough away. Then she gathered a jug of wine, bread, and a basket of dates and pomegranates and dragged out the ladder to set it up once more.

The men on the roof were silent. Could they have fallen asleep? Setting down the food she had brought with her, she crossed the roof quietly, took up a bundle of flax, and set it aside. She didn't want to startle them.

"The soldiers are gone now. It's safe to come out."

The taller man sat up first. When he looked at her, she felt the impact of his gaze. He was curious about her, and he was disturbed by his attraction to her. He said nothing as his companion stood up and brushed himself off. "We heard shouting."

She wanted to put them at ease. "The soldiers have left the city in pursuit of you." When she stretched out her hand, she realized she was shaking badly enough for them to notice. "I have bread and wine."

She understood their hesitation. She was a Jerichoan and a harlot. Why should they trust her? They must be wondering why a Canaanite would protect them. They might even wonder how she'd managed to get rid of the soldiers so quickly, without their even searching the house. Why should these Israelites believe anything a harlot had to say? But believe her they must. So many lives depended on it.

Rahab lowered her hand and lifted her chin. "I know the Lord has given you this land," she told them. "We are all afraid of you. Everyone is living in terror. For we have heard how the Lord made a dry path for you through the Red Sea when you left Egypt. And we know what you did to Sihon and Og, the two Amorite kings east of the Jordan River, whose people you completely destroyed. No wonder our hearts have melted in fear!"

She wondered why they'd even come here. Surely they knew better than she that the land was theirs! Why should they come to spy out a land the Lord had already given them? Did they doubt? Did they need encouragement?

"No one has the courage to fight after hearing such things. For the Lord your God is the supreme God of the heavens above and the earth below." Her eyes filled with tears, for her heart ached deeply to be counted among the chosen people of this God.

Swallowing hard, she stepped forward and spread her hands. "Now swear to me by the Lord that you will be kind to me and my family since I have helped you. Give me some guarantee that when Jericho is conquered, you will let me live, along with my father and mother, my brothers and sisters, and all their families."

The taller man glanced at his companion, who stared at Rahab. There was enough moonlight that she could see his consternation. The taller man looked at her again, his expression curiously excited. "My name is Salmon, and this is Ephraim. We offer our own lives as a guarantee for your safety."

Her heart soared with relief and thanksgiving. She looked at the other for his response.

"I agree," Ephraim said with less enthusiasm, giving Salmon a disgruntled look. He looked at her again. "If you don't betray us, we will keep our promise when the Lord gives us the land."

She smiled broadly, elated. She would trust these men with her life and the lives of those she loved. She had made them swear to her by the Lord. They wouldn't dare break such an oath. The faith they had in their mighty God would make them uphold it.

"Please," she said, extending her hand toward the cushions in one corner of the flat roof. "Sit. Make yourselves comfortable. You're my guests." She busied herself with the food she had brought with her. "What can I serve you? I have dates, almonds, honey and raisin cakes, bread, wine ... "

"Nothing," Ephraim said coldly.

"But thank you," Salmon added, as if to ease the rejection.

Rahab turned and studied them. Though they had promised to save her life and the lives of her family members, it seemed all too clear they wanted no part of her. Especially the man called Ephraim. He made her feel like a bug that had crawled out from under a rock. The other young man studied her with open curiosity. She sat down on a cushion and looked at him. "Ask whatever you want."

He looked into her eyes intently. "How did you come by your faith in our God?"

"I've heard stories about Him since I was a girl."

"So has everyone else in Jericho."

She blinked. "I know that all too well, and I can't explain why I believed when everyone else didn't."

"Your people are afraid," Ephraim said. "We heard enough at the gate to know that much."

"Yes, they're afraid of you, as they would be any conquering army. But they don't understand that it is your God who gives you victory."

Salmon's eyes shone as he studied her face. Then his eyes moved down over her and back up again as though taking her in all at once. She could see plainly enough that he liked what he saw. So did she. He was a very handsome young man.

Ephraim seemed determined to keep her in her place. "You have gods of your own."

"Wooden statues of no earthly use," she said disdainfully. "Did you see any in my chamber?" Ephraim looked uncomfortable. "Go on down," she said, gesturing toward the ladder. "Open the cabinets. Look behind the curtains, under the bed. Search anywhere you wish, Ephraim. You will not find any idols or talismans among my possessions. I lost faith in the gods of my people long ago."

"Why?"

The Hebrew seemed intent upon testing her. So be it. She was more than willing to comply. "Because they couldn't save me. They're just things made by men, and I know how weak men are." She spread her hands in a gesture of appeal. "I want to live among your people."

Ephraim frowned slightly and looked at Salmon.

Salmon leaned forward slightly. "You must understand that we have laws, laws given to us by God Himself."

"I would like to know these laws." She had felt some message pass between the two men and sensed it would affect her greatly.

Salmon considered her for a moment and then said quietly, "There are laws against fornication and adultery."

Ephraim was not so gentle in his condemnation of her profession. "Prostitution is not tolerated. Anyone found practicing it is executed."

Rahab remembered how she had hung out her window and called down to them as she had a hundred others before them. The heat poured into her face. Never had she felt such self-loathing. No wonder they had hesitated. No wonder they wouldn't eat food from her table or drink so much as a drop of water. She was filled with shame.

"I didn't choose this lifestyle," she said in quick defense. "I was presented to the king by my father when I was a girl and had no say – " She stopped when she saw Salmon's grimace. What did it matter how she had come to be what she was? She had sensed from the beginning that it was wrong. What did it matter that she had been just a girl and had to do what she was told? Did that excuse continuing in her profession these past years and gaining wealth from it? No! She frowned and looked away, feeling the Hebrews' perusal. She looked at them again, calm and accepting. "If God loathes prostitution, then I'm done with it."

Salmon rose and walked to the edge of the roof. He stared out across the city for a long moment and then turned and looked at her again. "It's time for us to leave," he said. "We've served our purpose in coming, Ephraim."

Rahab rose abruptly. She knew they had to act quickly now. She hurried down the ladder into the house, followed by the two men. Crossing the room, she untied and yanked free the crimson rope that held her curtains back from her bed. "You can't go by way of the gate. I can lower you from the window with this." Looping it up, she went to the window, brushed Salmon aside, and dropped one end over the sill. She peered out as the crimson cord snaked down the wall. "It reaches to within ten feet of the ground."

"Close enough." Salmon took the rope from her hand and set her aside. You first," he said, nodding to his friend. Ephraim lifted himself up and swung his legs out the window.

"Wait!" Rahab said. "Escape to the hill country," she told them. "Hide there for three days until the men who are searching for you have returned; then go on your way."

Ephraim nodded, grasped the rope, and went out the window. Rahab heard a soft cascade of loosened mortar, then a thud as he hit the ground. Salmon handed the rope to her and sat on the windowsill.

"Listen to me, Rahab. We can guarantee your safety only if you leave this scarlet rope hanging from the window. And all your family members – your father, mother, brothers, and all your relatives – must be here inside the house. If they go out into the street, they will be killed, and we cannot be held to our oath. But we swear that no one inside this house will be killed – not a hand will be laid on any of them."

She bit her lip as gratitude filled her.

He swung one leg out and looked back at her. "If you betray us, however, we are not bound by this oath in any way."

"I accept your terms," she replied.

The look in his eyes changed subtly. Letting go of the rope, he reached out and cupped the back of her head, pulling her close. Her heart stopped, for she thought he meant to kiss her.

"Don't be afraid. I'll be back for you."

"I hope so."

He released her and took up the rope. "Are you strong enough to hold me?"

She laughed. "I'll have to be!" She held on with all her strength, and when she thought she'd fail, she found strength she didn't know she had.

When Salmon let go of the rope, she stood on her tiptoes and looked out the window. Both men stood below her. Ephraim was looking around cautiously, but Salmon grinned up at her. He raised his hand in a gesture of salutation and promise. She waved for him to go quickly.

She smiled when she saw they took the road leading to the hill country.

three

SALMON and Ephraim followed the road over the mountains into the hill country. It was well past dawn when they rested near a small stream. Kneeling, eyes alert, they drank and drank their fill.

Ephraim trapped several fish in a pool and flipped them onto the bank, where Salmon had built a small fire. After cleaning them, Salmon roasted the fish on a stick. Salmon had never eaten anything but manna and found the fish a new and interesting taste to his palate. Replete, they saw a Canaanite shepherd bring his flock of goats to drink downstream. The man glanced their way, then drove his flock west.

"He's afraid of strangers," Ephraim said.

"The fear of the Lord is upon the land." Exhaustion caught up with them. Salmon stretched out on his back, a soft blanket of grass beneath him. He could hardly keep his eyes open. "Our days in the wilderness are almost over." He filled his lungs with the rich, fragrant scent of the land. The sky was cerulean with wisps of white. *Oh, Lord, my God, You are bringing us home to a land You have prepared for us. You have laid out this gift before us. Give us the courage to take it.* Closing his eyes, Salmon drifted off to sleep while listening to the stream of living water.

And as he did so, he dreamed of a beautiful woman peering down at him from a window, her luxurious curly, black hair rippling in the wind.

<hr />

Rahab saw Cabul and the king's men returning late the next afternoon, while the gates were still open. Even from a distance, they looked weary and defeated. She drew back so Cabul wouldn't see her as he passed below her window, heading for the gate.

"Rahab!"

She ignored him. She hoped he wouldn't come and question her or seek solace in her company. She wanted no further discourse with the fellow.

The king had summoned her yesterday, and she had repeated her lie about the spies and her directions to his men. He believed her, and that had been the end of it.

Later that evening, Cabul knocked at her door. Hiding her fear, she opened the door long enough to find out if the king had thought the matter over further and become suspicious. When Cabul made it clear he had come for personal reasons, she told him she was ill and needed to be alone. It was no pretense. She was sick – sick of him, sick of the life she led, sick at the realization that everyone in this city would be dead soon because of their stubborn hearts and stiff-necked pride. She did not rejoice that destruction would come upon them, but she wanted to separate herself from them. She wanted to close herself in and stand at the window, waiting for her deliverance.

But there were others to consider, others to protect.

She let another night pass. On the third day, she ventured out of her house to shop in the marketplace, where she knew her father would be selling dried dates, raisins, and parched grains. When she approached him, he smiled briefly before returning his full attention to a patron standing at the booth. Her heart softened, for her father had never condemned her for the choices she made. Groveling for a living himself, he'd understood her reasons and never stopped loving her. Her mother had had grand hopes for her when the king had summoned her to his bed, but she'd put too much confidence in her daughter's physical beauty. Rahab had had no such illusions. Men were fickle, especially when they held positions of power, and she hadn't expected the affair to last long. She'd only hoped it would last long enough for her to make a place for herself in the king's service. It had, and now she had a livelihood and could help provide for her family – when their pride would allow it.

Neither her father nor her brothers had condemned her when she entered the king's chamber. Nor did they pity her when she left the king's house. They'd treated her with sad tolerance, until she showed she could manage independence and prosperity beyond their own. She'd been the one able to give money whenever it was needed, and she'd always made sure her mother, sisters, and sisters-in-law shared in the gifts she received from patrons. She'd never done so out of a feeling of compulsion or pride but out of love for them.

"How goes the day for you, my daughter?"

"It is a day of hope, Father."

"Hope is a good thing. Come and sit with an old man and tell me what news you've heard these past weeks." He set two stools out and sat on one, gesturing for her to take the other. Rahab watched him rub his leg. The years of hard work showed on him, and he seemed to be in more pain today. But he would not thank her for mentioning it. "How is Mother?"

"In her glory, tending three grandchildren while your sisters beat and strip the flax."

"And my brothers?"

"At work on the ramparts."

No wonder he was rubbing his leg and pinched with pain. "You've been climbing the date palms again." What choice had he if the king summoned her brothers to work on the wall defenses and left an old man to carry the work of his sons?

"I've been training a grandson."

"Oh, Father. You're lucky you haven't broken your neck!"

"The king is in greater need than I."

"He can add all the fortifications in the world, and they won't help."

His hand stopped rubbing and his head came up. "The Israelites have settled in Shittim," he said.

"Not for much longer."

"No?"

"No. The Lord has given them this land."

His eyes flickered as he studied her face. "I heard that spies entered the city several nights ago."

"By now, they will have given their report."

His eyes filled with fear. "Did you help them get away?"

She leaned forward and took his gnarled hands in hers. "I have seen the truth, Father. I know what's going to happen, the only thing that can happen. But I can't talk about it here. Come to my house before you leave the city. I have news that will give our family cause to celebrate." His hands were cold as they tightened on hers. He searched her eyes. "What have you done, Daughter?"

"It's what will be done for us, provided we act in good faith. Come tonight and I'll tell you everything."

"They will come against Jericho?"

"Yes, Father, and they will destroy it." She stood and leaned down to kiss his cheek. "But our salvation is at hand."

Rahab's father brought her two brothers with him. She greeted them warmly and seated them on cushions set around a low table. She poured wine for them and encouraged them to eat. "I'm not hungry," Mizraim said tersely. "Father said you summoned us."

"It wouldn't hurt to eat while we talk."

"Should we have an appetite when the Israelites are camped across the Jordan?"

Her youngest brother, Jobab, afraid and angry, looked up at her. "Father said you took in the spies. What possessed you to risk everything we've worked for? If the king finds out – "

"The king knows the spies were here at my house," she said, seeing three faces blanch. "He sent soldiers to take them, and I told his men they'd already left the city."

"Then they must have escaped," Mizraim said. "If they'd been captured, their bodies would be hanging on the wall by now."

Rahab smiled. "They weren't captured, because I hid them on my roof."

"You ... what?" her father said weakly.

"I hid them, and then I let them down from my window and told them to hide in the hill country for three days before crossing the Jordan."

Her father and brothers stared at her. Mizraim came to his feet. "By the gods, what have you done to us?"

Jobab held his head in despair. "We'll all be destroyed for your treason."

"I've chosen the side that offers life," Rahab said.

"Life?" Mizraim said, his face red with anger. "You don't know what you're talking about! What of us? Are we not able to choose?"

She restrained her anger. How many times had she come to the aid of her family, and Mizraim could still accuse her so? "That's why you're here." She set the jug of wine firmly in the middle of the table and sat with them. "Years ago, Father, you met an Israelite spy in the palm grove. You said you could see in his eyes that he would return."

"They did return and were defeated."

"Yes, but they came back without the Ark of their God. Isn't that what you told me?"

"Yes." Her father frowned, thinking back. "And Moses didn't lead them."

"I've heard Moses is dead," Mizraim said, taking a seat again.

"Do you think that matters?" Rahab was determined to make them understand that the arrangements she had made with the spies were their only chance for survival. "For all his greatness, Moses was only a man. It is the God of all creation who protects these people. The first time they came into the land, they entered like a band of thieves scattered across the ridges of the hill country. They were defeated because God was not with them. This time the Israelites stand together. There's a new generation of Israelites out there across the river. They're waiting for their God to instruct them. Do not speak, Mizraim! Listen to what I'm telling you. When the time is right, the Israelites *will* cross the Jordan, and they *will* be victorious."

"They'll never take Jericho," Mizraim said, picking up his cup of wine. "I've been working on fortifications since the last full moon. You know yourself how tall and wide these walls are. No army can break through them!"

"You boast, but I see the fear in your eyes." She was not cowed by his angry glare. "What are these walls to a God who can part the seas? We've all heard the stories. God laid waste to Egypt with ten plagues. He spoke through Moses, and a nation was delivered from slavery. He opened the Red Sea so the Israelites crossed over on dry land. Have you ever heard of such power? Truly, He is God, the *only* God. You *must* know this! I've always told you everything I've heard. Think on what you know. Why else do you think our people quake in terror? You, among them."

"But this is *our* land!" Jobab said. "They have no right to it! We built these walls! We planted the crops and built the houses! Our father's father and his father before him harvested dates from the palm grove just beyond these walls!"

She wanted to shake them all. "We've bowed down to the baals all these years, thinking they were the owners of the land. But this land belongs to the God out there, and He's going to take it." She gave a bleak laugh. "Do you think we'll be safe because we've sacrificed to statues we carved and molded? What power have they over the elements?" She sneered. "They've never been anything more than mindless, heartless stone and clay idols." She slammed the palm of her hand on the table. "Well, now, the true landlord has revealed Himself. The God of the Israelites owns the land. He owns the palm trees and terebinths and grapevines; He owns the bees that make the honey; He owns the locusts that destroyed Egypt! Everything is His, and He can give the land and all that's on it to whomever He chooses. *And He has chosen those people across the river in Shittim!*"

They sat in stunned silence. Her father looked up at her. She could see he was trembling. "This is the news we came to hear, Daughter?"

"We should gather our families and have a feast together," Jobab said dismally. "We'll lace the wine with hemlock and be spared the agony of being hacked to pieces by the swords of Israel."

"Bravely spoken," Mizraim said in disgust.

"We will live," Rahab said.

Mizraim picked up his cup of wine again. "How? The Israelites leave no survivors."

"I helped the spies escape, and they've promised to spare our lives when they take the city!"

"And you believed them?" Mizraim said. "Everyone knows they annihilate every living thing."

"They swore an oath to me."

"An oath is no better than the man who swears it!"

Rahab tipped her chin. "I know that better than you, my brother. I've had dealings with men since I was a girl."

"And brought shame upon us for it."

Her father slammed his fist on the table. "You'll listen to your sister! She is older than you and wiser in the world than all of us."

Mizraim winced and lowered his head.

"They were strangers," her father said. "Why should you trust them?"

"I asked the men to promise by the Lord, and they did so. Would any man dare swear a vain oath before this God? If they fail to keep their word, they'll answer to Him for it."

"Not that it'll matter much to us," Jobab said, still gloomy. "We'll be dead."

Rahab reached out and put her hand over her brother's. "You must decide where to place your faith, Jobab. You can have faith in the king of Jericho, who is but a man. Or you can put your faith in the King of Kings, the God of Israel. It's true, I don't know these men who came as spies, and I've only heard the stories about the Lord. But I believe what I've heard. Each time I heard of Him, I've experienced a quickening inside me, an assurance. I can't explain it any more than that, but I *know* this is God, the only God, and I've chosen to put my faith and hope in Him." She leaned back, looking at them. "You must decide for yourselves whether you choose life or death."

"We choose life," her father answered for them.

"We have one chance," Rahab said, "and that chance rests in the Lord God of Israel." Her heart beat strongly with excitement and thanksgiving. "We must make provisions for the days ahead. When the Israelites rescue us, we don't want to go to them empty-handed. Sell sparingly in the marketplace, Father, and bring most of the grain, raisins, and dates here. I'll store them so that we have food when the siege begins and gifts for later."

She nodded toward the far corner. "I've purchased a large storage jar for water, and I've gone to the spring each day in order to fill it. Have my sisters fill skins so there will be water enough for everyone."

She rose and went to the window, looking out toward the desert. "We'll make ourselves ready now. Have your possessions packed and ready to move. Stay girded and keep your weapon beside you at all times. When the Israelites cross the river, gather your wives and children and come here to my house." She turned. "Waste no time. We must separate ourselves from everyone in this city, for they are all marked for destruction. The two men from God promised me that everyone who's inside my house will live. Anyone outside it will perish."

Her father leaned forward, clasping his hands on the table. "There are a dozen windows in the wall, Rahab. How will the Israelites know this house from all the rest?"

Smiling, she lifted the crimson rope she'd tied in her window. "They will know us by this sign, and death will pass us by."

"There are twenty of us, Rahab. How're you going to make room for all of us and the provisions we'll need to survive?"

"Oh, Mizraim, you worry about so many things. You worry about what you're going to eat and where you're going to sleep. Only one thing is necessary. Obey the instructions we've been given! If you want to live, pack your belongings and come to my house." She smiled. "And in your haste, don't forget to bring Basemath and the children with you."

※※※

After three days, Salmon and Ephraim left the hill country and crossed the Jordan. Stripping off the Amorite garments, they donned their own clothing and ran the rest of the way to Shittim, where they found Joshua and Caleb together.

"The Lord will certainly give us the whole land," Ephraim said, panting heavily, "for all the people in the land are terrified of us!"

"Be at ease and rest." Joshua nodded for them to sit close to the fire. He was calm, his gaze steady, as though nothing they told him had changed anything.

Salmon's excitement was roaring within him so that he felt he could run through the entire camp, shouting the news to the thousands who waited to go into battle. "The land is ours, and it's rich beyond anything we've ever imagined! God has kept His promise. The hearts of the Canaanites have melted before the power of the Lord."

"A harlot in Jericho told us," Ephraim said, still breathing hard.

A harlot. Salmon didn't like the way Ephraim described Rahab.

Salmon had always thought it was Joshua's and Caleb's faith that had singled them out from all others among the chosen race, but a single evening in the company of a Jerichoan whore had made him realize that God could write His name upon the heart of anyone He chose – even a Canaanite prostitute! Out there in the darkness, across the Jordan inside the wall of a pagan city was a woman of contemptible reputation who'd never seen a miracle, tasted a bite of manna, or heard a single word of the Law. And yet her faith was strong enough that she had greeted, welcomed, and protected those who were coming to destroy her and her people. "The Lord your God is the supreme God of the heavens above and the earth below," she had declared.

"The woman's name is Rahab," Salmon said to the two venerable old warriors. "She called down to us from a window in the wall and met us just inside the gate, then took us into her house. She hid us on her roof before the soldiers came, then told them we'd left the city."

Ephraim quickly took up Rahab's defense as well. "The soldiers believed her lie and went chasing after shadows."

"She welcomed us with kindness and recommended we wait in the hill country for three days before returning to give you our report. It was this woman who said the Lord has given us the land. She said, 'The Lord your God is the supreme God of the heavens above and the earth below.' And she asked us to give an oath to save her family from death, an oath by the Lord."

Joshua's eyes narrowed slightly. "And did you give this oath?"

Salmon felt the sweat break out on the back of his neck. Had he overstepped himself and gone against the will of the Lord? "Yes, sir, we did give our oath." He swallowed hard. "If I have done wrong in this, I pray the Lord will hold me alone responsible and not punish this woman. We did swear before the Lord our God that anyone inside Rahab's house would be spared."

"Then it will be so," Joshua said.

Salmon breathed easier.

"How will we know her from the others?" Caleb asked.

Salmon turned to him eagerly. "We gave her a sign to use so that we'll know where her dwelling is. She used a scarlet cord to let us down to the ground, saving our lives and giving us a way of escape. I told Rahab to leave that same cord tied in her window. It will be easily seen from outside the walls."

Joshua rose. "The Lord protects those who belong to Him."

"Blessed be the name of the Lord," Salmon said, relieved.

Caleb tossed a branch onto the fire, sending up a burst of sparks. He stared into the flames, his hands clasped. Joshua glanced at his old kinsman and then came around the fire to Salmon. He put his hand on Salmon's shoulder. "You and Ephraim will both see to the safety of this woman and her family. The Lord spoke to me this morning, and I've given His instructions to the commanders of the tribes. You will hear them now. We cross the Jordan in three days. Make your preparations."

Ephraim watched Joshua walk away. "Our mission wasn't necessary. He had already decided what to do even before he heard our report."

Caleb snapped a branch in half. "Never question the ways of the Lord or the servants He has put over the people!" He glared at Ephraim and then at Salmon. "Joshua is God's instrument."

Salmon didn't share Ephraim's disappointment over lost glory for their deed. He'd been honored that Joshua had felt enough confidence in him to send him to Jericho at all. What did it matter that the Lord spoke to Joshua before they returned? Did God need their report? It seemed to Salmon that he and Ephraim had been sent to Jericho for another reason, a reason no one had known about except the Lord: God had sent them so they would find Rahab and open the way for her deliverance.

Caleb looked between them. "Which of you intends to take charge of the woman?"

"I will," Salmon said.

Caleb's eyes darkened.

"Blessings upon you, my brother," Ephraim said. "I'd be hard-pressed explaining to Havilah how I came to be in the company of a prostitute!" Laughing, he slapped Salmon on the back.

"I'm certain your brothers and sisters await your safe return," Caleb said.

Ephraim's amusement evaporated. "Yes, sir." He gave Salmon a quick, sympathetic glance as he strode off to rejoin his relatives.

Salmon waited for Caleb to speak his mind. Since the death of Moses, there was no man other than Joshua whom Salmon respected more than this patriarch of his tribe, the tribe of Judah. Caleb was one of only two men to be found faithful among the slaves who had been delivered from Egypt.

The old man raised his head, his expression challenging. "She is a foreign woman. You know the warnings about foreign women."

"She wants to be one of us." Salmon wanted this man's confidence and approval. He debated within himself, and then decided the best course of action was to speak the truth about his feelings and seek Caleb's counsel. "I want to take this woman into my tent."

"One battle at a time, my son."

Salmon met his look. "I thought it best to discuss it now."

"She must be beautiful," Caleb said wryly. Salmon could feel the heat climbing into his face. The old man's smile turned cynical. "You blush like a boy."

Anger stirred Salmon to speak more boldly. "I'm twenty-six years old, and I've never met a woman who has so inclined me toward marriage."

Caleb shook his head, angry and aggrieved. "It's ever thus, Salmon. It's always the pagan women who draw our men away from God."

"Rahab isn't a pagan!"

"She is a Canaanite."

"This woman has acted with more faith than my father or mother. But let's lay out all the objections at once. She's older than I, and she's made her living as a prostitute!"

Caleb's eyes shone strangely. "And you would choose such a woman to be your wife?"

"Rahab is a woman of excellence."

"Excellence?"

"She proclaimed her faith by her actions."

Caleb poked the fire with a stick. "Perhaps she's merely a cunning liar who's betrayed her people in order to save her own skin."

"Who are her people?"

When Caleb raised his hand as though to wave Salmon's words away, Salmon plunged ahead in his defense of Rahab. "It is God's will we are to follow. You and Joshua are the ones who have taught me that. And that's what I seek to do: *God's will.* Help me find it where this woman is concerned!"

Caleb let out his breath slowly and rubbed his face. "Joshua has already given the command. You will see to the woman's safety and that of those who are with her. And if you choose, she will belong to you by right of conquest."

Salmon's heart beat strongly. He felt he'd been handed a precious gift, despite the coolness of Caleb's proclamation.

Caleb lowered his hands and looked at him gravely. "You will leave this woman and her relatives outside the camp. Perhaps she will go her own way and take her family with her."

"She will want to become one of us."

"How can you be so certain?"

Salmon hunkered down. "I saw her eyes. I heard her voice."

He wanted Caleb to trust Rahab as he did. "Were we not slaves when God delivered us? I believe God sent Ephraim and me into Jericho to find this woman. It's the only reason that makes sense to me, considering that God spoke to Joshua before we returned to give our report. The Lord wants this woman delivered from the evil of the Canaanites, just as He delivered us from Egypt."

"Be careful not to add to what the Lord has said, Salmon. You must align yourself with the will of God – not the desires of your own heart. My generation thought they could have their own way, and they all died in the desert."

"The will of God is ever in my mind. From the time I was a small boy, you've taught me the truth and lived it before my eyes. One thing has always been clear to me. It was not because we had merit or deserved freedom that the Lord delivered us from Egypt. The Lord saved us out of *His* great mercy." Salmon held his hands out. "Would the Lord not extend His mercy to anyone who yearns to belong to Him? I saw this yearning in Rahab. I heard it in her voice. She *believes* the Lord is God, and she declared her allegiance to Him by saving us, His servants." He paused, weighing his next words carefully. Finally he spoke the question that had been burning on his heart for the past three days. "Could it not be that God has aligned the desire of my heart with His good purpose toward this woman?"

Caleb considered his words. "You're only guessing about the desires of this woman's heart, Salmon."

"It is a sign of wisdom that she is in awe of the Lord. Could Rahab truly declare that the Lord is the only God – the God of the heavens above and the earth below – if God Himself had not written His name upon her heart?"

"If you seek a quick answer from me, my son, I have none. We must both pray and seek God's will in this matter."

Salmon struggled against the urgency he felt. "If anyone finds out she's given aid to Ephraim and me, she may not survive long enough to be rescued. I should go back – "

"Did she ask this of you?"

"No, but – "

Caleb's eyes blazed. "Then I would ask you this: where is *your* faith, Salmon? If it is indeed God's plan to deliver this woman, *He will do it.*"

Salmon started to say more but was silenced when he looked into Caleb's eyes. He had said enough already. The lines in the old man's face showed wisdom earned by years of suffering. The sins of others, including those of Salmon's own father and mother, had caused Caleb and Joshua greater heartache than he would ever know. It had been almost forty years since Joshua and Caleb had received the promise that they would be the only ones of their generation to set foot in the Promised Land. Two out of an entire people. All because the others had refused to believe the promise God had given them.

"I believe the Lord will protect her," Salmon said, lowering his head. "May God forgive my unbelief."

"I was young and impetuous once," Caleb said more gently. "You must learn to be patient. God doesn't need our help."

Salmon raised his head and smiled. "When you meet Rahab, you'll understand what I see in her."

"*If* I meet Rahab, I'll know it is by God's will – not by your efforts – that her life has been spared." He stood. "It's late, and we both need to rest. There is much to do tomorrow. We must make our preparations for the days ahead."

Salmon rose with him, but didn't move away from the fire. He wanted Caleb's blessing for his plans regarding Rahab. "Then you have no objections to my taking Rahab into my tent?"

Caleb gave him a rueful stare. "It would be wise to wait and see what choice *she* makes."

"She's already made her choice."

"Indeed, and if God delivers Rahab from Jericho, it will be left to her to decide what to do with the life God grants her." His mouth tipped up in a gentle smile. "If she is as wise as you say, she will prefer an older man."

Salmon laughed, all the tension falling away. Had Caleb merely been testing him? "You said she belonged to me by right of conquest."

Caleb laughed with him. "Ah, that's true, but a woman with her faith and courage will have a mind of her own." He clamped his hand upon Salmon's shoulder, his expression serious again. "When the battle is over, Joshua will decide her fate. Her true motives will be put to the test." He let go of him. "If she is as you say she is, then you needn't concern yourself over the outcome."

Salmon felt less than satisfied. He'd wanted a firm answer, and instead he had been told to wait.

Would Rahab prove to be the woman he thought she was? If not, it would no doubt fall to him to make sure she didn't trouble Israel again.

four

RAHAB poured grain into the pottery bin Mizraim's son had brought her. Two more baskets, and the jar would be full. Three large storage jars contained water. She had two baskets full of dates and two more of raisins. Over the past few days her mother, her sisters, and her brothers' wives had brought beans, lentils, onions, garlic, and leeks. Her house was beginning to look like one of the booths in the marketplace, loaded with foodstuffs for sale. But would there be enough if the siege lasted longer than a week? She looked around again, taking mental inventory of what she had and what more she might still need to take care of her family until the Israelites could break through the gates and come to their rescue. Time was short, and each day that passed increased her feelings of urgency – and excitement.

Jobab and Mizraim came to her each evening after their labor on the walls. As she served them a meal, they told her what they'd heard. Every bit of information she could glean might become important later. Most important was to encourage her father and brothers to trust in the God of Israel and not to put their confidence in the king's plans.

"The king's convinced we're all safe," Mizraim said one evening. "The Israelites have never faced a wall so high and thick as this one."

Jobab tore off a piece of bread and dipped it in the lentil stew Rahab had prepared. "They may not even be able to reach the walls. The king has thousands of arrows made and ready for the attack. The entire army will be standing on the battlements, ready to shoot any man who dares come close."

"Don't fool yourself, brother." Rahab replenished his wine. "Don't put your trust in that man to save us. I know him better than you, remember? Besides, he and all his soldiers and weapons won't mean a thing when the Israelites come against us. They have God on their side. Do as I've told you. Drop everything and come here when the Israelites step foot on the west bank of the Jordan."

"But how are they going to get to the west bank?"

"I don't know!" Rahab set the jug down and put her hands on her hips.

"Maybe they'll build rafts. Maybe they'll swim across. Maybe they'll *walk* across!"

Mizraim laughed. "Maybe eagles will come and carry them across. Or better yet, maybe they'll sprout wings and fly!"

"You dare laugh?" Rahab smacked him on the back of his head. "If God can part the Red Sea, do you think that river will stop Him? He could dry it up with one breath! The only safe place outside the camp of Israel is right here where you're sitting." She took the jug and glared at her two brothers in frustration. Why wasn't it as clear to them as it was to her? "God is coming! And you'd better be ready when He gets here!"

Jobab pushed his stool back and stood. He looked around the room at the storage jars, the rush mats stacked in the corner, the blankets piled on her bed. "What more do we need?"

She closed her eyes tightly, trying to still the trembling inside her. "Patience." If the Israelites crossed the Jordan at this very moment, it would not be too soon for her.

While the Israelites remained camped in Shittim, manna continued to rain down from heaven, though it lessened each day until only a soft sprinkling appeared like dew as the sun rose.

Salmon went down onto his knees with the thousands of other men, women, and children who gathered their share for the day. He made a cake of the coriander-like flakes of manna and placed it on the camp stove his parents had brought out of Egypt. He thought of his parents often now, praying he wouldn't make the same mistakes, praying he would stand in faith, praying he would not weaken in the face of battling the enemy, praying he would be a man of God, not just a man.

Breathing in the wonderful, sweet aroma as the manna cake sizzled in olive oil, he took a pronged stick and carefully turned the cake. His stomach clenched with hunger. When the cake was finished, he rolled it up and sat back to eat it slowly, savoring its sweetness. Soon the manna would disappear altogether, for the people would have no need of it when they entered Canaan, a land of milk and honey. Milk meant herds of cattle and goats; honey meant blooming fruit trees, vines, and crops of grain and vegetables, foods his generation had heard of but had never tasted. The Lord had said they would take possession of orchards and vineyards they hadn't planted, harvest the wheat and beans and lentils another nation had sown, shepherd herds and flocks left by the fleeing enemies of God. Yet Salmon couldn't help but feel a deepening sadness.

He'd never known anything but the taste of manna. The first time he had tasted anything else was the day he and Ephraim had camped alongside the stream in Canaan, where they'd caught and roasted fish. Though the meal had been delicious, it couldn't compare with what God had given them and what God would soon take away.

Salmon held the bread of heaven reverently. All his life he had taken it for granted; now he realized how precious it was. As he ate of it, tears came, for he knew this bread had come from the very hand of God, a free gift keeping him alive. Could there ever be anything as sweet? Could anything else be as nourishing?

Soon the people would cease to be children wandering in the desert and stand as men and women of God in the land of promise. And like mother's milk, the manna would be taken from them. He and the others would plow, plant, tend herds and flocks, and harvest crops. They would have children, build homes, build cities.

Oh, God, keep us faithful! he prayed. *Don't let us again become whining infants! Don't let us become arrogant in the victories You will give us. The sins of our fathers are ever before us. If only they could be wiped away once and for all time, so that we could stand in Your presence the way Adam and Eve did, when first You created them.*

And the shofar blew, calling the people to gather.

The time had come to move forward and receive the gift God had so graciously prepared for them.

❧❧❧

Officers came through the camp, calling down the orders from Joshua. "When you see the Levitical priests carrying the Ark of the Covenant of the Lord your God, follow them. Since you have never traveled this way before, they will guide you. Stay about a half mile behind them, keeping a clear distance between you and the Ark. Make sure you don't come any closer."

Salmon quickly took down his tent, rolled the leather around the poles, and secured it to his pack. He shouldered his load and stood waiting with thousands of others from the tribe of Judah. He felt a rush of strength and longed to run to the river, but he held his place, keeping the heat banked within him.

The Ark of the Covenant passed before them, and he felt tingling excitement in his soul. The priests carried the Ark toward the Jordan River. At the prescribed distance, the tribes began to follow. The land was alive with the moving populace, thousands walking with an assurance of victory.

They camped near the Jordan, and Joshua spoke to the people. "Purify yourselves, for tomorrow the Lord will do great wonders among you."

Men separated from their wives and washed their garments. Salmon was among the multitude of men. He fasted from everything but the small portion of manna he had gathered that morning and spent the evening inside his tent, alone and in prayer.

When the sun rose, Salmon stood once again among the thousands, waiting to hear Joshua proclaim the Word of the Lord. *"Sons of Israel, come and hear the words of the Lord your God!"*

Salmon moved forward with his brothers and cousins so they were shoulder to shoulder. Joshua raised his hands, his voice strong and carrying to the farthest members of the congregation. "Come and listen to what the Lord your God says. Today you will know that the living God is among you. He will surely drive out the Canaanites, Hittites, Hivites, Perizzites, Girgashites, Amorites, and Jebusites. Think of it! The Ark of the Covenant, which belongs to the Lord of the whole earth, will lead you across the Jordan River! The priests will be carrying the Ark of the Lord, the Lord of all the earth. When their feet touch the water, the flow of water will be cut off upstream, and the river will pile up there in one heap."

At Joshua's command, the priests carrying the Ark started out once again toward the river.

Salmon stretched his neck to watch. His heart pounded. He feared God as much as he loved Him. Whenever the Ark was carried before Salmon, he trembled with an inexplicable excitement. His skin tingled. The hair on the back of his neck rose. He'd grown up seeing the cloud lift from the tabernacle, giving the sign that the people were to move their camp. He'd seen the pillar of fire at night. But he hadn't been born yet when his people left Egypt. He hadn't seen the miracles done there or the parting of the Red Sea so that the Israelites could cross on dry land. He trembled, his breathing shaky, anticipating how the Lord would enable His people to cross the rushing torrent of the Jordan.

The Ark was far ahead of the people. Was God showing them that He didn't need their protection? Had the people been allowed, they would have clustered tightly around the Ark as it moved, but it was out there ahead, the gold shimmering in the sunlight and showing them the way.

As they came closer to the river, everyone grew quieter. No one moved, no one spoke as they watched and waited for the command to go forward.

The priests reached the bank of the Jordan. They didn't hesitate but walked straight into the flooded Jordan. And as they did, there was a roaring sound such as Salmon had never heard in all his life. The hair stood on the back of his neck as he saw the water draw back, a hiss of steam billowing up. Walking in faith, the priests carried the Ark of the Covenant of the Lord to the center of the riverbed and stopped there, planting their feet. The golden Ark glistened in the morning sunlight.

And thousands upon thousands followed.

When the people were safely across the river, Joshua announced that the Lord had told him to choose twelve men, one from each tribe. As head of the tribe of Judah, Caleb called out the name of the man who would represent them. Jedidiah pressed forward. He was easily seen, taller and stronger than all the rest, and the men of Judah slapped him on the back and gave him room to walk to the front of the tribe and stand beside Caleb. The old man put his hand on Jedidiah's shoulders, spoke to him softly, and released him. Jedidiah ran ahead and joined the eleven other tribal representatives near Joshua.

"Go into the middle of the Jordan, in front of the Ark of the Lord your God," Joshua called out to the twelve representatives of the tribes. "Each of you must pick up one stone and carry it out on your shoulder — twelve stones in all, one for each of the twelve tribes. We will use these stones to build a memorial. In the future, your children will ask, 'What do these stones mean to you?' Then you can tell them, 'They remind us that the Jordan River stopped flowing when the Ark of the Lord's covenant went across.' These stones will stand as a permanent memorial among the people of Israel."

Joshua and the twelve men strode forward.

Rahab heard someone screaming and ran to the window. Leaning out, she saw a soldier running up the road. *"They're coming! They're coming! The Israelites are heading for the river!"* On the east side of the Jordan, a cloud of dust rose as a mass of people headed for the river, but what caught her attention was something ahead of them, something that shone brightly and sent shafts of light in all directions! Was it the Ark of the Lord that she had heard about?

Her lips parted as she saw two lines of steam shoot into the air and move back from the small figures now moving down into the riverbed. Her skin tingled as a rush of emotions took hold of her. Fear. Exaltation. Awe. She was laughing and crying at the same time. Her heart galloped. She leaned so far out the window, she almost toppled. *A miracle.* She was seeing a miracle! "What a mighty God He is!" she cried out as men shouted from the ramparts.

Steam continued to rise, forming a cloud over the river. Panic-stricken, people outside the walls were screaming and running toward the city like a stampeding flock. Did she hear, or only imagine, the sound of a ram's horn? The army of Israelites was crossing the Jordan. There were thousands upon thousands of them spreading out across the plains of Moab. They were as many as the stars in the heavens. They moved quickly but in order.

Rahab looked away and craned her neck toward the grove of palms. "Come, Father, come on. Where are you?" Farmers and workers were running toward Jericho. She slapped her hands on the windows, fighting against her impatience. Finally she saw him. Her mother followed, and both were struggling beneath burdens of belongings.

"Leave everything!" Rahab shouted. *"Come as you are!"*

It was useless to yell. They couldn't hear her above the din of panicked citizens descending upon the already overcrowded gates. She waved frantically. Her father saw her but dropped nothing. Tiring, her mother slid her heavy bundle to the ground and began dragging it behind her.

"Run!" Rahab gestured wildly. "Everything you need is here!"

They plodded along, stubbornly hanging on to everything they owned. Rahab cursed in frustration. A crowd was pressing through the gates. Someone was shrieking. Someone had probably fallen and was now being trampled. They sounded like a mob of wild animals, fists flying as those who were stronger tried to beat their way ahead of everyone else.

Someone banged on her door. "Rahab!" Mizraim called. "Let us in!"

She yanked the bar up and opened the door so that he and his wife, Basemath, could enter. They were carrying their two children. Jobab and his wife, Gowlan, were hurrying down the street, shouting for their children to hurry ahead. They all looked wild-eyed and pale with fear, and everyone carried something. Rahab shook her head at their choices as they entered her house: a pot; a painted urn; a basket containing a kohl bottle, tweezers, an ointment box, jewelry, and a horn of oil.

Mizraim's baby boy screamed until Basemath sat on Rahab's bed and nursed him. When footsteps raced across Rahab's roof, Mizraim's daughter dropped the urn. It shattered on the floor. Mizraim shouted at her. Crying hysterically, the little girl ran to her mother and clung to her.

"Hush, Mizraim. You're behaving as badly as those madmen at the gate. You're only frightening the children more." Rahab scooped up the little girl and hugged her. "We're all safe here, Bosem." She kissed her cheek. "Everything will be all right." She waved her hand, beckoning the others. "Come on, children. All of you. I have some things for you." She set Bosem on her feet and put out a basket of painted sticks and knucklebones. "Awbeeb, my sweet, come play with your cousins."

Rahab's sisters, Hagri and Gerah, and their husbands, Vaheb and Zebach, arrived with their children in tow. "People are going mad out there!" Seeing the others, the boys and girls joined their cousins in their games of knucklebones and pickup sticks.

"Where are Father and Mother?" Jobab said.

"I lost sight of them when they joined the crowd at the gate," Rahab answered, nodding toward the window as she took the baby from Basemath. "See if you can spot them, Mizraim." She lifted the child to her shoulder and held him close, patting his back and pacing.

"I heard the guards are going to close the gate," Jobab said.

"They'll let everyone in," Rahab said calmly. "The king will want every able-bodied worker inside before the gates are closed. If his army perishes, he'll have the citizenry standing on the walls and throwing rocks." She was angry that her father hadn't done as she told him. He and her mother should have dropped everything and come running with the first cry of that soldier running up the road. Had they listened, they would have been spared the violence at the gate. She hoped they wouldn't be hurt in the pushing and shoving mob trying to get inside the city walls.

"I'll go out and find them," Mizraim said. "Bar the door behind me, Zebach."

When an hour passed and he hadn't returned, Basemath began weeping.

"As soon as Father and Mother make it into the city, he'll come back," Rahab said, trying to stay calm for the children's sake. She could see the throng from her window and knew the city was filling with those who lived outside the walls. Even traveling merchants and caravans were clamoring to be let in.

"Let us in!" It was Mizraim. The women all sighed in relief as Zebach threw the bar off and yanked it open. Basemath ran to her disheveled husband and sobbed against his torn tunic. Rahab's father was just behind him, his face bleeding.

Rahab poured some water into a bowl and then saw her mother dragging her bundle into the house. Thrusting the bowl into Hagri's hands, Rahab strode across the room. "What's so important you'd risk your lives to bring it with you?" she demanded, reaching for the bundle.

"No!" Her mother slapped her hands away, crying out. "No, no!"

Rahab fought tears of exasperation. She was so relieved to see them safe and yet so angry at their foolishness. She forced herself to display a calm she was far from feeling. "Here. Let me take it. I'll be careful. Let go!"

Weeping, her mother sank to the floor, exhausted. She covered her head with her shawl and sobbed.

Her father brushed away Hagri's attempts to aid him and stumbled wearily to the window. "Did you see it? Did you see what happened? The water rolled back like a carpet, toward the town of Adam and the Salt Sea."

"I saw," Rahab said. "The hand of God has come upon the land, and He will brush away His enemies like stones on a game table."

Her father turned away from the window and sat heavily on the step she'd built. Rahab had never seen him so exhausted. He was trembling, and his face was sweating profusely. "You're right, Rahab. They will destroy us. They're coming across the plains of Moab like locusts, and they'll destroy everything in their path."

"Hush, Father." Everyone was frightened enough without his fanning the flames of doom. She took the bowl of water from Hagri and knelt down before her father. She spoke loudly enough for all to hear. "As long as we stay inside this house, we're safe." Squeezing out the cloth, she dabbed his face gently.

"Never have I seen such a thing in all my life." Still shaking, he closed his eyes and swallowed. "Never have I even dreamed of seeing such a thing as happened today." He made fists on his knees, his body rigid with fear. "Never have I beheld such a terrifying God as this!"

"And the men who serve this God have promised to spare us." Setting the bowl aside, Rahab put her hands over his, gripping them tightly. "Remember the crimson cord that hangs out of my window. When the day of destruction comes, we will not perish."

❧❧❧

The multitude stood on the west bank in Gilgal, east of Jericho, and watched as each of the twelve tribal representatives shouldered the largest stone he could carry and brought it into the midst of the camp. There the stones were set upright in a line, side by side, as a memorial of what God had done that day. Joshua took twelve men back down into the dry riverbed, where they piled up twelve more stones to remember the place where the Lord had brought them across the Jordan.

When the priests carried the Ark of the Covenant forward out of the dry riverbed, the sound of many waters came rushing. The river rumbled, racing down the riverbed from north and south, smashing together over the twelve stones. Once again, the Jordan overflowed its banks.

Joining thousands of others, Salmon cried out with joy as the Ark of the Covenant of the Lord came into the camp called Gilgal. The multitude raised their hands and voices in worship to the Lord God of Abraham, Isaac, and Jacob, the God who had brought them into the Promised Land.

Inside the walls of Jericho, the people waited, paralyzed with fear. Those who hadn't been able to get inside the city before the gates were shut and the beams rammed into place had fled over the mountain road to find protection among the kingdoms in the hill country. Some would go as far as the Mediterranean. And everywhere they traveled, they spread the news: The God of Israel dried up the Jordan River so the Hebrews could cross over!

The Israelites are in Canaan!

five

CALEB gathered all the men and boys of Judah. "We have entered Canaan on the day of preparations for Passover, and Joshua has received these instructions from the Lord: the entire male population of Israel must be circumcised."

All those present knew that their fathers, who had been circumcised upon leaving Egypt, had lived under God's wrath because they continued to think and act like slaves rather than as free men chosen to be a holy nation. Thus, the fallen generation had not been allowed to circumcise their sons. But now the promise was about to be fulfilled. The hand of God would bring the seed of Israel safely into the land of Canaan. But before that could happen, God wanted His people to become a circumcised nation once again.

Salmon stood waiting among thousands of his brethren. There were males of all ages, from babes in arms to men ten years older than his twenty-six years. To keep himself from thinking about the knife, he looked at the walls of Jericho. Would it matter if the enemy knew he and all the rest of the warriors would be incapacitated for a few days? They would be vulnerable and easily defeated, just as the Shechemites had been four centuries ago when Jacob's sons took vengeance over the rape of their sister. Yet Salmon felt no fear. God had performed a miracle before Jerichoan eyes. They wouldn't dare open the gates and come out against Him. No, they would stay tightly holed up in their walled city. They were paralyzed with fear. The enemy would watch as Israel was circumcised. Let them watch, tremble, and do nothing. Passover was coming, and all Israel would remember the night the angel of death had passed over the Hebrew slaves who'd painted their door lintels with the lamb's blood, moving on to strike down all the firstborn of Egypt.

A boy cried out in pain. Salmon winced in sympathy. Six men went ahead of him before it was his turn.

"Salmon," Caleb said solemnly as he approached. After performing the rite, Caleb blessed him. "Just as you have entered into the covenant, so may you enter into marriage and good deeds."

"May the Lord make me His servant!" Salmon steadied himself before standing. For one second, he was sure he would faint and humiliate himself, but the light-headed sensation passed quickly. He returned to his tent and knelt on his mat. Bowing his head to the ground, He thanked God that he was one of His chosen people.

By the end of the day, he lay upon his mat, every movement causing pain. Every male had been circumcised. The Israelites were now freeborn children of God, no longer tainted by the idolatry of Egypt.

The covenant had been renewed.

❧❧❧

"Give me that!" Rahab yanked a clay idol from her sister's hand and marched to the window.

"What are you doing?" Hagri cried out, getting up and racing after Rahab. "No!"

"What do you mean by bringing this wretched thing into my house?" Rahab hurled the false god out the window and watched it explode into pieces on the rocky ground below.

Hagri blanched. "The gods will avenge your disrespect!"

"If that thing held any power, would it have let me toss it out the window? Use the head you were born with, Hagri. Do you think that idol can bring us harm? It's nothing but clay. There is only one God, and He is the God of heaven and earth. He's the God who rolled back the Jordan a few days ago! Have you forgotten so quickly? Bow down to *Him*!"

Her father and mother and sisters and brothers and their children were all staring at her in frightened confusion. She was so angry she was shaking, but shouting at them wasn't going to make them understand. Why were they so stiff-necked and foolish? Why were they so stubborn?

She strove to speak calmly. "Our only hope is in the God of the Hebrews. We must get rid of everything that insults Him. Have you any other idols hidden among your possessions?" When they just stared at her and said nothing, she almost erupted in fury. "Spread out your things! Let me see what abominations you've brought into my house!"

Grudgingly, they began spreading out their possessions a few at a time. Vaheb, Hagri's husband, set out a clay-filled skull with shell eyes. "My father," he said when Rahab looked at it. "He was a wise man."

"Wise and *dead.*"

"Our ancestors advise us!"

"To do what? Become like them? Do you think that skull filled with dirt can tell you the way to escape the coming judgment? *Get rid of it!*"

"It's my father!"

"Your father is dead, Vaheb. A pity his head wasn't buried with him."

"Rahab!" her father said. "You've said enough!"

"I will have said and done enough when these things are thrown out that window!" Her brothers and sisters protested, but she outshouted them. "Should I have your deaths upon my conscience? Listen to me! All of you! That skull filled with dirt is nothing but a filthy idol and an insult to the God of the Hebrews. Get rid of it! *Get it out of my house!*"

"Abiasaph!" Vaheb appealed to Rahab's father. "Do you agree with her?"

Rahab felt the heat rush into her face as they turned away from her leadership. She pointed to the window. "Look out there! How many thousands do you see? And they all *walked* across the Jordan River, which is now flooded again. Do you wish to trust the God who brought them to the plains of Jericho, or do you want to trust a dead man's skull?"

No one said anything for a moment. Then her father spoke. "Do as Rahab says."

Vaheb pleaded, "What if I hide it among my things and keep it out of sight? Then it won't offend you."

"You and that idol you cling to can get out of my house."

"You'd put us out?" He looked up, stricken and angry. "Your own sister and our children? You are a hard woman!"

Her eyes burned with tears. "They can follow you and your dead ancestors out that door, or they can trust almighty God to save them and stay here with me." She looked around at the others. "And that goes for the rest of you, too. You must decide. Our people sacrifice day and night in the hope that their gods can protect them if the walls cannot. Clay idols cannot fight a living God."

She pointed at the skull in Vaheb's hands. "Look into those shell eyes, my brother. Can they look back at you? Has that jaw ever opened and spoken words of wisdom? Can that skull *think*? It's a dead thing! Three days ago, we saw a true miracle. Put your hope in the God who brought the Israelites across the Jordan, the God who dwells in their camp. That God is going to give them Jericho."

"I'm afraid!" Gerah wept against her husband, Zebach.

"We're all afraid," Rahab said more gently. "But fear the Lord who has the power to destroy us rather than these *things*. We've clung to useless, lifeless idols for too long. Do you think the God of heaven and earth will show mercy if we dishonor Him by having these things in our midst? We've separated ourselves from everyone in the city, and now we must remove all the unclean things from among us. Get rid of your false gods, Mama. Look to the God of Israel for salvation, Vaheb!"

Rahab's father rose slowly and came to her mother. "We must do likewise, Dardah. Give the idols to me."

"But, Abiasaph ... "

"They almost cost us our lives getting into the city. Rahab is right." When he held his hands out, she opened the bundle she had dragged into the city, displaying an idol case and six round objects carefully wrapped in sheepskin. Rahab shuddered. As a child, she'd been afraid of the skulls of her ancestors with their dead eyes. They'd always held a place of prominence in her father's house, gruesome reminders of the past generations.

"Surely we could keep the box," her mother said.

"Why?" Rahab said.

"It's costly and beautiful. This is ivory and these stones are – "

Rahab wasn't willing to compromise. "It will only serve as a reminder of the unclean thing it held."

Her father dropped it out the window. The box cracked open and the stone statue bounced out and rolled down the slope. Next, her father dropped the skulls. One by one, they were smashed on the rocky ground below.

Rahab looked around again. "Remove the talismans from the children, Gerah."

Gerah did so and handed them to her to toss out the window. Rahab's spirit lifted and warmth filled her. Her relatives searched the room for anything that might be offensive to the God of the Hebrews. She turned away, overcome with emotion. If only she could throw away all the experiences of her life, leaving them behind like those broken idols on the hard ground outside the window. Her life was fraught with idols – her quest for money and security, her ability to mentally stand outside herself as she allowed her body to be used by countless men, her willingness to serve a king who saw his people as possessions meant to serve him. Oh, if only she could start afresh, be a new creation before this living God. If only she could be cleansed of all unrighteousness so that she could bow down before Him in thanksgiving instead of shame.

Blinking back tears, Rahab gazed out the window again. She stretched out her hands toward the tent in which the golden box had been placed. *God of Israel, how I long to kneel before You. Whatever offering You require of me, I will give it, even my life. I have opened the gates of my heart and soul, for only You are worthy of praise, only You.*

Mizraim caught her around the waist and drew her back inside. "The guards might see – "

"Let them see." Shoving his hands away, Rahab stepped up again and stretched out her hands. Let *Him* see.

※※※※

After the solemn rite of circumcision, the children of Israel celebrated the Passover – a feast marking the anniversary of their exodus from Egypt.

Salmon girded his loins, donned his sandals, and joined his older brothers, their wives and young children. His unmarried sister, Leah, would complete their family circle. Amminadab, the eldest, killed the Passover lamb at twilight. His wife prepared the bitter herbs and unleavened bread. As the lamb roasted over the fire, the family gathered close for the traditional retelling of the events leading up to the deliverance from slavery.

"Why is this night different from all others?" the youngest boy said, leaning against his father, Salmon's second brother.

"Forty years ago, our fathers and mothers were instructed by God to paint the blood of a lamb on their door lintels." Amminadab spoke carefully so the children would understand. "That way, when the angel of death came to strike down all the firstborn of Egypt, he would pass over the people of Israel."

Another child settled into the lap of her mother. "Were we always slaves?"

"Our father, Jacob, was a wandering Aramean long before our people went to Egypt. Jacob had two wives and two concubines, who bore him twelve sons, the patriarchs of the tribes who are gathered here now. Ten of these sons, including our father, Judah, were jealous of their younger brother, Joseph, so they sold him to a band of Ishmaelites traveling to Egypt. Joseph became the slave of Potiphar, captain of the palace guard, but the Lord blessed him in all he did. Even when Potiphar's wife falsely accused Joseph of a terrible crime and Potiphar sentenced him to prison, God continued to bless Joseph. And during the time of his slavery and imprisonment, God was preparing Joseph to deliver his father and brothers from death."

The children came and sat closer around Amminadab, drawn into the story of their history.

"After a time, Pharaoh was plagued by bad dreams. One of his servants told him Joseph could explain them, so Pharaoh had Joseph brought to him. The Lord revealed to Joseph the meaning of the dreams: a great famine would come upon Egypt and all the surrounding nations. The Lord also told Joseph how to save Egypt from starvation. When Pharaoh saw that Joseph was the wisest man in all the land, he made him overseer of all Egypt."

Amminadab's wife turned the spitted lamb slowly as he continued.

"It was during the famine that the sons of Jacob came to Egypt to buy grain. Joseph forgave their sins against him and told them to come to Egypt to live. Pharaoh gave them the land of Goshen, the most fertile land in all Egypt."

He sat the youngest boy on his knee. "In time, Joseph and his brothers died, but their descendants had many children and grandchildren until Israel became a strong nation. A new pharaoh arose who didn't remember how Joseph had saved Egypt. This pharaoh saw our people as a threat and made them slaves. He put brutal slave drivers over us because he wanted to destroy our people by heavy work. But the Lord blessed us even in our oppression, and we thrived. The Egyptians became afraid and made our slavery even more bitter. They forced us to make bricks and mortar and work long hours in the fields. Even this didn't satisfy Pharaoh. So he gave the Hebrew midwives orders to kill all the baby boys as soon as they were born. But these women feared God more than Pharaoh, and they refused to do it. Then Pharaoh gave orders that all the young Israelite boys be killed."

Amminadab put his hand on one of the boys close to him. "Thousands of children were thrown into the Nile River. Little babies like your brother Samuel. But there was a brave woman named Jochebed who hid her son for three months. When she couldn't hide him any longer, she covered a wicker basket with tar and pitch, and placed him in it. Then she set it afloat among the reeds. And that's where the daughter of Pharaoh found him."

"Moses!" the children all said at once, laughing and clapping their hands.

"Yes, the child was Moses," Amminadab said quietly. His solemnity made the children go quiet again. "Moses was the chosen servant of the Lord, the one who brought Israel the Law God wrote upon the stone tablets with His own finger on Mount Sinai, the Law for which the Ark of the Covenant was made." He ran his hand gently over the hair of his daughter and looked at the other boys and girls. "It is because our fathers and mothers broke faith with God that we've wandered almost forty years in the wilderness. It is because they refused to believe and obey that they all died in the wilderness. The Law is written so that we can study it and know how to live to please God."

"The Law is meant to be written upon our hearts as well," Salmon said.

His brother glanced up at him. "If such a thing is possible."

Salmon thought of Rahab. She didn't know the Law, and yet she was exhibiting the heart of it. *Love the Lord your God with all your heart, all your mind, and all your strength.* How could Rahab have such faith unless God Himself had given it to her as a gift? Could anyone grasp the ways of God with human understanding? Could anyone account for His great mercy? Rahab was a pagan, marked for death, and yet the Lord was seeing to it that death would pass over her.

"The Lord sent Moses to Pharaoh. Moses told Pharaoh to let our people go," Amminadab went on, "but Pharaoh wouldn't listen."

Another brother, Nahshon, stepped forward with a glass of wine. He hunkered down and began to pour the wine slowly onto the ground. "The Lord God poured out his wrath upon Egypt in ten plagues: water became blood; frogs and lice came; beasts of the field died; disease, boils, hail, locusts descended; darkness came when it should have been day; and finally came the slaying of all the firstborn of Egypt." The last of the wine stained the ground.

"Before each plague," Amminadab said, "the Lord gave Pharaoh another opportunity to repent and let our people go, but each time his heart grew harder and more arrogant, more defiant. When the last plague was coming upon Egypt, the Lord instructed us through Moses to kill a perfect lamb and paint our door lintels with its blood. That night when the angel of death came, he saw the blood and passed over all Israel."

"Why do you cry, Mama?"

"I cry over the suffering of our fathers and mothers under slavery, but I cry, too, for all those who died because Pharaoh held power over them."

"All Egypt was laid waste because Pharaoh's heart was hard," Amminadab said. "He had no mercy upon Israel, nor did he have mercy upon his own people."

"Some of them came with us," Nahshon said.

Amminadab's eyes flashed. "And most died in the desert because they couldn't give up worshiping their idols." He looked at Salmon. "They led our people astray!"

Heat poured into Salmon's face. Everyone had heard about Rahab. "Our own nature leads us astray," he said gently. "The Lord says, 'Hear, O Israel!

The Lord is our God, the Lord alone. And you must love the Lord your God with all your heart, all your soul, and all your strength. And you must commit yourselves wholeheartedly.'"

"I know the Law."

"She doesn't know the letter of the Law, but she obeys the heart of it. She has repented and made God first in her life."

"Who?" a child said, only to be ignored.

Amminadab was not mollified. "We shouldn't have foreigners among us. They bring their foreign gods with them. They bring trouble!"

"I agree," Salmon said quietly. "Foreigners do bring trouble. But they cease being foreigners when they cast off their false gods and worship the Lord God with all their heart, mind, and strength."

Amminadab's eyes flashed again. "And how do you know if they are sincere in what they say? How can you trust a woman who has prostituted herself to other gods – not to mention other men?"

"Who?" another child piped in.

"As our fathers and mothers prostituted themselves to the golden calf?" Salmon said, restraining his own rising anger. "How quick you are to forget our own weaknesses and see those of others who have not had the blessing of God's very Presence."

Setting his nephew aside, Amminadab rose. "You risk us all by saving this woman and her relatives!"

The children looked back and forth, confused and frightened. Salmon looked from them to his older brother. "God has given us Jericho, Brother. I don't know how He'll do it, but He will hand it to us. If Rahab and her relatives survive what is to come, it's because death passed over them just as it passed over us. The red cord hanging – "

"Red is the color of a harlot," Nahshon said.

Feeling attacked from all sides, Salmon refused to withdraw. "Red is the color of blood, the blood of the Passover lamb."

"You are so sure of her, Salmon?"

"Leave it to Leah to ask the gentle question," Amminadab mocked when their sister quietly spoke up.

Salmon faced Amminadab again. "The heart of this woman belongs to the Lord; I'm sure of it. She declared her faith as strongly as Miriam, the sister of Moses, did. And do you not wonder? Of all the thousands in that city, the Lord singled out Rahab for our attention. Why would God do that unless He meant to rescue her?"

Salmon spoke to the children. "The Lord didn't save our people because we were worthy. Look how our fathers and mothers turned away from God! They witnessed the ten plagues; they saw God open the Red Sea! They were still faithless and rebelled. And some of our own people turned away to bow down to the baals of Moab. No, *we* are not worthy. Only the Lord is righteous. No other but the Lord is worthy of praise."

"And yet, God saved *us,*" Amminadab said firmly.

Salmon rose and faced the others. "Yes, God saved us. The Lord delivered us because of *His* great mercy. *He* plucked us out of Egypt just as *He* will pluck Rahab out of Jericho. This night we must remember *the Lord our God* freed us. *The Lord* delivered us. *The Lord* redeemed us. *The Lord* took us to be His people. Our salvation depends not on who we are but on who *He* is."

"Who's Rahab?" the children persisted.

"No one important, dear ones," one of the women said softly.

"Just an Amorite woman in Jericho," Nahshon said.

Salmon restrained his anger. "Rahab is a woman of faith. She hid Ephraim and me when the king of Jericho sent his soldiers to capture us. She told us that the Lord our God has given us the city." He smiled at the children and at his sister. "And you'll meet her soon."

"God willing," Amminadab said.

Rahab looked out at the plains of Jericho, where thousands of campfires flickered beneath the starry night. Jobab came and stood beside her. "What is that sound?"

"Singing."

"They're celebrating as though they're already victorious."

"They *are* victorious. Their God is on their side." And soon, she hoped, soon, she and her relatives would be with them, aligned with the Lord God of heaven and earth.

"Why do you think they wait?"

"I don't know. Perhaps their God told them to wait."

"Why?"

"I can't answer, Brother. I'm in the darkness as much as you."

"Maybe they've changed their minds now that they've seen the height and breadth of the city walls," Mizraim said from across the room, where he had been dozing against some cushions.

"They will do to Jericho what they've done to the other Amorite cities,"

Rahab said, "but the men who came here will rescue us."

"I'm hungry," Bosem whined.

Smiling, Rahab stepped down from the block. "I'll make bread." She added small pieces of wood to the hot coals in the brazier and put the sheet of metal over the top. She and her sisters had ground flour that morning. She poured some into a bowl, added water and seasoning, and worked the dough.

"I hope it will be as you say, Rahab," Mizraim said. "I hope we will be saved."

"God will hold them to their oath." She flattened a piece of dough and turned it round and round until it was thin. She laid it carefully on the hot metal. The dough bubbled and steamed. Using a pronged stick, she watched it briefly and then turned it over carefully. Her house filled with the aroma of roasting grain.

Awbeeb squatted beside her, watching her cook.

"The bread will be ready shortly, little one. Why don't you ask your father to pour wine?"

By the time the first loaf of flat bread was made, she had prepared another to cook. She placed the first on a reed mat to cool and began a third. Her father broke off a piece and passed it to his eldest son. The men ate first, then the children. Rahab broke a round of flat bread into quarters for her sisters. There was enough dough left in the clay bowl to make one small portion of unleavened bread for herself.

Mizraim replenished his father's cup of wine. "Maybe they'll simply wait until we run out of food and water."

"That will take months!" Jobab said. "They're probably looking for a way to break through the gate or set fire to it."

"They won't be able to get close. The king has archers on the wall."

"You still don't understand," Rahab said. "Do you think God will waste the lives of those who honor Him? The God of Israel isn't like the gods of Canaan. He protects His people. He doesn't demand their blood. You waste your time worrying."

Mizraim ignored her. "When the battle begins, there will be confusion."

"Confusion *within* the city, Brother," she said hotly. "There's no confusion out there. They are calm. God is making them ready for battle."

"Why must you go on and on about their god?" her mother cried out.

"There must be something we can do," Jobab said. "Perhaps we should try to get out of the city now, before the battle begins."

"We will wait, as we were told to do," Rahab said, frustrated. "If we try to protect ourselves by our own means, we're doomed right along with everyone else in this city. No. We will trust in the men of God. They will see the red cord and remember their oath. Inside this house, we are safe." She broke off a piece of her bread. Dipping it into the wine, she ate it.

Still, her brothers grumbled and whined and worried. Why did men have such difficulty with inaction? She tried to be patient. She tried to be compassionate. Her father and brothers had been cooped up in this house for days. They were beginning to wear on one another. The women were no better. All this talk of war disturbed them. As much as Rahab loved her relatives, they were a trial to her. No matter how many times she reminded them of the promise and encouraged them, they kept worrying over the future. They were like dogs chewing a bone.

"Why don't we eat our bread and go to sleep?" she suggested. "Let tomorrow take care of itself." She needed some peace and quiet.

When everyone was settled for the night, Rahab went back to the window. With a sigh of contentment, she propped her chin in her palms and watched the Israelite encampment. The night was so still; it was as though everyone and everything around Jericho waited for the Israelites to move forward into battle. She ran her hand over the thick red rope that hung from her window. After a long while, she lay upon her mat. She put her arm across her eyes, fighting her tears.

Come, Lord of heaven and earth! Please come! Break down the gates and take the city! Send Your men to rescue us from this place of desolation! Oh, God of all creation, I'm begging You for mercy. Let the day of our deliverance dawn!

When the battle was won, would the Hebrews allow her to become part of their nation? Ephraim had been far from friendly, quick to judge her. If her future were left up to men like him, what hope had she? He would keep his promise to save her and her family, but that would be the end of his obligations. And she hoped for so much more. Should she have asked for more? begged for more? She would drive herself mad worrying about it. All she could do was wait ... and hope that God was more merciful than the men who followed Him.

She rose first in the morning as she always did, eager to see if there was any movement in the Israelite camp. She stepped over Mizraim and Basemath and around Vaheb and Hagri. The stars still shone, only the hint of dawn coming.

Startled, she saw an old man of regal bearing standing within arrow shot of the city wall. He was staring up at it. Who was this man dressed for battle, all alone, seemingly without fear of the danger in which he had put himself? Was he studying the walls to find some weakness? He had the bearing of a leader, a man diligent and responsible. Was he contemplating the defenses of the enemy? Surely, if this was the Israelite commander, he should have soldiers with him to act as his bodyguards. Lifting her head, Rahab looked for others who might be keeping watch over this man, but all was quiet in the camp behind him.

When she looked at the man again, another was with him, a soldier, his sword drawn. Where had he come from? Surely she would have seen his approach. The old man went to the soldier quickly, his manner both challenging and eager. He was close enough to the walls of Jericho that she could see his lips move.

Rahab's heart pounded as the old warrior fell to his knees and then prostrated himself before the soldier. Then he rose just enough to remove his sandals! Her skin prickled strangely. Who was the man standing before the elder? Why would the elder bow down to the younger?

Mizraim groaned behind her and rolled over, startling her. She glanced back.

"Mizraim," she said softly. "Get up! Quickly!" She motioned to him frantically. "Come see what is happening outside the walls!"

When she turned back, the soldier was gone and the old man was striding back toward the Israelite camp, head high, shoulders back. She felt a shiver run through her body.

"What is it?" Mizraim said sleepily, standing beside her, looking out the window as dawn spilled light across the plains of Jericho.

Rahab leaned out the window as far as she could. The soldier was nowhere to be seen. She felt a strange excitement rush through her blood. "The day has come, Mizraim. God is bringing His people into their land!"

six

"THE commander of the Lord's army has given me the Lord's instructions," Joshua called out to the throng of Israelite men of war. He'd already gathered the priests and stretched out his arm toward them. "Take up the Ark of the Covenant, and assign seven priests to walk in front of it, each carrying a ram's horn." He faced the men of war again. "March around the city, and the armed men will lead the way in front of the Ark of the Lord."

Salmon was troubled, as were others around him. They all began talking in low voices. Shouldn't they dig trenches? Shouldn't they erect earthworks? How could they break down the gates of Jericho without a battering ram?

Joshua raised his hands, and the men fell silent again. "Furthermore, do not shout; do not even talk. Not a single word from any of you until I tell you to shout!"

A fast of silence.

The tribes formed ranks, and the captains of hundreds repeated the orders. Then all fell silent again as the vast army started out in obedience to the Lord's command. The only noise Israel made was the rhythmic pounding of marching feet, accompanied by the sounding of the rams' horns.

Rahab heard the king's soldiers shouting from the watchtower on either side of the gate. *"They're coming! The Israelites are coming!"* Footsteps pounded across her roof as soldiers took their duty stations along the wall.

Mizraim flew to the window. "What do we do? Do we wave the red cord? Do we – ?"

"We wait," Rahab said calmly, watching the massive Israelite army marching across the Jericho plain. They were coming straight for the city. The deep, resonant sound of the rams' horns came from the distance, but it was the sound of thousands of marching feet that made her heart quicken. *Thump, thump, thump ...* On they came, thousands upon thousands. Closer and closer. *Thump, thump, thump.* She could feel the earth tremble beneath her. Or was it her own ecstatic fear that this was the day the Lord would come? She saw the priests with rams' horns, the Ark of the Lord, and the marching soldiers coming toward her.

"Is that their god?" Mizraim said, standing beside her. "Is it?"

She had never seen anything so beautiful as this object with its strange winged creatures facing one another on the top. "The God who created the heavens and the earth cannot be kept in a box of any size."

"Then what is that thing they carry?"

"I've heard it's called the Ark of the Lord. Their leader, Moses, went up Mount Sinai, and God with His own finger wrote laws upon stone tablets. Surely, that is what they carry."

"If that Ark was captured, would the power pass to others?"

She knew her brother well enough to see where his thinking was taking him. "God chose the Israelites to be His people, and He gave them His laws. I don't know why. But the power isn't contained, Brother. Was it men who struck Egypt with ten plagues or opened the Red Sea? Was it men who rolled up the Jordan like a carpet? Power belongs to the Lord. And the Lord is ... " She spread her hands, at a loss for words. "The Lord is."

"They don't have any battering rams," Jobab said, looking over her shoulder.

"Or siege works," her father said as he approached the window.

The men were crowding her, pushing her aside in their eagerness to see the advancing army. And they saw it with men's eyes.

"How do they expect to break down the gates and get into the city?" Mizraim said.

"They will rush the walls soon," her father said grimly.

"They're close."

"Almost close enough for the soldiers on the walls to shoot them with arrows," Jobab said.

The first ranks of the Israelite soldiers turned in formation and continued marching along the wall.

"What are they doing?" Mizraim said.

"Maybe they intend to attack from the other side," her father said with a frown.

All morning, they watched as soldiers marched past the window. When the Ark came back around, Rahab closed her eyes and lowered her head in respect as the last of the long phalanx snaked around Jericho.

"They're leaving! The Israelites are leaving!" came the cries from the wall as the Israelite army marched back toward the plains of Jericho. The

Jerichoan soldiers were shouting and laughing and jeering.

Rahab winced as she heard the insults being flung after the retreating army. Did the men on the wall not know they were debasing those who would conquer them? She wanted to plug her ears as their crude taunts were flung at the God of Israel. She was ashamed of her people, ashamed of their arrogance, ashamed of their disdain toward the almighty God. If her people had possessed any wisdom, they would have sent ambassadors bearing gifts! The king would have gone out and paid homage to the God of Israel! The king and the people would have thrown open their gates and welcomed the King of Glory! Instead, these hard-hearted, senseless, proud people had shut up the city and made it a tomb.

"They've left us!" Mizraim said. "The Israelites are going away!" He turned, his face red in anger. "What do you suppose will happen to us now?"

"You were wrong, Rahab!" Jobab focused his fear and disappointment upon her as well. "The walls *are* high enough and strong enough to protect us!"

"If the king ever finds out you hid the spies and lied to his guards, we'll all die for your treason!" Mizraim added.

"And how will he find out unless one of us tells him?" her father said, now afraid of the king. "Listen to me, all of you. You will keep this to yourselves for the sake of your sister! She thought she was saving your lives!"

Gerah lifted one of her children. "We've been locked up in this house for days, all for nothing!"

Rahab refused to admit she was disappointed. She'd hoped today would be the day of their deliverance, but it seemed God had another plan. She was certain of only one thing. "The walls will not stand against them."

"You said they would come today!"

"They did come today, Basemath," she said quietly, "and I've no doubt they'll come back again tomorrow." She spread her hands. "Don't ask me why it's being done this way. I don't know. Am I God? I can only guess." Why was she saddled with these rebellious people?

"What do you guess?" her mother asked.

Rahab turned to comfort her, for her mother had wept at the sound of those marching feet and now sat distressed and watching her children argue among themselves. "I believe something strange and wonderful will happen here, just as it happened in Egypt and at the Red Sea and at the Jordan only days ago. I'm certain of it, Mother." She looked at the others. "I'm so certain. Haven't I staked my life on Him?"

"And ours," Mizraim said grimly.

Why couldn't her family see God as she did? Did they have scales over their eyes and plugs in their ears? "Yes, I've staked your lives as well. I admit it. But you're still free to choose. You're free to be like the others outside my door who've put their faith in walls instead of the living God. As for me, I'd rather wait and watch and see what God will do. I will stay here. We have been *promised* salvation if we remain in this house!"

"But Rahab," Jobab said, "they can't succeed. They don't even have battering rams!"

How soon men forget! She threw her hands into the air. "Did they need *rafts* to cross the Jordan River?" Calming herself, she continued, "Just wait, my beloved ones. Be patient. Be *still!* Soon you will see and know that God is master of this city and all the land beyond it. The world is His, if He chooses to lay claim to it. And there is nothing anyone in this city can do to stop Him."

"I believe," Awbeeb said.

Laughing, Rahab held her arms out to the child and he leaped into them. "May the others be as wise, my sweet." She settled him on her hip and stepped up to keep watch at the window.

≈≈≈

Salmon entered his tent, dismayed at how tired he was. Surely marching a few miles shouldn't deplete him so much.

He knelt and prayed silently, thanking God he hadn't needed to fight today. He doubted he would have had the strength to raise a sword. He winced as he lay down. The scar of his circumcision was not fully healed. Or was he merely weary from the inactive days of the Passover celebration?

The camp was silent.

Stretching out on his bed, Salmon frowned as he crossed his arms beneath his head. He wondered what Rahab was doing right now. Had she convinced all her relatives to enter her house and stay there? What if someone had seen her lowering two men from her window? The king could have had her executed by now. Salmon's stomach tightened at the thought, but he forced himself to relax. Surely God would protect a woman who had not only professed, but had also proven, her faith in Him. Salmon had been shaken by her physical beauty when she'd hung boldly out her window and called down to him, but even that did not compare with the courage and conviction she displayed when she put her life at risk to save him and Ephraim. Faith *and* courage.

He had to get his mind off Rahab.

The silence surrounded him, pressing in upon him until it rang in his ears. What better way to end grumbling, questioning, and discussion than by imposing a fast of silence? The Lord God knew the tendencies of His people. It seemed the inclination of all men and women to question and argue and rebel against any command. The rumble of it had begun before the words of command were fully out of Joshua's mouth.

His father and mother were dead in the wilderness because their generation had rebelled against the Lord. Joshua was wise. Keep the people silent. They became impatient too quickly, thinking they could march in and take the land by themselves. Once before, they'd made that devastating mistake.

Oh, Lord, I look at those massive walls and tremble. How many of us will die when we charge them and batter down the gates to do battle against that evil city? We'll be easy targets for those soldiers on the wall. Will I die before I'm able to fulfill my promise to Rahab?

Drowsy with exhaustion, he closed his eyes. He could still hear the echoes of marching feet in his head. Hour upon hour, mile upon mile. As they had turned away from Jericho, he'd heard taunts and smarted at the insults shouted from the wall. But he'd clenched his teeth and kept marching back to Gilgal.

Is this the reason for Your strange plan, Lord? To humble us? Are You teaching us again to wait upon You? Whether we succeed or fail doesn't depend upon our efforts but upon Your power. Is that what You're trying to get into our thick skulls and hardened hearts?

No answer came.

When Salmon arose the next morning, he fell in among the armed men of Judah as they took their position among the tribes of Israel. The day's order had been passed down from Joshua and disclosed by the captains of hundreds.

The armed warriors of Reuben, Gad, and the half-tribe of Manasseh led the phalanx across the plains of Jericho, followed by the tribes of war-ready men, some priests blowing the rams' horns and others carrying the Ark of the Covenant. They marched around Jericho once and returned to Gilgal, just as they had done the day before.

The orders stood on the third day ... and the fourth.

Each day the taunts from the soldiers and people on the walls of Jericho grew worse, as they mocked God and laughed and shouted insults. With each circumference, Salmon glanced at the wall and saw the crimson cord hanging from a window in the wall – Rahab's house. Twice he saw someone framed in the window, but the person didn't lean out so that he could see if it was Rahab or one of her relatives. But he knew she was there. The crimson cord told him she was safe. *God, protect her when the battle begins.*

Salmon knew wrath was being stored up in the hearts of his countrymen marching around the city with their shoulders back and their heads held high. His own heart burned within him.

With increasing determination, the people obeyed. They kept silent. They picked up their feet and set them down firmly upon the earth, waiting for the Lord's day of retribution. When it came, they'd be unleashed with swords in hand.

By the fifth day, Salmon was in full strength. The army of Israel was fully healed, rested, conditioned ... and ready to annihilate those who were blaspheming the Lord God.

⋙⋘

"I can still hear them marching," Basemath said after the Israelite army had marched around the city, then left, for the sixth time. "My head is pounding with the sound of it. All those thousands of men and their pounding feet."

"It seemed louder today than yesterday," Gerah said.

"Every time the Israelites march around the city, the earth seems to tremble a little more. Can you feel it?" Zebach said. "Or am I imagining things?"

Rahab watched Mizraim run his hand over a wooden cabinet that was covered with dust that hadn't been there at dawn, when the Israelites began marching around the city. He rubbed his fingers together and then brushed his hands off. Frowning, he looked around at the ceiling and the walls. "There's a crack in the wall by the door." He glanced at her.

She smiled tightly. "Perhaps tomorrow will be the day of our deliverance, Mizraim. Maybe tomorrow we'll be free, with no walls around us." Not even those of their old way of thinking.

⋙⋘

At dawn on the seventh day, the Sabbath day that belonged to the Lord, the marching orders changed. Salmon breathed hard, for it took all his strength to keep still and silent and not raise his fists in the air in exultation. His heart pounded a battle beat as he and the multitude of his brethren maintained discipline.

Today, the battle would begin. Today, he would fight his way into the city, find Rahab, and get her and her family to safety before destruction came upon them.

For today, *Jericho would fall!*

THEY'RE not leaving this time," Mizraim said, standing at the window. "They're going around the city again!"

Jobab joined him, leaning past Mizraim to see for himself. "It's true!"

Rahab checked the water supply. Satisfied there was plenty, she filled a bowl and motioned for Awbeeb. "We must get ready." She soaked a piece of linen and wrung it out. "We want to look our best when they come for us." She washed Awbeeb's dusty face.

He winced as she cleaned his ears. "Will they come soon?"

"We will be ready and hope this is the day the Lord has chosen."

"How will the soldiers get into the city?"

"The Lord their God will let them in. Now go and ask your mother if she has a fresh tunic for you. Bosem, come and wash your face and hands." She glanced at her mother and sisters, who sat staring at her. She couldn't suppress the excitement and joy she felt bubbling up inside her. "Get up! Wash yourselves! Brush your hair. Let's dress in the best we have! Should we greet those who deliver us with dour, dusty faces and dirty clothing?" She laughed. "We will dress as though we are attending a wedding!" She opened her cabinets and took out robes she had purchased over the years. "Today all Canaan will see that walls cannot prevail against the Lord our God. Today is the day of our deliverance!"

Someone moaned. "That's what you said yesterday."

"And the day before," another added.

Three times the Israelites marched around the city. Then a fourth, and a fifth, and a sixth. It seemed each time Salmon rounded the city, his strength grew, for it was the day of the Lord, and the Lord would take the day. The red cord hung from a window not far from the east gate. Salmon fixed his eyes upon it as he headed around the city for the seventh time, Ephraim marching beside him.

Then the command came. Joshua called out, "Shout! For the Lord has given you the city! The city and everything in it must be completely destroyed as an offering to the Lord. Only Rahab the prostitute and the others in her house will be spared, for she protected our spies. Do not take any of the things set apart for destruction, or you yourselves will be completely destroyed, and you will bring trouble on all Israel. Everything made from silver, gold, bronze, or iron is sacred to the Lord and must be brought into His treasury."

As the seventh round began, Salmon's heart beat harder and faster. His feet came down more firmly, joining the thousands of others so that the sound of Israel marching seemed to reverberate against the mountains to the west.

Then the massive army stopped and faced the city. The horns sounded their blast, joined by a million voices in a ferocious battle cry.

Rahab's heart trembled at the horrifying sound. As a low rumble sounded, she heard screaming from the men in the gate tower, and she clutched the windowsill as everything around her shook. Screams of terror followed from her mother and sisters, and even her father and brothers were shouting, "The walls!"

Dust billowed up as stones broke loose and tumbled down. An entire section of the wall between her house and the gate was collapsing, stones pouring in an avalanche onto the roadway. Men and women spilled out and were crushed beneath the crumbling fortress.

Then the Israelites broke ranks and came running, their battle cry raising the hair on the back of her neck. Thousands raced toward her, swords drawn and raised. Some who had fallen from the walls were wounded and tried to rise. They were cut down by the first line of Israelites.

Rahab jumped down from the step by the window. "Gather your possessions. We must be ready when our rescuers get here! Quickly, Basemath! Children, stand behind me!" She stepped forward as the screaming of the Israelites grew louder. The outer wall of her house cracked, one section breaking free. "All of you, stand behind me. Quickly!" she cried out above the din. "Don't be afraid! Stand firm!"

~~~~~

"Keep your promise!" Joshua shouted to Salmon and Ephraim as they all ran. "Go to the prostitute's house and bring her out, along with all her family!"

Zeal for the Lord swelled in Salmon until his blood was a fire within him, retribution in his hand. Screaming the battle cry, he ran with all the pent-up rage from days of listening to insults and blasphemies shouted from the battlements. He looked neither to the right nor the left, but ran straight toward the fallen gate, leaping onto it. Swinging his sword, Salmon cut down a Jerichoan soldier who was clamoring to get out of the path of the avenging army of God.

"This way!" Salmon shouted above the din of enraged soldiers and terrified foes. "This way, Ephraim!"

They turned to the right, running along the street down which Rahab had taken them the day they first entered the city. Israelite soldiers by the thousands were pouring over the collapsed walls while Jerichoans fought in confusion, their voices a babel of terror and chaos. Salmon parried a blow and brought his sword down and around, so that the attacker's weapon flew out of his hand. Slicing through him, Salmon freed his sword and ran on.

There were screams all around him as the vanquished fell before the swords of the victors. "Rahab!" he shouted, racing past the crumbled houses containing their crushed inhabitants. Where was she? One portion of the wall of her house was still standing, though parts of it were crumbling into the street. *"Rahab!"*

"We're here!"

His heart did a strange flip at the sound of her voice. The door of her house lay split in two in the stone-strewn street. Salmon entered the open section of her wall and found her standing in the middle of the house, more than a dozen others behind her. Her arms were outstretched, as if to shield her family. Her lovely face was pale, but her eyes were bright. Ephraim ran in behind him.

Rahab inclined her head in greeting and respect. "Welcome!"

Lowering his sword, Salmon stepped forward and extended his hand. "Come with me." Her fingers were cool when she took his hand. Studying her, he saw the pulse beating wildly in her throat. She was not as calm as she appeared. "You are safe now, Rahab. We'll get you out of here." He drew her toward the gaping doorway.

"If you want to live, follow us!" Ephraim said to the others behind them.

Rahab felt the heat rush into her face as the young man separated her from her family. She looked back and extended her hand toward them, then saw that her father, mother, brothers and sisters, and their children were obeying Ephraim's command, and he was taking up a protective position behind them.

Across the street, a fire blazed. The bodies of her neighbors lay in their doorways. Screams came from the center of the city. She could hear stones cascading into the street behind her. When she glanced back, she saw her house collapsing.

Salmon released her hand and caught her around the waist. "This way," he said sternly, urging her forward. "Hurry!" He lifted her over some rubble. Over his shoulder, she saw her relatives hastening after them.

When Salmon turned to help the others, Rahab held her arms out to Awbeeb. He scrambled over some fallen rocks, and she caught him up into her arms. Awbeeb clung to her, his face buried in her neck. Everywhere she looked, there was carnage. They picked their way hurriedly through the crumbled wall. She looked back at the others. "Keep going, Rahab!" Salmon commanded her. "Don't look back! We'll see to the others. Now go! Wait for us beneath the palms."

When Rahab reached the outer edge of the rubble, she ran. She didn't stop until she reached the shade of the palms. She set Awbeeb on his feet and turned to encourage the others. Dragging air into her burning lungs, she called out to her mother and sisters, who were running from the rubble with the rest of the children. Her father and brothers came more slowly, heavily burdened with family possessions. Salmon and Ephraim brought up the rear, swords drawn and ready to protect them if need be.

Her mother's face was ashen as Rahab helped her sit against the palm. Basemath, Gowlan, and Gerah were weeping and holding their children close. Hagri was blinking back tears and staring back toward the city. Rahab followed her gaze.

Jericho looked as though a hand had come down from heaven and flattened it against the earth. The walls and towers were scattered stones that had collapsed and rolled outward. Screams still rent the air as smoke and fire rose.

"This way," Salmon said, grasping her arm. He turned her toward the Israelite encampment at Gilgal.

By sunset, the once great trading center of Jericho was burning. The air was acrid, smoke billowing into the darkening sky.

Red and orange tongues of fire licked up the last bits of wooden rubble within the circle of tumbled stone. The cloying scent of burning flesh was heavy.

Shuddering, Rahab clasped her knees to her chest. She was weary with exhaustion, greatly relieved to have survived the destruction and yet saddened as well. All those thousands of people were now dead because they'd foolishly put their trust in man-made walls rather than in the living God who had created the stones. They'd heard the stories just as she had. Why had they refused to believe?

Salmon and Ephraim guarded her and her family as the Israelites returned from battle.

"None of your men are carrying any plunder," Mizraim said in surprise.

"Jericho is accursed," Ephraim said.

Salmon seemed more hospitable and willing to explain. "The Lord commanded through Joshua that every living thing in the city was to be killed: man, woman, child – young and old, ox, sheep, and donkey. Whatever silver, gold, brass, or iron that remains after the fire will be brought into the Lord's treasury. We take nothing for ourselves."

Rahab lowered her head against her knees. She didn't want Salmon or Ephraim to see her tears. They might misunderstand and think she grieved over the fallen city or that she wasn't grateful that they had fulfilled their vow. Her heart was filled with thanksgiving toward the Lord God of heaven and earth, who had held these men to their promise. She and every member of her family were alive and safe.

Yet she had hoped for more. Oh, so much more.

Someone gripped her shoulder. She glanced up sharply to see her brother Jobab bending over her. "I'm sorry I ever doubted you, Rahab."

"I, as well," said Mizraim. "The god of the Hebrews is a mighty god, indeed." He sat with his wife and children, putting his arms around them and holding them close.

The last of the Israelites returned to Gilgal.

"You will be safe here," Salmon said. He inclined his head to Rahab and then turned and walked away. Ephraim went with him.

Rahab rose quickly and followed to the edge of darkness. She stopped there and watched the two young men head back to the Israelite encampment. Behind her, no one said anything. When the two men disappeared among the tents of Israel, Rahab closed her eyes and fought despair.

After a long while, her father came out to her and put his arm around her shoulders. "We are all relieved, my daughter. Because of your wisdom, we are alive and safe."

She lowered her hands angrily. "We are all alive because of God." Tears coursed down her cheeks.

"Yes, of course."

Cautious words, not faithful ones. Rahab shook her head sadly. None of those she loved would understand her sorrow. Even now, after all they'd heard and seen, they didn't share her faith or the desire of her heart. Nor would they understand her desolation. She was unworthy to be counted among the Israelites. God had rescued her from destruction. He had shown mercy upon her and her family members. But that didn't mean she was acceptable in His sight. That didn't mean she could assume a place among His people. She saw in the faces of the men who had come to represent their people that she was still just "the harlot from Jericho."

Her shoulders shook, and she covered her mouth to hold back the sobs.

"Do you cry for those who died, Rahab?"

"No," she said raggedly.

She wept because her dream of being a follower of the true God was turning to dust. She was still outside the camp of Israel.

≈≈≈

Rahab slept fitfully that night and rose early in the morning. She stood in the predawn twilight, watching the Israelite camp awaken. As the sun rose, three men approached. Her heart leapt, and she immediately awakened the others. They all rose quickly and stood with her. Rahab moved to stand beside her father.

She recognized Salmon and Ephraim immediately, but not the older man with them, who walked with grave dignity. She and her family members bowed down before them.

"It is *him*," her father said quietly. "The man I met in the palm grove forty years ago!" He knelt and put the palms of his hands and his forehead to the earth. "I would recognize him anywhere."

It was the man she'd seen studying the walls before the march began, the man who had bowed down to the soldier with the drawn sword.

"Arise!" the elderly man said, hitting his staff against the ground. "Bow down before God, not man."

Rahab rose quickly and helped her father to his feet. She could feel how he was shaking. And no wonder, for when she looked into the commander's eyes, she trembled as well. Never had she seen such fierceness in a human face.

"I am Joshua."

"You and I met once many years ago in the palm grove," her father said. "I knew you would return."

"I remember you, Abiasaph."

Her father bowed his head again. "I thank you for taking pity upon my family and sparing our lives."

"It is God who has rescued you from destruction, Abiasaph, not I," Joshua said. "But now it is left to you to decide what you will do with the lives you've been given. Have you considered your future?"

"Our only desire is to live."

"Your lives are granted you," Joshua said. "No one in Israel will do you harm. Where do you wish to go?"

"If it is as you say and we can decide for ourselves," her father continued cautiously, "then I would ask that we be allowed to return to the palm grove so that we might live there safely and make a living for ourselves."

Heart sinking, Rahab closed her eyes.

Joshua inclined his head in agreement. "You may go, Abiasaph, you and yours, and peace be with you!"

Afraid he would leave and she would never have another opportunity to speak for herself, Rahab stepped forward. "I don't wish to go!" All eyes focused upon her – her father's and brothers' in warning, her mother's and sisters' in fear.

Salmon's eyes glowed and he seemed ready to speak on her behalf, but she turned her face from him. She could only imagine what had been said to him for giving his oath to rescue her and her family. She would not risk shaming him now. Besides, her hope rested on no man. Let God be her judge. If He were an eagle and she a mouse scurrying for shelter, she would still seek refuge beneath His mighty wings.

Joshua considered her enigmatically. "You are Rahab, the prostitute who hid our spies."

"I am Rahab."

"What is it you want, woman?"

Her father had chosen for the family, but she had this one chance, this one brief moment when opportunity lay within her grasp.

"Don't be afraid," Joshua said. "Speak."

"I want to become one of the people of God, no matter what it takes."

Joshua turned his head and looked at Salmon. Rahab held her breath, studying the two men. Was Joshua giving Salmon a silent reprimand for sparing her and her relatives and bringing this bother upon him? Was he blaming the young man for her outrageous plea? She could almost imagine what he was thinking: *How dare this brazen harlot think she deserves to be among God's people! Isn't it enough that the Lord spared her life? What right has she to ask for more? Be off with her!*

"If I cannot be grafted into God's own people, then it would have been better had I died among the rest of those lost souls in Jericho!"

Her father grasped her wrist and gave her a hard jerk. "Be silent, Daughter. Be thankful for your life!"

She yanked free and appealed to Joshua again. "I am thankful to God for my salvation, but you have said we can choose, and so I choose not to go back to my old life. I want to start afresh. Would that I could be a new creation under God!"

Her father said quickly, "She knows not what she says."

"Indeed, she does," Salmon said.

"She is only a woman and foolish," Mizraim said, clearly angry with her, his expression warning her to silence. *This, from a man who would have put his hope in the walls of Jericho and the wooden idols now ash in the rubble,* she thought angrily, refusing to be cowed.

Joshua raised his hand for silence. "The Lord has shown pity toward all of you," he said, "but toward this woman, He has shown compassion beyond measure. Abiasaph, your request has been granted. Take your family and go in peace. Live in the palm grove as you wish. But be warned: Jericho is accursed. Any man who rebuilds the city will do so not only at the expense of his firstborn son but of his youngest as well."

"What of my daughter?"

"If Rahab wants to remain behind, she may."

As Joshua and the two spies walked away, her eyes filled with tears. She hung her head in sorrow.

"You see how it is," Mizraim said, while his wife began repacking their possessions. "They think they're better than we are. They don't want a woman like you among them."

She didn't answer. She knew what he said was true, but she refused to let him see her pain.

"We'll build you a house near the road, Rahab," Jobab offered. "You can have a lucrative business – "

"I'm staying here." She sat down.

"Stubborn woman! Show some sense!"

"Sense?" She glared up at him. "What sense is there in walking away from a God who protects His people?"

"He didn't protect *our* people!" Mizraim pointed out, gesturing toward Jericho. "You can still smell their burning flesh on the wind."

"Those are my people," she said and pointed toward Gilgal.

"I want to go home," her mother said, weeping. "When can we go back to our house in the grove?"

"Will you go back to worshiping your little wooden idols as well?" Rahab asked bitterly.

"The god who destroyed Jericho isn't for us," her father said gravely. "We're alive, and that's all that matters."

"No, Father. It isn't enough to be alive but not serve the God who rescued us."

"Not for you, perhaps," Mizraim said. "But enough for us."

"Then go!"

"Please come with us, Daughter," her mother pleaded. "What will become of you if you stay behind? The Israelites will never allow you to live among them."

"I'll make her come," Mizraim said angrily, reaching for her.

She slapped his hand away. "I've had stronger men than you try to bend me to their will! Don't try it!"

"Leave her alone," her father said, hefting a bundle onto his back. "Give her a few days to think things over. She'll come to her senses."

"When will you come to yours?" she cried out. "How can you turn away after you've seen the truth?"

"What truth?" Jobab said.

"That it was God who saved you!"

"It was you, Rahab," her father said. "And we're grateful."

"But you all know the stories about God just as I do. Haven't I told you each and every one as I heard it?"

"Yes, this god has great power."

"*All* power!"

"All the more reason to go, my dear. Such a god is best avoided."

"And how do you propose to do that, Father? Where can you hide from Him?"

He looked troubled, but remained firm. "We will dwell quietly among the palms as Joshua has said we can. We will go about our business and not interfere with theirs. And, in this way, we will have peace with the people of Israel and their god."

Shaking her head, she looked away toward the Israelite encampment of Gilgal and wept.

"Come with us," Hagri said. "Please, Sister. You'll be all alone here."

"I'm staying."

"And if they break camp and leave?"

"I'll follow."

"Why?"

"Because I have to." How could she explain that she yearned for God, like a deer panting for water?

Crying softly, Hagri kissed Rahab on the head and then walked away.

≋≋≋

Salmon stood with Joshua at the edge of the encampment.

"I told you she wouldn't go with them."

"Leave her alone for three days. Give her time to consider her choices. If she remains, you may go and bring her in among the tents of Israel."

"She is a woman alone. Shouldn't a guard be posted?"

Joshua smiled at him. "She already has one."

≋≋≋

As the sun rose on the fourth day of her solitude, Rahab saw a man walking toward her. It was Salmon. He was unsmiling as he came near, and she wondered what dour message he had to give her. Perhaps Joshua had sent him to warn her away.

"You've remained here for three days," he said, standing on the opposite side of her fire.

"Joshua said I was free to choose, and I choose to stay here." She poked the fire. She had enough grain to make bread for today only; tomorrow she'd go hungry.

"How long do you plan to stay here?"

"As long as Israel remains in Gilgal."

"We will be moving soon."

"Then I suppose I'll be moving, too."

He straightened, and she thought he would walk away. "I will take you into my tent and cover you with my mantle."

Her face went hot at his proposal of marriage. "You?" She covered her cheeks with her hands.

He frowned slightly. "You refuse?"

"You're so young!"

He grinned. "I'm old enough."

She gave a bitter laugh. "Marriage to someone like me? You don't know what you're saying. Didn't you hear Joshua the other day? I am Rahab *the prostitute*, a prostitute in the eyes of all Israel and anyone else who hears of me."

"Ah, yes, the woman with a past to whom God has given a future."

"Do not jest about such things," she said angrily, struggling against the tears. If only she could live her life over, she would change so many things.

"I do not jest, Rahab." He came around the fire. Reaching down, he took her hand, drawing her firmly to her feet. "Why do you suppose Ephraim and I came into Jericho?"

"To spy out the city."

"So we were told."

"So you *said*." Frowning, she looked up at him.

"So we thought, but I've been wondering ever since I met you."

He had the most beautiful, tender brown eyes.

"Wondering what?" When he touched her cheek lightly, her heart quickened.

"If God didn't send us to find you."

"Why would God take note of an unworthy woman like me?"

"Because the Lord knows His people wherever they are, even when they're inside the walls of a pagan city. He knew *you*, Rahab, and He answered the prayer of your heart. God saved you from death, and God is now offering you a way to be grafted into His people."

She shook her head and stepped back from him. As much as the idea might appeal to her, this would not do at all. "I know God is my Savior. I also know He is God of all there is and thus master of my life."

"Then accept the blessing He offers you." Salmon smiled and placed his hand against his heart. "A young husband."

She laughed bleakly. "Young and impulsive." Jerking free, she turned away. "Give yourself a few days, and you'll be glad I said no."

"I made up my mind the day I met you."

She turned back and arched a brow at him. "Oh, really?" How many times had she heard such nonsense? The king of Jericho had said such words to her. "When did you know, Salmon? When I was hanging out the window and brazenly calling out to you?" She touched her hair. "Was it my streaming black tresses that set your heart afire?" She touched her throat. "Or my other 'character attributes'?" Her fingers teased the neckline of her dress.

His eyes never left hers. "When I first looked up at you in the wall of Jericho, I saw you as a harlot. Bold. Filled with iniquity. But when I came into your house and you spoke to us, I saw you for what you are – a woman of wisdom, a woman worthy of praise."

"Oh, Salmon ... " When she started to turn away, he caught hold of her and turned her around to face him.

"Almost from the moment you proclaimed your faith in God, I loved you."

"Love?"

"Yes, *love*. In all my life, I haven't met a woman among all Israel who is more worthy of praise than you. All the young women I know have seen the pillar of fire, the cloud that rises and leads us across the desert wasteland. They have drunk water that streamed from a rock and eaten manna from heaven. And still their faith does not match yours. From you will come prophets ... perhaps even the Messiah."

"*Messiah?*" What did the word mean?

He smiled again. "There is so much to teach you, so many things you don't know. The history of our people, the Law, the promises of God ... " He cupped her face tenderly. "Be my wife, and I will teach you."

"And what will your family say?"

"That I am prudent in selecting such a wife. Caleb has already given permission."

"Who is Caleb?"

"Leader over my tribe, the tribe of Judah. He was with Joshua when Moses sent men to spy out Canaan forty years ago. He and Joshua are the only two survivors from my father's generation. Caleb is held in high esteem by all." His mouth tipped wryly as he ran one hand over her hair. "He suggested that he be the one to marry you, but I told him he already had one wife too many."

She swallowed back her tears, amazed at the mercy of God. First He rescued her, and now it seemed He was providing a man of God to be her husband. Her *husband!* Never had she dreamed of such a thing.

"You are the woman I've waited for," Salmon said quietly. "Come with me."

She put her hand up so he would know she needed a moment. She couldn't speak a word past the lump in her throat. He frowned, dismayed, and she knew she had to show him she had decided. Stepping away from him, she knelt and scooped dirt over her fire. Gathering her possessions into a bundle, she straightened, tears of joy trickling down her cheeks.

Smiling once more, Salmon stepped forward and wiped them away. If she had doubted his words of love before, she did no longer, for his gaze shone with the joy of someone who had just been given exactly what he wanted.

Salmon picked up her bundle, took her by the hand, and led her home.

epilogue

RAHAB and Salmon had a son, Boaz.
Boaz was the father of Obed;
Obed, the father of Jesse;
Jesse, the father of King David.
And from the line of King David of the tribe of Judah
came the promised Messiah,
Jesus Christ our Savior and Lord.

seek and find

DEAR READER,

You have just read the story of Rahab as perceived by one author. Is this the whole truth about the story of Rahab and the fall of Jericho? Jesus said to seek and you will find the answers you need for life. The best way to find the truth is to look for yourself!

This "Seek and Find" section is designed to help you discover the story of Rahab as recorded in the Bible. It consists of six short studies that you can do on your own or with a small discussion group.

You may be surprised to learn that this ancient story will have applications for your life today. No matter where we live or in what century, God's Word is truth. It is as relevant today as it was yesterday. In it we find a future and a hope.

Peggy Lynch

THE VISIT

SEEK GOD'S WORD FOR TRUTH

Read the following passage:

> *Then Joshua secretly sent out two spies from the Israelite camp at Acacia. He instructed them, "Spy out the land on the other side of the Jordan River, especially around Jericho." So the two men set out and came to the house of a prostitute named Rahab and stayed there that night.*
>
> *But someone told the king of Jericho, "Some Israelites have come here tonight to spy out the land." So the king of Jericho sent orders to Rahab: "Bring out the men who have come into your house. They are spies sent here to discover the best way to attack us."*
>
> *Rahab, who had hidden the two men, replied, "The men were here earlier, but I didn't know where they were from. They left the city at dusk, as the city gates were about to close, and I don't know where they went. If you hurry, you can probably catch up with them." (But she had taken them up to the roof and hidden them beneath piles of flax.) So the king's men went looking for the spies along the road leading to the shallow crossing places of the Jordan River. And as soon as the king's men had left, the city gate was shut.*
>
> — JOSHUA 2:1-7 —

✢ Joshua secretly sent two men to spy out Jericho. What things in this passage indicate that this mission was not a secret to the citizens of Jericho?

✢ Where did the spies go?

✢ Who is Rahab? How does she make her living?

✢ According to this passage, how did the king of Jericho view these two "visitors"?

✢ How did Rahab perceive these visitors?

✢ Contrast the king's and Rahab's responses to the visitors.

FIND GOD'S WAYS FOR YOU

✛ Most of us will never face an invading army as Rahab did, but we do face overwhelming situations of other kinds. What kinds of problems are you facing right now? What kinds of choices do you have?

Read the following passage:

> *If you need wisdom – if you want to know what God wants you to do – ask him, and he will gladly tell you. He will not resent your asking. But when you ask him, be sure that you really expect him to answer, for a doubtful mind is as unsettled as a wave of the sea that is driven and tossed by the wind. People like that should not expect to receive anything from the Lord. They can't make up their minds. They waver back and forth in everything they do.*
>
> *– JAMES 1:5-8 –*

✛ What does this passage tell you to do?

✛ What warning do you find?

STOP AND PONDER

✛ How are you wavering in your decisions?

THE STAND

SEEK GOD'S WORD FOR TRUTH

Read the following passage:

> *Before the spies went to sleep that night, Rahab went up on the roof to talk with them. "I know the Lord has given you this land," she told them. "We are all afraid of you. Everyone is living in terror. For we have heard how the Lord made a dry path for you through the Red Sea when you left Egypt. And we know what you did to Sihon and Og, the two Amorite kings east of the Jordan River, whose people you completely destroyed. No*

wonder our hearts have melted in fear! No one has the courage to fight after hearing such things. For the Lord your God is the supreme God of the heavens above and the earth below. Now swear to me by the Lord that you will be kind to me and my family since I have helped you. Give me some guarantee that when Jericho is conquered, you will let me live, along with my father and mother, my brothers and sisters, and all their families."

"We offer our own lives as a guarantee for your safety," the men agreed. "If you don't betray us, we will keep our promise when the Lord gives us the land."

— JOSHUA 2:8-14 —

✝ List the reasons that the people's hearts had melted in fear and no courage remained.

✝ What declaration does Rahab make about God?

✝ What does Rahab ask of the spies?

✝ Rahab asks the men for a promise. Upon whom is that promise based?

✝ How do the spies respond?

FIND GOD'S WAYS FOR YOU

✝ What fears grip you? Why?

✝ What do you do when you are fearful?

✝ What kind of advice have you given to others who are fearful?

King David, one of Rahab's most famous descendants, wrote of God: "Even when I walk through the dark valley of death, I will not be afraid, for you are close beside me. Your rod and your staff protect and comfort me" (Psalm 23:4).

✝ What does God offer you?

STOP AND PONDER

✦ Where is God in relation to you right now?

THE ESCAPE

SEEK GOD'S WORD FOR TRUTH

Read the following passage:

> *Then, since Rahab's house was built into the city wall, she let them down by a rope through the window. "Escape to the hill country," she told them. "Hide there for three days until the men who are searching for you have returned; then go on your way."*
>
> *Before they left, the men told her, "We can guarantee your safety only if you leave this scarlet rope hanging from the window. And all your family members – your father, mother, brothers, and all your relatives – must be here inside the house. If they go out into the street, they will be killed, and we cannot be held to our oath. But we swear that no one inside this house will be killed – not a hand will be laid on any of them. If you betray us, however, we are not bound by this oath in any way."*
>
> *"I accept your terms," she replied. And she sent them on their way, leaving the scarlet rope hanging from the window.*
>
> *The spies went up into the hill country and stayed there three days. The men who were chasing them had searched everywhere along the road, but they finally returned to the city without success. Then the two spies came down from the hill country, crossed the Jordan River, and reported to Joshua all that had happened to them. "The Lord will certainly give us the whole land," they said, "for all the people in the land are terrified of us."*
>
> – JOSHUA 2:15-24 –

✦ Where was Rahab's house located?

✦ How did she help the spies escape?

✦ What instructions did she give the spies? Why?

✛ What warning and conditions of rescue did the spies give Rahab?

✛ What was Rahab's response?

✛ What signal was Rahab to use?

FIND GOD'S WAYS FOR YOU

✛ Like Rahab, we have opportunities to help others. List some ways you have helped others.

✛ What advice have you given?

> Jesus said, *"Don't worry about having enough food or drink or clothing. Why be like the pagans who are so deeply concerned about these things? Your heavenly Father already knows all your needs."*
>
> – MATTHEW 6:31-32 –

✛ What instruction and what promise does Jesus offer here? What is the condition?

STOP AND PONDER

✛ Who has first place in your life?

THE WAIT

SEEK GOD'S WORD FOR TRUTH

Read the following passage:

> *Now the gates of Jericho were tightly shut because the people were afraid of the Israelites. No one was allowed to go in or out. But the Lord said to Joshua, "I have given you Jericho, its king, and all its mighty warriors. Your entire army is to march around the city once a day for six days. Seven priests will walk ahead of the Ark, each carrying a ram's horn. On the seventh day you are to march around the city seven times, with the priests*

blowing the horns. When you hear the priests give one long blast on the horns, have all the people give a mighty shout. Then the walls of the city will collapse, and the people can charge straight into the city."

So Joshua called together the priests and said, "Take up the Ark of the Covenant, and assign seven priests to walk in front of it, each carrying a ram's horn." Then he gave orders to the people: "March around the city, and the armed men will lead the way in front of the Ark of the Lord."

After Joshua spoke to the people, the seven priests with the rams' horns started marching in the presence of the Lord, blowing the horns as they marched. And the priests carrying the Ark of the Lord's covenant followed behind them. Armed guards marched both in front of the priests and behind the Ark, with the priests continually blowing the horns. "Do not shout; do not even talk," Joshua commanded. "Not a single word from any of you until I tell you to shout. Then shout!" So the Ark of the Lord was carried around the city once that day, and then everyone returned to spend the night in the camp.

Joshua got up early the next morning, and the priests again carried the Ark of the Lord. The seven priests with the rams' horns marched in front of the Ark of the Lord, blowing their horns. Armed guards marched both in front of the priests with the horns and behind the Ark of the Lord. All this time the priests were sounding their horns. On the second day they marched around the city once and returned to the camp. They followed this pattern for six days.

– JOSHUA 6:1-14 –

✝ Why was Jericho "tightly shut"?

✝ What proclamation does the Lord give Joshua?

✝ List the battle instructions given by God.

✝ What instructions does Joshua give to the people?

✝ How do the priests and army respond?

✝ Rahab and her family members are also tightly shut up within the walls of Jericho, waiting for the impending battle. They must have been watching from the wall. What indications do you find that no one knew when the day of victory/rescue would be?

FIND GOD'S WAYS FOR YOU

✝ Rahab and her family members were locked up inside her house within the walls of Jericho – waiting for the promised rescue. In what ways are you locked up?

✝ What kind of waiting place are you in?

Psalm 27:14 says: "Wait patiently for the Lord. Be brave and courageous. Yes, wait patiently for the Lord."

✝ What instruction is given in this verse?

✝ What does it mean to you?

STOP AND PONDER

✝ On whom do you rely for strength and courage?

THE RESCUE

SEEK GOD'S WORD FOR TRUTH

Read the following passage:

On the seventh day the Israelites got up at dawn and marched around the city as they had done before. But this time they went around the city seven times. The seventh time around, as the priests sounded the long blast on their horns, Joshua commanded the people, "Shout! For the Lord has given you the city! The city and everything in it must be completely destroyed as an offering to the Lord. Only Rahab the prostitute and the others in her house will be spared, for she protected our spies. Do not take any of the things set apart for destruction, or you yourselves will be completely destroyed, and you will bring trouble on all Israel. Everything made from silver, gold, bronze, or iron is sacred to the Lord and must be brought into his treasury."

When the people heard the sound of the horns, they shouted as loud as they could. Suddenly, the walls of Jericho collapsed, and the Israelites charged straight into the city from every side and captured it. They completely destroyed everything in it – men and women, young and old, cattle, sheep, donkeys – everything.

Then Joshua said to the two spies, "Keep your promise. Go to the prostitute's house and bring her out, along with all her family."

The young men went in and brought out Rahab, her father, mother, brothers, and all the other relatives who were with her. They moved her whole family to a safe place near the camp of Israel.

Then the Israelites burned the city and everything in it. Only the things made from silver, gold, bronze, or iron were kept for the treasury of the Lord's house. So Joshua spared Rahab the prostitute and her relatives who were with her in the house, because she had hidden the spies Joshua sent to Jericho. And she lives among the Israelites to this day.

— JOSHUA 6:15-25 —

✢ In the previous lesson we learned about the plan during the six days of waiting. What new instructions were carried out on the seventh day?

✢ What instructions were given regarding Rahab?

✢ Whom did Joshua send to rescue Rahab and her family? Where were they taken?

✢ What happened to the city and its contents?

✢ What items were spared and why?

✢ Rahab and her family were spared. What reason is given?

FIND GOD'S WAYS FOR YOU

✢ When your world is falling apart and things are not going as you planned, what do you do to try to regain control?

God says, "My thoughts are completely different from yours ... And my ways are far beyond anything you could imagine. For just as the heavens are higher than the earth, so are my ways higher than your ways and my thoughts higher than your thoughts" (Isaiah 55:8-9).

✣ What do you learn about God's ways and thoughts from these verses?

Jesus said, "For God so loved the world that he gave his only Son, so that everyone who believes in him will not perish but have eternal life. God did not send his Son into the world to condemn it, but to save it" (John 3:16-17).

✣ What is God's rescue plan for the world?

✣ Why does He want to rescue you?

STOP AND PONDER

✣ Whom have you chosen to rescue you?

THE OUTCOME

SEEK GOD'S WORD FOR TRUTH

So Joshua spared Rahab the prostitute and her relatives sho were with her in the house, because she had hidden the spies Joshua sent to Jericho. And she lives among the Israelites to this day.

— JOSHUA 6:25 —

✣ Of those rescued, how many made their home in the midst of Israel?

✣ What reason is given?

The story does not end here. We are not told what happened to Rahab's family members, but we do know what happened to Rahab. She married an Israelite named Salmon and bore him a son. Rahab is considered a woman of great faith, and she is held in high esteem in the Bible. The following passage about Rahab was written centuries after her death:

What is faith? It is the confident assurance that what we hope for is going to happen. It is the evidence of things we cannot yet see ... It was by faith that Rahab the prostitute did not die with all the others in her city who

refused to obey God. For she had given a friendly welcome to the spies.
— HEBREWS 11:1, 31 —

✝ Based upon what you've learned about Rahab, how does this definition of faith apply to her?

✝ How did she demonstrate her faith?

The apostle Paul wrote: "God saved you by his special favor when you believed. And you can't take credit for this; it is a gift from God. Salvation is not a reward for the good things we have done, so none of us can boast about it" (Ephesians 2:8-9).

✝ From this, what else do you learn about faith?

The apostle Paul also wrote: "I did this so that you might trust the power of God rather than human wisdom" (1 Corinthians 2:5).

✝ Upon whom did Rahab base her faith?

And finally, the outcome of Rahab's story is the honor given to her in the first chapter of the Gospel of Matthew, where she is listed in the lineage of Jesus Christ, the Messiah (see pages 581-582).

FIND GOD'S WAYS FOR YOU

Your story does not end here, either. What have you learned about yourself from this study?

✝ What changes, if any, have you made?

✝ How would you describe your relationship with God and why?

✝ How do you choose to live out your life?

STOP AND PONDER

✝ How have God's ways become your ways?

Unshaken

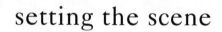

setting the scene

RUTH 1: 1-4

In the days when the judges ruled in Israel, a man from Bethlehem in Judah left the country because of a severe famine. He took his wife and two sons and went to live in the country of Moab. The man's name was Elimelech, and his wife was Naomi. Their two sons were Mahlon and Kilion. They were Ephrathites from Bethlehem in the land of Judah. During their stay in Moab, Elimelech died and Naomi was left with her two sons. The two sons married Moabite women. One married a woman named Orpah, and the other a woman named Ruth ...

one

RUTH walked down the narrow, crowded streets of Kir-hareseth, her mind and heart in turmoil. Her beloved husband, Mahlon, was dying of a lingering illness that had come upon him months earlier. She fought the sorrow and fear stirring in her. How would she live without Mahlon? She'd dreamed of living a long life with the man she loved, bearing his children, growing old with him. And now, she suffered watching him suffer. She grieved that there would never be children to carry on his name.

But it was the new moon, and her mother was expecting her for her monthly visit. They would drink tea, eat the delicacies of her father's table, and talk about family matters. Ruth dreaded this visit. She couldn't keep her mind from her troubles. And she didn't want to hear what her mother thought was the cause of them.

Poor Naomi! How could her mother-in-law bear another loss? Fifteen years ago she'd lost her husband, Elimelech; and her younger son, Kilion, had died last spring. Would Naomi's faith in the God of Israel continue to give her peace, or would she finally crumble beneath the crushing grief of losing her last son?

Oh, Lord God of Israel, hear our cry!

From the time Naomi had told her about the true God, she had believed because she saw such peace in her mother-in-law. It was a peace that defied circumstances. Ruth had never seen such peace, certainly not in the house of her mother and father. She and Naomi had spoken often of God, especially when questions had arisen in Ruth's heart. And the answers had always come down to trusting God, obeying Him, accepting His will, knowing there was a purpose in what was happening even if they couldn't see it. But sometimes the pain seemed unbearable.

And Ruth was afraid.

Would she be inconsolable like her sister-in-law, Orpah, had been when Kilion died last year, wailing and rocking and refusing to eat until Ruth and Naomi were afraid for her health?

Oh, Lord God, don't let me be a burden to Naomi. Give me the strength to help her.

When she reached her father's house, she took a deep breath, squared her shoulders, and knocked. A servant opened the door and smiled brightly. "Ruth! Come," she beckoned eagerly. "Come."

It was difficult to enter her father's grand house with its expensive furnishings and not make comparisons to the humble abode of her husband. Here, everywhere she looked was the conspicuous evidence of wealth – fine urns, rugs, beautifully colored linen curtains, low tables inlaid with ivory. She had grown up in this house and taken her father's wealth for granted. Then she met, fell in love with, and married a young Hebrew merchant who was having difficulty keeping the family business going and, sometimes, keeping food on the table.

Her father and mother took great pride in their possessions, but over the years of living with Naomi, Ruth had come to recognize her own parents' poverty of spirit. There was a richness in Naomi's life that had nothing to do with the house she lived in or the material possessions she had.

"Ah, my beautiful daughter." Ruth's mother entered the room and embraced her. They exchanged kisses. "Sit, my love." She clapped her hands, gave quick orders to a maiden, and sat on one of the plump scarlet-and-blue cushions. "Do you notice anything new?"

Ruth glanced around. Was there a new table or wall hanging or rug? When she looked back at her mother, she saw her fingering a gold necklace.

"What do you think? It's beautiful, isn't it? A gift from your father. It's from Egypt."

"He's always been generous," Ruth said, her mind drifting back to Mahlon. He'd insisted she come today, insisted she leave him for a while. His mother was with him. Everything was fine. *"Go. Go and enjoy yourself."* But how could she? All she could think about was Mahlon and how quickly she could leave this place and go home to him, where she belonged.

A servant entered with a tray laden with fruit, bread, two goblets, and an urn of wine. A second servant set down a platter of cooked grain with bits of roasted lamb. Ruth's stomach cramped at the tantalizing aroma of the well-seasoned food, but she didn't extend her hand, even when her mother pressed her. How could she take a bite when Mahlon was too ill to eat anything at all? How could she enjoy the delicacies her mother spread out on the table before her when her mother-in-law had nothing in the house but bread, olive oil, and sour wine?

"You must keep up your strength, Ruth," her mother said softly. "You're so thin."

"Perhaps in a while, Mother."

"Orpah's mother spoke with me in the marketplace yesterday. Has everything been done that can be done?"

Unable to speak, Ruth nodded. Naomi, insisting there was always hope, continued to pray and beseech God. She and Ruth both prayed. Prayer had become an unceasing habit.

"Oh, my darling. I'm so sorry you're going through this." Her mother reached out and placed her hand over Ruth's. For a moment, she was silent. "What will you do when he dies?"

Ruth's eyes filled with tears at the blunt question. "I will grieve. I will comfort Naomi. Beyond that, I don't know. And I can't think about it now."

"But you must."

"Mother," Ruth said softly in protest and then drew in a sobbing breath as she covered her face.

Her mother rushed on. "I didn't ask you here to cause you more pain. I know how much you love Mahlon. If your father didn't love you so much, he would have insisted you marry Kasim, and you wouldn't be facing such anguish now. Your father wants you to know that you're welcome to come home. And you know how much I'd love to have you here with me again, even if only for a little while. You needn't stay with Naomi if Mahlon dies. Come back to us."

Ruth dropped her hands into her lap and stared at her mother through her tears. "After all Naomi has been through, could I leave her? My duty is to my husband's household, Mother. You know that."

"Naomi would be the first to tell you to return to us. Do you think she'll want to stay here when her last son dies? She will go home to her own people where she belongs."

The words cut into Ruth's heart. Her mother spoke as though Mahlon was already dead and Naomi best forgotten. "I must go, Mother." She started to rise.

Her mother caught her hand. "No, please, listen to me. Naomi's husband was eager to adopt our customs and become one of us, but your mother-in-law has always held herself aloof. She still dresses like a Hebrew. She's never set foot in one of our temples nor given a single offering to any one of our gods. Perhaps that's why she suffers so. Our gods are angry with her."

"She has a God of her own."

"Oh yes, and what good is he? What has he given her but poverty and grief?" She made a sweeping gesture. "Look around you, Daughter. See how the gods of Moab bless us. Look at what we have to show for *our* faith."

"But you're never satisfied, Mother."

Her eyes darkened. "I'm satisfied."

"Then why do you always want more? Possessions don't matter to Naomi."

Her mother released her hand angrily. "Of course not. Why would possessions matter to someone who will never have them?"

"You don't understand, Mother."

"I understand that you've turned away from the gods of your own people to worship hers. And what good has come from it? You're being punished for it. Turn back to the gods of our people, Ruth. Leave that house of sorrow and come home."

Home to what? Her father and mother had never been content. The more wealth her father accumulated, the more he wanted. Their appetites were ever whetted for increase. Nothing satisfied. In a few days, her mother would tire of the gold necklace she wore, and she would hunger for something new, something about which to boast.

Naomi boasted in nothing but the God of Israel. And she found peace even in the midst of chaos when she went to Him in prayer.

God, oh God, help me! There are so many things I don't understand. I have no answers for my mother. Can you hear the voice of a frightened Moabitess? I don't want my faith to die if You choose to take Mahlon from me. My mother's words are like spears in my heart. Shield me.

She wept.

"We know you must stay with Mahlon to the end, Ruth. And we understand that you'll want to stay for a few weeks after that and comfort Naomi. Fulfill your duty to her. Then come home to us, my love. Come home where you belong and where life will be so much easier for you. Everyone will understand. Naomi loves you. She'll want the best for you, just as we do. There's no need for you to live in poverty. You're young and beautiful. You have your whole life ahead of you."

But Ruth couldn't imagine her life without the man she loved or the mother-in-law who had opened her heart to her. How could staying a few weeks fulfill her obligation to Naomi? Duty was not the only bond between them. There was also love. Not just love for one another but love for the God they both believed in.

"I can't leave her, Mother."

"But what about your own family? What about your father? What about *me?* Come home, Ruth. Please come home to us. How can I bear to see you live in such poor circumstances when … "

Ruth felt torn between her love for her mother and father and her love for Naomi and Orpah. If Mahlon did die, could she turn her back on them and walk away? Could she go back to living the way she had before, bowing down to the statues representing the gods of her mother and father, gods she no longer believed even existed? The bond she had with Naomi was deeper than a relationship by marriage. Ruth had come to embrace her mother-in-law's beliefs in an unseen God. She had explained her new beliefs to her mother and father, and heard them laugh and shake their heads. *"How can you believe such nonsense? An unseen god?"* She loved her mother and father deeply, but she wouldn't turn her back on Naomi or the truth she had come to realize through her.

"Mahlon, Naomi, and Orpah are my family, Mother, just as Father became yours when you married him."

When her mother's face crumpled in tears, Ruth embraced her. "You know I love you, Mother. I'll always love you. But I must do what's right."

"This isn't right! You're throwing away your life!"

Ruth saw that her mother refused to understand. Things could never be the same as they had been when Ruth was a child in her father's household. She was a woman now, with a husband and a mother-in-law and responsibilities toward both. Her life didn't belong to herself anymore. And even if it did, would her decision be any different?

Oh, Lord, give me strength. I feel like a broken jar with all the oil spilling out.

She had to tell her mother the truth. It wouldn't be fair to leave her with false hopes.

"I won't leave Naomi, Mother. You have Father. You have my brothers and their wives and children, and my sisters and their families. If Mahlon does die, who will Naomi have left?"

"She will have Orpah," her mother said stubbornly. "Let Orpah stay with her."

Orpah didn't believe in the God of Israel. She still worshiped idols and burned incense to Ashtoreth. "Orpah is a kind and loving daughter-in-law, but she doesn't share Naomi's faith."

Her mother's eyes darkened in anger. "How can you persist in believing in this unseen god of hers after all that's happened? It's not fair that you give up your life for this ill-fated family! If Naomi decides to leave, *let her go!"*

Ruth refused to be drawn into another argument about whose god had grander temples or the most elaborate and pleasurable worship services. She drew back and stood. "Mahlon needs me. I must go."

Her mother rose with her, weeping again as she followed her to the door. "Please consider carefully what you're going to do, Ruth. I beg of you! Don't throw your life away!"

Ruth's emotions warred within her. Love ... grief ... impatience ... confusion. She turned and embraced her mother quickly. "I love you," she said in a choked voice. "Tell Father I love him, too." She released her hold, turned away, and hurried out the door.

As she sped along the narrow city streets, she covered her face with her shawl so those passing would not see her anguish.

⟨⟨⟨⟨⟨⟨

Grief is deeper when the sun goes down and memories rise up with the moon and stars. The streets of Kir-hareseth were deserted now, everyone home and asleep, but Naomi's mind was whirring as she sat at the end of her pallet, her back against the cold stone wall of her small house. She felt alone, even though her two beloved daughters-in-law lay sleeping within a few feet of her. They were worn out with sorrow. Each had lost a husband, Orpah first and then Ruth. But they would never experience the deeper grief of losing their children, for they had none.

My sons are dead! My sons, oh, my sons ... Naomi wanted to scream out her pain, but for the sake of the young women sleeping nearby held it in instead.

It was dark now, so dark the night closed in around Naomi, bringing with it fear and doubt. She tried to pray, but her whispered words seemed to bounce off the ceiling and land back in her lap unheard. And she began to wonder. Had God ever heard her prayers? Had the Lord ever listened to her pleas?

Like the approach of locusts ready to feast upon her faith, the silence hummed inside her head. She pressed her hands over her ears and clenched her teeth. Why was the night like this? Sometimes the darkness was so still she could hear her own blood rushing through her veins. The sound was like a heavy rain washing open the doors of her mind, flooding her with memories she wanted to forget.

The room echoed with her dead husband's voice. "We're going to Moab whether you like it or not, Naomi! There's no famine there."

"But, Elimelech, we mustn't leave Bethlehem! It's our home."

"Our home is turning to dust!"

"If we trust and obey God, He will provide."

"Are you blind? Look around you, woman. God has abandoned us!"

"Because you and others bow down to baals!"

"I bow down to Baal because he's the lord of this land!"

"Moses told our fathers the Lord is God and there is no other!"

"And what good has God done for us lately?" Elimelech argued. "How long since rain last fell on our land? When was the last time our crops produced even a little more than what we need to fill our own stomachs?"

"But you are saying it yourself, my husband. The Lord has provided what we need to survive."

"I'm sick of hearing you say that! *I'm* the one taking care of us, Naomi. I'm the one working my flesh to the bones on this rocky ground and watching my crops die! Don't tell me God is taking care of us! Look at my hands! Look at the calluses and tell me it's God who takes care of you and our sons. God stands far off and watches while everything I own turns to dust. He's abandoned us! You're just a woman. What do you understand of these things? I'll do what's right in my own eyes."

That same day, Elimelech had mortgaged the land he'd inherited from his father. He'd come home, packed their possessions on two donkeys, and taken Naomi and their sons, Mahlon and Kilion, away from Bethlehem. She'd barely had time to bid good-bye to her friends and few remaining family members. Elimelech had been so certain he was making the right decision! What man wanted to hear the constant dripping of a nagging wife? So she did what she felt she could do: she kept silent with her doubts and she prayed.

She prayed in the morning when she first awakened. She prayed throughout the day as she worked. And she prayed when she lay down upon her pallet at night. She prayed and prayed and prayed – and watched her life turn to ashes.

Elimelech found work in Moab at Kir-hareseth. He cut off his locks of hair, shaved off his beard, and donned Moabite clothing to make his way easier. There were other Israelites sojourning in Moab and living in Kir-hareseth. They, too, had come to wait out the famine in the Promised Land, and they, too, quickly embraced the ways of the people around them and forgot the Law of Moses and the promises of God.

It was summer when Elimelech died.

"I just need to rest." He'd come home complaining of pain in his chest.

"I'll be fine in the morning." He'd sat right where she was sitting now, rubbing his arm, up and down, up and down, grimacing. "Naomi?" The strange catch in his throat had brought her to her knees before him.

"What, my love?" She took his hand and covered it with her own, wanting to comfort him.

"Naomi," he said again, the sweat beading on his forehead. He'd looked terrified. "I only did what I thought was right." His lips were blue. She'd wanted to comfort him. She'd held him in her arms and tried to soothe him. But nothing had helped ease his torment.

Even now, after fifteen years, the grief rose up in her again, renewed by Mahlon's untimely death, just as her grief had been renewed and deepened last year when Kilion died. There was no escaping the pain, no hiding from it, no pushing it down deep inside her anymore. She remembered everything so acutely, especially her unanswered prayers. She'd prayed so hard that God wouldn't take her husband from her, prayed that God would have mercy upon him, and kept praying even as she watched the light ebb from Elimelech's eyes. Then she prayed for mercy and saw death take him.

Her sons had buried their father among Moabites. At first, she could scarcely believe Elimelech was gone. She kept thinking she would awaken from this nightmare and he would be there, complaining as always. When full realization had sunk in that she would never see him again, she had become angry with him. But that, too, passed. She had been too busy helping her sons put food on the table.

It had been fifteen years since Elimelech died, and still the grief would rise up unexpectedly. It was never as sharp as those first weeks, but it never fully dulled. She had thought the pain of losing her husband was the greatest of all, but that was before she had lost sons. Now, she was drowning in a sea of sorrow.

She couldn't even pray anymore. She had always had a glimmer of hope and a sense of God's presence. Now she felt God was beyond reach, His mercy not meant for her. All her prayers were like smoke blown away by an angry wind. Every one of them. Perhaps Elimelech had been right after all. God was standing far off, watching her suffer.

God, where are You? How do I find You?

She wanted to defend herself against His judgment. Hadn't she pleaded with her husband to stay in Bethlehem? Hadn't she begged him to trust in God? Hadn't she prayed that God would change Elimelech's mind and they would go home? Hadn't she wanted to return to Bethlehem when Elimelech died? When God had taken Elimelech, hadn't she tried desperately to convince her sons that they should go back to the land God had promised them? But Mahlon and Kilion had been old enough by then to decide for themselves.

"What is there for us, Mother? This is our home."

Their hearts had been turned away from God and the Promised Land years ago. Their home in Bethlehem was nothing more than a bad memory to them, a place of hardship and heartache. Their father had never said a good word about it. Why should her sons want to return? They knew little of Hebrew customs and laws, for Elimelech had neglected his duties. He'd never taught his sons the history of the Israelites, the Law of Moses, the way of righteousness. Her sons had watched how Elimelech lived and done as he had done. When their father died, they listened to the elders of Kir-hareseth. They listened to the priests of Chemosh. They listened to their own desires and thoughts and did as they pleased, even unto taking Moabite wives for themselves. Oh, the grief her sons had caused her!

Nothing she had said to them had mattered. They loved her, but she was just a woman. What did she know? So they said. So they'd been taught to believe by their father before them.

Naomi looked at her daughters-in-law sleeping nearby. How strange that they were her only consolation now, these young women she'd grieved over when first she heard about them. Foreign wives! The shame of Israel! Oh, how she had despaired. Yet she'd managed to put on a smiling face when Mahlon brought Ruth home, and Kilion brought Orpah. What else could she do? She could not bring herself to risk losing the love of her sons. And she'd hoped to have some small influence upon their young wives.

Now they were widows like her, and as dear to her as if they had come from her own womb. *Nothing brings people closer together than shared suffering.* She remembered in the beginning, she had accepted them and tried to build a relationship with each of them in order to keep peace in her house. And secretly, she'd prayed that Ruth's and Orpah's hearts would be softened toward the God of Israel. If she could teach them about the Lord, perhaps there would be hope for the next generation. But now her last hope for the future was lost.

A sudden fever had taken Kilion last spring. Then a lingering illness had brought Mahlon down. Kilion had died in the space of a few days, suffering little discomfort, but poor Mahlon had received no such mercy. When he fell ill, the suffering went on and on. She could do nothing but watch her eldest son, the first fruit of Elimelech, be eaten alive by disease. She'd prayed countless times for God to ease his suffering, for God to put all the sins of her husband and sons upon her, but the days wore on and on. Poor Ruth, poor faithful, loving Ruth. How many nights had the girl sought to ease Mahlon's pain and ended up weeping over her helplessness? Sometimes Naomi wished she could escape the city and run out into the fields and scream and tear her hair and throw dust over herself. She had wept when Mahlon looked up at her with the eyes of a wounded animal in agony, hounded by terror.

Her own grief had almost consumed her during those long, terrible months, but she had spoken to Mahlon often and gently of the mercy of the Lord. *Mercy!* Her heart had cried within her. *Mercy! Lord God, mercy!* While Ruth had ministered to her husband's physical needs, Naomi sat by and told him about the signs and wonders God had performed in Egypt and in the wilderness, and in the land of Canaan. He couldn't resist her now, but was he ready to repent and seek the Lord? She told Mahlon how God had delivered the Israelites from Egypt, not because they deserved it, but because He had chosen them to be His people. She told him about Moses and the Law and how the people were stubborn like Elimelech and rebelled. She told him about the blessings and the cursings. And she told him about the promises. When he slept, she bowed her head and prayed. *Oh, Lord, Lord ...* she couldn't find the words. *Oh, Lord, search my heart ...* She prayed and prayed and prayed.

And still Mahlon had died.

Ruth had been sitting with him and holding his hand when he died. She let out a long, anguished cry when he stopped breathing, then wailed and covered her head.

Had it been only twenty-two days ago?

Orpah had tried to comfort her and Ruth by saying Mahlon would be at peace now; his pain was over. Naomi wanted to believe these words, but they seemed hollow, without foundation. What did Orpah know of God?

Naomi's sorrow was so deep that she felt paralyzed by it. All she could do was wait for the sun to rise so she could go on sitting in this dusty, dank corner and listen to the rush of people going past her door. How dare life go on as it always had, when her sons were dead! She resented the laughter of neighbors outside her door. She was embittered by the changeless activity. Were her loved ones so unimportant they might have been mere grains of sand cast into the Dead Sea, leaving hardly a ripple? Only Orpah and Ruth shared her anguish.

Naomi hated Moab and Kir-hareseth more with each day that passed. She hated these foreign people. And she hated herself for hating them. It wasn't their fault Elimelech, Kilion, and Mahlon had taken up ways displeasing to God. *Men decide their own path, but it is God who judges, God who prevails.*

The sun rose, and Naomi wished she could close her eyes and die. Instead, she found herself alive and aware of what was going on around her. She could hear Orpah and Ruth weeping together and talking in soft voices so they wouldn't disturb her. She ate when they asked her to do so and lay down when they pleaded with her to rest. But she felt lost and angry and hopeless and afraid.

She wallowed in memories, thinking back over the early years of marriage with Elimelech. Oh, how they'd laughed together and dreamed of a fine future brought by hard work and dedication to the land. Naomi, his merry one, he'd called her. She remembered the joy when she found she was with child, the anticipation, the celebration when a son was born – first one, then another. She had sustained them with her body, nursing them until they were able to walk. She had rejoiced in their childish exuberance, laughed at their antics, relished their presence. Life had been full then. She'd felt God's presence in every blessing.

What do I have now? Nothing! I will never know joy again.

Things had been bad in Bethlehem, but everything got worse when they left. She'd tried – and failed – to have influence over Elimelech. She had wanted to raise her sons in the ways of the Lord, but Elimelech felt the Laws of Moses were too rigid, too intolerant. "Our way is not the only way, Naomi. Look around you and see how the Moabites prosper. Those in Bethlehem are still reduced to scraping out a living from the earth." In her heart, she'd known Elimelech was rejecting God, but she could never find the words to convince him he must turn back.

Is that why I'm being punished? Should I have been more determined in reasoning with Elimelech? Should I have gone to the elders for help instead of being too ashamed to admit what was happening in my home? Should I have gone to his brothers? I should have found someone he respected who might have been able to dissuade him from leaving the land God gave us! Perhaps if I'd refused to leave Bethlehem, everything would have turned out differently. Perhaps if we'd stayed, my husband and sons would still be alive.

How she tormented herself wondering if she could have done things differently, worrying that she had failed those she loved so much.

Oh, why didn't I teach Kilion and Mahlon the importance of the Law? I should have been a better mother. I should have made them sit down and listen. I should have worried less about losing their love and more about losing their souls. And now I've lost them forever. I've lost my sons ... Oh, my sons, my sons ...

She didn't speak the words aloud, but she was scourged with self-recriminations day after day and night after night.

Father, forgive me. I was weak. I was foolish. I took the easy way and followed Elimelech because I wanted peace in our family. I didn't want to be a contentious wife. I wanted to support him in his endeavors. I wanted to be his helpmate. But You warned us of the cursings to come if we were unfaithful. Oh, Father, I wanted to be faithful. I tried to be faithful. Every day, I felt torn, my husband on one side and You on the other. I didn't know what else to do but pray in silence and hope in secret and walk alongside Elimelech and then my sons. I hoped and prayed everyday they would come to their senses and we'd go home to the land You gave us. Oh, God, I've prayed and prayed all these years, and not one prayer has been answered. My husband is dead. My sons are dead! You have stripped me bare! You have poured me out! Who is left but You, Father? What do I have to cling to now but You?

She rocked back and forth, moaning.

Ruth rose and put her arms around her. "Mother, I'll take care of you." The girl's tenderness broke Naomi's heart. She wept in her daughter-in-law's arms, allowing herself to be held and rocked like a baby. But it was no comfort, for other thoughts rushed into her tortured mind and made her cry all the harder.

There would be no children to carry on the names of her sons. It would be as though they never lived at all. *Their names will go down into the dust along with them. No children ... There will be no children ...*

❧❧❧

Seventy days passed before Naomi went outside the door of her small house. The sunlight hurt her eyes. She was weak from grieving, having wept enough tears to fill a cistern, and it was time to stop. Crying would not bring the dead back to life. She must think of the living. Ruth and Orpah were young women, too young to spend the rest of their lives mourning over Mahlon and Kilion, or taking care of an old woman whose life was over.

She sat on the stool outside her door and watched someone else's children. They raced down the street, their laughter echoing back as they rounded a corner. Children were life, and hers were no more. But there was still a chance for her daughters-in-law, if she did what she knew she must.

If she remained in Kir-hareseth, Ruth and Orpah would continue to live with her. They would spend their youth looking after the mother of their dead husbands. How could she allow these sweet girls to waste their lives on her? She loved them too much to continue to see them begging for a handful of grain from strangers or living off charity from friends and relatives. But if she left Kir-hareseth and Moab, her daughters-in-law could return to their families, who would welcome them. Naomi had no doubt their fathers would find husbands for them quickly, for they were young and beautiful. Then Ruth and Orpah would have the joy of children. Naomi wanted that for them more than anything.

As for her, she wanted to go home to Bethlehem. She didn't know if any of her relatives or friends remained there or had survived the famine, but she had heard that the famine had finally ended. Perhaps the Midianite raids had also come to an end. Even so, what did it matter? She longed to go home, and she was willing to accept whatever she found when she reached Bethlehem. If she must be reduced to spending her last years as a beggar, so be it. At least she would feel the Promised Land beneath her feet again. At least she would be where others worshiped God as she did.

Oh, Lord, make it be so. Bring me safely home before I die. Oh, Father, have mercy on me, for I'm alone and in deep distress. My problems go from bad to worse. And I want to do what's right in Your eyes. Help me!

Neighbors greeted her as they passed by. She smiled and nodded her head while her mind raced on. *Why am I sitting here? Am I waiting for God to speak to me audibly as He did to Moses? Who am I that God would speak in such a manner? Do I expect Him to write a letter to me on that wall over there telling me what to do? I know what I must do! I will repent and return to my homeland.*

Naomi put her hands on her knees and pushed herself up. Lowering her shawl to her shoulders, she went back into her house. Ruth was kneeling, flattening bread dough and laying it over the metal stove, while Orpah was mending a garment. Both young women glanced up and smiled at her. She paused, gazing between them, trying to find words to explain, and failing. She turned away and began gathering her few things.

Ruth rose. "What are you doing, Mother?"

"I'm packing."

"Packing?" Orpah said. "But where are you going?"

"I'm going home."

Naomi had known that Ruth and Orpah would insist on accompanying her to Bethlehem. Impetuous youth. She didn't argue with them; she knew they would soon understand the immensity of leaving Moab and their families behind. She was sure they would be ready to go home again by the time they reached the Arnon River. It would be far easier to dissuade them at the boundary of their country than to waste her breath arguing with them now. She would enjoy their company awhile longer and then send them home. She didn't want to ponder the fact that she would never see them again after they left her. She would never forget them, and she would pray for them everyday for as long as she lived.

As they prepared to leave the house, Naomi wondered if they would even make it down the hill with all the things Orpah had decided to bring. The poor girl. She couldn't bear to leave anything behind. She was loaded down with everything she had accumulated during her marriage to Kilion, including a small stool. Orpah moaned in distress. "Oh, I wish we could bring the table and rug ... "

Ruth, on the other hand, had only a pack full of colorful sashes she'd made, a skin of water, and enough grain and raisin cakes to last for several days. "Where are the rest of your things, Ruth?" Naomi asked her.

"I have all I need. Let me carry the cooking pan, Mother. It's too heavy for you. We'll travel farther today if I carry it."

Naomi had spoken to the family next door, telling them Orpah and Ruth would be returning in a day or two. She wanted to be sure no one bothered what was left in the house. When the young women returned to Kir-hare-seth, they could sell everything, including the house, and split whatever came of it. Naomi didn't care about any of the belongings she was leaving behind. She preferred the plain things of her people to the finery of the Moabites, Philistines, and Egyptians. It was Elimelech who had placed such importance on the gifts he gave her, and they would be out of place in Bethlehem.

She suspected that Ruth would give everything to Orpah. Dear Ruth – she had such a generous heart, not to mention a wealthy father who would want her to return to his house. Naomi knew him well enough to suspect that he already had another husband in mind for Ruth, a rich merchant's son or an official in the king's court. Her heart sank at the thought of Ruth married to someone other than her son. Curiously ... the same wasn't true of Orpah.

Perhaps it was because Ruth had responded to her teachings about the true God. How Naomi had rejoiced as she watched the slow budding of the girl's faith.

"Did you see your father and mother yesterday, Ruth?"

Ruth shook her head.

"Why not? They should know you're leaving the city."

"They will know that I'm with you."

"Do they know I'm going back to Bethlehem?"

"My mother said you would, and I told her that even if you did, I belong with my husband's family."

Naomi said no more about it. She started off, carrying only a small sack of parched grain, a skin of water, and a leather bag in which was a sandalwood box containing crystals of frankincense. She would give it to the priest when she reached Bethlehem, an offering for the Lord.

She felt a sense of relief as she walked through the gates of Kir-hareseth and saw the road before her. Whatever hardships came, at least she was on her way back to Canaan. She didn't look back. Orpah did look back, weeping softly, but Ruth merely smiled and gazed off toward the King's Highway to the Dead Sea. "It's a good day to begin our journey, Mother."

The day wore on and the sun rose, hot and oppressive. Naomi felt despair creeping into her heart. Soon she would say good-bye to these daughters. *Lord, give me the strength to place their needs ahead of my fear of being alone. Father, bless them for their kindness to me. Take them safely home, and give me the courage to go on alone.*

At midday they stopped to rest beneath a terebinth tree. Naomi accepted the raisin cake and cup of water Ruth offered, but Orpah declined food. She was quiet, her eyes downcast. Ruth sat down and wiped the perspiration from her face. She looked weary but was more concerned about her sister-in-law than herself. "Are you not feeling well, Orpah?"

"I'll be all right after a rest."

Naomi knew what was wrong, but the knowledge gave her no satisfaction. She must send them back now. There was still time enough for them to be safely back inside the city walls before nightfall. She finished eating quickly and rose, lifting to her own back the bundle Ruth had insisted upon carrying to this point.

"What are you doing?" Ruth said, rising as well.

"I'm going on alone."

"No, Mother!"

Orpah came to her feet and joined Ruth in protest, weeping profusely. "Don't go! Please don't go."

Naomi's heart broke, but she knew she must remain firm. "Go back to your mothers' homes instead of coming with me. And may the Lord reward you for your kindness to your husbands and to me. May the Lord bless you with the security of another marriage."

Ruth wept. "No." She shook her head. "No, *no* ... " She stepped forward. "We want to go with you to your people."

"Why should you go on with me?" Naomi said, striving and failing to keep her voice from becoming strident with restrained emotion. "Can I still give birth to other sons who could grow up to be your husbands? No, my daughters, return to your parents' homes, for I am too old to marry again. And even if it were possible, and I were to get married tonight and bear sons, then what? Would you wait for them to grow up and refuse to marry someone else? No, of course not, my daughters! Things are far more bitter for me than for you, because the Lord Himself has caused me to suffer."

Ruth and Orpah wept harder. Orpah embraced her. "I shall never forget you, Naomi. May you have a safe journey home."

"Nor I you," Naomi said and kissed her. "And a safe journey to you as well!"

Orpah took up her bundles and started back toward Kir-hareseth. She paused after a little way and looked back, perplexed. "Aren't you coming, Ruth?"

"No." Ruth shook her head, her eyes awash with tears. "I'm going with Mother."

Orpah dropped her things and ran back to embrace her. "Are you certain, my sister?"

"Never more certain."

"Please ... "

"No. Go back without me. I will go on with Naomi."

With one last look back, Orpah started off again. Naomi watched Orpah walk quickly away and then looked at Ruth. She stretched out her hand and pointed toward Kir-hareseth. "See. Your sister-in-law has gone back to her people and to her gods. You should do the same."

Tears slipped down Ruth's face, but she didn't move. "Don't ask me to leave you and turn back, for I won't."

"But how can I not tell you to go?" Naomi came closer. "You heard what I said, Ruth. Should I take you back to Bethlehem with me so you can have the same bitter existence I'll have? Should you grow old without a husband and children? Go after Orpah! Return to your mother and father!"

"No," Ruth said, weeping. "I *won't* leave you. Make me your proselyte."

Naomi's heart squeezed tight. "Oh, my sweet one, think of what you're saying. The lives of my people are not as easy as what you've known. We're commanded to keep Sabbaths and holy days, on which we may not travel more than two thousand cubits."

"I will go wherever you go."

Naomi knew she must speak the truth, even if it hurt Ruth's feelings. "We're commanded not to spend the night with Gentiles."

"I will live wherever you live."

"We're commanded to keep over six hundred precepts!"

"Whatever your people keep I will keep, Mother, for your people will be my people."

Naomi kept on. "We are forbidden to worship any strange god. Chemosh is an abomination!"

"Your God will be my God."

Naomi spread her hands. "We have four sorts of deaths for malefactors, Ruth: stoning, burning, strangling, and slaying with the sword. Reconsider your words!" When Ruth said nothing, she went on, beseeching Ruth to see the many ways their people were different. "Our people are buried in houses of sepulchre."

"Then let it be so for me as well, Mother." Falling to her knees, Ruth wrapped her arms around Naomi's waist. "I will die where you die and will be buried there." When Naomi tried to press her back, Ruth clung more tightly. "And may the Lord punish me severely if I allow anything but death to separate us!"

Weeping now, Naomi placed her hands on Ruth's head and stroked her hair. Naomi looked up at the heavens. She had never hoped for this, never expected that this young Moabitess would be willing to give up everything in order to go with her. She looked down again, stroking Ruth's head absently. "You will never see your mother and father and brothers and sisters again, Ruth. Do you realize that?"

"Yes." Ruth raised her head. Her face was streaked with tears.

"Your life will be easier if you return."

"Oh, Naomi, how can I go back to my old life when you hold the words of truth?" Her arms tightened again as she began to sob. "Please don't plead with me to leave you. Don't lead me into temptation. I'm going with you!"

Your God will be my God.

How could Naomi say no to such words? Hadn't she prayed that Ruth's heart would be softened toward the God of Israel? One prayer had been answered, one prayer among thousands. "Be at ease," she said gently and loosened Ruth's arms from around her waist. Cupping Ruth's face, she smiled down at her. She smoothed away Ruth's tears. "As God wills. Whatever comes, we'll face together."

Ruth's eyes shone as she smiled in relief. "I will heed your every word, for I know you'll teach me what I need to know."

"Everything I learned at my mother's knee I will make known to you. All I have is yours. I give it to you with pleasure." For Naomi knew now there was more than marriage to her son that had grafted this girl into her life and heart. And now she would pray that Ruth would be grafted in among her people as well.

You have not forgotten me, Lord. You knew I couldn't make it home alone. You have not abandoned me.

"Come," Naomi said, taking Ruth's hand and helping her up. "We must make a long journey before we reach home."

Ruth didn't dwell on what hardships she and Naomi might encounter when they reached Bethlehem. Each day of travel was enough trouble to bear without fearing what might come when they reached their destination. Ruth had lived in fear all during the months of Mahlon's illness, and it had accomplished nothing. She'd loved her husband, but she couldn't save him. All her efforts to make him better had failed, and the fear of losing him hadn't prevented death from coming anyway. Nor had fear helped her face the difficulties of surviving without a man to provide for the household. After Mahlon's death, she decided she would never again allow her mind to dwell on things beyond her control. The future was one of these things. She would face whatever came and do the best with whatever life God gave her.

Naomi often comforted her without even realizing it. "The Lord will take care of us," she'd said last night, and Ruth had lain awake on the hard earth, staring up at the stars and thinking about those words. *The Lord will take care of us.* After all Naomi had suffered, she still clung to her faith. Ruth was comforted by Naomi's strength. *The Lord will take care of us.* She chose to believe it because her mother-in-law said it was true.

From the time she had entered Mahlon's home, Ruth had known there was something different about Naomi. First there was the outward sign: her clothing. Even after years of living among the Moabites, her mother-in-law continued to dress as a Hebrew. She didn't do so with an air of pride, as though she was better than those living around her. It was simply who she was. Ruth had also seen her deep faith in God. At first, she'd worried that Naomi's long silences meant she didn't like Mahlon's choice of a wife. But Mahlon had said that wasn't so.

"She's just praying," Mahlon had told her with a shrug. "She's done it for as long as I can remember. Don't let it upset you. It doesn't do any harm. Just ignore her."

But Ruth hadn't ignored her mother-in-law. She could see that prayer meant a great deal to Naomi, and Ruth wanted to understand more about it. So she had surreptitiously watched Naomi. Sometimes her mother-in-law would look so peaceful when she talked to her god, and at other times, anguished. Every morning, often at midday, and always during the evening hours, Naomi would draw her shawl over her head, sit in the corner of the house, and become still and quiet. Ruth asked her once what she prayed about, and Naomi had smiled and said, "Everything." Her eyes had grown sad. "Mostly about my sons." She'd reached out and put her hand over Ruth's, her eyes softening. "And my daughters."

The kind words had brought tears to Ruth's eyes. Naomi's good opinion had mattered very much, for Ruth admired her greatly. Naomi was kind and pleasant, fair in her division of chores, and she always worked as hard as everyone else. She loved both of her sons deeply and equally, and despite their cultural differences, she embraced Ruth and Orpah as daughters. Love was a gift Naomi had in abundance. And though Mahlon seemed unimpressed, Ruth sensed a deep, abiding knowledge and wisdom in her mother-in-law, knowledge and wisdom she longed to share.

Yet Ruth sensed her sorrow as well. Naomi was never quite settled in Kir-hareseth, never quite at ease with the world around her. It had to do with her God. Ruth had been afraid to approach Naomi and talk with her about it. So she approached her husband instead.

Mahlon had never had much to say about the God of his people. In fact, he seemed to know very little about Him. "Why are you so interested in God?"

"Shouldn't I be able to teach your sons about Him?"

"Teach them about Chemosh if it pleases you. It doesn't matter to me. I'm sure my mother will teach them about Yahweh. The important thing is for them to be tolerant of all religions. That's the only way they're going to succeed in Kir-hareseth."

In Mahlon's eyes, one god was no better than any other, but Naomi could not compromise. She was respectful, never disdaining others' beliefs, but she held to her faith in Yahweh with quiet tenacity.

Ruth looked at her mother-in-law now, curled on her side, her head resting on a stone for a pillow. She'd fallen asleep within minutes after eating the bread Ruth prepared for her. The sun was down and the air was cooling quickly. Ruth rose and carefully draped her shawl over Naomi. The journey was already very difficult for her mother-in-law. She had eaten very little during the weeks following Mahlon's death. Ruth had feared that Naomi would waste away in grief. So she had prepared savory stews in an effort to entice her mother-in-law's appetite. Now it was the physical exhaustion that dampened Naomi's appetite. She was so tired after walking all day, she could barely keep her eyes open long enough to eat anything. It was strange, but Ruth felt as though they had traded positions. Naomi had become the child, and she the caring mother. "But I don't mind," she whispered, leaning down to kiss Naomi's cheek. She smoothed the tendrils of black hair back from her mother-in-law's sunburned brow.

Ruth rose and hugged her arms close to her body, shivering slightly. Mount Nebo stood in the distance. Naomi had told her this morning that Moses had gone up onto that mountain and died there after putting Joshua in charge of God's people. They had crossed the Jordan River soon afterward and claimed Canaan. She loved it when Naomi talked about what God had done for the Hebrews. She felt a strange stirring within her as she learned of His mighty feats and His unfailing love.

She closed her eyes and lifted her face to the heavens. "Lord, help me to take care of Your servant Naomi," she whispered. "It's because of her that I've come to believe in You. Please guide our steps and bring us safely home to Bethlehem. And, Lord, if it isn't too much to ask, let there be old friends to greet Naomi upon her return, people who loved her in days gone by and who will continue to love her in the difficult days ahead."

two

THE days were long and hot and dry. Ruth rose early and awakened Naomi. "The sun's coming up, Mother," she would say. "We should travel now in the cool of the day." Silently, they would walk until the sun reached its zenith and then find shade where they could rest. Weary, Naomi usually dozed. Ruth more often looked off down the road, wondering what the future held for both of them.

They reached the Wadi Arnon, which marked the southern boundary of the Reubenite territory, and followed the King's Highway to Dibon, Heshbon, and Abel Shittim. In each city they passed through, Ruth bartered her woven sashes in the marketplace to buy food, while inquiring about the road ahead.

"Oh, you're not going over the Jericho road," said a woman selling onions and garlic. "Robbers hide out up there in the mountains and attack the caravans. You won't be safe alone."

"I'm not alone. I'm traveling with my mother-in-law."

"Two women? Well, you'd better go down to the camel market and see if you can find a traveling merchant who will allow you to travel with his caravan. No one travels the Jericho road without protection. You'd find yourself snatched up and sold into slavery."

When Ruth returned to their little camp near the city wall, she found Naomi cooking unleavened bread on the metal bowl placed over the fire. She turned the bread skillfully with a two-pronged stick. "I've been worried," Naomi said without looking up.

"I'm sorry, Mother," Ruth said, hunkering down. "I should have come back and told you what I was doing. A woman in the marketplace told me robbers attack people going over the mountains, so I thought it wise to seek assistance. We're going to join a caravan tomorrow morning and travel with it over the Jericho road. The man is a Benjaminite, and he has armed guards. We'll be safe with him."

Naomi's body relaxed. She hooked the edge of the bread and lifted it

from the bowl, laying it aside to cool. "I should have thought of that myself."
She sat back on her heels and covered her face.

Ruth took the bread and broke it. She handed Naomi half. Naomi shook
her head. "You must eat, Mother. You need your strength."

Hands still covering her face, Naomi wept. "Why didn't I think of the
dangers? I never even considered what could happen to you. What was I
thinking to let you come on this journey? I'm a selfish old woman!"

"You tried to turn me back," Ruth said with a smile. "It did you no
good. Try not to worry. We're going to be safe."

Naomi raised her head. "There's more danger for a young woman like
you than an old widow like me."

"There's danger for both of us, and we're taking every precaution. The
man seems trustworthy."

"No one can be trusted these days."

Ruth picked up the bread and held it out to her again. Naomi took it
and broke off a little piece, eating slowly, still frowning.

Ruth smiled at her. "How often have I heard you say 'the Lord watches
over those who love Him'?"

"And punishes those who reject Him." Naomi's eyes welled with tears,
and Ruth knew she was thinking of Elimelech, Kilion, and Mahlon. Her
own grief rose sharply as she thought of her husband. He'd been so young,
with years ahead of him. How she wished she'd given him a child! A son to
carry on his name.

"I'm so tired," Naomi said, her voice tear-choked. "I don't know if I can
even make it home. Those mountains, I remember them so well now. How
could I have forgotten how hard the journey was?"

"We will rest when we need to."

"And the caravan will go on without us," Naomi said dismally.

"Then we'll join another."

"If we aren't robbed and ... "

"Don't!" Ruth said with a sob. She rose and went to Naomi, kneeling
down and taking her mother-in-law's hand. "Don't even think of such things,
Mother. If you do, we're defeated. Think about what's on the other side of
the mountains: *Bethlehem*. Our home. If we dwell on all the things that
could go wrong, we'll be too afraid to take another step. *Please*. Tell me
about the Lord again, Mother. Tell me how He fed thousands of people in
the desert. Tell me how He brought water from a rock. And pray." She
wept softly. "Pray He has mercy upon us."

Naomi winced, her expression filled with regret. She touched Ruth's face. "Sometimes I forget." Her eyes were still awash with tears. "I think about what I've lost instead of thinking about what I have."

"We have each other," Ruth said. "And we have God. That's more than enough to face whatever comes. You taught me that."

"Keep reminding me."

※※※

They crossed the Jordan River with the caravan late the next afternoon. Naomi wilted beneath the trees on the other side. "I can't go any farther."

Ruth settled her comfortably and brought some water. "Rest here while I thank Ashir Ben Hadar." The last of the camels were crossing the river when Ruth approached the caravan owner and bowed her face to the ground. "Thank you for allowing us to travel in your company."

"You're leaving the caravan so soon?"

"My mother-in-law has gone as far as her strength can carry her. We'll camp here by the river and continue on in the morning."

"A pity. We'll be camping for the night at the oasis. You'd be safer with us."

"May the Lord bring you safely to your destination and bless you for your kindness toward two widows."

He frowned heavily. "May the Lord protect you." Turning away, he mounted his camel, whacked the animal's neck with a stick, and shouted orders in Egyptian to one of his servants. The camel rocked forward and then back as it came to its feet. Ruth bowed again as the man rode toward the front of his caravan. She'd almost reached the trees by the river when one of Ashir Ben Hadar's servants ran up to her and thrust a sack and a bulging skin into her hands. "Gifts from the master," he rasped and raced off again.

Smiling, Ruth knelt down by Naomi. "Taste and see how the Lord provides for those who love Him."

Tipping the skin cautiously, Naomi took a small sip. Her eyes grew wide. "Fresh goat's milk!"

Ruth laughed and opened the leather, displaying the fullness of their bounty. "And raisin cakes, Mother. Enough for several days. With the grain we have left, we have enough to sustain us until we reach Bethlehem."

They ate and then rested as the sun slipped over the mountains behind Jericho. "It wasn't far from here that the Lord rolled back the water of the Jordan so that Joshua could bring our people across," Naomi said, replete and relaxed. "My mother told me when Moses went up Mount Nebo to Pisgah Peak and died, the people mourned for thirty days. Joshua was filled with the Spirit of God and led the people over there," she said and pointed from Nebo along the way they had come, "to Acacia. He waited there until the Lord told him what to do. Joshua brought the people to the banks of the Jordan. The Lord rolled back the water, and the people crossed on dry land. My mother and father were among the people who came into Canaan that day. They camped at Gilgal and celebrated the Passover."

Ruth was standing beneath the shade following with her eyes the course Naomi said her people had taken. "What are the stones over there?"

"The standing stones?" Naomi rose. "Everyone who passes by them will remember what the Lord did for His people. There are twelve, each stone carried by a member of one of the tribes who descended from our father, Jacob. Do you see where the water ripples over there? There are twelve more stones on the spot where the priests stood with the Ark of the Covenant while our people crossed over." She stood beside Ruth, pointing back the way they had come. "Over there is the altar the sons of Reuben, Gad, and Manasseh built. The tribes on this side almost went to war over it."

"Why?"

"Because the tribes on the west bank thought it to be an altar for burnt offerings and sacrifices to other gods. But it stands as witness that the tribes of Reuben, Gad, and Manasseh have an inheritance in the Lord; it is a monument to remind us that we are brothers."

Naomi repeated the stories her father and mother had told her, until the sun went down and the stars shone. Ruth listened hungrily to everything Naomi said about the years in the desert and the mighty deeds the Lord had done to save and discipline His people. When Naomi fell asleep, Ruth looked up into the heavens and felt reassured. Surely if the Lord had watched over His rebellious people in the wilderness, He would watch over Naomi now. Ruth believed that the Lord would bring them both safely home to Bethlehem.

The next day they walked as far as the oasis and spent the night beneath the palms. The jagged silhouette of Jericho stood out against the base of the mountains, the once-great city now blackened rubble inhabited only by lizards and snakes. However, there was a small but thriving community not far away, encamped around the spring. They earned a prosperous living from travelers using the Jericho road across the mountains to Jerusalem.

As they began the arduous journey up the Jericho road, Ruth prayed continuously, while keeping watch for dangers along the way. *God, pro-*

tect us. Watch over us and guide our steps.

A caravan came up behind them. Ruth spoke with the overseer and was given permission to camp near them the first night. She made no effort to hurry Naomi the next morning, but set her pace by her mother-in-law, even though the caravan went ahead and disappeared from sight.

"Lord, please help us get over these mountains," she whispered each night before she closed her eyes.

And each day the road was steeper and more difficult, the days hotter and their supplies shorter. Naomi weakened, so Ruth took her load. When her mother-in-law became despondent, Ruth asked her questions about Bethlehem and her childhood, hoping to revive her determination to reach their destination. "Each day we're closer, Mother."

"And what awaits us? Everyone I knew may be gone by now."

"Perhaps there will be friends you've forgotten."

"And who have forgotten me." She wept as she often did when she was close to complete exhaustion. "I'm bringing you home to poverty. There will be no one to welcome us." She covered her face and sobbed.

"Look back and see how far we've come," Ruth said, breathing hard beneath her burdens.

"Look how far we've yet to go. Up, up, forever up."

Ruth looked around. There was no place to camp where they were. They had no choice but to go on. She was close to crying along with Naomi. Her back ached from carrying the full load all day, her eyes were gritty and her throat parched. She clasped the small bottle she wore on a cord around her neck. It was filled with tears she had shed for Mahlon, a sign of her respect and love. Letting go of it, she shut her eyes tightly. "The Lord sees our sorrow, Mother. He knows our needs."

"Then where is He?"

Ruth pressed her lips together to keep from crying out in frustration and despair. She couldn't allow herself to give in to it. If she did, where would they be?

"I can't go on, Ruth. It's too hard. I can't. Just leave me here to die. I don't care anymore. I'm too tired to care!"

Ruth shifted the packs and looped her arm around Naomi, giving her support. "You have to go on. Just a little way. We'll find a place and rest for the night."

"I'll be just as tired in the morning. I'm sick and tired."

"We'll make it, Mother."

"And what will be there if we do?" Naomi said bitterly, feet dragging as she leaned heavily upon Ruth. "I have no land. I have no house. I have no husband, no sons. What will be there for us?"

Fighting tears, Ruth said, "I don't know, but whatever it is, God will help us."

After that, she could speak no more. She had only strength enough to keep them moving until they found a place of rest. *Oh, please, God, please help us!*

As they came around a bend in the road, Ruth noticed a large crack in the stone mountainside. "Just a few more feet," she said, urging Naomi on. The crevice was large enough to shelter both women for the night.

Naomi sank down with a groan and leaned back against a boulder. Ruth winced as she shrugged off her bundles and sat beside her. She rolled her shoulders to ease her aching muscles. "We're almost to the summit," she said, leaning her head back against the cold stone. "We will reach Jerusalem tomorrow."

Naomi said nothing. She was breathing heavily, her eyes closed, her face pale with exhaustion.

Ruth rose again and unrolled the bedding. She broke the last raisin cake in half. "You'll feel better after you've had something to eat." Naomi took the food and ate slowly. Ruth saw the sheen of tears in Naomi's eyes.

"God willing, we will be in Bethlehem early tomorrow," Naomi said, folding her hands in her lap. "It is only a short distance beyond Jerusalem."

Ruth smiled and put her hand over Naomi's. "You're almost home, Mother."

Naomi closed her eyes, but not before tears slipped down her dusty cheeks. Ruth sat closer and put her arm around her mother-in-law. Naomi leaned her head against Ruth's shoulder, and within moments was asleep.

Lord, Lord ... Ruth didn't know what to pray anymore. She was too weary to think but not to fear. *Thank You for bringing us this far. Please do not leave us now.*

Ruth knew the real trial of her strength was only just beginning. With each day of travel, Naomi had become increasingly dependent upon her. Ruth did not mind, but she was plagued by worries.

What would become of them when they reached Bethlehem?

three

WITH Bethlehem so close, Naomi became eager to reach home. Rising before the sun, the two women set out on the final leg of their journey. Naomi's strength was renewed. Ruth didn't have to urge her on as before. "It's not far now. Not far at all," Naomi said. With the rising sun, they followed the road past Jerusalem. It was still morning when they entered the town of Bethlehem. Women were gathered at the well in the center of town, talking and laughing as they drew up water for the day's household needs. They noticed Naomi and Ruth, and drew in closer together, lowering their voices. Ruth could feel Naomi's tension. "Come, Mother. Perhaps there will be someone you know, and I need to fill the skins."

One woman, older than the rest, separated herself from the others. "Is it really Naomi?" She frowned heavily, tilting her head as though she couldn't see clearly.

Ruth touched her mother-in-law's arm gently. "You aren't forgotten. You still have friends in Bethlehem."

"It is Naomi!" She came toward her, arms outstretched. "Naomi, you have returned!"

The women cried out in excitement, hastening toward her mother-in-law. Ruth stepped back to allow them room, giving silent thanks to God that Naomi was remembered and welcomed so warmly. Perhaps the enthusiastic greeting of these women would raise her mother-in-law's spirits.

"Naomi, you look as though you've traveled hundreds of miles!"

"Where have you been all these years?"

"We heard you went to Moab."

"What's happened to you?"

Ruth saw Naomi's distress growing. Her mother-in-law looked this way and that as though seeking an escape from this throng of interrogators.

"I remember the day you left with mules loaded down with your possessions."

"What's happened to you?"

Ruth could only imagine what her mother-in-law was thinking. Naomi was home in Bethlehem, but she was destitute. She was among friends but was clearly the object of their pity and curiosity. Aching for her, Ruth was uncertain what to do. Should she press her way into the center of the circle and try to rescue her? Or would that only make matters worse? The women had made a tight circle around Naomi, while presenting Ruth their backs. In fact, no one had given her more than a hostile glance. The women made no effort to hide their shock at Naomi's appearance.

"Where is your husband, Elimelech?"

"Such a tall, handsome man."

The women pressed in upon Naomi from all sides, asking questions that would only stir up the grief of recent tragedies.

"You had sons. Where are they?"

"Surely they haven't remained in Moab!"

"Where are Mahlon and Kilion?"

They were all speaking at once, their piqued interest focused on Naomi's misery. Ruth was not surprised or hurt because the women chose to ignore her. Naomi had warned her she would not be welcome. "My people will see you as a foreigner. And worse, they'll know you're a Moabitess." Everything about Ruth's appearance declared her nationality. Her clothing was distinctive, and her skin was darker. She had no money to change the one, and no ability to change the other. It would take time for these people to accept her.

"Don't expect to be invited into anyone's house," Naomi had said. A Hebrew could not invite a foreigner inside his home without defiling it.

"Oh, Naomi," the women said, hearing about the death of Elimelech, Kilion, and Mahlon. "Oy, your sorrow is too much to bear!" They seemed to withdraw slightly, embarrassed, uncertain. Were they afraid Naomi's misfortune might somehow be transferred to them if they offered her assistance? Ruth moved forward, edging her way through the women until she was close enough to Naomi to be seen.

"Don't call me Naomi," Naomi cried out. "Instead, call me Mara, for the Almighty has made life very bitter for me."

She began to weep and wail. "I went away full, but the Lord has brought me home empty. Why should you call me Naomi when the Lord has caused me to suffer and the Almighty has sent such tragedy?"

Perhaps the women had been too long separated from Naomi to share her grief. Though offering words of sympathy, they seemed ill equipped to comfort her. They stood uneasy, looking at one another, distressed and silent. Ruth moved forward again, and when Naomi's gaze fell upon her, relief flooded her mother-in-law's face. "Ruth, oh, my Ruth, come here to me."

As Ruth pressed her way forward, the women moved back from her, drawing away so she wouldn't brush against them. They no longer ignored her, but stared openly, contemptuously. Heat poured into Ruth's cheeks. Had the Moabites stared at Naomi the same way when she first came to Kir-hareseth?

"This is my daughter-in-law. This is Mahlon's widow, Ruth," Naomi said, taking her hand. Ruth could feel how Naomi was shaking. Was this the moment her mother-in-law had most dreaded? Introducing her Moabitess daughter-in-law to her friends? Was Naomi ashamed of her? She was all the proof these people needed that at least one of Naomi's sons had turned away from God and taken a foreign wife. Ruth was filled with sorrow at the thought of causing her mother-in-law more grief.

"She's a Moabite." The words came out like a curse.

"By birth," Naomi said.

"Does she expect to stay here?" Never had Ruth felt so unwelcome.

Naomi lifted her chin, her hand tightening around Ruth's. "Yes, she will stay. She and I will live together."

"But Naomi, think of what you're doing!"

"I would not have survived without Ruth."

"You're among your own people now, Naomi. Send the foreigner back where she belongs. You know what the Law says."

Naomi turned slightly, her body rigid. "There were Egyptians who came with us out of Egypt."

"And look at the trouble they caused!"

"Foreign women are cursed of God!"

"They turn our men's hearts away from the Lord!"

"Enough!" Naomi cried out. "Should I cut off what God has grafted in? Ruth chose to come with me. She turned her back on her mother and father and her brothers and sisters, all she has ever known, to come to Bethlehem and worship God with me."

Everyone fell silent for a moment, but Ruth knew words could not convince these women that she was worthy of acceptance. She would have to live an exemplary life before them in order for them to believe she had chosen Naomi over her father and mother, and God over the idols of her people. Time. It would take time.

"You have returned in time for Passover, Naomi. It is good to have you back among us."

And with that said, the women began to disperse, leaving Ruth and Naomi alone at the well.

Ruth wept softly. "I have brought shame upon you. I have made your homecoming even more difficult than it might have been otherwise."

"No," Naomi said wearily. "They remember the way I was before I left. My husband prospered and I had cause to rejoice. I could laugh and sing with them. Now my wretchedness makes them uncomfortable. If it could happen to me, they think, it could happen to them. It's not a comforting thought."

"You will laugh and sing with them again, Mother."

Naomi shook her head. "I didn't expect to find anyone," she said softly. "But this ... " She bent her neck, staring down at the ground. "Not one offered us so much as a loaf of bread or a sip of watered wine."

"Because of me."

"Should you take all the blame? I lived in Moab for twenty years. I dwelt among idol worshipers and opened my home to the foreign women my sons took for wives. In Hebrew eyes, I am as defiled as you. Perhaps more so because I *knew better.*" Naomi's eyes welled with tears. "Oh, my dear. You're all I have. You're God's blessing to me. We are not going to be welcome in their homes, Ruth. It is the way things are. We will have to make our own way." Tears spilled down her cheeks. "And tomorrow is Passover. I'd forgotten. How could I forget a day so important? The most important celebration of my people and I ... "

Ruth embraced her. She held Naomi close, stroking her as she would a hurt child, all the while aware of several women watching them from their doorways. When Naomi regained control over her emotions, Ruth kept a protective arm around her. "We will find someplace to stay, Mother. Everything will look better after a good night's sleep."

Ruth took a coin from the small cache she kept deep in her pack, but when she offered it to an innkeeper on the edge of town, he shook his head. "There's no room in the inn for you."

As Ruth turned away, she saw how haggard and dejected Naomi looked. Truly, Naomi was "Mara," for Ruth had never seen her look so bitter. "We will go on," Ruth said. There will be another place farther down the road."

But there wasn't. As the morning wore on, Ruth realized there would be no room for them anywhere in Bethlehem. "We have slept under the stars before," she said, trying to remain hopeful for her mother-in-law's sake.

"The land that belonged to my husband is not far from here," Naomi said as they walked beyond the borders of the town. "There are caves near it. The shepherds use them as folds for their sheep during the winter months, but the flocks will be gone by now. They will have contracts with the landowners to graze in the fields after harvest."

The larger caves were still occupied by members of the shepherds' families. Leaving a cave unattended was an open invitation for the destitute to take residence. But not far away was another cave that was empty, one not large enough to be of use as a sheepfold, but more than big enough to shelter two tired, lonely women from the elements. Naomi entered and looked around as Ruth unpacked their bedding and few possessions.

The difficult days of travel were over, but Ruth could see her mother-in-law's grief was deeper and more acute now than it had been during the grueling days of their journey. All the years her mother-in-law had dreamed of coming home, only to find herself here in such mean surroundings with nothing but the clothes on her back and a few necessities for survival – cookstove, blanket, water. Night was falling. It was going to be cold. They had little food left and no relative to show pity on them.

Naomi moved farther into the cave and sat with her back against the stone, staring into the shadows. Her face was filled with despair. Ruth wondered if she was thinking back to the way things had been before she and her husband and sons left this city. Were regret and guilt being added to grief over her losses?

"I went away full, but the Lord has brought me home empty ... " she'd said at the well.

Ruth looked out and wondered what it had been like when Mahlon was a little boy. Memories of her husband flooded her. Poor Mahlon. He'd been so young when he died, all his hopes and dreams dying with him. And there would be no son to carry on his name. But she could not allow herself to dwell upon these thoughts. It would only weaken her and make her of no use to Naomi, who needed her desperately. Being needed and of use was a good thing.

She drew in her breath. "It's spring, Mother. Can you smell the flowers?"

"We haven't what we need to celebrate Passover," Naomi said grimly.

"I'll go back to Bethlehem and buy whatever we need."

"With what? Will you beg? Will you prostitute yourself? They won't give you anything. You saw how they looked at you. You know how they acted."

"We have a few coins left."

Naomi glared, her eyes awash with tears. "And what will we do when those run out?"

"The Lord will help us."

"The Lord has forgotten us!" Naomi looked around the cave. "He has forgotten me!" She drew her shawl over her face and wept bitterly.

Ruth pressed trembling lips together until she knew she wouldn't weep along with her. She must be gentle but firm. "We are home, Mother. We are back among your people. God *will* help us. He helped us get here, and He will help us survive." She put her hand on Naomi's knee. "You said we should trust in God and so we shall. You said we should love Him with all our heart, our mind, and our strength. And so we shall." Her voice broke softly. "Now, please tell me. What do we need for Passover?"

Naomi lowered her shawl, her face ravaged by tears. "I can't even remember, Ruth. After the first few years in Moab, Elimelech stopped celebrating the feasts of the Lord. And I couldn't."

Ruth sat beside her and took her hand. She stroked it. "It will come back to you. Tell me about the way it was when you were a little girl."

As Naomi talked, she relaxed and remembered. "We'll need a shank bone from a lamb, bitter herbs, an onion, a candle, and grain. The Feast of Unleavened Bread begins the day after. It will take everything ... "

"We have enough."

"What will we do when everything is gone?"

"We will live this day alone. God will take care of tomorrow."

Naomi shook her head, weeping. "Where did you learn such faith?"

Ruth smiled at her. "Where else? From you."

Ruth returned to Bethlehem, purchased what they needed with the few coins she had left – the coins that had decorated her wedding headdress – and headed back. On the way through town, she filled the skin with water.

Water was free.

The day after Passover, Ruth gave Naomi the last of the parched grain. " I'm going back into Bethlehem to buy some supplies."

"With what? We have nothing."

"I have these." She removed two thin gold bracelets.

"Oh, no. Mahlon gave those to you!"

"As long as I live, I will never forget Mahlon." She kissed Naomi's pale cheek. "Would your son want us to go hungry? Rest now. I'll return as soon as I can."

All through the day, worry plagued Ruth. How would she provide for her mother-in-law when money ran out and she had nothing more to sell? She prayed unceasingly as she walked through the marketplace. *Lord, I don't know what to do. Help me take care of my mother-in-law.* Ruth bargained with four merchants before she got the price that she wanted for her bracelets. Then she bargained even harder for the lowest price for dates, a jar of olive oil, an ephah of parched grain, and an extra blanket for Naomi, who had shivered through the night. Her purchases took everything she had.

She knew that other women in her situation had resorted to prostitution, but she would rather die than bring such shame on herself or Naomi. Would she and her mother-in-law have no recourse but to sit at the city gate each day and beg others for charity? She was young and able-bodied. Perhaps she could sell herself as a slave and give the money to Naomi. But what would happen to Naomi when the twenty shekels ran out? There must be another way.

Lord, what must I do? I will do whatever is in accordance with Your Law for the sake of Your servant, Naomi. But we have only enough to sustain us for a few more days. Show me the way to provide for my mother-in-law and not bring further shame upon her.

When Ruth stopped at the well to refill the skin, she noticed several women decorating their doorways. Though they glanced her way frequently, no one greeted her. Ruth shifted the things she was carrying so she could manage the skin of water and headed back to the cave.

"The women were hanging garlands of greenery," she told Naomi upon her return.

"They're preparing for the Feast of First Fruits."

"Are there many feasts?" Ruth wondered aloud. Silently, she worried about how she would provide what was needed. *Oh, Lord, Lord, what must I do? I am defeated already.*

"Sit with me awhile, and I'll tell you about the feasts of the Lord," Naomi said.

Ruth sat just inside the mouth of the small cave, where she was sheltered from the sun.

"We've arrived in Bethlehem in time to celebrate four feasts of the Lord," Naomi said. "There are seven each year. We've celebrated Passover and are now beginning the six days of the Feast of the Unleavened Bread. The barley is the first grain crop to be harvested, and it's ready now for reaping, so the women are making preparations for the third feast, the Feast of First Fruits. Men will be chosen to cut stalks of barley for the procession. The stalks will be brought to the priest, who will present them before the Lord. Fifty days after that, we'll celebrate the fourth feast, the Feast of Weeks, when the wheat harvest begins. We'll bake two loaves of bread with fine flour and leaven to be presented to the Lord by a priest on the high place."

Wheat cost dearly. Ruth looked away, not wanting her mother-in-law to suspect her distress. Naomi mustn't know how bad their situation was. It would only add to her grief.

"There will be three more feasts of the Lord later," Naomi said. "The Feast of Trumpets, the Day of Atonement, and the Feast of Tabernacles." She went on to explain.

Ruth tried to be attentive and absorb everything Naomi was teaching her, but her head was swimming with details, her mind clouded by worries. In fifty days, she and Naomi wouldn't have to worry about how to prepare a feast because they would be starving. She had nothing left to sell, no way of making money, no opportunity to work. There would be no wheat to make bread for the Lord, let alone bread to eat.

"The Law guides our lives," Naomi said. "When we fall away, the Lord disciplines us. As I have been disciplined."

Ruth wanted to cover her face and weep. Instead, she sat silent, gazing outside, hiding her inner turmoil. *Oh, Lord, Lord* ... She didn't even know how to pray. Perhaps there were special words, ablutions, offerings, *something* that would help her prayer be heard. *Oh, God, have mercy. I want to please You. I want to serve this woman I love who loves You so much. Please, I beseech You. Show me what to do.*

Naomi stretched out her hand. "Do you see this fallow field? Once it was thick with wheat. Elimelech put his hand to the plow and the land prospered. I remember how the wind would blow gently over the stalks so that the field moved in golden waves. We had so much. Life was so good. During those early years, there was so much, Elimelech did not begrudge the gleaners. It wasn't until later that he wouldn't let them come and work, but gathered every stalk, right to the edge of his land." Naomi frowned. "Perhaps that's why ... "

"Gleaners?" Ruth leaned forward.

Naomi leaned back against the stone. "The Lord commanded that no one reap to the edges or corners of their fields. The grain that grows there is set aside for the poor to gather." She looked out at the field again, troubled and deep in thought. "When all is done according to the ways of the Lord, no one goes hungry."

Ruth closed her eyes in relief and bowed her head. *Oh, Yahweh, You are truly a God of mercy.* Her heart filled with so much gratitude, her throat closed hot with tears. She hadn't realized how afraid she was of the future until this moment when she felt hope surge again. God had not forsaken them! She almost laughed at her ignorance. She had grown up in a city and knew nothing about the ways of farmers. She had grown up in the shadow of Chemosh, a false god who took and never gave back. And now, here was the God who loved His people and provided for them – even the poorest of the poor, the broken-hearted, the broken in spirit.

Truly, Jehovah, You are a merciful Redeemer and gracious Protector! I should have remembered how You protected us every step of the way from Kir-hareseth over the mountains to Bethlehem. Forgive me, Lord; forgive Your foolish handmaiden. How could I have believed You would bring us so far only to let us starve?

Smiling, Ruth lifted her head and filled her lungs with air, her heart swelling with gratitude and a strange sense of complete freedom.

⫘⫘⫘

And the women were saying ...

"Poor Naomi. Do you remember how she used to laugh and be so confident?"

"*Too* confident, if you ask me."

Elimelech wasn't the only man who wanted to marry her."

"Do you remember how handsome he was?"

"Naomi is a year younger than I am, and she looks so old."

"And thin."

"Grief does that. A husband and two sons dead. Oy."

"God must be punishing her."

"All she has to show for the years in Moab is that girl who came with her."

"She looks so foreign."

"Such dark eyes."

"You've heard about Moabite women ... "

"No, what did you hear?"

They clustered together, whispering, gasping, shaking their heads.

"Naomi should send that girl home to Moab where she belongs. We don't want her kind around here."

"Yes, I agree. But who among us will take Naomi in?"

"Well, I can't!"

"I've barely enough to feed my own family."

"I have no room."

"Then what will happen to her?"

"God will take care of her."

The day after the Feast of First Fruits, Ruth rose and asked Naomi for permission to go out into the fields and gather leftover grain.

"Not everyone will welcome you, Ruth," Naomi said, alarmed.

"But the Law allows – "

"Not everyone heeds the Law. My own husband and sons – "

"I must go, Mother. This is the only way."

"But I'm afraid for you. There are men in the fields who will try to take advantage of you. They'll see nothing wrong in assaulting a Moabitess."

"Then I will work alongside the women."

"They'll be no better. I don't know what I'd do if something happened to you."

Ruth embraced and kissed her. "I will pray that the Lord protects me, that He is a shield around me." She smiled into Naomi's frightened eyes. "Perhaps God will lead me to the field of some kind man who will allow me to glean the free grain behind his reapers. Pray for that."

"You must watch out."

"I will."

"Don't turn your back on anyone."

"I'll be careful."

"All right, my daughter, go ahead," Naomi finally relented.

Ruth walked along the road and entered the first field where reapers were at work, but she didn't stay more than a few minutes. Another gleaner hurled a stone. Ruth uttered a cry as it struck her cheek. She stumbled quickly from the field, hearing the woman shouting. "Get out of here, you Moabite harlot! Go back where you belong!" Staunching the trickle of blood on her cheek, Ruth went on. The reapers in the next field were no kinder.

"Moabite whore! Go back to your own kind and stay out of our fields!"

"And stay away from our men!"

When she started to enter another field, the workers leered at her. "Come here, my pretty one!" an overseer called to her. "I'm in need of a roll in the hay." The other men laughed.

Ruth ran back onto the road, her face aflame as the men and women laughed. They continued to call out insults and make jokes about the Moabites as she hurried away.

She walked on and on, passing fields of wheat not yet ripe for harvest. Finally she came to another barley field, where the men were girded and hard at work with their scythes. Women worked behind them, gathering the stalks of barley and bundling them. There were no gleaners. Dejected, Ruth wondered if it was a sign of the owner's attitude toward the destitute. She could only hope the absence of gleaners was due to the field's considerable distance from Bethlehem. She looked around cautiously. Surely the owner had some compassion, for he had erected a shelter where his workers could rest. Some of the men and women in the field sang as they worked.

Swallowing her fear, Ruth approached the overseer standing near the shelter. He was a tall man, a powerfully built man with a solemn demeanor. Clasping her hands and keeping her eyes downcast, she bowed before him. "Greetings, sir."

"What do you want, woman?"

Heart pounding, she straightened and saw how his gaze moved down over her grimly. Would he deny her the right to glean because she was a foreigner? "I've come to ask your permission to pick up the stalks dropped by the reapers. " She would beg if necessary.

Frowning, he stood silent, considering her request. Then he nodded and pointed. "There will be more grain for you if you glean at the corners of the field and along the edge."

Relief swept through Ruth. She let out her breath sharply and smiled. "Thank you, sir!" She bowed once more. "Thank you!" He looked so startled, she blushed and lowered her head quickly.

"Stay clear of the workers," he said as she left him.

"Yes, sir." She bowed again. "Thank you for your kindness, sir." She felt him watching her closely as she hurried away. The reapers took notice of her as she hastened toward the farthest corner of the field. One woman gathering the stalks behind the reapers glanced at her and smiled. No one cast an insult or threw a stone. No one called out lewd propositions or insults. The workers in this field left her alone. They kept on with their own work and began to sing again.

Relieved and thankful, Ruth set to work. Without tools, she had to break off the stalks of barley with her bare hands. Soon her fingers were blistered. Hour after hour she worked while the sun beat down hot and heavy. She became light-headed from the heat and labor and sat in the shade of a tree near the boundary stone until she was rested enough to begin work again. *I will be like an ant laying up stores of grain through the spring and summer months so there will be food to last through the winter,* she thought, smiling as she worked. Each hour was important, and she threw herself into the labor, grateful she had been given freedom to do so.

The songs of the reapers lifted her spirits. "The earth is the Lord's in all its fullness ... maker of heaven and earth ... ruler of all ... who delivered us from Pharaoh ... holy is Your name ..."

Ruth hummed as she worked, and when she learned the words, she sang with them.

※※※

Boaz had checked the work in all of his barley fields but one. He rode his horse along the road, raising his hand in greeting to those he recognized overseeing or working in the fields. Some elders at the gate shook their heads at him, asking why he always felt it necessary to spend so much time in the fields with his workers. His overseers had proven themselves trustworthy. Why not leave the work to them and sit and talk with those of his station? They never understood why he enjoyed being a part of the harvest, and not just showing up for the celebration at the end.

He had worked in his father's fields as a boy when the crops had come in fourfold. And he had worked in the fields as a young man when famine was upon the land. Surely it was through the mercy of God alone that he'd prospered while many others had struggled. Many had sold their land and sought a better life elsewhere. Rather than repent and turn to God again, they had despaired and moved on, necks stiff with pride as they continued to bow down to the baals and Ashtoreth.

Elimelech had left that way. Boaz had tried to reason with him, but the man had never been one to listen, even to a close relative. "What good is the Promised Land when it won't yield grain?" It seemed beyond Elimelech's reasoning to see that God had turned away because His own people had proven themselves unfaithful. "Stop bowing down to the baals and stay here, Elimelech. Think of what is best for your sons. Work your land. Surely the Lord will bless you if you're faithful," Boaz had urged him.

"Faithful? I've given sacrifices. I've given offerings."

"What God wants is a contrite heart."

"Why should I be contrite when I've done everything I was supposed to do? What good has it done me? Here you stand, Boaz, thinking you're a better Jew than I am. All you have over me is better land."

Elimelech never could see his blessings.

Boaz didn't want to think about the past, but it was there stirring long-forgotten feelings inside him, feelings he thought he'd smothered by hard work. But they were like the hyssop that grew from a stone wall. What use was there in going over hard words exchanged twenty years ago? What use in reliving the pain and frustration of trying to help another before he brought disaster on his own head? Elimelech had failed to realize how richly he'd been blessed by God, even during those famine years. Mightily blessed, but blind to see it. Boaz had talked long and hard and succeeded in accomplishing nothing but a broken relationship and hard feelings on his cousin's side. All these years later, Boaz could still remember as though it were this morning when he stood at the city gate watching Elimelech take Naomi and their two sons away from Bethlehem.

Ah, Naomi, sweet, vibrant Naomi ...

He'd wept that day, though no one had known the fullness of his grief.

Since then, the Lord had poured bounty into his hands, so much bounty that it naturally overflowed into the hands of others in need of it. The long years had been filled with purpose and thanksgiving, if not the joy he had hoped for. He'd always had more than he needed and knew he had God to thank for it. Even though the Lord had denied him the one thing he'd prayed for with such fervent longing, Boaz praised His name. God was sovereign, and it wasn't for a man to question or grieve for what he could not have. Boaz found contentment in accepting his life as it was and thanking God for it.

As he rounded the curve, Boaz saw the field of ripe grain stretching out before him. The workers were singing as they worked. He smiled, for he wanted his servants to be happy in their labor and not just going through the motions to receive what they needed to sustain life. Life should be bounteous, and he did what he could to make it so for those who worked for him. Surely the pleasure men and women received from food and drink and the work of their hands was a gift from the hand of God.

A young woman worked in the farthest corner of his field. He'd never seen her before, but he knew by her dress that she was not from among his people. A Moabite. Most gleaners stayed within easy walking distance of the city. Why had this one come so far? He dismounted and tied up his horse near the shelter. "Good day, Shamash. The work is going well, I see."

"Indeed, Boaz. The crop is even better than last year."

"Who is that girl over there?"

"She is the young woman from Moab who came back with Naomi. She asked me this morning if she could gather grain behind the harvesters. She has been hard at work ever since, except for a few minutes' rest over there in the shelter."

Naomi's daughter-in-law! He had heard about her soon after the two women arrived in Bethlehem. People had been talking about the young Moabitess ever since.

"She has come a long way to glean."

"She looked as though she'd had a hard time at another field."

Boaz glanced at him. "Then she did well to come here." He put his hand on Shamash's arm and smiled. "Talk with the young men, and make sure no one bothers her." He went out into the field among his servants and spoke to them. "The Lord be with you!"

"The Lord bless you!" they said in return.

When he went to the young woman at the corner of the field, she stopped working and bowed her head in respect. She didn't look into his eyes, but she greeted him like a slave would greet a master. She showed uncommon respect. His heart softened when he saw how the stalks of barley in her hand shook slightly. "Listen, my daughter," he said gently. "Stay right here with us when you gather grain; don't go to any other fields. Stay right behind the women working in my field. See which part of the field they are harvesting, and then follow them. I have warned the young men not to bother you. And when you are thirsty, help yourself to the water they have drawn from the well."

She glanced up in surprise. "Thank you." Her smile made her quite beautiful.

He felt an odd sensation in his chest as he looked into her dark eyes. *Here now, what is this?* He felt a twinge of embarrassment at his attraction, for he was more than twice her age.

"Why are you being so kind to me?" she asked, her voice sweet and thickly accented. "I am only a foreigner."

And clearly had been treated as one, for there was a bruise and an abrasion on her cheek. "Yes, I know. But I also know about the love and kindness you have shown your mother-in-law since the death of your husband." His voice deepened as his emotions rose. "I have heard how you left your father and mother and your own land to live here among complete strangers. May the Lord, the God of Israel, under whose wings you have come to take refuge, reward you fully." Surely the Lord had shown great mercy to those who belonged to Him. As Naomi always had. And now, this young woman.

Ruth's cheeks turned red. "I hope I continue to please you, sir," she replied. "You have comforted me by speaking so kindly to me, even though I am not as worthy as your workers."

Noticing the bruise again, he asked gently, "Did someone hit you?"

She frowned slightly and then looked startled. She raised her hand instinctively to cover the mark and lowered her head as though to hide it. "Only a small stone. No great harm done. I suppose it's to be expected."

As though that would excuse such treatment. "It had better not happen in *my* field," he said darkly.

"Oh, it didn't happen here," she said quickly. "No one has bothered me since I arrived."

Boaz felt shame that any of his neighbors would treat her so cruelly.

He wanted her to feel safe, but he didn't want her to misinterpret his intentions. She was a comely young woman, and no doubt had received the attentions of much younger men than he. "Be at ease among us, Ruth. You're safe here."

He left her to her work, thinking as he walked away that young Mahlon had shown uncommon wisdom in choosing a girl like this one to be his wife. Not all foreign women were a curse on Hebrew men, drawing them away from the true God into lustful pagan worship. Some foreign women had been grafted in among God's chosen people because of their great faith.

His mother, Rahab, had been such a woman. She'd welcomed two Hebrew spies into her house in the wall of Jericho. Unashamed, she had boldly declared to them her faith in Yahweh, the God of the Hebrews. She'd risked her life to be aligned with God and His people. One of those spies had been his father, Salmon. And God had blessed both his parents, for they had loved one another throughout their lives.

Nevertheless, God had warned His people against the miseries of yoking themselves to foreigners. Men were too easily seduced away from God by the wiles of women. But what constituted a foreigner? Surely this young Moabitess was one of God's people. She had declared her faith by turning her back on life in Moab and coming to Bethlehem with Naomi. This girl was like his mother, who had been a standing stone of faith among a mountain of loose gravel. Boaz often wondered if it wasn't faith – not just Hebrew blood – that declared one chosen by God. For surely it was and always had been God who selected those who would belong to Him.

But perhaps that was merely the old hurt rising within Boaz, rationalizing and justifying the match his father had made. Even after all these years, he felt the pang of rejection. Hadn't he been turned away as a suitor because he was half Canaanite? There were those among God's people who thought the bloodline to Abraham was all that God counted as righteous, and faith a mere by-product of blood.

Boaz paused at the edge of his field, gazing back at the young woman gleaning behind his reapers. She gathered a stalk here and a stalk there, cradling them in her arms. Her attire proclaimed her a young woman of the city. Yet, here she was in his field, doing backbreaking work in the heat of the day, and grateful for the opportunity. And why did she work so hard? To provide for her Hebrew mother-in-law. Were there any young women among his people that would do such a thing for someone not of Abraham's blood?

Something stirred within him, pain and pleasure at the same time. How long since he had felt this yearning? He smiled in self-mockery and turned away.

A pity Ruth was so young, and he so old.

≈≈≈≈

Ruth heard a man call her name. When she glanced up, she saw Boaz standing before the shelter, motioning for her to come. "Come over here and help yourself to some of our food. You can dip your bread in the wine if you like."

Her heart thumped heavily as she placed her gleanings in a careful bundle and left them where she had been working. She was amazed that a man of his station would take notice of a dirty, sweating foreigner at all, let alone invite her to share a meal with his workers. Before entering the shelter, she washed her hands in the water provided. She was embarrassed by the curious looks of his workers. The men perused her from the hem of her dress to the top of her head, while the women whispered among themselves.

"May I sit here?" she said at an open place among his maidservants.

The girl sitting closest moved over. "Should I say no when the master has invited you?"

Ruth's face went hot. When she sat down, she noticed how the girl beside her shifted again, increasing the distance between them. Folding her hands in her lap, she bowed her head and closed her eyes as Boaz blessed the food. When he finished, those around her began to talk among themselves again. They made no effort to include her in their conversation, nor did she expect it of them. She was surprised to see the master himself serving his workers. When Boaz came to her, he gave her a double portion.

She glanced up in surprise and saw him frowning down at her hands. She drew them back and clasped them beneath the table again. Had she committed some breach of etiquette? When she dared look up, the others glanced away, talking among themselves. She was so hungry her stomach rumbled loudly, embarrassing her even more. Boaz had given her more than enough to satisfy her hunger. She put half of the double portion of bread into her shawl for Naomi, and then tore off a piece of the second portion and dipped it into the wine.

Gradually, the whispering curiosity lessened as the young women around her talked and laughed, as did the young men on the other side of the enclosure.

Ruth watched Boaz surreptitiously as he sat with his overseer. Despite the disparity of their positions, the two men talked with the ease of good friends. The overseer was young enough to be Boaz's son. He was a handsome man, powerfully built with dark hair and eyes. Boaz was plain. His hair and beard were streaked with gray, the two thick curls at his temples white. He was not attractive in any way that would draw attention. Yet his kindness made her heart soften toward him. His tender care touched some deep place within her. When he turned his head slightly and looked her way, she lowered her eyes again. It was not proper for her to study any man, let alone one who was so far above her station. As she looked away, she encountered the open stares of several young men. One grinned at her. She looked away quickly so that he would know his attentions were unwelcome.

She did not linger over the meal but returned quickly to the field, gleaning in the distant corner where she would neither offend the maidservants nor attract unwanted interest from the reapers.

~~~

Boaz took Shamash aside before the reapers returned to the fields. "The young men have taken notice of the Moabitess."

He laughed softly. "Any man breathing would take notice of her."

"See that no one takes advantage of her."

Shamash's grin faded. "Of course." He nodded.

Boaz put his hand on the overseer's arm. "I know you wouldn't allow her to be mistreated, but there are those, even among our workers, who are clearly disturbed by the presence of a Moabitess."

"The young women." His mouth tipped.

Boaz removed his hand from Shamash. "Did you notice her fingers are raw and bleeding?"

Frowning, Shamash looked out into the field where Ruth was working. "She hasn't the tools for the work."

"Precisely. When I've gone, go out and tell her to glean behind the workers. Give this young woman time and opportunity to prove herself."

Then Boaz called the younger men to him. When they gathered around him, he looked each in the eye. "You have all noticed the young gleaner among us. Her name is Ruth, and she's providing for her mother-in-law, Naomi, wife of our brother Elimelech. Let her gather grain right among the sheaves without stopping her. And pull out some heads of barley from the bundles and drop them on purpose for her. Let her pick them up, and don't give her a hard time! Whatsoever you do to this young woman, you do to me."

Thus advised, the reapers returned to the field. Boaz mounted his horse.

"Be at ease about the young Moabitess, Boaz," Shamash said. "Everything will be carried out according to your will."

Boaz looked out over his field and the reapers and harvesters cutting and gathering the sheaves. He loved those who belonged to him, and he wanted them to behave with honor toward those less fortunate. Ruth worked alone. "Perhaps God will shine His countenance upon her and give her a young husband from among our people."

He looked down at Shamash and smiled. "May God be with you, my friend."

Shamash smiled. "And with you, my lord."

As Boaz rode away, he kept his eyes straight ahead on the road back to Bethlehem, refusing himself the pleasure of looking back at the young Moabitess working in his field. Instead, he thanked God for giving him the opportunity to help her, and thus help another who mattered greatly to him.

Sweet, vibrant Naomi, the girl he had once sought for his wife.

Ruth straightened and watched Boaz ride away. "Lord, please bless this man for his kindness toward me and my mother-in-law. Give him joy in his old age." Smiling, she bent to glean again.

The overseer came out to her. She paused in her labor and inclined her head in respect. "I'm to give you instructions from Boaz," he said. "You are to glean among the workers. They won't bother you."

She looked off toward the road down which Boaz had ridden. "I've never known anyone so kind."

"There are few like Boaz." His mouth tipped ruefully. "The Lord brought you to his field. And may the Lord continue to watch over you." He nodded toward the other workers. "Go and join them."

The women sang as they worked. "The Lord is my strength, my song, and my salvation. He is my God, and I will praise Him. He is my father's God – I will exalt Him. The Lord is a warrior – yes, Jehovah is His name ... " Ruth quickly absorbed the words and began to sing with them. They glanced at her in surprise. Several smiled.

One made a point of snapping off the heads of barley and dropping them for her. Ruth put her palms together and nodded deeply in gratitude.

She worked until evening and then beat out the barley. She had a half bushel of grain! "Surely it is You, Lord, who has provided so much." Filled with a sense of joy and satisfaction, she tied the corners of her shawl and lifted the grain to her back, heading home toward the city of Bethlehem and the small cave where Naomi waited.

⬿⧓⬾

And the men were saying ...

"That's the first time I've ever known Boaz to take such interest in a gleaner."

"He's always been kind to gleaners."

"It took courage for her to come out here."

"It looked to me like she may have tried some other fields. Did you see the bruise on her face?"

"Did you know she's gleaning for one of our own widows?"

"No."

"There are probably a lot of people who don't know why she's here."

"And that's an excuse for throwing rocks at her? The Law is clear about gleaners."

"And clear about foreign women."

"Boaz's mother was a foreign woman."

"I suggest we concentrate on our work and mind our own business."

⬿⧓⬾

And the women were saying ...

"Do you see how the men are cutting stalks and tossing them over to her?"

"When a girl is pretty, men turn helpful."

"Boaz spoke to them before he left. He probably told them to give her extra grain."

"So even the master is interested in her. Look there. Do you see?"

"See what?"

"Shimei is looking at her again."

"Well, if you weren't staring at Shimei, you wouldn't know that."

"I don't like her."

"Why?"

"Do I have to have a reason?"

"Well, I like her."

"Why?"

"Unlike some I know, the girl works hard and minds her own business."

❈❈❈

"So much!" Naomi exclaimed, rising as Ruth entered their dwelling place and lowered the bundle of grain from her back. The girl was smiling brightly, her eyes aglow. "Where did you gather all this grain today? May the Lord bless the one who helped you!"

"I've been saying prayers of thanksgiving for the man all the way home, Naomi. His field is some distance from the city."

Naomi didn't ask why Ruth had ventured so far, seeing the bruise on her cheek. She was afraid she knew the answer. "What was the landowner's name?"

"The man I worked with today is named Boaz."

Naomi put her hand to her throat. "Boaz?"

"Yes, Boaz." Ruth took the bread she had saved and handed it to Naomi. "He invited me into the shelter where his maidservants and reapers ate the midday meal, and gave me a double portion!" She held out a piece of bread. "I've never heard of a man in his position stooping to serve his workers."

Naomi took the bread with trembling fingers. She hadn't given a thought to Boaz when she returned to Bethlehem. She had forgotten all about him. Or maybe the truth was that she had deliberately put the man out of her mind. Just thinking about him made her cringe with shame. Many years ago, he had come to her father and made an offer of marriage for her. How she had carried on as soon as he left the house! How she'd wept and pleaded that her father accept Elimelech instead.

"But he hasn't even offered for you!" her father had said, red-faced with anger.

"He will. His sister told me he has spoken to his father about it."

"Boaz is a man of unquestioned virtue, my daughter."

Indeed, but he was not a man to make a girl's heart beat with love. She wanted a tall husband, ruddy and handsome with laughing eyes and winning ways. She wanted Elimelech. His name meant "my god, a king." Surely that was an indication of his character. The love she saw in Boaz's eyes had embarrassed her. She had been impatient with his attention, repulsed by it. Why wouldn't he go away? Why wouldn't he look for some other girl, one as plain as he?

She had known none of those reasons would sway her father against Boaz, but one thing would – a fact he seemed to have forgotten. "Boaz has unquestioned virtue, Father, but questionable blood." His mother was Canaanite. And a prostitute.

Naomi lowered her head and closed her eyes tightly. *Oh, Lord God, that Boaz of all men should be so kind!* What shallowness she had shown toward this man. And to look down upon his mother, who had proven herself a woman of such strong faith! Unthinkable! Unpardonable! Yet, despite Naomi's sins against him, Boaz welcomed Ruth and poured a double blessing out for her. "Praise the Lord for a man like that! May the Lord bless him!" she said, her words choked with tears. She deserved his condemnation but received his compassion. She hadn't recognized his worth when she was young, but life had taught her hard lessons. She was older now and far wiser.

A tiny spark of hope came to life within her.

Raising her head slowly, she looked at Ruth. "He is showing his kindness to us as well as to your dead husband." She saw confusion in the girl's eyes. There were so many things yet to teach her about Hebrew ways and the Law. What would be her response if she were to tell Ruth the fullness of Boaz's obligations to them? Would Ruth respond the same way she herself had all those years ago, seeing only the outer shell of the man and not his lion heart? She had never known a man to be more bent upon pleasing God than Boaz. Sadly, a young woman's heart was not often won by a man's character.

"That man is one of our closest relatives, one of our family redeemers, Ruth."

"No wonder he was so kind to me."

"No," she said quickly, not wanting her daughter-in-law to misunderstand. "Boaz is not the sort of man to limit his kindness to family members, Ruth. He has always been kind to anyone in need."

"Even foreigners?"

"His mother was a Canaanite. In fact, she was a prostitute who lived in the wall of Jericho." When Ruth's eyes widened, Naomi hastened to explain. "She was a woman of great faith, but there were many people who looked down upon Boaz when he was a young man because he was of mixed blood. Hebrew on his father's side, and Canaanite on his mother's. Rahab hid two spies sent out by Joshua before our people took the land promised us by God. She declared her faith in Yahweh and saved the men's lives by letting them down from her window by a rope. They went back for her and brought her out when the city was being destroyed, and she lived among our people from that time on. One of the spies took Rahab as his wife."

"Then perhaps Boaz was kind to me for his mother's sake."

Naomi was certain that was not the only reason. "He would understand better than anyone that God calls whom He chooses." If God had called Rahab to be of His own people, then He could call a young Moabite widow as well. She leaned forward. "Did he say anything else to you?" Had Boaz mentioned her?

"Boaz even told me to come back and stay with his harvesters until the entire harvest is completed."

Naomi felt a rush of relief. Surely Boaz wouldn't have encouraged Ruth if he held the ill will of a long-ago rejected suitor. "This is wonderful! Do as he said, Ruth. Stay with his workers right through the whole harvest. You will be safe there, unlike in other fields."

As she ate the bread Boaz had given Ruth, Naomi smiled to herself. She watched her daughter-in-law pour the barley into a basket, careful not to lose a single seed of grain. It seemed all was not lost after all. There was one door left to open so that Ruth could walk through into a future and a hope. And, if God was willing, the door would stay open for her as well.

≈≈≈≈

Naomi awakened when she heard a soft cascading of rocks just outside the cave. The sun was barely up and Ruth was coming up the slope, carrying a large skin of water. "You're awake early," Ruth said, smiling.

"I thought I would go into Bethlehem today and talk with some of my old friends."

Ruth poured the water from the skin into a large earthen jug. "Good.

I'm sure they've missed you and will have plenty to talk about with you." She hung up the empty skin and swung her black shawl over her hair and shoulders. "I'll try to be back before dark."

"God be with you, Ruth."

Ruth smiled brightly. "And with you, Mother."

Naomi rose. Dragging a blanket around her shoulders, she went to the mouth of the cave and watched Ruth head down the road.

Naomi stood amazed that God had blessed her with such a daughter-in-law.

Ruth had left behind opportunities and possibilities. She had turned away from a secure future in Kir-hareseth so that she could come here to Bethlehem and live in this cave with a tired, despairing, complaining old woman. At any time, her daughter-in-law could have returned to the home of her affluent parents, but instead she went off every morning to do the work of the poorest of the poor. Not once had she uttered a word of complaint. Every evening, she returned with a smile, grain, glad tidings, and a grateful heart.

A man of discernment like Boaz would appreciate a young woman with Ruth's virtues, Moabitess or not.

Naomi drew herself up before she allowed her thoughts to run rampant. It wouldn't do to make plans for Ruth's future before learning the facts. Naomi had no intention of rushing into Bethlehem, seeking out the elders, and making a case. No, she would move slowly. There was no hurry, now that she and Ruth had shelter and food. She would take time to observe, take time to let people get to know her daughter-in-law ... for who could not respect her when they did? Was there a finer young woman than her precious Ruth? Above all, Naomi would take time to pray for God's guidance, even though it was surely God Himself who had planted this seed of hope in her mind.

For the first time since burying her last son, Naomi saw what life could hold in the future instead of what life had held in the past.

⋙⋘

And the women were saying ...

"I think she's pretty."

"That's because you like her."

"You're just jealous because Rimon, Netzer, and Tirosh were trying to talk with her today."

"Have you noticed how she never works near the men?"

"She never even gives them a second glance."

"She must have loved Mahlon very much."

"She's certainly loyal to her mother-in-law."

"My mother said Ruth comes to the well early every morning and takes water back to her mother-in-law before she comes to the fields."

"Then she must be up well before dawn."

"Shamash keeps an eye on her."

"So do all the men!"

"No one's going to marry a Moabitess who's already had a husband."

"I would be sorry to see Ruth and her mother-in-law live out their days in that cave."

"They live in a cave?"

"The one just below town where the shepherds keep their flocks in the winter. Didn't you know?"

"I thought they lived in the city."

"Naomi spends her time in the city, visiting with friends and bartering."

"What about the house that belonged to her husband?"

"I heard my father say Naomi's husband mortgaged it and all his land before taking the family to Moab."

"Everybody is talking about them."

"Especially about Ruth, I would imagine."

"You're jealous!"

"I'm not jealous!"

"Then why do you dislike her so much?"

"Foreign women rouse the worst kind of interest in our men."

"Foreign women don't make a habit of going to the synagogue."

"Now you're telling me she's a proselyte?"

"Ruth attends every Sabbath with her mother-in-law, drinking in every word the priest reads from the Law. They stand at the back with the other widows. That's probably why you haven't noticed them. You're up front near the screen where you can look through and see Netzer."

"How you talk, Tirzah, when you're no better, gawking at Lahad all day."

"Can I help myself? He's so handsome."

The young women entered Bethlehem laughing together.

～～～

"He's not married?" Naomi said in surprise, feeling a pang of guilt at this bit of information given to her by Sigal, a friend from years past. "What's wrong with the man that he's not taken a wife by this age?"

"Nothing." Sigal poured grains of wheat onto the grinding stone. "He probably never had time to seek a wife. He's poured his life into building up his estate. Boaz isn't like other landowners. He's out there in the fields every day. And when he's not, he's at the city gate helping settle disputes."

"What good is an estate without sons to inherit?"

"He's not in the grave yet, Naomi. He can still look for a wife, if he has a mind to do so. Believe me, there are plenty of fathers who would throw their daughters at Boaz if he broached the subject of marriage. He's become the wealthiest man in Bethlehem."

"And probably the loneliest."

Sigal gave a snort of laughter. "The man has no time to be lonely."

"Still, it's a pity he isn't married."

"Maybe he's waiting for the perfect woman, someone beautiful and intelligent and who has the faith of his mother. Some men have expectations so high they can never be met."

"Some men want a wife who will love them."

"Boaz is loved and respected by everyone in Bethlehem."

"I mean he might be waiting for someone to fall in love with him."

"I doubt that. Most men know love takes time. As long as the girl respects her husband, there's every reason to hope for a happy marriage."

"You are a wise woman, Sigal."

"I always was."

Naomi couldn't help wondering. Had she hurt Boaz so badly he never dared ask another woman to marry him? She felt grieved at that thought. Surely that wasn't the reason he had remained without a wife. Boaz was too sensible to give up marriage just because of one foolish girl.

Should she ask him about it?

Her heart lurched. No! Never! She couldn't say a word about the past without embarrassing Boaz and possibly jeopardizing the future. She wanted to make up for the pain she had caused him so many years ago. Whatever his reasons for not taking a wife, it made her sad to think of him living out his life alone. A man was not meant to be alone. And certainly not a man like Boaz. God had blessed him with land and possessions, but surely it was a sign that He had not blessed the man with the one thing he needed to fulfill his life: a wife who would bear him sons. The man should have a family of his own.

"I remember a rumor I heard years ago," Sigal said, continuing to grind wheat. "About you and Boaz." She gave Naomi a teasing smile.

"Rumors aren't worth the sand we walk on," Naomi said. If the rumor was revived, it would only serve to humiliate a good man. "Elimelech paid my father the bride-price when I was fourteen."

"All the young women were envious of you. Elimelech was very handsome."

"Were they envious of me when he mortgaged the land and took me and our young sons away from Bethlehem?"

Sigal blinked in surprise.

Naomi grimaced at her own harshness. "I'm sorry, my friend. Even after all these years, I still remember the bitterness of that day."

Sigal stopped her grinding and placed her hand over Naomi's. "I thought of you many times over the years."

Tears filled Naomi's eyes. "I longed for home every day I was gone." She drew in her breath and released a contented sigh. "But for all that, the Lord blessed me with Ruth."

"Truly," Sigal said. "She loves you as though you were her own mother."

"I could not love her more if she were from my own flesh."

"God has comforted you through her, Naomi. Everyone says she is a young woman of excellence."

Naomi was pleased. Ruth was no longer looked upon as "the Moabitess ... " Surely the Lord Himself had seen that her virtues had not gone unnoticed by those who dwelt in Bethlehem.

The question remained: Had Boaz noticed?

four

BOAZ came by the barley field every day to see how the work progressed. And every day, he took cautious notice of the young Moabitess working close behind his reapers. He didn't speak to her, concerned that his attentions might cause his workers to gossip. When he stayed to share a meal with his workers, he made sure he kept his gaze away from the young woman. Never had he found anything more difficult to do!

The barley harvest was over, and the wheat stood tall and ripe, ready for the reapers. In another few weeks, all the grain would be harvested. Had Ruth gleaned enough to carry herself and Naomi through the year? He knew they lived in the cave within the boundaries of Bethlehem. Elimelech had owned the field near it. But did they have enough stored to carry them through until next harvest? Boaz looked out at the workers. "Has the young Moabitess made any friends among our people?" he asked his overseer.

"All of them look upon her with respect and admiration."

That was not what he'd asked, but Boaz understood the implication. Ruth was admired from a distance, much as his mother had been.

"What about the young men? Has she taken interest in anyone in particular?"

"She never leaves the company of the maidservants. She pays no attention to the men. Unlike some of our other young women, I've never seen Ruth do anything to draw attention to herself. She comes early to the field and works late. And she seems content with the work. I hear her singing with the maidservants." Shamash smiled. "She always asks me to extend her thanks to you. Is there a reason you don't speak with her yourself?"

"You know how people talk." Boaz mounted his horse. "You like her, don't you, Shamash?"

"Everyone admires her, Boaz. I've never known a young woman more worthy of praise. I haven't heard a word said against her, even in the city." Shamash looked out at the young woman working in the field. "She would make a good wife."

Boaz felt a pang of discomfort. Was Shamash falling in love with Ruth? Boaz didn't like the sinking feeling in his stomach. Should he begrudge another man happiness? Who knew better than he that a man alone was often lonely, even among friends. "A good wife is worth more than her weight in gold, Shamash. She is a crown on her husband's head. The young woman out there would bring honor to any man." He saw Ruth look up and averted his gaze. He was startled to find Shamash staring at him with an odd smile. Frowning slightly, Boaz gave a nod. "May the Lord bless you in your endeavors, Shamash."

Shamash bowed. "And may the Lord grant you your heart's desire, Boaz."

It was a long ride back to Bethlehem. Boaz gave charge of his horse to a waiting servant and talked with the elders at the gate. He was occupied with various disputes and business affairs of the city until he saw the maidservants returning to the city. His pulse quickened when he saw Ruth among them. She was walking along the road with his girls, listening and smiling over their carefree chatter, but not joining in. He was startled when he saw Naomi pass by. She went out the gate to meet her daughter-in-law. They kissed one another in greeting and talked briefly as the other young women walked through the gate into Bethlehem. When Ruth and Naomi turned toward their humble home, Ruth glanced his way. She smiled and bowed her head respectfully. Naomi was looking at him. He looked away from the two women and forced himself to listen to the elders. What fine point of the Law had they been discussing? Closing his eyes for a moment, he pretended to be deep in thought, when in truth, he was trying to calm the wild gallop of his heart.

⤜⤜⤜

Naomi studied Ruth's manner each day when she returned home from gleaning in Boaz's fields. She relished every detail Ruth told her about her time with the maidservants and reapers, and she was hungry to hear her every thought about Boaz. But Ruth said nothing about the landowner. She talked about the work and the pleasant maidservants. Sometimes she sang the songs she'd learned while working among them.

But now, Naomi had cause for hope. Today she had stood just inside the gate waiting for Ruth. Boaz hadn't noticed her there, but she had been in a good position to watch the man. Oh, how his head had come up as his maidservants returned. She knew the moment he spotted Ruth.

"Does Boaz come often to the field?"

"He came four times this week and three times the week before that."

Oh! Naomi thought with deepening satisfaction. *The girl keeps count of the landowner's visits!* That was a good sign. "Does he speak with you each time?"

Ruth shook her head. "He hasn't spoken with me since the first day when he gave me permission to glean. He's a very busy man."

"Ha. Not so busy he couldn't show you a little courtesy." She watched Ruth closely to see her reaction to such talk and was satisfied when Ruth protested.

"Oh, Mother, no. Boaz has shown me courtesy beyond measure. Was it not Boaz who made my work easy by telling his reapers to drop grain for me to glean? We're both indebted to him for his kindness. Every grain of barley and wheat we have is due to his kindness."

"You like him?"

Ruth lowered her eyes. "No more than all those who work in his fields." She sat at the mouth of their cave, gazing out at Elimelech's fallow field. "I wonder why he never married, Mother. How is it God has blessed this man with such prosperity but not given him a wife and sons?"

Naomi smiled to herself. Ruth saw past the plainness of the man to the lion's heart of faith that beat in his breast. Why not test her a little more and see if her compassion could not be refined into tenderness of another kind? "There was never anything in his appearance to commend him." When Ruth glanced back in surprise, Naomi hastened on. "A pity he is so homely."

"He's not handsome the way Mahlon was, but I don't think he's homely."

"Did you find him the least attractive when you first saw him?"

Ruth blushed. "I never considered ... " She shook her head. "Surely you're not saying you think Boaz ugly."

"Would I call a man ugly who puts grain in my hands? May it never be! But I won't pretend to be blind either. Boaz is a good man, a man who lives the Law and doesn't just preach it. But he's wanting in the assets that would win a girl's heart."

"He has dignity and character."

"Was it dignity and character that made you fall in love with my son? If Mahlon had been plain, short, and thin, would you have been attracted to him?"

"Mahlon was more than a handsome face, Mother. You know that as well as I."

"We aren't talking about love growing in the bonds of marriage, my dear. We're talking about what you thought the first time you saw Mahlon striding along the streets of Kir-hareseth. God was merciful to my son. At least Mahlon knew the love of a good wife." She shook her head. "Poor Boaz." She clucked her tongue. "He has no one, and it's too late now."

Ruth looked troubled. "Why should it be too late?"

"He's old."

"Oh, Naomi!" Ruth laughed. "You were telling me yesterday that Abraham fathered Isaac when he was one hundred years old, and Boaz can't be more than half that age."

What a jewel Mahlon had received in this girl. If only Mahlon had given her a son, Naomi would not have so many worries. As it stood now, Mahlon's name and the name of Elimelech would die out. Naomi couldn't sit by and let it be so.

Oh, Elimelech, had you been stronger in faith, your sons would be gathering in the wheat from that field down there. You would be enjoying the inheritance God gave you. You would have claimed the promises and lived by the Law and been blessed like Boaz. Instead, my beloved husband, you took us away from our inheritance and gave your life to dreams of wealth. And everything you worked so hard to gain for yourself is gone, used up, blown away like dust. Your life was as fruitless as that fallow field out there. There's nothing to show for all the work you did. Even the fruit of your loins has died. You left nothing behind that will last.

And I'm angry, so angry with you, Elimelech. My very blood cries out against you for wasting our lives. I'm angry with myself because I was so easily swayed by your handsome face, your winning ways, your sweet words that went down and turned sour. You'll never know the full extent of the pain you caused because you wanted to take the easier road rather than the right one.

But as God has forgiven me for my sins and brought me home, I forgive you, too. Because I loved you to the end, no matter the manner of man you were. And besides, you suffered more than anyone for the choices you made.

As much as Naomi had loved her husband, she knew better than anyone that Elimelech had never been the man Boaz was. Her husband had rejected the promises of God, left his land, brought up his sons in a foreign country. When Elimelech had died in Moab, he'd left his family stranded there. His two sons, the fruit of his loins, had taken foreign wives and died in Moab. Through eyes of love, Naomi could see the truth. Elimelech had sinned against God, cast blame on Him for the consequences, and looked out for himself rather than repent. Her husband had believed he could prosper by his own power.

Oh, the foolishness of man.

Boaz was the other side of the coin. He'd chosen to stay in Bethlehem during the hard years when God was punishing His stiff-necked people for bowing down to the baals. He'd claimed the promises of God and lived an upright life before the Lord. And God had blessed him for his steady, stubborn faith. Boaz was wealthy now, a man of high standing in Bethlehem. He sat at the city gate with the elders and made decisions that affected the entire city. Yet he hadn't become puffed up with pride because of his exalted position. Humility was his mantle. He looked out for others less fortunate, even a young widow from Moab.

The cry of Elimelech had always been "God has abandoned us, so *I* will provide!" Boaz's life made his declaration: "God is my provider, and I will trust in Him."

Surely the wife of such a man would have cause for rejoicing. Naomi wanted Ruth to be happy. She wanted this precious girl, who had given up everything to take care of an aging mother-in-law, to have *joy!*

But there was a problem.

Boaz was not the only relative left. Naomi had learned during her visits in town that there was another man more closely related to her than Boaz. A younger man that made the women roll their eyes and smile.

A man like Elimelech.

〰〰〰

Ruth was disturbed by what Naomi had said about Boaz. When he came to the field the next day, she watched him surreptitiously and felt a strange tenderness for him. Everyone respected him and had great affection for him, but it was the kind they would have for a father or an older brother.

Had any woman ever looked upon Boaz with love? Had the mere sight of him walking by stirred any woman's heart with passion the way hers had been stirred for Mahlon? She couldn't imagine it, and that saddened her. How old was Boaz? Fifty? Sixty?

The poor man. For all his wealth, what did he have that would last?

Oh, Lord, God of Israel, don't let the name of Boaz die out.

She watched him talking with Shamash and thought he looked so solemn. Did he ever laugh? What did he do when he wasn't checking on the progress in his fields, seeing that his servants were well cared for, or serving the community by making heavy decisions at the gate? He had friends, but could he confide in them as he would a woman who loved him? What were his dreams? She had seen the sorrow in his eyes. Was it a sorrow born of having no one who cared enough to look beneath the rugged casing of the man into his heart and spirit?

He must have sensed her attention, for he glanced her way. Her feelings of tenderness swelled, and she smiled, giving him a nod of respect, and quickly looked down. She had cause to be thankful that God had led her to this field and this man. When she glanced up, sensing his perusal, Boaz looked away. One of the maidservants noticed the silent exchange and gave her a curious look. When she spoke to another close by, Ruth felt the heat climb into her cheeks. Did these young women think she was showing an inappropriate interest in their master? He was a rich man, after all. There were women who would want to be his wife for that reason alone, without thought to his feelings.

Shaken, Ruth kept her attention on her work for the rest of the day. She didn't want her interest in Boaz to be misinterpreted. Gossip could destroy her reputation and cause him embarrassment. She would keep her eyes off the man and pray for him instead.

Oh, Lord, God of mercy, remember this man for his kindness toward the less fortunate. Let his name be held in esteem not for this generation only, but for generations to come, for surely Boaz is Your faithful servant. He proclaims Your name with every opportunity. He is a man who desires to please and obey You. Oh, Jehovah-jireh, this lonely man has been a tool of Your mercy and provision. I know You are enough, but surely a man such as this one was not meant to be alone. May it please You to give him whatever his heart desires ... Oh, Lord, oh, Lord ...

She prayed unceasingly for her benefactor. She thought of little else but Boaz while she worked in his field.

And the more she prayed for him and thought about him, the more she saw his goodness.

※※※※

Naomi prayed fervently as well. She set her grief aside in favor of her love for Ruth and a desire to see her daughter-in-law settled somewhere better than in this cave. Naomi knew it was time she stopped grieving and started to live again, no matter how painful the effort. It was time to take a good hard look at her own life instead of attending Elimelech's mistakes. Nothing she supposed would happen had happened. Hadn't she left Kir-hareseth expecting to travel back to Bethlehem alone? And Ruth had come with her.

Hadn't she expected to be destitute? And Ruth worked in the fields to sustain her. Hadn't she expected all her friends and family to be dead or gone away? And she'd found half a dozen women she'd known and Boaz, as well as another relative.

Boaz was attracted to Ruth. Anyone who bothered to study the man would know. Naomi also knew him well enough to realize he wouldn't speak up and make any attempts to win her. The man's hair would go white and fall out entirely before he allowed his feelings to show openly.

And Ruth would go on dedicating her life to providing for her poor old mother-in-law. She would work until her back was bent and her womb dry. She'd slave away until Naomi had gone the way of her ancestors. Then what would happen to the poor girl? Should Naomi sit by and watch Ruth dedicate her life to gleaning rather than running a household and raising up children for the Lord? Should she do nothing about Ruth's future? Wasn't it a mother's place to stoke the fires a little? Who else but her and God would care about the future of this precious young woman?

So, Lord, what are we going to do about her? How do we shake up that quiet old man and get his blood moving again? If we wait on him, what chance is there?

Supposing she did think up a plan that would turn Boaz's head. Would Ruth agree to carry it through – whatever it was? Ruth would have to agree!

Naomi spent the next days and nights thinking about Ruth's future and what a good husband Boaz would make. Toward the end of the wheat harvest, she thought of a plan so bold it was certain to capture Boaz's attention. Just imagining his reaction made Naomi laugh. But would Ruth trust her judgment? Would her daughter-in-law heed the advice of an old woman who'd made so many mistakes it might seem a way of life?

In the confusion of her feelings, Naomi could not be sure about her motives. She knew only that the Lord could sort it all out and make things right. She loved Ruth as she would a daughter of her own womb and wanted to see her happily settled, but she also wanted a grandson to claim Mahlon's inheritance and carry on his name. She wanted to make amends to Boaz for the pain she had caused him when she was a young girl. And what better way to do that than by offering him a beautiful young wife with many years of childbearing ahead of her?

Was it right to ask so much of God when she'd spent most of her life walking behind Elimelech?

Ruth and Boaz. Boaz and Ruth. Don't You think they're right for each other, Lord? I grant she is much younger than he, but what better blessing to give a righteous man like Boaz than a quiver full of children in his old age? And what children they would have! You would not see their sons and daughters bowing down to baals!

She pleaded their case to the Almighty and longed for an answer. How fortunate Moses had been to hear The Voice from a burning bush. Naomi knew better than to expect God to give her an audible answer, but she couldn't trust any of her friends with the questions tormenting her. Was this plan right before God? If it wasn't, what might be the cost to Ruth?

Let the cost be on my head, Lord.

～～～

When the harvest came to an end, Naomi knew the plan had to be put into action now or never. Boaz had been given plenty of time to notice Ruth's virtues, and Ruth had great respect for him.

"My daughter, it's time that I found a permanent home for you, so that you will be provided for. I intend to find a husband for you and get you happily married again."

Ruth laughed. "And who would marry someone like me?"

"The man I'm thinking of is Boaz."

"Boaz!" Ruth spilled some of the grain she was pouring into an earthen container and stared at her. "You can't be serious!"

"I know he's old ... "

"He's not *old.*"

"Homely, then. Is that why you object?"

"Mother, he's the most respected man in all Bethlehem! He stands among the elders at the gate! He's a rich man with land and servants!"

"All the more reason to consider him."

Ruth shook her head, half in amusement, half in consternation. "I know you love me, Mother, but your esteem for the widow of your son is beyond bounds. How can you possibly think I would be worthy of Boaz? The idea is ludicrous."

"You were good enough for my son. You're good enough for Boaz."

Ruth went back to pouring grain into the earthen container. "Not even if I threw myself at his feet would the man notice me."

"You don't think he's noticed you? Ha. He noticed you long ago."

"In kindness."

"More than in kindness. Have you no eyes in your head? He admires you. From too much a distance, but admire you, he does."

"You're mistaken. He thinks no more of me than he does any other gleaner in his fields."

"I've made it my business to study the man's manner around you, Ruth. Shouldn't I look out for your future? His eyes tell the whole story when he sees you returning from the fields."

"He greets me in the same manner he does all his maid-servants. 'God be with you,' he says."

"Do you think a man in his fifties can court a young widow from Moab without tongues wagging? The women would think you a harlot and him an old fool. And the men ... well, we won't talk about what they would think. Boaz won't show himself under any circumstances other than those called upon by our Law." Leaning forward, Naomi clasped Ruth's hands and smiled broadly. "But the Law is on our side."

Ruth looked confused. "I don't understand."

"Boaz is a close relative of ours, and he's been very kind by letting you gather grain with his workers. He is a compassionate man and would show mercy to anyone in need. But because he is also our close relative, he can be our family redeemer."

"Family redeemer?"

"God provided a way for widows under His Law. As our family redeemer, Boaz would take you as his wife and give you a son to carry on the name of Mahlon and inherit Elimelech's portion of the land God promised."

Ruth's face flooded with color. "After all he's done for us already, should we ask him to give me a son to carry on another man's name? What of his own inheritance?"

"Would it change anything to leave the man be? Boaz has no sons, Ruth. Nor any prospects for begetting them."

"And you think I should ... " She stopped, stammered, blushed. "H-he's one of the elders! Surely he already knows he holds the position of our family redeemer. He hasn't offered because it isn't a responsibility he wants."

"The man is too humble to offer. What would he say to you, my dear? 'I want to offer my services ... '? Never in a million years would he say such a thing, nor God allow it. I know Boaz better than you do. I remember him from years past, and I've listened to all that my friends have said about him in the years between. He will *never* approach you about this matter."

"Because I'm not worthy to be the wife of such a man!"

"No. Because he's more than thirty years older than you. And because, if I know him at all, he's waiting for a young man, handsome and with a charmed tongue, to offer you marriage instead." God forbid. Boaz had stood back and allowed Elimelech to claim her because she'd been swayed by physical appearance and charm. Was Boaz standing back again and waiting until the other relative realized Ruth's worth? Boaz might even make himself a matchmaker! "Boaz wouldn't put himself forward if his life depended on it." Which in Naomi's eyes it did. "The man would not risk embarrassing you with an unwanted proposition."

Ruth looked away, her brow furrowed. When she looked back at Naomi, her discomfiture was clear.

"Should I help you find a husband, Ruth? Could you be happily married to Boaz?"

Ruth considered for a long moment. "I don't know."

"Saying you don't know is better than saying a flat no," Naomi said, satisfied. "Will you trust me if I tell you that Boaz could make you happy? He would do everything in his power to make sure of it." She saw moisture build in Ruth's eyes. Before her daughter-in-law could protest, Naomi began explaining her plan. "I happen to know that tonight he will be winnowing barley at the threshing floor. Now do as I tell you – take a bath and put on perfume and dress in your nicest clothes. Then go to the threshing floor, but don't let Boaz see you until he has finished his meal. Be sure to notice where he lies down; then go and uncover his feet and lie down there. He will tell you what to do."

Ruth's face was white, her eyes wide. "Should I do such a bold thing?"

"Trust me, my daughter. Unless you make it known to the man that you want him for a husband, he'll live out his life the way he is. Should such a man go down to Sheol without sons of his own?"

"And what of you?"

"Me? What about me?"

"If Boaz does take me for his wife, what will happen to you? Should I leave you alone in this cave?"

Naomi's heart softened. Precious girl! Ruth was a jewel with many facets. Naomi was all the more determined to see her in the proper setting. "Boaz gave you a double portion the first day he met you. Do you think he would leave me out in the cold to fend for myself?" She shook her head and smiled. "If all goes as I've prayed, we will all have a future and a hope, Ruth. If the plan succeeds, it will be because God makes it so and not because an old widow has done a bit of matchmaking."

Ruth let out her breath slowly. "All right," she said slowly and inclined her head. "I will do everything you say."

Lowering her head, Naomi was silent a moment, disturbed by Ruth's solemnity. Ruth was in the springtime of her life; Boaz, autumn. Naomi could understand Ruth's hesitation, but she was certain Boaz could make her daughter-in-law happy. Still, she pondered. Would this please God, or was she making plans of her own as she had done before?

What am I to do, Lord? Many are the plans of women, but Your will prevails.

Be merciful, Jehovah-rapha. Let us all be healed of our grief and know love again. Let the homeless have a home again, a home where You are master. Boaz will teach my daughter the way of life and uphold her on her journey. I see the loneliness in the man's eyes, Jehovah-jireh. I see the love there, too. If it be Your will, soften his heart toward Ruth and her heart toward him. If they come together only out of mutual respect and duty, if it please You, Lord, let those feelings grow into love. Build a fire in each of them that will warm them for a lifetime.

〰〰〰

Boaz had the sheaves of barley loaded onto donkeys and carried to the high place near Bethlehem that he'd turned into a threshing floor. Shamash and the young men broke the bundles open and cast the stalks onto the hard-packed earth, where a pair of oxen were driven in a circle, dragging behind them a heavy wooden sledge.

The stones fastened to the underside of the sledge crushed the stalks and loosened the grain. Girding his loins, Boaz joined his servants in the work. The air filled with the scents of crushed stalks, oxen, and the hot sun and earth. When the floor was heavy with broken stalks of barley, the oxen were led away and the men took up their winnowing forks.

Boaz pitched grain into the air. The afternoon breeze caught the straw and chaff and whiffed it away while the heavier kernels of barley dropped back to the threshing floor. It was hot, hard work. Over and over, he dug his fork into the piles of threshed grain. Sweat soaked through his tunic and beaded on his forehead. He paused and tied a cloth around his head to keep the perspiration from dripping into his eyes. Bending to his labor, he raised a song of celebration and his servants joined in.

As the threshing progressed, he set workers to gather the straw into piles to be stored and used through the year to fire stoves and feed his animals. When the bits of straw and chaff were too small to be pitched by fork, the men set aside their winnowing forks and used shovels instead. They paused to eat and drink and then returned to work. When the breeze died down, some of the servants waved woven mats to blow the chaff from the barley. Other workers began to purify the grain by sifting. As the grain passed through, bits of rubbish were caught in the sieves and thrown away. The darnel grains were removed, for if these weed and tare seeds were left, they would be eaten and cause dizziness and sickness.

The harvest was so plentiful, the work would last for several days. "Enough for today, men!" Boaz called out. His cooks were ready with savory dishes of bean-and-lentil stew. Trays of fruit were set out, along with plenty of bread and wine. The men relaxed, talked, sang, and laughed as the stars came out.

No lanterns were lit, for the risk of fire was too great.

Ruth sat some distance from the threshing floor and watched Boaz sing, laugh, and drink with his servants. When the stars came out, she moved closer as the celebrating slowed. When Boaz rose, the gathering broke up. His servants spread out and found places to cover themselves with their mantles for sleep. Work would begin again early in the morning. Ruth watched Boaz lie down beside the pile of grain.

She remained concealed in an outcropping of rocks for another hour. She wanted to be certain all of Boaz's servants had settled down for the night and were asleep before she came out of her hiding place. She couldn't risk being seen here. Gossip would spread through Bethlehem like a fire, burning up her reputation. That thought tortured her as she moved slowly, cautiously, toward the place where Boaz slept. Her heart thumped until she felt sick with tension.

When she finally reached him, she hesitated, studying the man in the half-moon light next to the mound of grain. He looked younger, his many responsibilities forgotten in sleep. He lay with one arm flung over his head. Trembling, Ruth knelt at his feet and drew his mantle back carefully so she wouldn't disturb him. He moved restlessly. Her pulse jumped. She curled up quickly at his feet without making a sound and drew his mantle over her so that the cool night air would not awaken him. Then she released her breath slowly, wishing her heart would slow its wild, erratic pace.

She tried to make herself relax, but how could she with this man so close she could hear his breathing and feel his warmth? She could smell the sweat of his body mingled with the scents of earth, straw, and barley. She remembered how the odor of sickness and fear had clung to Mahlon during the last months of his life. The scent of Boaz's body was that of life – hard work, the fruit of his labor, the land God had given him. His essence was at once provocative and soothing.

She swallowed and closed her eyes, disturbed by the emotions this great man stirred within her. Putting her hand beneath her cheek, she listened to the sound of her own heart racing in her ears and the slow, even breathing of the man so close his feet were against her back.

Boaz awakened in the middle of the night and lay still, wondering what had startled him. A dream? He couldn't remember it. He listened for a long moment, but nothing moved. In fact, there was an uncanny stillness around him. He heard one of the men snoring loudly from the other side of the mound of grain and relaxed.

Inhaling deeply, he closed his eyes, intending to go to sleep again, but instead he came more fully awake as he smelled a sweetness in the air he breathed. He frowned slightly, attentive to it. He breathed in again and thought he had never smelled anything so luscious. Where did it come from? Was an evening breeze bringing the scent of flowers? No, it was too rich and evocative. Like perfume.

When he stretched out his leg, he brushed against someone. The interloper was small and curved. He drew in his breath sharply. Pulling his foot back abruptly, he sat up and threw off his mantle. Who but a harlot would dare come to the threshing floor?

The woman sat up quickly and turned her head toward him. It was too dark to see her face. "Who are you?" he whispered roughly. He didn't want to awaken anyone.

"I am your servant Ruth."

His heart began to hammer. "*Ruth?*" His voice came out choked and confused.

Her voice shook. "Spread the corner of your covering over me, for you are my family redeemer."

A flood of heat swept through his entire body beginning with the foot that had brushed against her body. He could hardly breathe for the nearness of her and the request she made. Never in the solitude of his wishful thinking had he ever dreamed Ruth would make such a request of him. Did she know his heart had yearned for a wife to love and care for, a wife to walk with him and give him children?

Lord, Lord, how do I ever dare hope for a girl like this? There are obstacles. Is this a test? I must do what's right rather than do what I want. And You've known since the first time I heard about this girl that my heart was softened toward her. Such a woman ... but Lord, surely Naomi is aware of the other relative. She must know it's not my right to fulfill this duty, unless ... oh, God, give me the strength to do what I should, even if it means seeing another woman I love walk away with another man.

"The Lord bless you, my daughter!" His voice was husky with emotion. He was glad of the darkness so she wouldn't see the longing and astonishment he felt. Did she understand the kindness she was showing him by coming to him? His head swam. He'd surrendered his hope of ever having a family of his own years ago. God was God, and for whatever reason, He had chosen not to give the blessing of a wife to him. And yet, here, in the middle of the night and cloaked in darkness, a few whispered words from Ruth made Boaz's hope for a wife and children spring to life again. He forced himself to think, to consider her actions and motives. Surely she had done it for Naomi!

"You are showing more family loyalty now than ever by not running after a younger man, whether rich or poor."

"You have been kinder to me than anyone, Boaz. Will you put your mantle over me?"

He could hear the tremor in her voice and wanted to reach out to her and reassure her. It was beyond reason that she might love him, but his heart had been fixed upon her firmly from the beginning. He wanted nothing more than to take her as his wife, but was this God's will?

"Now don't worry about a thing, my daughter. I will do what is necessary, for everyone in town knows you are an honorable woman." *None more than I,* he longed to say. "But there is one problem."

"A problem?" she said softly, distress clear in her tone.

"While it is true that I am one of your family redeemers, there is another man who is more closely related to you than I am."

"Another man?"

There was no mistaking the disappointment in her tone. When she moved closer, her hand brushed his leg. She drew back quickly, but not before his body had caught fire. He wasn't such an old man after all. The power of his feelings for her shook him. He looked around, wondering if anyone had heard them speaking. What disaster would befall her if she were to be discovered here on the threshing floor! His mind raced unwillingly toward advantages to himself if that happened. The other relative would have cause to question her purity. He might then refuse to fulfill his obligations to her on the grounds of her ruined reputation. The entire city would gossip about her and speculate on what had happened between them here tonight. There would be talk for years to come. As much as Boaz wanted her, he would not dishonor her in such a way.

Could he stand before the Lord if he allowed such a thing to happen to Ruth? Could he look into her eyes if he allowed shame to be poured on her because he wasn't vigilant to do what was right? No! He must protect her reputation, even if it meant giving her up to another man. His heart sank at the thought. Gritting his teeth, he struggled with his desire to have her for himself. But how could he overlook the Law? No matter how much he wanted Ruth, he must obey the Lord.

You know I want her, don't You, Lord? Is that why You're testing me now? Oh, Jehovah-tsidkenu, give me strength not to give in to my desire to have her. Keep me to Your path, for if I step off, I am lost! Help me show Ruth the kindness she has shown me, and establish her.

"Yes," he said to her. "There is another relative who must be consulted. Stay here tonight, and in the morning I will talk to him. If he is willing to redeem you, then let him marry you. But if he is not willing, then as surely as the Lord lives, I will marry you! Now lie down here until morning. No one must know that a woman was here at the threshing floor."

Ruth lay down at his feet again. Boaz felt her presence so acutely, his stomach hurt. He wondered if she slept, for she made no sound at all. Nor did she move. He longed to touch her, to talk with her, but withheld his hand and kept his silence.

He prayed instead.

Oh, Lord, Lord ...

He didn't even have words for the feelings stirring so strongly in him. He was shaken by her presence, shot through with hunger for her to be his wife. How many years had it been since he'd felt like this? Not since he'd thought himself in love with Naomi. *It's been more than twenty years!*

The hope of loving Ruth made him afraid for the first time in years.

Ruth came abruptly awake when a gentle hand brushed the hair back from her forehead. *"Shhhhh."* Boaz put his finger over his lips. He was down on one knee beside her, and it was light enough to see his smile. "Everyone's still asleep," he mouthed. Dawn was coming. It was time for her to leave before any of his servants awakened and saw her there.

"Bring your cloak and spread it out," he whispered. She followed him to the pile of barley that had been purified of all the tare seeds. "I can't send you home without a present."

He shoveled grain into her shawl until there was more than a bushel and a half. Then he tied it and laid it on her back. "For Naomi."

His generosity never ceased to amaze her. She could not have carried any more. "Thank you," she whispered and looked up at him. When her eyes met his, she felt the jolt of recognition and connection. He wasn't just looking at her the way a man looked at a woman he found attractive. He looked at her as though she already belonged to him. The way he studied every detail of her face made her heart quicken. She blinked, stunned by the realization that this man, so far above her station, wanted her.

When Boaz reached out, she drew in a trembling breath. Though she stood still, waiting for his touch, he withdrew his hand. His smile became almost fatherly, his tone faintly reproving. "May it be as God wills."

※※※

As soon as Ruth was out of sight, Boaz awakened Shamash.

"I'm going into the city. I don't know when I'll be back."

Shamash started to rise. "Is there trouble?"

Boaz put a hand on his shoulder. "No trouble, my friend. There's a matter of business I need to take care of this morning. It can't wait."

"It must be important. I've never known you to leave the threshing floor."

Boaz had no intention of explaining. He didn't want anyone speculating about Ruth's visit to the threshing floor. By the end of the day, she would have a husband. He intended to do all he could to make certain it was him. Whether he succeeded would be up to God. He squeezed Shamash's shoulder. "Pray for me, my friend. Pray what I want is what God intends."

A quick frown flickered over Shamash's face, but he responded quickly. "May the Lord give you wisdom in every circumstance."

"From your mouth to God's ears."

Boaz strode down the road toward Bethlehem, his mind racing with the plan that had been forming in his mind.

※※※

Ruth was home before the sun had risen and surprised to find Naomi up and watching for her. "Have you been waiting all night for me?"

"Could I sleep on such a night? Well? What happened, my daughter?"

Uttering a mirthless laugh, Ruth lowered the grain. "It's not settled yet, Mother. Boaz told me there's another relative more closely related than he is." She kept her face averted, for she didn't want Naomi to see how disturbed she'd been by that news. "But he said not to worry; he'll take care of all the details. He said if this other man won't marry me, then he will. Boaz swore by Jehovah that he would." She couldn't hide the sudden rush of tears. "What if he can't work it out and I have to marry this other man? I don't even know who he is!"

Frowning heavily, Naomi tapped her fingertips against her lips.

Wiping the tears from her cheeks, Ruth stared. "You knew, didn't you? You knew about this other man and still sent me to Boaz?"

"I want you to have the best of men."

Did Naomi know something about this other man that made him undesirable as a husband? "Who is this man?"

"He is a man like any other man, but not the man I would have for you."

"Oh, Mother. What does it matter what you and I want? It's out of our hands now." Ruth wept, the tensions of the night taking their toll on her resolve. She wished she had never agreed to go to the threshing floor. "Weren't we doing all right by ourselves? Wasn't God providing for us each day?"

Naomi embraced her. "Oh, my sweet girl, you needn't worry. Boaz wants you!"

"How can you know that?" Perhaps she had been mistaken by what she thought she saw in his eyes.

"Look at all this! Do you think the man would have sent so much grain home with you if he were indifferent to the outcome? Just be patient, my daughter, until we hear what happens. The man won't rest until he has followed through on this. He will settle it today."

Boaz strode quickly through the city streets until he came to his house. Several of his servants were up and doing chores. The house was in good order; it smelled of bread baking. "Bring me water, Avizemer, and have Yishmael bring me a new tunic, mantle, and sash."

He washed carefully and donned fresh clothing. Drawing his prayer shawl over his head, he prayed again, beseeching God for wisdom and strength to do what was right. He didn't hurry in speaking with the Lord, but remained in a chamber by himself until the sun was well up and he knew he would be at peace with the outcome, whatever it was.

When he came out of his inner chamber, his servants were huddled together, whispering. They glanced up in concern. "Yishmael, I have an errand for you." Boaz smiled at the others. "Everything is fine. Go back to your work."

They did as he bid them, but he could sense their curiosity. His mouth curved in a rueful smile. It wasn't every day their master came racing into his house in the manner he had. No wonder they were concerned. They were more accustomed to seeing him come home late in the afternoon, dusty from work, ready to wash, eat, pray calmly, and go to bed. Every day had a sameness about it.

But today was different!

He gave Yishmael the names of ten of the chief men in the city, men who were good friends and honest in their dealings with everyone. "Ask them to meet me at the gate of the city." Most of the men would be easily found at the synagogue. They often met in the morning before they began their business transactions for the day. Several might already be sitting in the gate, hearing and helping to settle disputes between citizens. "As soon as you've spoken to them, go to Naomi and Ruth, the Moabitess. They live in a – "

"I know where to find them, my lord."

"Good. Bring them to the gate right away."

Boaz went down to the marketplace to find Ruth's and Naomi's relative. He knew more than he wanted to know about the man's reputation but was determined not to judge him on gossip. He intended to present Ruth's case in a way that would test the man's character. He walked among the booths until he spotted Rishon, son of Oved, brother of Elimelech, talking with several young men while his wife scooped barley from an earthen container and poured it into an old woman's woven basket. The two women argued. Scowling, Rishon turned, said something to the older woman, and gestured impatiently. The woman turned away with a defeated frown.

Stiffening, Boaz stood still for a moment, breathing in slowly and reasoning with himself. What he witnessed was not necessarily all it seemed to be. He needed to keep his mind clear for the discussion ahead. Rishon's children were in the booth with his wife. He counted three, including the baby cradled in Rishon's widowed mother's arms.

"Rishon," Boaz called, going no closer. When the younger man turned, he beckoned. "Come over here, friend. I want to talk to you." He kept his voice casual, as though what he wanted to discuss was of no great importance to him.

Rishon came readily, blushing and looking faintly guilty. "I take it you saw that woman. She's always expecting more than – "

Boaz raised his hand to stop the flow of excuses. "It's another matter I would discuss with you."

Rishon looked visibly relieved. "Another matter? What matter?"

"Come," Boaz said, holding his hand out in welcome. "Sit with me where it's cooler."

He caught the glint of speculation in Rishon's eyes when he sat down in the shade of the city gate. Rishon sat down with him. Boaz called the names of the ten men who had gathered in the gate. "Will you agree to be witnesses to whatever is decided here today?"

Each agreed and took a place close by to hear out the case and act as a witness to what was decided between the two men.

Rishon looked around at them, frowning, and then faced Boaz again. "What's this all about, Boaz?"

Boaz glanced around cautiously and saw Naomi standing in the shadows. His heart thumped heavily as he saw Ruth standing behind her. When he looked at Naomi again, she raised clasped hands before her heart, smiled faintly, and nodded.

"You know Naomi," Boaz said, extending his hand toward her. Rishon glanced at her indifferently and gave a curt nod of acknowledgment before returning his full attention to Boaz. "Naomi, who came back from Moab," Boaz said.

"So I'd heard."

And yet have shown no mercy or familial consideration, Boaz thought grimly. "She is selling the land that belonged to our relative Elimelech." Rishon's eyes started to glow, for it was prime land, close to the city. "I felt that I should speak to you about it so that you can redeem it if you wish. If you want the land, then buy it here in the presence of these witnesses."

"All right," Rishon said with a full sigh of greedy anticipation. "I'll redeem it."

~~~

Ruth had never seen a more handsome man than Rishon. He was much younger than Boaz, well built, ruddy, with dark curling hair and beard. He was dressed in a fine tunic and mantle and had the manner of a man eager to find any advantage. He surveyed the gathering of elders with caution, his eyes gleaming with speculation. There was a proud tilt to his head. Though he tried to take on the posture of confidence, she sensed his discomfort, as though he expected them to confront him for some error. He was wary of this meeting with Boaz and was deferential in his manner toward the older man. Ruth had the feeling Rishon's manner was not from the heart but from the head.

Nor did she like the way her relative looked at Naomi. The man barely glanced at her mother-in-law before dismissing her from his mind, as though she was of no import.

Her heart dropped when Boaz said Naomi wanted to sell her husband's land. She clutched Naomi's arm, wanting to protest for her sake, but her mother-in-law leaned close and whispered, "Boaz knows what he's doing. Trust him."

"If you want the land, then buy it here in the presence of these witnesses," Boaz was saying. "But if you don't want it, let me know right away, because I am next in line to redeem it after you."

"All right, I'll redeem it," Rishon said eagerly.

"Good," Boaz said. Ruth felt the blood drain from her face. Had she misunderstood his feelings toward her, his desire to take her for his wife? He didn't even look in her direction or seem concerned that she would become the property of Rishon.

"It's good land," Rishon said. "It's a pity it's remained fallow for so long."

"Of course, your purchase of the land from Naomi also requires that you marry Ruth, the Moabite widow. That way, she can have children who will carry on her husband's name and keep the land in the family."

Rishon's expansiveness evaporated. "The Moabitess?" He made no attempt to hide his disappointment. He looked from Boaz to the elders gathered. His mouth tightened. "So ... " His face darkened. "Then I can't redeem it because this might endanger my own estate."

"Such is his excuse," Naomi whispered in disgust to Ruth.

Ruth wondered what bothered Rishon most: Having to do his duty to her and provide Mahlon with an heir, or risking that any fraction of his property might go to a child she might conceive? The people who had come to watch whispered among themselves.

"His wife wouldn't like it," someone near Ruth said.

"He should do his duty by Naomi."

"He covets the land but doesn't see any point in buying it if he has to give it back as an inheritance to Elimelech's family."

Rishon glanced around at the gathering and appeared discomforted. He untied his sandal hastily and handed it to Boaz, publicly validating the transaction. "You redeem the land; I cannot do it. You buy the land." He rose quickly and pushed his way through the gawkers.

Naomi grasped Ruth's hand tightly. "He did it!" She gave a soft laugh of pleasure. "I knew he would."

Ruth caught her breath when Boaz looked at her. Though his expression was solemn and respectful, his dark eyes held a light she had never seen before. He seemed to catch himself, for he blinked and glanced away. He stood, Rishon's sandal gripped tightly in his hand. He addressed the ten elders and the crowd that had gathered to see what was going on. "You are witnesses that today I have bought from Naomi all the property of Elime-lech, Kilion, and Mahlon. And with the land I have acquired Ruth, the Moabite widow of Mahlon, to be my wife. This way she can have a son to carry on the family name of her dead husband and to inherit the family property here in his home town. You are all witnesses today."

The ten men rose with Boaz, looking majestic in their long robes and prayer shawls and phylacteries. "We are witnesses," they said.

"We are witnesses!" the crowd joined in.

Naomi pressed Ruth toward the men. "Go," she whispered, her face aglow with excitement. "Go to him, dear."

The oldest of the elders held out his hand to Ruth. The crowd parted as she walked forward and placed her hand in his. Boaz moved to stand on the other side of him. The elder smiled at Boaz and then inclined his head to Ruth. "May the Lord make the woman who is now coming into your home like Rachel and Leah, from whom all the nation of Israel descended!" He drew Ruth forward as Boaz held out his hand. When her hand was placed in his, his fingers closed warmly around hers. The elder put his hands lightly upon their clasped hands. "May you be great in Ephrathah and famous in Bethlehem. And may the Lord give you descendants by this young woman who will be like those of our ancestor Perez, the son of Tamar and Judah."

The servant who had come for her and Naomi pressed his way hastily through the throng of people and ran down the street. People were calling out blessings to Ruth and Boaz. Men and women pressed in on them in their excitement, the men slapping Boaz on the back while the women took turns embracing Ruth and offering her fervent blessings. Boaz laughed and talked to everyone. Naomi was smiling broadly, gesticulating as she talked excitedly to the friends who surrounded her. Ruth was still stunned at the outcome. Boaz kept his hand locked around hers, keeping her close by him as the people swarmed around them offering their blessings and congratulations. The crowd followed as he brought her into the city and along the street. Overwhelmed by the throng of people celebrating around them, Ruth glanced back over her shoulder, her cheeks flushed, her heart racing. Where was Naomi? Was she coming with them?

"Ruth!" Naomi called, pushing her way through the many well-wishers, several women accompanying her. "We must prepare for the wedding," she said, embracing her and drawing her to one side as she playfully slapped Boaz's hand. "Your bride will be ready for you this evening." Ruth found herself hustled away by Naomi, her friends, and Boaz's maidservants from the fields, all of them talking at once. Ruth could scarcely catch her breath.

She was taken to the home of Abigail, a childhood friend of Naomi. Water was brought into an inner chamber where Ruth was stripped of her worn dress. She was washed thoroughly and rubbed with scented oils, her waist-length hair brushed until the thick, curling mass shone.

A young serving girl came for Naomi. "Boaz has sent gifts for Ruth to wear." They disappeared from the room, returning within moments. Naomi carried a carved box inlaid with ivory. "Look," she said as she opened it for Ruth. "Jewels! See how he prizes you." She lifted out a necklace set with red sardius, emeralds, sapphires, and diamonds. "And he's sent wedding clothes as well."

Naomi gave the box to Abigail and helped Ruth dress. "You will look like a queen." When the long white tunic was slipped over her head, Ruth sighed. She had never felt anything so soft in her life. There was an overdress as well, embroidered in vibrant colors, and a sash made from the finest gold, blue, purple, and scarlet linen thread woven into an intricate design. There were bracelets and earrings, with stones of every color of the rainbow, and a narrow crown of gold on which were loops of chains with circles of gold.

One of Abigail's handmaidens braided Ruth's hair with the precious stones Boaz had sent. Last, a diaphanous veil edged with embroidered grapes and leaves and bundles of wheat was draped over her head. The cloud-light material hung all the way to her knees.

"The men will be coming soon," Naomi said, holding Ruth's hand and kissing it. Her eyes were shiny with tears. "I am so happy for you."

Ruth grasped Naomi's hand in both of hers. "For both of us."

Naomi caressed her cheek. "Don't be afraid of him, dear. I would not have sent you to him if I weren't convinced he could make you happy."

Quick tears filled Ruth's eyes. "But will I make him happy?"

"Oh, my sweet one. Did you not see his face when Rishon handed him the sandal? Gold and silver couldn't have pleased him more. You are his treasure, my daughter, a gift from God."

Ruth bowed her head and closed her eyes. She was shaken by Naomi's words. Could Boaz truly love her so much? Surely a man like Boaz deserved to be loved in return. But was she capable of giving him what he must long for more than anything? Would her heart soften toward him as it had toward Mahlon? Would she tremble at his touch?

Would she come to yearn for the sight of him? She admired Boaz. She had the greatest respect for him. But love? Could she give her heart and her body without reservation? Would she respond to him in a way to bring him joy? Or would she always see him as a kindly father or an older brother whom she admired?

Oh, Lord God, I don't want to cause Boaz grief. Please mold me into the woman intended for this man. I have seen this wholehearted love for You. Please fill me with whole-hearted love for him! Mold me into a wife who will add to his crown. I would rather die than cause this man pain!

She felt Naomi's hands upon her head, light and reassuring, and heard her pray in a soft but fervent whisper, "Oh, God of Israel, still the fears of my child. She belongs to You as I do. Please bless Ruth for her love and obedience to me. And if it be not too much to ask, give her a love for Boaz that will exceed the love she had for Mahlon ..." her voice broke softly, "my son." She kissed Ruth on the head.

≈≈≈≈

Boaz had never been more nervous. He tried to hide it, but he noticed the smiles his servants exchanged and knew he was doing a bad job of it. He laughed in self-mockery. "I cannot even tie this sash properly!"

Shamash stepped forward. "If you will allow me, my lord?" Boaz relinquished the sash thankfully and sighed in relief when his overseer finished securing it. Another servant held a white mantle with purple, blue, and red trim. Boaz fixed the gold brooches linked by a gold chain to hold the mantle in place. Last, a gold crown studded with precious stones was placed upon his head.

His friends were gathering and filling the house. Some took delight in teasing him while others took this opportunity to praise his bride.

"It's about time you got yourself a wife, Boaz!"

"He had to trick a relative to do it!"

"Ruth is a young woman worthy of praise, my friend."

"She will fill your house with children."

"A pity such a pretty girl has to marry such an old goat!"

Boaz laughed with them, but he did not possess the confidence he displayed. How did Ruth perceive him? He wasn't young and he had never been handsome. He could think of nothing to commend himself to a young woman of virtue. Doubts assailed him from all sides, despite the joyous atmosphere surrounding him.

"Do not frown so, Boaz," Shamash said. "You'll scare the poor girl."

Boaz forced a smile. His house was overflowing with friends, including the chief men of the city. He had given orders for all the preparations, even seeing that those less fortunate had festive clothing to wear for the occasion. Everything was in readiness, except for him.

"What troubles you, Boaz?" Shamash said.

Boaz had chosen his overseer to act as his companion for the wedding ceremony. Shamash had proven himself a trusted friend over the years. Boaz drew him aside and confessed his gravest concerns. "I compelled her into this marriage. What was I thinking? I should have arranged a better match for her than – "

"A better match? There is no better match! Is it not enough that the girl respects you?"

Should he be encouraged by such words? "I want more for Ruth than that."

"Many men begin with less." Shamash smiled wryly. "Besides, it's too late to worry about all this. You *are* her husband. The covenant between you was witnessed by everyone at the gate. It's dusk and time to go and get your bride." His eyes filled with compassion. "Ruth is a young woman of wisdom, Boaz. I think you will be happily surprised at the future God has prepared for you both."

Boaz laughed nervously. "I am already happily surprised, my friend. I never thought to have a wife, let alone a wife such as Ruth."

Before leaving, Boaz made sure all the preparations for the wedding feast had been finished. The canopy was set up and decorated with flowers and boughs of greenery and lined with cushions for comfort. The house was filled with the aroma of roasting meat, fresh-baked bread, spices, and flowers. Woven mats covered the floor. Trays were already laden and ready to be presented to the guests. Boaz counted the earthen containers against the far wall. "Is there enough wine?"

"Enough, my lord," Shamash said, "and the best in all Bethlehem!"

Boaz did not ask about the bridal chamber. His hand-maidens had seen to its preparation.

Shamash stepped closer. "All is in readiness, Boaz. If you delay any longer, Ruth might think you've changed your mind."

Boaz walked straight from his house, and his friends fell in beside and behind him. The procession wove through the streets of Bethlehem. His companions sang. Some played double-reed pipes, lutes, and lyres. Others danced.

When Boaz reached the house of Abigail, he didn't even have to knock before the door was opened. Naomi stood before him, her face transformed. He hadn't seen her smile since she had come home from Moab. She almost looked young again, and he was reminded of the past when he had thought to make her his wife. "I have come for my bride," he said. His heart stopped when he looked past Naomi and saw the women in festive dress bringing Ruth to him in her wedding veil. He couldn't speak another word. When he reached out to her, Ruth took his hand. He felt her fingers tremble against his as he guided her to his side. He wished he could raise the veil and see her eyes. Perhaps then, he would sense what she was feeling.

Ruth and Boaz were pressed along again as the women joined the men in the procession back through the dark streets of Bethlehem. Some of the men carried torches. The women played tambourines, beat small hand drums, clinked finger cymbals, shook tingling bells, and sang with the men. Many carried oil lamps to light the way.

When Boaz entered his house, he raised his mantle and held it over Ruth as he drew her up onto the dais beneath the canopy. He was surprised and pleased that she knew exactly what to do. He walked her in a full circle several times for all the witnesses to see that she had his covering of marriage. When he stopped, Ruth didn't hesitate. She drew off her veil and draped it over his shoulder according to custom. The people declared, "The government shall rest upon his shoulder!" Naomi was smiling proudly.

Ruth settled herself beside Boaz on a cushion beneath the canopy. "I have never seen you look more beautiful, Ruth."

She glanced up at him and he smiled. Fascinated, he watched the color mount into her cheeks. "Nor I you," she said and lowered her head again.

He gave a soft laugh. "I was sorely in need of new plumage."

She took his hand in both of hers. The warmth of her touch went up his arm and spread through his body. "May God bless you for your kindness toward me."

His throat tightened. "He already has."

When they were escorted to the bridal chamber and left alone, Boaz felt like a callow youth standing in the middle of the room. He didn't know what to say to Ruth. He wanted to put her at ease, but how could he when he'd never been more nervous in his entire life? He was ill equipped to know how to please her and wished he had talked with one of his married friends. There hadn't been time! He started to pace and stopped himself. He combed his fingers through his beard. Catching himself at this nervous activity, he put his hand at his side. Thankfully, Ruth had turned away and had not seen his fumbling ineptness.

When she drew off the embroidered overdress, he felt shock at the power of his desire. "We can wait, Ruth."

"It's expected of us."

Was it resignation or willing acceptance he heard in her voice? "We can wait," he said again.

She glanced over her shoulder. Frowning slightly, she turned fully to look at him. She said nothing for a long moment, her doe-brown eyes searching his face. He wanted to hide himself from that perusal but didn't. She blinked in surprise. She came to him then, each step across the room tightening the pain in his chest. He was more vulnerable than he had been when he had sought Naomi's hand, for he hadn't loved her as deeply as he loved this young woman.

She took his hand. He couldn't find his voice. When she kissed his palm and put it against her cheek, he couldn't move.

"It's not necessary to wait, my husband," she said softly. "I came to you without compulsion."

"Naomi sent you."

She looked up at him solemnly. She searched his eyes, her own filled with strange confusion. "I chose to obey. I hoped, but never dared believe, you would find me acceptable."

He let his breath out sharply. "I hoped," he said hoarsely, "but still don't dare believe ..." He could not finish. This girl could destroy him with a word.

Her eyes glistened with moisture. She reached up and cupped his face. "So that you will know I belong to you, my lord." She drew his head down and kissed him.

~~~

And the women were saying ...

"It's about time Boaz took a bride."

"And such a lovely girl."

"I've never seen a girl more dedicated to her mother-in-law."

"I should be so lucky!"

"Ruth is better than a son."

"Don't I know it. A son marries and forgets all about his poor old mother."

"That's some roof Ruth's put over Naomi's head."

"I should be so lucky!"

"A girl like that, I've been praying for one for my son, but he's more interested in what a girl looks like than her integrity."

"What a pity if Boaz has no real love for Ruth."

"A marriage of obligation is a cold bedfellow."

"May God give them every happiness."

The women agreed and each went her own way, returning to her own house and family.

~~~

And the men were saying ...

"I knew by Boaz's manner that it was something of great importance to him. He was in a great hurry to settle the matter without delay."

"Rishon didn't have a chance."

"Rishon had all the chance he deserved. He wanted the land but not the responsibility that came with it."

"Don't be so quick to cast stones. Rishon's wife has born him three daughters. Would you be so eager to give up your firstborn son for another man's inheritance? And what if his first wife bears no sons at all? What then?"

"All that aside, Rishon still neglected his duty to Naomi and Ruth."

"She is a fine girl."

"May God grant her many sons."

"Boaz has remained all these years without a wife. It will be a difficult adjustment."

"I should be so lucky!"

Some laughed.

"She is very young. I wouldn't want to see my friend's heart broken at this stage of his life."

"Your fears are without cause. Ruth is young, but her character is proven."

"I don't doubt her character. I merely pray she will love him as he most evidently loves her."

"May the Lord God of Israel warm her heart toward our friend."

five

RUTH gave birth nine months after the wedding festivities. Sinking back and resting against the bedding, she watched Naomi take the infant and wash him, salt him, and carefully wrap him in swaddling clothes. "He is beautiful," Naomi wept, holding him close. "So beautiful." She carried him from the room and Ruth turned her face to the wall, tears spilling silently.

Boaz came to her later. She had risen from her bed, dressed, and was sitting in the doorway to the garden, watching Naomi walk around with the baby. Boaz drew up a stool and sat beside her. "Naomi will no longer be called Mara."

Ruth looked at him. He was gazing into the garden as she had, but she couldn't read the expression on his face. "Thank you," she said softly.

He didn't look at her. "Don't thank me for doing what was right." His voice was rough with emotion.

"You have given up your firstborn son to be heir for another man's family."

"It is our way, Ruth."

"No. It wasn't Rishon's way. It is your way, Boaz. You have put others ahead of yourself."

He looked at her. "Do not praise me too highly, Ruth. I struggle between my duty and my desire." He looked away. "I am a man like any other."

She blinked back tears, wanting to cry out that he wasn't anything like others she had known. Not even Mahlon, whom she had loved so much, would have done what Boaz did.

"Do you want his name to be Mahlon?" Boaz said quietly, still watching Naomi sitting on a stone bench beneath an olive tree.

"Let his name be Obed." A servant.

"So be it. Naomi will never have to fear being alone in her old age," Boaz said.

"Nor will you."

Boaz rose. He touched her head lightly and then turned away, leaving her alone to watch Naomi with their son.

She kept the infant at night and rose every few hours to nurse him. She savored those times when the stillness surrounded her and she held her son close and felt his mouth tug at her breast. She caressed his soft cheek and let his fingers close tightly around her finger. Tears welled, but she blinked them back. When she was finished nursing him, she kept him close beside her on her bed. Each morning, Naomi entered her chamber, leaned down to kiss Ruth, and then took Obed in her arms and tended him throughout the day, surrendering him for feedings only.

≈≈≈

"I shall never be called Mara again," Naomi said, laughing at the expressions crossing Obed's face. "Never again."

"He is beautiful!" the women exclaimed as they admired the baby. Every phase of Obed's growth was met with proclamations by the women of the town who often gathered at Boaz's house to watch the baby progress. "Praise the Lord who has given you a family redeemer today!"

"May he be famous in Israel."

"May this child restore your youth and care for you in your old age."

"And no doubt he will, for he is the son of your daughter-in-law who loves you so much."

"Ruth has been better to you than seven sons!"

Ah, yes, Ruth, her precious Ruth. Naomi smiled, lifting Obed to her shoulder and rubbing his back, delighting in the way the baby nuzzled against her neck and melted against her. She couldn't remember a happier time in her life than now, with this child in her arms. God had stripped her bare and now was rebuilding her house on a firm foundation. This child who had been born to replace her sons and husband would be brought up by Boaz, a man of faith, who studied the Law with diligence and passion, a man who sat in the city gate and ruled his people with wisdom and loving-kindness.

"Ah, my little one," she said, lifting Obed and kissing him beneath his chubby chin. "May you grow to be the man your father is." She delighted in her grandson's baby chuckles. As she turned, she saw Ruth watching her from the doorway, and the mother hunger was plain to see. Naomi felt a pang of conscience at the gift she had been given so willingly. Had she ever thought of the cost to Ruth and Boaz? Her daughter-in-law smiled and then turned away to some chore within the house. Naomi frowned slightly as she nestled Obed against her shoulder once more.

Something was missing. Naomi knew what it was, but she could do nothing about it. And so she prayed and prayed and prayed unceasingly for that which only God could give to the two who had given up so much.

～～～

Ruth found it a consuming job to run Boaz's considerable household, but she was thankful for the work that occupied her time and her mind. Boaz encouraged her to make all the decisions involved in running the home, and she sought Naomi's advice frequently, gradually adapting to her new role as the wife of one of Bethlehem's leading men. She learned to delegate duties to the servants rather than try to do everything herself. She praised their work, thankful for their increasing efforts. They seemed eager to please her, and she was equally eager to see to their needs. She rose before dawn to prepare breakfast for her household and to make plans for the day's work for the servants. She watched for the best bargains in the marketplace and was generous to those in need. No one in her household went wanting. Her hand was always open, for everything Boaz touched seemed to bring forth bounty.

When Boaz had come for her at Abigail's house and taken her home with him, almost two years ago now, she'd been afraid she would disappoint him, that she would be unable to love him as he deserved to be loved. But all that had changed when he treated her with such tender respect on their wedding night. Who would not love such a man? Over the months, her feelings had blossomed and deepened even more until a miracle had happened. Having never expected to love again, she now found herself so deeply in love with Boaz that she had to remind herself he had married her only to raise up a son for her first husband.

She and Naomi spent many hours together combing flax and weaving cloth so they would have material to sew clothing for the poor, while Obed played on the floor close by. They laughed at his antics, for he was a delightful, happy baby. He kept them both occupied when he began first to crawl and then to toddle about the house, his hands ready to touch anything and everything within his reach. Sometimes Boaz would come home and watch him play, but he only held him when Naomi placed the child in his arms. It was as though Boaz waited for permission to hold his own son.

Even with all she had to do, Ruth felt a vague disquiet, an aching loneliness. She had been married to Boaz for almost two years and knew as little of his inner thoughts now as she did on the day she met him in the field of barley. He was her husband, and yet he withheld himself from her.

"I don't think he's happy," she said to Naomi one day when her mother-in-law chanced to mention how much time Boaz was spending with the other elders at the city gate.

"What gives you such a thought?"

"He rises before I do, prays alone in the garden, and leaves for the rest of the day. He spends more time with the other men than he does in his own house, Mother. Sometimes I wonder … "

"Wonder what?"

"If he's avoiding me."

Naomi rose and hurried over to pick up Obed before he could pull over a pile of dried flax. She laughed and scolded him, before turning back to Ruth. "Have you talked with Boaz about this?"

"How dare I speak to Boaz about anything, Mother? After all he's done for both of us, should I expect more of him?" She concentrated on her weaving, afraid to confide too much to Naomi. The last thing she wanted to do was risk hurting her mother-in-law by admitting how much she loved her husband. Would Naomi feel she was being disloyal to her dear Mahlon?

Naomi smiled slightly, balancing Obed on her hip. "Things have changed, haven't they?"

"Changed?"

"You agreed to go to Boaz so he might give you a son to claim Mahlon's inheritance. You went to Boaz so I would have a roof over my head. You went because I sent you."

"I agreed to go to him." Ruth's mouth trembled. She didn't want her mother-in-law to think she had been completely selfless in her actions. If she hadn't admired Boaz, she would not have agreed so readily to offer herself to the man. She pressed her lips together. "You know how much I loved Mahlon, Mother. You know, don't you?"

Naomi looked bemused for a moment, and then her eyes cleared suddenly and widened. "Oh, my dear." She set Obed down. She came and sat close beside her. "You were a wonderful wife to my son. I know that better than anyone."

Ruth's hands shook as she clasped them in her lap. "I don't want to hurt you."

Naomi put her hands over Ruth's. "If you're trying to tell me you love

Boaz, I can assure you I won't see it as any disloyalty to my son. In truth, I will rejoice over an answered prayer!"

"You will?" She searched Naomi's face and saw no pain at all, not even a hint of it.

Naomi cupped her cheek. "Oh, Ruth, I love you as I would a daughter of my own flesh. I want you to be happy. And Boaz is a good man, a very good man."

Ruth smiled tremulously. "A wonderful man." She felt relieved of her guilt, but it didn't change the dilemma in which she found herself. "But I think he married me for no other reason than to fulfill his duty as our relative."

"I'm sure you are mistaken. Boaz loves you. Didn't I tell you so before I sent you to him?"

"He scarcely looks at me. He hasn't touched me since ... " She shook her head, disheartened. She swallowed hard and continued bluntly. "Boaz has succeeded in performing his duty as our relative, Mother."

"Ah," Naomi said, her eyes revealing her understanding.

Ruth glanced away. What of Boaz's inheritance? If he died without additional sons, all of his property, as well as Mahlon's, would go to Obed. A good and loving man like Boaz deserved sons to carry on his own name.

He withheld himself from her in so many ways, and she longed to know everything about him. She wanted to share his thoughts, his pain, his struggles, his hope. But he seemed to retreat to his work, his obligations to the people of Bethlehem, his service to the Lord, anything and everything that kept him away from his own home – and his own wife. Yet how could she complain? Everyone benefited. Boaz's good deeds extended to everyone, including her and Naomi. He poured himself out for her sake and Naomi's and expected nothing for himself. He didn't seem to expect – or even want – her love.

Ruth felt confined, trapped in silence. She was so confused, her emotions in such turmoil. She hadn't felt this uncertainty when she left Moab. She had come to Bethlehem, content to spend the rest of her life taking care of her beloved mother-in-law. Instead, God had taken her beneath His mighty wing and provided for her through the kindness of Boaz. Why should she, the lowest of the low in Bethlehem, a foreigner, be elevated before all eyes and made the wife of the kindest, most generous, most righteous man in all the city? She rejoiced daily over the blessings God had poured upon her, even while feeling increasingly unworthy of them.

So why this unending sorrow? How dare she ask for more? And yet ...

how she longed to make her husband happy!

Oh, Boaz, my Boaz!

She spent her days waiting for him to return home. She melted when he smiled at her, even if it was a fatherly smile. Just the sound of his voice made her heart sing. When he touched her, she trembled.

But Boaz was at home less and less. And she could think of only one reason why he would absent himself so much of the time. He could not return her feelings and felt uncomfortable in her company. For surely he had sensed how deeply she loved him.

She had prayed that God would make her content to spend the rest of her life on the periphery of her husband's life, content in his contentment. She wanted to be a part of Boaz's life, wanted him to trust her enough to share his struggles and triumphs, wanted to be part of *him*. But it seemed that Boaz didn't share her desire.

"What is it, my daughter?" Naomi said, holding Ruth's hand between her own. "What is causing you such grief?"

"I love him. I love him so much it hurts." She loved him more than she had ever loved anyone, even Mahlon.

"And you haven't told him."

"I don't want to embarrass him."

"Embarrass him? Is it better if he thinks he's failed as a husband?"

Ruth drew back. "He hasn't failed!"

"Anyone can see you're unhappy."

"Because he stays away, Mother." She rose from her loom and moved away, restless. "Because he's never home."

"My dearest Ruth, a man who marries late in life has little knowledge of how a woman thinks, let alone a young woman in love. He probably stays away because he believes it will make you happy."

Ruth blinked and looked back at Naomi. She'd never considered that.

"Boaz is only a man, my dear, and men are not always as strong as they portray themselves. I imagine Boaz thinks of himself as a much older man than his lovely young wife, too old for her to love. You could crush his heart with a word."

"I want to make him happy."

Naomi smiled. "Then accept this old woman's blessing, and *do so*."

Naomi was not content to leave things as they were. Her daughter-in-law had been bold once for her sake, but Naomi doubted she would have the confidence to reach out and grab hold of anything for herself. Naomi left the house soon after speaking with Ruth. She said she was going to visit a sick friend. She made her way straight to the city gate, where she knew she would find Boaz. He was there, as usual, and in his usual place. He saw her coming and looked troubled, even more so when she beckoned him. With a word to the other chief men, he rose and came to her. "Is something wrong?"

"All is well," she said.

"Then why do you look the way you do?"

"What way do I look?"

"Like a woman ready to do battle."

He was blind only when it came to his young wife. "Can we walk together and talk somewhere that people won't be listening to our every word and watching our every move?"

Frowning, Boaz fell into step beside her, matching his pace to hers as she walked out of Bethlehem. She said nothing for a long time.

Let him stew and wonder. Let him *ask*.

"Did Ruth send you?"

"No, she didn't send me. I came of my own accord. Someone has to light a fire under you."

"A fire?"

She stopped and looked up at him. "There are times when a man can safely put his heart above his head, Boaz."

He stepped away uneasily. "What are you talking about, Naomi?"

"What do you think I'm talking about? You love her, don't you?" The color that poured into his face was all the answer she needed. She crossed her arms over her chest and glared at him. "When do you intend to tell her you married her for reasons other than honor and legal obligations?"

"She knows," he said dully.

Naomi threw her arms in the air. "And how would the girl know?" She paced back and forth in front of him. "You managed to stay home with her for the seven days of the wedding celebration, but then you dove back into your life as usual. You spend every waking hour overseeing things your overseer gets paid to oversee. And if you're not about your own business, you're tending everyone else's business at the gate. You treat Ruth like a guest in your house! She is *your wife!*"

She stopped reproaching him, satisfied with his stunned look. She pulled her shawl tightly around her and glared up at him. "I knew about Rishon,

Boaz. Did you think I could spend a whole month in Bethlehem and not know about every living relative and friend I'd left behind? I didn't want Rishon to have Ruth! Would he hold her in the esteem you do? Would he love her? I watched you sitting at the city gate, and I saw the way you looked at my daughter-in-law when she was coming in from your fields. And I praised God for you and the feelings you had for her! That's why I sent Ruth to you. I sent her to you because *you loved her*."

"Yes, I love her," he said roughly. "And now you have a son to carry on Elimelech's name. What more do you want from me, Naomi?" He turned away and raked a hand back through his hair.

She let out her breath. Compassion filled her, along with an aching regret. "I want you to be happy, Boaz. I want you to accept the gift I gave you."

"I have accepted Ruth."

"No, you haven't."

He turned and looked at her, his eyes dark with pain. "Her son will have everything I own. Is that not acceptance? Does that not show how highly I esteem her – and you?"

"Ruth is in love with you, Boaz."

He stared at her. "What?" She'd never seen a man look more astounded. "What did you say?"

"I said ... Ruth ... is ... in ... love ... with you." She spoke slowly, as she would to a child slow to understand.

"She can't be."

"Why?" Though it would hurt, she needed to speak plainly. "Because I was blind to your beauty? And you are beautiful, Boaz, beautiful in all the ways that count, all the ways that last. Ruth sees you more clearly than I ever did, my dear, dear friend. Now, it's you who must open your eyes and see the girl you married."

"Should I believe the impossible?"

"Is anything impossible with God? I have prayed for this to happen. I know a dozen others who have prayed as well. Half of Bethlehem prays for you and Ruth! Does God not hear our prayers? Do you know how many people in Bethlehem watch and wait for the Lord to bring the greatest blessing of all upon you both? *Love*. And now He has."

"I can't believe it."

"You can say this with the same mouth that praises God who performs miracles? I know of what I speak. I left her, weeping, not long ago."

"Weeping?"

"Because you're never home where you belong."

He stood a moment, silent, and then he laughed, amazed.

It was good to hear him laugh, even better to see the light in his eyes, a light she had never seen shine so brightly.

His smile softened, his eyes searching hers. "It is strange, isn't it, Naomi? I loved you once."

"And I was a thoughtless, shallow, young girl." She came close and put her hand upon his arm. "Now I'm your mother-in-law," she said with a sly grin. She gave his arm a playful slap. "So show some respect for an old woman. Go home, *my son*. Go home to my daughter, Ruth, who loves the ground you walk on."

Boaz leaned down and kissed her cheek. "May God bless you, Naomi," he said hoarsely.

Naomi watched him stride away. She shook her head in wonder that Ruth and Boaz could have so little confidence in themselves. Ah, but they had unshaken faith in God. And that was a good thing. No, it was the best thing of all. For God would never disappoint them.

Turning her back, Naomi blinked back tears as she looked out over the harvested fields. She thought of Elimelech. She thought of Kilion and Mahlon and ached with her losses. And yet, she thanked God as well, for despite their many sins, as well as her own, their names would not die out after all.

⨯⧓⧓⨯

Boaz's throat was tight, his heart pounding, as he entered the house. "Ruth?"

"I'm here!" She sounded surprised. When he entered the main chamber, he saw her rise and step out from behind her loom, tense and wide-eyed. "Boaz." She blushed. "You're home early."

"Do you mind?"

"Oh, no. Of course not."

He walked toward her, searching her face. Her cheeks were deeper pink than usual. Her eyes widened even more as he came closer. She lowered her head. Was he making her uncomfortable? She reached out and fingered the cloth she was weaving, then put her hand quickly at her side. He'd never seen her more nervous. But then, she was no less nervous than he.

"Have you spoken to Naomi?" Her voice was strangely constricted.

"Yes, though I can scarcely believe what she said."

She looked up at him. "What did she say?"

He was afraid of saying too much, so he said cautiously, "She said ... you wanted to speak with me." This time there was no doubting the color in her cheeks. "I apologize. I've embarrassed you. I think she misunderstood, or I did, or – "

She interrupted. "No. I hoped she would talk to you."

He stared at her. "You've only to say what you wish, Ruth. Obed can have my portion."

"You have land enough for many sons, Boaz."

His heart began to pound.

Her smile was shy after saying something so bold. But she wasn't finished. She stepped closer, looking him full in the face. "I would give you as many sons and daughters as you and God will allow."

"Oh, my love." Her eyes flickered in surprise and then filled with so much hope that he no longer doubted her feelings. He gave a soft laugh. "When I heard people talking about you, when you and Naomi first arrived, I knew you were something very special. And then when you came to my field ... it gave me pause that a man of my age could be so stirred."

She wrapped her arms around his waist and pressed herself against him, crying. Perplexed, he held her closer. She was trembling and weeping. What had he said to bring on such grief? Breathing in the incense of her hair, he thought of the night she had come to him on the threshing floor. She had worn perfume then, but he preferred her as she was now. She smelled like springtime, and she made him feel young again. "What can I say or do to make you happy?"

"I *am* happy!"

"But you're weeping."

"Yes, I am, aren't I?" She looked up and laughed, tears streaming down her cheeks. "I've never been more happy! I want to laugh and sing and dance, all because you love me."

He laughed with her, relishing the outpouring of her feelings. "I would have spoken sooner if you had given me some small hint of your own feelings."

"How could I, when I was convinced you would be embarrassed?"

"So. Are you going to tell me now that you fell in love with me at first sight?"

"No, but I admired you from the first day when you were so kind to me."

"Like a father," he said dryly.

"Only because you persisted in calling me 'daughter.'"

He cupped her cheek tenderly. "I had to remind myself daily that I was too old for you, and that it was far from appropriate for me to feel the way I did."

"So I had to come to you and propose on the threshing floor."

"And you wouldn't have done so if Naomi hadn't pressed you into it."

"I'm glad she did. May the Lord bless her forever for it!" Ruth shook her head and let out her breath softly, her smile softening. "I never thought I could love another as I did Mahlon, and what I feel for you now is so much more. Oh, Boaz, God is merciful! He is kind and generous." Tears streamed down her cheeks as she gazed up at him with adoring eyes.

Boaz cupped her face and drank in the sight of her love. "The Lord is all that and more, my love." *Oh, Lord God, You amaze me! Never would I have dared dream of having such a treasure as this.*

Leaning down, Boaz kissed Ruth with all the love he had stored for a lifetime.

⟨⟨⟨⟨⟨

And the women were saying ...

"I thought she was pretty before, but even more so now. Have you ever seen a more beautiful woman than Ruth?"

"It's love that's done it."

"It's the clothes. It's got to be the clothes. Anyone can be beautiful when you're married to the richest man in town."

"If you put sackcloth on that girl, she'd still shine."

"She's a lamp on a stand."

"Have you seen the way she looks at Boaz?"

"Have you seen the way *he* looks at *her?*"

The women giggled.

"I should be so lucky."

"Naomi must be proud of her matchmaking."

"A word here, a nudge there."

"Boaz didn't need much prodding."

"Are any among us more deserving? Has anyone been more generous to the poor than Boaz?"

"Has anyone shown more devotion to her mother-in-law than Ruth?"

"Ah, but it is God who has poured His blessings upon them."

"Blessed be the name of the Lord."

And the men were saying ...

"I rejoice at our brother's happiness!"

"As do we all, brother!"

"Boaz waited a long time for the Lord to answer his prayer."

"A good wife is more precious than rubies."

"Beauty doesn't last."

"True, but Ruth is a young woman who fears God and respects her husband."

"And loves him. Anyone with eyes can see."

"She is to be highly praised."

"May our brother's household increase."

"May their sons be like Boaz, and their daughters like Ruth!"

"From your mouth to God's ears."

And the assembly at the gate all said, *"Amen!"*

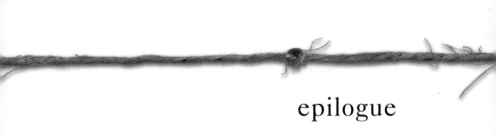

epilogue

THIS is the family tree of Boaz, beginning with his ancestor Perez: Perez (whose mother was Tamar), Hezron, Ram, Amminadab, Nahshon, Salmon, Boaz, Obed, Jesse, and David, who became king of Israel. And from the line of King David came the Christ, the anointed One of God, Jesus, our Savior and Lord.

seek and find

DEAR READER,

You have just read the story of Ruth as perceived by one author. Is this the whole truth about the story of Ruth, Naomi, and Boaz? Jesus said to seek and you will find the answers you need for life. The best way to find the truth is to look for yourself!

This "Seek and Find" section is designed to help you discover the story of Ruth as recorded in the Bible. It consists of six short studies that you can do on your own or with a small discussion group.

You may be surprised to learn that this ancient story will have applications for your life today. No matter where we live or in what century, God's Word is truth. It is as relevant today as it was yesterday. In it we find a future and a hope.

Peggy Lynch

DECLARATIONS

SEEK GOD'S WORD FOR TRUTH

Read the following passage:

In the days when the judges ruled in Israel, a man from Bethlehem in Judah left the country because of a severe famine. He took his wife and two sons and went to live in the country of Moab. The man's name was Elimelech, and his wife was Naomi. Their two sons were Mahlon and Kilion. They were Ephrathites from Bethlehem in the land of Judah. During their stay in Moab, Elimelech died and Naomi was left with her two sons. The two sons married Moabite women. One married a woman named Orpah, and the other a woman named Ruth. But about ten years later, both Mahlon and Kilion died. This left Naomi alone, without her husband or sons.

Then Naomi heard in Moab that the Lord had blessed his people in Judah by giving them good crops again. So Naomi and her daughters-in-law got ready to leave Moab to return to her homeland. With her two daughters-in-law she set out from the place where she had been living, and they took the road that would lead them back to Judah.

But on the way, Naomi said to her two daughters-in-law, "Go back to your mothers' homes instead of coming with me. And may the Lord reward you for your kindness to your husbands and to me. May the Lord bless you with the security of another marriage." Then she kissed them good-bye, and they all broke down and wept.

"No," they said. "We want to go with you to your people."

But Naomi replied, "Why should you go on with me? Can I still give birth to other sons who could grow up to be your husbands? No, my daughters, return to your parents' homes, for I am too old to marry again. And even if it were possible, and I were to get married tonight and bear sons, then what? Would you wait for them to grow up and refuse to marry someone else? No, of course not, my daughters! Things are far more bitter for me than for you, because the Lord himself has caused me to suffer."

And again they wept together, and Orpah kissed her mother-in-law good-bye. But Ruth insisted on staying with Naomi. "See," Naomi said to her, "your sister-in-law has gone back to her people and to her gods. You should do the same."

But Ruth replied, "Don't ask me to leave you and turn back. I will go wherever you go and live wherever you live. Your people will be my people, and your God will be my God. I will die where you die and will be buried there. May the Lord punish me severely if I allow anything but death to separate us!" So when Naomi saw that Ruth had made up her mind to go with her, she stopped urging her.

– RUTH 1:1-18 –

✢ There are many life-changing events that come into our lives. List all the life-changing events you find in the above passage.

✢ How many of these events were the result of Naomi's choices?

✢ What is her response to these events?

✢ What do you learn about Naomi's daughters-in-law?

✢ What choices did they make?

✢ With whom do you identify?

FIND GOD'S WAYS FOR YOU

✢ What life-changing events have you experienced?

✢ Who helped you through these events?

✢ What kind of counsel did you receive?

Naomi and Ruth needed wisdom to make their decisions. Contrast worldly wisdom and godly wisdom from the following passage:

If you are wise and understand God's ways, live a life of steady goodness so that only good deeds will pour forth. And if you don't brag about the good you do, then you will be truly wise! But if you are bitterly jealous and there is selfish ambition in your hearts, don't brag about being wise. That is the worst kind of lie. For jealousy and selfishness are not God's kind of wisdom. Such things are earthly, unspiritual, and motivated by the Devil. For wherever there is jealousy and selfish ambition, there you will find disorder and every kind of evil.

But the wisdom that comes from heaven is first of all pure. It is also peace loving, gentle at all times, and willing to yield to others. It is full of mercy and good deeds. It shows no partiality and is always sincere. And those who are peacemakers will plant seeds of peace and reap a harvest of goodness.

– JAMES 3:13-18 –

STOP AND PONDER

✛ Based on your contrast of wisdom from the passage you have just read, which kind of wisdom do you seek? Which kind of wisdom do you impart to others?

PROVISIONS

SEEK GOD'S WORD FOR TRUTH

Read the following passage:

So the two of them continued on their journey. When they came to Bethlehem, the entire town was stirred by their arrival. "Is it really Naomi?" the women asked.

"Don't call me Naomi," she told them. "Instead, call me Mara, for the Almighty has made life very bitter for me. I went away full, but the Lord has brought me home empty.

Why should you call me Naomi when the Lord has caused me to suffer and the Almighty has sent such tragedy?"

So Naomi returned from Moab, accompanied by her daughter-in-law Ruth, the young Moabite woman. They arrived in Bethlehem at the beginning of the barley harvest.

– RUTH 1:19-22 –

✛ When Ruth and Naomi arrive in Bethlehem, how are they received?

✛ What is Naomi's attitude? Whom does she blame for her misfortunes?

Read the following passage:

Now there was a wealthy and influential man in Bethlehem named Boaz, who was a relative of Naomi's husband, Elimelech.

One day Ruth said to Naomi, "Let me go out into the fields to gather leftover grain behind anyone who will let me do it."

And Naomi said, "All right, my daughter, go ahead." So Ruth went out to gather grain behind the harvesters.

And as it happened, she found herself working in a field that belonged to Boaz, the relative of her father-in-law, Elimelech.

— RUTH 2:1-3 —

✣ Describe Ruth's plan to take care of her mother-in-law.

✣ Who owned the field where she worked? Who was he?

Read the following passage:

Boaz went over and said to Ruth, "Listen, my daughter. Stay right here with us when you gather grain; don't go to any other fields. Stay right behind the women working in my field. See which part of the field they are harvesting, and then follow them. I have warned the young men not to bother you. And when you are thirsty, help yourself to the water they have drawn from the well."

Ruth fell at his feet and thanked him warmly. "Why are you being so kind to me?" she asked. "I am only a foreigner."

"Yes, I know," Boaz replied. "But I also know about the love and kindness you have shown your mother-in-law since the death of your husband. I have heard how you left your father and mother and your own land to live here among complete strangers. May the Lord, the God of Israel, under whose wings you have come to take refuge, reward you fully."

"I hope I continue to please you, sir," she replied. "You have comforted me by speaking so kindly to me, even though I am not as worthy as your workers."

— RUTH 2:8-13 —

✣ What did the landowner offer her and why?

✣ What is Ruth's response?

FIND GOD'S WAYS FOR YOU

✢ When you are faced with life's misfortunes or even the everyday "calamities," how do you respond?

✢ Whom do you blame? Why?

✢ Do you identify with either Ruth or Naomi? Why?

Read the following verse:

Work with enthusiasm, as though you were working for the Lord rather than for people.

— EPHESIANS 6:7 —

✢ Ruth accepted the circumstances that had placed her in a humbling, subservient position. What does Ephesians 6:7 say about serving?

STOP AND PONDER

✢ Read Ephesians 6:7 again. What kind of servant are you?

REPUTATIONS

SEEK GOD'S WORD FOR TRUTH

Read the following passage:

Boaz arrived from Bethlehem and greeted the harvesters. "The Lord be with you!" he said.

"The Lord bless you!" the harvesters replied.

Then Boaz asked his foreman, "Who is that girl over there?"

And the foreman replied, "She is the young woman from Moab who came back with Naomi. She asked me this morning if she could gather grain behind the harvesters. She has been hard at work ever since, except for a few minutes' rest over there in the shelter."

At lunchtime Boaz called to her, "Come over here and help yourself to some of our food. You can dip your bread in the wine if you like." So she sat with his harvesters, and Boaz gave her food – more than she could eat.

When Ruth went back to work again, Boaz ordered his young men, "Let her gather grain right among the sheaves without stopping her. And pull out some heads of barley from the bundles and drop them on purpose for her. Let her pick them up, and don't give her a hard time!"

Ruth gathered barley there all day, and when she beat out the grain that evening, it came to about half a bushel. She carried it back into town and showed it to her mother-in-law. Ruth also gave her the food that was left over from her lunch.

"So much!" Naomi exclaimed. "Where did you gather all this grain today? Where did you work? May the Lord bless the one who helped you!" So Ruth told her mother-in-law about the man in whose field she had worked. And she said, "The man I worked with today is named Boaz."

"May the Lord bless him!" Naomi told her daughter-in-law. "He is showing his kindness to us as well as to your dead husband. That man is one of our closest relatives, one of our family redeemers."

Then Ruth said, "What's more, Boaz even told me to come back and stay with his harvesters until the entire harvest is completed."

– RUTH 2:4-7, 14-21 –

✛ In the previous lesson, we read that Boaz was "a wealthy and influential man." What evidence do you find in this passage to support that statement?

✛ What report did Boaz receive from his foreman regarding Ruth?

✛ What did Boaz offer Ruth and why?

✛ Why do you think Boaz gave special orders to his young men regarding Ruth?

✛ How did Naomi respond to Boaz's provision?

FIND GOD'S WAYS FOR YOU

✛ What does it mean to you to have character?

✛ Difficult situations in life reveal our real character. What kind of report could be given about you?

✝ What opportunities have you had to encourage people less fortunate than yourself? How have you treated them?

Read the following passage:

Dear brothers and sisters, what's the use of saying you have faith if you don't prove it by your actions? That kind of faith can't save anyone. Suppose you see a brother or sister who needs food or clothing, and you say, "Well, good-bye and God bless you; stay warm and eat well" – but then you don't give that person any food or clothing. What good does that do?

So you see, it isn't enough just to have faith. Faith that doesn't show itself by good deeds is no faith at all – it is dead and useless.

Now someone may argue, "Some people have faith; others have good deeds." I say, "I can't see your faith if you don't have good deeds, but I will show you my faith through my good deeds."

– James 2:14-18 –

✝ According to this passage, how important are your actions toward others in need?

STOP AND PONDER

"For I was hungry, and you fed me. I was thirsty, and you gave me a drink. I was a stranger, and you invited me into your home. I was naked, and you gave me clothing. I was sick, and you cared for me. I was in prison, and you visited me. And the King will tell them, 'I assure you, when you did it to one of the least of these my brothers and sisters, you were doing it to me!'"

– Matthew 25:35-36, 40 –

✝ What would the King have to say about you?

COLLABORATION

SEEK GOD'S WORD FOR TRUTH

Read the following passage:

One day Naomi said to Ruth, "My daughter, it's time that I found a permanent home for you, so that you will be provided for. Boaz is a close relative of ours, and he's been very kind by letting you gather grain with his workers. Tonight he will be winnowing barley at the threshing floor. Now do as I tell you – take a bath and put on perfume and dress in your nicest clothes. Then go to the threshing floor, but don't let Boaz see you until he has finished his meal. Be sure to notice where he lies down; then go and uncover his feet and lie down there. He will tell you what to do."

"I will do everything you say," Ruth replied. So she went down to the threshing floor that night and followed the instructions of her mother-in-law.

After Boaz had finished his meal and was in good spirits, he lay down beside the heap of grain and went to sleep. Then Ruth came quietly, uncovered his feet, and lay down. Around midnight, Boaz suddenly woke up and turned over. He was surprised to find a woman lying at his feet! "Who are you?" he demanded.

"I am your servant Ruth," she replied. "Spread the corner of your covering over me, for you are my family redeemer."

"The Lord bless you, my daughter!" Boaz exclaimed. "You are showing more family loyalty now than ever by not running after a younger man, whether rich or poor. Now don't worry about a thing, my daughter. I will do what is necessary, for everyone in town knows you are an honorable woman. But there is one problem. While it is true that I am one of your family redeemers, there is another man who is more closely related to you than I am. Stay here tonight, and in the morning I will talk to him. If he is willing to redeem you, then let him marry you. But if he is not willing, then as surely as the Lord lives, I will marry you! Now lie down here until morning."

So Ruth lay at Boaz's feet until the morning, but she got up before it was light enough for people to recognize each other. For Boaz said, "No one must know that a woman was here at the threshing floor." Boaz also said to her, "Bring your cloak and spread it out." He measured out six scoops of barley into the cloak and helped her put it on her back. Then Boaz returned to the town.

When Ruth went back to her mother-in-law, Naomi asked, "What happened, my daughter?"

Ruth told Naomi everything Boaz had done for her, and she added, "He gave me these six scoops of barley and said, 'Don't go back to your mother-in-law empty-handed.'

Then Naomi said to her, "Just be patient, my daughter, until we hear what happens. The man won't rest until he has followed through on this. He will settle it today."

– RUTH 3:1-18 –

✛ According to this passage, what is Naomi's concern for Ruth?

✛ Describe Naomi's plan.

✛ What evidence do you find that Ruth trusted the advice of her mother-in-law?

✛ What did Ruth ask of Boaz when he discovered her at his feet?

✛ What was Boaz's response, and what does he reaffirm about Ruth?

✛ What surprising information did Boaz tell Ruth, and what did he plan to do about it?

FIND GOD'S WAYS FOR YOU

✛ What concerns do you have for your loved ones?

✛ What plans have you tried to make for them? How did they turn out?

✛ How have you handled awkward situations with loved ones? What was their response?

✛ Share how you have carried out special promises.

STOP AND PONDER

Trust in the Lord with all your heart; do not depend on your own understanding. Seek his will in all you do, and he will direct your paths.

– PROVERBS 3:5-6 –

✛ Who directs you?

OBLIGATIONS

SEEK GOD'S WORD FOR TRUTH

Read the following passage:

So Boaz went to the town gate and took a seat there. When the family redeemer he had mentioned came by, Boaz called out to him, "Come over here, friend. I want to talk to you." So they sat down together. Then Boaz called ten leaders from the town and asked them to sit as witnesses. And Boaz said to the family redeemer, "You know Naomi, who came back from Moab. She is selling the land that belonged to our relative Elimelech. I felt that I should speak to you about it so that you can redeem it if you wish. If you want the land, then buy it here in the presence of these witnesses. But if you don't want it, let me know right away, because I am next in line to redeem it after you."

The man replied, "All right, I'll redeem it."

Then Boaz told him, "Of course, your purchase of the land from Naomi also requires that you marry Ruth, the Moabite widow. That way, she can have children who will carry on her husband's name and keep the land in the family."

"Then I can't redeem it," the family redeemer replied, "because this might endanger my own estate. You redeem the land; I cannot do it."

In those days it was the custom in Israel for anyone transferring a right of purchase to remove his sandal and hand it to the other party. This publicly validated the transaction. So the other family redeemer drew off his sandal as he said to Boaz, "You buy the land."

— RUTH 4:1-8 —

✢ According to this passage, where does Boaz go and what does he do?

✢ Initially, what does Boaz tell the next of kin? What is the relative's response?

✢ What information does Boaz withhold at first?

✢ What excuse does the relative offer for his change of mind?

✢ What does the relative finally tell Boaz?

✛ How was a transaction of this kind legalized?

FIND GOD'S WAY FOR YOU

✛ How do you go about making major decisions?

✛ From whom do you draw support and wise counsel?

✛ What excuses do you offer people when you don't want to do something?

✛ How would you speak the truth in love? Give an example.

STOP AND PONDER

Don't copy the behavior and customs of this world, but let God transform you into a new person by changing the way you think. Then you will know what God wants you to do, and you will know how good and pleasing and perfect his will really is.

– ROMANS 12:2 –

✛ Have you let God transform you?

CELEBRATIONS

SEEK GOD'S WORD FOR TRUTH

Read the following passage:

Then Boaz said to the leaders and to the crowd standing around, "You are witnesses that today I have bought from Naomi all the property of Elimelech, Kilion, and Mahlon. And with the land I have acquired Ruth, the Moabite widow of Mahlon, to be my wife. This way she can have a son to carry on the family name of her dead husband and to inherit the family property here in his hometown. You are all witnesses today."

Then the leaders and all the people standing there replied, "We are witnesses! May the Lord make the woman who is now coming into your home like Rachel and Leah, from whom all the nation of Israel descended!

May you be great in Ephrathah and famous in Bethlehem. And may the Lord give you descendants by this young woman who will be like those of our ancestor Perez, the son of Tamar and Judah."

So Boaz married Ruth and took her home to live with him. When he slept with her, the Lord enabled her to become pregnant, and she gave birth to a son. And the women of the town said to Naomi, "Praise the Lord who has given you a family redeemer today! May he be famous in Israel. May this child restore your youth and care for you in your old age. For he is the son of your daughter-in-law who loves you so much and who has been better to you than seven sons!"

Naomi took care of the baby and cared for him as if he were her own. The neighbor women said, "Now at last Naomi has a son again!" And they named him Obed. He became the father of Jesse and the grandfather of David.

This is their family line beginning with their ancestor Perez:

Perez was the father of Hezron.
Hezron was the father of Ram.
Ram was the father of Amminadab.
Amminadab was the father of Nahshon.
Nahshon was the father of Salmon.
Salmon was the father of Boaz.
Boaz was the father of Obed.
Obed was the father of Jesse.
Jesse was the father of David.

– RUTH 4:9-22 –

✛ Boaz is sitting with the elders, and the relative has declined any right to Naomi's property. What does Boaz announce to this assembly of elders?

✛ What further claim does he extend regarding Ruth?

✛ The elders respond by saying, "We are witnesses!" What is their blessing for Boaz?

✛ Finally, Ruth and Boaz marry. When they have a baby son, how do the townswomen react? How do they bless Naomi?

✛ Who would this new baby's grandson be?

FIND GOD'S WAYS FOR YOU

Read the following passage:

> *Then Jesus said, "Come to me, all of you who are weary and carry heavy burdens, and I will give you rest. Take my yoke upon you. Let me teach you, because I am humble and gentle, and you will find rest for your souls. For my yoke fits perfectly, and the burden I give you is light."*
>
> — MATTHEW 11:28-30 —

✛ Who has offered to give us rest from the burdens that weary us?

✛ A yoke is used to help oxen share a burden. What kind of yoke does Jesus offer?

✛ What is the weight of the burden Jesus will give us?

✛ What is the nature of Jesus' character?

STOP AND PONDER

> *Jesus told him, "I am the way, the truth, and the life. No one can come to the Father except through me."*
>
> — JOHN 14:6 —

✛ Are you yoked to Jesus? If not, what hinders you?

Unspoken

setting the scene

THE powerful and mighty King Saul of Israel was jealous of a shepherd boy. The reason was simple: The Lord God had anointed this young man, David, as His chosen king. And more than that, David held the hearts of the people in his hands. When David spoke, people inclined their ear. When he danced, maidens swooned. When he sang, the hearts of men, women, and children rose in praise to God.

And when David fled into the wilderness to escape Saul's murderous envy, hundreds of men followed him, camping with him in the caves of Adullam and En-gedi. Some were discontented men. Philistine raids had hounded others. Some were men overtaxed by a king in whom they had lost confidence. And scattered among the honorable men, who longed for the days when God was Israel's supreme Commander, were men of violence and vengeance, men who simply loved shedding blood and grasping plunder.

War ripped the nation into factions as the king's jealousy mounted against his imagined enemy. But David was ever submissive to the king's authority. Refusing to wrest the crown from Saul by violent means, David was content to wait for God to act on his behalf.

Meanwhile, the company who gathered around David swelled steadily, from two hundred to four hundred to six hundred. Among them were thirty mighty men, an elite group of warriors of proven valor and loyalty. David's courage and integrity rallied them, and they held together like a family, fiercely intent upon protecting its own against all enemies, be they the king of Israel who had turned his back on God or the armies of the idol-infested nations surrounding them.

These valiant fighting men did not come alone to fight for David. They brought their wives and sons and daughters with them.

Traveling among the growing throng of David's followers was a little girl named Bathsheba ...

one

PERCHED on her grandfather's knee, Bathsheba tore off a piece of bread and offered it to him. Laughing, Ahithophel ate it from her hand. "She's becoming more like your mother every day, Eliam."

Her father watched her with a faint frown. "It's hard to believe she's growing up so fast. Eight years old already. It won't be long before I'll have to find a husband for her."

"A mighty man to protect a pretty young maiden."

She looked across the fire at the man who appeared to her like an angel from heaven. Tugging on her grandfather's tunic, stretching up, she whispered her heart's desire, "I want to marry David."

He laughed out loud and looked across at the handsome young man sitting across the fire. "David, here is another who has set you upon a pedestal." Heat flooded into her cheeks as the man she idolized looked back at her grandfather with embarrassed tolerance. Her grandfather kissed her cheek. "Forget David, Bathsheba. He has three wives already, my sweet." As he looked into her eyes, his amusement faded. His expression softened. "Better to be the only wife of a poor man, than one woman among many in a king's harem."

"Come inside, Bathsheba!" Her mother beckoned. Her grandfather lifted her from his knee and set her firmly on her feet, sending her off with a light swat on her backside. When Bathsheba paused to look back at David, her mother caught her by the arm and yanked her inside the tent, flipping the flap down behind them. "It's time for bed." She followed Bathsheba and drew up the blanket as the girl lay down on her pallet. Kneeling, she leaned down and kissed Bathsheba. Troubled, she stroked the wisps of black hair back from Bathsheba's forehead. "Some dreams can only bring heartbreak."

"But I – "

Her mother put her fingertip over Bathsheba's lips. "Hush, child." She leaned back upon her heels and rose gracefully. "Go to sleep."

Bathsheba lay awake, listening to the men's voices rumbling quietly outside. Others had joined them. She recognized Joab's voice and that of his brother Abishai. Both were commanders of David's army, and they often came to talk war with her grandfather, who had earned David's respect for his shrewd tactical advice. He knew a great deal about the Philistines and Ammonites and their methods of battle. He also knew the land of Canaan as well as the lines in the palm of his own hand.

"Saul was in our hands, David," Joab said. "You should have killed him when you had the chance."

Joab's brother, Abishai, was quick to speak in agreement. "Yes, you need to kill Saul! God gave him to us in the Cave of the Wild Goats. I would have slit his throat for you."

"And I told you why I didn't want him killed," David said. "He is the man the Lord God anointed as king."

"He'll keep chasing you," Joab said. "He'll never stop until one of you is dead."

"It would be better for the nation if you took the crown from Saul now," another said, and Bathsheba heard the rumble of agreement among several other men sitting at her father's campfire.

"Strike the shepherd and the sheep will scatter," Joab insisted.

"What am I to do with you sons of Zeruiah?" David said harshly, and she knew his impatience was directed at Joab and Abishai. "How many times must I tell you I will not raise my hand against the Lord's anointed!"

She heard his footsteps moving away.

"I don't understand him," Joab said in frustration. "Speak sense to him, Ahithophel!"

"What would David have gained by murdering the king while he had turned his back to relieve himself?" Her grandfather spoke calmly in the face of the younger men's hot tempers. "When Saul heard David call to him from the cave, he knew David could have killed him – yet David allowed him to walk away with only his pride injured. Would a man who coveted his kingdom have done that? Of course not! Every man riding with Saul now knows David is in the right! And they know David was giving King Saul the chance to repent!"

"Repent! The fire in Saul's belly will be back soon enough, and we'll be on the run again. Should we spare a man who ordered the murder of eighty-five priests and their families at Nob?"

"Leave judgment to the Lord. David's course is a righteous one."

"You know as well as I that as long as there is breath in Saul's body, he will hunt David!"

"I know, too, that God will prevail, Joab. It will be by His efforts, not yours, that David will one day be king. The Lord is in command. Every day, more men join us. Why? Because they believe as we do: that God is with David wherever he goes. The Philistines, Ammonites, and Amalekites cannot defeat a man who has the Lord God of Israel as his shield."

"I want to see the crown on David's head!"

"So do we all, Joab. But let it happen in God's time and not before."

The men went on talking. Bathsheba's eyes were heavy with sleep. She dreamed of David dressed in royal robes, holding out his hand to her. Startled awake, she lay still, listening. Men were shouting in the distance. Probably another argument. She heard familiar voices outside, and rising to her knees, she peered between the stitches of the tent seam. David had returned and was sitting in the flickering firelight, talking with her father and grandfather.

"We'll join forces with the Philistines." David was saying. "When the fighting turns against Saul, we'll be in a position to turn the battle in his favor."

Her grandfather frowned in concentration. "How many do you plan to take?"

"All of them."

"Who will protect our women and children ... ?"

Bathsheba gazed at David, her head full of dreams. She loved the way he tilted his head as he listened intently to what her grandfather had to say. She studied every line of his face.

Men shouted again. Her mother moaned softly, rolling over on her pallet. Bathsheba looked out again. David had his head turned toward the disturbance. A muscle in his jaw clenched. "These men are too much for me to manage!"

Her grandfather sat with his hands clasped between his knees. "They are a flock of sheep in need of a strong shepherd."

"Sometimes they behave more like a pack of wolves!" He shook his head and rose. "I guess I should do something." Sighing, he walked away.

"I don't understand him," her father said, tossing a rock into the darkness. "Why is he always coming to Saul's rescue even when it could mean his own death?"

"Have you forgotten that Saul's son, Jonathan, is David's closest friend? And his first wife is Saul's daughter."

"Jonathan has chosen sides, Abba, and Michal is defiled. Saul gave her to another man. David lives in hope that everything will change back to the way it was before Saul went mad with jealousy. It'll never happen."

Her grandfather poked the fire. "Joab's advice is shrewd. Saul's death would put an end to this war and place David on the throne. But there would be no blessing for David if he kills the Lord's anointed. Ah, my son, David lives to please God. His passion is for the Lord." He looked up, his face aglow. "If every man among us had the heart David has, what a kingdom God would build for us!" Tossing the stick into the fire, he rose. "Come, let's stand with our friend and hear what the Lord has given him to say this time."

Bathsheba knew David wouldn't shout orders at the fighting men, nor interfere with their arguments. Instead he would simply sit near them and sing. She waited, and after a little while, she could hear the sound of his harp amidst the shouting – a soothing melody played quietly against angry, discordant voices. Already the angry voices were dying down. Pulling at the seams, Bathsheba tried to see more from within the narrow view of her father's tent. Her grandfather always said God gave David's words and music the power to lift hearts and minds from petty differences to God's majesty and the blessings He had poured upon His chosen people. She had heard David play and sing many times before, and she never tired of it.

Her mother was asleep. What harm if she snuck out and crept close enough to watch and listen? She slipped through the flaps and hastened toward the gathering, staying at the edge of firelight. Hunkering down, arms wrapped around her knees, she sat and listened. Her young heart trembled at the sight of David, his handsome face bronzed in the firelight. No one in the entire world could be as perfect as David, her beloved.

"O Lord, our Lord, the majesty of your name fills the earth!" his voice rang out in the night air. His words grew indistinct when he turned away. So she rose and crept closer. One by one, men sat and reclined, gazing up at David as they listened, captivated as he worshiped God more openly than any priest. David stopped in the midst of his men and lifted his head, singing a wordless melody that made her heart ache. Then lyrics came again to him.

"When I look at the night sky and see the work of your fingers – the moon and the stars you have set in place – what are mortals that you should think of us, mere humans that you should care for us?"

Everyone was silent now, waiting as David bowed his head and plucked the strings of his harp. The sound and words pierced her so deeply that Bathsheba felt he was plucking the strings of her heart. "For you made us only a little lower than God, and you crowned us with glory and honor.

You put us in charge of everything you made, giving us authority over all things – the sheep and the cattle and all the wild animals, the birds in the sky, the fish in the sea, and everything that swims the ocean currents." David shook his head in wonder and looked up at the stars again, his face rapt. "O Lord, our Lord, the majesty of your name fills the earth!" He played a few more chords on his harp and then lifted his hand slowly above his head, offering his words of praise to the God of all creation.

And the camp was quiet; so quiet, Bathsheba could hear her own heartbeat.

"Sing another psalm, David," her grandfather, Ahithophel, said.

Others joined in his appeal. "Sing to us of the Lord!"

Bathsheba rose and crept in among the gathering, slipping in next to her doting grandfather, seeking his warmth. "What're you doing up?" he whispered gruffly and put his arm around her, snuggling her close.

"I had to hear, and I was getting cold." Shivering, she looked up at him pleadingly. "Please, Grandpapa, just for a little while ... ?"

"You know I can't say no to you." He pulled his cloak around her. "One song."

David sang another psalm, one she had heard many times before. His handsome face glowed in the firelight and his words poured forth upon her thirsty soul. Unlike so many around her, David's heart wasn't turned toward war. He longed for peace. He appealed to God for help and mercy and deliverance from his enemies. What would it be like to live without fear of a pursuing king, of Philistines and Ammonites, of the raiding Amalekites? She looked at her father and saw his eyes were moist as he leaned forward, listening intently. How many times had she heard her papa say God would uphold their cause? God would hide them in the cleft of the rocks and inside the caves of En-gedi and Adullam. God would sustain them with food and water. God would give them victory against every enemy. Why? Because they were with David and David did nothing without inquiring of the Lord. David prayed his songs, and God listened.

David walked a few steps and stood for a moment with his head bowed. His eyes were closed. She watched his hands move gently over the strings, strumming softly and making her heart ache. He raised his head and looked from face to face. Would he look at her? Would he notice her sitting between her father and grandfather?

"The Lord is my shepherd; I have everything I need ..."

When his gaze fixed upon her, her heart leaped into her throat. She held her breath, staring back at him, but his gaze moved on, touching each person there as though they were all equally precious to him. She felt crushed beneath the pressure of her love for him, and dejected that he hardly noticed her among his throng of devoted followers.

You are my shepherd, David. You make me want something I can't even name. You lead us through the wilderness, but I'm not afraid, because you are with us. And I would do anything for you ...

Someone gripped her shoulder tightly, startling her. "Bathsheba!" her mother whispered angrily.

"So you've been caught again," her grandfather whispered, unfurling his cloak and lifting her from his lap. Scowling, her mother scooped her up and carried her away, setting her on her feet when they were halfway back to the family tent. "You're lucky I don't take a rod to you!" Lowering her eyes, Bathsheba followed her mother through the darkness. Her mother swished the flap back. "Get inside!" Once past the opening, her mother gave her a swat on her behind. "Since I can't trust you to stay where you belong, you'll sleep beside me until your father returns." Her mother drew her close. "You know better than to disobey."

Bathsheba sniffled. "I'm sorry, Mama. It's just that I love him."

Her mother sighed. "I know you do. We all love David."

"Not like I do. I'm going to marry him someday."

Her mother's arms tightened. "Oh, my sweet one. Every girl among us wishes for the same thing. You must listen to me, Bathsheba. What you hope for is impossible. It's the idle dream of a child."

"Why?"

"Because David is too far above you."

Her throat tightened. "He was a shepherd."

"He still is a shepherd, but not in the way you mean. You must understand. David is destined to be *king,* and as such he will marry the daughters of kings. You're only the daughter of one of his soldiers."

"Abba is a warrior, one of David's *best* warriors, and one of his *closest* friends. And Grandpapa ..."

"*Hush!* Remember he's still married to Saul's daughter, Michal, even though Saul gave her to someone else. And David is married to Ahinoam and Abigail."

"Abigail isn't the daughter of a king," Bathsheba said stubbornly.

"No, but Abigail kept David from committing a great sin. He was grateful for her wisdom. And she is very beautiful."

"Do you think I'll be beautiful someday, beautiful enough – "

"Someday, you'll be very beautiful, and wiser than you are right now, I hope. At the very least, wise enough to understand some things are not meant to be. Your father will find a good husband for you, and you'll forget you ever thought yourself in love with David."

Never! Never, never, never! Bathsheba blinked back tears and turned her head away.

"When you grow up, my love, you will understand the wisdom of worshiping God and not a man."

Bathsheba lay still until she heard the sound of her mother's deepened breathing. Then she eased out of her arms, crawled to the other side of the tent to peer into the night once more. Her father and grandfather had returned to the fire, and David had joined them once again. They spoke quietly of battle plans. Bathsheba closed her eyes and listened to the sound of David's voice. Content, she fell asleep.

When she awakened the next morning, Bathsheba found herself on her pallet, under her blanket. Her father snored beside her mother. Bathsheba rose quietly and left the tent. David would be up by now. He was always up before everyone else, and he always went off by himself to pray. She had seen him several times coming back from the stream, and she hurried toward it now. Her heartbeat quickened when she spotted David hunkered by a rippling pool, washing his face, arms, and hands. Her father and grandfather always did the same thing before they prayed.

Her footfall caused a soft cascade of pebbles to spill down the slope and David turned sharply, eyes intent, hand on the hilt of his sword. When he saw her, he relaxed.

"You're up early, Bathsheba. Aren't you a little far from camp?"

Her heart hammered as she came closer. "I came to get water."

"Then you have a problem, little one."

"What problem?"

He smiled. "You have no jug."

Heat surged into her cheeks. When he started to turn away, she spoke quickly before she lost all her courage. "Could we talk a while, David? I came all this way to see you."

He turned and looked at her. "You shouldn't be so far from camp. It's dangerous. Go on back to your tent where you belong."

"But ..."

"You know your mother wouldn't be happy you strayed so far. I don't think she'd be pleased if she had to come searching for you a second time."

Crushed by his reprimand, Bathsheba bolted up the slope, ducked behind some rocks, and sat down heavily. Trembling, she put her cold palms against her burning cheeks. Then she took a breath and peered out from her hiding place. David was still standing by the stream, his hands now on his hips. "Go home before you're missed! And don't leave the camp again!"

Sucking in a sob, Bathsheba clambered up and ran all the rest of the way back to her father's tent, thankful no one was awake to see her tears – or ask the cause of them.

⊱⊰⊱⊰

Word came that the Philistines were going out against Saul. Bathsheba's grandfather and father laid out their armor and weapons. Bathsheba helped her mother prepare parched grain and raisin cakes for them to take with them. Her mother was silent, as she always was before the men left. So, too, was Bathsheba as she listened to them talk.

"We go tomorrow and join the ranks of Philistines," her grandfather said. Bathsheba remembered the plan she had overheard David talking about. His men would only be pretending to help the Philistines. Really they were waiting for a chance to help King Saul defeat this enemy army.

"Surely they'll suspect David's offer as pretense," her father said tightly. "It's only through God's mercy we haven't been caught raiding the Geshurite and Amalekite villages these past years."

"We've timed our raids carefully and left no survivors."

"Rumors spread ..."

"David wants to be in a position to help Saul. If the Philistines reject our offer of aid, there'll be nothing we can do."

"Saul's fate is in God's hands already, and I don't like leaving our women and children on their own."

As the sun rose the next morning, Bathsheba watched her father and grandfather leave camp with David. As soon as they were out of sight, her mother went inside the tent and wept. She was quickly herself again. She sat in the shade of the tent carding wool and sent Bathsheba off with the sheep.

The day after the men had left, Bathsheba was bringing water up from the stream when she heard yelling and screaming. Dropping the skin, she ran up the bank. Amalekite raiders were charging into the camp while women fled in a dozen directions, grabbing up their children as they ran.

Defenseless, they were quickly rounded up like a scattered flock.

When Bathsheba saw a man knock her mother to the ground and try to tie a rope around her flailing hands, she shrieked and ran at him in a fury. Jumping on his back, she clawed his forehead and yanked his hair. "Let her go! Let my mother go!"

With an angry shout, the man caught hold of her hair and hurled her over his shoulder. She hit the ground hard. Gasping for breath, she made it to her hands and knees, but someone looped a rope around her neck. Rolling over, she grabbed it and kicked the man. He uttered a harsh groan and bent over, his face going white while one of his company called out a laughing insult. "Is that little flea too much to handle?"

Enraged, the Amalekite gave the rope a hard yank. As she choked, he dragged her up by her arm and shook her violently. "Fight me and I'll drag you to your death!" He sent her flying into the line of women and children.

Sobbing, her mother quickly loosened the rope and clasped her close. "Bathsheba! Oh, Bathsheba!"

Bathsheba coughed violently and wretched and dragged in a full, painful breath. "David will ..." Her mother clapped a hand over her mouth and shushed her. She'd never seen terror in her mother's face before this day.

The Amalekite guard turned on her. "*No talking!*"

The women and older children were tied and led away. Younger children were carried. The band of raiders and captives walked for hours, the midday heat boring down hard upon the women and children, who were given only enough water to keep them going. They stopped as the sun was setting. Most of the women collapsed, too tired even to whimper. Each captive was given a handful of parched grain.

Bathsheba ate ravenously, but her stomach still ached with hunger. Her neck was bruised and burned from the rope. Her throat hurt from the hard yank she'd received early that day. Her feet were raw from walking across dusty, rocky ground. Her body ached all over. When she began to cry her mother pulled her close and shared her body warmth as the moon and stars appeared and the temperature plummeted.

"I'm afraid, Mother." Bathsheba cried softly.

Her mother stroked her hair back from her sunburned face. "It does no good to cry. We need to save our strength for whatever lies ahead."

"David will come looking for us, won't he?"

"We will pray he and your father return quickly." She held Bathsheba tighter. Bathsheba felt her mother trembling, and asked no more questions. "Pray, my daughter. Pray hard." And Bathsheba did. *David, oh,*

David, come and find us. Come and save us!

The Amalekites kept the women on the move, hastening them toward a future of slavery, prostitution, and death. Exhausted, the women and children collapsed each night, too bone-weary to cause their captors trouble of any kind. After the first two nights, they were left unbound while the men sat around the campfire, drinking and laughing. No guards watched over them. There was no need after so many miles of travel. When the sun rose and set on the third day, hope waned.

≈≈≈

Bathsheba awakened abruptly to the sound of battle cries. The air around her reverberated with shouts and screams. Confused and terrified, she tried to rise, but her mother grabbed her. "Stay down!" She pulled her back and down as a nearby Amalekite grabbed for his sword. He fell back with a scream, his arm severed, and then his head as well. Horrified, Bathsheba looked up at the warrior who jumped across the lifeless body. Her father's friend, Uriah! Shouting his battle cry, he charged on. If Uriah was here, surely, her father was also, and her grandfather.

"Abba!" Bathsheba screamed. "*Abba!*"

The Amalekites fell back and tried to run, but they were cut down without mercy by avenging fathers, husbands, and brothers. Bathsheba saw Ittai the Gittite, hack, from shoulder to sternum, the guard who had choked her. The roar of battle was terrifying. Israelites cried out in wrath, Amalekites screamed in terror. The crash of swords and thunder of men's feet were all around her as she cowered against her mother.

And then it was over. As quickly as it started, it had ended, and the silence was a shock. The bloodied bodies of the Amalekite raiders lay sprawled around the camp while the men standing were no less terrifying in their stained garments, their hands and arms and weapons splashed with red.

Bathsheba heard David call out. "Ahinoam! Abigail!" Other men cried out names as well, searching for their wives and children. "Here! I'm here!" women cried out. All was still in confusion.

"Eliam!" Her mother let go of her and ran into her father's arms, sobbing against his chest.

"Bathsheba," he said raggedly and held out his arm, but she couldn't move at the sight of him covered in blood. His eyes were so fierce he looked like a stranger. "Come, daughter," he said more gently, still breathing hard.

"Come to me. I won't hurt you." Trembling violently, she looked away and saw the carnage around her.

Her grandfather was there suddenly, catching her up in his arms, holding her close. "You are safe, my little flower." Over his shoulder, Bathsheba saw David speaking with Ahinoam and Abigail. She lost sight of him again when her grandfather put her back on her feet, his hand firmly upon her shoulder, keeping her against his side. "War is always worse for the children," he said gruffly.

"I didn't think you'd be able to find us," her mother said, her arms still around Bathsheba's father. "Oh, Eliam, you would've been proud of your daughter." She told him everything from the day the Amalekites had raided the camp.

Bathsheba closed her eyes, but even then she couldn't block out the picture of the slaughter around her. She was cold and couldn't stop shaking. She understood now why her mother cried every time her father left camp with David.

"The Philistines turned us away," her father said. "If they hadn't, we might not have been able to track you so quickly."

Her mother frowned. "Saul?"

"He's outnumbered."

"What will David do?"

"The only thing he can do. Nothing."

On the way back to camp, some of the men argued over the share of spoils they'd taken from the Amalekite camp. They were not willing to share with those who had been too tired to cross the river. David commanded that the spoils be divided equally among all the men, with gifts to be sent to the elders of Israel's cities.

And so it was done, but not without grumbling.

An Amalekite came into David's camp, bearing news of Israel's defeat. Bathsheba was listening when he told David that Saul and his son Jonathan had been killed by the Philistines at Mount Gilboa. Their bodies were hanging on the wall of Beth-shan, while Saul's weapons had been placed in the temple of Ashtoreth. When the messenger stepped forward and stretched out his arms, murmurs issued from David's men who stood by watching. The Amalekite smiled broadly, triumphant, as he offered David Saul's crown.

David looked at it and began to shake with rage. Bathsheba wondered why he was so angry. David took the proffered crown. "How do you know that Saul and Jonathan are dead?" he demanded.

The man's eyes flickered. Perhaps the Amalekite sensed something ominous in David's tone. "I happened to be on Mount Gilboa," he answered. "I saw Saul there leaning on his spear with the enemy chariots closing in on him. When he turned and saw me, he cried out for me to come to him. 'How can I help?' I asked him. And he said to me, 'Who are you?' I replied, 'I am an Amalekite.' Then he begged me, 'Come over here and put me out of my misery, for I am in terrible pain and want to die.' So I killed him," the Amalekite told David, "for I knew he couldn't live. Then I took his crown and one of his bracelets so I could bring them to you, my lord."

Even from her vantage point, Bathsheba could see the blood drain from David's face. "Were you not afraid to kill the Lord's anointed one?" he cried. As the man shifted his weight, David said to one of his men, "Kill him!" And the man thrust his sword into the Amalekite.

"You die self-condemned!" David spoke into the impaled man's face. "For you yourself confessed that you killed the Lord's anointed one." He yanked the sword from the Amalekite and watched him crumple to the ground.

David must have felt the eyes of all upon him, for he looked around at the silent men, women and children staring at what he'd done. Bathsheba longed to understand, to share his grief. His emotions burst forth and he cried out, "Your pride and joy, O Israel, lies dead on the hills! How the mighty heroes have fallen! O King Saul!" He sobbed, dropping the sword and holding his head. "Oh, Jonathan! Jonathan, my brother!"

David's grief infected the entire camp as everyone mourned the death of King Saul and David's best friend, Jonathan. David sang songs of tribute to them, reminding the people of the good days when Saul had loved the Lord and served Him.

And when the period of mourning came to an end, he obeyed the Lord and moved his army to Hebron.

≈≈≈

It was at Hebron that Bathsheba watched David marry Maacah. Through the years she watched him marry Haggith, Abital, and Eglah, and with each wedding, she heard he made important alliances. He needed allies, for despite Saul's death, the house of Saul continued to wage war upon David. "He has an eye for beautiful women," she heard her grandfather say. Amnon was born to Ahinoam, Chileab to Abigail, Absalom to Maacah.

Messengers came from Abner, commander of the army of Saul's son Ishbosheth, proposing an alliance. Bathsheba's grandfather advised David to be cautious and test Abner's sincerity and strength. So David sent word he would not agree to anything unless his first wife, Saul's daughter, Michal, was returned to him.

"He must love her very much," Bathsheba said. She still could not look at David without feeling a quickening inside her, but she was more clear-sighted now than she had been as a small child. She no longer clung so tenaciously to her fantasies of marrying the man of her dreams.

Her mother shook her head. "Love has nothing to do with it. What rightfully belonged to David must be restored. He will take Michal into his house, but she will never have children."

"All of his other wives have had children. She will also."

"Your grandfather will advise against it. She's been defiled by adultery. King Saul gave her to another man years ago, when you were just a baby. Besides that, should David beget a child by her and build the house of Saul? May it never be! David will listen to your grandfather. He will provide for Michal and protect her, but he will never touch her again."

Bathsheba felt pity for Michal. "It would have been kinder to leave her with the other man." And David would have one less wife, one less beautiful woman in his household.

"Perhaps," her mother said quietly. "I heard that the man followed her for miles, weeping and wailing. Abner had to order him away. But David is a king, Bathsheba. He is not an ordinary man."

"No one could ever have called David ordinary, even before he was king."

Her mother looked at her solemnly. Bathsheba smiled. "Don't worry, Mother. I know I am only the daughter of a humble warrior." Something flickered in her mother's eyes. Bathsheba turned away. "If David will never have children with Michal, why is it so important she be returned to him?"

"He must prove himself strong. A king who cannot keep possession of the women who belong to him cannot hold a kingdom together."

Bathsheba knew he was strong enough. What strength he lacked God would provide. She looked toward David's tent. "Do you think she loves him?"

"She did once. She even saved his life. But that was years ago. I don't think he loves her anymore. I don't think he's ever given his heart to any woman, not completely."

"Oh, my dear." Her mother sighed heavily. "It is wiser for a woman to fall in love with a poor man who can only afford one wife." Bathsheba's throat closed hot and she blinked back tears as her mother rose and came to her, turning her around and tipping her chin up. "You became a woman a month ago. I spoke with your father and he says someone has already spoken to him regarding you."

Bathsheba's heart pounded with trepidation. "Who?"

Her mother smiled. "A good man. A strong one."

"Who is it?"

"I won't say until it's settled, but if it comes to be, you will have a husband you can respect."

"Respect, but not love."

"In time, love, too. If you allow it."

Bathsheba's father and grandfather accepted the bride price from Uriah the Hittite, and all, in their minds, was settled. Her mother, in an effort to encourage her, explained their many reasons for choosing him. Uriah had saved her father once in battle; Uriah was counted among David's thirty mighty men; Uriah had proven himself valorous and dependable in hard times. Ahithophel had seen Uriah charge into the hottest battle without fear in order to defend David. He was admired and respected by all, and the friend of the king. Such a man would be able to protect her and provide for her and the children she would give him.

"He's a courageous man, Bathsheba, and he's loyal. He's been wise with his possessions. Unlike others, Uriah hasn't squandered the spoils he gathered in battles against the Philistines and Amalekites."

"But he's so much older than I am!"

Her mother looked her in the eyes. "He's a year younger than David."

Bathsheba sat heavily, covered her face, and wept in defeat. She was a woman, albeit a young one, and had no say in the matter. The decision of whom she would marry had never been hers, and she'd always known in her heart that David was as far beyond her reach as a star in the heavens. She was nothing but a foolish earthbound child clinging to her dreams, but, oh, how it hurt to have them wrenched from her. Years ago, David had been chosen by God and anointed by Samuel to one day be king of Israel. Who was she to think she was worthy to be his wife – or even his concubine? What wretched misery to fall in love with a man who was a king!

"If only he'd been an ordinary shepherd ..."

Her mother stamped her foot. *"Enough of this foolishness! Enough dreaming!* I will not have my daughter act like a selfish child! You should thank God David is more than a shepherd! Where would our people be if he'd never left the pastures and his father's flocks? Even if you were the daughter of a king and worthy to marry him, what then? Could you bear to watch him take more wives and concubines? A king must build a strong house and preserve the kingdom. You would have to put your own desires aside for the sake of a nation that depends upon him."

Her mother grasped her shoulders tightly. "Your father has chosen a fine man for you. Uriah is good and decent, and you will be his *only* wife. David has never so much as glanced at you, Bathsheba, but Uriah looks upon you as though you were a pearl of great price. You will be his most prized possession."

Bathsheba felt ashamed. "I have nothing against Uriah, Mother. It's only that I ... " Tears streamed down her face. She knew it was useless to say another word. Could she change the inevitable?

Her mother let go of her abruptly and moved away. "No one expects you to love Uriah right away, Bathsheba. In time, you will. If you give him a chance." She turned and looked at her. "But for now, you *will* show Uriah the respect and obedience he deserves as your husband. If you don't, I will take a whip to you myself!"

Bathsheba raised her chin. "I will marry Uriah, Mother, and I will show him the respect and obedience he deserves. But love cannot be commanded."

For as long as she could remember, her heart and soul had belonged to David. And she knew that would never change, no matter what others demanded of her.

~~~

Bathsheba never expected David to come to her wedding. When she saw him through the colored gauze of her veils, she almost wept at the pain, knowing he had come not to see her become a wife, but to honor his friend, her husband.

Uriah was dressed like a king for the ceremony. Even then, her husband paled in comparison to her true sovereign lord, who wore a simple tunic and leather girdle. David outshone every man at the ceremony! And even though he placed a groom's crown upon Uriah's head, there could be no comparison between them. There was a nobility about David that proclaimed his place among men. No one was more handsome and graceful. No one could surpass his gifts of music and dance. No one held a position of greater power, nor had a more humble, tender heart. David asked for no special treatment, but everyone deferred to him out of love and respect. God had blessed David in every way.

The wedding feast proceeded with Bathsheba in a haze. She was relieved when Uriah left her side to greet David. They laughed together and shared a goblet of wine while she sat on the dais and watched. It was David who drew her husband back to her side. It was David who took up a pitcher and replenished Uriah's cup and then filled hers. She brushed his fingers with her own as she took the goblet, sensing his surprise. Did he think she was bold?

"May the Lord bless your house with many children, Uriah," David said grandly, and in a voice loud enough to carry. He raised his cup high. She raised her eyes and looked into his, and for an infinitesimal moment, she felt something change between them. Heat spread over her skin. "And," he continued, "may all your sons and daughters look like your wife and not like you." He looked into her eyes as he sipped, his own strangely dark and perplexed.

The men around them laughed, Uriah loudest of all. David blinked and then laughed as well, slapping Uriah on the back and saying something to him that was lost in the din surrounding her. Uriah nodded and looked at her proudly, his eyes glowing. David's eyes met hers again, and her stomach fluttered strangely. The moment was both enticing and terrifying. When Uriah looked at her, she felt nothing. But David's look made her cheeks burn and her heart hammer. She lowered her eyes, startled by the powerful feelings surging inside her. She glanced around cautiously, wondering if anyone had noticed the effect David had upon her. She was trembling. Afraid, she looked at her mother, but she was dancing and laughing with the other women, and her father and grandfather were drinking with the men.

Turning her head shyly, she encountered David's stare. It shook her deeply, for she instinctively understood its meaning. Exaltation was overwhelmed by despair.

Why does he look at me as a woman now, when it's too late? Why couldn't he have noticed me a new moon ago?

Uriah came and sat with her upon the dais. He took her hand and kissed it, his eyes bright from admiration and too much wine. "I am blessed among men," he said thickly. "There is not a man here, including our king, who does not envy me such a beautiful young wife."

She smiled back tremulously, embarrassed by his impassioned compliment.

The wedding feast wore on until she was emotionally exhausted. She forced a smile until her cheeks ached. She pretended to be happy, pretended she wasn't drowning in a sea of sorrow. Twice more, David looked at her. And twice, she looked back at him, fighting against the tears. He always looked away quickly as though caught doing something that made him ashamed. And that made her suffer all the more.

Oh, David, David, what a wretched woman I am. I love you! I'll always love you the same way I have since I was a little girl. Do you remember how I followed you to the stream of En-gedi and watched you pray? I was just a child, but love caught me and held me tight in its grip. Nothing can kill it. And now I'm married to a man I can never love because I gave my heart to you years ago!

When he rose and left, she was almost relieved.

※※※

Uriah was a man hardened by years of fighting the Philistines, Amalekites, and King Saul, but Bathsheba found him surprisingly kind as well. "I don't know anything about women, Bathsheba. I've spent my entire life training for battle and fighting alongside David. And that won't change. My allegiance will always be to David first, for he is God's anointed. But I promise I will take care of you. And if anything should happen to me, you will have enough so that you will always have a roof over your head and food to eat." His hands were callused from using his sword, and he shook when he touched her. "Please don't cry."

She wept because Uriah deserved to be loved and she had no love left to give him.

※※※

As the months passed, Bathsheba gave up her dreams and fulfilled her duties to her husband. She carried water from the well. She washed, cooked, cleaned, and carded wool. She wove cloth and made garments for her husband. She did everything she knew how to make her husband's life comfortable and pleasant. And though she did come to respect him, she could not *will* herself to fall in love with him.

Uriah spent most of his time with the other mighty men, training David's army, sparring, talking, and planning late into the night. Sometimes he brought soldiers home with him. He told her to keep her face covered so the men wouldn't stare when she served them. He told her to cover her face when she left the house. "There are rough men among David's army, men who have no respect for women."

"I've known such men all my life, Uriah. No one has ever bothered me before."

"Before, you were a child, Bathsheba. Now, you're a beautiful young woman. And you are my wife. Obey me." He tipped her chin and looked into her eyes. "It is always wise to avoid trouble."

Uriah and the other mighty men talked freely while they ate and drank, and by listening Bathsheba learned much of what was going on in Canaan. She knew within hours that Joab, David's commander, had murdered a man in vengeance. She heard how furious David was, and how he mourned the murdered man. She was among the people when David condemned Joab's actions as evil. She was afraid for David because Joab was a powerful man, and a proud one as well. Why would David retain Joab as commander over his army?

Nothing came of David's reproach, but soon more news changed the course of Bathsheba's life. Ishbosheth, son of Saul and heir to the throne of Israel, was murdered. The men who came with news of the assassination thought David would be pleased to have his rival removed. Now the way was clear for David to assume his rightful place as king over all of Israel! They even brought the head of Ishbosheth with them to prove their foul deed. Rather than rewarding them, though, David had them executed. He ordered their hands and feet cut off and their bodies hung up beside the pool of Hebron.

Many of the men Uriah brought home were violent, more comfortable in war than in peace. Her house was constantly filled with stories of intrigue surrounding David. Why was there such cruelty in the world? And if David were ever crowned king over all Israel, would there be those who would try to assassinate him, just like Saul and Ishbosheth before him?

Often, she would remember her mother's words: *The life of a king is never easy ... Better to love a poor man ...* It was not easy to be the wife of a warrior either, for she never knew from one battle to the next whether she would be left a childless widow. "I live in fear every day, wondering if I'll lose your father," her mother admitted when they talked at the community well.

What would happen to Uriah's household if he died now? Bathsheba had no children, but not for want of trying. She wondered if her husband was disappointed in her, but if he was, she saw no sign of it. Two years had come and gone since their wedding feast, and he still treated her with kindness.

All the tribes of Israel gathered at Hebron, appearing before David and declaring that he was God's anointed. "We are all members of your family," the high priest said to him before the people. "For a long time, even while Saul was our king, you were the one who really led Israel. And the Lord has told you, 'You will be the shepherd of my people Israel. You will be their leader.'"

Bathsheba's heart swelled with pride as she stood among the crowd and watched David make a covenant with the people and be anointed King of Israel. He was only thirty years old, and yet the elders of all the tribes bowed down before him. And Uriah stood nearby, one of David's bodyguards and closest friends, raising his hands to heaven and shouting in exaltation.

And then David went to war again, Uriah at his side.

⋙⋙⋙

Bathsheba waited with the other wives to receive word about the battle for Zion, and when it came, she cried out in joy with all the rest.

"They've taken Jerusalem!"

But neither David nor Uriah came home to Hebron. Instead, they sent a contingent of warriors to bring the families to the newly conquered mountain stronghold. Building commenced all around the City of David, strengthening Zion for defense. Walls were built. Hiram, king of Tyre, sent cedar trees and carpenters and stonemasons to build a house for David. And Uriah chose a stone house near the site of the the king's palace.

Still, peace was elusive. The Philistines gathered against David, spreading out across the valley of Rephaim. And once again, Uriah was called away to war. Bathsheba cried this time, for she had come to care very deeply for him.

"Don't fear for me. The Lord is on our side!" was his parting exhortation. His words were of no comfort to her. She had no son to carry on Uriah's name or to take care of her when she was old.

Word returned that the Philistines were defeated at Baal-perazim. When Uriah came home with an idol, Bathsheba protested. It was the first time in their marriage that she dared argue with her husband. But she knew how detestable idols were to the Lord God. "Would it please God to know you have set that loathsome thing in our house?"

"It means nothing. Everyone carried something from the field of battle. It's a memento of our triumph. Nothing more."

"David wouldn't bring something unclean into *his* house. You should've destroyed it!"

His eyes darkened with the fierce pride of a victorious warrior. "Don't tell me what I should've done! What are you afraid of, woman? It's nothing but clay. Did it save the man who owned it?"

"It's a thing of evil, Uriah!"

He tossed his armor aside and glared at her. "Do you think I don't know there is only one God? It's the Lord who has given David victory on every side! And you'll leave that idol where it stands as a reminder of a battle *I* fought alongside my king, the battle *I* helped win!"

Ashamed of having spoken out so forcefully, Bathsheba said no more.

The Philistines regrouped, and again, Uriah was called away to war. The Philistines were like a plague that lingered. The Lord gave David victory again, and the Philistines were struck down from Geba as far as Gezer. But Bathsheba knew it would never be over. Men's hearts seemed bent upon war. Uriah's most of all.

Uriah didn't return home. It was her mother who told her that her father and Uriah had gone with David to Baalah of Judah to bring the Ark of God back to Jerusalem. Bathsheba ran down the road with the other women and wept in relief when they returned. Her joy was quickly dampened by their manner, for the Ark was not with them. David looked neither to the right nor the left, as he rode by on his mule. His face was dust-covered and tense. When she spotted Uriah, Bathsheba kept pace with him along the road. An air of defeat hung over them. David gave orders to disperse the men and went up to his house and his wives.

Uriah came to her then. She'd never seen him so tired. She lowered her shawl from her face and searched his eyes. "What's happened, Uriah?"

"David's afraid to bring the Ark to Jerusalem."

"David's never been afraid of anything."

His jaw clenched. He took her arm and turned her toward home. "He's afraid of God. We all are. Uzzah, the priest's son, is dead. He laid hands on the Ark when the cattle stumbled and the Lord struck him down. I've never seen a man die so fast." His hand loosened. "He went down as though hit by a thunderbolt."

"Where's the Ark now?"

"At the house of Obed-edom of Gath, where it will stay until the Lord tells David otherwise."

With Uriah home, the house became a gathering place again as soldiers came often to pass time with Bathsheba's husband. Sometimes they lingered late into the night. They could talk of little else but the continuing reports of how God was blessing the household of Obed-edom. After three months of such tidings, David summoned his mighty men and went down for the Ark. Uriah was among them.

From a great distance came the sound of trumpets and shouting, announcing their return. Women swept out into the street and ran to meet the procession. Jubilant, Bathsheba raced down the mountain road with them. Sunlight shone off the Ark and she thrilled at the sight of it. Each time the men who were carrying it had gone six steps, they stopped and waited so David could sacrifice an ox and a fattened calf. Trumpets sounded. And David danced with all his might. Men, women and children sang and wept. Stripping off his outer garment, David continued leading the procession, dancing in his tunic. The people caught his zeal for the Lord. Men sang out praise after praise to God as women joined David in dancing.

The hard years were over at last. God had protected David and given him victory on every side! God had made him king over all Israel! The nations could not stand against him because God was on his side! The Lord had strengthened him and built an army of mighty men around him, and now the Ark would rest upon the mountain where Abraham had once been ready to sacrifice his only son, Isaac, to God!

Bathsheba's racing blood sang with joy. She could not stand still and watch. If she didn't cry out in praise and dance, she would go mad. Laughing and weeping, she tore away her shawl, lifting it high like a canopy over her head as she twirled, dipped, twisted and was caught up in the ecstasy of the moment.

Peace would reign at last! No enemy could defeat them.

Yet, crouched at the door was a greater enemy than those who camped around Israel. And a greater battle was coming, one that could tear a nation to pieces. The battle would not take place in the mountains, valleys, or plains of Israel. It would take place in the wilderness of the human heart.

two

"HANUN did *what?*"

David leaned forward, scarcely able to believe the news he was hearing. He'd sent ambassadors to show respect for Nahash, the old king who'd allowed his father and mother to live among the Ammonites during the years King Saul had pursued him. He'd intended to make clear to Hanun, Nahash's son, that he had no intentions of invading. Yet now, he learned his ambassadors had been insulted. Far worse, they'd been humiliated!

The dust-covered, sweating young messenger stepped closer and repeated his news in an embarrassed whisper. "King Hanun accused your ambassadors of being spies, Sire!" He grimaced as he rasped, "He had half their beards shaved off and their tunics cut to their buttocks. While his entire court laughed, he ordered them out of his palace!"

David shot to his feet, and the men clustered in small groups around the court, fell silent an instant before the room buzzed with whispered questions and speculations.

Joab had watched the exchange between David and the messenger with narrowed eyes while Ahithophel and Eliam left their companions and strode across the room.

"Quiet!" Ahithophel shouted above the din. "The king speaks!"

David wished he hadn't shown his anger. He should have left the room with the messenger and heard the news in private. Then he could have heard everything and thought over what course he would take before the men knew what had happened.

Joab's face was rigid. David knew he was ready to go to war, hungry for battle. Looking around the court, David saw they all were. Often he despaired at being around such violent men. Yet, what right had he to grumble to God, when his own blood was hot and crying out for revenge against Hanun?

The fool! Did he think he could insult Israel with impunity? Did he think there would be no repercussions? David would not ignore what had been done to his men. He couldn't afford to ignore Hanun's foolishness and risk losing the respect of his men. Worse, the nations around them would hear of any leniency shown and take it for weakness instead.

If David didn't act soon, the Ammonites would think Israel was ripe for invasion. He didn't need to ask Ahithophel for advice. He knew what he had to do: teach this arrogant Ammonite king a lesson so that no one else would dare insult or attack Israel!

They will know there is a God in Israel!

He'd just defeated the Philistines, he'd crushed Moab and the Arameans under King Hadadezer, and he'd established garrisons in Edom to maintain control of the land. And now, Hanun threw oil on a banked fire. Hanun would burn in the blaze he set!

How long, oh, Lord, how long must I be at war? How long will I have to raise my sword in battle before the nations know there is a God in Israel? I long for peace! I would rather spend my life writing psalms and singing praise to You, my Lord and King, than leading these men of violence into war again. They are too much for me to manage! I'm tired. When will I have rest?

"David," Ahithophel said quietly.

Gritting his teeth, David shut his eyes, struggling for control over his rage and frustration. He knew what his men wanted: war! How they loved battle! How they delighted in shedding blood! Joab and Abishai were like wild donkeys, kicking and fighting the restraints of peace. And many of his mighty men were as bent upon violence as they. They stood restless, discontented with peaceful pursuits, eager to go out into battle where they could unleash their passions. They sought any excuse, and now Hanun had given just cause!

Oh, Lord, how I yearn for the days of my youth!

He wanted to weep as he remembered the freedom of tending his father's flocks. In those days, he had spent countless hours meditating on God's precepts and the Law. He'd walked over pasturelands by day and gazed at the stars by night, experiencing God in everything around him. No one had interfered with his thoughts. No one had distracted him from his praise. Hour after hour, he delighted in the Lord and felt the presence of God all around him.

Now, burdened with responsibilities, he had to struggle to find time alone. He ached to write psalms for God and set them to the music of his harp. He longed for the days when he'd been no more than a shepherd over his father's flock, responsible merely for finding food and water for his sheep and protecting them from predators. Now, he found himself surrounded by predatory men!

Bowing his head, he gripped the back of his neck. *O Lord! Will there ever be an end to war? I am so tired of living among people who hate peace!*

"Sire," Ahithophel said, stepping closer.

David raised his head. He felt bone-weary and depressed. Every decision he made cost human blood. And yet, what other choice had he? He was the king!

"We're going to war again, Ahithophel." He saw the man's dark eyes catch fire. "Come into the inner chamber and we'll discuss it." David motioned to the messenger to accompany him. "Joab, Abishai. Both of you as well!" He saw the eagerness in them.

He drew the dusty messenger close. "Rest tonight and then go back. Tell my ambassadors to sojourn in Jericho until their beards grow back."

He was going to make Hanun regret he'd ever laid eyes on them.

≈≈≈

King Hanun hired Aramean mercenaries to come to his aid, and David went out against them, defeating them and moving on the Ammonites without mercy. They fell by the thousands, and the following spring, David gave Joab orders to lay siege to Hanun's city, Rabbah.

Bathsheba stood with her mother at the city gates as the men mustered yet again. David remained astride his mule as he spoke to his commanders and captains. Uriah stood among them, and she felt pride in her husband's position. The thirty mighty men dispersed and returned to their units.

Every time the Ark was carried out of the city and into battle, Bathsheba felt strangely vulnerable. She knew that God could not be put into a box, and yet the Ark represented His presence among the people. And God's presence was going with the army.

Her mother wept when Bathsheba's father marched by. "Each time he leaves, I wonder if I'll ever see him again," she said through her tears. All the women were solemn as fathers, brothers, and husbands went off to war.

Bathsheba wept as well. Uriah had given her a home of her own on the street beside the palace, although the palace itself was where he spent most of his time. Sometimes Uriah surprised her with gifts of jewelry to show he loved her. She was proud of the respect he commanded, even more proud that he had earned the respect of her father and grandfather. Many men were courageous in battle, but few had the integrity of her husband. Uriah was a man of his word and a favorite among the king's captains, many of whom had spent an evening in her home, eating a meal she had prepared while she sat in her private chamber with her maid.

If only she loved him ... If only she could feel more for him than just affection and respect.

She had only to look at David to know her feelings for him had not diminished with time.

Her mother took her hand. "I pray Uriah will come home to you safely."

"God protect him." She noticed that David was turning his horse away, riding back into the city instead of going out with the men. "David isn't going with them?"

"No. Your grandfather hoped he would change his mind, but David said he's tired, and tired men make poor decisions."

Uriah had said nothing about this.

"Your needn't worry about your husband, my dear. Joab and Abishai have proven their ability to command. I suppose the king didn't feel his presence was necessary."

Bathsheba heard the gravity in her mother's voice. Was she criticizing David after all these years of thinking him above reproach? "Is it so wrong for him to remain behind?"

"Unwise. But who am I to say what a king should or shouldn't do?" Her mother turned her face away and spoke wistfully. "If only all men were sick of war! But it seems that will never be. Men live to fight, and women live to bear sons for a king's army."

Bathsheba took her mother's hand and squeezed it. "Perhaps it will not always be so. Perhaps God will allow David to conquer all our enemies and we'll have peace on all sides."

"No good comes from an idle king."

Bathsheba let go of her. "David has never been idle!"

Her mother looked at her. "No, he hasn't. But whom can he conquer inside his own palace walls?" She walked away.

The days passed slowly for David. He couldn't recline for a simple meal without hearing constant bickering and whispered complaints from wives and children. His daughters and sons competed for his attention until all he wanted to do was escape to a quiet place and be alone. And when he was alone, restlessness took hold of him. He was discontented and uneasy. Was this all there was to life? He tried to write psalms, but no words would come. Every note he plucked on his lyre was discordant. He tried to rest, but the more he slept, the more tired he felt. Soul tired.

A messenger came with news that Joab and Abishai had defeated the Arameans and were laying siege to Hanun's city, Rabbah. David felt no jubilation. He knew months would pass before the Ammonites would be starved into submission. Attacking the walls might hasten their destruction, but it would needlessly cost lives. He was sick of war!

Bored and melancholy, the king walked the palace walls, gazing out over the city named in his honor, desperate for distraction.

※※※

The days crawled by as Bathsheba waited for Uriah to come home from the war. When word came that the army had laid siege to Rabbah, she had no illusions that this meant the war was over. Many months could pass before the Ammonites surrendered and Uriah returned home. *If* he returned home. Each time he marched away to war, she lived with the uncertainty that he might be marching out of her life forever, leaving no son behind to carry on his name. She longed to have children. But how could she conceive when her husband was seldom home?

Loneliness became her greatest enemy. It grew to an intolerable ache inside her. Sometimes she sat in the quiet of her chamber and wept over her plight. Yet, what choice had she? Happiness was out of reach.

The city felt empty, populated only by women and children, a few men too old to go into battle, and a king who had decided to remain home, while the war raged on elsewhere.

When she looked up at the wall of David's palace, she imagined him surrounded by doting wives and concubines. A dozen sons and daughters would be delighting him with their attention. Who could be unhappy with so many family members surrounding them? But here she sat, childless and alone, her husband away. How many months had it been since she had laid eyes on Uriah? How many months since she had felt his arms around her? How many more months would come and go, her chance for having a child passing with each?

She cupped water and pressed it to her flushed cheeks. She knew what was wrong. Every time her menses passed and it was time to take the ritual bath of purification again, self-pity took hold of her. What was the point of making herself ready for a husband who was never home? Another month would pass and another and another, and her arms would remain empty of children. Tears welled. Anger stirred. Frustration abounded.

"Your bath is ready, my lady."

Bathsheba removed her gown and stepped into the basin prepared for her in the privacy of her courtyard. Beneath the gauze canopy that protected her from the harsh afternoon sun, the handmaiden slowly poured water over her body, while Bathsheba washed. She stepped out of the basin and stood waiting as her handmaiden emptied it. Enjoying the coolness of the drying droplets on her body, Bathsheba lifted the heavy mass of curling hair from her back and shoulders. Her handmaiden returned and Bathsheba stepped into the basin again. She drew in her breath as the refreshing water cascaded over her heated flesh. Bathsheba closed her eyes and lifted her head as she stroked the water from her body.

The city was quiet, so quiet she felt a strange sense of expectancy.

Her skin prickled strangely. She sensed someone looking at her. Disturbed, she glanced up and saw a man standing on the wall. Gasping, she covered herself with her hands and ducked beneath the gauzy shelter that did little to hide her. It was afternoon, a time when most people were inside their homes resting and avoiding the heavy heat. What was the man doing on the palace roof?

Angry, she leaned forward to see if she recognized the guard intruding upon her privacy. Uriah would hear of it, and when they returned so would her father and grandfather. As she peered up, her heart jumped.

It was not a palace guard staring down at her, but a man in a white linen tunic with purple trim. *David!*

Her heart pounded as she hid beneath the transparent canopy. Yearning flooded her. Even the sound of the canopy flapping gently in the wind made her senses spin. She remembered how David had looked at her the day she was given to Uriah in marriage and felt all over again the shock of attraction she'd seen in his eyes. If he had noticed her sooner, he could have taken her as his wife instead of looking at her like a starving man.

She knew she should flee to the privacy of the house and complete her bath later, but hurt and resentment filled her. Why not let him see what he had let slip through his fingers? Let him think back to the skinny, sunburned child who had followed him about like an orphaned lamb after its shepherd! She boldly looked up. Would he wish now he'd asked for her instead of leaving it to her father to find a husband for her?

As David stared down, Bathsheba's anger dissolved in a wave of sadness. Why was he standing on the wall and looking down into her courtyard? Why look at her at all with all the beautiful women at his beck and call?

"My lady?"

Startled, Bathsheba turned away, heat surging into her face. Her hand-maiden glanced up at the wall. Bathsheba felt a wave of relief when she glanced up and saw David was no longer there.

"Are you all right, my lady?"

"I was praying." Shame rose inside her. Mortified at what she'd done, she snatched the cloth from the girl, wrapped it around her body and ran inside the house. Slamming the bedroom door, she leaned against it, holding the damp cloth tightly. She gulped in air as she crossed the room and sank down onto her bed.

What had she done? What could she possibly have been thinking when she allowed the king to gaze upon her? She pressed her hands against her chest, wishing she could calm the wild beating of her heart. Her feelings tumbled one over another – shame, excitement, sorrow, anger, self-loathing. What must David think of her now?

Curling on her side on the bed she shared with her husband, she covered her face and wept.

≈≈≈≈

David had seven wives and numerous concubines, and yet, not one could compare in beauty to the woman he had just seen bathing in a house near the walls of his palace. He had found himself mesmerized by the curves of her body and the grace of every movement. Eve could not have been more perfect!

He knew the moment the woman sensed his presence above her, for she had paused and cocked her head like a hart ready for flight. She looked around slowly and then raised her head. Seeing him on the roof, she drew back quickly beneath the gauzy canopy.

For an instant, he was embarrassed to be caught staring at her during such private ablution. But only for a moment. He was the king, after all, and it was his roof. He had every right to stroll it whenever he pleased. She could have bathed inside her house instead of setting up a canopy in her courtyard. What possessed her? His breath had caught in his throat when she looked up at him. He'd never seen a more beautiful woman.

Pushing back from the wall, David strode the battlements until he spotted one of his guards. "Joram!" When the soldier glanced up, David beckoned him.

"My lord the king?"

David took him by the arm and pointed. "There is a woman in that house. Find out who she is."

Startled, the guard quickly left to do his bidding.

David expelled his breath slowly. Gripping the edge of the wall, he watched until the guard appeared on the street below. David turned away and went down the steps hurriedly. Waving away several of his children, he summoned another guard. "When Joram returns, send him to my private chambers immediately."

"Yes, my lord the king."

Alone in his bedroom, David waited. As the minutes passed, he drummed his fingers impatiently. Uneasy, he rose and raked his hand back through his hair. He had never felt such fierce desire for a woman. He was troubled, but he chose to ignore the niggling discomfort. Closing his eyes, he imagined the woman again, her small hands open, her head lifted up as though in prayer, and her body, oh, her body ...

He bolted from his seat. "What's taking so long?" He paced, agitated and annoyed by the delay. He wanted her and he would have her, whatever the cost.

Someone tapped at the door. "Enter!" Joram stood on the threshold. "Come in and close the door behind you." David waited, hands on his hips. "What did you find out?"

"The woman's name is Bathsheba."

"Bathsheba?" Why did that name sound so familiar? "Bathsheba ..."

"She is Bathsheba, the daughter of Eliam and the wife of Uriah the Hittite."

Oh, no! David felt his stomach drop. He remembered a skinny little girl who had sat on Ahithophel's knee and stared at him across the fire. No! It couldn't be! Little Bathsheba who, as a child, had worshiped him and followed him to the stream at En-gedi. "*I want to talk with you.*" Her heart had been in her eyes. Bathsheba, married to one of his best and most reliable friends, daughter of a man he trusted and who trusted him, granddaughter of Ahithophel, Israel's most able military adviser. Could anything be worse? He remembered looking into her eyes on her wedding day and feeling as though someone had punched him in the stomach. He'd made sure from that day on never to look at her again!

He expelled a hoarse laugh. Turning his back, he gripped the back of his neck. The old weariness and depression rose up once again. "You may go, Joram."

"Is there anything you wish for, my lord the king?"

David clenched his teeth. "Nothing I can have."

"Nothing is out of your reach, Sire. You are the *king*. Whatever you want is yours."

David lowered his hand and raised his head. He *was* the king. Furthermore, his army was miles away at Rabbah. Uriah, Eliam, and Ahithophel had been gone for months and would not return for many more to come. His heart began to pound. What if he did summon Bathsheba to his private chambers? What if they did find pleasure in one another's arms? What harm could one night do? Who would ever know?

His desire for Bathsheba burned hotter.

"What is your wish, Sire?"

"Bring her to me." He felt a pang of guilt as he spoke his lust aloud, but he quickly squelched it with thoughts of the night ahead. Still, he must be prudent. "Wait until dark before you go for her, and take another soldier you know can keep a secret."

"And if the woman resists?"

"She won't." Bathsheba had loved him for years. She'd followed him around the camps at Adullam and En-gedi. He'd thought she was a pesky little fly then, but now ...

"But if she does ... ?"

She was a common woman and he was a king. "My order stands." Joram bowed and left. David knew Bathsheba would come to him. She had been extending him an invitation when she had so boldly met his eyes during her bath. If she regretted her impulse, he would take pleasure in swaying her.

It would be hours yet before Bathsheba was brought to his bedchamber. Time enough to bathe and anoint himself with scented oils. Time enough to order a small feast prepared. Time enough to burn incense to tease her senses. Time enough to think about the pleasures of the night ahead.

Time enough for sin to conquer him.

≈≈≈

Bathsheba spent the rest of the afternoon in her chamber weeping and wondering how she would ever have the courage to show her face before the king again. She dressed in a loose embroidered robe that hid every curve of her body. She brushed her hair until her scalp hurt. Then, holding the brush against her chest, she rocked and sobbed. Time hadn't dissolved her love for David. This afternoon when she realized he was the one on the roof looking down at her, all the old feelings had risen up and swept over her again.

Someone tapped at her door. "My lady?" came the muffled voice of her maid.

"Go away!"

"There's a soldier at the door, my lady!" The girl's voice was shaking with alarm. "He said you must come!"

A soldier? Bathsheba rose quickly. She could think of only one reason a soldier would come to her door. Uriah was wounded or dead! Uttering a sob, Bathsheba threw open her door, brushed past her maid and hurried through the house, her handmaiden on her heels.

The soldier stood just inside her door, but he wasn't dusty from travel. And he wore a palace guard's uniform. Startled, Bathsheba stopped. "Why are you here?"

The corner of his mouth tipped up. "The king has summoned you, Lady Bathsheba."

"Summoned me?" Confused, she stared back at him. "The king?"

"Yes. *The king.*" He stepped back and extended his hand toward the open front door. Another soldier was standing outside looking in at her. Bathsheba began to shake. She was a little girl again, crouching behind a boulder as David reprimanded her. Her cheeks caught fire.

"My lady." The handmaiden moaned. "Oh, my lady."

Bathsheba turned to her quickly and grasped her hands. "Hush, now. The king won't harm me, Hatshepsut. He's known my father and grand-father for many years." Could that be the reason he was summoning her? "Perhaps he has news of them. Go quickly and bring me my shawl."

The girl ran to do her bidding while Bathsheba stood filled with anxiety before the palace guard. His hand rested on the hilt of his sword as he waited, head up, eyes straight ahead. Was it bad news from Rabbah? "Has the king summoned my mother as well?" Why would the king stoop so low as to inform two women they had lost loved ones in the war?

"Your mother?" The guard spoke wryly. "I think not."

"Then can you tell me why the king wishes to see me?"

He looked at her then, and the expression in his eyes made heat rise into her cheeks.

Her handmaiden returned with a shawl. Heart pounding, Bathsheba took it and draped it over her head and across one shoulder so that her face wouldn't be seen. As she went out the door, the guards fell in on either side of her. It didn't occur to her until she was near the palace entrance that she was still wearing the loose embroidered robe she normally wore only inside her own house.

"This way!" The guard jerked his head and led her toward a pathway around to a side entrance used only by servants. If there had been any question in her mind as to the clandestine reason for the king's summons, or her social standing in his eyes, she had none now.

Tears of shame pricked her eyes. She had only herself to blame for this situation. She kept her head down and her face covered as she came in through the servants' entrance. She walked through the palace kitchen, servants' quarters and corridors, and up a flight of stairs, looking neither to the right nor the left. The guards stopped before a door. One knocked lightly, and the other stood to one side.

The moment the door opened and she looked up, she forgot all about the guards. David's gaze was fixed upon her.

When he smiled and held out his hand, she took it, her breath catching when his fingers closed warm and firm around hers. He drew her into his private chamber as he gave orders to the guard to keep watch. "No one is to disturb me." And then David closed the door behind her. Her heart leaped and bounded like a rabbit fleeing for its life. He still had hold of her hand, and there seemed no indication that he intended to let go. "I'm glad you came."

"Did I have any choice?"

"You did choose."

He kissed her hand, his eyes smiling into hers. "Why do you cover your face, when you're more beautiful than the sun or the moon?"

When she raised her hand to hold her shawl in place, he inclined his head slightly. "Come. I've had a meal prepared for us. Let me serve you."

The air was filled with the sweet scent of incense. Cushions were scattered on the floor. A large bed loomed across the room. Food was spread over a long table. "How many were you expecting?"

He laughed, and the throaty sound made her tremble. "Only you, my sweet."

"I'm not very hungry." Gathering her courage, she looked at him. "Do you know who I am?"

"Of course." His eyes caressed her face. "You're the little girl who used to stare across the fire at me. Do you remember following me to the stream at En-gedi?"

"I'm not a little girl anymore. I'm – "

"The most beautiful woman in the kingdom." He searched her eyes.

"You said you wanted to talk to me that morning. I told you to go home." He tucked his finger into her shawl and drew it down from her face. "Talk to me now, Bathsheba." He stepped closer and lifted the shawl from her hair. "Say whatever is on your mind." The shawl slipped down from her shoulders and pooled around her feet.

"Why do you call for me *now?*" Her voice was thick with tears. All the years she had dreamed and hoped. She had never wanted to come to him like this. Summoned in the middle of the night ...

"You know." He breathed against her neck.

Her skin tingled. "It's too late."

"You're here with me now."

She drew back and lifted her chin scarcely able to see his face through her tears. "Summoned like a harlot and brought to you through the servants' gate!" She shook her head and bowed her head again. "And I've no one else to blame considering the way I behaved this afternoon. I'm sorry. I – "

"You took my breath away."

"I did?" Her child's heart trembled and swelled with pride. "Oh, David. Send me back."

"Not yet." He tipped her chin firmly. "You aren't happy, are you?"

Tears trickled down her cheeks. "How can you ask such a question?"

"I want you to be happy." He searched her eyes and his expression changed. He looked troubled. "Do you remember your wedding feast? When I looked into your eyes in Hebron, my stomach dropped to my feet. I couldn't take my eyes off of you."

"Is that why you left so quickly?"

"Why else?" He put his arms around her.

She put her hands against his chest. She knew she should say something to stop him. She should be like Abigail and make him aware of the sin he was about to commit. But her resolve weakened when she felt his heart pounding faster and harder than her own. He wanted her. *I'll let him kiss me once, just once, and then I'll say something to stop him. I'll have his kiss to remember. Just one.*

When his mouth took hers, Bathsheba felt herself being pulled down with him into a vortex of desire. His fingers raked through her hair. He moaned her name, and the words of warning died in her throat. As her body caught fire, she clung to him and didn't say a word.

She knew that if she did, David would remember himself and send her home where she belonged.

Hours later, David stood beside his bed watching Bathsheba sleep. She was so beautiful she made his heart ache. But it would be dawn soon. He had to get her out of the palace before anyone knew she'd been here. When he'd awakened and seen her lying beside him, he thought of Ahithophel, Eliam, and Uriah and what they would make of this clandestine affair. *What was I thinking! They could turn the army against me!*

Putting his knee on the bed, he leaned down and kissed her. Her eyes opened slowly. Still clouded with sleep, she smiled. "David," she sighed, and his pulse quickened. Shaken by his feelings, he straightened.

"It's almost daylight, Bathsheba. You have to go."

Her smile died.

David's stomach squeezed tight at the wounded look in her eyes. Turning quickly away, she dragged a blanket up and covered herself. Shame hadn't been in attendance last night, only unbridled passion. But now, morning had come and light streamed in upon the true situation. "My guards will see you safely back to your house." Why should he feel guilty? They had a right to some happiness, didn't they?

She sat up quickly. "I know my way home." When he heard the soft sound she made as she groped for her discarded robe, he went down on his knees on the bed and reached for her.

"Bathsheba," he said, his voice hoarse with pent up emotion. She jerked from his touch. He caught hold of her shoulders and pulled her back against him. She struggled to be free. He locked his arms around her. "Bathsheba," he said raggedly and buried his face in her neck. How could he let her go after last night? He breathed in the scent of her and knew he was undone.

"I thought last night would be enough." She put the heels of her hands against her eyes. "I thought I could live on the memories of being with you. But now ... I feel ... I feel ... unclean!" She shuddered.

Her words so mirrored his own feelings, he was disturbed. "Do you think I *want* to send you away?" He felt torn and frustrated. "I'd keep you with me if it wouldn't raise a cry across the city. Your father ... your grandfather."

"My husband!"

"I have to get you out of here before anyone knows what's happened between us."

Her body was tense against him. When he kissed her neck, she tipped her head back with a shaky sigh. "It's no use. Someone will find out. And I'll die for it."

He went rigid. "No one's going to find out!"

She turned in his arms, and he saw the fear in her eyes. "People already know, David! Your guards, my handmaiden. Any one of a dozen people who saw your men bring me in through the servants' entrance last night."

He dug his fingers into her hair. "And who are they to dare speak against the king? My men will keep silent, and you will tell your maid she'd better hold her tongue if she values her life!" He saw the shock in her eyes and spoke more gently. "You didn't realize what a ruthless man I could be, did you?" He tried to smile, but there was a fierceness inside him that claimed her for his own. "Listen, my love. Supposing someone did whisper of our night together, would any priest confront me?"

"Nathan would."

"Nathan knows me. He would dismiss any gossip as ugly rumor and nothing more. And besides, who would take the word of a guard or handmaiden over that of a king?" He kissed her tears away. "Trust me. I won't allow any harm to come to you. I swear it!"

"I've always trusted you, David. My father said you've always been a man of your word."

David winced inwardly, but anger rose quickly in self-defense. Why should he feel guilty over having spent one night with the woman he desired? What harm could come of something done in secret? He was the king. Didn't he deserve some happiness? Kings had always taken whomever they wanted. Why shouldn't he? Who had done more in bringing the tribes together? Who had killed Goliath and rallied the Israelite army to victory? Who had led the kingdom to victory after victory? Who had been wrongly accused and pursued for years all because the people loved him? And during those hard years, who had been the one man to praise God? Besides, it was no one's business but his own what he did in the privacy of his chamber!

Still, he knew it was wiser to keep his own counsel in this particular matter. He thought of Eliam, his long-time friend. He thought of Ahithophel, his adviser. He thought of Uriah's courage and ferocity in battle. If they found out Bathsheba had spent the night in his bed, there would be trouble. Both were men of God and would want to follow the letter of the Law. And the Law of Moses demanded that an adulteress be put to death.

Fear gripped David's belly as he realized the danger to Bathsheba. He shoved it away and reminded himself he was the king! Who would dare touch a woman he loved?

"No stone will ever strike you." He would kill any man who tried to harm her.

It never once occurred to David that it was he who was shattering her life.

~~~

Bathsheba waited for David to summon her again, but he didn't. She watched for him on the wall, but the king didn't appear. She listened for word of him, but all she heard was, "The king is resting in his palace while our husbands are off at Rabbah fighting his war with the Ammonites!"

"It's our war," she said in his defense. "If the Ammonites get away with insulting David's ambassadors, they might think him weak and attack Jerusalem. Better to have the battle at Rabbah than Jerusalem."

She tried to tell herself that David was busy with matters of state, but jealousy and hurt crept in. Her imagination tormented her. *Whom is he holding in his arms tonight? Ahinoam? Abigail?* Or had he lost all interest in his wives and concubines? *How many other women in this city have looked up at the handsome king strolling along the battlements and yearned to warm his bed?* She remembered the girls in the camps, girls exactly like her who'd gazed at David with adoring eyes and dreamed dreams about him.

David could have anyone he wanted! Even before he was king, women were falling in love with him.

She was stricken with regret and fear as the days passed. If only she had fled to the privacy of her house that day. If only she hadn't brazenly continued her bath, exposing herself to this endless heartache. She had no one to blame but herself for what she suffered now. She'd gone willingly to David's bed. She'd told herself love was reason enough to give herself to him. David, her god.

Why hadn't she thought about the Law before she gave herself to him? He had assured her that no stone would touch her. But what could he do if the priests cried out against her? For if their affair became known, she had no illusions about who would bear the blame. David was a beloved king. She was a powerless woman.

Adultery! She'd committed adultery! How could she have done such a thing after being brought up by her mother, father, and grandfather who held to the Law of Moses with such fierce devotion?

If they ever find out, they'll kill me!

A week passed and then another and another, and she received no summons from the palace, no message, no hint of David's concern. How easily he had abandoned her!

The time for her monthly show of blood came and went, and terror filled her. After all the years of trying and failing to conceive with Uriah, she was pregnant after one night in David's arms! Why now? Why under these circumstances? What could she do now?

Had she only imagined the tenderness in David's touch? Had her hope deceived her into believing she saw love in his eyes? If he loved her, wouldn't he have summoned her by now? Or at the least sent a message of some kind?

Nothing! He cares nothing about me!

She pressed her hands against her temples. Seven wives and ten concubines! What need had he of her? Would he even care that she was with child as a result of her night with him? In a few months, everyone was going to know she'd committed adultery. Her handmaiden had already guessed she was pregnant – and by whom. Soon, her mother would notice the changes in her. Soon every man, woman, and child who laid eyes upon her would guess her secret.

Trembling, she placed her hands on her abdomen. She was torn between terror and exultation. Within her womb was the child of a king – not just any king, but King David, hero of her childhood dreams. David, singer of songs, conqueror of nations! He had been like a god to her.

Anger filled her. She looked up at the wall of his palace where David had stood on that fateful day of her undoing. She'd always thought she would rejoice when she was with child, anticipation of the happy event of bearing a son to her patient, loving husband.

Never in her life had she felt such despair and fear!

Was it the love she'd felt for David all these years that had made the soil fertile enough to accept the seed?

Only the king could protect her from suffering the consequences of their sin.

But would he?

She grieved over David's silence and was terrified at what Uriah would do to her when he found out how she'd betrayed him. What defense had she? David hadn't dragged her into the palace kicking and screaming!

She'd never wanted to hurt Uriah. He was a good man, a kind and generous husband. But Uriah's touch didn't make her burn. David's embrace made her soar and melt. Was it so wrong to crave the caresses of a man she'd loved for as long as she could remember? Wasn't she entitled to one night of happiness without having her entire life destroyed by it?

Life was unfair!

She'd never been meant for Uriah. She'd been meant for David. Surely that made it all right for them to steal a few hours together. She'd thought she would have wonderful memories of their night together, to last a lifetime, but she was tormented instead. The fire David had built in her was turning her life to ashes. She felt abandoned and terrified of the future. She'd been filled up with love for him. She'd poured herself out like a drink offering for David, her king. David, her idol. And now, she was consumed by fear, her loneliness worse than ever. It was too late to go back and undo anything. What price would she pay for that one night? What cost to others she loved and who loved her? Uriah, her mother, her father, her grandfather. She couldn't bear to think of it. She would rather die than have them know. But did she have the courage to take her own life?

Shaking, she put her hands over her belly again. If she died, so would David's child. Part of her rejoiced over the life growing within her. Part of her wished the evidence of her sin would be swept from her body with a stream of blood before anyone else knew of it.

Everyone was going to know this child was conceived in adultery. How could she defend herself when her husband had been away at war for months? She imagined the angry shouts of a mob closing around her, taking up stones. She imagined the condemnation in her mother's eyes, the hurt, the disappointment. A mother knew a daughter's heart better than anyone. Her mother had known for years that she was in love with David. Hadn't she counseled Bathsheba to give up her childish fantasies, her unrequited love? The blame wouldn't be put at the feet of the king, but laid firmly upon her head. Hadn't her mother told her to guard her heart?

No one could help her now. No one but David. But would he?

Lowering her hands, she clenched them in her lap. Silence did not always mean indifference. Hadn't he promised no harm would come to her? Hadn't he sworn it? Hadn't David always been a man of his word?

She cut a piece of papyrus from Uriah's accounts. David would help her. He had to help her! She wrote him a brief message. Rolling it tightly, she tied a string around it. Then she summoned her handmaiden. "Take this to the king."

"What if the guards won't let me through the gate?"

"Ask for Joram. Give him the message. Tell him it's from me and meant for the king's eyes only."

"Yes, my lady."

Bathsheba closed the door and pressed her forehead against it. All types of fearsome possibilities swirled in her mind. Surely David would be honor bound to help her. Surely he wouldn't forsake the daughter of Eliam, the granddaughter of Ahithophel. Surely he would try to do something for her so that Uriah would never find out she'd betrayed him. But what could he do? What? He could secret her away so that she could have his child in another city. Where would he send her? Where? Where!

Oh, David help me! Please help me!

She refused to believe he was indifferent. How could he be after the risks he'd taken to bring her into the palace? But what would David do to solve this problem?

Exhausted by worry, she sat. She had no choice but to wait, for her life was in the king's hands.

David felt an ominous premonition when his guard whispered, "The handmaid of Bathsheba, wife of Uriah, has come with a message." The mere mention of Bathsheba's name was a jolt to his senses, arousing feelings he knew were better forgotten. He'd never wanted a woman as much as he'd wanted her. How many times over the past weeks had he denied himself the pleasure of summoning her again because he knew it would increase the risk of exposure? He'd had to remind himself repeatedly that she was the wife of a friend, the daughter of one of his most valued captains, the granddaughter of Ahithophel, a man he'd respected for years! He had enough trouble in the kingdom without turning friends into enemies!

"Bring the maidservant to me."

He felt curious eyes upon him as he untied the string around the small papyrus. He read Bathsheba's brief message, and his stomach dropped. Heat climbed up his neck and spread across his face. Three words, enough to shock him from his complacency and trumpet disaster.

I am pregnant.

He felt the accusation in those three words and heard Bathsheba's desperate cry for help. He brushed his fingers lightly over the words and frowned. Guilt gripped him.

Oh, Bathsheba. He remembered his promise and wondered how he could fulfill it. Her handmaiden stood in the doorway, waiting for his reply. He saw heads leaning toward one another, whispering. Speculation already!

He could hear the soft buzz. Would it grow into screams for blood? His *and* hers? Disaster stretched ahead for both of them if word spread of their affair. He needed time to think, time to find a way out of this mess!

Crumpling Bathsheba's message in his hand, he leaned back indolently and smiled, beckoning the next case be brought before him. He listened impatiently and made a decision he saw was ill-received. What did he care about their petty differences when Bathsheba faced certain death? He had to find a way to rescue her from the mess she was in. If he didn't find a way to cover their sin, there would be trouble in the ranks of his fighting men. They would lose faith in him, possibly rebel.

"Enough!" He stood. He waved his servants away. "I need to be alone."

When he entered his chamber, he closed the door and put Bathsheba's crumpled message in among the embers of burning incense, watching as it burned.

He sat for an hour with his head in his hands before a plan came to him. He knew it would save them both from exposure and would even give cause for celebration among his closest friends. He smiled at his own cleverness as he summoned Joram.

"Send a messenger to Rabbah and tell Joab to send me Uriah the Hittite."

Joram bowed and left.

Strangely agitated, David removed his crown and tossed it on his bed. He raked his fingers back through his hair. Temptation gripped him to summon Bathsheba and explain his plan, but he squelched the impulse. Why take any more risks when, in less than a week's time, there would be no cause for fear of reprisals? Uriah would return to Jerusalem, where his king would treat him with the respect of an emissary. David intended to find out what was happening at Rabbah.

And then he would send the Hittite home to his wife.

Bathsheba was the granddaughter of Ahithophel. Surely she would be quick to see the means of her salvation and fulfill her part in the plan. He would even send food and wine as reward for Uriah's service. Any man who'd been gone as long as Uriah would be eager for his wife.

David clenched a fist as jealousy gripped him. The plan was repugnant, but he could see no flaw in it. Whatever he felt now about Bathsheba lying with another man, the act would save her life as well as that of his child. The plan would also save him embarrassment.

If all went accordingly, Uriah would never know he'd been betrayed by his wife and cuckolded by a friend. David found grudging satisfaction in knowing that this child of his loins would be brought up by an honorable man who had adopted the ways of Israel.

He raked a hand through his hair again. He would allow the Hittite *one* night to get the deed done, and then he'd order him back to his duties at Rabbah. In a few weeks, Bathsheba could send word to her husband that she was with child, and Uriah could celebrate with his friends in the army while finishing the job of taking Rabbah.

The matter thus resolved in his mind, David stretched out on his bed and slept for the rest of the afternoon.

≈≈≈≈

When her maid opened the door at last, Bathsheba jumped to her feet. "What news?"

The girl's eyes flickered in discomfort. "The guard took me to the king's court."

"The king's court?" Bathsheba felt weak and light-headed. How many courtiers had been in attendance when her message was delivered? How many tongues were now wagging with speculations? She didn't ask. She didn't want to know.

"Joram demanded to know who had sent me." Her handmaiden started to weep. "I had to tell him, my lady. I had to. But I said it quietly. I said it so quietly, he had to bend forward and tell me to repeat what I'd said. And then he went forward and informed the king."

"For all to hear?"

The girl's face was pale. "No. He whispered into the king's ear."

Somehow that made everything worse. Bathsheba shuddered. "Did he take my message?"

"Yes, my lady."

"Did he give it to David?"

"Yes, my lady."

"And did the king summon you then? Did he give you a message to bring back to me? Did he say *anything* to you?"

"No, my lady, no, no, but how could he say anything with so many around to hear and wonder? He called for ... "

"Called for ... ?"

"The next case."

Bathsheba turned her face away. "You may go."

"Oh, my lady ... "

"*Go!*"

Alone, Bathsheba sank to the floor and covered her face. It was too late to regret loving David, too late to regret giving herself to him without a word of protest. All she could do now was wait and see if David would remember his promise to her.

For now, it appeared he'd chosen to remember her not at all.

three

DAVID assessed Uriah as he walked toward him. He was a tall man with broad shoulders, his skin weathered and ruddy from years in the sun, his mouth an uncompromising line. He'd removed his leather helmet and tucked it beneath his arm. David noticed the streaks of gray at the Hittite's temples. He stopped in front of the throne, hit his fist against his heart and bowed low before David. "My lord the king!"

When the Hittite straightened, David inclined his head with the respect due a man of proven loyalty and courage, well-respected by captains as well as commanders, and even the king. No sign of curiosity lit Uriah's eyes now. He was a consummate soldier, who obeyed his supreme commander without question. David knew that whatever he commanded, Uriah would do.

Relaxing, David leaned back. This was going to be easy. "How does Joab fair? Tell me about the people and how the war prospers."

"All goes well, my lord the king." Uriah gave detailed information on how Joab and Abishai had employed the captains and the soldiers beneath their command. Uriah gave a full picture of the situation. He spoke of skirmishes in which the Ammonites had been chased back inside the city " ... like dogs with their tails between their legs." David laughed with him. Uriah spoke of the fear upon the land since David had defeated Hadadezer and his allies the previous year. "Hanun is alone. It's only a matter of time before Rabbah falls and Hanun's crown will be placed in your hands."

Nodding, David smiled. "Good news, indeed. Is it not so?" He looked around at the other men in court who received the news eagerly. He returned his attention to Uriah. The time to show magnanimity was right. "You may take your leave, my friend. Go down to your house and relax."

A frown flickered across Uriah's brow. "My lord the king!" With a fist against his heart, he bowed low again, straightened, stepped back and turned with the precision of a marching man. David stifled his jealousy as he watched the Hittite stride from the throne room.

"Joram." He beckoned his guard. "I want a meal prepared for Uriah and his wife, something special, something that will bring back fond memories of their wedding feast." He gripped the arm of his throne tightly. "Have it prepared and delivered to Uriah's house immediately."

"Yes, my lord the king."

Good food would help Uriah relax and make the transition from battlefield to a peaceful night in the arms of his beautiful young wife.

David spent the rest of the day hearing various cases brought before him by the people. The trifling disputes tried his patience, but the time he spent resolving them kept him from dwelling upon the thought of Bathsheba in the arms of another man.

He would give Uriah one night to do what was expected, and then the man was going back to Joab at Rabbah.

Bathsheba was feverish when her mother greeted her in the marketplace with news that Uriah had been seen entering Jerusalem. "He must have news from Rabbah," her mother said, going on to make a dozen speculations while Bathsheba felt the sweat break out on her body. What could David possibly be thinking? Was he going to confess to her husband? Would he claim she'd seduced him by parading naked in front of him? Or had he other plans? Would he offer gifts to absolve his guilt? She told her mother she wanted to prepare to see her husband and hurried home, where she remained, pacing in agitation.

When Joram and several servants of the king came to her house laden with trays of succulent food, enough quantity and variety to please a king, she was alarmed. "What is all this?" Surely David wasn't intending to come into her house. Her neighbors would see and talk. The whole city would know of their affair!

"Tell Uriah the king sends his best wishes for a pleasant evening," Joram said with a mocking smile.

"Uriah has been serving in Rabbah."

"Indeed, until he was summoned from Rabbah to report to the king about the war. My lord the king gave him leave to return home and spend the night with you."

She felt the heat come up from her toes to the top of her head as she understood the full implication of what Joram was saying. "Uriah isn't here."

And even if he had come home, he would not put a hand upon her. Did David know his men so little? Had he forgotten the Law? When a man was called out to war, he was to remain abstinent from sexual relations. He was to save his strength for battle against the enemies of Israel rather than spend it on his own pleasure.

"Then I will find him," Joram said. "I will inform him of what the king has done to honor him." He waved the servants out and left.

Honor Uriah? Shame swept over Bathsheba as she realized the way David had chosen to help her. He was attempting to hide their sin of adultery by enticing her husband to sleep with her and believe he was the father of her child! Was this the fulfillment of David's promise to help her? He was drawing her into deeper sin, pulling her down further into sorrow and shame. If Uriah gave in to his fleshly nature, David expected her to lie and pretend to rejoice that she was with child, for everyone would naturally assume the child was Uriah's. Uriah would have to bear the embarrassment of having broken his vow of abstinence.

Oh, she saw everything so clearly now. David, commander of the army of Israel, rested in his palace while his army fought the war. The king, restless and bored, peeping at her bathing and summoning her for his own pleasure. He hadn't cared that she belonged to another man, a man who'd been his friend through the hard years of running from King Saul, a man of proven loyalty, a man both valorous and honorable! And she had gone to him, her heart in her hands, giving everything of value to him. She'd prostituted herself to her idol-king who took his leisure while men like her husband risked their lives to win his battles against Israel's enemies!

How would she face Uriah when he came home? How would she look into his eyes and survive the anguish? How could she have betrayed him like this? She'd succumbed to her childish fantasies and made a fool of herself, imagining that one night of passion meant anything lasting to a king! She'd served to sate his desire for a night. She meant nothing to him. He'd probably forgotten all about her until she sent him that message! Did he curse the inconvenience of her conception?

"What have I done?" She groaned, her arms hugging herself as she rocked back and forth. "What have I done?"

Joram returned. "Your husband is sitting at the door of the king's house with all the servants of David. I told him of what the king sent in his honor." He stepped forward. "You must go to Uriah, my lady. Go to him and do whatever you must to bring your husband home to you for the night. It is the king's wish that you do so."

The king's wish.

If she fulfilled her part in the abominable plan, the king's reputation would be unblemished by scandal, she would live, the child would live, and Uriah would never know the truth. She could go on pretending she was the dutiful, loving, faithful wife. She could have the child she'd longed for. The people would be spared the same anguish she now felt, realizing the man she'd loved and worshiped for so many years was deeply flawed. He was no longer the charismatic boy who had killed Goliath and rallied the nation. He was a king whom power had corrupted, for he had become selfish, cunning, and capable of deceit.

Bathsheba felt unclean and helpless. David was presenting her with a way to survive. If she didn't go through with it, she'd die. So would the child she carried.

"Go," she said softly. "Just go and leave me to do what I must." She closed the door behind Joram. Dismissing her maid for the night, she took up her shawl and went out of the house. She stood in the darkness for a long time, feeling it press in around her. She wished she could think of another way out the mess she'd stepped into when she had freely allowed the king to gaze upon her in her bath. As she walked along the moonlit street, she looked up at the wall of the palace where David had stood gazing down at her as she bathed. And she realized, even now, her feelings for him hadn't changed. How was it possible, with her eyes wide open, she could still love David so much?

She saw the palace gate, closed for the night. Guards were still posted. She approached slowly, her heart in her throat. Would they ask her name, ask her purpose in coming? Or would they be among the many soldiers she'd met at her father's campfire, or served in the house of her husband?

Two soldiers stepped forward. "Woman, why do you come at this hour?"

"I am Bathsheba, wife of Uriah. I was told my husband has returned from Rabbah."

"Uriah is bedded down inside the gate with the king's servants. He is among *friends.*"

She felt the cold wind blowing.

Did men talk among themselves as women did? Were rumors circulating among the palace servants? Even if they were, who would dare tell Uriah that his friend, the king, had cuckolded him?

"I will tell him you're here," the other guard said and left them. The guard who had spoken first returned to his position without a word. He didn't look at her. Bathsheba understood the implications of his rudeness. He knew about her affair with the king.

How many others knew?

She kept her face covered as she waited. The city slept and only the guard was present, but she could feel eyes upon her, eyes that saw through her subterfuge and into her heart. She wanted to cower and hide, but knew she would never escape.

The gate was opening. The guard reappeared and her husband followed.

As Uriah walked toward her, her heart hammered. She turned slightly and took a few steps away from the gate so that they would have privacy to talk. When he stopped before her, she raised her eyes and saw his troubled expression. He searched her face intently, but didn't speak.

"The king sent a feast to our house to welcome you home." Her voice trembled.

His eyes flickered, and then an expression spread across his face that made her go cold. Something had been confirmed. His face went taut as though he had been struck. "So," he said and said no more.

He knew!

She saw the moist sheen build in his eyes and wanted to curl up at his feet and die. Could anything hurt a man more than to learn the wife he loved had betrayed him in another man's bed – especially a king he'd loved so much and served so long? She might as well have drawn Uriah's sword from his belt and stabbed him through the heart. Her throat closed tight and hot. *What can I do? How can I show him how sorry I am?* Her hands relaxed, and the shawl slipped down around her shoulders as her eyes filled with tears. "Oh, Uriah ..." She could say no more. She shook with sorrow and shame.

"They expect me to kill you where you stand," he said hoarsely.

"And so you should." What excuse had she? What defense could she offer? As much as David's callow treatment hurt her, she couldn't cast all the blame at his feet. She'd been willing and eager for him. Now, she saw the cost to a man who truly loved her. Heart sick, she went down on her knees and found a stone large enough to fill her palm. Straightening, she extended her hand. "You have every right."

A muscle jerked in his jaw as tears spilled down his cheeks and into his beard. He took the stone and made a fist. She could see him struggling with his emotions. After a long moment, he shook his head and dropped the stone at her feet. When he lifted his hand, she waited for the blow, but he merely laid his hand gently against her cheek. He stroked her tear-dampened skin with his thumb as he gazed into her eyes, his own filled with sorrow and forgiveness. She put her hand over his and closed her eyes in anguish, and felt him slip his hand from beneath hers.

She watched him walk slowly away, his shoulders bent. A guard opened the palace gate just enough for him to pass through to the inner gate, where he would spend the night with other soldiers like himself, men who had dedicated their lives to the service of the king. Then the gate was closed behind him, and the guards resumed their posts.

Bathsheba never saw Uriah again.

≈≈≈

David clenched the arms of his throne. "What do you mean, Uriah spent the night with my servants at the gate?" He strove to keep his voice calm while his insides tensed and roiled in anger as he thought of the hours of torment he'd suffered the night before, imagining that Hittite caressing Bathsheba. How dare Uriah disobey his command! "I told him he could go down to his house."

"He slept with your servants at the gate, my lord the king."

"Bring him to me." When the servant left, David fought to regain control of his emotions so that others in the court wouldn't be curious over his reaction. He would be magnanimous and give the Hittite another opportunity to make things right.

When Uriah entered the court, David dismissed the others and smiled as Uriah walked forward. "What is this I hear, my friend?" he said in the cajoling manner of two men who had been friends for years. "What's the matter with you? Why didn't you go home last night after being away for so long?"

Uriah's dark eyes were inscrutable. "The Ark and the armies of Israel and Judah are living in tents, and Joab and his officers are camping in the open fields. How could I go home to wine and dine and sleep with my wife? I swear that I will never be guilty of acting like that."

David felt the heat come up into his face. Was the Hittite reprimanding him? Was he saying the Ark and the army were encamped in tents while the king was at his leisure inside his palace walls? David felt the sting of reproach. Breathing slowly to cool the hot blood racing through his veins, he leaned back and considered Uriah. "Well, stay here tonight, and tomorrow you may return to the army."

Uriah turned.

David's teeth clenched as he watched Uriah walk from the throne room. The Hittite hadn't addressed him properly as "my lord the king." Had the soldier forgotten to make obeisance? Or had the omission been deliberate?

Joram reported on Uriah's movements the next morning. The Hittite remained in Jerusalem as commanded, but did not go down to his house. Impatient and frustrated, David ordered a sumptuous feast prepared for two and summoned Uriah to be his guest. He sat on the dais, eating and drinking before the Hittite, encouraging the Hittite to do likewise. Food and drink always relaxed a man and helped turn his thoughts to other sensual delights. The evening proved torturous, for Uriah scorned food while he drank freely and talked – talked of the glorious battles they'd fought together. His words were like bee stings, pricking David's conscience, and swelling his resentment. He didn't need to be reminded how the mighty men had served him. But who had led them? David had! The mighty men would have been no more than a band of marauders without him!

Raising his cup, Uriah toasted David. "To the shepherd boy we made a king." He wept as he drained his cup.

David was disgusted by the man's display of emotion. The Hittite couldn't hold his wine. David was eager to see the back of him. He rose and came down from his dais. Gripping the Hittite's arm, he hauled him to his feet. "Enough for tonight, my old friend." He slapped his back. "Go home."

David watched him walk unsteadily from the chamber.

Joram came to him shortly afterward. "He sleeps at the gate, my lord the king."

"I'll deal with him in the morning." Angry, David retired, but his sleep was troubled. Someone was trying to speak with him, and he knew he didn't want to hear what the Voice had to say. Groaning, he awakened drenched with sweat. He sat on the edge of the bed he'd shared with Bathsheba and thought of the promise he'd made. Raking his hands back through his hair, he held his head. Uriah hadn't cooperated, so he would have to think of another way to help her. A pity the Hittite hadn't been killed at Rabbah. Then there'd be no problem. He could ...

His head came up. Another plan developed, one final and perfect, and one that would give him what he wanted most: Bathsheba.

David rose and went to the writing table where he had composed some of his most beautiful psalms. He prepared the ink in its small pot, dipped his brush, and began to write orders for Joab, commander of his army:

"Station Uriah on the front lines where the battle is fiercest. Then pull back so that he will be killed."

David knew that Joab, of all men, would understand the need for secrecy. He would also understand the passions of a man's heart. After all, Joab had once murdered a man in vengeance. He would do whatever David told him without question – and without condemnation. In fact, he would probably admire the king's cunning.

Rolling the small scroll, David melted wax and pressed his ring into it to seal the message. Then he rose, washed, dressed, and went to the court. "Bring me Uriah the Hittite."

Within a matter of minutes, Uriah entered the courtroom. David saw that he had washed as well. He walked forward with regal bearing, no sign of ill-effects from the night of drinking. He stopped before the throne, but he said nothing. Nor did he bend his knee or put his hand against his chest and bow as he had done the day of his arrival. He stood silent, waiting.

David held out the small sealed scroll. "Give this to Joab." His heart beat ten times before Uriah came forward, reached out and took the scroll from his hand. When Uriah's fingers lightly brushed against his, David retracted his hand and glared into the Hittite's eyes. What he saw there gave his heart a jolt. An expression of sorrow. And acceptance.

The man knew he was receiving his death sentence.

Uriah tucked the small scroll inside his armor, against his heart. Then he turned and walked from the court with the bearing of a valorous soldier going out once again to prove his loyalty to the king.

✀✀✀

Bathsheba was unprepared for the news that came to her door. "Your husband, Uriah, has been killed in battle at Rabbah."

She stood gaping at the soldier standing before her. "What?"

"Your husband is dead."

"No. No!" As her legs buckled, her handmaiden embraced her. "Oh, my lady, my lady … " Bathsheba rocked back and forth, wailing and keening. Women came out of their houses up and down the street as Bathsheba sat in her doorway tearing the neckline of her dress and throwing dust upon her head.

As the day wore on, other women were heard mourning their dead, but Bathsheba was too immersed in her own sorrow to wonder why so many grieved. Not until her mother came to her did suspicion sink its talons into her. For Bathsheba had not heard *all* the news from Rabbah, nor did she know of the rumors and gossip overflowing the king's court and palace, spilling into the streets of Jerusalem.

"Your cousin Miriam's husband is dead! And so is the husband of Havalah. Your husband, Uriah, was not the only man to die before the walls of Rabbah." She hunkered in front of Bathsheba and glared at her. "Tell me what this means, Daughter. Tell me!"

Confused and frightened, Bathsheba drew back from the cynicism glittering in her mother's eyes. What was her mother implying? Why would these deaths have anything to do with her? "How would I know what happened in Rabbah, Mother?" Why was her mother blaming her for a battle that had happened miles away from Jerusalem? It made no sense!

"Don't you know how people talk? Things done in the dark always come out into the light. Tell me about the message from the king, Bathsheba."

Bathsheba's alarm grew. "What message?"

"The one Joab received just before he sent men forward to the walls! And Joab didn't choose a weak spot where victory was certain. He chose a place where valiant Ammonites were positioned. They came out of the city and fought, and the servants of David fell." Her hand gripped Bathsheba's arm tightly. "Your father's cousin who serves the king thought David would cry out at the news of such needless loss of lives. But he didn't! Nor did he seem surprised by the news. Tell me why, Bathsheba!"

"*I don't know!*" Bathsheba gasped, face flushed. "Why should I know anything?" She tried to pull free, but her mother's fingers dug into her flesh. "Mother! You're hurting me!"

"Tell me, wretched girl! Why would a commander as wise in the ways of battle as Joab send men so close to the wall?" She gave Bathsheba a hard jerk. "Joab knows as well as everyone how King Abimelech, son of Gideon, was killed by a piece of millstone thrown down upon him by a woman on the wall. He even mentioned it in the message he sent to the king! There is no humiliation worse for a man than to be destroyed by a woman! Oh, my daughter, what have you done?"

Bathsheba felt the coldness in the pit of her stomach seep into her blood. "Nothing! I've done nothing!"

"Nothing!" Her mother sneered. "The messenger said, 'Uriah the Hittite was killed, too,' as though this was the news the king waited to hear!"

Bathsheba felt the blood drain from her face. "No," she choked. "*No.*" She shook her head, refusing to believe the accusation leveled against David. "They were friends," she stammered. "David would never ..."

"*'David'* is it? Do you know what *David* said about the news of your husband's death? He said to tell Joab not to be discouraged, for the sword kills one as well as another!" She spat the words bitterly, her face ravaged. "Your father is in Rabbah!"

"I didn't know this would happen! How could I know?"

Her mother let go of her and drew back. "So the rumors are true!" She looked ill and pinched with pain. "I threatened a woman who said she saw you being taken into the palace over a month ago. I prayed the rumors about you and the king were false. I told the woman not to repeat her lies. *Lies!* I should've known what you'd do if you ever had the chance!"

Crying, Bathsheba bent over, covering her head.

"Ohhh." Her mother moaned and rocked. "What have you done to us all? Ohhhhh ..."

Gasping between her gulping sobs, Bathsheba confessed. "David saw me bathing from the roof of the palace. He sent for me. What could I do? He is the king!" Her mother slapped her hard across the face. Bathsheba recoiled, raising her arm to protect herself.

"And what did you do?" Her mother spat. "Did you cover yourself? Did you call me for help? When he summoned you, did you do as Abigail did and tell him he would bring sin upon himself? You did none of those things! I can see the guilt written all over you, you wretched, stupid girl! *You harlot!* You've ruined us all!"

Bathsheba shook before her mother's fury. "I didn't mean to hurt anyone."

"I told you years ago David was not for you! I told you and told you! Why didn't you listen? *You've murdered your own husband!*"

"I didn't murder Uriah! *I didn't!* All I wanted was one night in the arms of the man I love, the man I've *always* loved. You knew! Did you try to help me? You always knew! I didn't mean for anyone to be hurt!"

"And you think *love* makes what you've done forgivable? Men fought with Uriah near the walls of Rabbah! Men died because of what you want!" She struck Bathsheba again, sobbing with anguish and rage. "You've brought shame upon my household! Shame upon your father! Shame upon Ahithophel! Do you think they'll ever forgive you? It would better for me had I died in childbirth than give life to such as you! Disobedient daughter! Better had you been born dead!"

Bathsheba blocked another blow. "I carry David's child!"

Her mother uttered a broken sob and sank to her knees. "Ohhhh ... " She wailed, her hands clenched over her ears. "Ohhhh ... "

Bathsheba sobbed. "I didn't mean for this to happen, Mother! You have to believe me!"

"What does it matter what I believe? Fool! How many have died because of you? It will all be on your head. Do you think others won't learn of what the king has done for your sake? There are widows all over the city now who will curse you, and the king, too. And do you think the sons left fatherless today will rise up to praise David's name? Do you think they will take up arms for him? They will hate him with every breath they take! They will seek his destruction. And what of the thirty mighty men who fought with Uriah on David's behalf? What of your own father and all the others who've stood by David during his years in the wilderness? What will they think of their king now? Is he worthy of their loyalty and their life's blood? What will your father and grandfather do when they learn David murdered Uriah to have you? You are their flesh and blood, and you've betrayed them. They will never look at you again. People will spit on the ground when you pass by. They will never speak your name aloud! They will curse the day of your birth! And they will seek revenge upon the man who has ruined the reputation of their household!" Her mother tore the neckline of her dress. "You are dead to me, dead to us all!"

Horrified, Bathsheba stretched out her hands, weeping and pleading. Her mother slapped her hands away and stood. Bathsheba rose to her knees and grasped her mother's dress. "Mother, please! Speak reason to them!"

Her mother shoved her away. "Reason? *You* dare speak of reason?" She kicked her.

Afraid for the child, Bathsheba cowered and curled into a ball, but her mother didn't strike her again. "You are cursed among women! Your name will be a byword for *adulteress!* Your name will be unspoken as long as I live!" She spit on her and went to the doorway. She stood there, her back to Bathsheba. "May the Lord God of Israel strike me down if your name ever crosses my lips again! May God do to you what you have done to others!" She fled into the street, leaving the door ajar behind her.

Scrambling over to it, Bathsheba closed and locked it.

Over the days that passed, she grieved the loss of her husband, the loss of the others who fought beside him, the loss of her family, the loss of her reputation as well as that of the king she still loved so desperately. She grieved over the chaos she knew would come because of her sin with the king and the murder of her husband. She fasted and wept for Uriah, collecting her tears in a small bottle she wore around her neck. She covered her head with ashes.

The formal mourning period of seven days ended, but the sorrow and shame would not lift. Her fears deepened, withering her soul. During the dark hours of night, Bathsheba understood why purity was so highly praised. She was paying the cost of disobedience now, and the price was higher than she ever could have imagined. One night of passion would cost her a lifetime of despair.

And the cost to others ...

Soldiers entered her house eight days after Bathsheba had received the news of her husband's death. "We are under orders to bring the wife of Uriah the Hittite to the palace."

The wife of Uriah.

Bathsheba clutched against her heart the bottle filled with her tears.

The captain of the guard stepped forward. "You must come." Bathsheba left her house with nothing. She walked down the middle of the street with six soldiers as her escort. She wondered if David was showing her honor or merely protecting her. Women came to their doorways to watch the procession. One spit in the dust as she passed by. It seemed the eyes of Jerusalem were upon her, eyes of suspicion, eyes of hatred. She heard people whispering.

The guards didn't take her through a side entrance this time. They escorted her through the main entrance of the palace. The king was taking to wife the widow of one of his fallen mighty men. Perhaps it was meant as a show of great magnitude, for she was, after all, only a common woman, the daughter of a warrior, the granddaughter of a military advisor.

No one was fooled.

Except, perhaps, the king.

four

DAVID eagerly awaited the arrival of his newest wife. When the knock came upon his door, he opened it himself. Joram stood before him. He stepped aside and David saw a figure in black, head bowed. His pulse was racing. "The wife of Uriah the Hittite, my lord the king," Joram said smoothly.

David's head came up sharply. "Do not refer to her in that way again." He jerked his head in dismissal. He wanted no reminder that she'd belonged to another man before him. She belonged to *him* now. Nothing else mattered. As Joram's footsteps receded, David calmed himself. "Bathsheba." His voice came out rough. She stood with eyes downcast like a shy virgin. "Ah, my love," he whispered. He took her hand. "I've missed you." She shivered slightly as she stepped hesitantly over the threshold. Her fingers were cold. Was she trembling with the same need he felt? He drew her into his bedchamber. "You've no need to be afraid anymore." He closed the door behind her. "You're with me now and always will be. Our child will be born with no cloud over him."

She said nothing.

Disturbed by her silence, David turned her to face him and tipped her chin. Her face was thinner, and she was as pale as alabaster. He removed the veil and jealousy gripped him as he saw the small bottle on a string. He lifted it mockingly. "Did you love him so much?"

"I loved Uriah," she said softly. She raised her head, and her eyes were dark with pain. "But not as I've loved you. You were always the man of my dreams." She held out her free hand, palm up. "The man who held my heart in the palm of his hand." She clenched her fist, her eyes filling with tears.

David touched her cheek, marveling at the softness of her skin. She was the most beautiful woman in his kingdom, and she belonged to him now. "You'll never know how much I love you, Bathsheba." He saw her shudder and cupped her face. "You are *my* wife now." Ignoring the distressed look in her eyes, he removed the bottle of tears and tossed it aside. "Forget him. I will treat you like a queen." He leaned down and kissed her, gently at first until he felt her respond. "All other women pale when compared to you." He dug his fingers into her hair.

≈≈≈

David stood just outside his door and read the note Joram had brought from one of his advisors. Matters of state beckoned. He crumpled the message impatiently. He didn't need to be reminded that he was responsible for the lives of his people, and it was time to return to matters of state. Joram waited, silent, eyes straight ahead.

"Summon the eunuch in charge of my harem," David said quietly so that Bathsheba wouldn't be disturbed from her sleep.

"Yes, my lord the king."

David went back into his bedchamber and closed the door quietly behind him.

He crossed the room and stood beside the bed looking down at his wife. She was exquisite. He'd never seen a more beautiful woman, and he knew she would always be so. Like Abraham's Sarah. He smiled, taking a tress of black hair and rubbing it between his fingers. It was like thick silk. He would no longer be tormented by her absence. She belonged to him now. He could summon her any time he pleased.

Smiling, he sat on the edge of the bed. Leaning down, he kissed her and watched her awaken. She stretched and sighed softly. When she looked up at him, he realized she no longer had the look of starry-eyed adoration that she'd had as a young girl. Her love was mixed with troubled awareness. He didn't ask why. She reached up and touched his brow. He took her hand and pressed a kiss into her palm. "I don't want to leave you, but I must."

"You are the king."

"A chamber has been prepared for you." He stroked a tendril of curling black hair back from her brow. "If there is anything you need or want, you've only to tell the master of the harem. He will see to it."

A blush spread across her cheeks. He saw the moisture building in her eyes.

Stricken with emotions he couldn't identify, he grew impatient. "Up, my love." He had no time for teary brides! "We can't spend the rest of our lives in bed." He rose and moved away. The covers rustled behind him and he glanced back, intending to enjoy the pleasure of watching her dress. She reached for her widow's garb. "*No!*" He wrenched the garments from her, rolled them into a ball and flung them into the corner. Shaken by the power of his emotions, he glared at her.

"Am I to enter your harem naked, my lord the king?"

He strode across the room, grabbed one of his own tunics. "Wear this!" He thrust it into her hands. She trembled violently as she put it on. The purple hem pooled around her feet. She looked so young and vulnerable; he was reminded of the little girl who'd followed him to the stream of En-gedi. "Bathsheba, I'm sorry."

A knock sounded on the door, startling them both. He knew the eunuch had arrived to take her to her quarters. "Come!" he called out and the door opened. Bathsheba looked at the servant, but didn't take a step toward him. "I will call for you again soon," David said pointedly. Why should he feel guilty? Didn't she understand he was a king?

Her eyes flickered. Her cheeks filled with color as she bowed low. "I am yours to command, my lord the king." When she straightened, he saw a tear slip down her cheek before she turned quickly away. She followed the eunuch from the room.

David rubbed his chest, wondering why his heart should ache so much when everything had turned out exactly as he'd planned.

≈≈≈

Bathsheba's quarters were sumptuous, her new life one of leisure and luxury. She had beautiful clothing, plenty to eat and the protection of the king. She was never alone, for more than two hundred people lived in David's palace – six of his other wives, their numerous handmaidens, his children, servants, secretaries, craftsman, laborers, nannies, caretakers, cooks, guards, porters, stewards, and artisans. There were also many faithful elderly retainers and old soldiers who could no longer carry arms. A stream of visitors came and went into the palace as David's wives visited with their family members and entertained.

No one came to visit Bathsheba.

When David's wives gathered for the evening meal, they did not include her in their conversation, nor even acknowledge her presence. His older sons did look at her, pointedly; Amnon, the eldest, with·lasciviousness, Absalom with contempt. These women and their children were her family now, and Ahinoam had spoken for most of them the day Bathsheba had been shown into the women's quarter: "So this is the king's whore!"

She remembered overhearing her grandfather say to her father years ago, "Never trust anyone outside your own family." But Bathsheba knew she could never trust any of these women or their sons, and her child would always be in danger.

The days wore on her like a windstorm over stone. Whispered words blew harsh, rubbing painfully, reshaping her. Bathsheba sat alone, consoling herself with love for the child she carried. When her son came, she wouldn't give him up to a wet nurse or a nanny. She would keep him with her and love him. And if the child were a girl, she would watch over her and train her into womanhood herself rather than entrust her to the care of others. And she hoped. *Let the child be a son to make David proud!*

She waited a month before letting the news be known that she was carrying the king's child. There were some in the palace whose loyalty toward David ran so deep they refused to think ill of him, no matter what others whispered. They rejoiced that the king's household was about to grow by another child. However, there were many who cast side-long glances at her, lips sneering. Some would not look at her at all.

The wives spent every day entertaining themselves with games, music, conversation. Some did handwork to while away the hours. Whenever word came that the king would spend the evening with them, they focused all their energies on preparing for his visitation. Each tried to outdo the others in beauty preparation. They primped and fussed, sending handmaidens hither and yon for whatever they thought might attract David's attention. Ahinoam put on Egyptian kohl and Persian mascara. Maacah painted her toenails with henna and wore anklets. They all braided their hair and anointed themselves with perfume. Bathsheba bathed, brushed her hair until it shone and rippled over her shoulders and down her back, and wore the simple dress of a commoner. Let David remember her as she had been, not as she had become.

When David entered the room, her heart leaped. She watched as he looked around. His gaze settled briefly upon her and his eyes glowed warmly. But he looked away, speaking to Ahinoam, who caressed his arm and smiled up at him as though he were the moon and the stars. Though he did not linger long, David wandered the room, pausing here and there, giving each a measure of attention. Bathsheba observed his every movement with increasing anguish. He greeted each woman with a smile, talked amicably, charmed them with a touch. He was so handsome, who would not love him? She felt a shaft of pain each time he brushed his knuckles against an upturned face, took a hand and kissed it, spoke a soft word or laughed.

The women flirted boldly, some so boldly Bathsheba wanted to scream and tear their hair out. But she remained in her seat, pretending a calm she didn't feel. When David sat upon a cushion, he was surrounded and caressed. He looked at her only one more time, but she took little comfort in the darkening of his eyes, for his attention was drawn away almost immediately.

So this was the pain her mother had warned her against! Hadn't her mother tried to tell her what it would be like to be David's wife? *"One among many."* Could there be any agony worse than seeing the man she loved pampered and petted by six other women? She shifted her body so that she wouldn't have to endure it.

David came to her then. "Are you well, Bathsheba?" She was too distressed to answer, afraid if she spoke she would give the women fuel for further torment when David was gone. "Bathsheba?" He spoke in a hoarse whisper and hunkered down as he turned her face so that she had to look at him. He searched her eyes, his own hungry and troubled. "Try to understand. I can't give in to what I want and forsake all these others."

The irony of his words made her look away. Hadn't she forsaken all others for him? Wasn't her husband now dead because she had given in to what she wanted without thought of the consequences?

"Bathsheba," he said again, her name a soft groan. The others watched like a pride of lionesses.

"Of course, I understand," she whispered, looking into his eyes and hoping he didn't sense her despair. Understanding increased her suffering. He was a king, above all. And a king must have many wives so that he could build up his house with sons. Now that it was known that she was already with child, what need had he to call her to his bed? She remembered her mother's words. *"When you grow up, you will understand the wisdom of worshiping God and not a man."*

She must grow up and throw away her fantasies! She must face her circumstances! There would be worse scandal if the king summoned her now that her pregnancy was known. Everyone knew the only reason the king visited a wife was to beget more children. They couldn't be alone together until after the child was born and she'd fulfilled the rites of purification – forty days for a boy, eighty for a girl. *Oh, let it be a boy!*

Her heart sank as she faced the months of loneliness ahead of her. For she was despised among these women, the object of their jealousy, the victim of their constant gossip. But what right had she to resent them? Everything they said was true!

David brushed his fingers against her cheek and rose. She watched him walk away with a sinking heart. Bowing her head, she took up her embroidery and kept her gaze away from him for the rest of the evening. Her heart fluttered and her forehead broke out in cold sweat. She knew exactly how long he spoke with each wife. Never had she thought her sweet dreams of David could turn into such a nightmare! She was torn between relief and dread when the king finally rose to leave the company of his wives. She knew when he looked at her, but she didn't look up. She kept thinking of how he'd sung to his men around the fire, looking from one to the next. She was no more or less regarded by the king than any other woman in this room. She was just one of many who lived to be in his company. Her mother had told her so time and again, but life was her teacher.

The women relaxed as soon as the doors were closed behind the king. They no longer competed for his attention. Some talked. Some lounged indolently. Others returned to their handwork. When the eunuch entered the chamber, they fell silent. "Abigail," he said, and she rose quickly, cheeks flushed as she followed him out of the room.

Never had Bathsheba felt such pain! Her heart felt as though it were being torn from her! Maacah smirked. Haggith whispered behind her hand to Eglath, who laughed and looked across the room at Bathsheba. Did her anguish show? She wanted to leap up and run. She wanted to lock herself in her private chamber and scream out her pain.

Ahinoam sniffed. "Why is he calling for Abigail? He hasn't called for her in months. Besides, she's too old to bear him another son."

"Better her than another whose name I won't mention."

Maacah glared at Bathsheba. "Perhaps David craves the company of a *virtuous* woman."

Words of retaliation rose like bile in Bathsheba's throat, but she swallowed them. Why pour oil on the fire? Besides, what defense had she? She *was* faithless. She gathered her sewing, rose, inclined her head and walked sedately from the room, refusing to give them further opportunities to stab her heart. When her chamber door was firmly closed, she crumpled to the floor and stifled her sobs with a pillow.

She slept little that night, tortured by thoughts of David and Abigail. She rose early and walked alone in the inner garden. She sat beneath an olive tree and bowed her head, afraid to pray. Why draw God's attention when the price for sin was death? She moved her hands slowly over her abdomen, love distracting her from her anguish. She would pour her life out for her child. David's child.

"Bathsheba?"

Startled, she glanced at Abigail.

"I've come from the king," the older woman said.

Bathsheba's heart twisted. She clenched her hands in her lap, her stomach tighten. Did Abigail mean to gloat over the night she'd spent in David's arms? With an effort, Bathsheba kept silent, refusing to show her feelings. David's third wife studied her for a moment. "May I sit?"

"If it pleases you."

Abigail took a seat beside her. "I'm not here to cause you more sorrow, Bathsheba." She looked down and brushed imaginary dust from her dress. "David asked me last night if you are adjusting to life in the palace. I told him you've shown great dignity. He asked if you've been well, and I told him I haven't heard you utter a word of complaint. He asked if you've received visitors, and I said not to my knowledge." She gave a soft broken laugh. "I suppose our husband felt he could speak with me about these things because I'm older than he and was married to another before him. I suppose he thought I would understand your feelings better than anyone else in the palace." She drew in her breath and released it slowly. "He also asked me if you still grieved for Uriah."

Fighting tears, Bathsheba stared straight ahead.

Abigail lifted her head and turned to look at her. "I've never known David to ask so many questions about a wife, or to show jealousy over one. He's always been very careful to treat each one equally to preserve peace in the household. We all vie for his attention, but he has never before found distinction between us. Last night, he let his heart be known. Not because he wanted everyone to know, but because he can't help himself. He has a special regard for you."

Bathsheba sucked in a sharp breath as joy caught her off guard. She quickly dampened it when she recognized the pain in Abigail's eyes. How many others were in love with him? "I'm sorry, Abigail."

Abigail understood her meaning and smiled wryly. "It is never wise to fall in love with a king."

"My mother told me that years ago."

"Your mother is wise." She lifted her eyes. "I think David is in love with you. I don't think he could've done the things he's done otherwise."

Heat surged into Bathsheba's cheeks, but strangely she heard no condemnation in Abigail's tone, nor saw it in her eyes. She trembled. "I'm the one who sinned." It was better for all if she took full responsibility.

Abigail shook her head. "We've all sinned."

"*You* didn't. You warned David against sinning." She didn't have to add the rest – that she'd unwittingly encouraged him to do so.

"I called my husband a fool before witnesses."

"You remained faithful."

"And waited until Nabal was sober so that I could tell him what he had done and have him understand completely. I knew his greed. I knew his arrogance. I also knew his cowardice. I spoke and watched the terror come upon him. I watched him die, and thanked God for my deliverance. And when David sent for me to be his wife, I packed in all haste and came to him because I'd loved what I'd heard about him and loved him still more when I laid eyes upon him." Her eyes were shiny with tears. "I love him still."

Bathsheba was deeply touched that Abigail trusted her enough to be so open. "You did nothing deserving of condemnation. Everyone spoke of your wisdom and quick actions. You saved countless lives that night, Abigail." Whereas Uriah was dead because of her, and all the men who had stormed the walls of Rabbah with him.

"Do not praise me. God sees the heart, Bathsheba, and God will judge us all."

Bathsheba felt a chill in the pit of her stomach. Closing her eyes, she hung her head. "That's what I fear most of all." *I've broken the Law. How can I ever undo what has happened because of my sin? Oh, Lord God of Israel, be merciful. Please pull me up from the pit I dug for myself and change the direction of my life!*

Abigail put her hand over hers and squeezed it gently. "God is also merciful to those who repent." She rose, leaving Bathsheba alone to wonder how repentance would change anything now. No matter what she did from here forward, people would remember her as an adulteress.

The child she carried would be the evidence held against her.

When the child came, Bathsheba saw in the eyes of those who assisted her that her sins were now revealed. The eighth wife of the king, a mere six months after entering the palace, had born a fully developed child with strong limbs and lungs. As her baby screamed in the midwife's arms, Bathsheba felt the woman's repugnance. She looked from face to face and was afraid. Ignoring the pain and summoning her strength, she reached out quickly. "Give me my son!"

The midwife dumped him into her arms as though he was an unclean thing. Shocked by such careless handling, Bathsheba drew back from the woman and held her son close. If she'd ever wondered what treatment her child would receive, she knew now. The entire population of the palace, nay, the nation, would know her son had been conceived in sin!

The midwives left, but Bathsheba heard their voices buzz just outside her door.

Abigail entered soon afterward. "Would you mind if I stayed with you for a while?"

Bathsheba wept at her kindness. "I understand their hatred of me, but my son is *innocent!*"

Abigail brushed the hair back from her face. "Hush now, for the child's sake." She tucked her hands beneath the infant. "Let me have him. I'll wash him and rub the salt in gently so he'll be safe from infection. Then I'll swaddle him and present him to the king."

Where her grandfather, Ahithophel, would see and know ...

David had offered him many gifts upon his return from Rabbah. David assured her all was well between them, but she knew David would be dead by now if he were not king. Her grandfather was shrewd, but he was also as unforgiving as Joab. She feared what went on in the mind of her grandfather. When David returned at the head of his army with Hanum's crown upon his head, she'd watched her grandfather from the palace wall as he came into the city at the head of the military advisors. He looked up and saw her where she stood. He didn't smile and raise his hand. His eyes fixed upon her like a target.

Bathsheba could only hope her father hadn't been told the whole story when he'd been transported home after being wounded in Rabbah. Had her mother taken pity upon her as her father lay suffering? Surely she would not have been so cruel as to tell him his daughter had committed adultery with the king and caused the murder of her husband! It would have been an act of kindness to tell him simply that his daughter had been taken into the palace as the king's wife after news of Uriah's death – and omit the rest of the sordid tale.

She had frequent nightmares, awakening in a cold sweat and expecting to see her grandfather leaning over her with his curved knife. Sometimes she dreamed she was standing at the door of her father's house, hearing her grandfather swear to his son in her hearing, "Oh, my son, my son! They will not go unpunished! Though David be king, I will lay him low! And if I meet failure, may my life be forfeit!"

She tried not to think of what the future might hold. She tried to forget the bad dreams and separation from David as she held her son in her arms and nursed him. Perhaps this would be enough.

David was pleased with her son. He sat with her and cupped the child's head tenderly, then looked into her eyes. She decided to live for each infrequent moment in David's company, basking in his love, even if it proved inconstant. Her son would be different. She relished his warmth in her arms, the tug of his mouth at her breast as he took his sustenance from her. Never had she loved anyone as much as she loved this child of her body. She dedicated herself to him. Night and day, she watched over him, entrusting his care to no one else. She kept him close, aware of his every movement and sound. A child existed to be loved, and she poured her love out like an offering upon him.

And then the prophet Nathan came to set things right.

※※※

David was informed the moment Nathan approached the palace, and he came into the court to offer the elderly man a warm welcome and greeting. He tensed when he saw the fire in the old prophet's eyes and realized Nathan had come with less than pleasant words to impart. "What brings you to the palace?" David said, taking his seat and resting his hands on the arms of the throne. "What can I do for you?"

Nathan stood before him, feet planted. He was far older than David's forty years, but life shone brightly in his eyes. The presence of the Lord could be felt in the room the moment he opened his mouth and spoke in a deep, clear voice for all to hear.

"There were two men in a certain town. One was rich, and one was poor. The rich man owned many sheep and cattle. The poor man owned nothing but a little lamb he had worked hard to buy. He raised that little lamb, and it grew up with his children. It ate from the man's own plate and drank from his cup. He cuddled it in his arms like a baby daughter. One day a guest arrived at the home of the rich man. But instead of killing a lamb from his own flocks for food, he took the poor man's lamb and killed it and served it to his guest."

David slammed his fist upon the arm of his throne. "As surely as the Lord lives, any man who would do such a thing deserves to die! He must repay four lambs to the poor man for the one he stole and for having no pity."

Nathan's eyes blazed. "*You are that man!*"

David went cold, his skin prickling.

Nathan stepped forward. "The Lord, the God of Israel says," he said in a voice all the more powerful because of its quietness, "'I anointed you king of Israel and saved you from the power of Saul. I gave you his house and his wives and the kingdoms of Israel and Judah. And if that had not been enough, I would have given you much, much more.'"

Fear gripped David until he shook.

"'Why, then, have you despised the word of the Lord and done this horrible deed? For you have murdered Uriah and stolen his wife.'"

All those in the court gasped and stared at David. Drops of sweat formed on his brow and dripped down his temples. His ears were opened! For he heard the truth Nathan spoke. His eyes were opened fully to the evil he'd done, and he cried out in horror. How could he have been so blind? How was it possible to love God so much and be captured so completely by sin? David bolted out of his throne and threw himself at the feet of the prophet, his heart thundering as he felt the eyes of God upon him.

"'From this time on,'" Nathan went on, "'the sword will be a constant threat to your family, because you have despised Me by taking Uriah's wife to be your own. Because of what you have done, I, the Lord, will cause your own household to rebel against you. I will give your wives to another man, and he will go to bed with them in public view. You did it secretly, but I will do this to you openly in the sight of all Israel.'"

Sorrow filled David. "I have sinned against the Lord!" He deserved death. He remembered the look in Uriah's eyes before he turned away and went to face his death. *How could I have done it?* David wept. *My friend! My friend!* He waited for God to strike him down where he lay. Instead, he felt Nathan's hand gentle upon his head.

"The Lord has forgiven you, and you won't die for this sin."

David's head came up in amazement. Nathan stroked his hair as though he were a child, his eyes grieved. "But," he said sadly, straightening, "you have given the enemies of the Lord great opportunity to despise and blaspheme Him, so your child will die."

David's stomach dropped. He stared into Nathan's eyes and saw there would be no compromise. His chest tightened as he thought of the cost to Bathsheba. Shutting his eyes, he bent over and covered his head as Nathan turned and walked from the court.

～～～

Bathsheba was alarmed when her baby wouldn't nurse, then frightened when he became feverish and cried pitifully. She did everything she knew to bring the fever down, but it raged unabated, sapping the child of strength. She held him and rocked him. She walked with him in her arms. When she became too exhausted to hold him, she lay upon her bed with the baby nestled against her. And she wept, hour on unending hour, for fear of losing him.

"Where is David? Does he know ...?"

"He knows, my lady," the eunuch told her. "He's fasting and inquiring of God for the child."

Bathsheba felt a flicker of hope at this news, for hadn't the Lord always heard David's prayers? Hadn't God always helped David?

She didn't dare beseech God herself.

Each day, the child lost strength. On the seventh day, while Bathsheba was holding him and pleading softly, the baby stopped breathing. For a long moment, Bathsheba felt as though her own heart had stopped. She didn't cry out or tear her hair or rent her clothing. She lay quietly upon her bed and curled her body around her dead child, and closed her eyes.

God, I know you've taken my son. Why didn't you take me instead?

Some of the women who'd lost children pitied her. But others took cruel pleasure in God's judgment upon Bathsheba's baby and her anguished silence. "She deserved it," they whispered. "See what God does to sinners!" they gossiped. "She's getting a taste of the bitterness she's caused others."

Abigail sat with Bathsheba, weeping and stroking her hair, but saying nothing. The older woman simply held her as the little body was taken from her. Bathsheba wept hysterically.

Finally, exhausted and heartsick, Bathsheba lay staring at nothing. "David never came. Not once. I sent word. He knew our child was dying. And he never came. I thought he loved us."

Abigail put her hand on Bathsheba's shoulder. "He's been fasting and praying for seven days. He beseeched God's mercy continuously, Bathsheba. The priests were afraid to tell him that your baby has died. They thought he might kill himself."

Bathsheba sat up, frightened.

Abigail shook her head quickly. "Don't be alarmed. I was told David knew what had happened when the men came to speak with him. He arose from the ground, washed, anointed himself, changed his clothes, and went into the house of the Lord to worship. He returned to the palace and is taking a meal."

Bathsheba sank down again and turned her face away. "God is so cruel."

"You mustn't say that."

"Why shouldn't I say it? He should've struck *me* down instead of killing an innocent child! Let God strike me now!" She pulled her hair, her chest heaving with the rising sobs. "It was *my* sin, *mine!* Why take out His wrath on a helpless baby?" She gulped breath as she cried. "My son ... oh, my son ... "

Abigail cupped Bathsheba's cheek. "You'll become sick if you go on like this."

"Let me be sick unto death!" Weeping, Bathsheba drew her knees into her chest and covered her head. "Why did God let my son suffer for my sins? Why?"

"I don't know," Abigail said.

Desolate, Bathsheba turned her face to the wall and said no more.

David's advisers were quick to give their opinion, speaking to him hurriedly as he finished his meal. "It would be wise, my lord the king, to establish separate quarters for the wife of Uriah. You must see no more of her."

David raised his head, seeing the way the wind blew. It was always easier to attack the weak.

"The people," another said. "You must think of the people."

He *was* thinking of his people, and the impact of his sin upon them weighed heavily on his mind and heart. How could he have been so blind? How could he have done the things he did without seeing the evil in it? The men surrounded him like old hens, looking for someone to peck to pieces.

"Of course, you must assign guards to protect the woman from those who will want to take justice into their own hands."

"Cloister her as you have cloistered Michal."

"It might serve you better if you sent the woman to live in Hebron or Jericho."

David shoved his plate away and stood. "I've listened to your advice." He glared at his advisers. "Bathsheba will not be punished for sins I committed. I confessed before God and repented. And I will make the truth known to the people."

Those who loved him quickly capitulated, but there were others who merely bowed their heads and pretended obedience. David knew them well. Hadn't he spent years in the desert with these men? Fine clothes and houses hadn't changed them. There would always be those inside the palace who crouched like hungry lions, seeking an opportunity to devour their prey.

"Nathan said God has forgiven me for my sins."

"Yes, my lord the king. The Lord has forgiven *you*. God said nothing in regard to the woman."

The woman. Amazing how two words could show such contempt. "Bathsheba is innocent of Uriah's death."

"Is a woman ever innocent, my lord the king? Was it not the woman in the Garden of Eden who drew the man into sin?"

He looked into their eyes and was chilled by their lack of mercy. How quick they were to absolve him because he sat upon the throne but pour blame for everything upon a defenseless woman.

"You are beloved by all Israel," one said, and David knew his flattering tongue was dipped in poison.

"I was the shepherd who led the lamb astray."

"You are king, and the nation is at stake, my lord. Isn't it an unblemished lamb that is offered as atonement for sin?"

His eyes filled with tears at the hardness of their hearts. "The Lord chose the lamb. He took our son." He turned his back on them and went straight to the women's quarters. He had neglected Bathsheba for too long, serving these men who devised evil plans against her.

His heart broke when he entered her room and saw her curled on her side facing the wall. He dismissed her handmaiden with a nod of his head and sat on the edge of the bed. "Bathsheba." Her body jerked and she covered her head. "Bathsheba." He turned her and pulled her into his arms. "I'm sorry."

"Our son ... our son ..." She clung to him sobbing, her fingers clutching at his tunic.

David pressed his face into the curve of her neck and wept with her. "The sin is upon my head," he said hoarsely.

She pulled away from him violently, her face ravaged by grief. "No, no. It was me."

"Bathsheba ... "

"Who was it who followed you around the camp? Who was it who could look only at you when her groom sat beside her? Who was it who stood naked in her courtyard so that you could see her? Who was it who went into your arms without a thought for her husband?" She beat her fists against her heart. "Me! It was me!"

David caught hold of her wrists. "God didn't punish our son, Bathsheba. He took him out of the reach of evil men." Like those he had just left. Like others within his own house that would use this to rise against him. "How many would've used the circumstances of our son's birth to blaspheme against God? The Lord has kept our son from harm."

"I want my son! I want to hold my son!"

David gripped her head and looked into her red-rimmed, tear-drenched eyes. "He's in the Lord's hands, my love. I can't bring him back to you." He pulled her close again, rocking her as though she were a child in need of comfort. "Someday we will go and be with him."

Bathsheba relaxed against him. "The Lord must hate me."

"No." He tipped her face and tenderly combed the dark lank hair back from her face. His heart squeezed tight at the pallor of her cheeks, the suffering in her eyes. "I misused my authority, Bathsheba. When I saw you, I asked who you were. Did I have a thought for your husband or your father or grandfather? I remembered the little girl who had followed me about the camp with her heart in her eyes. I saw the beautiful woman you'd become, and I wanted you. Nothing mattered but to satisfy my own lust. I gave no thought of the cost to others, especially the cost to you."

"I should've been like Abigail, warning you ... "

"I was a different man when Abigail confronted me, Bathsheba. Young and on fire for the Lord. I was running for my life in those days. Look around you. You see the way I live now. When I saw you from the roof, I was a king blinded by pride." Pain filled him as he saw himself clearly. He had shirked his duty as commander of the army. He'd grown bored and restless while living his life of leisure in the palace. When he saw a woman of unusual beauty bathing, he sent soldiers to bring her to him. Why shouldn't he take whatever he wanted? He was *king!*

What a fool he'd been.

"I was so conceited! I thought I held all power in my hand. I thought I could have whatever I wanted. So I stole you from another, sired a child, then tried to use my friend to hide the evidence of my sin. Uriah proved himself more righteous than I." He felt her shudder in his arms.

"He knew," she said softly.

"Yes. He knew." He shut his eyes, stricken again. "The judgment is on my head, Bathsheba, because I shed innocent blood." He was filled with self-loathing and grief. "After all the Lord has done for me, I allowed lust to control me and turned away from the One who had given me victory on every side."

"I share the blame. I used love as an excuse to sin."

"You didn't kill Uriah."

"A man's heart can die before a spear ever pierces him." Tears streamed down her pale cheeks. Uriah had been a good husband, an honest man, and she'd crushed his heart and been the motive behind his murder.

David pressed her head against his heart, unable to speak. How was it possible for two people to know and love the Law and yet sin so abominably? How and when had sin first crept into their lives and spread like a plague until it killed their consciences? Had the seeds of sin been planted years ago, when he'd realized she was no longer a child and wished he had asked for her before Eliam gave her to another man? Had the seeds planted then been watered with his own fantasies?

Yet, what he felt for Bathsheba wasn't lust. Not entirely. He *loved* her.

Tipping her chin, David kissed her. Her lips trembled, and he sensed her hesitation. He kissed her again and felt her respond. When he lifted his head, she leaned against him again with a soft sigh. "God has forgiven us," he said, closing his eyes and giving silent thanks. "The Lord has shown His great mercy in giving us our lives. And He did *not* say I had to give you up."

"But how shall we live, knowing what we've done and the harm it's brought to others?"

"We will live one day at a time and face whatever comes."

"It'll never be over. Oh, David, I see so clearly now, and it hurts so much. We won't be the only ones to suffer." She drew back, looking up at him. "If only we were the only ones ... "

He cupped her cheek. "Nathan proclaimed the word of the Lord. I know what is to come."

She went into his arms and clung fiercely. "I love you, David. I've always loved you. No matter what happens, I always will."

"I know," he said with a sad smile.

Love was never the issue between the two of them. He loved her too, more fiercely than he had ever loved a woman. But he was deeply grieved when he remembered the loyal friends he'd betrayed because he thought his love for Bathsheba provided adequate excuse: Uriah, who had fought beside him in more battles than he could remember; Eliam, who'd shared his fire and food; Ahithophel, his brilliant military adviser. Would they still stand with him? Love betrayed turned to hate. Now, Ahithophel never spoke Bathsheba's name; her mother hadn't attended her during the birth of her child. Bathsheba had been abandoned by her family, though she hadn't once complained.

David vowed silently to do all he could to mend the broken relationships, to renew trust, and glorify God's name.

"I'm sorry," he said, heartbroken at the pain he had caused her. He prayed that the honor he showed her as the woman he loved would eventually soften the hearts of those he'd hurt and humiliated.

"Our son." Her body shook violently as she began weeping again. "Our son ... "

David gathered his young wife into his arms and comforted her the only way he knew how. And as he did, he prayed God would show them even more mercy by granting them another child to replace the one who had paid the price for their sin.

five

WHEN Bathsheba realized she was with child again, she was afraid to rejoice. Would God take this child also? Would she have another baby only to have it die in her arms like her firstborn son?

Cloistered in luxury, favored wife of an absent king, she lived a life of sorrow and loneliness, shunned by family and friends. David was in Rabbah with the army, leaving her vulnerable and unprotected from the enemies that surrounded her. People outside the walls judged her a harlot and condemned her, just as her mother had. How could she hope for God's mercy when her own mother hated her? How could she believe God had forgiven her sins when no one else had? The prophet Nathan told David that God had forgiven him, but did that forgiveness extend to her as well? David had claimed so, but Bathsheba would make no assumptions. She lived in constant fear, for she had no possessions of her own, no money to buy sacrifices. All she had to offer God was a contrite heart and the desire to do right for the rest of her life.

How she longed to go back in time, to be a child again, safe in her mother's arms. How she longed to be on her grandfather's knee, listening to him dispense wisdom to those who came to visit at their fire. Once she had been an innocent girl with unrequited love for a handsome warrior, a singer of psalms, the charismatic leader of a growing army. Now she was David's eighth wife, known far and wide as the adulteress who had enticed a beloved king into murdering her husband so she could live in the palace. The people forgave David, but used her as their scapegoat.

She did not resent the people's lenience with David. Someone had to bear the blame, and it was better laid upon her head than have the people turn on him. She was just a woman, but he was their king.

But, oh, how can I ever hold my head up again? When I sing praises to the Lord, people glare at me as though I'm blaspheming. They come to worship You and see me among the women, and their hearts are turned away from You as they nurture thoughts of vengeance.

Bathsheba begged God to blot out her transgressions, to cleanse her from all sin. "Give me a heart that will be pleasing to You, Lord. Don't cast me out into the darkness." But even as she prayed, she felt overwhelming shame at being so presumptuous. What right had she to ask for mercy?

Fear attacked most often at night when she was alone in her chamber. What right had she to hold a baby in her arms? None! How many mothers wept over the loss of sons who had died with Uriah? How many wives grieved husbands or brothers or cousins? She had no right to happiness.

But the child, oh, the child.

"Oh, God of mercy, only You can deliver me from my guilt. O Lord, comfort those who mourn. Give them joy in the morning. Do with me whatever You will, but please spare my baby, who is innocent of the sins I committed."

With so many pointing fingers and shaking their heads, Bathsheba didn't hope for mercy.

The baby came easily, and her son was strong and healthy and beautiful. Bathsheba held her second son and wept. Overwhelmed with tenderness, yet still afraid, she gazed at her baby as he nursed. The fingers of his right hand clasped tightly around her thumb. "I promise to raise up my son to be a man after Your own heart. I will teach him to love Your Law." Tears streaked her face, she raised her son's tiny hand and kissed it. "And I give him the name Solomon, for it is through his birth that I have come to experience *God's peace.*"

Please, please, let it be so between us, Lord. Forgive me.

A message came within a few hours, written by the hand of Nathan the prophet. "*Your son shall have the name Jedidiah – 'beloved of the Lord.'*"

Bathsheba laughed. *O, Lord, You have washed me clean and warmed me in Your loving kindness.* Even when all those around her scorned her and failed to celebrate the birth of her son, God looked with favor upon him and gave His blessing. She was filled with amazement and gratitude. "My son ... my son ... " She wept with joy. She kissed his small face. "I took my troubles to the Lord. I, so unworthy, cried out to Him for deliverance, and He has answered from His throne." She laughed joyfully, tears of exaltation dripping like a baptism upon Solomon's brow. She smoothed them over his soft skin. "Jedidiah." She kissed each cheek and nestled him against her shoulder. "Jedidiah." She savored the feel of his body tucked close. "My cup is overflowing with God's blessings," she whispered, rubbing his back.

Jedidiah. The Lord had named *her* son "*beloved of the Lord.*"

~~~~

Rabbah fell, and the defeated Ammonites were set to work with saw, iron threshing boards and iron axes, tearing down the temple and altars of the Ammonite god Molech and the walls of the city. Before leading his army away, David left orders for the Ammonites. When the demolition was done, they were to turn their work to the brick molds and rebuild the conquered cities according to his specifications.

David led his army into Jerusalem, wearing the crown of the Ammonite deity Molech upon his head to show that false gods could not stand against the Lord. The people cheered as he rode through the gate, leading the way for wagons loaded with booty. His commanders and advisers followed, and the troops came marching home.

Bathsheba saw her grandfather among David's advisers and hoped there would be peace between them. Perhaps Ahithophel would forgive her when he learned he had a great-grandson. Still, she was chilled by what she'd heard from Joram. David had not gone to Rabbah on his own. Joab had sent for him to come, for he'd won the battle and the crown was waiting for David. Joab might as well have said: *You are king and will wear the crown, but never forget I am the one who conquered Rabbah!*

She was afraid for David.

Joab and his brother Abishai were both fierce warriors given to quick insult and long-lasting plots for revenge. Bathsheba remembered hearing in Uriah's home about Joab's vengeful murder of Abner, one of the most powerful men in King Saul's army. Abner had killed Joab's brother Asahel just after the contest held at the Pool of Gibeon. Joab had then taken the life of Abner in revenge. Bathsheba recalled hearing how furious David had been and how he mourned Abner's death. She had been among the people when David condemned Joab's actions as evil. At the time, she had been afraid for David. And now Joab was even more powerful, more evil.

Was it not Joab's idea to send other men with Uriah to their deaths? Although attempting to cover David's orders to murder Uriah, he'd added tenfold to the consequences of David's sin. Even the message he'd sent to David after Uriah's death was a challenge: He had reminded David that Gideon's son Abimelech was killed by a piece of millstone thrown down upon him by a woman on the wall. She knew Joab had been pointing an accusing finger at her, predicting that she would cause David's downfall.

Joab was a threat to David, even if David was unable – or unwilling – to see it.

※※※

And how many other enemies were rising within David's own ranks and within his own family? How many would whisper lies and make secret plots to destroy him? How many would set snares and lay in wait, devising schemes to bring him down? Nathan had warned him.

The palace was fraught with tension and hostility, rampant with jealousy and ambition. She saw how David's other wives were bringing their sons up to be contenders for the throne. They were hungry to grasp power for their offspring. They saw David's love for her as a threat. David's sons ran wild with pride and arrogance, and he did nothing to dissuade them.

Bathsheba feared her grandfather most. She had grown up among fighting men. She had listened to the conversations around her grandfather Ahithophel's campfire. She had listened to her father talk about enemies and allies. Was her grandfather now pretending forgiveness while plotting revenge? Could she believe Ahithophel would forgive and forget the humiliation she and David had brought upon his house? Her grandfather was brilliant in the tactics of warfare. He would know how to destroy a king.

When she spoke with David of her concerns, he dismissed her fears. "I've spoken with Ahithophel at length. He swore his allegiance to me. Besides, my love, I've given him gifts, more than twice the bride-price of Ahinoam. So don't worry yourself about things a woman can't possibly understand."

She understood that David had tried to show her grandfather that he valued her more than any other and would show her the honor of a first wife. But the gift could easily be seen as a bribe, and her grandfather had always been uncompromising. A man's hatred could run deeper than any gift could reach. But nothing she could say would convince David to be cautious when heeding the military advice of her grandfather. He refused to look upon Ahithophel as a possible enemy.

It was the first time she and David argued, and the first time David left her bed before sunrise. Nor did he speak to her during the next visitation.

When Bathsheba learned that David had taken another wife, a girl several years younger than she, the daughter of a powerful merchant of the tribe of Benjamin, Bathsheba felt betrayed. Weeping, she went before the Lord and prayed. She spent hours thinking about her situation and finally realized she was being childish again. David was *king* and would never belong entirely to her. If she didn't accept her station in life as one of his many wives, she would make herself and him miserable.

David would take more wives and concubines in the years ahead. She would have to learn to live with the pain that would come each time his eyes drifted to another. When David's young bride was ushered into the women's quarters, Bathsheba mastered her jealousy and greeted her as she would have wished to be greeted.

In the midst of her suffering, Bathsheba grew up. She'd loved David since she was a little girl. She had placed him on a pedestal like an idol. But she knew now that David wasn't a god. He was an ordinary man who'd been made extraordinary through the tender mercies of God. David was a man capable of great victories, but also of horrendous defeat. Hadn't his lust for her almost destroyed him? Her weakness might yet destroy her. If David were to die, she and her son would be at the mercy of men like her grandfather and Joab, or whichever of David's sons could wrestle power from the hands of the others.

When fear threatened to overwhelm her, she set her mind upon the Lord, comforting herself with thoughts of what God had already done for her. She sang her husband's psalms to her son, and clung to the promises in them. And every time she did these things, she felt an inner peace. The Lord was her shield, her deliverer, the lifter of her soul. Not David. David was only the man she loved, not the God she now worshiped.

Knowing her husband's faults and weaknesses didn't diminish him in her sight. Strangely, she loved him all the more because of his vulnerability. Two years of suffering had awakened her. Power was in the hand of the Lord! And so, she went down on her knees daily, bending her head to the floor each morning when she first awakened so that she could thank God for His blessings and ask for His guidance. She prayed constantly that God would protect David and give him wisdom. And whenever she was in David's company, she did all she could to give comfort, pleasure and joy. She knew a contentious wife was worse than a constant dripping and submitted herself to his needs, even those he didn't realize he had – especially to listen.

She was no longer a child filled with dreams, but a woman tempered by hardship and sorrow. She spoke often with the Prophet Nathan, seeking his wisdom, because she knew it would come from God. When she lay down at night, whether in David's arms or alone in her private chamber while he was in bed with another woman, she praised God for all the day had held, both good and bad.

Every time David added another wife or concubine to his harem, the hurt would rise in her again. But she learned not to expect perfect love from David, for to have those expectations increased her suffering. She refused to give in to the emotions tearing at her heart and remembered the source of love. She turned her attention from David's wandering eye to God and His faithfulness to His people. Her husband could still arouse her physical passion, and she could still feel suffering, betrayal, confusion, and loneliness. But she was no longer in despair, no longer without hope. The Lord God of Israel taught her about love, faithfulness, forgiveness, provision, protection, peace, and compassion. Every time David wounded her, she turned to God for healing and comfort. And the Lord was always there. For His love *was* perfect.

"The Lord is our shepherd," she whispered to Solomon. "We have everything we need. He lets us rest in green meadows; He leads us beside peaceful streams. He renews our strength. Oh, may He guide us along right paths, bringing honor to His name. Even when we walk through the dark valley of death, we will not be afraid, for God will be close beside us. His rod and staff will protect us and we will be comforted by His presence. The Lord will prepare a feast for us in the presence of our enemies. He will welcome us as His guests, anointing our heads with oil. Our cup overflows with blessings." She kissed Solomon. "Surely God's goodness and unfailing love will pursue us all the days of our lives, if we give ourselves wholeheartedly to Him. And we will live in the house of the Lord forever."

David summoned her more often than any of his other wives or concubines. Each time he professed his love for her, she knew he spoke from his heart. She knew also his deepest desire was to please God and walk in all His ways, and she knew how often he failed and grew depressed. Was it any different for her? The more she tried to live a perfect life for God, the more she recognized her failings. Why else were the sacrificial fires burning from morning to night?

She rested in her husband's arms during one of the evenings she was privileged to spend with him and listened to him. "I wonder what God would've done to help us if I'd poured my heart out to him that day on the wall? What would He have done if I had prayed to Him when I saw you bathing, rather than taking matters into my own hands?" He combed his fingers through her hair.

She closed her eyes. Considering how greatly God had blessed her despite her grievous sin, she couldn't imagine what His plan might have been had she been faithful and obedient. What if David had never seen her bathing? What if he'd never called for her and she'd remained faithful to Uriah? Yet having experienced God's discipline, she knew she had gained a life-changing understanding of redemption and restoration. She now knew beyond a shadow of a doubt how great were God's mercy and lovingkindness, and for that she was oh so thankful. The sweet incense of faith was released when her life and will were crushed.

Lord, I thought I could live my life and be happy without You. I was wrong, so terribly wrong. Forgive me.

And God did.

Everyone knew David loved her, for he treated her with the honor of a first wife. He didn't seem to notice or care about the problems his partiality caused inside the palace. Men and women alike feared her influence and vied for David's attention. David was proud of all his sons, especially Absalom, but the king seemed to have a special affinity for Solomon, who shared his intense love for God. And Bathsheba knew that affinity was a danger. She remained watchful.

God's blessings continued to rain down on Bathsheba, and she bore David a third son, Shimea, and a fourth, Shobab, and a fifth, Nathan. David's wives treated her with grudging honor, for no one wanted to share the same fate as Michal, David's first wife, who was cloistered and given charge over her brother's children, doomed never to have children of her own.

Yet, some of the women found their own revenge. Ahinoam and Maacah planted seeds of suspicion and dissension in their sons. They nurtured the young men's pride and arrogance. They fanned the fires of their ambition, and they failed to instruct their sons in the Law.

Of all those around her, there were only a select few Bathsheba trusted: David, Abigail, her handmaiden, and the prophet Nathan, after whom she had named her fourth son. The prophet had become her friend as well as her counselor.

Caught up in the duties of raising four sons, she had no time for hollow flattery and less time to worry over the manipulations of the other women in the palace. Or of the antics of David's other offspring. Her duty was clear: to raise up her sons to be men of God. She had no power over David and what he did, and she grieved when she saw him shirk his kingly responsibilities. Each year, he seemed to delegate more of his duties to others: her grandfather, Ahithophel; his commander, Joab; his eldest sons, Amnon and Absalom. He spent more and more time writing beautiful songs of praise and worship, pouring his heart out before the Lord, and making plans to build a magnificent temple for the Lord. She knew all these things were good, but what of Israel? What of the people who needed him? What of those who looked to him to lead?

David failed to see the gathering storm.

The prophet Nathan had told her of the cursing to come. She took the Word of the Lord to heart and was watchful of what was happening around her. One sin set others in motion. The first stone had tumbled years ago, and an avalanche was coming. She kept her sons close, teaching them about God as she walked with them, teaching them as she sat with them. She tucked them into bed with stories of creation, the flood, the patriarchs, the Egyptian enslavement and God's deliverance. "Remember the Lord," was her litany.

She knew her sons would face the brunt of the prejudice against her. When they asked painful questions, she answered with the devastating truth. "Yes, your father and I committed adultery. Yes, men died because of me." She had compromised once; she couldn't afford to compromise again. She took every opportunity to speak to her sons of repentance and responsibility, of consequences set in motion when one gives in to sin, of the power of the Lord to uphold the righteous. And she told them of the Lord's great mercy and lovingkindness toward her.

"Whenever you sin, for sin you will, you must repent. You must turn your back on evil and seek God's face. If you do that, God will forgive you."

"And God will make it right," Solomon said.

She smiled sadly. "He will forgive you, but he won't remove the consequences."

"Why not?"

"We must learn to obey."

When Nathan sent word that he wanted to instruct her sons in the Law of the Lord, she seized the opportunity with thanksgiving and sent them off with instructions, "Listen with your hearts, my sons." Once again, God had reached down. And this time He was lifting her sons from a palace of intrigue and setting them down beside His chosen prophet.

Shouting and screaming reverberated in the palace as news spread that Amnon, David's eldest son and heir to the throne, had raped his half-sister, Tamar. David tore his robe, for he realized he'd believed the tale his son had concocted to gain permission for the girl to attend him in his private chamber. David had sent Tamar to Amnon, never suspecting the young man had improper intentions towards her.

Now Maacah, Tamar's mother, was screaming at him for justice, demanding that Amnon be punished for his crime. How could he agree, when the punishment for rape was death? Could he execute his own son, his heir? When Tamar had cried out in the streets, her brother Absalom had silenced her.

"Woman, if Absalom isn't demanding his brother's blood, why should you? He's taken our daughter into his house and told her to say no more of the matter."

"He's waiting for you to do something!"

"And would you be so quick to demand justice if it were your son who sinned?"

"My son would never take a woman in sin!" She wept hysterically. "This is your fault! It started with your taking that woman!" She could not be silenced. "Your brother's son Jonadab suggested the plan to Amnon, and *you sent my daughter* to Amnon! You sent her, and now she's ruined! What will become of Tamar now? Amnon's sin is on *your* head!"

David wept because he knew she was right.

Those who wanted David to prosper advised him to follow the Law, but David didn't listen.

"How can you ask me to stone my own son? Did I not sin when I took Bathsheba into the palace? Did I not sin when I murdered Uriah? God showed mercy upon me!"

"You repented, my lord the king. Amnon ... "

"How can I show less mercy to Amnon, my own flesh and blood?"

"My lord the king ... "

"I will not pass judgment upon another, when I myself have sinned so grievously. I forgive him and demand that you do likewise!"

Bathsheba covered her face and wept in the privacy of her chamber.

What could a son learn from a father who stole another man's wife and murdered her husband – what else but to believe he could do as he pleased? He had learned to take what he wanted when he wanted it, without counting the cost to anyone.

Oh, God, thus does my sin come to rest again upon me! If not for Your love and mercy, how could I bear to stand and witness what my sins have caused?

Bathsheba mourned for Tamar. She mourned for Maacah, who was inconsolable and embittered. She mourned for Amnon because she knew God would judge him for what he had done. And in the midst of her grief, she felt the accusing glances, saw the whispering. She knew what people were thinking. *What you did all those years ago is the cause of our misery now!*

Absalom's silence made her tremble, for he was no less arrogant than Amnon. In fact, he was even more proud. He'd been praised for his looks and petted since he was a little boy. The older he grew, the more he strutted like a peacock. Would a man like that forgive the rape of his beautiful sister?

Solomon noticed her distress. "What do you fear, Mother?"

"I fear what happens when sin is overlooked." *When the sentence for an evil deed isn't executed quickly, the hearts of men are given fully to evil.*

Months passed, and nothing happened. David considered the matter resolved and never spoke of it. Bathsheba continued to watch. She hoped David was right, but she continued to do all she could to guard her sons from corruption.

A year passed, and another, as the weeds grew taller among the wheat.

⋙⋘

"Absalom invited me to his sheep shearing," David told her one evening as they took supper alone together. "He's invited all his brothers."

Though alarmed, she kept silent about her misgivings. Absalom had not invited *her* four sons, but she was relieved he hadn't. Absalom hated her because David preferred her over his mother. And he saw her sons as a threat, even though he was next in line as heir to the throne after Amnon. She poured more wine. "Are you going?"

He shook his head, caressing her fingers as he took the cup. "I'd rather stay here. Besides, why should I burden Absalom with the cost of my retinue? It's better for him if I remain in the palace. The young men will have their fun without me. Amnon's already agreed to go as my representative."

She shuddered. "I'm glad my sons won't be going."

"Why aren't they?"

"They weren't invited."

David frowned and thought for a moment. Then he shrugged. "Perhaps Absalom didn't think they'd be interested in such festivities, since they spend so much time with Nathan."

A few days later, Bathsheba was startled by the sound of screaming and wailing. She ran from her room, terrified that something had happened to David. Solomon intercepted her, his face pale, his eyes wide with shock and fear. "A messenger just came and said that Absalom has struck down all the brothers who attended the sheep shearing. Not one of them remains!"

She went cold, her mind racing. If Absalom had dared such a thing, she knew what he would dare next. "Find your brothers and go to your father. Stay at his side!"

Absalom was after the throne, and the only way to take it would be to wage war against David.

The palace was in an uproar, women screaming and wailing, men standing about in torn garments while David lay prostrate and weeping upon the floor.

More news arrived. Only Amnon was dead. One by one, David's sons rode home on their donkeys, repeating the story of how David's heir had been merry with wine when Absalom set his servants upon him, watching in glee as his brother was stabbed repeatedly until dead.

David gathered men to go after Absalom, but his son fled to Geshur and took refuge in the home of his mother's father, King Talmai.

Bathsheba often thought about what had happened at the sheep shearing. She tried to think as her grandfather would. There were three reasons why Absalom would murder Amnon: to avenge his sister, to openly defy his father, and to declare himself heir to the throne of Israel. David's remaining sons were now stricken with fear of Absalom. They knew he was ruthless in his quest for vengeance and power.

Would Absalom have killed David if he had gone to the sheep shearing? Surely a son would stop short of murdering his own father! David talked continually about going out against him. He talked and talked ... but did nothing.

≈≈≈

Three years passed. Consoled over Amnon's death, David dismissed the notion of war, for his spies reported that Absalom had not gathered an army around him in Geshur. David concluded that Amnon's murder had been an act of revenge over Tamar, not a bid for the throne. Bathsheba knew David's mind was still fixed upon Absalom. Her husband was torn by love for this wayward son and anger over the young man's actions.

"Your son waits to be forgiven," Joab told the king, and Bathsheba sensed that her husband was waiting for any excuse to welcome Absalom home again. Without an army and allies, he wouldn't succeed in taking the crown from David, but Bathsheba still didn't feel he was trustworthy. She said nothing against Absalom, of course, knowing anything she said would be misconstrued. What good would come of her speaking her mind when

David still grieved over his absence and listened so eagerly for any news of him? No, all she could do was to make certain he knew he did have sons who sought God's favor and would stand with their father against all enemies. Whenever David sent word he wanted to spend an evening with her, she made certain Solomon and his brothers joined them for a time. David always enjoyed talking with them, and she wanted him to see and take comfort in his only godly sons.

⚬⚬⚬

The palace was changing.

David ordered several houses built in an attempt to keep peace among his women. Ahinoam continued to mourn Amnon while Maacah pleaded Absalom's cause so long and loud that David finally refused to see her any more.

Solomon and his brothers often spent their afternoons with Bathsheba. She loved to hear them talk over the things they were learning from Nathan. They were astute in other areas as well. They knew what was happening in Jerusalem while she, dwelling within the walls of the palace, knew so little. It was her sons who informed her that Absalom would soon be returning to Jerusalem.

"Has your father pardoned him?"

"Not exactly," Solomon said. "I was in court the other day when a Tekoite widow came forward, claiming a clan wanted her to hand over her son who had killed his brother. She said if she did so, they would kill him as well and she would have no sons. Abba agreed to protect the heir. Then he realized the story was a ruse."

"A ruse?"

"Joab put the words in her mouth."

Disturbed, Bathsheba stood and moved away. Joab again. Was Joab sending the king another message: *Bring Absalom back or I stand with him against you?*

"My father would be wise to keep Absalom close so he can watch him," Solomon said.

"Yes, he would." She looked back at him. "Speak with Nathan about this. See what he has to say!" She intended to pray that David would not give in to his volatile emotions again. Joab had manipulated him, but retaliation would serve no purpose.

When David was told Absalom was coming up the mountain to

Jerusalem, he struck a blow against Joab. "Absalom may go to his own house, but he must never come into my presence." The Word of the Lord given through Nathan so many years before stood: the sword would never leave his house. David had slammed the door of reconciliation in his son's face in order to put Joab in his place.

When Bathsheba heard what David had done in anger, she grieved. How long before Absalom's pride demanded retribution? And how many would die when he lashed out again?

⨯⨯⨯

It took two years for the fire in Absalom's heart to come out into the open.

"Absalom set fire to Joab's field," Shobab told Bathsheba.

Solomon shook his head. "It's only a matter of time now before Joab comes to Abba and pleads our brother's case," Solomon said grimly.

"If your father reconciles with Absalom, it can only be good for the nation." She wished for an end to familial hostilities. The breech with his eldest surviving son depressed David and divided the people. Many felt Absalom justified in killing Amnon because the king had not acted according to the Law in avenging the rape of Absalom's sister. Others said David's inaction was a sign of indecision, not mercy. An indecisive king was a weak king, open to the schemes and machinations of enemies, and David had enemies on all sides. Only God could protect him and keep him on the throne.

"No good will come of this, Mother," Solomon said. "If Absalom dares to set fire to Joab's field, what more will he dare besides?"

"Are you implying he will stand against the king?"

"He's too shrewd to be so open. And he needs allies. Joab won't stand with him now. But you know better than I how proud Absalom is."

Shimea laughed. "I heard he weighs his hair every time he cuts it!"

"His beauty has made him vain," Bathsheba said quietly.

"Everyone is charmed by his good looks, but he's filled with deceit. Abba ordered him to his own house two years ago, and that command hasn't changed. Two years is more than enough time to stoke the fires in Absalom's belly."

Bathsheba searched for reasons to hope for peace. "Absalom is heir to the throne. He needs to be patient. He has nothing to gain by dividing a nation he will one day rule."

Solomon laughed without humor. "The only time I've seen my brother show patience was during the two years he plotted the murder of Amnon."

She rose. "We will speak no more of this now." She couldn't bear it. "Keep your eyes open and tell me what you see and hear." She knew if Absalom ever challenged David and won, her life and the lives of her sons would be forfeit.

Solomon bowed his head. Bending down, he kissed her cheek. He started to say something more, but she put her fingers over his lips. "Speak with Nathan about your concerns," she said. "Seek the counsel of the Lord."

"Yes, Mother."

She kissed him and each of her sons and watched them leave.

Lord God, protect my sons. Let the sins of the past fall on my head and not theirs.

⊱⊰⊱⊰⊱

David heard Joab's plea and allowed Absalom to come before him, but the kiss he bestowed upon his son was less in affection than official pardon. Soon after, Bathsheba heard that Absalom had taken to riding in a horse-drawn chariot with fifty men running before him as though he were already a king. He rose early and went down to stand by the gate road, intercepting those who came to Jerusalem to have their cases heard before the king, telling them he was the only one who would listen and judge justly, and making promises only a king could fulfill.

When he came before David and asked to go to Hebron to fulfill a vow he'd made in Geshur to worship the Lord, David let him go, too preoccupied with his own comforts and pleasure to sense Absalom's true motive.

Absalom left Jerusalem with two hundred invited guests and declared himself king in Hebron. "All Israel has joined Absalom in a conspiracy against you," David was told by messengers.

And Absalom was on his way to Jerusalem, with an army, to take the throne from his father.

⊱⊰⊱⊰⊱

Women and servants scrambled around the palace, gathering what they would need for a journey. David had given orders that his household was to leave Jerusalem before Absalom could arrive with his army. Only ten concubines would stay behind and keep the house in order.

Bathsheba kept her sons close by her side as David led them out with all his people after him. As they stopped on the outskirts of the city, six hundred men joined forces with them, foreigners who had come to see the king. David told them they should leave, that this wasn't their battle. Bathsheba was relieved when they swore allegiance to him and remained. David would need all the men he could muster if they were to survive.

Men and women were weeping and wailing as they crossed the stream of Kidron, heading out toward the wilderness. Zadok, the high priest, and all the Levites followed David with the Ark of the Covenant, but when David heard about it, he told them to go back to Jerusalem.

"If the Lord sees fit, He will bring me back to see the Ark and the Tabernacle again. But if He is through with me, then let Him do what seems best to Him." He walked barefoot and wept, keeping his head covered as he grieved over his rebellious son.

As he led his people up the Mount of Olives, a messenger came, dusty and exhausted. "Ahithophel is among the conspirators!"

Bathsheba dropped to her knees and cried out. She covered her head with dust. She wept, remembering her grandfather, the man she'd loved as a child and a young woman – his laughter, his love, his tender devotion to his family. Ahithophel was at last taking his vengeance against her and David. She felt David's eyes upon her and put her head against her thighs, ashamed of what her love for him had caused. She put her hands over her head when she heard David cry out in anguish and wrath.

"O Lord, let Ahithophel give Absalom foolish advice!"

Counselors and advisers surrounded David, all speaking at once, drawing him away from her. Bathsheba felt strong arms lift her and heard Solomon's fierce whisper, "God will protect us."

"My fault," she choked. "This is all my fault."

He embraced her, protecting her from those who stared. "Should the sins of everyone be laid at your feet?"

She shook with grief. "The avalanche started years ago, my son, and the whole mountain is coming down on us this time!"

"Each man makes his own decision, Mother. Ahithophel's sin will rest upon his own head."

She shook her head. "He's your great-grandfather."

"He requested leave and went home to Giloh years ago, using the excuse that Israel was at peace. Now we know the real reason for his departure. Treachery!" He drew back while still giving her support. "If there's anything I've learned from all this, Mother, it's not to trust anyone, even someone of your own blood."

"You can trust me. You can trust your father."

"I love you, Mother, and I trust you, but what power have you? And I love my father, but the king lost touch with his people years ago."

Bathsheba didn't reprimand her son for his words because he said them with sorrow and not condemnation. She thought of her grandfather again, and her heart quaked. All these years he had pretended to be at peace with David while seeking an opportunity to destroy him.

Oh, if only I'd been stronger and wiser ...

She stopped the thought. *If only ... if only ...* What was the use in such thinking? It was too late to wish she'd done things differently. They were all stained with sin, and sacrifices merely covered it with another's blood.

Oh, God of mercy, how I long to be free of my sins, to be an innocent child again, as white as snow.

Had Ahithophel thought through his vengeance? Could he hate her and David so much that he would destroy himself to get even? If he succeeded in setting Absalom on the throne, David would die. She would die. And the lives of Ahithophel's four great-grandsons would be forfeit as well! Angry and desperate, she prayed with every step that her husband's prayer would be answered and God would confuse her grandfather's advice to Absalom. For without God's favor, all would be lost. Ahithophel knew more about waging a successful war than any man in the kingdom, including Joab who now marched with David, protecting him against the son with whom he had once schemed. Joab with his murderous pride. Joab with his hidden motives and deadly ambition! He'd pulled David in a dozen directions over the past three decades!

She looked up at Solomon. "You and your brothers must go and stand with your father."

"We are standing with him."

"No. Stay *close* to him. Protect him from Absalom and anyone else who might harm him. If the king falls, we all fall." Tears blinded her. "Show David he has sons he can trust!"

As she walked alone among the throng leaving Jerusalem with David, she remembered conversations from years past around her father's campfire at En-gedi. *"Kill Saul,"* Abishai had once said. *"Strike the shepherd and the sheep will scatter,"* Joab advised. David had left the fire, refusing to listen, and her grandfather had discussed the matter with her father after the others followed. *"Joab's advice is shrewd. Saul's death would put an end to this war and place David on the throne. But there would be no blessing for David if he kills the Lord's anointed."*

No blessing.

The last thing her grandfather would want was blessing on the House of David. And what better way to avenge his so-called honor than by setting son against father? He would destroy a nation because of his pride. Were all men so evil-bent, so lacking in the ability to forgive? What right had man to judge what God redeemed? Her mother had warned her years ago that her grandfather would never let the matter go. She had hoped and prayed that he would take a different course. She wept now as she saw that Ahithophel had only pretended to forgive. She knew he would advise Absalom to pursue and kill David. And if successful, Absalom's kingdom would be cursed as well, for what nation could prosper through a son's shedding his father's blood? The House of David would fall.

Oh, Lord, Lord, that one night of sin could bring such sorrow!

No matter what happened, someone she loved was going to die.

Let it be Ahithophel, Lord. She wept at uttering such a prayer. *Let it be my grandfather and not my husband and sons.*

❧❧❧

As David lead his people to Bahurim, a man named Shimei from the family of Saul came out and shouted curses at him. The man kept pace, picked up stones and hurled them along with his bitter words at David and his servants. "Get out of here, you murderer!" he screamed in rage. "You scoundrel! The Lord is paying you back for murdering Saul and his family. You stole his throne, and now the Lord has given it to your son Absalom. At last you will taste some of your own medicine, you murderer!"

Abishai drew his sword. "Why should this dead dog curse my lord the king? Please, let me go over and cut off his head!"

David cried out in anger and despair. "No! What am I going to do with you sons of Zeruiah? If the Lord has told him to curse me, who am I to stop him?" He wept and shouted. "My own son is trying to kill me. Shouldn't this relative of Saul have even more reason to do so? Leave him alone and let him curse, for the Lord has told him to do it. And perhaps the Lord will see that I am being wronged and will bless me because of these curses."

David continued along the road, wincing at every word Shimei laid upon his head. He felt stones strike him. He tasted the dust the Benjamite kicked up.

When the people grew too weary to go further, he gave orders to camp. He'd done all he could. He had sent another of his military advisors, Hushai, to pretend allegiance to Absalom. Hushai had been instructed to counter whatever counsel Ahithophel gave. David had also sent Zadok the priest and his sons back into Jerusalem to act as messengers for Hushai. If there was any hope for escape, Hushai would see that David got word. Everything rested in God's hands. The outcome would be according to God's will.

I will die if my son pursues me now, Lord. I'm too tired to go on, and my people need rest. Help me. Oh, God, help me!

He took off his crown and held it in his hands. "Oh, Lord, hear me as I pray," he whispered. "Don't hide Yourself from my plea. Please answer my prayers. Trouble is all around me because of a grudge held against me for sins I committed long ago. My heart is anguished." Closing his eyes, he gripped the crown tightly. "God, I'm terrified of death. Mine and all those I love. I'm shaking like a boy untried by battle. I wish I had wings like a dove so I could escape." He swallowed. "Confuse Ahithophel's tongue. All these years I thought he was my friend, and he's been plotting against me." He wept as he raked one hand back through his hair, dangling the crown in his other hand. "Ahithophel. My friend. My companion all these years. We had sweet fellowship together during those years in the wilderness."

He ground his teeth, running his hand around the back of his neck. "All these years his words have been as smooth as butter, and war has been in his heart. He talked of peace with a drawn sword behind his back. He has fanned my son's ambitions and set him against me." He shook as rage heated his blood. "Send them into the pit of destruction, Lord! Let him go down alive into Sheol!"

He let out his breath slowly, striving for control of his emotions. He must be calm to give the people courage. He must think. He must act wisely. *What a fool I've been, allowing myself to become soft and letting others run the kingdom!* He turned the crown slowly in his hands and placed it back on his head, then rubbed his face, feeling the dust and grit of travel rubbing his skin. *Oh, God, I never asked to be king.* He would have been happier as a shepherd singing psalms and looking at the stars in the heavens. He would have been happier as a poor man with only one wife.

Men plan, but God prevails.

With a sigh, David stood. "I will trust in You, oh, Lord. I will trust in You. Do with me as you will."

Hushai reported to Zadok, and the priest sent his two sons to David. "Quick!

Cross the Jordan tonight! Ahithophel is advising Absalom to pursue immediately, overtake you, and kill you. Hushai advises you not spend the night in the plains of the wilderness, but speedily cross over lest you and all the people with you be swallowed up!"

And there was more news, bitter and reminiscent of Nathan's prophecy so many years before.

"Acting on Ahithophel's advice, Absalom has taken your ten concubines up onto the roof. He is sleeping with them before all Israel."

David felt the hair on the back of his neck rise. He could imagine Ahithophel's face ravaged by hatred, could imagine his thoughts. *Remember all those years ago when you stood upon your roof and looked down upon my granddaughter? Remember how you took her and defiled her? How you brought shame upon my household? Now I will watch your son defile your women and bring shame upon your household before all Israel!*

David roused the people and they traveled on to Mahanaim, where they were met by men from Rabbah and Ammon and offered beds, basins, and earthen vessels filled with wheat, barley, flour, parched grain, beans, lentils, parched seeds, honey and curds, sheep and cheese from the herd. David's people ate their fill and rested.

David counted his men. He set up captains over thousands and captains over hundreds. Dividing his army into three parts, he sent one third of his fighting force with Joab, one third with Abishai and one third with Ittai the Gittite. Then, with a heavy heart, he prepared to go out to war against his own son.

The people protested loudly against his going out with them. "You must not go. If we have to turn and run – and even if half of us die – it will make no difference to Absalom's troops; they will be looking only for you. You are worth ten thousand of us, and it is better that you stay here in the city and send us help if we need it."

David listened and once more stepped down. "If you think that's the best plan, I'll do it." He gave orders to Joab, Abishai, and Ittai in front of the army. "For my sake, deal gently with young Absalom." Then he remained standing at the gate as the men passed by him and went out to battle.

Once again, David remained behind while others fought for him. But this time he did it because it was what the people wanted and not what he wanted for himself.

The watchman from the tower called down. "A runner is coming!"

David paced. "If he is alone, he has news," he muttered to himself. When the watchman shouted down again that another man was spotted coming swiftly after, David's heart quickened in dread.

"The first man runs like Ahimaaz, son of Zadok!" the watchman called again.

David clenched and unclenched his hands. "He is a good man and comes with good news."

Ahimaaz called out before he reached the open gate, "*All is well!*" David's heart leaped as the young man fell to his knees before him and bowed his face to the ground. "Blessed be the Lord your God," he gasped, "who has handed over the rebels who dared to stand against you."

"What about young Absalom? Is he all right?"

Ahimaaz raised his head in surprise. His eyes flickered and he bowed his head again. "When Joab told me to come, there was a lot of commotion. But I didn't know what was happening."

Why did Ahimaaz hide his face? David's heart beat harder. He raised his head as the watchman cried out again. Another messenger raced toward them. "Wait here," David ordered Ahimaaz.

The second messenger arrived, breathless and dusty. "I have good news for my lord the king. Today the Lord has rescued you from all those who rebelled against you."

"What about young Absalom? Is he all right?" David demanded.

The Cushite's eyes flashed. "May all of your enemies, both now and in the future, be as that young man is!"

David's heart turned over, for he knew. "My son! My son is dead!" He cried out in anguish. "O my son Absalom! My son, my son, Absalom! If only I could have died instead of you! O Absalom, my son, my son!"

Stumbling up the stairs into the chamber above the gate, David collapsed in grief.

❦❦❦

David didn't rouse himself when the door of his chamber opened. He didn't raise his head until Joab's voice raked over him in a rage.

"We saved your life today and the lives of your sons, your daughters, and your wives and concubines!" Joab's face was red, his hand clenched on the handle of his sword. "Yet you act like this, making us feel ashamed, as though we had done something wrong. You seem to love those who hate you and hate those who love you. You have made it clear today that we mean nothing to you. If Absalom had lived and all of us had died, you would be pleased!"

David hated him and saw in the man's eyes that he had been behind Absalom's death. And was glad of it. "He was my son, my heir!" Had he not ordered Joab before witnesses to treat his son gently? But Joab always did what he thought best, with no regard for others – or for what was right. He was a man who served his own ambitions.

And David saw death in the man's hot eyes.

"*Get up!*" Joab shouted at him. "Now *go out there* and congratulate the troops, for I swear by the Lord that if you don't, not a single one of them will remain here tonight. Then you will be worse off than you have ever been!"

Anger filled David. His body shook as he strove to calm himself, to control the impulse to attack the man. If he didn't do what Joab said, what cost to the kingdom? He looked into his commander's eyes and knew that if he didn't get up, Joab would be the one to strike, for he made no attempt to hide his anger or disgust.

David rose and crossed the room. He stood in front of Joab and stared into his eyes. "Did you kill him because he burned your field?" A muscle jerked in Joab's cheek as he glared back, silent. David's lip curled. Even if he hadn't, Joab had still ignored the command of the king.

And David knew there was nothing he could about it. Not now. Once again, it had been Joab who led the army to victory, while the king waited within the city walls.

Joab stepped back and inclined his head. He had the eyes of a coiled snake.

David didn't give him the chance to strike. Stifling his anger and grief, he went out and sat by the gate. One by one, his warriors came out to see him, and he thanked each of them properly for saving his kingdom.

And then David took his household back to Jerusalem.

≈≈≈

Bathsheba sat in her chamber and waited. Would David blame her for the death of his son Absalom? Her grandfather had been behind the conspiracy to kill David and take the throne. Did he blame her now?

Days passed and she didn't see him. Nor did the king summon any other woman.

Then, one day, the door opened, and without being announced he entered her room. She rose, her heart in her throat. He looked thinner, his face lined with suffering, streaks of gray at his temples. She took several steps toward him and then went down on her knees, bowing her head until her forehead touched the floor. "Oh, David, I'm so sorry." She began to weep.

His hand rested gently on her head. "I don't blame you for Ahithophel's actions."

She raised her head and looked into his eyes. Amazed, she saw he still loved her. "Oh, David." She went into his arms, both of them on their knees. He held her so tightly, she hurt. She put her head against his chest and felt him kiss the back of her neck.

"I have news," he whispered against her hair, his arms tightening. "When Absalom took Hushai's advice to wait, Ahithophel went home and hanged himself."

She trembled violently. God had heard and answered her prayers. *"Ahithophel's sin will rest upon his own head,"* Solomon had said to her as they fled from Absalom. Her grandfather had judged and, by his own measure, been judged.

David nuzzled her neck, kissing the sensitive curve and making her tremble. His breath was warm against her flesh. She heard the hard swift pounding of his heart.

"I've decided Solomon will be heir to the throne." She drew back sharply and looked up at him, afraid. He cupped her face. "I've decided. Do you want to know why? The others have nursed their sons on ambition and made them hungry for power." She saw the grief in his eyes. "I swear to you, Bathsheba, it will be *your* son who wears the crown."

"But who am I that you would – "

"Of all my wives and concubines, only you have wholeheartedly sought the Lord."

Her eyes filled. "Where else could I go after what I'd done and all the pain that's come from it?"

David kissed the tears that streaked her face. "Maybe it's only those who've made such chaos of their lives who can understand the heights and depths of God's mercy." He kissed her lips. "I was fond of you because you were the daughter of my friend. I lusted after you and took you because of your beauty. I have loved you for the pleasure you've given me and the peace I feel in your company." He drew back and took her hands.

They stood together. His gaze never left hers as he lifted her hands and kissed each palm. "But I love you most of all for the loving wife you've been and the mother you are to my sons. You have raised up four men who love the Lord and seek His face, sons I'm proud of, sons I ... " His voice broke.

She put her arms around him and comforted him, knowing what he wanted to say but couldn't.

She had raised up sons he could trust.

six

JUST before David's return to Jerusalem, another rebellion had threatened to tear the nation into factions as Sheba, a Benjaminite, called the men of Israel to war against David. His call to arms ignited the discord that had been festering between the ten tribes of Israel and David's own tribe, Judah. Only the men of Judah clung to their king. Now David instructed Amasa to mobilize his army, but Joab murdered him and took command of David's army once again, leading the warriors out against Sheba. Trapping the rebel at Abel-beth-maacah, he laid siege to the city until a woman gathered the elders and convinced them to toss Sheba over the wall, saving the city from Joab.

Years later the Philistines came out against Israel, and David led the nation into battle again. He was old and weary, and the men protested. "You are not going out into battle again! Why should we risk snuffing out the light of Israel!"

David relented, and his men went into battle without him. During the war that ensued, his mighty men struck down Goliath's brothers, thus wiping out the last sons of the titan.

Even while David wrote psalms of praise for the Lord, his strong tower and mighty fortress, he sinned against the Lord by taking a census of his fighting men. His pride and ambition led him to count the people so that he could glory in the size of his army, its power and defenses – rather than trusting in God's ability to give them victory regardless of their number. Was it by man's strength his kingdom stood? When he recognized his sin, he begged for God's forgiveness. The Lord gave him a choice: three years of famine, three months of fleeing from his enemies, or three days of plague. "Let us fall into the hand of the Lord," David said, "for His mercy is great." He chose the plague.

Seventy thousand people died because David had counted his men and gloried in their numbers. Then the Lord relented and said, "Stop! That is enough!" David saw God's death angel sheathe his sword on the threshing floor of Araunah the Jebusite and shook in awe. David bought Araunah's threshing floor and oxen and built an altar there, presenting burnt offerings and communion sacrifices to the Lord, who had stopped the destruction of Israel.

One day the Temple would stand on the same spot.

≈≈≈

Bathsheba watched her beloved husband growing older. His hair was gray, the lines deepening in his still handsome face. His shoulders drooped as though the weight of Israel were on his shoulders. He walked more slowly through the corridors of his palace, and he seldom visited his concubines. His wives continued to come to him with their complaints, pressing their sons forward for his notice until David allowed some to assume duties.

On occasion, David would come to her quarters and spend an afternoon with her.

"I was once as swift as an eagle, and now my legs weigh like tree trunks, keeping me planted firmly on the ground."

She smiled up at him as she rubbed his feet. "We're all getting older, my love." When he shivered, she put a blanket around his shoulders.

He took her hand and kissed it. "You're as beautiful to me now as you were as a young woman."

"And you're as charming as ever." She rose and kissed him with the affection of a couple that had weathered many storms over the decades. "You're still shivering."

"The hot blood of my youth has grown cold."

"I don't love you any less."

"My servants have found a way to keep me warm."

She smiled wryly. "So I heard." They'd scoured the land to find the most beautiful young virgin to sleep with him. "Did you plant the idea in their heads, you old rogue?"

"Abishag is beautiful to behold, but that's all I do – look. I'm past all the rest."

"If I could've held you to me alone, I would have."

"And if I'd been wiser at a younger age ... " He sighed. "If, if ... " He shook his head. "I knew the Law as well as any man could. I dare say that even if we had the Law written upon our hearts, we would still be incapable of staying out of trouble."

"Nathan said you were a man after God's own heart."

"I'm beset by failure on every side. An adulterer, a murderer, a – "

She put her fingers over his lips. "God loves you because you repented every time you realized you'd sinned. You *grieved*. You *tried* to do right. God knows you are only a man, my love."

"A man who has hurt everyone he loves and cost the lives of countless thousands." He shook his head, his eyes filling with tears. "Why did God do it? Of all the men in Israel, why did God choose *me* to be king?"

She knelt in front of him and rested her head in his lap. She smiled and closed her eyes as he combed his fingers through her hair. "Because you're the only man who would ask that question."

〜〜〜

Bathsheba knew Haggith was encouraging her son, Adonijah, to claim his rights as the next heir, for he had been born next after Absalom. When Adonijah procured chariots and horses and recruited fifty men to run in front of him, behaving before all Israel as though he was already king, just as Absalom had done all those years before, she became afraid. Was another rebellion brewing?

David said nothing about Adonijah's activities, and Bathsheba held her tongue. But she wondered. Had David forgotten his promise to make Solomon king? If Adonijah became king, she and her sons would die the day David did, for Adonijah was as arrogant as Absalom had been in his public posturing. When she heard from her sons that Adonijah parlayed with Joab and Abiathar, the priest, and they were lending him their support, she knew it wouldn't be long before he proclaimed himself king and had the backing to uphold his claim.

She took her fear of the future before the Lord. She fasted and prayed, and waited for Him to answer.

Adonijah went to the sacrificial feast of sheep, oxen, and fattened calves near En-rogel. He invited all of David's sons to go with him – all but Solomon and his brothers, the prophet Nathan, the priest Benaiah, and the warriors who remained loyal to the king. Bathsheba knew war was again at hand. Perhaps this was God's final judgment upon her and David for their sins.

Nathan came to her, grim of countenance, his eyes fierce and alive in his ancient face. "Did you realize that Haggith's son, Adonijah, has made himself king and that our lord David doesn't even know about it?"

"I've been praying."

"If you want to save your own life and the life of your son Solomon, follow my counsel. Go at once to King David and say to him, 'My lord, didn't you promise me that my son Solomon would be the next king and would sit upon your throne? Then why has Adonijah become king?' And while you are still talking with him, I will come and confirm everything you have said."

"I will do it," she said, trembling at what might happen if David had forgotten his promise. Would he think she was just like all the other women in his life, scrambling for power for her sons? Yet, what choice had she? Power in the wrong hands would bring death to her entire family.

She prayed feverishly as she hurried along the corridor to the king's chambers. "I must speak with the king on a matter of great importance," she told his guard. He bowed his head to her and went to seek the permission of the king, returning soon after and opening the door for her. As Bathsheba entered, she saw the beautiful Shunammite girl, Abishag, serving the king his morning meal. The girl looked up, her lovely face lighting with a sweet smile, inclining her head in respectful greeting. Bathsheba had liked her from their first meeting. Abishag had been a shepherdess over her father's flock before she'd been brought to Jerusalem to serve the king. The loving young Shunammite had many things in common with the old king, especially her faith.

Bathsheba went down on her knees, bowing her face to the ground before her husband, the king.

David roused himself. "What can I do for you, Bathsheba?"

Her heart thundered as she prayed, *Oh, Lord, don't let David see me as he does the others.* She lifted her head and trembled as she spoke. "My lord, you vowed to me by the Lord your God that my son Solomon would be the next king and would sit on your throne. But instead, Adonijah has become the new king, and you do not even know about it. He has sacrificed many oxen, fattened calves, and sheep, and he has invited all your sons and Abiathar the priest and Joab, the commander of the army."

David sat up, his eyes suddenly fierce.

"But he did not invite your servant Solomon. And now, my lord the king, all Israel is waiting for your decision as to who will become king after you. If you do not act, my son Solomon and I will be treated as criminals as soon as you are dead."

"My lord the king," the guard said from the doorway. "Nathan the prophet is here to see you. He said it is a matter of gravest import."

"Let him enter!" David said, breathing heavily, his face tense and red.

He waved Abishag away impatiently. "Go, Bathsheba. Leave me!"

Striving to control her emotions, she hurried out of his chamber. She paced and prayed while she waited outside. *Oh, Lord of mercy, let him heed Your prophet.* She clenched her hands and stood, eyes closed. *Oh, God, move David's heart to remember his promise. I know I'm unworthy, I know I'm unworthy, but please save my sons. Set Your servant Solomon upon the throne.*

"Call Bathsheba!" David roared, and her heart stopped. It began pounding hard and fast as she hastened toward the door. The guard opened it for her. "I am here, my lord the king."

David was standing. "As surely as the Lord lives, who has rescued me from every danger, today I decree that your son Solomon will be the next king and will sit on my throne, just as I swore to you before the Lord, the God of Israel."

Bathsheba dropped to her knees and bowed her face to the ground, weeping as she spoke from her heart. "May my lord King David live forever!"

David called for Zadok the priest, Benaiah, and Nathan the prophet and gave them instructions. "Take Solomon and my officers down to Gihon Spring. Solomon is to ride on my personal mule. There Zadok the priest and Nathan the prophet are to anoint him king over Israel. Then blow the trumpets and shout, 'Long live King Solomon!' When you bring him back here, he will sit on my throne. He will succeed me as king, for I have appointed him to be ruler over Israel and Judah."

"Amen!" the priests said, their eyes glowing as they glanced at one another.

The old lion had finally awakened.

Bathsheba's heart was in her throat as she stood with members of David's household and watched Zadok take the horn of oil from the Tent, anointing her son king. David was smiling, two men giving him support while Abishag stood nearby. Nathan spoke for all the king's servants. "May your God make Solomon's fame even greater than your own, and may Solomon's kingdom be even greater than yours!"

As Nathan turned toward him, David removed his crown and held it out. "Give it to Bathsheba."

The old prophet's eyes lit up. As he handed the crown to Bathsheba, her eyes welled with tears at being honored so before the people. David smiled and inclined his head toward her. She smiled back, turned, and placed the crown on their son's head. The people shouted joyfully. "*Long live King*

Solomon!" Over and over again, they cried out their blessings.

Bathsheba laughed and cried, her heart so full she felt it would burst. She looked from David to her son. The anointing oil dripped down Solomon's face into his beard. *"Beloved of the Lord!"* Who would have ever thought *her* son would be king over Israel!

Oh, Lord God of Israel, merciful redeemer, lifter of my soul, look what You have done for me! Look what You have done! She put her hands over her heart and bowed low.

All the people went up after Solomon. Some played flutes. Thousands danced in the streets and sang, making such revelry the earth shook with their jubilee.

When Solomon was seated on the royal throne, David, near exhaustion, bowed down to him. "Blessed be the Lord, the God of Israel, who today has chosen someone to sit on my throne while I am still alive to see it."

A messenger came, informing David that Adonijah's guests had fled when they heard the people celebrating Solomon's coronation. Now, out of fear for their lives, all were clamoring to be first to sing Solomon's praises and bow down before him. David rose. When Bathsheba started to rise, he shook his head. "Enjoy this day, my love. See what God has done." He was assisted from the room by two male attendants with Abishag following.

Another messenger came, throwing himself on his face before Solomon. "My lord the king!"

"Rise, and speak your message."

"Adonijah is afraid of you and has caught hold of the horns of the altar. He said, 'Let Solomon swear to me today that he will not kill me!'"

Bathsheba held her breath as she saw Solomon's eyes darken and his hands tighten on the arms of the throne. "If he proves himself to be loyal, he will not be harmed. But if he does not, he will die." She breathed easier as her son sent guards to take his brother down from the altar and bring him to the throne room. The elder brother bowed to her son, but he didn't throw himself on the floor as others had done before him. He inclined his head, but did not bend his back. Her son watched Adonijah closely, his eyes narrowed. "Go on home, Adonijah. Go and remember my warning."

There was a hushed silence as Adonijah turned and walked out of the throne room. Bathsheba knew there would be trouble ahead if a way to peace between the brothers could not be found.

As Solomon took over the responsibilities of kingship, David's health declined. Bathsheba came each morning to sit with him, but it was Abishag who was in constant attendance, seeing to his most basic needs. Bathsheba's heart ached as she watched the man she loved slip away. She knew it was close to the end when he summoned Solomon from his duties. The king brought his brothers Shobab, Shimei, and Nathan with him.

Solomon bowed down before his father. David put his hand on his son's head. "My son," he rasped, tears in his eyes. "Sit and we will talk as we used to." He smiled at the four men surrounding him. Reaching out, David took Bathsheba's hand.

"I am going where everyone on earth must someday go."

Solomon and his brothers began to weep.

"Take courage," David said, directing his words to Solomon, "and be a man. Observe the requirements of the Lord your God and follow all His ways. Keep each of the laws, commands, regulations, and stipulations written in the Law of Moses so that you will be successful in all you do and wherever you go. If you do this, then the Lord will keep the promise He made to me: 'If your descendants live as they should and follow Me faithfully with all their heart and soul, one of them will always sit on the throne of Israel.'"

Bathsheba closed her eyes, her throat constricting as she heard the encroaching weakness in David's voice. She was losing him. After all these years, he was leaving her.

David took his hand from hers and stirred on his couch, restless, hurried. "And there is something else. You know that Joab son of Zeruiah murdered my two army commanders, Abner son of Ner and Amasa son of Jether. He pretended that it was an act of war, but it was done in a time of peace, staining his belt and sandals with the blood of war. Do with him what you think best, but don't let him die in peace!"

"Yes, Abba."

"Be kind to the sons of Barzillai ... "

"Yes, Abba."

"And remember Shimei son of Gera, the man from Bahurim in Benjamin. He cursed me with a terrible curse as I was fleeing to Mahanaim. When he came down to meet me at the Jordan River, I swore by the Lord that I would not kill him. But that oath does not make him innocent. You are a wise man, and you will know how to arrange a bloody death for him."

Bathsheba shuddered, but she said nothing as David sank back, breathing heavily. Turning his head, he looked at her, pain etching his face. "Ah, my love," he said softly. His breath came out in one long, deep sigh of peace and his body relaxed.

Bathsheba rocked back and forth, her anguish so deep, the tears gathered like a hot stone in her chest. When Abishag leaned forward and gently ran her hand down David's face, closing his eyes, Bathsheba's grief broke free. Kneeling, she ripped the neckline of her dress and pressed her hands over her chest, feeling as though her heart had been torn from her. "David! *Daaaa … vid!*"

Her sons rose and surrounded her like sentinels. And King Solomon's hand was gentle upon her shoulder.

⪻⪼⪻⪼

David was buried with great ceremony in the city named after him. As the people mourned him, Bathsheba prayed they would remember the good he had done for them and the heart he had for God rather than the mistakes he had made.

Solomon sat easily upon the throne, his mind trained in administration by Nathan and the priests. But his throne was not yet secure. Enemies were gathering.

One afternoon, Adonijah came to see her. "My mother sends you greetings," he said, bowing to her for the first time she could remember.

Haggith had always been as ambitious for her sons as Maacah. "Have you come to make trouble?" Should she remind him to heed the warning Solomon had given for his own sake, or hear him out to know better what was going on in his mind?

"No," he said quickly. "I come in peace. In fact, I have a favor to ask of you."

A favor? She tilted her head. "What is it?" she said cautiously.

"As you know, the kingdom was mine."

She stiffened, her heart thumping. Did he mean to remind her that he had been next in line after Absalom? Or was he referring to his rebellion? He had managed to gain the backing of powerful men in the kingdom, men who had encouraged him to declare himself king. They'd all mistakenly thought David too tired and ill to notice. And even if the king did know, they figured he would not be able to muster enough strength to stop the rebellion.

Adonijah spread his hands as though to show he had no weapons. "Everyone expected me to be the next king. But the tables were turned, and everything went to my brother instead; for that is the way the Lord wanted it."

She watched his face for some sign of subterfuge, but he seemed to accept David's wishes. *The Lord wanted it.* The Lord had chosen Solomon to reign – Solomon, her son. *I am still amazed, Lord, amazed that you would choose the son of an adulterous woman ...*

"So now," Adonijah said, drawing her attention back to him, "I have just one favor to ask of you. Please don't turn me down."

"What is it?"

He stepped closer and went down on one knee, his face taut, his eyes dark. "Speak to King Solomon on my behalf, for I know he will do anything you request. Ask him to give me Abishag, the girl from Shunem, as my wife."

Abishag! She searched his face and thought the emotions she saw there must be love, for she could feel his intensity and could see his hunger.

Oh, Lord, is this the way to bring peace between brothers? If Solomon gives his brother Abishag, will there be peace between them? Will that tender girl soften this man's heart? Oh, let it be so!

"All right," she said slowly and saw his eyes catch fire. "I will speak to the king for you."

Adonijah said not another word, but when he rose, his lips curved in a strange smile of triumph.

⤬⤬⤬

Bathsheba dressed in her finest attire before going to her son, the king. She waited while he was told she requested an audience with him. When she was admitted, Solomon rose from his throne and came down the dais to her. She blushed as he bowed down before her, his entire court watching him. Smiling, he took her hand and took her up the steps with him. "Bring another throne for my mother," he commanded.

"You show me too much honor, my son," she whispered as a second throne was set to the right of his.

"The people must understand my respect for you." He smiled as he seated her first. "Does the Law not say, 'Honor your father *and* mother'?"

Tongues would never be silenced where she was concerned, and she would not be able to protect him against the prejudice held against her. Hadn't her sons been scorned and excluded over the years? It would be best if she went into seclusion. Perhaps if she were not seen, she would be forgotten, and the stains of her sin would not seep into Solomon's reign. "I hold no grudges, my son."

"Nor do I, Mother." His eyes glittered. "But boundaries need to be established. My father loved you and treated you as his queen, and so shall you be treated by all." He let out his breath and smiled again. "Now, tell me what it is on your mind, for I know you wouldn't have come without good reason."

She laid her hand upon his. "I have one small request to make of you." She hoped it would bring peace between him and his brother as well as kinder feelings between her and the other widows of David. "I hope you won't turn me down."

"What is it, my mother? You know I won't refuse you."

She relaxed. "Then let your brother Adonijah marry Abishag, the girl from Shunem."

Silence followed her words, and such a look of shock and growing wrath on Solomon's face that her heart stopped. When he jerked his hand from beneath hers, she drew in a startled breath, confused by the growing wrath upon his face.

"How can you possibly ask me to give Abishag to Adonijah?" His voice was low and intense. "You might as well be asking me to give him the kingdom! You know that he is my older brother, and that he has Abiathar the priest and Joab son of Zeruiah on his side!" He bolted from the throne. "May God strike me dead if Adonijah has not sealed his fate with this request!"

Oh, no! Oh, God, what have I done now?

"The Lord has confirmed me and placed me on the throne of my father, David." Solomon spoke for all to hear. "He has established my dynasty as he promised. So as surely as the Lord lives, Adonijah will die this very day!"

Bathsheba uttered a soft cry. She held her hand out to stop Solomon before he could say more, but he ignored her and called out for his most trustworthy servant, Benaiah. "Go *now* and execute Adonijah."

"Yes, my lord the king!" Benaiah drew his sword and strode from the room.

Bathsheba lowered her hands to her lap and bent her head as Solomon called for another of his servants and commanded him to bring Abiathar the priest to him at once. When Solomon turned to her, she raised her head, her eyes awash with tears. "I didn't know. I never thought this would happen."

"Return to your chamber, Mother." His voice was gentle again. "Rest. I'll talk with you later."

Thus dismissed, she rose trembling. Frowning, he put his hand beneath her arm. "Mother," he said softly.

"I will be all right," she said in a quavering voice.

"Take my mother to her chamber," he told his servant and released her into another's care.

Bathsheba felt everyone's eyes upon her. Lifting her head, she walked with grave dignity from the room. She said nothing as she walked along the corridors. Her son's servant released her to the eunuch in charge of the women's quarters. "My lady," he said, frowning. She shook her head and walked away from him, entering her private quarters.

Her handmaiden came to her. "My lady! What is it? What's happened?"

Bathsheba put a hand to her forehead. "Leave me."

"But you look ill."

She shook her head. "I just need to be alone. Please go! I'll be all right."

Distressed, the girl withdrew. The door closed and Bathsheba crumpled to the ground. Stifling a cry, she stretched out flat on her face, arms outstretched. "Oh, Lord God of Israel, have mercy ... have mercy upon me." She wept violently.

She had cost the life of yet another of David's sons.

seven

SOLOMON acted quickly to destroy his enemies. Adonijah's execution sent Joab running to the sacred tent of the Lord, where he caught hold of the horns of the altar. King Solomon sent Benaiah out again. "Kill him there beside the altar and bury him. This will remove the guilt of his senseless murders from me and my father's family. Then the Lord will repay him for the murders of two men who were more righteous and better than he!"

Solomon then deposed Abiathar as priest before the Lord and sent him home to Anathoth to live out his life in disgrace.

The king summoned Shimei and ordered him to remain within the boundaries of Jerusalem. "On the day you cross the Kidron Valley, you will surely die; your blood will be on your own head!" Solomon set guards to watching, knowing it would be only a matter of time before Shimei disobeyed. The day he did, Solomon would execute him for daring to curse God's anointed, King David.

Everyone knew Solomon had his eyes wide open. He'd given notice to all that this king would be watching and holding the reins of the kingdom firmly in his own hands. He would not be manipulated by lesser men.

Bathsheba felt relief rather than joy. Perhaps this bloodshed would now bring peace in Israel. Perhaps the men would no longer need to go out to war against the nations surrounding them. Perhaps there would be a time of plenty in Canaan. Men would toil and enjoy the work of their hands. Surely that would be a great blessing from the Lord.

She'd been born into a time of war. Peace had come infrequently, like a breath of spring in the midst of a long, cold winter, a sweet aroma hinting of what one day would come, but it wouldn't last.

Not in her lifetime.

She was old now, and tired, so very tired. Strange how the past came back so vividly. Poignant memories often gripped her and made her heart ache. Ahithophel, holding her upon his lap, smiling. Her father laughing, his face bronzed by firelight. Her mother holding her close. Uriah dropping the stone she gave him and walking away. And David, always David. He lived in her dreams, agile as a deer leaping to high places, singing songs to his men and leading them out to build a kingdom for God's people. Oh, how she had loved him – and loved him still.

"Mother," came a gentle voice, drawing her back to the present. She blinked and turned her face toward it, smiling. She brushed Solomon's cheek. The crown rested firmly upon his regal head. He was shrewd and would watch over and protect his brothers. He would seek the Lord's guidance in how to make Israel a beacon to all nations. She need not worry about her sons. Hadn't God put a protective hedge around them from the time they were babies? Hadn't God kept them safe within the walls of a palace torn by intrigue? Whoever would have thought God would put the son of an adulteress on the throne? Who would have imagined *her* son would take the reigns of this unruly nation and make it the center of civilization?

Lord, Your mercy is beyond anything I will ever understand. Far beyond anything I deserve. Help me to give my sons what they need before I go the way of all flesh, back to dust.

"Listen to me, my sons," she said as they gathered around her bed. "Remember your father's instructions, and don't forsake what I've taught you. Fear the Lord, for He holds all power and you will accomplish nothing without Him. Treasure the Lord's commandments more than gold or jewels. Be attentive and incline your heart to understand them. Remember the blessings and the cursings and make wise choices."

She looked at Solomon. He was as handsome as David, but there was a shrewdness about him his father had lacked, an edge of cynicism that made her sad. Perhaps it was the way he had grown up, among power-hungry brothers. She held out her hand and he sat on her couch. Taking her hand, he kissed it. Shobab, Shimea, and Nathan moved in closer, tears in their eyes.

"You all know how much I loved your father," she said in a trembling voice.

Solomon's hand tightened. "Yes, Mother. No one could doubt your love for David."

"Then please listen with that understanding and save yourselves sorrow."

"She's in pain," Shobab whispered.

"Perhaps we should call her maidservant."

"No," Solomon said, his eyes never leaving hers. "Let her speak."

She sensed there was little time left. "When you marry ... " She looked around at each of her sons, and then held Solomon's gaze. "Choose a wife carefully from among the maidens of Israel. Find a young woman who fears the Lord, a girl who is trustworthy, who works with her hands and has joy in it, can manage a household wisely and with compassion, a girl who cares for the poor. Let her be physically strong and attractive so she will be able to give you healthy sons and raise them up to be men after God's own heart. But don't go after a woman simply because she's beautiful." She smiled sadly. "Beauty is often deceitful and vain. You've all grown up with beautiful women around you. You know how treacherous they can be." Hadn't it been her beauty David first lusted after? Hadn't she sensed that with her woman's heart and opened the door for him to sin? Oh, the price they'd both paid for that. She was still paying.

Oh, Lord, let it not be so for my sons. Let them be wise and choose women of virtue, women who love You more than the things of this world, women who love You with all their heart, mind, soul, and might!

She smiled at Solomon. "A woman of virtue will be an excellent wife and a crown for your head. A crown you will look upon with more delight than the one you wear, my son."

She looked at Shobab, Shimea, and Nathan. Fine sons, all of them, each an unexpected blessing from the Lord and evidence of His grace and mercy. *Oh, God, let them hear my instruction.* "A good wife will increase your honor at the gates. She will discipline your sons and raise them up to follow in the ways of the Lord your God. Sons like that will strengthen the House of David and bless our nation."

There was so much more she wanted to say, but she knew better. The longer a mother spoke, the less inclined her sons were to listen. Besides, she had said it all many times before. She had been teaching them from the time they were babies at her breast, boys on her knees, or young men she'd sent away to learn from a prophet of God. *Oh, Lord God of Israel, that You should choose my sons. Your mercy never ceases.* She had done all she could to raise up her sons to love the Lord and serve Him with all their strength. She wanted these young men to be better than their father, David, whom she had loved so much. And still loved. Death could not diminish love.

"I'm very tired." She drank in the sight of each son as he bent down and kissed her, straightened, and walked out the door, returning to his own life and choices.

Solomon lingered. "You were an excellent wife to Abba," he said softly, tears in his eyes. "You didn't honor him in word only, like the others. You honored him in truth and in deed."

"I brought great harm to him."

"And great blessing, too." He smiled. "Four sons, one of whom will be a great king."

"With God's help, my son." She kissed his hand. "Don't ever forget who has the real power."

Her mind drifted. She heard her mother's voice in a distant memory. *"A king must build a strong house and preserve the kingdom."* She gripped his hand tightly. "The life of a king is more difficult than the life of a shepherd, my son. Your father drank from another man's cistern and poisoned his own well." Solomon frowned. His lips parted, but she spoke quickly. "Have you ever loved someone, Solomon, truly loved her?"

"Abishag."

The hair stood on the back of Bathsheba's neck. She thought of David's sending orders to kill Uriah. She remembered Solomon's wrath the day she had gone to ask that the Shunanite be given to Adonijah as a wife.

Solomon leaned down. "No, Mother, I did not order my brother's execution over a woman. I had Adonijah killed because he was intent upon evil. He wanted the throne. Rebellion would've cost thousands of lives and brought chaos to Israel. There is a time for war, Mother. God used King David to subdue the enemies that surround us. It was left to me to destroy the enemies that have dwelt among us. Now, it is time for peace."

Let it be so, Lord, oh, let it be so.

She felt herself growing weaker. "Then keep the well clean," she said softly. "Take Abishag for your wife, for she is everything I've described to you. But remain faithful to her. I know you are a king and can have as many wives and concubines as you want. I know it is the practice of kings, but don't turn your freedom into an opportunity to sin. Rejoice in the wife of your youth."

"I must build my house."

Her heart sank. "No, my son. Let God build your house."

Solomon leaned down and kissed her cheek, and she knew he was a man withdrawing from her woman's counsel. He had entered the courts of men. *Oh, God, will he make the same mistakes his father did? Are men and women all destined to sin? Is it simply their nature to do so? For so it seems. We have the Law, but we can't seem to keep it.*

Solomon rose and stepped back. She stretched out her arm, holding fast to his hand as long as she could. "I love you, Mother," he whispered hoarsely. "I love you, but I must go." She relaxed her hand and his fingers slipped from hers. Her handmaiden opened the door for him and he went out.

Bathsheba sank back against her bed cushions and closed her eyes. *Oh, Lord, only You can save us from ourselves. Come, Lord, come and save us. Come and dwell among us. Walk with us again as You did in the Garden of Eden. Speak with us face to face as you did with Moses. Take us up to live with You as You did with Enoch! Change our sinful hearts.*

"My lady," her handmaiden said, her voice tinged with grief.

Bathsheba opened her eyes. "There's nothing to fear." The girl adjusted the covers, briefly covered Bathsheba's hand with her own, and sat again. Bathsheba closed her eyes again and let her mind wander back over the past.

She remembered her mother's angry, embittered words flung in a prophetic curse on her head. *"You've brought shame upon my household! ... Fool! How many have died because of you? It will all be on your head. ... People will spit on the ground when you pass by. ... They will curse the day of your birth! ... You are cursed among women! Your name will be a byword for adulteress! Your name will be unspoken as long as I live!"*

The pain of rejection stabbed her as fiercely now as it had the day her mother had turned her back and walked out the door. Bathsheba had only seen her mother one time after that – when she lay on her deathbed, too weak to move or speak. Bathsheba had nursed her for several days, praying silently for some way to restore their relationship. But at the last, her mother had turned her face away and died without ever saying a word to her.

And now, she lay quiet upon her couch waiting for her own life to end. She hoped it would be soon. She didn't want to live long enough to see her sons fail. And fail they would because they were, after all, only human. What chance had they to live perfect lives before God with David's hot blood running in their veins? David's blood mingled with her own.

"Your name will be unspoken!"

Only the Lord forgets sin. Only God can take it and send it as far away as the east is from the west. Man remembers. Man recounts. Man condemns.

How many years would come and go after she was dust when men and women would still hold up her sins and wave them like a bloody banner? *Will anyone ever see more in me than that one fateful day when David saw me from his roof and called me to his bed?*

She felt warm breath upon her face and a gentle kiss on her forehead.

I see.

Bathsheba's heart raced in joy. She opened her eyes. When had it grown so dark? Her handmaiden slept in the chair beside her bed, but no one else was in the room.

She drew in her breath and smelled incense drifting in the air. It reminded her of the Tent of Meeting; sweet, so sweet her soul drank it in.

She relaxed, her mind drifting again, gently this time, as though floating in a cleansing stream.

I know they will remember my sins, Lord, but when they look upon my life, let them see what You did for an unworthy woman. Let them see the hope born from despair. If they must recount my sins, let them count Your blessings more so. You protected me. You raised me up. You gave me sons. Let my name be unspoken, Lord, for what am I that anyone should remember me? But, oh, Lord God of Israel, if they do remember me, let them open their mouths and sing praises for Your great mercy toward me. Let them see Your infinite grace and Your boundless love. And let them ...

She sighed deeply.

... be encouraged.

seek and find

DEAR READER,

You have just read the story of Bathsheba as perceived by one author. Is this the whole truth about the story of David and Bathsheba? Jesus said to seek and you will find the answers you need for life. The best way to find the truth is to look for yourself!

This "Seek and Find" section is designed to help you discover the story of Bathsheba as recorded in the Bible. It consists of six short studies that you can do on your own or with a small discussion group.

You may be surprised to learn that this ancient story will have applications for your life today. No matter where we live or in what century, God's Word is truth. It is as relevant today as it was yesterday. In it we find a future and a hope.

Peggy Lynch

THE TEMPTATION

SEEK GOD'S WORD FOR TRUTH

Read the following passage:

> *The following spring, the time of year when kings go to war, David sent Joab and the Israelite army to destroy the Ammonites. In the process they laid siege to the city of Rabbah. But David stayed behind in Jerusalem.*
>
> *Late one afternoon, David got out of bed after taking a nap and went for a stroll on the roof of the palace. As he looked out over the city, he noticed a woman of unusual beauty taking a bath. He sent someone to find out who she was, and he was told, "She is Bathsheba, the daughter of Eliam and the wife of Uriah the Hittite." Then David sent for her; and when she came to the palace, he slept with her. (She had just completed the purification rites after having her menstrual period.) Then she returned home. Later when Bathsheba discovered that she was pregnant, she sent a message to inform David.*
>
> – 2 SAMUEL 11:1-5 –

✢ In the spring, kings go off to war. Where was King David this particular spring?

✢ What did David do when he could not sleep?

✢ What did David find out about "the woman" he was watching? List everything he knew *before* he sent for her?

✢ David still had time to change the course of events. However, what course does David take?

✢ From the same verses, list what you learn about "the woman."

✢ From what little is told about the woman, would you describe her as a seductress, a victim, or something in between. Why?

FIND GOD'S WAYS FOR YOU

Read the following passage:

Remember, no one who wants to do wrong should ever say, "God is tempting me." God is never tempted to do wrong, and he never tempts anyone else either. Temptation comes from the lure of our own evil desires. Then evil desires lead to evil actions, and evil actions lead to death.

– JAMES 1:13-15 –

✛ Where do temptations come from and where do they lead?

Read the following passage:

Remember that the temptations that come into your life are no different from what others experience. And God is faithful. He will keep the temptation from becoming so strong that you can't stand up against it. When you are tempted, he will show you a way out so that you will not give in to it."

– 1 CORINTHIANS 10:13 –

✛ What does God say about temptation and what does He offer as a solution?

✛ Look again at 2 Samuel 11:1-5. List the ways of escape you can see that David ignored. Do the same for the woman.

✛ Think about times when you have been tempted. How have you responded and what kind of pattern do you see?

STOP AND PONDER

✛ Look back at 1 Corinthians 10:13. Do you look for ways of escape?

THE COVER-UP

SEEK GOD'S WORD FOR TRUTH

Read the following passage:

So David sent word to Joab: "Send me Uriah the Hittite." When Uriah arrived, David asked him how Joab and the army were getting along and how the war was progressing. Then he told Uriah, "Go on home and relax." David even sent a gift to Uriah after he had left the palace. But Uriah wouldn't go home. He stayed that night at the palace entrance with some of the king's other servants. When David heard what Uriah had done, he summoned him and asked, "What's the matter with you? Why didn't you go home last night after being away for so long?"

Uriah replied, "The Ark and the armies of Israel and Judah are living in tents, and Joab and his officers are camping in the open fields. How could I go home to wine and dine and sleep with my wife? I swear that I will never be guilty of acting like that."

"Well, stay here tonight," David told him, "and tomorrow you may return to the army." So Uriah stayed in Jerusalem that day and the next. Then David invited him to dinner and got him drunk. But even then he couldn't get Uriah to go home to his wife. Again he slept at the palace entrance.

So the next morning David wrote a letter to Joab and gave it to Uriah to deliver. The letter instructed Joab, "Station Uriah on the front lines where the battle is fiercest. Then pull back so that he will be killed." So Joab assigned Uriah to a spot close to the city wall where he knew the enemy's strongest men were fighting. And Uriah was killed along with several other Israelite soldiers.

Then Joab sent a battle report to David. He told his messenger, "Report all the news of the battle to the king. But he might get angry and ask, 'Why did the troops go so close to the city? Didn't they know there would be shooting from the walls? Wasn't Gideon's son Abimelech killed at Thebez by a woman who threw a millstone down on him?' Then tell him, 'Uriah the Hittite was killed, too.'"

So the messenger went to Jerusalem and gave a complete report to David. "The enemy came out against us," he said. "And as we chased them back to the city gates, the archers on the wall shot arrows at us. Some of our men were killed, including Uriah the Hittite."

"Well, tell Joab not to be discouraged," David said. "The sword kills one as well as another! Fight harder next time, and conquer the city!"

When Bathsheba heard that her husband was dead, she mourned for him. When the period of mourning was over, David sent for her and brought her to the palace, and she became one of his wives. Then she gave birth to a son. But the Lord was very displeased with what David had done.

– 2 SAMUEL 11:6-27 –

✛ Bathsheba sent a message to the king informing him she was pregnant. How did King David respond? What instructions did he give Uriah?

✛ What was the motivation for Uriah's actions?

✛ David writes a letter to Joab. In your own words, describe David's new plan and his attitude.

✛ How did Bathsheba react to her husband's death? What do you gather from her reaction?

✛ What happened to Bathsheba after her time of mourning was over?

✛ Contrast the actions and attitudes of David, Uriah and Bathsheba.

FIND GOD'S WAYS FOR YOU

Bathsheba chose to rely on David to take care of "the problem." David chose to handle things himself. And Uriah became the scapegoat.

✛ When you make wrong choices, what kind of pattern do you fall into?

✛ How have you helped cover up for other people?

✛ What impact have your choices had on others?

✛ What impact have other people's choices had on your life?

STOP AND PONDER

There is path before each person that seems right, but it ends in death.
— PROVERBS 14:12 —

✛ Where are you headed?

THE CONFESSION

SEEK GOD'S WORD FOR TRUTH

Read the following passage:

So the Lord sent Nathan the prophet to tell David this story: "There were two men in a certain town. One was rich, and one was poor. The rich man owned many sheep and cattle. The poor man owned nothing but a little lamb he had worked hard to buy. He raised that little lamb, and it grew up with his children. It ate from the man's own plate and drank from his cup. He cuddled it in his arms like a baby daughter. One day a guest arrived at the home of the rich man. But instead of killing a lamb from his own flocks for food, he took the poor man's lamb and killed it and served it to his guest."

David was furious. "As surely as the Lord lives," he vowed, "any man who would do such a thing deserves to die! He must repay four lambs to the poor man for the one he stole and for having no pity."

Then Nathan said to David, "You are that man! The Lord, the God of Israel, says, 'I anointed you king of Israel and saved you from the power of Saul. I gave you his house and his wives and the kingdoms of Israel and Judah. And if that had not been enough, I would have given you much, much more. Why, then, have you despised the word of the Lord and done this horrible deed? For you have murdered Uriah and stolen his wife. From this time on, the sword will be a constant threat to your family, because you have despised me by taking Uriah's wife to be your own.

"'Because of what you have done, I, the Lord, will cause your own household to rebel against you. I will give your wives to another man, and he will go to bed with them in public view. You did it secretly, but I will do this to you openly in the sight of all Israel.'"

Then David confessed to Nathan, "I have sinned against the Lord."

— 2 SAMUEL 12:1-13A —

✛ How does the Lord confront David?

✛ How does David view the man in the story?

✛ Why do you think Nathan had to bluntly tell David, "You are that man!"?

✝ As God lays bare the extent of David's sin, what does He say will happen to David's house and why?

✝ What further consequences will befall David's family?

✝ What is David's confession?

FIND GOD'S WAYS FOR YOU

✝ Remember a time when someone confronted you about your actions or words or choices. How did you respond or react, and why?

✝ How quickly do you recognize sin in your life?

✝ What kind of consequences are you living with because of your own wrong choices or the wrong choices of someone close to you?

✝ When you face your own sin, do you hide it, handle it, or confess it?

STOP AND PONDER

Search me, O God, and know my heart; test me and know my thoughts. Point out anything in me that offends you, and lead me along the path of everlasting life.

— PSALM 139:23-24 —

✝ What do you need to confess to God right now?

FORGIVENESS

SEEK GOD'S WORD FOR TRUTH

Read the following passage:

Then David confessed to Nathan, "I have sinned against the Lord."
Nathan replied, "Yes, but the Lord has forgiven you, and you won't die for this sin. But you have given the enemies of the Lord great opportunity

to despise and blaspheme him, so your child will die."

After Nathan returned to his home, the Lord made Bathsheba's baby deathly ill. David begged God to spare the child. He went without food and lay all night on the bare ground. The leaders of the nation pleaded with him to get up and eat with them, but he refused. Then on the seventh day the baby died. David's advisers were afraid to tell him. "He was so broken up about the baby being sick," they said. "What will he do to himself when we tell him the child is dead?"

But when David saw them whispering, he realized what had happened. "Is the baby dead?"

"Yes," they replied. Then David got up from the ground, washed himself, put on lotions, and changed his clothes. Then he went to the Tabernacle and worshiped the Lord. After that, he returned to the palace and ate. His advisers were amazed. "We don't understand you," they told him. "While the baby was still living, you wept and refused to eat. But now that the baby is dead, you have stopped your mourning and are eating again."

David replied, "I fasted and wept while the child was alive, for I said, 'Perhaps the Lord will be gracious to me and let the child live.' But why should I fast when he is dead? Can I bring him back again? I will go to him one day, but he cannot return to me."

– 2 SAMUEL 12:13-23 –

✛ What does God do with David's sin? And what is the good news about David's life?

✛ What shocking news does Nathan give David?

✛ What does David do and for how long?

✛ How does David react when the child dies?

✛ Where does he go and what extraordinary thing does he do?

✛ David's servants were baffled by his actions. What comfort and hope motivated David?

FIND GOD'S WAYS FOR YOU

Read the following passage:

If we confess our sins to him, he is faithful and just to forgive us and to cleanse us from every wrong.

– 1 JOHN 1:9 –

✢ From this Scripture, what is God's promise? What is the condition of that promise?

✢ Have you experienced forgiveness? How do you know you've been forgiven? How willing are you to forgive others?

Read the following passage:

The Lord is merciful and gracious; he is slow to get angry and full of unfailing love. He will not constantly accuse us, nor remain angry forever. He has not punished us for all our sins, nor does he deal with us as we deserve. For his unfailing love toward those who fear him is as great as the height of the heavens above the earth. He has removed our rebellious acts as far away from us as the east is from the west. The Lord is like a father to his children, tender and compassionate to those who fear him. For he understands how weak we are; he knows we are only dust.

– PSALM 103:8-14 –

✢ List everything you learn in this Scripture about how God deals with you and sin.

STOP AND PONDER

Read the following passage:

So now there is no condemnation for those who belong to Christ Jesus. For the power of the life-giving Spirit has freed you through Christ Jesus from the power of sin that leads to death.

– ROMANS 8:1-2 –

✢ Who owns you?

RESTORATION

SEEK GOD'S WORD FOR TRUTH

Read the following passage:

Then David comforted Bathsheba, his wife, and slept with her. She became pregnant and gave birth to a son, and they named him Solomon. The Lord loved the child and sent word through Nathan the prophet that his name should be Jedidiah — "beloved of the Lord" — because the Lord loved him.
— 2 Samuel 12:24-25 —

✛ David confessed to God. David waited on God. David worshiped God. David believed God for the future. These steps lead to a restored relationship with God. What does David now do concerning Bathsheba?

✛ What did God do for Bathsheba?

✛ Who named the baby Solomon?

✛ What message did God send to Bathsheba through Nathan the prophet?

✛ God sent Nathan to confront David regarding his sin. What was the purpose of Nathan's visit to Bathsheba?

✛ From the above passage, what evidence do you find that Bathsheba also experienced a restored relationship with God?

FIND GOD'S WAYS FOR YOU

✛ What does *restoration* mean to you?

Read the following passage:

Dear brothers and sisters, if another Christian is overcome by some sin, you who are godly should gently and humbly help that person back onto the right path. And be careful not to fall into the same temptation yourself. Share each other's troubles and problems, and in this way obey the law of Christ.
— Galatians 6:1-2 —

✛ What role do we have in helping one another be restored to God?

✛ What attitude are you to have when others need to be restored?

✛ Are you seeking restoration? What steps do you need to take?

STOP AND PONDER

God saved you by his special favor when you believed. And you can't take credit for this; it is a gift from God. Salvation is not a reward for the good things we have done, so none of us can boast about it. For we are God's masterpiece. He has created us anew in Christ Jesus, so that we can do the good things he planned for us long ago.

— EPHESIANS 2:8-10 —

✛ Are you a new creation?

BLESSINGS

SEEK GOD'S WORD FOR TRUTH

Traditionally, Bathsheba is remembered for her adulterous affair with King David and is referred to as "the wife of Uriah." But let's recount how God remembers her. Read the following passages:

Then David moved the capital to Jerusalem, where he reigned another thirty-three years. The sons born to David in Jerusalem included Shimea, Shobab, Nathan, and Solomon. Bathsheba, the daughter of Ammiel (Eliam), was the mother of these sons.

— 1 CHRONICLES 3:4B-5 —

✛ What did God do for Bathsheba?

Then Nathan the prophet went to Bathsheba, Solomon's mother, and asked her, "Did you realize that Haggith's son, Adonijah, has made himself king and that our lord David doesn't even know about it? If you want to save your own life and the life of your son Solomon, follow my counsel. Go at once to King David and say to him, 'My Lord, didn't you promise me that my son Solomon would be the next king and would sit upon your throne? Then why has Adonijah become king?' And while you are still talking with him, I will come and confirm everything you have said."

– 1 KINGS 1:11-14 –

✢ List everything that shows God's continued care for Bathsheba.

"Call Bathsheba," David said. So she came back in and stood before the king. And the king vowed, "As surely as the Lord lives, who has rescued me from every danger, today I decree that your son Solomon will be the next king and will sit on my throne, just as I swore to you before the Lord, the God of Israel."

Then Bathsheba bowed low before him again and exclaimed, "May my lord King David live forever!"

– 1 KINGS 1:28-31 –

✢ How did David continue to support and comfort Bathsheba?

All the royal officials went to King David and congratulated him, saying, "May your God make Solomon's fame even greater than your own, and may Solomon's kingdom be even greater than yours!" Then the king bowed his head in worship as he lay in his bed, and he spoke these words: "Blessed be the Lord, the God of Israel, who today has chosen someone to sit on my throne while I am still alive to see it."

– 1 KINGS 1:47-48 –

✢ How did God keep His promise to Bathsheba? And what was David's response?

Young Woman: "Go out to look upon King Solomon, O young women of Jerusalem. See the crown with which his mother crowned him on his wedding day, the day of his gladness."

– SONG OF SONGS 3:11 –

✢ What further joy did Bathsheba have?

Jesse was the father of King David. David was the father of Solomon (his mother was Bathsheba, the widow of Uriah). Jacob was the father of

Joseph, the husband of Mary. Mary was the mother of Jesus, who is called the Messiah.

— MATTHEW 1:6, 16 —

✛ What ultimate blessing was bestowed upon Bathsheba?

FIND GOD'S WAYS FOR YOU

✛ How do you think you'll be remembered?

✛ How would you like to be remembered?

✛ How has God blessed you?

✛ Trace God's hand of mercy in your life.

STOP AND PONDER

"For I know the plans I have for you," says the Lord. "They are plans for good and not for disaster, to give you a future and a hope. In those days when you pray, I will listen. If you look for me in earnest, you will find me when you seek me. I will be found by you," says the Lord.

— JEREMIAH 29:11-14A —

✛ Jesus has found you. Have you found Him? He's waiting.

Unafraid

setting the scene

YOU have another daughter." The midwife held the squalling infant up as Anne collapsed back on her pallet, exhausted after hours of labor.

Anne's heart sank at the news. She turned her face to the wall, not watching as the midwife cut the cord, washed the baby, and rubbed salt over the quivering little body to prevent infection.

"Your daughter," the older woman said.

Anne took the tiny wizened infant tenderly in her arms and wept, knowing her husband would be bitterly disappointed. He had been fasting and praying for a son.

Kissing the baby, Anne held her up to the midwife. "Give the child to her father, so that he may bless her." As the woman left the house, Anne shifted on the pallet, wincing at the pain. She strained to hear what her husband had to say, but it was the excited voice of their older daughter, Mary, she heard.

"Can I hold her, Father? Please. Oh, she is so sweet."

Joachim spoke too softly for Anne to hear. When he entered the house, she searched his face. Though he did not look at her with reproach, she saw his disappointment. Leaning down, he placed their newborn firmly in her arms once again. What could he say to ease both their hearts? God had not seen fit to give them a son.

"I love her," Mary said, coming into the house.

"We all love her," Joachim said quickly.

Ah, but Anne understood. A son would work alongside his father. A son would go to synagogue and give distinction to his father. A son would provide for his mother if his father died. A son might one day grow up and stand against Israel's oppressors. Or even turn out to be the long-awaited deliverer, the Messiah for whom all Israel prayed.

But a girl? What use was a girl, other than to share in the daily chores? She would simply be another mouth to feed until the time came for her father to find her a proper husband.

"I've been considering the name Deborah," Anne said quietly, head down. This baby was more delicate than her first, but there was a sweetness in her face that gripped Anne's heart.

"We will call her Mary."

"But Mary is *my* name," their older daughter said, looking between them.

Joachim put his hand on her head and spoke gently. "Your sister shall be *little* Mary."

Anne reached out to her older daughter. "Don't be distressed, dear one. Go outside so that I may speak with your father." When she was alone with Joachim, she looked up at him. "Won't you please consider another name, my husband? Deborah is a strong name. And there are so many Marys. It has become the most common name in all Israel."

"And when there are enough, perhaps the Lord will finally hear our cry!" Joachim's voice broke. Color seeped into his cheeks as he looked away. "Her name shall be Mary." He left the house. Anne overheard him tell their older daughter to play with her friends and leave Mama alone to rest.

Anne studied her newborn's face. "Mary," she whispered. "My precious little Mary." Her heart was heavy, for both of her daughters now bore a name that meant "bitterness and suffering." The name *Mary* declared the depth of every Jew's despair under the oppression of Roman conquerors. *Mary* was a cry to the Lord for rescue.

Raising her knees slightly, Anne cradled her baby on her thighs. She unwrapped the cloth and stroked the small arms, studied the legs bowed from nine months in the womb. Tears streamed down Anne's cheeks as she kissed the tiny hand that clasped her finger. Little Mary's skin was softer than a baby rabbit's. "Lord, Lord, please let her name come to mean more than 'bitterness and suffering.' Let it come to mean 'strength is from the Lord.' Let it come to mean 'God's love upholds us.' Let it mean 'trust in God, and let nothing defeat faith in you.' Oh, Lord ... " She wept softly as she lifted her baby to her breast. "Let the name *Mary* remind us to obey without fear."

one

MARY sat alone beneath a mustard tree, her hands covering her face. Did all brides feel this way when the contracts were signed, gifts given, and futures sealed by the will of others? She trembled at the prospect of life with a man she hardly knew, other than as a man admired and befriended by her father upon his arrival in Nazareth three years ago.

"He's of our tribe, Anne," Joachim had announced after meeting Joseph at the synagogue. "And descended from the royal line of David."

"Is he married?" Her mother cast an eye toward Mary.

Thus had plans for her future been set in motion, for her father was quick to find out that Joseph was looking for a wife from the tribe of Judah, a descendant of David, a young woman of unquestioned virtue and faith. Mary knew their ambitions. Mary's older sister was married to a Nazarene, and her parents hoped to marry their younger daughter to another man of their own tribe. And of course he must be devout, kind, and able to provide a good home for her and any children she might give him. So they invited the carpenter to their home frequently, and Joseph was receptive to their hopes.

"Why did he not seek out a young woman in Bethlehem?" Mary had asked her mother once.

"Why ask such questions?" Her mother had been impatient. "Just accept that God sent him here to Nazareth."

Her father had been less inclined to believe that God would be intimately involved in the personal life of a humble carpenter or a poor man with failing health and a daughter soon of marriageable age. "Joseph needs work like anyone else, and Sepphoris is growing. Carpenters and stoneworkers can earn more money there than in Bethlehem."

The men had begun to discuss a match, but when her father died, Mary's future was left for her mother to settle. And she intended to settle it sooner rather than later.

"Your father wanted to give you more time, Mary," she had said, "but time can be an enemy. You are ready to marry, and, considering our circumstances, there's no time to waste. I've already spoken to Joseph, and he has agreed to take you as his wife. All will be well now, Mary. We will not be left to fend for ourselves."

Now, sitting beneath the mustard tree, Mary buried her face in her arms. Would they have been left to fend for themselves? God promised to care for those who put their faith in him. Mary believed the Lord's promises.

All she had ever wanted was to be close to the Lord. Her heart yearned for him. She longed for him as a deer panted for streams of water. How she wished she'd been among the people delivered from Egypt. How blessed they'd been to see God's miracles, to hear the Law for the first time, to see water spring from a rock, and to taste the manna from heaven. Sometimes she almost wished she had been born a man. Then she could have gone to the desert cliffs of Qumran and dedicated her life to God.

Was it youth that made her restless? Her deep thirst for the Lord frustrated her. How could she love the Lord God with all her heart, mind, soul, and strength if she was to be given to a man? How could she love God fully and still give proper honor to her husband?

And yet she understood the practicality of marriage. Women were vulnerable. How often she heard the hoofbeats of Roman soldiers approaching her little village of Nazareth. Countless times she had seen them at the well, filling their waterskins. Then they took whatever food-stuffs they needed from the resentful, downtrodden citizenry. Sometimes they took young women as well, leaving them abused and ruined. Life could become unbearable for an unprotected woman, especially a young one. Mary's mother had taught her to run and hide when she heard the sounds of horses or marching feet. Her heart squeezed tight with anxiety, for she could hear them coming closer now.

Pax Romana had brought anything but peace to Israel, for Mary's people fought Rome's control. Wouldn't it be wiser for her to remain unwed rather than to marry and bring children into such a world? Many Hebrews fought against Hellenistic influences with all their being, nursing their grievances, fanning their hatred into violence. Others turned traitor, rejecting the God of Abraham, Isaac, and Jacob, and adopting the customs of their conquerors.

Where was God in all this? Mary knew he was as powerful now as he had been when he created the world. Was she disloyal to wonder if her people had brought this wretchedness upon themselves? She knew the history of her people. She knew how God had disciplined them in the past in order to make them turn back to him. Why must Israel repeat her cycles of disobedience, generation after generation? And how much longer would it be until God once again sent a deliverer?

For as long as Mary could remember, she had heard her people crying out for rescue from Roman oppression.

Someday the Lord would send *the* deliverer, the one promised after Adam and Eve's fall from grace, the one who would make all things right, all things new. The Messiah. Every day Mary prayed for him to come ... as she prayed now, sitting beneath the shade of the mustard tree, struggling with questions beyond her ability to understand. Torn by the turbulent world around her as well as her own now-settled future, Mary cried out for a savior.

Oh, Lord, when will you send us a deliverer? Rescue us from the foreign oppressors who carry golden idols, arrogantly proclaiming their capricious emperor a god!

She must cease this struggling. She would be wed to Joseph. The matter was settled. Mary honored her mother and would obey.

Oh, Lord God of Israel, I don't understand these things. Is it wrong to want to belong to you? My soul longs for you. Help me to be obedient, to be a proper wife to Joseph, for you are sovereign and must have chosen this man for me. Make me a woman after your own heart. Create in me a clean heart, and renew a right spirit within me.

A strange tingling sensation spread over her skin. Her hair prickled as she raised her head and saw a man standing before her. Heart thumping with terror, she stared at him, for she had never seen anyone like him before. Was it merely the sun at his back that made him look so terrifying?

"Greetings, favored woman! The Lord is with you!"

Trembling, she sat still and silent, wondering at his words. She shut her eyes tightly and then opened them again. He was still standing there, looking down at her with kind patience. What did his greeting mean? Were not all God's chosen people favored? And why did he say the Lord was with her? Was he the Lord? Fear filled her, and she closed her eyes again, for surely anyone who looked upon the Lord would die.

"Don't be frightened, Mary, for God has decided to bless you!"

A sob welled up inside her throat, catching her off guard, for she wanted nothing more than to please God! But the Lord knew how undeserving she was. She blushed, remembering that only the moment before, she had resisted the idea of marrying Joseph, though he loved God as much as she. And now, this man said precious words that filled her with joy!

The stranger drew closer, his head inclined toward her. "You will become pregnant and have a son, and you are to name him Jesus."

Jesus. The name meant "the Lord saves."

The angel was still speaking. "He will be very great and will be called the Son of the Most High. And the Lord God will give him the throne of his ancestor David. And he will reign over Israel forever; his Kingdom will never end!"

Mary swallowed, her mind whirling with the implications of his words. He was telling her she would bear the Messiah! As soon as the words were uttered, she felt attacked by a chorus of dark voices.

You? Why would the Lord choose anyone so low? The Messiah will not come from some Nazarene peasant girl. What evil is this, that one so unworthy should dare imagine she could bear the Messiah! Ignore this madman. Look away from him! Reject what he says. Close your eyes! Say nothing!

Yet another voice spoke, a quiet voice, a voice her heart recognized.

What is your answer, Mary?

She stood, tilting her head as she looked up at the angel. "But how can I have a baby? I am a virgin."

The angel smiled tenderly. "The Holy Spirit will come upon you, and the power of the Most High will overshadow you. So the baby born to you will be holy, and he will be called the Son of God. What's more, your relative Elizabeth has become pregnant in her old age! People used to say she was barren, but she's already in her sixth month. For nothing is impossible with God."

Mary drew in her breath with a smile and clasped her hands. Oh! She knew how Elizabeth had always longed for a child. Nothing was impossible with God! Elizabeth would be like Sarah, who bore Isaac in her old age. She would be like Hannah, dedicating her son to the Lord. The news made Mary's faith leap. She wanted to race to Elizabeth and see this miracle for herself, but the angel stood in front of her, silent, waiting for her answer.

If she said yes, she would become the mother of the long-awaited Messiah. Why the Lord had chosen her to be part of his plan she couldn't even guess. She was uneducated, poor, and lived in an obscure village that most Jews disdained. Yet she also knew from listening to Scripture readings in the synagogue that God often used the most unlikely and unworthy to fulfill his purposes. It didn't matter who she was. God would accomplish his purposes in his way. The angel of the Lord was asking her to be part of God's plan. And everything within her heart and soul cried out a joyous yes.

Do you really think you can be the Messiah's mother? Do you think you will know how to rear God's Son to be king over Israel? The dark voices again.

No. I won't, her heart answered. *But God will.*

Gathering her courage, Mary looked up. "I am the Lord's servant." She spread her hands. "And I am willing to accept whatever he wants. May everything you have said come true."

As soon as she made her decision, the angel was gone. She uttered a soft gasp of dismay. She would have thought she imagined the entire episode, had not the air still trembled around her. Shaken, she clutched her hands against her chest until she remembered the angel of the Lord had said not to be afraid. Letting out her breath softly, she knelt and lifted her face to heaven. She lifted her hands, palms up. *Lord, your will be done.*

Her skin tingled strangely as she saw a cloud coming down. She placed her hands over her heart as she was overshadowed. Closing her eyes, she breathed in the scent of spring flowers, earth, and the heavens. Her skin warmed as her body was flooded with sensation. She drew in her breath and held it. For one brief space in time, nothing moved; no sound was heard as all creation paused.

Within the womb of a poor peasant girl from an obscure village in Galilee, God the Son became one with the seed of Adam.

Joseph glared at Mary. "How can you expect me to believe such a story?" All his hopes for a bright future were demolished. He would never have thought a girl like Mary – so young, so sweet, so devout – could betray him in so foul a manner. *Pregnant!* He was attacked by emotion, shaken by it. He shut his eyes, fighting against the violent thoughts filling his mind: **Denounce her! Cast her aside! Report her to the rabbi! Have her stoned!**

"No!" he cried out, putting his hands over his ears. He opened his eyes and saw Mary's mother, Anne, cowering and weeping in the corner.

Only Mary was calm. "You will believe, Joseph." She looked up at him, her dark eyes innocent. "You will. I know you will."

How could she appear so calm when, with one word, he could have her killed?

"There is only one way a woman conceives."

"With God, anything is possible."

"And God would choose *you* to bear the Messiah?"

She laughed at his sarcasm, her face filled with joy. "Hasn't God always chosen the weak to confound the strong? Oh, Joseph." She clasped her hands, excitement radiating from her. "Think of him. God never chooses as man would choose."

"I can't believe this. *I can't!* It defies all reason!" He had to get out of this house. He couldn't look at her and think clearly.

"Joseph!" Anne rose and came after him. "Joseph! Please!" She cried out as he went out the door and left it ajar behind him. *"Joseph!"*

He ducked around the corner and walked quickly away, heading up a narrow street toward the end of town. He didn't want people noticing he was upset and asking questions. He had to think!

Out of sight of Nazareth, he wept. What should he do now? Forget she was the daughter of a man who had befriended him, a man who was of his own tribe? Could he ignore the fact that she was pregnant with another man's child? She had committed a sin of abomination! She was unclean! If he married Mary now, people would point the finger at him. Both their reputations would be ruined. The gossip would circulate for years to come. And when the child was born, what then? Everyone would know he was conceived before the wedding ceremony, and would whisper behind their hands as he passed.

Why were women such weak vessels, so easily deceived? He kicked the dirt angrily. Who could have done this to her? Who would dare take advantage of an innocent, fatherless girl? And why would she concoct such a ridiculous, outlandish lie to cover up her sin? He grimaced. An angel came and told her she was to bear the Son of God! What man in his right mind would believe such a story?

When Joachim had offered Mary to him, Joseph thought he'd been offered a future and a hope. Now, he held disaster in his hands. If he exposed her, he would have to stand by and watch the daughter of Joachim stoned to death for the sin of fornication. And the child she carried would die with her.

Yes! Do it! rasped the dark foreign voice. *Why shouldn't she die for betraying you and her father? Why shouldn't she be cut off from Israel for rejecting the Law you live by? Kill her! Kill the child!*

The violence in his thoughts frightened Joseph and he cried out, "Oh, God, help me! What should I do? Why do you throw this catastrophe at my feet? Haven't I tried all my life to do right, to live according to your law?" He sat, dragging his fingers through his hair. Gritting his teeth, he wept angrily. "Why, Lord? Make me understand!"

The sun set, but he was no closer to an answer. Weary, Joseph rose and walked back to town. The streets were empty, for it was late and everyone had returned home. He entered his workshop and sat at his worktable. He'd never felt so alone. "Where are you, God? Where are you when I need your counsel?" He considered going to the rabbi for advice, but rabbis could not always be trusted to keep confidences. Joseph wanted no one else to know about Mary until he had decided what to do. He ran his hand over the yoke he had been carving, then picked up his tools. Perhaps work would ease his mind.

Who was he to condemn Mary?

Joseph followed the Law, but he knew in his heart that it was only on the surface. Beneath the dutiful hours in synagogue, the giving of tithes and offerings, his heart was rebellious against the yoke of Rome, the yoke of corrupt rabbis, and the weight of the Law itself. How could any man help it? Sin taunted Joseph every time he saw a Roman soldier mocking a woman at the well, or a rabbi haranguing some poor widow for her tithe, or a rich patron who ignored what was owed for work rendered, or a beggar who cursed him when he had no money to give. Though Joseph had taken countless lambs to the Temple in Jerusalem for sacrifice over the years, he had never felt completely cleansed of sin. The blood of the sacrificial lamb covered it over, and then he'd sin again. He wanted to do right, but he found himself failing again and again.

Stretching out on his pallet, Joseph flung his arm over his eyes, still undecided what action to take regarding Mary. The Law was clear, but his heart was torn. He closed his eyes, hoping sleep would enable him to think more clearly in the morning. But his sleep was tormented by nightmares. He heard angry voices and a girl screaming. He cried out, but when he tried to run, his feet sank into sand. As he struggled, darkness surrounded him and someone spoke from it. *Kill the girl. Kill her and the spawn she carries!*

"Joseph, son of David," came another voice he'd never heard before, but knew instantly. A man in shimmering white stood above him. "Do not be afraid to go ahead with your marriage to Mary. For the child within her has been conceived by the Holy Spirit. And she will have a son, and you are to name him Jesus, for he will save his people from their sins."

Joseph absorbed the words, his soul trembling with delight. All his life he had heard people talk of the coming Messiah. Since the time of David, the Jews had waited for another king to triumph over Israel's enemies. And more than that, the promised Messiah would reign over all the earth. Now the time had come, and God was sending the Anointed One. And Joseph would see him. He would stand at the side of the Messiah's mother and protect the Chosen One as his own son.

You, a simple carpenter, stand as guard? Dark laughter surrounded him, and Joseph moaned in his sleep. *I will kill them. And you, if you stand in my way.*

Joseph groaned again and rolled onto his back. He opened his eyes and felt the darkness around him. Fear gripped him, until a whisper pierced it.

He will save his people from their sins ...

Joseph's longing for righteousness welled up in him like the thirst of a man lost in the desert. And he remembered the words of his ancestor, David, whispering them into the darkness: "Those who live in the shelter of the Most High will find rest in the shadow of the Almighty ... I will *not* be afraid of the terrors of the night, for God will order his angels to protect his Son. The Lord himself will guard him."

The darkness rolled back, and Joseph saw the stars through his window. He stared at them for a long while. Smiling, he went back to sleep.

Anne wept in relief, but Mary seemed not the least surprised by Joseph's decision to marry her quickly. In fact, she crossed the room and put her hand on his arm, surprising him with a demand. "I must go to my relative Elizabeth."

Her mother protested. "Why would you want to go there? The hill country is a hard journey – "

"Oh, Mother, it doesn't matter. Elizabeth is with child!"

"Don't be ridiculous! She's long past her time of bearing children."

"The angel told me she's with child."

"And what do you suppose people will say when you suddenly marry Joseph and then go off to the hill country of Judea?"

"What does it matter what people say if it's the Lord's will I go?"

Joseph saw how the journey could solve several problems. The angel had said nothing about announcing to the citizenry of Nazareth that Mary had conceived by the Holy Spirit and would give birth to the Messiah. What if the news did get out? What sort of dangers might present themselves to the child? When Mary's pregnancy became apparent, there would be gossip. However, if they went on this journey together ...

"As soon as we are married, I will take Mary to visit her relative."

"People will talk," Anne said.

Yes, people would talk, but the condemnation would be aimed at him rather than Mary.

❧❧❧

When Mary's pregnancy became apparent, some in Nazareth thought they now understood the reason for Joseph's haste in marrying her. Women whispered at the well while the men shook their heads and clucked their tongues in the synagogue. What did anyone really know about Joseph, other than that he was a carpenter come from Bethlehem? Poor Joachim. The man had trusted the carpenter because he was a relative, a descendant of David. Surely Joachim's bones were crying out now that it was evident Joseph had taken conjugal rights before those rights were due. Some went to the rabbi and insisted the couple be disciplined so that other young people wouldn't think such behavior was condoned in Nazareth! The rabbi said Joseph had acted within his rights under the contract, gifts having been exchanged and documents signed.

A voice came out of the shadows at the back of the synagogue. *"Will you not destroy the evil among you?"*

The rabbi raised his head from the Torah. "Who speaks?"

"Does Scripture not say the Lord hates haughty eyes and a lying tongue?" The voice was deep and dark and familiar to many. *"We must destroy the wickedness among us."* Men glanced at one another and voices began to swell as the accuser remained in the shadows. *"Who is this carpenter who defies the Law? Who is this girl who plays the harlot?"*

A man stood, face flushed. "He's right!" Others joined in agreement.

Chilled, the old rabbi raised his hands. "The Law also says there shall be two witnesses. Let them come forward."

A low rumble moved through the gathering of men, but no one moved. Men looked about. Trembling, the rabbi rolled open the Torah. "The Lord also hates a false witness who pours out lies, a person who sows discord among brothers." He spoke quietly, but the words carried.

The accuser departed.

Soon after, all gossip regarding Joseph and Mary died when Roman soldiers arrived in Nazareth carrying a decree from Caesar Augustus. A census of all who inhabited the earth was being taken. Men cried out in dismay. Did this Roman "god" realize what chaos his decree would create? For the order was that everyone must return to the village of his birth in order to be counted.

two

JOSEPH had dreaded this moment since he'd heard the decree read. He looked between the two women at the table — one so young and lovely his heart turned over, the other older and aggrieved over the cruel things said about her daughter during the past few weeks. "We must go to Bethlehem," he said into the silence. He explained the situation to both women. Mary glanced at her mother, but Anne sat shaking her head.

"Mary's time is close, Joseph."

"We must obey the law."

"Whose law must we obey? Should you risk my daughter for the sake of a Roman emperor, a pagan idolator who thinks he is a god?"

Joseph leaned forward and put his hand over Anne's. "Scripture is being fulfilled, Mother." He had heard from the time he was a little boy that Bethlehem would one day be the site of the Messiah's birth. "The prophet Micah said, 'But you, O Bethlehem Ephrathah, are only a small village in Judah. Yet a ruler of Israel will come from you, one whose origins are from the distant past. ... And he will stand to lead his flock with the Lord's strength.'"

Mary's eyes lit up as she looked at Joseph. She turned excitedly to her mother. "You can come with us, Mother. Come and see the great day of the Lord being fulfilled."

"Yes," Joseph said, pressing Anne's hand slightly. "Come with us."

"No." She jerked her hand from beneath his. "I belong here in Nazareth. And so does Mary!" Joseph watched her rise and turn her back. She wrapped her arms around herself and raised her head. "How can you even consider such a journey when Mary is so close to her time?"

He understood Anne. She was a mother and did not want to let her favorite daughter go. "If you cannot see this as fulfillment of Scripture, look upon it as a means of escaping the gossip surrounding our marriage."

Anne turned on him. "So you're thinking only of yourself! You care nothing about the dangers to her."

"Mother!" Mary said in surprised protest.

Her mother looked at her beseechingly. "You can't even consider it, Mary. And you," she said, glaring at Joseph again, "I can't believe you'd think of taking Mary from me now when she will need me more than ever."

Mary blinked and looked at Joseph. He lowered his eyes, searching himself frantically to find any truth to Anne's words. Was he wrong in the way he saw this decree? Was he jeopardizing Mary's life for the whim of a foreign emperor? Should he discount the prophecy about Bethlehem and delay the journey another week?

Mary tilted her head. "I must go where my husband goes."

"You must stay here and wait until the child is born."

"Have you forgotten Ruth?"

"Don't speak to me of Ruth," her mother said angrily. "That was a long time ago. And she was leaving pagan parents for the sake of her mother-in-law, who had taught her about the Lord."

"Mother, please listen," Mary said gently.

"No!" Anne covered her face, her shoulders shaking as she wept. "I thought there would be no greater honor than for my daughter to bear the Anointed One, but my heart is being torn from me. How will I know that you're well and safe?"

Mary took her mother's hand and pressed it to her cheek. "Will the Lord himself not watch over his own Son? Has the Lord ever made a promise he did not keep?"

Joseph saw anguish in Anne's eyes as she cupped her daughter's cheek. Joseph had heard that giving birth was an excruciating process, one that endangered the mother as well as the child. Who would act as midwife? "Please, Anne. Come with us."

His mother-in-law considered a moment and then shook her head slowly, decisively. "Joachim was born here, Joseph, and so was I. I must remain here, as surely as you must return to Bethlehem. Perhaps this is the Lord's way of making me let go of my daughter." Her lips curved sadly. "Does not Scripture say a man and woman are to leave their fathers and mothers and be joined to one another?" She tipped Mary's face. "You are right, my precious one. You must go with your husband. Your sister and her husband will watch over me."

Mary's expression brightened. "Of course. And you will come with them to Jerusalem for Passover. We will see each other then."

Anne's eyes grew moist, but she said no more. She forced a smile and then turned away in anguish as Mary turned to Joseph and grasped his hands. "We will go to Bethlehem, Joseph. We will register for the census, and then we will dwell within sight of the walls of Jerusalem, in the shadow of the Most High God."

Joseph felt a surge of joy at her words, until the dark voice dampened it.

Ah, yes. Come to Bethlehem, where the child will be born in the shadow of my servant Herod.

⬖⬗⬖

After much thought, Joseph decided it would be wise to purchase a place with one of the Mesopotamian caravans passing through Nazareth. Since Mary was near her time to give birth, they must take the quickest way south. Rather than taking the easier plains of the Mediterranean and the Way of the Sea or traveling through the Jordan Valley, they would go by way of the old trade route through the rocky highlands. He didn't like the idea of traveling with foreigners, but at least they would be under heavy guard and therefore safe from bandits and mountain lions.

Grieving over Mary's tears, Joseph spoke not a word the day they left Nazareth. They descended the high Galilean hills, Mount Tabor rising in the east. Every few minutes, Joseph would glance back at his young wife riding on their donkey. She kept her head bowed, but he noticed she held the saddle with tighter hands as the hours passed. Not once did she utter a word of complaint, and only once did she lift her head and look at him with silent desperation, the mounting strain and discomfort clear on her face. "Oh, Joseph, let me walk." But when he did, she was quickly exhausted.

When they stopped for the night, she ate sparingly before curling on her side. Smiling for the first time that day, she put her hand protectively over her unborn child and went to sleep immediately. Joseph sat by her and prayed. When night fell and she shivered, he lay down behind her and drew his mantle over her to keep her warm.

The next day, they traveled through the beautiful plain of Jezreel. "Drink in the air, Joseph," Mary said, smiling, for they were passing through green forests. Joseph drew the donkey aside so she could rest in a meadow of wildflowers. His heart turned over when she tucked a lily of the field behind his ear. "Does not the earth cry out, Joseph?" Her eyes shone as she stretched out her hand to the cloudless blue sky. "O Lord, our Lord, the majesty of your name fills the earth! Your glory is higher than the heavens!"

Joseph took her hand and kissed it. How he loved her!

Over the next few days, they camped by fresh running water. Then began the long, hard climb into the mountains. On the seventh day, Joseph watched grimly as the caravan moved away from them while he and Mary remained behind to observe the Lord's Sabbath. He knew they would catch up the next day, for the string of heavy-laden animals could not move as quickly as a strong donkey whose only burden was a small girl and food enough for travel. Still, Joseph worried.

Mary broke bread and handed him his portion. Her fingers brushed his hand tenderly. "God is watching over us, Joseph." Her eyes were as soft as a doe's, her faith as strong as a lion's.

They caught up with the caravan the next afternoon, then slowed their pace to match that of the slow, plodding animals. They passed by Mount Gilboa, where King Saul and his son Jonathan had been slain by the Philistines. They traveled through Dothan, where Jacob's son Joseph had been sold into slavery by his brothers. They spent the day talking about his life and the Israelites' slavery in Egypt. More than four hundred years had passed before the Lord spoke to Moses from the burning bush and used him to deliver Israel. And another forty years had passed while the disobedient generation had wandered in the desert, until finally their children had entered the Promised Land.

"Soon the Promised Land will belong to us again," Mary said, her hand caressing the curve of her belly. "God will make everything right."

Each day proved more difficult for Mary as her time approached. Every time Joseph saw her bend over, fear gripped him. She said little, but he saw her lips move as she prayed as hard as he that they would reach Bethlehem soon and find rest and shelter before the baby came.

The caravan camped outside the walled city of Shomrom-Sebaste, and Joseph prayed that the caravan merchants would sell their wares quickly so they could move on. There were Samaritans who would gladly kill a Jew and take no pity on his pregnant wife. They traveled ten miles south to Shechem, another wealthy Samaritan city filled with arrogant, uncircumcised men. To think that Jacob's well was in the midst of them! Joseph shook the unclean dust from his feet when he and Mary left Samaria.

The caravan traveled around Shiloh. Once it had been the home of the

Ark of the Covenant. Now it was a new city built up from broken-down buildings and shattered altars. Joseph and Mary turned aside from the caravan to say prayers in the synagogue at Bethel, for it was there Abraham had offered his sacrifices to God and Jacob had dreamed of angels climbing up and down a ladder to heaven. It wasn't until they reached Ramah that they could see the holy city of Jerusalem and the pinnacles of the great Temple shining in the setting sun.

"Only one more day, Mary," Joseph said, worried over her increasing discomfort.

When they arrived in Jerusalem, the paved streets were crowded. Joseph pulled at the donkey's reins while a group of Roman soldiers watched them pass. Above them were the Roman fortress named for Mark Antony and the Temple, with its eaves and pinnacles covered with gold. Cupping Mary's hand, Joseph kissed her palm. "The ways of God are beyond my under-standing, for I would have thought the Messiah should be born in the City of Zion, in the Holy of Holies."

It was dusk when they finally arrived in Bethlehem. Normally a small town inhabited mostly by shepherds and farmers, it now teemed with members of David's tribe come home for the Roman census. It was easy to find the line for registering, and he stood with Mary leaning against the donkey until it came his turn to give his name and the number of his household. "Joseph, of the tribe of Judah, and my wife Mary." The Roman raised his head enough to see Mary's condition. He added one check in the column for children, the better for gaining more taxes. "Next!" he said im-patiently, dismissing them without a glance.

"Oh, Joseph," Mary groaned, her hands spreading white over her swollen belly as she bent forward.

"I'll find us a place." He put his arm around her and helped her walk.

Men stood on every corner, grumbling about the emperor's decree and the throng of sojourners. Joseph set Mary upon the donkey again, but each step increased the pain he could see in her eyes. He stopped half a dozen times, only to hear the same response from each innkeeper: "There's no room here. Now move along!"

"Joseph!" Mary gasped, bending over again. "Oh, Joseph." He'd never seen a look of panic in her eyes before, and it shook him deeply. Her fingers clutched the donkey's mane, trying to keep herself from falling. Joseph quickly lifted her from the animal and carefully set her down against the wall of the last inn. He pounded on the door. "Please!" he said as a man opened the door. "Please, can you make room for us? My wife has reached her time."

The man peered past Joseph and grimaced as he saw Mary. "There's no room for you here. Go away!"

"Have mercy!" Joseph grabbed the edge of the door before it was closed. "Please! I beg of you!"

"Beg all you want," the man growled, "but it won't change anything!" Regret flickered as he glanced at Mary again. "A curse upon the Roman dog who put people like you on the road." He shoved Joseph back and slammed the door. There was a loud thud as he dropped the bar, denying entrance to anyone else.

Shaking, Joseph turned to Mary. Her eyes grew huge. "Ohhh ... " Her voice was taut with pain, her arms around her belly, her knees drawing up.

He knelt down quickly and gripped her arms. "Hold on. Oh, Mary, hold on."

The pain eased and she looked at him with tear-washed, frightened eyes. "He will come soon, no matter where we are."

Oh, Lord, help us! Joseph looped the donkey's reins into his belt and lifted Mary in his arms. *Lord, Lord, show me where to go!* "The Lord will help us, Mary," he said as he carried her. "He will help us." He fought back the doubts attacking him. Mary groaned and her body tensed in his arms. Fear filled him as he looked around, frantically searching for help.

An older woman sat, leaning against a wall, a worn blanket wrapped snugly around her. "Try the caves down there." A gnarled hand appeared from beneath the soiled blanket, a bony finger pointing. "The shepherds keep their flocks there in winter, but they'll be out in the hills now."

"May the Lord bless you!" Joseph carried Mary down the hill and across a flat stretch. He saw the mouth of a small cave above him and headed for it. He wrinkled his nose as he entered the dark recesses, for the air was dank and fetid from the odors of dung and smoke. The donkey followed him into the cave and headed straight for the manger near the back.

Mary tensed in his arms again and cried out. Fear washed over Joseph as he looked at the filthy floor of the cave. *Is this the place where the Messiah will be born?* Tears filled his eyes. *Here, Lord?*

"He's coming ... ," Mary said. "Oh, Joseph, Jesus is coming."

What did he know about helping a woman bear a child? Was there time to find a midwife? Even if he had time, where would he go to look for one, and what of Mary in his absence? "You must stand here a moment." He set her gently on her feet. "Use this post for support while I prepare a place for you."

He found a pitchfork and spread straw in the stable near the back, then yanked his blanket from the pack on the donkey and spread it over the straw. He helped Mary lie down. "Try to rest while I build a fire and find water." Kindling and firewood were stacked to one side of the entrance of the cave, and a cask of water stood near a trough. He tasted it and found it surprisingly fresh.

Within a few minutes, he had a small fire going in the pit near the center of the cave. Above it, the ceiling was blackened by years of soot, the floor caked with the packed dung of hundreds of animals who had been sheltered here over the years. "I'm sorry, Mary." He knelt beside her, tears running down his cheeks into his beard. "I'm sorry I couldn't find a better place for him to be born."

She took his hand and pressed it against her cheek. "God brought us here." Her fingers tightened and she began to pant and groan. He felt her pain as though it were his own. For the first time in his life, Joseph wished he was something other than a carpenter who knew nothing of these matters. He prayed fervently, asking God for wisdom, for help, for Mary's intense pain to be over, and for the child to be safely delivered. And then, Mary uttered a sharp gasp, and Joseph saw water spread a stain over the blanket beneath her hips. "Tell me what I can do to help you!"

"Nothing." Her grip eased on his hand, but she smiled through her pain. "Haven't women been going through this since the Garden of Eden?" She closed her eyes as another contraction came rolling over the first, her fingers tightening painfully around his. When the pain passed, she panted heavily. "My mother gave me a small bag of salt, a piece of sharp slate, some yarn, and strips of cloth. They're in the pack." He found them for her. "I'll need water, Joseph."

"There's fresh water in the cask. I'll fill the skin."

"Place it beside me and then go outside."

"But, Mary ... " She was only fourteen, a mere child herself. How could she manage on her own?

She spoke with authority. "Go, Joseph! I know what to do. Mother gave me instructions before we left Nazareth. And surely the Lord will guide me in this as he has guided us in everything thus far. Go now." She clenched her teeth, her shoulders rising from the ground. *"Go!"*

Joseph went outside. Too tense to sit, he paced, praying under his breath.

He heard Mary moan and paused, listening intently in case she changed her mind and cried out for him. He heard the hay rustling and paced again, staring up at the points of light in the dark sky. He sensed forces gathering around him as though invisible beings had come to witness this event. Angelic or demonic, he didn't know. Heart pounding, Joseph beseeched God for help and stepped back so that he was standing in the entrance of the cave. The wind came up and for an instant he thought he heard laughter and a dark voice speaking: *Do you really believe you can protect them from me?*

Joseph fell to his knees and raised his hands to the heavens, where God was upon his throne, and he prayed fervently. "You are the Lord our God, the maker of the heavens and the earth. Protect Mary and your Son from the one who is trying to destroy them both."

And he stretched out his arms as though to take the full force of whatever would come against them.

The cold wind stopped and the air around him grew warm again. His heart slowed as he heard the sound of wings. Scriptures flooded his mind. *Don't be afraid, for I am with you. I am with you.*

≈≈≈≈

Squatting, Mary uttered a last fierce cry as the Son of God, bathed in water and blood, slid from her body. Sagging to her knees, Mary lifted him and held him against her breast, welcoming him into the world with soft joyous tears. He cried in the cold night air, and Mary worked quickly, using the yarn to tie off the cord before cutting it. She gazed at her son in adoration as she washed his slick, squiggling body with water and rubbed the salt over his skin to prevent infection.

She was surprised that he looked like any other baby. There was no hint of Shekinah glory, or of the majesty of his Almighty Father. Ten fingers, ten toes, a thatch of black hair, skinny little legs and arms and the wizened face of a newborn who had dwelt in water for nine long months.

She laughed as she wrapped him snugly in strips of cloth and held him again, kissing his face and cradling him tenderly in her arms. "Jesus," she whispered, "my precious Jesus." She was filled with emotion. She held in her arms the hope of Israel, the Anointed One of God, Son of Man, God the Son, the Son of God. Closing her eyes, she prayed fervently. "Help me be his mother, Lord. Oh, help me."

When all was accomplished as her mother had said, Mary rose on trembling legs. "Joseph," she called softly, "come and see him."

Joseph entered the cave immediately, his face pale and sweating as though he had been the one in travail and not her. She laughed softly in joy and looked down at Jesus sleeping in her arms. "Isn't he beautiful?" Never had she felt such love for any human being. She felt she would burst with it.

Joseph came close and peered down at the baby, a look of surprise on his face. Mary's knees were trembling with exhaustion, and she looked around for a warm, safe bed for her son. There was only the manger. "Add more straw, Joseph, and he'll be warm." As Joseph prepared the manger, Mary kissed her baby's face, knowing that one day this baby would grow up and hold the destiny of Israel in his hands.

"It's ready," Joseph said, and Mary stepped over and placed Jesus in the manger filled with straw. When she turned, she felt light-headed.

Joseph caught her up in his arms and placed her in a bed of fresh straw. Her eyes were so heavy. "I'm sorry, my love," Joseph said in a choked whisper. "There's no one here to help you but me." He removed her soiled dress, washed her gently, dressed her like a child in a soft woolen shift her mother had made for her, and covered her with blankets, tucking the edges around her the same way she had tucked Jesus into his humble, warm bed.

Mary sighed, content. "All is well, isn't it, Joseph?"

He kissed her softly. "Yes, my love. All is well."

⧓⧓⧓

Joseph rose and went to stand by the manger. His heart beating fast, he stared down at the child. Tucking his finger into the edge of the blanket, he drew it down so he could gaze on the face of the one who would save his people. "Jesus," he whispered. "Jesus." He touched the velvet-soft skin of the infant's face and brushed the tiny palm. When the baby's fingers closed around his finger, his heart raced even faster. Never had he felt such encompassing joy – and spreading terror.

Am I to be his earthly father, Lord? A simple carpenter? Surely your Son deserves better than I!

Joseph looked around at the dark walls of the shepherds' cave, and tears filled his eyes. Filled with shame, he looked down again and swallowed hard. "Forgive me." This child deserved to be born in a palace. "Forgive me." Tears streamed down his cheeks.

The baby's eyes opened and looked up at him. Joseph's shame melted away as love filled him. Leaning down, he kissed the tiny hand that gripped his finger, and everything in him opened to the will of God.

When a footfall sounded behind him, Joseph turned sharply, placing himself firmly in front of the manger. An old shepherd stood at the entrance of the cave, a younger man just behind him. They peered in with expressions rapt and curious. "Is the child here?" The older man stepped inside the cave. "The child of whom the angels spoke?"

"The angels?" Joseph saw other shepherds behind these two, and beyond them, a flock of sheep in the grassland below the hillside cave.

"An angel of the Lord appeared among us, and the radiance of the Lord's glory surrounded us," the shepherd said as others crowded the entrance. "We were terrified, but the angel said not to be afraid."

Another said, "He told us, 'I bring you good news of great joy for everyone!'"

Another pressed forward. "'The Savior – yes, the Messiah, the Lord – has been born tonight in Bethlehem, the city of David!'"

The older shepherd looked from Joseph to Mary, asleep in the hay, and then to the manger at the back of the cave. His eyes glowed with hope. "'And this is how you will recognize him: You will find a baby lying in a manger, wrapped snugly in strips of cloth!'"

"Suddenly, the angel was joined by a vast host of others – the armies of heaven – praising God: 'Glory to God in the highest heaven, and peace on earth to all whom God favors.'"

Tears streaming down his face, Joseph turned and lifted Jesus from the manger. "His name is Jesus."

At the sound of Jesus' name, the shepherds fell to their knees, their faces aglow in the firelight.

Mary awakened. Startled at the gathering of strangers, she pushed herself up. Joseph came to her and hunkered down, with Jesus in his arms. "The Lord has announced Jesus' birth, Mary." He explained how the shepherds had come to find them.

Smiling at the shepherds, Mary sank back wearily. She smiled serenely as Joseph placed God the Son in her arms. Joseph and the shepherds watched as she and Jesus fell asleep together.

"The Lord is come," Joseph said quietly.

The old shepherd closed his eyes, tears blending into his beard. "Blessed be the name of the Lord."

≈≈≈

Mary awakened in the wee hours of morning at Jesus' cry. She drew him close and nursed him, marveling at what God had done for her. Each tug at her breast filled her with a sense of wonder and bonded her more strongly to her son. The night was still and silent as she cuddled Jesus close. She could see light streaming into the entrance of the cave and wondered at it. When Jesus finished feeding, she rose carefully, wincing at the pain in her loins, as she carried him back to the manger and snuggled him into the blanket cradled by hay.

Taking up her shawl, Mary went to the cave entrance and gazed up at the night sky. Was it her imagination that one star shone more brightly than all the others? It was like a shaft of light breaking through the floor of heaven and shining down on the City of David. Had not the prophet Joel said the Lord would display wonders in the sky and on the earth when the Savior came?

Lifting her shawl, Mary covered her hair. "Lord Most High, Creator of all people, you who dwell in heaven so far above us, you who are holy, I love you." She pressed her clasped hands against her heart. "I adore you. There is no other like you in all the universe." She closed her eyes, her heart filled with confident hope. "You have made me the vessel for your Son. Your kingdom will come. Through him, you will reign upon the earth as you do in heaven." She looked up again. "Blessed be the name of the Lord, and blessed be the name of your Son, Jesus."

The cold evening breeze rippled her thin dress. She hugged her arms around her. Though chilled, she remained at the cave entrance a moment longer, thinking about the day the angel of the Lord had come to her with the announcement that she would bear God's Son. She thought of Joseph's dream and his acceptance of her and the miracle child she carried. She thought how even a Roman emperor unwittingly obeyed the will of the Lord by commanding the census that called Joseph home to Bethlehem, so that the prophecy about the place of the Messiah's birth would be fulfilled. She thought about the shepherds who had received the news of the Messiah's birth from the angels.

And the more she thought about the things that had happened, the more she realized her mind could not fathom all that the Lord had planned and would accomplish through her son.

Her gaze drifted over the landscape. She looked up at Herod's palace on the mount overlooking Bethlehem. Up there dwelt an earthly king so jealous of his power that he had murdered his wife, Mariamne, and two of his sons. Shuddering, she stared at the lighted windows of the great castle. They seemed to stare down at her.

Weariness swept over her and she turned away from the mouth of the cave. She must rest so she would be ready when Jesus needed to be nursed again. Yawning, she returned to the bed Joseph had made. The hay rustled as she sat, and her husband awakened. He started to rise, but she put her hand against his shoulder. "Everything is fine, Joseph. Go back to sleep." As she lay down, he drew her close and pulled the blanket over them both. He asked her if she was warm enough and tucked her closer.

⁂

Outside, God's sentinels stood guard against the one who would destroy the child. Finding no way to enter into the humble sanctum, Satan turned away in a cold blast of fury.

I will find another way to kill the one who threatens my domain!

His minions came to report that men were traveling from the ends of the earth to see the king the new star announced.

I will draw them off the track to Herod, for then my will shall be accomplished on earth. Dark laughter echoed in the night while Mary and Joseph slept.

Only Jesus awakened and heard.

three

MARY held Jesus close to her heart as she and Joseph entered the Temple. They had traveled to Jerusalem to offer a sacrifice for their son, in accordance with the Jewish Law. Joseph went from booth to booth until he found two turtledoves he deemed perfect enough to take to the priest.

Eyeing the two small birds, Joseph sighed with regret. "If only I had enough money for a lamb."

Touched deeply by her husband's humility, Mary smiled up at him. "It was a dove who bore the message to Noah that God had stayed his hand of judgment."

Joseph's face softened as he put his arm around her. As they went up the steps together, she stared in awe at the immensity of the temple Herod had built. The deep beckoning sound of the shofar pulled her attention upward, where she saw the priests standing on their platforms holding the long rams' horns to their lips. Mary trembled as she heard the sound. Her throat closed. Masses of pilgrims moved in and out of the courts, filling the corridor with the rumble of a thousand voices. Lambs bleated; cattle lowed. Money changers vied for business, coins clinking into trays as men argued over percentages of exchange.

"Do you think the Lord does not see how you're robbing me?" someone cried out angrily.

"If you don't like it, see if you can do better!"

"May the Lord judge between you and me!"

Joseph hastened Mary past the disturbance and escorted her along the corridor to the entrance to the women's court, where other women and children waited. He left her there with Jesus and went to present the turtledoves to a priest for sacrifice.

An old man wandered among the women holding babies, pausing to peer down into each infant's face and give a soft blessing to the proud mother before moving on to another. Mary heard an older woman address him. "Simeon ... " They spoke briefly before he turned away again. She felt his gaze fix upon her.

"What child is this?" he said in the quavering voice of advanced age.

"His name is Jesus." Mary tipped her son proudly, drawing the blanket down enough so the old man could admire him. Could anyone guess she held the Messiah in her arms? She, a mere peasant girl from Nazareth?

"Jesus," Simeon repeated softly. "'The Lord saves.' A common name in Israel, for it is the desire of every devout girl to bear the one who will save his people from their sins."

Mary's heart fluttered strangely as she looked into the venerable man's opaque eyes. Though he was almost blind, he seemed to be looking for something with great longing. She felt impelled to say more. "I did not give him the name. It *is* his name."

Frowning slightly, the old man fixed his gaze upon her son again. He leaned closer that he might see him better. Mary smiled as Jesus made a soft mewling sound and awakened. The old man's face flushed. "May I hold him?" He held out trembling hands.

Mary hesitated only briefly before relinquishing Jesus. She studied Simeon's face while he held her son, gratified by the man's increasing excitement. Jesus reached up, his tiny fingers grasping the long white curl at Simeon's temple. Simeon drew in his breath sharply and uttered a sob.

Alarmed, Mary stood closer lest the old man drop her baby. Simeon raised his head, and Mary held her breath. She saw immediately the change in him. Simeon's eyes were no longer milky, but dark brown and alight with joy. Her heart raced wildly. When Jesus let go of the curl at Simeon's temple, the old man cupped Jesus' tiny hand and kissed his palm.

"Lord," Simeon said in a trembling voice, "now I can die in peace! As you promised me, I have seen the Savior you have given to all people. He is a light to reveal God to the nations, and he is the glory of your people Israel!" Smiling, he wept, staring and staring at Jesus as though he could not get his fill of seeing him. "Lord, Lord ..."

"Mary?" Joseph said softly, standing at her elbow.

"It's all right," she said, unaware until then of the tears pouring down her own cheeks. Here was a devout man who resided in the Temple, and he recognized her son as the Messiah.

Simeon raised his head and looked at each of them. "May the Lord watch over and protect you as you rear up this child in the ways of his Father. This child will be rejected by many in Israel, and it will be their undoing."

The word *rejected* struck Mary's heart. Who in Israel would reject the

Messiah? Didn't all crave for things to be put right between man and God? Surely the priests and elders would rejoice. Even the high priest would come out to greet him.

Simeon didn't explain. He looked upon Jesus again. "But he will be the greatest joy to many others." He placed Jesus back in Mary's arms. Then, surprising her, he reached out with both hands and cupped her face tenderly as one would a favored daughter. His face was filled with sorrow and compassion. "Thus, the deepest thoughts of many hearts will be revealed. And a sword will pierce your very soul."

Troubled by his words, Mary wanted to ask what he meant, but Joseph's hand was gently pressing against the small of her back. "We should go, Mary." Heeding his instruction, she bowed her head to Simeon and turned away.

As they came out into the corridor, Mary saw men and women drawing aside as an old woman, stooped with age and garbed in widow's black, hurried toward the women's court. People whispered close by: "It is Anna, the daughter of Phanuel of the tribe of Asher ... My mother said she came into the Temple when her husband died. ... She'd dedicated her life to serving God night and day with fasting and prayers ... She is said to be a prophetess ... "

Mary glanced back and saw Simeon standing in the corridor, his gaze still fixed upon Jesus. As she turned away, she saw that the old woman was heading straight for her and Joseph. "He is come!" The old woman gazed adoringly at Jesus in Mary's arms. Spreading her hands, she closed her eyes and lifted her head, speaking joyfully. "Out of the stump of David's family will grow a shoot – yes, a new Branch bearing fruit from the old root. And the Spirit of the Lord will rest on him – the Spirit of wisdom and understanding, the Spirit of counsel and might, the Spirit of knowledge and the fear of the Lord. He will delight in obeying the Lord. He will never judge by appearance, false evidence, or hearsay. He will defend the poor and the exploited. He will rule against the wicked and destroy them with the breath of his mouth."

Yes! Mary wanted to cry out. *My son will break the chains that bind us. Rome will no longer rule the world. My son will rule. My son will make all things right.*

Joseph's hand clenched Mary's arm, drawing her back. "We must go, Mary. We must go *now.*"

"But she is announcing the Day of the Lord."

"Yes, and Herod's spies are everywhere, even inside the Temple."

Mary understood his warning immediately. Herod had killed his favorite wife and two sons over an imagined threat to his throne. The Messiah was a rival, for he would one day remove the power of all earthly kings. "Yes, of course," she said, leaning into Joseph's lead as he drew her into the crowd. She must protect her son until he was old enough to take his proper place. They lost themselves in the throng who pressed in to hear the prophetess speak of the coming Messiah. Still, Mary's heart raced, for the Lord had seen to it that the Messiah's birth was announced in the Temple.

As they neared the doorway to the outside, Mary saw a man standing to one side. He looked straight into her eyes, his own so black they seemed to open into the black pit of his soul. She had never seen eyes so filled with hatred and violence. "Joseph!" she cried out in alarm, and her husband's arm came firmly around her. She held Jesus closer as they hurried down the steps.

"What did you see?" Joseph said as they hurried away from the Temple mount.

"A man, Joseph, just a man," she said, out of breath. *A man who had the eyes of death.*

≈≈≈

Joseph decided it would be best if they remained in Bethlehem, away from the gossip surrounding their hasty marriage in Nazareth. Soon after the visit to the Temple, Joseph found a small house on the edge of town in which they could live comfortably. There was enough room for him to set up shop and ply his carpenter's trade. They moved in with their few possessions. Joseph left for a few days with his donkey to dig up tree stumps so that he would have wood. Upon his return, he went straight to work making utensils, bowls, and dishes to sell in the markets of Jerusalem.

Each morning, Mary carried Jesus to the well in a blanket sling and drew up fresh water for the day's use. While at her household chores, she kept Jesus beside her in a cradle Joseph had made. Often, she would carry Jesus into Joseph's shop so her husband would see each change in their son. "He's smiling, Joseph! Look!" And Joseph would laugh in delight with her.

Jesus was sitting up at six months and crawling at seven. At ten months, he gripped Joseph's fingers and pulled himself up. Joseph loved the sound of his baby chuckles and his intent interest in everything around him. At eleven months, he was toddling after Mary; at twelve months, he had his first skinned knee. Sometimes Jesus seemed like any other child, and at others, Joseph experienced a wave of awe when Jesus looked at him with eyes at once innocent and wise.

Each morning and evening, Joseph read to Mary and Jesus from the scrolls that had been in his family since the time of David. On one particular evening, Jesus played quietly on a mat, filling a toy boat with pairs of carved animals Joseph had made. Joseph paused in his reading to watch Jesus, his heart swelling within him. Jesus put two small sheep inside the boat, closed the door, latched it and clapped his tiny hands. Joseph lowered the scroll to his lap. "Do you ever wonder how much he knows, Mary?"

"Every day." She too, studied Jesus as he played.

Joseph smiled ruefully. "I wonder why the Lord didn't choose a more learned man, one who could provide a better home for Jesus."

"By better, you mean 'finer.'"

"Surely the Son of God deserves finer."

"Hasn't God always chosen things the world considers foolish in order to shame those who think they are wise? Maybe God chose a peasant girl to be his mother and a carpenter to be his earthly father because the Messiah is meant for *all* our people, not just those who dwell in the fine houses of the provinces or the palaces of Jerusalem."

A knock startled them. "Who would come at this hour?" Mary lifted Jesus and held him close, while Joseph quickly rolled the scroll and put it back in the trunk against the wall. When Joseph opened the door, Mary heard strangers' voices speaking in stumbling, heavily accented Aramaic. She heard Joseph say yes, and the men cried out happily. Joseph glanced back at her, his eyes bright with excitement. "These men have come from the East."

"Who are they?"

"Learned men who study the heavens. They've been following a new star they say announces the birth of the King of the Jews. They've come to worship him."

Mary stepped forward. "Invite them in, Joseph."

"They're Gentiles, Mary, and will defile the house."

"How can they defile the house when the Lord himself has sent them?"

Joseph nodded. Turning back, he opened the door wider. Men in foreign dress began to crowd into the small house. Mary drew back to give them more room, for there were four, each accompanied by a servant. They stared at Jesus with a mingling of joy and awe. One by one, they knelt and bowed their heads to the ground before him.

Jesus pressed at her so that she knew he wanted down. She set him on his feet, keeping close watch over the strangers and her son.

"We have brought gifts," one said thickly. Turning to his servant, he took a carved box and opened it. Astonished, Mary saw it was filled with gold coins. She had never seen so much money, except at the table of the money changers in the Temple. It was more than Joseph would make in a lifetime. The next man handed her an embroidered leather bag. "Frankincense." The third man set down another box of coins, while the fourth placed a sealed alabaster bottle on the floor mat at her feet. "Myrrh."

Mary marveled at such gifts. They had brought gold as a tribute to her son who would be king, frankincense for him to burn as an offering in the Temple, and myrrh as a fragrant balm to anoint his body.

Jesus paid no attention to the gifts, but toddled among the men who had come to worship him, touching their faces and turbans, and peering into their eyes. He even went to the servants, who ducked their heads to the earthen floor rather than allow him to touch them. Jesus sat among them, opened the little toy boat, and spilled out the animals once again.

Joseph laughed. "Come. Be at ease. We don't have much, but what we have, we offer you." He poured wine and broke bread and listened with great interest as the men told them about their long journey to Judah. Mary sat on the mat with Jesus while he played with his boat and animals. She listened to everything that was said. When Jesus yawned, she took him up in her arms and put him to bed.

Only then did the conversation turn to the dangers surrounding her son.

"We went to Herod and asked, 'Where is the newborn king of the Jews?' We told him about the new star, and how we had traveled so far to worship this newborn king."

Joseph's face was suddenly pale. "And what did King Herod say?"

The oldest of the four sojourners leaned forward. "He called for the leading priests and teachers of your people and inquired of them. They said the Messiah was to be born in Bethlehem of Judah. For one of your prophets said, 'O Bethlehem of Judah, you are not just a lowly village in Judah, for a ruler will come from you who will be the shepherd for my people Israel.'"

"We were on our way out of the palace when Herod's servant came to us," said another. "He whispered to speak to us in private."

"King Herod told us to go and search carefully for the child, and when we found him to go back and tell him so that he too could come and worship him."

Mary saw the fear come into Joseph's eyes. "And when will you do this?"

"Don't be troubled, Joseph," the oldest of the company said. "King Herod's reputation is known among the nations." He leaned forward and clasped his hands between his knees. "And a messenger of God came to us and warned us against returning to the palace."

Mary looked at Joseph, but his attention was fixed upon the men.

"It is our habit to sleep by day so that we can follow the star by night," another said. "Yesterday, after leaving Herod's palace, we stayed at an inn in Jerusalem."

"And all of us had the same dream."

"The exact same dream."

The oldest man lifted his hand to calm the excitement of the others. "We were all told not to return to Herod, but to go home another way."

"Herod will seek you out," Joseph said grimly.

"He will send men to look for a company of magi with their servants, but he will not find us. Each of us will be heading in a different direction. Babylon, Assyria, Macedonia, Persia. You will have only a few days before the king realizes we have gone. Then he will begin hunting for the child."

Mary's heart pounded heavily with dread. She looked up at Joseph and saw the tension in his face.

"It is time," the oldest said, and they all rose. He grasped Joseph's arms. "May the God of your fathers watch over and protect your son." They went out into the night, and Joseph closed the door after them.

Mary stood up, trembling with fear. "What shall we do, Joseph?"

"We shall wait."

"You told me once that Herod has spies everywhere, even in the Temple. Wouldn't he have had those men followed? They know where we live."

He came to her and cupped her face. "Who's been telling me all these months that Jesus is from the seed of God?"

She was unable to stop the trembling. How could they protect Jesus if King Herod came searching for him?

Joseph drew her into his arms. "I'm afraid, too, Mary, but surely the Lord can protect his own Son."

"We should go back to Nazareth."

"No. We wait here." They both needed reminding. "God directs our steps."

Joseph heard the voice again that night while he lay upon his pallet with

Mary tucked against him. "Joseph," the angel said, luminescent and powerful, yet comforting. "Joseph."

"Yes, Lord," Joseph said in his sleep.

"Get up and flee to Egypt with the child and his mother," the angel said. "Stay there until I tell you to return, because Herod is going to try to kill the child."

Joseph awakened abruptly in the darkness. All was still in the street outside. He rose carefully so he wouldn't awaken Mary, took up the gifts the magi had left for Jesus and placed them carefully in the box with the scrolls that had been passed down to him. He went out to the stall he'd built at the back of the house and harnessed his donkey, tightening straps around its girth to mount burden baskets on each side. He tucked the box with the precious scrolls and gifts for Jesus in one and packed his tools, leather apron, and squares of olive wood in the other. Then he went to fill two skins with water and scoop enough grain into a bag to last the family a week.

"Mary," he whispered, leaning down to kiss her brow. "Mary, wake up." She sat up and rubbed her eyes like a little girl. He brushed the tendrils of hair back from her face. "An angel of the Lord came to me in a dream. We must leave Bethlehem *at once.*"

She glanced up, her eyes alight with hope. "Are we going back to Nazareth?"

"No, my love, we're going to Egypt." He saw alarm and dismay enter her eyes, but had no time to ease her fears. "Come, come," he said, taking her hand. "We must leave." As soon as she was standing, he took up the blankets and folded them quickly. "Make Jesus ready to travel." He took the blankets out and tied them on top of the pack.

Mary came outside soon after, Jesus bundled warmly and already asleep again in a sling she'd tied around her shoulders. She could nurse him easily as they traveled.

They set off into the night. Joseph felt no regret at the loss of the house he had purchased for his family or the business that had just begun to prosper. His only thought was to get Jesus safely out of Bethlehem before Herod sent his soldiers to find and kill him.

"Lord, give us strength for the journey," Joseph whispered. "Give us strength and courage for whatever lies ahead."

As they traveled along a byway widened by the onslaught of pilgrims coming up from the regions of Ashdod, Ashkelon, and Gaza, the sun rose in front of them. Jesus awakened and cried. "He's hungry," Mary said.

They stopped to rest so she could nurse him. "Did you ever think, Joseph, that we might be following the same road Joseph did when his brothers sold him to the Ishmaelites?"

Her sweetness pierced him. She thought about so many things, pondering them and wondering at possible hidden meanings. "No. I only thought to get us out of Bethlehem as fast as possible." He watched her set Jesus on his feet. She laughed as the little boy trotted happily toward a path of red poppies. Sometimes Joseph could hardly fathom that this child was the Son of God. Most of the time, he seemed like any other little boy of his age, fascinated by everything around him, needing protection and guidance. Yet there were times when a light would come into his eyes as though he remembered something. Was he merely human? Or wisdom incarnate, budding each day until full comprehension of who he was came upon him in all force? And then what would happen? Would this little boy whom Joseph loved like his own flesh and blood, become the warrior-king all Israel longed to see?

Or ... Joseph felt a strange sensation prickle along his spine. His throat closed hotly. Or would Jesus grow up to be the suffering servant of whom the prophet Isaiah had spoken?

Tears came as he watched Jesus. Sometimes Joseph had to remind himself that this child, who played like any other, was the Son of the God of Abraham, Isaac, and Jacob. Herod, the most powerful man in all Judah, was trying to kill him.

What kind of opposition would Jesus face when he became a man? Had not every prophet, but Moses and Elijah met with a violent death?

"Jesus! Come!" Joseph caught him up and held him close, love filling him until he ached with it. Eyes hot, he kissed Jesus and swung him up so that the child was perched on his shoulders. Jesus hugged him around the chin and Joseph felt a rush of pleasure. Taking the child's hands, he kissed each palm, then held both their hands outstretched. Jesus laughed.

Mary's eyes were aglow. "He looks as though he would like to embrace the whole world."

Yes, Joseph thought. *But will the world embrace him?*

⧉⧉⧉

Twenty long months passed. Although Joseph prospered, he felt uncomfortable dwelling among idol worshipers. The Law required that he take his family to Jerusalem for a pilgrimage at least once every two years, and that time was drawing near. And it was not just the Law that made him want to go. He longed to hear the sound of the shofar and the drone of voices speaking Aramaic in the streets. He prayed constantly that God would call them out of Egypt.

Every afternoon as the sun was setting, Joseph opened the box that held the precious scrolls and called Jesus to him. The boy climbed into his lap, and Joseph read aloud from the Torah or unfurled a scroll with the words of King David or the prophet Isaiah. And then he would hold the boy close and pray.

Joseph was resting in the afternoon heat when the angel of the Lord appeared to him.

"Get up and take the child and his mother back to the land of Israel, because those who were trying to kill the child are dead."

Joseph sat bolt upright, his heart pounding. "Mary!" He came to his feet and went outside, where she was sitting in the shade watching Jesus draw in the dust with a stick.

"Mary!" Elation filled him as he pulled her to her feet and kissed her. "We're going home!"

⋙⋘

Once again, Joseph and Mary left everything behind but their most precious possessions and went where the Lord led them. The journey back by the Way of the Sea went quickly for they traveled in haste, eager to return to their homeland. Joseph had it in his mind to take Mary and Jesus back to Bethlehem, where his ancestor David had lived. The town was close to Jerusalem, close to the Temple. Shouldn't the Son of God be close to the center of worship? Shouldn't he dwell on the mountaintop?

But when they came to a toll station on the southern boundary of Israel, where Joseph was required to pay a road tax, he spotted an insignia that troubled him. He frowned. "Who reigns in the place of Herod?" he asked.

The Roman soldier glanced up and gave a snort of derision. "Where have you been living, Jew? Archelaus, the son of Herod. Who else?"

Fear gripped Joseph.

Mary stood waiting for him, holding Jesus by the hand. When he approached, she peered up at him. "What's wrong, Joseph?"

Sometimes Joseph wished his wife was less perceptive. "Archelaus reigns in Jerusalem."

Her face paled. She knew as well as he that Herod's blood ran in

Archelaus's veins. Would this king also be a ruthless enemy? Mary lifted Jesus and sat him on her hip. "Should we go back to Egypt?"

He thought for a moment and took the reins of the donkey. "We go on."

"But Joseph, shouldn't we ponder this awhile until we know God's will?"

Joseph turned the beast toward Jerusalem. "Nothing has changed, Mary. God said to return to Israel, and to Israel we shall go until he says otherwise." He had only to glance at her to see her mind was going off in a dozen directions, considering all the possibilities. Mary pondered everything. "The Lord will protect us now, just as he did when we were in Bethlehem."

As they walked up the road, the excitement of returning home evaporated in the heat of anxiety. God had sent them running to Egypt because of Herod. Would Archelaus be any less protective of his power than his father had been? When they arrived in Bethlehem, would people remember the attention Jesus had attracted from Simeon and Anna in the Temple? Would they remember the strange visit of magi who had traveled hundreds of miles to see the child whose birth had been announced in the heavens? Word of such an event spread. Rumors would abound. The new king would hear. And, like his father before him, Archelaus would want to eliminate anyone who dared challenge his authority – even the Son of God.

Lord, Lord, I fear for the life of your Son and his mother!

Joseph was afraid to pray more than that, for the commandment of the angel had been clear. *Go back to the land of Israel.* Still, with each step, Joseph's apprehension grew. *Lord, Lord, I am afraid. Help me obey.*

"Joseph, can we rest awhile over there by those trees?" Mary said. He looked back at her and saw the sheen of sweat on her face. She hadn't put Jesus down since they left the toll station. He led the donkey off the road and let the reins dangle on the ground so the animal could graze while they rested in the shade. Mary set Jesus on his feet and sank to the ground with a sigh of relief. Closing her eyes, she filled her lungs with air and smiled. "Every land has its own scent."

While Jesus played nearby, Joseph fingered the knots on the strands of his prayer shawl. *Lord, Lord ...*

Mary sat down beside him. "Rest, Joseph."

He didn't want to share his worries with her. He wanted her to feel safe even when she wasn't. "I'm not tired."

She put her hand over his. "Close your eyes for a little while, Joseph. For my sake." She rose and walked toward Jesus. When they came back and lay down in the shade, Joseph relaxed. The heat of midday came down upon him like a heavy blanket. He was tired, so tired he felt he was sinking into the earth.

He heard the familiar voice again, speaking softly, so softly, his soul leaned closer. "Joseph, son of David, do not go back to Bethlehem, for Jesus will be in danger there. Go instead to the region of Galilee and live in Nazareth."

Awakening, he sat up. He saw by the position of the sun that several hours had passed. Jesus was still asleep in his mother's arms.

"Mary," Joseph said softly, heart pounding.

She opened her eyes sleepily and looked up at him. Blinking, she sat up. "The Lord spoke to you again. I can tell."

"We're to go to Nazareth and make our home there."

"Oh!" Her face lit with joy. She held Jesus close as he awakened. "We're going home, my love. Home to your grandma and your aunt and uncle. Home!"

≈≈≈

When Mary and Joseph arrived in Nazareth with Jesus, they found the modest village near the trade roads unchanged. But Mary's mother's house was deserted, weeds growing in the garden behind it. Distressed, Mary and Joseph hurried along to her sister and brother-in-law's house.

"Your mother died the year after the census," Clopas, her brother-in-law, told them, after joyful greetings had been exchanged.

"We all thought something had happened to you," Mary's sister said. "When we heard what Herod did, we thought you were lost."

"Lost? What do you mean?" Mary said, confused.

"What did Herod do?" Joseph said, standing beside her.

"He killed the male children in Bethlehem," Clopas said. "All of them! From newborn to two years of age. Every one of them. As well as any father or mother who stood in the way of the king's soldiers carrying out his orders."

Mary felt faint. She clutched Jesus tightly in her arms as realization struck her. Had Joseph not obeyed the Lord immediately, Jesus would have been among the children slaughtered by Herod's soldiers. That's why he had awakened her in the middle of the night and taken her and Jesus from the city. He hadn't known what was coming, only that God said, "Flee to Egypt." By God's great mercy, Jesus' life had been spared, and Herod's plans had failed.

Her throat closed in grief. God had saved her son, but what of those poor innocent children who had been slaughtered by Herod's order? What of their grieving mothers and fathers? How could such evil exist in the world? Mary ran her hands over Jesus as she wept.

"Mama?"

She wept into the curve of his neck.

Her sister came to her. "When you didn't return to Nazareth, we assumed you'd died in Bethlehem with your child." Weeping, she embraced Mary and Jesus. "But you are all here safe and sound. God be praised!"

"Your mother believed you'd all been killed," Clopas said. "She died believing that."

Mary heard the hint of accusation in her brother-in-law's voice and lifted her chin in defense of her husband. "God told Joseph we were to go to Egypt and wait there."

Clopas's brows came down as he looked at Joseph. "God told you to go to Egypt?"

Joseph's jaw tensed, but he said nothing. Distressed, Mary looked between the two men. Clopas's hostility was evident. Mary's anger mingled with embarrassment. Joseph would not defend himself or explain. Did her relatives think she had lied about the angel of the Lord coming to her and telling her she would bear the Messiah? Did they prefer the rumors that Joseph had seduced her before they were wed and that they had concocted a ridiculous story to keep from being stoned? Would the rumors about the child she bore revive now that she and Joseph had brought Jesus home to Nazareth?

Holding Jesus close, she turned to her sister. This woman knew her better than any other, save Joseph. Surely she would believe. "When Jesus was born in Bethlehem, shepherds came to see him. They told us that the angel of the Lord had appeared among them, and the radiance of the Lord's glory surrounded them. The angel told them not to be afraid, for he was bringing good news of great joy. For that night in Bethlehem, the Savior — the Messiah — had been born. And the angel said they would find the baby lying in a manger, wrapped in strips of cloth."

"A manger?" her sister said sadly.

Was that the only thing she heard? Did she not understand the fulfillment of prophecy?

Clopas made a sound in his throat. "The Messiah, born in a stable! And you expect us to believe that?"

Mary fought her tears. "Magi came to our house in Bethlehem, Clopas.

They said they had followed a new star that appeared in the heavens at the same time Jesus was born. They brought gifts. They went to the king first, to ask where the Messiah was to be born."

"Mary ... " Her sister tried to soothe her.

Clopas glared at Joseph. "How did you ever convince her of all this?"

"I'm telling the truth!" Mary cried out. "Why won't you believe?"

"Stop, Clopas," her sister said. "I beg of you."

"Don't tell me you believe it!"

"I know my sister." Her arms tightened around Mary. "She's never lied before."

"I'm not lying now!" Mary said angrily. "Jesus is the Messiah. He is!"

Clopas shook his head. "She's out of her mind."

"She speaks the truth," Joseph said quietly.

Clopas stared at him for a long moment and frowned. "Even if I did believe it, what would it matter? It's what everyone else in the village believes that matters." Clopas looked at Jesus and grimaced. "A son born too soon after the wedding ceremony – to a girl so full of herself she's convinced she's borne the Messiah – is a scandal. The Messiah, born to a peasant girl in Nazareth. No one will ever believe it."

Stunned, Mary could only stare at him in anguish. Joseph leaned down to her and took Jesus into his arms. "Come, Mary." He slipped his arm around her.

"I'm sorry," her sister whispered.

"Don't you dare apologize to him," Clopas said, glowering. "He's the cause of this trouble, and the reason for the shame that has fallen upon our family."

"You're wrong." Mary's mouth trembled. "Joseph is above reproach, and Jesus is God's Anointed One. Someday you'll see the truth for yourself!" One day she would be vindicated. They would all see her son on the throne, ruling with righteousness!

"I'll believe he's the Messiah when I see him with an army behind him, driving the Romans out of Jerusalem!"

Mary felt Joseph's arm tighten, pressing her through the doorway. She resisted, wanting to say more to her sister and brother-in-law. Anger coursed through her, but Joseph was firm. His arm encircled her protectively as they went out into the narrow street. "Oh, Joseph. I never expected it to be like this. Why do they prefer lies to the truth? Surely Jesus won't grow up beneath such a ... shadow."

"God brought us here, Mary. What will happen now, I can't say. We must live in God's strength, my love."

"Mama?" Jesus said, distressed by her tears of hurt and anger. Joseph ran his hand tenderly over Jesus' hair, his eyes troubled. When Jesus looked up at him, Joseph smiled and brushed his knuckles against the smooth round cheek. Mary saw the love in her husband's eyes and ached for him. His reputation had been ruined as much as hers. People believed he had seduced her.

Bless Joseph, Lord. Oh, please bless him for what he will suffer for the sake of your Son and me.

How many men would accept the loss of their reputation with grace, knowing their actions were by God's direction? How many men would rise at the first whisper of God's counsel and leave house and business and move to a foreign country? Or leave house and business and return to a town that thought they'd seduced a young virgin and filled her head with wild tales of angels and the coming Messiah?

Each day that passed increased Mary's love for the man God had chosen for her. She had liked him when she first met him. She had respected him more with each trial they had faced, and she loved him now more than she'd thought possible. *Oh, Lord, you have given me blessing upon blessing.*

Joseph set Jesus on his feet and Mary took his hand. As the three of them walked down the street together, Jesus reached up and took Joseph's hand. Mary smiled at her husband and felt the heaviness upon her heart lifting.

"Someday they will all see Jesus in power, Joseph. And they'll know then how they wronged us." Swallowing her tears, she lifted her head and walked on in silence.

Joseph's small house was the same as when they'd left it. He set up his shop and made a meager living making yokes, plows, and ladders. When no work came to him, he would rise early and walk to nearby Sepphoris, hiring himself out to overseers who needed good carpenters to build lattices, doors, and furniture for the wealthy.

Life fell into a routine of struggle and hard work. Each morning, Mary and Joseph rose together, washed their hands and eyes. Mary pronounced the blessing over the house and went out to feed and water Joseph's donkey before he went to work in his shop or started out for Sepphoris. Then she and Jesus went down to the common well to draw water for the day. She worked in the vegetable garden or small flower bed. She pressed oil for the lamps, pounded spices, gathered brushwood for the house fire, washed linen, worked spindle and loom, prepared meals, and laid out the pallets.

For Jesus' sake, Mary made no mention of the visitation of the angel of the Lord, his miraculous conception, the visit of the magi, or the gifts still held by Joseph in trust for him. She said nothing of the four times that the Lord had spoken to Joseph. Someday, when Jesus revealed his power and purpose, people would listen to how he came to be. But she would not speak of the miracles now. She would not give what was holy to unholy people and give opportunity to those who would mock God's Son.

Sometimes the ordinariness of their lives bemused her. In many ways, Jesus was like any other child she observed. He had crawled before he walked. He had stumbled when he took his first steps. He had chattered baby talk before he was able to pronounce words and put together sentences. He was curious, wanting to touch and hold everything within reach.

All the other mothers boasted about their sons, but Mary knew none could compare to hers. There was no child so perfect, so loving, so observant of the world and people around him. He watched and listened and was easily delighted. He never complained or whined, but simply stated his needs. He never tried to manipulate her with tears or tantrums.

Some said he looked like her. "Jesus has your chin, Mary. ... He has your nose ... "

But no one ever said Jesus had her eyes.

It was Joseph who sheared Jesus' curls when he was no longer a baby. They made the day a festival with all Mary's relatives and old friends, giving nuts and raisin cakes to the children who came to join in the special day.

Whenever Joseph went to Sepphoris to find work, Mary would walk with Jesus out to the edge of town as the sun was nearing the horizon. "There he is, Mother!" Jesus would point when Joseph appeared, coming up the road toward Nazareth. "Father!" He would run down to greet him and walk beside him as Joseph came up the hill.

Every evening, Joseph would set Jesus in his lap and read from the scrolls. He knew many of the psalms written by his ancestor King David by heart. Mary loved to listen to him. They ate the simple dinner Mary prepared and talked of the day's events.

She loved it when there was work enough to keep Joseph home in Nazareth, and he would take Jesus into his shop with him. She would bring them bread and water and stand watching for a few minutes. Joseph used every opportunity to teach Jesus how to use the tools of his trade:

hammer, chisel, mallet, and awl. He taught him how to use a smoothing block and cubit measure. When he was older, Jesus would learn how to use the adze and ax. They worked well together – Joseph a patient teacher, Jesus a willing and eager pupil. Jesus' brow would furrow in concentration as he chiseled out a pattern Joseph had drawn on a board: a curving vine with a cluster of grapes, a Star of David, or a pomegranate.

"When we go to the Temple again at Passover," Joseph said, "I will show you the great golden columns. Those columns are the work of skilled carpenters who carved them and then hammered thin sheets of gold over them so that they appear to be made of solid gold."

Working at her loom in the evenings, Mary would listen to Joseph as he read from the Torah, the prophets, the psalms of his ancestor, King David. It was Joseph who taught Jesus to read and write. And it was Joseph who took Jesus by the hand at the age of six and presented him to the preceptor of the synagogue so their son's education would be properly supervised.

Soon after, Mary's prayers were answered.

She stood in the doorway of Joseph's shop and watched him carving a drinking cup. "You have never once said you wished for a son of your own, Joseph."

He glanced up and shook his head. "Should I want for more than God has given me? Every day I look at Jesus and see the hope of Israel growing up."

"It would be good for him to have brothers and sisters who would love him as we do." There were still those in the village who whispered about Jesus' precipitant birth and looked down upon him, and taught their children to do likewise. "And what about you?" she said, not wanting to give up her secret too quickly. "Children are a blessing from the Lord."

He raised his head and smiled. "I would not ask for more blessings than what the Lord has already given me."

"The Lord blesses those who love him, Joseph. He blesses them abundantly."

Amused, she watched him whittle a curl of wood on the cup he held. She loved to watch him work, for he took such care with everything he did. He was a strong, kind, and loving husband and father. He leaned upon the Lord, seeking him in the morning, at noon, at night.

"Blessing upon blessing, Joseph." Her heart overflowed with joy. She was eager to see the same wonder and thanksgiving in his eyes.

Joseph looked at her again, frowning this time, his dark eyes filled with question. She knew then her husband had never asked God for more. But she had. She had asked for blessing upon blessing for this man God had placed at her side. And for Jesus. Should he not have the pleasure of brothers and sisters?

"Yes, Joseph. The Lord has blessed us." Her eyes welled with tears at the look of joy on his face. "Our child will be born when the wheat is ready for harvest."

She laughed in delight as Joseph caught her up in his arms.

four

MARY welcomed her second son with the same joy and anticipation with which she had welcomed Jesus. Her heart melted as she held this new baby close to her and nursed him. "Here he is, Jesus. Your brother, James." She nestled the baby in her firstborn's arms, laughing at the look of pleasure as he gazed at the new baby. She brushed Jesus' hair back. "He is blessed among children to have you for his brother."

Revelations came one after another during the next few months as Mary discovered the differences between her two sons. When Jesus was a baby, he'd cried only when he was hungry or wet. James cried whenever he wanted her attention. Even after ten months, James would awaken her several times in the middle of the night, crying until she rose and took him from his bed.

The women at the well were full of advice.

"If you don't put that baby down and let him cry it out, he'll be having tantrums for the rest of his life."

"Jesus never cried like this."

One of the women rolled her eyes. "She thinks the sun rises and sets on that one." The woman went off with her jug of water.

"Every child comes with trials, Mary," another told her. "Sometimes it's worse when you have an easy baby to begin with and then others that aren't so easily soothed later. No child is perfect."

Jesus is, Mary wanted to say, but she kept quiet, knowing it would sound like a boast rather than the truth. Having James had taught her that her mothering had nothing to do with Jesus' character. If he was a perfect son because of her training, wouldn't she be able to apply the same methods to bring up another son for the Lord? Both of her sons had strong wills. Jesus gave his full strength and attention to doing the will of God, while she could see James's will directed at getting his own way. If he was this trying as an infant, what would he be like as he grew into a boy, and then a man?

"I want James to be like Jesus," she told Joseph.

"That might be possible if he had the same Father." Joseph took her hand between his. "Mary, we will be diligent in teaching our sons the ways of the Lord. We will strive to live lives pleasing to God. Beyond that, James will decide."

Jesus still found time between school and working with Joseph to sit with her and talk awhile. He would take his little brother on his knee and play with him while he asked her a question. Often he wondered about things beyond her understanding. "Have you asked Joseph about this?"

Jesus was never satisfied when she tried to direct him in this way. "I'm asking you, Mother."

"All I know of the Law is what my father and mother taught me."

She repeated what she had been taught, but Jesus wanted to know the reason behind it. Once he had asked her why a group of boys had thrown rocks at an old leper. She had told him what she knew the Law said about lepers.

"Is that reason enough to throw stones at a sick old man?"

Mary's throat tightened at the pain she saw in her son's eyes. She cupped his cheek. "There is no reason in cruelty. It just is."

God opened her womb again, and James was followed by little Joseph, named after his father. Then came Anne, named for Mary's mother.

The children loved Jesus and were as envious of his attention as they were for hers or Joseph's. Anne especially wanted to sit in her big brother's lap whenever Jesus was in the house. She pleaded with him to tell her stories, and Mary would listen as he told his younger brothers and sister about Noah and the ark full of animals, Jonah and the big fish, Daniel in the lions' den. He sang psalms to the children in the evenings. Mary and Joseph sang with him when they were songs they knew, but sometimes Jesus would sing familiar words to a tune they had never heard before.

Each morning, when she kissed Jesus before he went off to study the Torah with other boys his own age, she felt a pang of sorrow that she didn't have him all to herself anymore. He was growing up, and her days were filled with a woman's duties to her household. When Jesus came home, he didn't sit and talk with her. He went straight to work alongside Joseph, filling orders for customers and helping put bread on the table for their growing family.

Is this really the Messiah? This quiet boy who says little and seems to have no ambition beyond learning the Law and Joseph's trade?

The thought came to her out of nowhere and she winced, disturbed by it. She pressed her fingers to her forehead, trying to rub it away. But it remained like a dark echo of someone else's voice.

Can this really be the Messiah who will deliver Israel? Is this the warrior-king who will deliver his people?

How could such a betraying thought come to her mind? She knew who Jesus was! She knew that her firstborn had been conceived by the Holy Spirit! She knew he was the long-awaited Messiah!

A clatter of noise and familiar voices drew her outside, where she saw James and Joseph having a sword fight with two sticks. She sighed. Those two seemed so determined to vie for position with their fists. She often found herself dreaming of the easier days when she and Joseph had had only Jesus. Loving, teachable Jesus, who drank in the world around him but never seemed a part of it. Her son of another world. Her son of the Holy Spirit. How could she help but favor him?

Her thoughts were cut short as James and Joseph's play grew more heated. James shoved his younger brother into the dirt and stood over him, stick pointed at his heart. "You're dead!"

Tears streaked Joseph's dusty face as he pushed himself up. "It's your turn to be the Roman."

"Stop it!" Mary cried out and then was immediately sorry for speaking so harshly. Why were boys so bent toward war? She knew it was the dream of every Jewish boy – including hers – to break the chains of Rome.

Jesus had come to do just that, but she wondered if it would happen in the way everyone expected. Jesus, her son. God's Son. Would Jesus one day march upon Jerusalem as King David had done? Why was that so difficult for her to imagine? What cost to this child who could look at his quarrelsome friends and siblings with such love?

She knew Jesus struggled, too. She remembered when he had been a little boy, disturbed by frequent nightmares. How many times had she taken him into her arms and asked him what was troubling him? He would never say. She saw the pain in his eyes when he came home from synagogue, the look of anger when he saw someone being treated unjustly. At times, there would be a sheen of sweat on his brow as he sat with his prayer shawl over his head, his face strained as he prayed.

One day she asked him, "Why do you look so distressed, Jesus? Tell me what's wrong."

"What good would it do to tell you?"

"It might ease your burden."

He looked at her, his dark eyes filled with compassion. "It's not ease I need, Mother. It's renewed strength. And it will come when I most need it."

She was about to press him further when Joseph entered the house, his shoulders stooped, his eyes downcast. Mary's heart sank. "Tobias didn't pay you for the chair you delivered?"

"He said he had unexpected expenses. He'll pay by the full moon."

Her skin went hot. It wasn't right that Joseph worked so hard and then was left to wait for his wages. Tobias could afford to pay his debt. He sat in the gate with the elders! Unexpected expenses! She'd heard only yesterday that he had bought a mule for his youngest son. She rose, her hands balled into fists. "I'll go talk with him."

Joseph looked up. "You will not."

"It's not right that he takes advantage of you! If you won't allow me to go, then let Jesus go down and speak to the man."

"Mary," Joseph said with pained expression, "Tobias will pay in his own time. He always does."

"And while we're waiting upon his time, how do we buy bread for our table?"

"There's plenty of work in Sepphoris."

"It's not right, Joseph," she said, tears springing into her eyes. "You work so hard."

"It's not Tobias who provides our livelihood, Mary. God always provides."

Joseph and Jesus left for Sepphoris the next morning. Late that afternoon, Anne became ill.

❧❧❧

Two days passed, and the fever raged, unabated by cool damp cloths that grew hot from the child's burning forehead. Anne cried incessantly while Mary paced with her in her arms. For once the boys were quiet. They loved their little sister and sensed Mary's fear. By the third day, Anne was unconscious.

When Joseph and Jesus returned from Sepphoris, Mary rose in a flood of tears and flung herself into Joseph's arms, for their youngest was dying.

Jesus laid his carpentry tools down and walked across the room. Joseph's hands tightened at Mary's waist and she turned.

Jesus stood over his sister for a long moment. Then he knelt down beside her pallet. "Anne," he said softly and brushed his fingertips across his little sister's forehead. She drew in a deep breath and opened her eyes.

Mary gripped Joseph's hand.

"Jesus," Anne said, smiling, her face filling with healthy color. "You're home." Mary's little daughter reached up to him. Jesus scooped her into his arms and straightened. Anne wrapped her arms around his neck and her legs around his waist, and rested her head against his shoulder. Jesus nestled his head into the curve of his sister's neck and closed his eyes.

Heart pounding, her skin prickling, Mary sat down heavily on the stool by the door. Joseph's fingers trembled as he gripped her shoulder. She started to laugh and covered her face, tears streaking her cheeks.

"Anne's well, Mama." James rose. "Can we go play now?" He rushed to Jesus, who shifted Anne enough so he could put an arm around his younger brother.

"Yes, she's well, James. Go on outside and play."

Young Joseph raced after him.

And Mary realized, though James and Joseph had seen, they hadn't understood.

⊗⊘⊗

Josiah, one of Jesus' friends, came into the woodshop with a message from the rabbi. "He wants you to come now. It's about Jesus."

"What about Jesus?" Joseph said, setting aside his adze and dusting the wood chips off the front of his tunic as he followed Josiah outside.

"The rabbi is angry with him again."

"I didn't know he'd been angry before." Joseph could feel the sweat beading on the back of his neck. "What happened, Josiah?"

"I don't really know," the boy said, shaking his head. "All Jesus did was ask him a question, but the rabbi's face got all red and he started shaking. Then he told me to come and get you."

They hastened along the street into the center of town to the synagogue. When Joseph entered, he felt the air crackle with tension and could hear the rabbi speaking in a taut voice about some aspect of the Law. As soon as he saw Joseph, he clapped his hands. "Enough for today. Remember what we've discussed as you go home. Think well on these things." He waved his hand in dismissal.

The boys rose and hurried from the synagogue, all except Jesus, who sat on a bench in the front. Heart sinking, Joseph came up beside him and put his hand on the boy's shoulder.

The rabbi shoved his hands into his sleeves and glowered at Jesus. "I'm tired of *him* questioning me!"

Joseph blinked. "Rabbi?" The synagogue was the place for questioning, the place for exploring the Law.

The rabbi shook his head, annoyed. "I don't mind questions. It's the manner of his questions I mind."

Confused, Joseph looked from the rabbi to Jesus and back to the rabbi.

"Speak with him!" The rabbi's eyes flashed. "Explain to your son that *I* am the rabbi, and if he persists in asking questions that make me look ... self-righteous, I will bar him from the synagogue. I will not have a mere carpenter's son undermining my authority."

Heat poured through Joseph's body. He let go of Jesus' shoulder and took a step forward, but Jesus caught his hand and stood. "I meant no disrespect, Rabbi," the boy said with quiet dignity and looked straight into the man's eyes and said no more.

All the bluster went out of the rabbi. He blinked. Then his eyes narrowed as he sought some hint of mockery. "You've been warned."

As Joseph left the synagogue with Jesus, he thought of asking him what question had caused such hostility. But when he looked at Jesus, he saw tears. Wincing, Joseph put his arm around the boy. "Did he humiliate you before the others?" Of course he had, Joseph thought, angry enough to go back and give the rabbi a piece of his mind.

Jesus shook his head, that faraway look coming into his eyes again. "Why are men so stubborn?"

Joseph knew Jesus was not asking him for an answer.

≈≈≈

When it came time for Jesus to read the Torah in the synagogue, Mary pressed forward in the women's gallery until she was able to see down into the gathering. The reader chanted the *Shema*. The children answered "amen." Facing Jesus on the platform was Nazareth's rabbi and the wealthy merchant who headed the congregation. Behind them sat the town's seven elders and then the men according to their trade. She spotted Joseph, Jesus, James, and Joseph among the carpenters.

Mary's fingers gripped the lattice. She had been waiting for this day, the day when her son would read before the congregation. Would he declare himself before the gathering? Would they finally see that he was the Anointed One of God?

The rabbi, followed by the head of the congregation and the chief of the court, approached the Ark of the Covenant and lifted out the sacred scroll of the Torah. The congregation rose and cried out, "And whenever the Ark set out, Moses would cry, 'Arise, O Lord, and let your enemies be scattered! Let them flee before you!'"

Jesus stepped out from the benches where the carpenters sat and walked forward, adjusting his prayer shawl across his shoulders. He walked with great dignity for one so young. Did others see the difference in his demeanor? Mary's heart pounded as Jesus ascended the platform. Would something happen today that would make his identity known to all in Nazareth who had whispered behind their hands about her and Joseph? Would they finally see that this son of hers *was* the Messiah? Would they gather around him and praise his name? Would they follow wherever he led them?

Let it be so, Lord. Let his time be now. Father in heaven, we have waited so long. David was anointed king as a boy. You gave David victory on every side.

Jesus took the place of the reader and held the scroll open. "The Lord Almighty says, 'The day of judgment is coming, burning like a furnace. The arrogant and the wicked will be burned up like straw on that day. They will be consumed like a tree – roots and all.'" As Jesus read, Mary's skin tingled. His voice was that of a boy, but it held an authority that had nothing to do with years. Did others hear it?

"'But for you who fear my name, the Sun of Righteousness will rise with healing in his wings. And you will go free, leaping with joy like calves let out to pasture. On the day when I act, you will tread upon the wicked as if they were dust under your feet,' says the Lord Almighty."

Her heart swelled with pride. Joseph glanced up at her smiling, his eyes shining.

"Remember to obey the instructions of my servant Moses, all the laws and regulations that I gave him on Mount Sinai for all Israel," Jesus read on. "Look, I am sending you the prophet Elijah before the great and dreadful day of the Lord arrives. His preaching will turn the hearts of parents to their children, and the hearts of children to their parents."

Jesus lifted his head, his gaze sweeping over the men listening and then up into the women's gallery. "Otherwise I will come and strike the land with a curse."

Mary felt the hair rise on the back of her neck. She was not afraid of the son she had borne for God, but of the future of her people. What of her other sons and daughter? Would they believe Jesus was the Anointed One of God and follow him no matter the cost? Or would they continue to witness his goodness, his love, his mercy, and still not understand that he was more than another child of her loins? He was God's Son sent from heaven to deliver Israel from bondage.

Ah, the son you bore is greater even than Moses. Your child will reign! Look at your boy, Mary. It's your blood that runs in his veins.

Her heart filled with a mother's pride as she stared down at Jesus. The men of Nazareth surrounded him and celebrated his first time reading the Torah before the congregation. It was a great and glorious day! The women around her pressed closer, congratulating her for such a fine son. "He reads so well, Mary. ... He has such dignity. ..." One of the elders began to sing a song of celebration, and the other men joined in until the sound of their voices swelled deep and strong, rising.

My son! My son!

Mary stared down at Jesus. When he looked up at her, she was surprised by the look of disquiet on his face. He looked straight at her, and she suddenly realized the direction of the thoughts racing through her head.

My son.

My blood.

My child will reign!

Staring back at Jesus, she pressed cold hands to her burning cheeks.

Oh, Lord God of Israel, forgive me! Jesus is your Son. He is a child of the Holy Spirit. I am only the vessel you used to fulfill your promise.

Jesus' face had already softened. His eyes shone as he raised his hands and spun around, laughing as he danced while the men of faith surrounded him, arms joined so they formed a circle.

⋙⋘

Mary sat on a small bench in the garden in the quiet of the evening. The children were all asleep on their pallets. Jesus and Joseph were talking after the day of celebration, poring over the Scriptures as they so often did. How many times had Mary heard Joseph say to their children that God's word was settled in heaven, and the truth of it would last to all generations? Jesus' brothers were too young yet to understand, but still their father would say, "Meditate on the Law, my children, for the Lord's commandments will make you wiser than your enemies."

She blinked back tears. A pity women were not allowed to study the Torah, to spend hours discussing the Law and the Prophets. She could drink in only what she heard from the women's gallery as the Torah was read. She could listen and savor only what Joseph read from the scrolls passed down to him through the line of David.

There was so much she didn't know, so much she didn't understand.

"Mary?" She felt Joseph's hand upon her shoulder. She put her hand over his, struggling against the tears that still threatened. Perhaps she was just too weary. "What troubles you, my love?" He sat on the bench beside her.

She swallowed, trying to find words. "So many things, Joseph." She bowed her head. She looked up at him. "I was so proud of my son today. He read so well. All the women said so." Even some of the ones who had whispered against her. "And the rabbi was smiling and ... " The same rabbi who had wanted Jesus expelled from the synagogue.

Joseph brushed a tear from her cheek. He said nothing, waiting patiently for her to speak her heart. He was so dear to her. She could speak freely with her husband. Perhaps he could unravel the emotions tormenting her, the niggling sense that something was wrong, something just beyond her understanding. "I know everything will happen in God's time, Joseph," she said quietly, "but sometimes I wish the time was now." She gazed at the stars. "Moses was eighty years old when the Lord called him out of the desert and told him to stand before Pharaoh." She looked down at her clasped hands, swallowing before she dared trust her voice to speak again. "His mother would have been long dead by that time."

"Are you afraid you won't live long enough to see Jesus come into his kingdom?"

"Is it wrong for me to want to see him in his rightful place?" She remembered Jesus' expression when he had looked up at her in the women's gallery. She felt again the flush of heat into her cheeks. Why should she be ashamed? Why shouldn't she be proud of her son? "Everyone in Israel longs for the Messiah to come and make all things right, Joseph. King David wrote that the Lord would summon the earth from the rising of the sun to its setting, and out of Zion, judge the people. Doesn't it say we will never have to be afraid of the terrors of the night or the dangers of the day or the plague that stalks in darkness? We will see how the wicked are punished." The Romans, the tax collectors, the Pharisees and scribes who piled more laws upon the backs of God's people until they felt crushed by the weight of them.

"Mary," Joseph said gently, "there are many Scriptures about the Messiah."

"David was a boy when God anointed him king."

"Jesus is more than a king."

"I'm his mother, Joseph. I know that better than you."

"Yes, my love. But think on this. Would the Lord come to judge the world before he made a way for us to be freed from the consequences of sin?"

"There is the Law, the sacrifices ... "

"Perhaps you feel cleansed of all sin, Mary, but I never have. Who can stand before the Lord on the day of judgment and not fall short of his perfect goodness?"

"We obey."

"With every breath? With every thought?" Joseph shook his head sadly. "Sometimes I think God gave us the Law just to show us how wicked we are. Every day, I hear men pray for the Messiah to come. But they pray for him to bring a sword to slaughter the Romans, a sword to drive every foreigner from our land." He looked into her eyes. "They pray to be vindicated for the hurt done to them. They long to see retribution." He brushed his knuckles softly against the curve of her cheek, his eyes tender. "Is it justice they want – or revenge? It's not judgment I long for, but a return to the relationship Adam had with the Lord in the Garden of Eden."

"Jesus will see that we have that, Joseph. And one day James and little Joseph will take their rightful places beside him." When Joseph said nothing to that, she peered up at him in the gathering darkness, anger stirring inside her. Surely he wanted the same things she did: Jesus on the throne, their sons beside him. "You know as well as I do that Jesus is the Messiah."

"Yes," Joseph said softly, "I know. But as you have often reminded me, God never does anything the way his people expect."

His words and manner troubled her. "Are you not impatient to see the promise fulfilled?" Why wouldn't he speak? Why did he look so pensive? "I have listened closely all these years from the women's gallery, Joseph. And I've listened to you as you've read the Scriptures to Jesus. What have we to fear? Moses said the Lord is a warrior, and the prophet Daniel said everything will be given to him. Jesus will have power, honor, and a kingdom. All nations, people of every language, will serve him, and his kingship will be an everlasting one that won't pass away. His kingdom will never be destroyed. I can only wish it would happen now!"

Joseph took her hand and held it between his own. "Daniel also said that the Son of Man would appear to have accomplished nothing."

She searched his eyes in the dimming light. "I don't understand."

"Nor do I, Mary, but Isaiah said the Messiah would be a man of sorrows, acquainted with the bitterest grief."

"No." Ever since the day the Lord had overshadowed her, Mary had faced rejection. Surely this would not happen to Jesus. Surely all things would be made known. The truth would finally be made clear for all to see. She turned toward Joseph and grasped both of his hands tightly. "No one will reject Jesus. He is so good, Joseph! So full of love for others. How could people not rejoice over him? When the time comes, the Lord will make it known to everyone that Jesus is the one we've been waiting for all these centuries. And Jesus will reveal himself to the nations."

"Mary, have you forgotten that God revealed himself to the nations when he delivered his people out of Egypt? And what happened? The entire generation of Israelites who crossed the Red Sea on dry land died in the wilderness because they rejected him."

"It won't be that way this time. I understand better than you, Joseph. I am his mother!"

"Yes, Mary, you are his mother. But it is his Father who will prevail."

She drew back from him. "Don't tell me the Lord would send his Son into the world to be rejected! Does that make sense?" The words Simeon had spoken in the Temple came unwelcomed into her mind: *"And a sword will pierce your very soul."* She stood and moved away. "No." She wrapped her arms around herself, chilled by the thought. She shook her head. "God is *merciful.*"

"Do you want *mercy* for all those who said you lied about how Jesus was conceived? Will you plead *mercy* for those who wanted to stone you? Is it *mercy* you want, Mary ... or vindication?"

His words cut deeply, but she knew he hadn't spoken in order to hurt her. Only to make her think more deeply. She put her hand over her trembling mouth. What did she want? For people to see the truth and be sorry for the pain they'd caused her and her family? Was it wrong for her to want to see Jesus end oppression and sorrow? Was it wrong to want everyone in Nazareth to know she had spoken the truth, that God had chosen her to give birth to the Messiah, that Jesus was born of God and would one day rule in righteousness and majesty? She wanted to see the day of the Lord! She wanted to see God's Anointed One on the throne! Tears blinded her. She wanted the world to be right again, the way it had been in the Garden of Eden.

Joseph rose and came to her. He took her hand and kissed the palm. He brushed the tears from her cheeks. "Somehow the Lord will bring mercy and justice together, Mary. I don't know how, but it will happen through Jesus. And the cost will be higher than anyone realizes."

"People will die," she said in quiet anguish. Whenever God disciplined his people, thousands fell.

"People have been dying since Adam sinned, Mary. I mean the cost of obedience. We know Jesus is the Messiah. But that's all we know. Not when or how he'll come into power, or who will stand beside him. God's plan is a great mystery. But I know this: All the faithful men and women before us longed for this day, and we are seeing the Son of Man grow up. But still, like them, we have to wait for the Lord. We have to trust him no matter what happens, no matter how things look." His voice broke. "This is what I see Jesus doing, from the moment he gets up in the morning until he lies down at night. Everything in him is fixed upon pleasing his Father."

Mary could see the sheen of tears in Joseph's eyes. "You're afraid for him, aren't you? You needn't be. God will protect him."

Joseph drew her into his arms and held her close. "Elijah is the only prophet who made it out of this world alive."

Mary watched Joseph lead Jesus, James, and young Joseph away while she took Anne's hand and headed for the women's court. They had come to Jerusalem to celebrate the Passover, as they had done every year since returning from Egypt. Today was the beginning of the celebration of how God had passed over the Jewish people and killed the Egyptian firstborns. Today was the beginning of the celebration of deliverance, of the Jewish people's liberation from slavery.

On the way back to the home of their relative Abijah, with whom they were staying, Mary saw the Roman soldiers marching through the streets and heard the grumbling of those around her. "Someday the Messiah will come and rout these filthy Roman pigs! He will be a king greater than Solomon, and all nations will bow down to him."

She and the other women in the household prepared the *matzoh shmurah* – the round, hard unleavened bread – for the Passover feast. They ground the horseradish and washed the parsley. They chopped fruits and nuts and mixed in spices and wine to make a pungent, rough paste.

And when they all sat on mats and reclined for the meal, it was Abijah who led the ceremonial meal. He was the younger brother of their relative Zechariah, who had recently died, as had Zechariah's beloved wife, Elizabeth. Mary wondered what had become of the couple's son, John. When Mary had visited Elizabeth soon after learning that she herself was pregnant with Jesus, Elizabeth's child had leaped within his mother's womb. Before Mary left for home, Elizabeth had leaned close and whispered, "When the time is right, my son shall announce to Israel that the Messiah has come."

Mary had been told that a member of the monastic order called the Essenes had come and taken John to their home in the cliffs above the Salt Sea. John had not been seen or heard from since. If he came to Passover each year with the Essenes, he made no attempt to find his relatives. Sometimes Mary would see a group of men, dusty from travel, emaciated from a life of self-denial. The orphan boys they tended were healthier than their benefactors, but she never saw one that resembled Elizabeth or Zechariah.

Had the Lord sent John into hiding just as he had sent Jesus to Egypt? Someday, John would appear again. And when he did, the Day of the Lord would be at hand. For surely God's hand was upon him, as his hand was upon Jesus. Someday John would herald Jesus' reign, just as Elizabeth had foretold.

Mary focused her mind on the Passover as Abijah's wife lit the candles, beginning the meal and providing light to the gathering. Abijah held up a cup of wine, and all gathered did likewise, as the venerable patriarch began the ritual prayers.

"Blessed art thou, O Lord God of Israel, king of the universe who has sanctified us with thy commandments and delivered us from Egypt ... "

At the appointed time, the youngest child, Abijah's granddaughter Leah, asked why there was an empty seat at the table. "We have left a place for Elijah," Abijah told her, "for the prophet Malachi said God would send the prophet Elijah before the great and dreadful day of the Lord arrives. Go and see if he is at the door." The child jumped up and ran to search for Elijah.

Mary's heart drummed as she looked at Jesus reclining at the table, flanked by his cousins. The rabbis said the Messiah would come at Passover. And she knew the Messiah was at this table. She turned and watched the door, wondering if this would be the night John would appear and proclaim Jesus' identity to all.

The child returned. "Elijah isn't here, Grandfather."

Abijah raised his cup. "Next year, in Jerusalem!"

※※※

Joseph saw the hope in Mary's face as she watched young Leah go and look for Elijah. And he saw the question in her eyes when the child returned and said Elijah wasn't there. He listened to the conversations around him as those present spoke with longing of the coming Messiah-king who would crush the evil from their midst and deliver the people from their bondage.

When he looked at Jesus, his throat closed, for each year the Scriptures from Isaiah came swiftly to mind. Sometimes Joseph wondered if Mary was like the rest – expecting the Messiah to come in might as David had and slaughter the enemies of God.

The rabbis said the Messiah would come at Passover. The Scriptures said the Messiah would be born of a virgin and would rise up to crush the head of the serpent, Satan. But what did it mean? How would it happen? Why this pain whenever he partook of the Passover feast? The answer was just beyond his reach, beyond his comprehension. Could anyone understand what God planned for mankind? But Joseph knew one thing without question: *The Messiah is here! He is at this seder! He is at this table! The one who would deliver us is eating of the lamb that was offered in sacrifice for the atonement of our sins! He is eating the unleavened bread and drinking the wine!*

No one realized. Everyone looked at Jesus and saw a twelve-year-old boy like any other, studying the Torah, working beside his father, growing up under the heel of Rome.

Jesus. Messiah. God with us.

Every year Joseph remembered the angel's words as though he had heard them just yesterday. He would shiver in awareness, and again it would strike him as the eight-day celebration progressed without John's appearing at the door. Passover was about a lamb sacrificed, a lamb whose blood marked for salvation those who believed what God said he would do. The lamb ... the blood-red wine ... the unleavened bread. His heart ached.

Jesus raised his eyes and looked into Joseph's, and for the briefest moment, Joseph imagined the boy slain. Shuddering, he closed his eyes and swallowed the anguish that welled up inside him as love for the boy gripped him. *Oh, Lord God ... Oh, Lord, Lord ...*

The meal passed in a mood of reverent celebration, and then Abijah brought out the hidden matzoh and removed the linen wrapping. He broke off a piece and passed it so that all could partake of it. As Joseph ate the morsel of unleavened bread, he wondered when the rest of the people would know what he and Mary had known for twelve years.

The Messiah is here! God is with us! Someday soon, he will set the captives free!

Mary walked with the women when they set off for home. Traveling with family members in a large caravan provided safety as well as camaraderie. James and Joseph ran ahead with the other boys. She hadn't seen Jesus all morning, but supposed he was with his cousins. She had given him freedom to wander Jerusalem with them over the past week and saw no reason to rein him in now that they were on the journey home. He had never given her cause to worry, and she was at ease as she visited with her relatives from Galilee. It would be another year before they saw one another again, and she wanted to enjoy their company while she could.

When they reached the Jewish estate a day out of Jerusalem, Mary didn't see Jesus among her nephews. "Have you seen Jesus?"

"Not since yesterday."

She went cold. "Yesterday? You mean he hasn't been with you all day?"

"No. He went off by himself and we haven't seen him since. Isn't he with Joseph?"

Mary raced off to talk with her husband, but found that Joseph hadn't seen him all day either. "James! Joseph!" She questioned her younger sons when they came running, but they didn't know where Jesus was either. "Oh, Joseph! He's never done anything like this before! Where could he be?"

"He must be in Jerusalem."

"Something must have happened to him! Oh, Joseph! Why didn't I keep better watch?" She saw the lines in Joseph's face deepen and knew he was as worried as she was. They went to her sister, Mary, and her husband and asked if they would watch over the other children while they went back to search for Jesus. They agreed readily, promising to keep James, Joseph, and Anne with them until Mary and Joseph and Jesus rejoined them.

"Jesus probably got caught up in the excitement of Jerusalem, Mary," her sister said. "He's probably on the road right now and will catch up with us by morning."

Mary spent a fretful night, sitting up each time she heard a noise. "Jesus?" Joseph slept no better than she did and was up before dawn, awakening Clopas to inform him they were leaving and the children knew to go with their uncle.

"Don't spare the rod when you find him," Clopas called after them.

They reached Jerusalem as the sun was setting, and entered the city before the gates were closed. They went straight to Abijah's house, hoping to find Jesus there. When they didn't, Mary wept, pleading that they begin searching the city right away.

"You won't find him at this hour," Abijah said. "And if you go out now, you'll end up being questioned by Roman soldiers."

"How can I rest when my son is missing?" Mary covered her face. "What could have happened to him?"

Joseph put his arms around her. "We'll start searching first thing in the morning."

She collapsed against him. "How could I have allowed this to happen?"

"Don't be afraid, my love. The Lord's hand is upon the boy."

She knew Joseph was right. All the things she had expected to happen hadn't. Why wasn't it more comfort? Simeon's words at the Temple came back to haunt her: *"And a sword will pierce your very soul."* Would she die by the sword before her son came into power? Or was this what the old prophet meant? For her heart was pierced by fear and shame that she hadn't kept better watch over the one God had given her.

"You must rest, my love," Joseph said, tender but firm. Though her mind rebelled, she knew she hadn't the strength to argue. She was so exhausted she could hardly stand, let alone search the city for her son. She wept.

God, forgive me for losing him! God, forgive me for not keeping watch!

≈≈≈

Abijah told them to search the marketplace, for that was the most common destination of boys visiting the great city. It was easy to become caught up in the excitement of activity as foreign merchants displayed their wares and patrons haggled for better prices. Mary and Joseph spent a full day searching through the maze of narrow passageways, lined by booths displaying everything from clay lamps to gold jewelry.

Jesus was not there.

They went to the synagogue, but they didn't find Jesus among the friends who had joined them for Passover celebration, nor did they find him among the boys watching the Romans go through their military exercises, or in the Temple court among the money changers or near the pens of animals. Thinking he might have found John, they went to the Essenes Gate, hoping to find him there among the desert dwellers who had not yet returned to the encampments above the Salt Sea.

Jesus was in none of these places.

Mary prayed unceasingly as she and Joseph hurried from place to place, looking for the son God had given her. Fear gripped her as she imagined all the things that could have happened to him. He was so young. So innocent.

"Yes, my love," Joseph agreed, "but he's not foolish."

Still, she couldn't eat or sleep. "I don't even know how long Jesus has been separated from us, Joseph. I'm so ashamed. I assumed he was with our relatives. I assumed he was with the caravan. The last time I saw my son was the morning Passover ended, and I was getting everything packed for the journey back to Nazareth. He must have said something to me. He must have. I just wasn't listening. Why wasn't I listening?"

"We were all distracted that day, making preparations for the journey home." He held her close. "Mary, Mary. The Lord is with him."

"I'm so afraid God will take him from me." She closed her eyes as she leaned against her husband. When she had become distracted by her many responsibilities for her other children, and for the child she knew she was carrying now, had the Lord decided it was time to hide Jesus away until his time came to take power? She knew in her heart that the Lord was with Jesus wherever he was, that his life rested in the hands of the Father. Still she grieved and pleaded.

Oh, Lord God of Israel, I want my son back. Please, give me my son back.

When they rose the next morning, Abijah told them he had spoken with his friends at the synagogue. "Eliakim said he saw Jesus at the Temple."

Heart leaping with hope, Mary threw on her shawl and headed out the door, Joseph on her heels. She ran until her side ached, walked until she could draw breath with less pain, and ran again. Pressing through the throng, she made her way up the steps to the Temple mount. She hurried along the corridor, peering between the columns, searching, praying.

And then she saw him sitting in the midst of the teachers.

Mary stood staring, her heart pounding, her lungs burning as she drank in air and gave silent thanks to God that Jesus was safe. Then, astonished, she realized that he was so intent upon what these men were saying that he didn't even notice her or Joseph standing nearby.

Does he even care about you?

The tears came, scalding, as she stood silent, watching her son. Had he been here the entire time? Had he made any attempt to contact his relatives or catch up with the family who loved him?

He is careless of your feelings. You don't matter to him. You're no longer important. How dare he put you through such pain and worry!

Anger welled inside her. How could Jesus do this to her and Joseph? She stepped forward, jerking her arm from Joseph's grasp. The men stopped talking when they saw her approaching. Glancing back, Jesus saw her. He smiled and rose. She was so angry, she wanted to shake him. Didn't he know how frightened she'd been? Hadn't he considered her feelings at all?

"Son!" she said, her voice trembling. "Why have you done this to us? Your father and I have been frantic, searching for you everywhere."

He searched her eyes intently, then looked up at Joseph as he stood beside her. "But why did you need to search?" Jesus said gently. "You should have known that I would be in my Father's house."

See how he defies you!

Mary shook her head. She saw no defiance in her son's eyes, but neither did she understand what he meant. His home was in Nazareth, not Jerusalem.

"Come," Joseph said, putting his arm around Jesus' shoulders. "Your Uncle Clopas and Aunt Mary have taken charge of your brothers and sister. They'll all be wondering what happened to you."

Mary took Jesus' hand as they left the Temple. She wove her fingers between his and held on tightly.

five

MARY gave birth to a daughter the following summer and named her Sarah. Anne pouted every time Mary nursed the baby. She began sucking her thumb because the baby did and stole the teething toy her father made for her baby sister. The boys squabbled with one another, drawing attention to themselves.

Eighteen months later, the twins, Simon and Jude, were born. By this time, Mary had come to realize a painful truth: Only Jesus was good. His brothers and sisters were incapable of obeying for any length of time. Even when they wanted to be good, they slipped into rebellion.

It was difficult to accept that Jesus' loving nature, faithfulness, obedience, and eagerness to learn and serve had absolutely nothing to do with her abilities as a mother.

James had come as a shock to her. Joseph, Anne, Sarah, Simon and Jude merely confirmed the nature of her purely human offspring. While Jesus found his own way through God's heart beating within him, nothing she tried with her other children changed their tendency to give in to sin! They fought with one another. They rationalized and justified their actions when caught doing wrong. They whined to get their way. When disciplined, they pouted and claimed she was favoring one over another. Their self-centeredness couldn't be soothed away with hugs and kisses or driven away with discipline. All of her children were strong-minded. While Jesus' mind was directed toward doing what pleased God, the others were bent upon pleasing themselves. Even when they were kind and thoughtful, there was an edge of self-satisfaction in their behavior. Mary couldn't count the times she'd bitten her tongue so that she would not cry out, "Why can't you be more like Jesus?" But who was she to cast hard words when she saw herself in each of them?

And yet, even in their disobedience, they were precious to her. And she loved them all equally. They were her children by Joseph. When she observed the other mothers in Nazareth, she saw that her plight was no different from others'. Life was a constant struggle. Each child came with joy, but added one more mouth to feed, one more body to clothe, one more mind to educate and train up in righteousness. And not even one among her own natural children by Joseph was righteous – not one! She had seen their will at work from the moment they left the womb. Then they had crawled and explored the world around them, reaching for things that would do them harm. "No, no," she would say. "No, no." And her son or daughter would cast her a beguiling smile and still reach out for what was forbidden.

Sometimes she couldn't help but laugh at her children's persistence, while at other times, she would weep. Sometimes they made her so angry, she wanted to cry out. She tried to be diligent in teaching them all she knew about the Law. She prayed for them constantly. She loved them fiercely. She lived each day with their development in mind. She was careful how she lived before them. After all, what good was it to teach God's ways and not live them?

With each year that passed, she watched Jesus and counted herself blessed among women for this one perfect son. She looked at him and her heart swelled with joy and anticipation. It never ceased to amaze her that the God of Abraham, Isaac, and Jacob had chosen her to be the vessel for the Messiah. She was a woman like any other, as imperfect as her children. Surely the Lord was teaching that lesson to her above all else. She laughed at herself and thanked God that he had given her other children so she would know it was not by her efforts and Joseph's that this son was so perfect, so blessed, so high above all others who walked the earth. He was God's Son through her flesh.

Every day held its own trouble, but she recognized that the difficulties of life rubbed away the rough spots of her faith just as Joseph smoothed and polished a cup. She struggled to show her sons and daughters the way of faith, accepting that God was refining and sifting her in the process.

Still, there were times when she had to fight her own inner rebellion, her own nature to want to see the fullness of God's plan played out before her eyes. *Oh, Lord, let me live long enough to see Jesus in his glory.* She had been quick to say yes to God, but that same impetuous faith made her impatient to see the Lord's plan played out and the world come under the reign of the Son of Man, God's Son on earth.

When, Lord? When will this Son of yours come into power? How long will we all have to wait before he makes things right and we are free? How long will your Son be content to work in the shop alongside my beloved Joseph, building tables and chairs, yokes and plows, doors and lattices, when there is a kingdom out there to build? How long will he sweep the carpentry shop clean of wood chips before the time comes for him to sweep the earth as clean as it was in the Garden of Eden? How long before he crushes the evil men who oppress Israel? Oh, Lord, how long? How long?

Finally the yearning became so strong, she gave in to it and one day asked Jesus, "Do you know who you are?"

When he didn't answer, she persisted. "Son," she said, "do you know?"

Why did he tense at the question? Why did he look at her with tenderness mingled with distress? She wasn't trying to vex him. She was only asking. ... Sometimes he would look at her as he did now, and she would feel that she was causing him grief. But how could that be? Who loved him better than she did? Who had been more devoted to him? She came close and took his hand, turning it in hers and running her fingers over the rough calluses. How could it be that the Messiah should have hands like a common laborer? "Oh, Jesus, should a king have hands like these? ... "

His hand stilled hers. "I am my father's son."

But when she looked into his eyes, she wondered. Did he mean Joseph or God? Should she tell him again how he came into this world? Should she tell him that all the world was waiting for him to come out of hiding? That *she* was waiting?

"You're my son, too, Jesus. I only want to see you receive the honor due you."

She had seen the signs of Jesus' power. Even when patrons didn't pay their debts or Roman soldiers came and took from their family provisions, there was always enough bread to fill empty stomachs, always enough fresh water to quench thirst, always enough oil to keep the lamp lit through the dark night. Even after the Romans had emptied the family's bins and jars and cruses, there was enough.

Still, life had not grown easier as Jesus increased in wisdom and stature. His struggles seemed more intense. Whatever battles he fought within himself were not easily won, nor did he share them with her or Joseph. Would life not be easier for all when he took his rightful place?

"David was a boy when the prophet Samuel anointed him king over Israel," she said.

"And it took more than ten years to develop his character so that he would be useful."

"Your character is perfect, my son. You are useful now."

Beads of sweat formed on his brow. "It is not my time, Mother."

"But when, Jesus? When will be your time?"

"It is not my time," he said again.

Why did he look so pressed? Anger rose. She wanted to shake him and make him tell her. Surely it was her right to know. "How long must I wait before I see what you were born to do?"

"You press me."

"Yes, I press you for your own good. Is it not for a mother to encourage her son to fulfill his obligations to his people? I love you, my son. You know how much I love you. Joseph and I have made sacrifices for you. But sometimes I wonder. Do you know who you are?"

"Mother ... "

"All I want is to see things made right. Is that wrong?"

"You must wait."

"I'm tired of waiting! Look around you, Jesus. See how your people suffer!" Her voice broke. She looked away, struggling with frustration. "When, Jesus? Just tell me when and I won't ask again. I won't press ... " She looked back at him through a sheen of tears. *"Please."*

His dark eyes were moist. Sweat dripped down his temples. "It is not my time," he said again. Something in his voice made her shudder inwardly. She sensed she had added to his travail by making demands of him, demands he had no intention of fulfilling. Perplexed and grieving, she said no more.

Instead, she went to Joseph and asked him to approach Jesus. They had always been able to talk. Surely Jesus would confide in him.

"You should not ask him."

"Why shouldn't I? I'm his mother."

"God will tell him when the time is come."

"How can you be so patient when you know all things will be made right when Jesus comes into power? Look around us, Joseph. We need him now."

"I don't have the right to ask why he doesn't make himself known now."

She heard something in his voice and turned to him in the darkness. "You don't think I have the right either, do you?" Eve had been deceived in the Garden. Was Mary being tempted now?

"No, I don't," Joseph said with gentle firmness. "Though you bore him, it was God who gave him life, and God will decide what he is to do with it. Let him be, Mary." He drew her close. "The Lord will tell him when. Don't be in a hurry."

She rested her head on his chest, listening to his heart beat. She let out her breath slowly and was silent for a long while, pondering the events of her life. The Lord had spoken once to her, but he had spoken four times to Joseph, directing their steps. Her husband lived with his eyes and ears open, seeking God's will. She saw every day how much he loved Jesus, how much he loved her and their own children.

The Lord had chosen Joseph to be her husband, to be head of the household, and she would listen to his counsel.

⟨⟨⟨⟨⟨⟨

Joseph loved to watch Jesus with his half brothers and half sisters. Their exuberance and antics often made Jesus laugh, and the sound of it made Joseph laugh also. "Quiet, my children. Give your brother a place to sit."

"Tell us again about David and Goliath!" James said.

"No! Tell us about Joshua and Jericho."

The boys never tired of hearing the chronicles of battles.

"Tell us about Noah and the ark again, Jesus," Anne said, leaning against him. "Please ... "

"You've heard that story over and over again," James protested. "I'm tired of it!"

Jesus sat his twin brothers on his knees. "We begin with the beginning ... "

Living with Jesus day to day sometimes made Joseph forget this young man was God's Son and not his own. Then he would remember and feel a surge of awe. Jesus didn't read the Scriptures, but spoke them naturally as if he'd written them himself. Sometimes he said more, so that he was relating what happened in a way that made it seem he was witness to the events of the Torah.

Joseph looked at his wife, smiling behind her loom, her head tilted as she worked, and listened to Jesus tell how the world was created. Joseph shivered as Jesus spoke of earth as formless and void, with darkness over the surface of the deep. Joseph's children sat around Jesus, flesh of his flesh, bone of his bone. Jesus had been conceived of the Holy Spirit, but exactly what that meant was beyond Joseph's comprehension. The boy was fifteen and had Mary's cheekbones and dark eyes. There were other men in Nazareth who were taller, others who walked with assurance, others who spoke Scripture word for word and claimed to know God's will for Israel.

How often had he heard men cry out for the Messiah to come! How often had he heard men arguing about what God wanted from Israel.

"God wants us to break the yoke of Rome from our backs!"

"It is God's judgment upon us that we suffer as we do!"

"Have we not suffered long enough? If we stand and fight, will not the Lord our God fight with us?"

"Fool! Who are you to say what God will or will not do?"

"So we sit on our hands and let the Romans take their provisions from our poverty?"

"We wait."

"How long must we wait? How long?"

Closing his eyes, Joseph leaned back. He was exhausted from the long trek to Sepphoris and back after a hard day's work. He was grateful for the denarius he'd received, though it barely stretched to cover the family's needs. He was grateful for the work God gave him, and even more grateful for the one who shared his load: Jesus.

His arm ached again. His fingertips were numb, but the pain raced up his arm and across his chest. He rubbed his arm and breathed slowly. Tomorrow was the Sabbath, and he could rest.

Joseph looked at his children gathered around Jesus, and it struck him again. The boy he loved most was not his own. *My son who is not my son. He has grown up in this small village like a tender green shoot, sprouting from a root in dry and sterile ground. He looks like any other boy. He isn't beautiful or majestic in appearance. People look at him and see a carpenter's son and nothing more. When he speaks, who but his brothers and sisters listen? And even they don't understand that Jesus is not one of us.*

He is the Son of the one who said, "I Am the One Who Always Is." God is in him. God is with us!

Will they recognize him when his time comes to proclaim himself to the nations?

Even as the question reared up in Joseph's mind, Isaiah's words came rushing in. *"He was despised and rejected – a man of sorrows, acquainted with bitterest grief ... Yet it was our weaknesses he carried; it was our sorrows that weighed him down ... a punishment from God. ... Yet the Lord laid on him the guilt and sins of us all."*

No.

"It was the Lord's good plan to crush him and fill him with grief. ... His life is made an offering for sin."

Joseph groaned, clutching at his chest.

"What is it, Joseph?" Mary said, suddenly at his side. *"Joseph!"* He felt her arms around him, but he could only look at Jesus and weep.

⋘⋙

Joseph felt Jesus lift him while the others were all talking at once, shaken by fear and confusion. "Hush, now," Mary said firmly. "Don't be afraid. Your brother is going to help."

As Jesus lowered him to the pallet, Joseph sensed the struggle going on inside the boy. Had there ever been a time in Jesus' life when he'd not come face-to-face with temptation and had to battle his human nature and crush it? Joseph saw the sweat bead on Jesus' brow now. "Oh," Joseph groaned, filled with anguish. Would Jesus fight and overcome evil only to be killed in the end? How could this be?

The pain in his chest increased, along with his conviction that he was dying. "Come close, my children. Come!" As they knelt beside him, he drew each down, kissing them and blessing them. "Listen to your brother, Jesus. Obey your mother. Trust in the Lord ... "

"You'll be all right, Joseph," Mary said, receiving his blessing, her eyes tear-filled but fierce. "I know you will. Jesus has only to – "

"Hush," Joseph said, putting his fingertips over her lips. Should they presume a miracle would be performed just because they wanted it? Should they expect Jesus, God the Son, the great *I Am*, to do their bidding? "God decides," he whispers. "We mustn't burden Jesus more."

Mary looked up at her son, her face pale and strained. Joseph saw how she pleaded with her eyes. "Mary, I must speak with Jesus."

"Yes, Joseph." Mary rose quickly.

Every breath he drew was painful. The fingers of his hand were numb and sweat soaked through his tunic. Mary quickly gathered the children and urged them from the room. Tears welled in her eyes as she looked at her eldest son. "I know you can help him. Do so. Please. Do so." She left the room.

Jesus sat close beside Joseph when the room was empty. Joseph smiled at him. Fighting the pain in his chest, he took Jesus' hand and placed it over his heart. "We don't make it easy for you."

"You weren't meant to."

Anguish clenched Joseph's throat. "Soften their hearts, Jesus. The children ... oh, please. Soften their hearts so they will understand and be saved."

"Each must choose."

"Even faith comes from God."

"Each must choose."

"But will they choose to believe you are the Messiah? Will they ... ?"

"Do you trust me?"

Joseph looked into his eyes. "Yes." He drew a sobbing breath. "I was thinking of Isaiah as you were speaking to the children." His eyes blurred with tears. "'As a lamb,' the Scriptures say, 'He was led as a lamb to the slaughter.'"

He searched Jesus' eyes and saw in them infinite love and compassion. The boy Jesus was only fifteen years old, but Joseph saw in him the Son of Man of whom the prophet Daniel had spoken. Joseph had seen the strength in him from birth and sensed the unending battle that went on around him. Not once in all his days had Jesus weakened and given in to sin. Not once had Joseph seen a sword in Jesus' hand, even when other boys his age played Zealot or King David. Not once had Jesus given in to the human desires that plagued everyone who entered the world. Who but God could withstand the onslaught of constant temptation?

"He was led as a lamb to the slaughter."

Weeping, Joseph closed his eyes. "You will take our guilt and sin upon you and be the offering. That's why you've been given to us, isn't it?" Joseph was overwhelmed with love for this boy he had reared from birth but never dared call his own. And he was torn by grief for what he feared would happen to Jesus. "They'll reject you."

Jesus said nothing. He merely laid his hand gently on Joseph's brow as Joseph held the other over his heart.

"I love you, Jesus. Save my children. And your mother. She doesn't understand." How could she, and still be in such a hurry to press him on?

"Don't worry," Jesus said. "I'm with them."

"I am so weak." Should he doubt God now?

"Rest," Jesus said softly. Joseph closed his eyes again and thought he heard Jesus whisper, "You have been a good and faithful servant."

The pain lifted as his children entered the room and gathered around him again. Mary knelt beside him and took his hand tightly in hers. Joseph smiled, but he had no strength to speak. He wanted to tell her she had been a good wife, a good mother, but he'd said those things to her many times before. She knew he loved her. Still, he saw the confusion in her eyes, the fear, the appeal when she looked at Jesus.

Joseph tried to speak. She leaned down, putting her ear near his lips. "Trust. Obey." When she laid her head upon his chest and wept, he looked up at Jesus. The only one they needed stood silent near the door, tears running down his cheeks as he obeyed the will of his Father, and did nothing to keep death away. Strangely, Joseph was no longer afraid. He sighed, relieved.

Closing his eyes, he entered his reward.

※※※

"Joseph!" Mary cried out when he stopped breathing. *"Joseph!"* She pulled Joseph's shoulders up and held him in her arms. How could this be? She looked up at Jesus. He was weeping. "Why?" she sobbed. *"Why?"* She knew he could have healed Joseph! She knew he had the power. Hadn't he healed Anne with a brush of his hand? Hadn't he multiplied their loaves of bread, filled their cruses with oil? Why had he allowed Joseph whom he loved to die?

Because he doesn't care. Because it serves his purpose.

No. She refused to believe it. She could see the sorrow in Jesus' eyes. She knew he loved Joseph. How many times had she seen them laugh together as they worked side by side in the shop or seen them with their heads close together as they read Scripture?

And now your son just stands there and watches him die. He does nothing. And now you're alone – a widow with seven children to feed and no man to provide for you. Is this the way God takes care of you?

No! She would not think such evil thoughts! She would not allow doubt to slither into her mind and sink its fangs into her, spreading poison.

"Jesus." She moaned. "Jesus!"

He was beside her at once, his hands upon her shoulders. "I am here, Mother."

She wept as she eased Joseph's body back onto the pallet and touched his face tenderly. How would she go on without Joseph's strength, his wisdom, his encouragement and love? Hadn't God spoken through him and guided them to Egypt, then back to Israel, and then here to Nazareth? And Joseph had been faithful, quick to obey when God spoke.

The children were all crying, confused, frightened, grieving. She understood how they felt, for she was caught in the same feelings, drowning in them. She tried to think what to do. Reaching up, she gripped Jesus' hand resting on her shoulder. As firstborn, he was now head of the family.

※※※

"I have no money to buy spices," Mary told her sister. How would she prepare Joseph's body for burial?

"We have spices, Mother." Jesus rose and went to the box Joseph had packed in Bethlehem that night so long ago when they had fled after the angel warned them Herod would try to kill Jesus. He opened it and took out the alabaster jar.

"What is that?" Mary's sister said.

"We can't use that," Mary said.

"Use it." Jesus held it out to her.

"But it was a gift to you, my son."

"A gift?" Her sister looked between them. "Such a jar? Who would give such a gift?"

"It is mine," Jesus said, "and I can give it to whom I choose." He placed it in her hands and left Mary alone in the room with her sister and the body of her husband, Joseph.

Weeping, Mary held the jar reverently. Removing the seal, she opened it and the room was filled with the sweet scent of myrrh as she obeyed her son.

⁂

In the months following the death of her beloved Joseph, Mary was torn by confusion and anger. Sometimes she felt she was surrounded by attackers, whispering doubts and accusations. It was all she could do to cover her head and pray.

Oh, Lord God, I don't know why you've taken Joseph from us, and why life must be so hard. I don't understand why your Son must labor like every other man, putting bread on our table by the blood and sweat of his brow. I don't know why so many years have passed and he still hides himself away.

But I dwell in your promises, Lord. ... You said Jesus will be very great and will be called the Son of the Most High. You said you will give him the throne of his ancestor David. You said his kingdom will never end. I remember it as if it happened yesterday. I remember. But, O Lord my God, it is so hard to wait to see the fulfillment of your promises.

⁂

Jesus worked hard to provide for the family, dealing with recalcitrant patrons who dragged their feet about paying their bills, or those who complained for no other reason than to hear the sound of their own voices. Mary never saw Jesus lose his temper.

When the time was right, Jesus arranged marriages for his sisters, finding for them young men who sought to please God above all others. Jesus continued to work with his brothers in their father's shop, teaching them the skills Joseph had taught him. Along the way, Jesus tried to teach them the ways of God. James was often difficult, and young Joseph followed his example, but Jesus remained patient, loving, firm.

"What use is studying the Torah when Rome crushes our people? I should be learning how to use a sword!" James cried out passionately, contending with Jesus yet again.

Jesus answered quietly. "Your work is to remain faithful to God."

James's face reddened. "I am faithful! How am I not faithful? I study. I recite."

"You study, but you don't understand. Your heart is given over to wrath."

"My heart is filled with righteous anger!"

"Where is the righteousness in following after those who would spill innocent blood?"

"Show me a Roman who's innocent!"

"James!" Mary tried to calm herself. "Listen to your brother."

James turned on her. "You always take his side. Just because Jesus is older doesn't mean he knows everything."

Angry, Mary rose. "You will show your brother the respect he's due as head of this family. Listen to what he says."

"I won't listen." James covered his face and wept in frustration. "I already know what he'll say, and I'm sick of hearing it."

Mary looked at Jesus, beseeching him to say something to turn the boy from living in resentment and anger. Jesus rose and went out to take another of his long walks in the hills.

Sitting with her boys, she pleaded with them. "You must listen to Jesus, my sons. You must allow him to train you as he desires, for one day you will see that he is more than your brother."

Joseph looked at her. "The rabbi told us every Jewish mother looks upon her firstborn son as the Messiah."

"And clings to that belief until proven otherwise," James said bitterly.

Mary's eyes filled with tears. Were they asking for signs and wonders? "Jesus healed your sister. He multiplied our loaves of bread. He kept the cruses of oil filled."

James glared at her. "You think so."

She went cold at their disbelief. "He brushed his fingertips across Anne's forehead, and the fever was gone."

"It's more likely Jesus picked her up just after the fever broke."

"I remember, Mother," Joseph said in agreement. "You were so tired you couldn't stand when Father came home. Anne was asleep."

"Anne was dying." She looked between these two headstrong boys who looked so much like their father, Joseph, and yet had so little faith. Anger filled her at their stubbornness. "Go out and sweep the shop for your brother. Go! Or must he do everything for you?"

She knew how hard it was to wait. But someday they would see Jesus lifted up in power, and then they would believe and stand with him. Someday!

But when? Oh, when will that day come?

❧❧❧

Year upon year passed.

Every spring, Mary's eldest son told her to make the preparations for the trek to Jerusalem for Passover. And every year, she would feel the rush of excitement as she looked up at him. "Is it time? Is this the year?"

Every step she took toward Jerusalem was one of anticipation. When all their relatives came together in King David's city and reclined together for the Passover meal, she prayed fervently that this would be the year Elijah would enter and proclaim that the Messiah had come. The bread was broken and passed, the wine sipped, the parsley dipped, the herbs eaten, and the youngest was sent to see if Elijah was at the door. Mary held her breath, her heart pounding.

"Elijah is not there, Grandfather."

Year after year. Jesus grew into manhood, and still the son of Zechariah and Elizabeth did not appear.

Every year, Mary raised her cup with the others and said: "Next year in Jerusalem." Then she bowed her head so Jesus would not see her tears of disappointment.

six

MARY carried her jar down the hill to the well and took her place in line to wait. She listened, only half interested, as the women talked about a new prophet at the Jordan River. There was always someone claiming to be a prophet of God.

"My son went down and heard him," one woman was saying. "He came back last night and told us this man speaks the words of Isaiah with power."

"Do you think he's the Messiah?" another asked.

"Who but God knows?"

"My husband left this morning to hear John preach. He took our sons with him."

At the mention of the man's name, Mary's heart leaped. She leaned forward. "Did you say his name was John?"

"He's called John the Baptist."

Containing her excitement, Mary filled her jar and lifted it to her head and plodded her way up the hill. She sloshed water as she set the water jar down and hurried through the house to the shop, where Jesus was working. "I just heard there's a prophet named John preaching at the Jordan River," she told him. "We must go and find out if this is Elizabeth's son."

Jesus continued filing a yoke. "I heard."

He knew? Why had he said nothing to her? She came closer. "We should go right away! I'll go at once and tell James and Joseph to make ready. They must come with us. And Simon and Jude, of course, and your sisters and their husbands. They should all come with us!"

Jesus raised his head and looked at her briefly, then returned his attention to the yoke he was smoothing.

Mary frowned. "Isn't this the sign we've been waiting for: John's appearance?"

"Everything in God's time, Mother."

Over the next few weeks, Mary strove for patience, but it seemed everyone in Nazareth except those of her family had gone down to hear John. The women at the well talked constantly about "the baptist."

"There are multitudes gathering at the river."

"I heard that some Pharisees went to hear him, and he called them a brood of snakes."

"Even the tax gatherers and Roman soldiers are going down to hear him."

"My son thinks John is the Christ."

The hair on the back of Mary's neck prickled.

"Everyone is wondering about him," another said.

Mary had to bite her tongue to keep from crying out in frustration that her son, Jesus, was the Christ, the Messiah. Each day added to her distress.

Finally she could bear it no longer. "I'm going to go, Jesus," she announced. "I want to see John." She was disheartened when he didn't offer to accompany her.

≈≈≈

The banks of the Jordan were teeming with men, women, and children when Mary and her younger sons arrived. The crowd was excited. Some called out questions to the wild-haired man who was sitting on a flat rock and was dressed in a garment of camel's hair and a leather belt about his waist. Was this unkempt man Elizabeth's son? It seemed everyone had come to hear this voice crying out in the wilderness, for there were gathered by the river prostitutes and priests, Roman soldiers and Hebrew scribes, farmers and fishermen.

"Prove by the way you live that you have really turned from your sins and turned to God!" John shouted, pointing at several Pharisees who stood near the water. "Don't just say, 'We're safe – we're the descendants of Abraham.' That proves nothing. God can change these stones here into children of Abraham."

Even from a distance, Mary could see how his words were received. The Pharisees' heads reared up and they turned their backs, stalking away. John shouted after them. "Even now the ax of God's judgment is poised, ready to sever your roots. Yes, every tree that does not produce good fruit will be chopped down and thrown into the fire!"

"Mama!" Jude pointed. "There's Jesus!"

Mary spotted him among the throng near the river, where men and women around him were crying out for John to baptize them. Her heart beat faster as her son came closer to the prophet. "I baptize you with water for repentance," John said, lowering a man beneath the waters and raising him. As the man got his footing and stepped away, John looked straight at Jesus standing on the bank. He stared at him and fell silent as Jesus walked into the water and came face-to-face with the one who had recognized him from the womb.

Mary took Simon's and Jude's hands and pressed through the crowd to get closer. John and Jesus talked briefly, and then John took hold of Jesus and lowered him beneath the waters, raising him up again. John looked up sharply as though something in the sky had caught his attention. Mary looked up, but saw nothing unusual. John stepped back and spread his hands as he stared at Jesus again, his expression rapt. Her son turned and waded out of the river and walked up the bank as several young men splashed their way into the water to get close to John.

"Come, my sons. We will do as your brother has done." Mary led her sons down to the river to be baptized, searching the crowd for a glimpse of Jesus. She thought she saw him once, but decided it couldn't be him because he was going off toward the east.

When Mary and her younger sons arrived home in time to begin the Sabbath, Jesus was not there.

Nor did he return.

⬚⬚⬚

A week passed, then another, and another, and Jesus did not come home. Where could he have gone? Had he been attacked on the way home and left bleeding beside the road? Surely not! But what else could have happened to him? James and Joseph were concerned and went off to seek word of him, returning a week later, unsatisfied and distressed. "No one has seen him, Mother."

"Jesus will come home when he's ready," Mary said, instilling more confidence in her words than she felt. Wherever Jesus was, she knew God was watching over him and keeping him safe from harm.

She was not afraid for him until she heard rumors that John the Baptist had been taken into custody by order of King Herod. Had her son gone to Jerusalem to argue for John's release?

"Where is your good son, Mary?" the women asked at the well. "My husband came by the shop yesterday to have his plow repaired and found only Simon and Jude there." When Mary told them he'd gone down to the

Jordan to be baptized, they shook their heads. "But that was weeks ago. It's not right that he leave you and the boys to fend for yourselves."

Even her sons objected to the way Jesus had gone off and left them without a word.

"He must do what his Father tells him."

"Our father is dead, Mother, and Jesus is the head of the household."

"Simon and Jude have read the Torah, and they've been apprenticed to Jesus in the shop long enough to carry on in their brother's absence." Even as she said the words, it occurred to her that Jesus might not come back at all. He was the Messiah! Why would he return to live in an obscure village in the district of Galilee? "Maybe he's gone to Jerusalem." If not Jerusalem, where?

What sort of son would leave a mother to worry like this?

She must not worry. She must trust in God.

The least he could have done is tell you where he was going and when he'd return! If he's so good, why would he turn his back on you and walk away without a word?

Should she make demands of Jesus? He'd never given her cause to worry before. He'd never done anything without reason and prayer.

He's your son. He owes you something for the suffering you've endured.

He is God's Son and owes me nothing! Mary covered her face and wept. Never had she felt so alone, even now with James and Joseph sitting on either side of her, Simon and Jude at her feet, her daughters close by. She hadn't felt such loneliness since Joseph died. Jesus had been her consolation, her strength.

It wasn't happening the way she'd expected.

Let him come, and watch how I crush him.

"No. The promise is being fulfilled." Mary raised her head. "The Lord is with us, and Jesus will make all things right."

"Mother," James said putting his arm around her.

She shook his arm off and stood. "The Lord is with us, and you will see the day come when the Messiah crushes Satan beneath his heel."

She saw her sons exchange looks of concern. Sorrow filled her. It would take more than her word to make them believe. It would take a change of heart.

⬦⬦⬦

The day before Mary left to attend a relative's wedding in Cana, Jude came racing up the hill into the house. "Jesus is coming! He's coming home!"

She ran down the hill to embrace him, weeping in joy. As soon as she put her arms around him, she was alarmed. "You're so thin!" she said in dismay. "And dark." She touched his sunburned face, seeing the signs of healing heat blisters. "Come, you must eat and rest."

Laughing, Jesus lifted her and kissed her cheeks as he set her on her feet again. "Woman, why are you always trying to tell me what to do?"

Mary laughed with him and cupped his bronzed cheeks. "Is it not like a mother to mother her son?" It was only then she noticed a group of men watching the exchange. "Who are these men?"

"They are my friends, Mother."

She peered around Jesus and recognized two of them. "James! John! How is my brother Zebedee?" She went quickly to greet them.

"He is well, Mary," John said, embracing her.

"But annoyed that we've left his household to follow Jesus."

She looked at the others and thought them a motley group. "Come. I have bread enough for all, and tomorrow we are invited to a wedding feast in Cana. And your friends are welcome to attend with us." Simon and Jude were vying for Jesus' attention as they all walked up the hill together.

She spent the evening joyfully serving her son and his friends. James and Joseph had come and drawn Jesus outside to talk with him earlier. She knew they were taking their older brother to task for worrying the family, and knew anything she might say would only add fuel to their fire. Still, she stood in the doorway, hoping her presence would still their critical tongues. Her presence did not ease their tension, but she was thankful Jesus listened as they listed their complaints. She had worried. She had slept fitfully.

"I must go where the Spirit leads," Jesus said when they allowed him to speak.

James's face was taut with frustration. "And what about Mother?"

Jesus put a hand upon James's shoulder and smiled tenderly. "I have not left our mother without provision." Mary understood as clearly as James and Joseph that it was their time to help provide for her, that the full responsibility would no longer be on Jesus' shoulders.

They left, annoyed when Jesus would not explain his absence or make promises regarding the future. She saw all too clearly the selfishness motivating their demands on him. Without their older brother to tend to everything, their lives would be less tidy, less convenient, less self-centered. She saw also their niggling jealousy of Jesus as the one who had captured and held her love. Perhaps she did favor Jesus over her other children, but how could she not when he was a perfect son and the others caused her endless trials and often, albeit unintentionally, hurt her feelings? She loved every one of her children, for they were her own flesh and blood. Would they never understand that Jesus was more than a child of her flesh? Would they continue to live in stubborn resistance? How was it these strangers who had come home with Jesus saw him more clearly than his own brothers did?

And what a diverse band of men they were – mixed in age, occupation, education, and district. Simon Peter, a fisherman with a graying beard, was near her own age, while Andrew, his younger brother, looked more like a scribe than a laborer. Nathanael, tight-lipped, listened to every word Jesus said without making comment, while Philip asked question after question about various points of the Law.

Still, unlike James, Joseph, Anne, Sarah, Simon, and Jude, these men hung on Jesus' every word, and hope spilled from their eyes.

As the sun set, Mary lit the lamps and went to bed content, for Jesus was home.

And all would be well now.

༺༼༻

Mary, Jesus, and his friends walked together to Cana the next morning. She longed to have Jesus to herself again, even if for just a few minutes. But he seemed intent upon encouraging these disciples to learn what he wanted to teach them. Perhaps later she could talk with him alone. She ran her hand down his arm, pleased that the tunic she had woven during his absence looked so fine on him. The work had kept her hands and mind occupied during the long, dark days she hadn't known where he was.

They arrived in time to join the procession through the small village as the bride was carried to her husband's household. The entire village was in attendance and the food and wine given freely to all. The music of harp, lyre, flute, and drum kept many dancing far into the night.

Mary had never seen so many at a wedding feast. Though the food was replenished from time to time, the wine flowed less freely as the celebration stretched to two, then three, days. On the fourth day, she overheard whispers of discontent. Jacob, the bridegroom, was so smitten with his new wife that he didn't even notice the look of growing strain on the servants' faces as they tried to see to the needs of his guests. One tried to gain the steward's attention, but failed.

Mary approached the servant. "What troubles you?"

"We have these pitchers of wine left, and then we have no more."

"Perhaps Jacob has a store of wine in his house."

The servant shook his head.

If the groom ran out of wine before the wedding celebration was over, he would be shamed before his guests. Poor Jacob would never outlive such embarrassment. "Come. I'll speak to my son. He can help you."

Jesus was deep in conversation with his friends when she approached. She entered the circle and knelt before her son, speaking softly. "They have no more wine."

"How does that concern you and me?" Jesus asked, not unkindly. "My time has not yet come."

She tilted her head and looked into his eyes with pleading. He knew as well as she that the lack of wine would pour humiliation on the groom's head and diminish his reputation before the community. She knew Jesus would not ignore the plight of this young relative, especially when he had brought friends with him to join in the celebration and increase the strain upon Jacob's supplies. Smiling, she took his hand and kissed his palm. Then she stood, stepped outside the circle of her son's disciples, and spoke to the nervous servants waiting. "Do whatever he tells you." Then she stood aside to wait upon Jesus' decision.

Remaining seated, Jesus looked at six large stone waterpots set against the wall. They stood empty now, but would be filled for the custom of purification. "Fill the jars with water."

Perplexed, the servants looked at one another. Mary could imagine them wondering what good that would do, for even the drunkest guest would know the difference between water and wine. However, they were so desperate they hastened to obey. They raced back and forth between the communal well and the big stone pots while Jesus returned his attention to his disciples. When the jars had finally been filled to the brim, the perspiring servants came quickly to Jesus.

"Dip some out," Jesus said, "and take it to the master of ceremonies."

Mary followed the servant, who dipped a pitcher into the water and carried it to the master of ceremonies. The water poured red into the man's cup, and she felt a wave of exultation. When he sipped it, his eyes brightened. She was close enough to hear him speak to the groom. "Usually a host serves the best wine first. Then, when everyone is full and doesn't care, he brings out the less expensive wines. But you have kept the best until now!"

Laughing joyously, Mary looked back at her son and saw astonishment on the faces of his disciples. Excited, the servants moved quickly among the guests, serving the new wine and spreading the news of what Jesus had done.

And Mary watched it all, tears of joy running down her cheeks.

Now they would believe! All the rumors that had surrounded her and Joseph would finally be laid to rest and her sons and daughters and friends would know the truth: Jesus was the one her people had cried out for over the centuries.

Jesus! The one who will save his people! Immanuel! God with us!

Soon, Israel would be free!

⨯⨯⨯

They all returned together from Nazareth and went to the synagogue to worship the Lord. Jesus sat near the front, his disciples around him. Mary, throat tight with excitement, strained forward to watch from the women's gallery as the Torah was read and the men began to talk about the meaning of the Law of Moses. When Jesus rose, there was a hush, for many had already heard he had been preaching along the shores of the Sea of Galilee. And it was rumored that he had turned water into wine at a wedding in Cana.

The old rabbi held out his hand in invitation to Jesus. Jesus drew his prayer shawl over his head and stepped up to the platform. The rabbi handed him the scroll. Jesus unrolled it and began to read. "'The Spirit of the Lord is upon me, for he has appointed me to preach Good News to the poor.'"

Mary's heart leaped. She remembered Joseph's words when, together, they used to marvel at Jesus' reading of the Torah. "His voice," Joseph would say, tears in his eyes. "His voice is like no other when he reads the Law. It doesn't pass over his tongue by years of practice, but comes out through his heart."

Now their beloved Jesus was proclaiming to all that he was the Anointed One, the long-awaited Messiah! Mary looked down at her other sons, sitting in the row Jesus had left. To her dismay, she saw their shoulders droop and their heads go down.

"'He has sent me to proclaim that captives will be released, that the blind will see, that the downtrodden will be freed from their oppressors, and that the time of the Lord's favor has come.'" Jesus closed the scroll and gave it back to the attendant. Then Jesus stepped down from the platform and took his seat again. The silence was deafening, every pair of eyes fixed upon him. Mary's heart was pounding faster and faster.

Jesus spoke with quiet authority into the pulsating silence around him. "This Scripture has come true today before your very eyes!"

A man came to his feet. "These Scriptures are about the Messiah! He blasphemes!"

Mary saw the one her son called Peter jump to his feet, his face flushed. "If you ask what he means, perhaps ... " He was drowned out by the rising voices.

"I hear he's performed miracles ... water into wine ... tells stories about seeds and sparrows ... has great wisdom ... "

"Where does he get his wisdom and his miracles?" a man in the shadows mocked. *"He's just a carpenter's son. What makes him so great?"*

Mary felt her face heat up, for she could feel the glances of the women around her as the mocking words roused in the minds of the Nazarenes, the foul rumors about her and Joseph and how Jesus was conceived. "No," she said softly. "No, no."

"We know Mary, his mother," someone joined in.

"And his brothers – James, Joseph, Simon, and Judas." Her sons, mortified, were pointed out.

"All his sisters live right here among us!" another called out.

Mary glanced back and saw Sarah blush and cover her face and Anne withdraw until she was near the doorway leading down and out of the synagogue.

"No ... no ... no." Mary shook her head, feeling eyes of pity and condemnation upon her.

She turned away, only to hear a woman whisper, "And I always thought Jesus was such a nice boy ... so good to his mother. ... She'll never live down the shame of this day."

Jesus remained seated. "A prophet is honored everywhere except in his own hometown."

"Now he's calling himself a prophet!" a man shouted angrily.

Jesus looked down the row at his cringing brothers. "And among his own family," he added. He stood and faced his accusers. "Certainly there were many widows in Israel who needed help in Elijah's time, when there was no rain for three and a half years and hunger stalked the land. Yet Elijah was not sent to any of them. He was sent instead to a widow of Zarephath – a foreigner in the land of Sidon. Or think of the prophet Elisha, who healed Naaman, a Syrian, rather than the many lepers in Israel who needed help."

"Who does he think he is, speaking to us like this?!"

"He's a blasphemer! Stone him!"

"No!" Mary screamed, seeing men laying hands upon her son, seeing the disciples enter the fray. She pressed through and raced downstairs. "Let him go! Let my son go!" The men below rose and pulled and shoved Jesus and his disciples from the synagogue. She tried to reach him as the mob propelled him up and up toward the brow of the hill on which the town had been built. "No!" she cried out. "You don't know what you're doing!"

A man shoved her back so that she fell to her knees, scraping her hands on the rocky ground. Gasping in pain, she scrambled to her feet and hurried after the crowd. Suddenly everyone stopped, and a strange hush fell over the mob. As Jesus walked back through their midst, each moved back from him as though being pushed back by unseen hands.

Panting, tears streaming down her cheeks, Mary ran to him and fell into step beside him, his disciples following. "Open their eyes, Jesus. Make them see. I know you can. Make them understand who you are!"

He stopped at the edge of town, on the road leading down the hill toward the Sea of Galilee, and looked at her. "They've hardened their hearts, Mother."

"Then soften them. Please, Jesus. For me." Never had she seen such sorrow in his eyes.

He reached out and tenderly cupped her cheek. "Mother," he said gently, "Nazareth is no longer my home."

Confused, she searched his eyes. "But, Jesus, how can you say that? I'm here. Your brothers and sisters ... "

Jesus drew her into his arms and held her tightly. She inhaled the scent of her son and put her arms around him as she had done so many times in the past. But now something was different. She felt engulfed by his love, upheld in it, and yet felt him withdrawing from her. She held on tighter, but he took her hands from behind him and stepped back. He spoke in a still small voice. "Each must choose." He searched her face for a moment and then turned from her.

As Jesus walked down the road, only his disciples followed.

⚬⚬⚬

Mary gathered her sons and daughters. "Your brother has left Nazareth and he won't be coming back."

"Even if Jesus wanted to come back, I doubt he'd be allowed back inside the synagogue." James was downcast.

Mary grasped James's hand and looked at the others. "He took the road down to the Sea of Galilee. I think he's going back to Capernaum. We should go there."

"It might be a good idea to leave Nazareth for a few days," Joseph said solemnly. "And let things settle down again."

"And we can talk to Jesus," James said.

"My husband needs me, Mother," Anne said. "I can't go without his permission."

Sarah looked as aggrieved as her sister. "After what happened at the synagogue, how do any of us dare go?"

Mary was stunned by their faithlessness. "Have you ever known your brother to lie?"

"No, Mother." James's eyes darkened. "But then, he never claimed to be God before."

"He *is* the Son of God." She saw how her children stared at her. She told them again how the angel of the Lord had come to her. She told them how she had conceived by the Holy Spirit. She told them how the angel of the Lord had appeared to their father in a dream, telling him that Jesus was conceived by the Holy Spirit, and how he had married her and kept her a virgin until after Jesus was born in Bethlehem. She told them about the star over Bethlehem, the visit of the magi, King Herod's decree to kill the children. When she finished, she looked from face to face and drew in a sobbing breath. "Why won't you believe me?"

James leaned forward, clasping his hands tightly between his knees, his face haggard with concern. "We know how children are conceived, Mother. He's our brother and we love him."

"You think I'm lying." They preferred the lies of gossips to the truth she spoke.

"We think – " he looked at the others and then back into her eyes – "that you're deluded."

Anger and hurt rose in her. "Deluded? How? By whom? Your father, Joseph? Other than Jesus, have you ever known such a righteous man so eager to please God? And Jesus. Hasn't he always done what is right and true and noble and ... ?"

James hung his head. "Just because he's obeyed the Law doesn't mean he's God."

She stood. She was angry, but she was even more afraid for them. What would become of her children if they rejected the Messiah? "We will go to

Capernaum. Your brother will make things clear to you."

~~~~

James and Joseph rose early one morning to speak with Jesus, but they were told Jesus had already gone off on one of his habitual solitary walks. "The men he calls his disciples refused to tell us, his brothers, where he went. They act like body-guards!" they complained.

Mary had hoped that her sons and daughters would recognize Jesus' true identity when they heard him preaching. But instead they were even more confused by Jesus' parables about wheat and weeds and choice pearls and mustard seeds. They were offended when Jesus did not separate himself from the others and treat them with more consideration than the hodgepodge band hanging around him day and night. There was never time to be alone with him because so many were pleading for his attention. Furthermore, they were frightened by the approach of priests and dismayed when Jesus welcomed *everyone*. He even ate with prostitutes and tax collectors!

Mary's daughters and sons-in-law left after two days, taking Simon and Jude back home with them. James and Joseph stayed another day, and then urged Mary to come home with them. "He doesn't need you, Mother. He's got a dozen men following him around like lost sheep." She felt torn between Jesus and her other sons, and was finally swayed by their arguments.

Passover was fast approaching, and she must prepare for the yearly pilgrimage to Jerusalem. Surely, Jesus would join them for the journey to the City of David.

It wasn't until the family came down from Nazareth that they heard from others that Jesus had gone on ahead without them.

~~~~

"Your son is in the city already," Abijah told Mary when she arrived in Jerusalem with her family. "He's been teaching in the corridors of the Temple." The elderly man wore a frown.

"Everyone has been talking about him," his wife, Rachel, said. "He seems to have a following."

Abijah shook his head. "The Pharisees are not pleased with his teaching."

"The Nazarenes weren't either," Joseph said grimly.

"I've heard that his disciples transgress the tradition of the elders."

"How?" Mary said.

"They do none of the ceremonial washing of hands before eating. It was on that very matter that the Pharisees questioned Jesus, and he called them hypocrites."

The hair rose on the back of her neck. "Hypocrites?" she said weakly, unable to imagine Jesus losing his temper.

"My friend said he told them straight to their faces that they honored God with their lips, but not their hearts. Your son said they worship in vain because they're teaching the doctrines and precepts of men." Abijah's face grew more and more flushed as he spoke. "Of course, the unwashed mob that follows him loved it." He glowered at Mary. "Where did your son get these ideas? You should speak to your son, and remind him of the respect due the men who take our sacrifices before God!"

Your son ... your son ... Mary could hear the accusation in her relative's voice. She felt the heat come into her face. Surely there was some mistake. Jesus had never been disrespectful to anyone.

"If he keeps on like this, he'll offend King Herod and end up like John the Baptist."

"Abijah," Rachel said in a hushed voice.

Mary felt her blood go cold. "What do you mean, 'end up like John'? What's happened?" She looked round at the faces of her sons and other relatives. What were they keeping from her? "James? Joseph?"

A muscle tensed in James's cheek. "He was beheaded."

Mary put her hand to her throat. "Beheaded?" Tears sprang to her eyes. John, the miracle child of Zechariah and Elizabeth, was dead? John, the child who recognized Jesus from the womb, was dead?

"It was only a matter of time," Abijah said. "He offended Herod and Herodias. You can't shout that the king and his wife are adulterers without expecting repercussions. He said it wasn't lawful for Herod to have Herodias because her husband is Herod's brother Philip and still alive."

She stared at him. "But that's true. Everyone knows it's true."

His face reddened. "Of course it's true, but it's foolish to proclaim it. King Herod had John arrested. I think he merely intended to keep John away from the people for a while, but Herodias held a feast for the king's birthday. Herod was drunk when Herodias's daughter danced for him, and he promised her anything up to half of his kingdom. And you can guess what happened. Herodias closed the trap, and told the girl to ask for John's head on a silver platter."

Mary slowly shook her head. "No. No! How can this be?"

Abijah seemed distressed at her reaction to his news, and turned to her sons in accusation. "How is it your mother has not heard any of this?"

"We didn't want to worry her," Joseph said. "John was arrested during the time Jesus was missing."

"Missing?" Abijah looked between her two oldest. "When was this?"

"After he went down to the Jordan and was baptized," James said.

Mary clutched her hands in her lap, struggling against the emotions that threatened to overwhelm her. Her sons must think she was weak and could not bear to hear what was happening around her. What else were they withholding from her? "John was a prophet of God," she insisted.

"Some say so," Abijah said sardonically.

She lifted her chin and looked at the men of her family. "A prophet of God speaks only the truth."

James frowned. "And every prophet who has done so has died for it."

Abijah leaned forward. "Your brother is going to get himself killed if he persists in offending everyone."

Mary's eyes glistened. "God brought Jesus out of my womb and made him trust in the Lord even at my breast. From conception, Jesus was cast upon the Lord. He can only do what God tells him to."

Abijah and Rachel stared at her, openmouthed. Abijah looked at James. "Is she claiming what I think she is?"

"She believes it," James said, glancing at her and bowing his head in shame.

"Woman," Abijah said in pity, "you are out of your mind if you think your son, the boy who has come every year to Jerusalem and sat at *my* table, is the ... the Messiah ... " He rose and moved away from her as though she were contaminated.

Mary felt Rachel's hand on her back. "Mary, Mary, my dear friend. You are a good woman, but do you really believe yourself worthy to be chosen to bear God's anointed? A poor woman from ... Nazareth, whose husband was a humble carpenter?"

"Our father was from the line of David," Jude said, pride-pricked.

"So are a lot of other men, in higher stations than your father," Abijah said and raised his hands. "We are not speaking against our relative. He was a good man, devout and faithful. But to be the father of the Messiah?"

"Jesus is not Joseph's son."

"Mother!" James said harshly, his eyes black with anger. "Everyone in this room knows what really happened."

Mary felt the blood surge into her cheeks. She looked around at them all. "God will keep Jesus safe. Jesus will not die!" He was the Messiah! He was the Anointed One of God, the Promised One who would save Israel! "The Lord's hand is upon him."

But she saw in their eyes that they didn't believe her and, consequently, would not believe in Jesus either.

❧❧❧

Mary returned home to Nazareth despondent. The tension in the family had increased over the Passover week. Their relatives had pressured her and her sons again and again to speak to Jesus before harm came to him. Mary had the distinct feeling that Abijah was less concerned with the welfare of her son than with the shame Jesus might bring upon his household.

When James and Joseph told her Jesus was back in Capernaum, she was not surprised that they wanted to go down and talk with him. She knew they feared for his life. But even more, they feared being excluded from the synagogue. The rabbi had been furious after Jesus' visit and said openly that anyone who believed Jesus was the Messiah would be cast from the congregation, just as the carpenter's son had been.

"We will go," she said firmly. "We will go and talk with Jesus, and then you will see."

But when she and her sons arrived in Capernaum, there was such a crowd around Peter's house that they couldn't even get close to the door. James shouldered his way through the crowd. "Make way for us! This is Jesus' mother and we are his brothers!" Hearing that, people touched them and exclaimed how blessed they were. Still, they were allowed no closer than the doorway. From there, they could hear Jesus, but not see him. Farther than that, they could not move.

James told the man in front of him to send word forward that Jesus' mother and brothers had come to speak with him. A few minutes later, Mary heard a voice call out. "Your mother and your brothers are outside, and they want to speak to you."

"Who is my mother?" she heard Jesus say. "Who are my brothers? These are my mother and brothers. Anyone who does the will of my Father in heaven is my brother and sister and mother!"

Mary felt the heat surge into her cheeks as those around her glanced at her and her sons, then looked quickly away.

Your son no longer needs you, and now he rejects you!

My son loves me. He loves his brothers. He would not reject us. He would not!

James's face was red and angry, Joseph's pale, Simon's and Jude's, confused and hurt. James leaned close to her ear. "You see how it is now, Mother. Now that Jesus has a following, he doesn't care for his own flesh and blood."

"We will wait for him."

"Why?" Joseph said. "To be further humiliated?"

James put his arm around her as if to shield her from the curious glances of the crowd. "We're leaving," he whispered harshly.

If she argued with her children, she would cause further disruption. She went with them a ways, and then she put her foot down firmly. "Are you all so proud you think Jesus must stop what he's doing the minute we appear?" She did not say again that Jesus was about God's work, for that would only incense them more.

"We came because we love him, and look how he treats us!" Simon said, tears running down his cheek. "We came because we don't want him to end up like John, with his head on a platter."

Mary embraced her youngest sons and looked up at James and Joseph. "Wait for him. Wait! Did you come all this way to turn your back on him?"

"He turned his back on us first." James turned away, but not before she saw the sheen of tears glistening in his eyes.

She refused to be swayed by hurt or confusion. She knew Jesus better than they did. Had she not been the one to suckle him at her breast and watch him grow into a man? Even as she walked away with them, she tried to turn them back. "Remember the parables your brother told us when he came home to Nazareth the last time. He's teaching the people about the kingdom of heaven. He is defining the children of God. He does not think as we think, my sons. His ways are not like ordinary men's. His ways are higher."

As she spoke her faith, assurance came, bringing comfort with it. "He is not excluding us, my sons, but *including* all those who have come to him to hear what pleases God." She looked back at those who craned their necks to hear her son's words of hope. "Those who realize they need God – the gentle and lowly, the sick, those who mourn, those who are hungry and thirsty for justice ..." She put her hand on James's arm, stopping him. "You know him. James. Joseph. Simon. Jude. You *know* him. Can you really say in your heart that Jesus has no love for you?"

They wouldn't listen.

She yearned to stay behind in Capernaum, but knew that if she did, these sons of Joseph would feel she had rejected them just as they were convinced Jesus was rejecting them. So, with sinking heart, she walked home with them. Every step away from Jesus made her feel more alone.

Each must choose.

The words echoed in her mind and made her heart ache. Jesus knew she loved him. Jesus knew she believed he was the Messiah. Jesus would understand that she couldn't leave her other sons.

Each must choose.

She had to stay with them and make them understand.

Each must choose.

If she left her other children, they would be hurt and angry, believing she had always favored Jesus over them.

Each must choose.

The farther she got from Capernaum and Jesus, the softer was the echo of her son's words to her ... and the deeper the ache in her heart.

Her sister, Mary, and Clopas stopped by Mary's house on their way out of Nazareth. "We've talked about it for months and decided to close our house and shut down our business so we can go with your son."

Mary's eyes spilled over with tears. At last, her sister and her husband believed! She had thought the day would never come. "Wait," she said and hurried to the box that held the last of the gifts from the magi. Mary put the incense and remaining pieces of gold into a bag and gave them to her sister. "For Jesus to use."

"Why don't you come with us?"

"I must try to sway my sons and daughters."

Soon after, Mary went once again with her sons and daughters to Jerusalem for Passover. She sat among her disbelieving relatives, overhearing rumors that King Herod was looking for Jesus because he thought he was John the Baptist come back to life. There was growing antagonism in high places against her son. Wisely, Jesus had crossed the lake to Gennesaret and was preaching in the surrounding district.

Upon her return to Nazareth, she heard that Jesus had departed from the district of Galilee and gone into the region of Judah beyond the Jordan. She heard rumors that Jesus had gone to Sidon and Tyre. But why would her son be among the Gentiles? It was Israel that awaited the Messiah.

With each day that passed, she felt the distance widen between her and Jesus, and the hearts of her sons growing harder.

"I want to go to him," Mary said, weeping. "I want to see my son!" All her efforts to save these stubborn children had failed. She was powerless to change their minds and hearts, powerless to turn them to the truth she knew: that Jesus was the Christ, the Son of the living God.

Oh, Lord God of Israel, God of mercy, why are they so stubborn? I can do nothing with them. Oh, Lord, I'm placing them in your mighty hands. Be merciful. Please be merciful.

"You tried to see him in Capernaum, Mother," her sons argued with her. "Do you not remember what happened? He has thousands of followers crying out his name. He has his inner circle of friends. He's famous throughout Judea. He doesn't care about us anymore."

It did no good to say Jesus loved them. It did no good to remind them of the years he had provided for them, held them in his lap, read to them, laughed with them, taught them. What would Jesus have to do to prove his love for them?

A year passed, and another, and Mary knew the time was fast approaching when she would have to do what Jesus said. She would have to choose. And she knew she must make the same choice she had made thirty-three years ago.

She must say yes to God and stop counting the cost. Even if it meant giving up her children.

seven

MARY traveled with her sons and daughters and their families to Jerusalem for the Passover. Everyone they met was talking about Jesus, telling stories of his miracles and preaching. He had not gone to Jerusalem for Passover the previous year, but had spent the week with his disciples in the desert after feeding a multitude on five barley loaves and two fish.

"Rumors, just rumors," someone near her said.

"I tell you, this man is a prophet of God!"

"He's my brother," Simon said proudly.

The strangers laughed at him. "Your brother!" They sneered. "Why aren't you following him?"

Her sons and daughters made no claims after that, but they talked a great deal among themselves, speaking softly, gravely concerned. Everyone they encountered was talking about Jesus, and all were hoping "the Nazarene" would come to Jerusalem this year so they could see him.

Mary was greatly disturbed and pondered what she was hearing. What exactly were these people expecting of Jesus? These people acted like children playing flutes, expecting Jesus to dance to their tune. They could talk only of the signs and wonders her son was performing, but retained nothing of the lessons he taught. They were eager to see Jesus perform miracles, greedy to eat bread that cost them nothing, hopeful to see their enemies crushed and humiliated.

Her son hadn't been born to do what men wanted, but what God willed.

How would Jesus do it? Mary wondered. How would her son bring redemption to these people who wanted to be entertained as much as the Roman mob did? If Jesus didn't do what they wanted or expected, they would turn on him.

Mary felt a cold chill down her back. Hadn't Jesus' own brothers turned on him when Jesus hadn't done as they wanted or expected? Could she expect more from strangers?

When they reached the gates of Jerusalem, Mary overheard someone say that the Nazarene was heard to be at Bethphage. "Let's go and join him there," she said to her children. "Let's find your brother and stay with him."

"He may need us," James said, looking as concerned as she felt. As head of the family, his opinion swayed the others. Simon and Jude were excited about the stories surrounding Jesus, as eager as everyone else to see what he could do, rather than hearing the word of the Lord and obeying it.

Before they had gone far, they heard shouting: "Praise God for the Son of David! Bless the one who comes in the name of the Lord! Praise God in highest heaven!"

The swell of voices grew until it was deafening. Mary's heart beat faster and faster as she hurried along, knowing they were welcoming her son into Jerusalem. The day had finally come for Jesus to be proclaimed the Messiah! She saw him coming up the road, surrounded by followers waving palm branches and crying out his name. Men and women were throwing garments down for him to ride over. Others were stripping branches from trees and spreading them on the road.

There were so many, Mary and her children could not get close.

"It's Jesus, the prophet from Nazareth in Galilee," people were saying around her.

"Not a prophet," she wanted to cry out. "He is the Son of God! He is the Messiah!" Overcome with excitement, Mary left the others and hurried along the outer fringe of the crowd along the road, crying out, "Jesus! Jesus!" She tried to keep pace, but lost sight of him as he entered the city. The crush of people drew her through the gates after him.

"Mother!" James called, pushing his way through the throng until he reached her. Shielding her, he drew her aside until Joseph, Simon, Jude, and the others caught up, and then they fell in with the multitude following Jesus.

"He's going to the Temple," Mary said, breathless. "He's going to declare himself!" Bumped and pushed, she was pressed forward through the streets of the city. They had almost reached the steps of the Temple complex when she heard shouts and saw wealthy merchants and priests darting out, covering their heads. Doves and pigeons flew out from among the Temple's columns and out across the city. Sheep bleated and ran among the crowd. She thought she heard Jesus' voice echoing: "Don't turn my Father's house into a marketplace!"

"What's happened?" people were crying out.

"He's overturning the tables of the money changers and those who are selling sacrifices!" someone called back, laughing.

"The Nazarene is driving the money changers out with a whip!"

James's face was pale, Joseph's strained. Simon and Jude wanted to get closer and see. Her daughters and their husbands looked alarmed by the mass of people pressing from all sides to get inside the Temple complex to see what was happening.

"If there's a riot, the Romans will come," James said. "And then what will happen to him?"

Mary scarcely heard. The Passover week had begun, and the Lord had said to remove all leaven from their houses. Once, years ago, Jesus had said he had to be in his Father's house – the Temple. And now, he was there, sweeping the evildoers out.

"Everything will be all right now," Mary said, tears of joy running down her cheeks. "The Day of the Lord has come!"

⟪⟫

By the time Mary and her family reached the corridor of the Temple, Jesus had gone. Everyone was seeking him. "He's gone back to Bethphage," some said. Others said he would go to Bethany to stay with a man he'd raised from the dead.

Exhausted, Mary went to Abijah's house and stayed with her relatives. Teary, she sat silently listening to their excited speculations about Jesus and what he might do next. She wondered where Jesus was, if he had managed to find a quiet place to collect his thoughts, what his plans were, and how long it would be before she could join him. Closing her eyes, she thought back over the many Passovers she and Joseph had spent with Jesus. Once before, she had been separated from her son.

She felt at peace again, for she knew Jesus would return to the city in the morning, and she would find him in the Temple.

⟪⟫

Mary sat all day in the women's court, hoping for a glimpse of her son. She prayed and watched men and women come and go, hearing clearly their heightened talk.

"The Pharisees say he casts out demons by Satan, the ruler of demons."

"But the Nazarene said a home divided against itself is doomed."

Priests stalked along the corridors, saying, "We ask for a sign, and he dares call us an evil and faithless generation!"

"Mary!" When she turned, she saw her sister running toward her, arms outstretched. They embraced, laughing joyfully.

"My son," Mary said, tearfully, "how is my son?"

"Oh, he's wonderful. You must come and listen to him, Mary. Are your sons here? Your daughters?"

Her sons had come to the Temple with her that morning, and left her at the entrance of the women's court while they went off to find Jesus and speak with him. She could only hope they would listen more than they talked.

"Come," Mary's sister said, her arm around Mary's waist as she drew her toward a gathering of women. "I want you to meet my sisters." She introduced her to Mary Magdalene, Mary the mother of James and Joseph, as well as others who had followed Jesus from Galilee. Each told Mary the story of how her son had saved her. Mary Magdalene had been possessed of demons while others had been sick or blind or hopeless. Mary wept with them, sharing the joy she saw in their faces.

Surely Israel would embrace her son as these women and the disciples had done. The Temple was filled with those who wanted to see the hope of Israel and hear the word of the Lord. Israel would repent and be united in devotion to the God of Abraham, Isaac, and Jacob.

"How terrible it will be for you teachers of religious law and you Pharisees. Hypocrites!" She went cold at the sound of her son's anger. "For you won't let others enter the Kingdom of Heaven, and you won't go in yourselves."

A low roar of voices was heard around her as Jesus walked among the pillars, his anger clear in his body and face. "You shamelessly cheat widows out of their property, and then, to cover up the kind of people you really are, you make long prayers in public. Because of this, your punishment will be the greater."

Her heart beat in fear, for she saw the rage growing on the faces of the men he confronted. They shouted at him, but Jesus' voice carried. "Yes, how terrible it will be for you teachers of religious law and you Pharisees. For you cross land and sea to make one convert, and then you turn him into twice the son of hell as you yourselves are."

She saw her sons, their faces pale and taut with fear. They were afraid of what people would say. She saw it in the way they looked around them, and then at her, beseeching. She could almost hear them plead, *"Do something, Mother. Stop him before we are all banned from the Temple."*

Her own cheeks were on fire as Jesus cried out in anger against the hypocrisy of the priests and elders. Everyone knew what he said was true, but no one had dared speak of it so boldly. Her heart hammered as she stared at Jesus striding along the corridor. Where was her quiet son, the one who sat meditating on Scripture beneath the olive tree in the yard at Nazareth, the one who sat soaking in the readings of the Torah at synagogue, the one who walked the hills above Galilee, praying? Her body shook at the power in his voice, for she was certain that if Jesus called for the stones of the Temple to fall, they would.

"You are careful to tithe even the tiniest part of your income, but you ignore the important things of the law – justice, mercy, and faith ... Blind guides! You strain your water so you won't accidentally swallow a gnat; then you swallow a camel!"

Mary had never seen Jesus angry, and she trembled at the sight of his wrath. He stood facing the rulers, his voice filled with authority and carrying through the corridors to the very heart of the Temple, though he did not shout as they did.

"Snakes! Sons of vipers! How will you escape the judgment of hell? I will send you prophets and wise men and teachers of religious law. You will kill some by crucifixion and whip others in your synagogues, chasing them from city to city. As a result, you will become guilty of murdering all the godly people from righteous Abel to Zechariah son of Barachiah, whom you murdered in the Temple between the altar and the sanctuary. I assure you, all the accumulated judgment of the centuries will break upon the heads of this very generation."

Jesus lifted his head and wept. "O Jerusalem, Jerusalem, the city that kills the prophets and stones God's messengers! How often I have wanted to gather your children together as a hen protects her chicks beneath her wings, but you wouldn't let me."

He faced the rulers once again, pointing at the the scribes and the black-clad Pharisees with their prayer shawls. "And now look, your house is left to you, empty and desolate. For I tell you this, you will never see me again until you say, 'Bless the one who comes in the name of the Lord!'"

Jesus turned and strode from the Temple.

For a moment, there was complete silence, as though all life had departed with him. And then there arose angry voices. Men shouted at one another, shoving, pushing. Mary saw her sons withdraw. The women with whom she had been talking scattered, rushing to the pillars and trying to follow their Master.

Mary was cut off, bumped, shoved. By the time she made it outside, her son was gone.

~~~~

Her children surrounded her when she arrived at Abijah's home, exhausted and depressed. "I couldn't find him. I walked to Bethphage and back, but I couldn't find him."

"If he's wise, he'll stay out of sight and leave after Passover," Abijah said grimly. "No good can come of what's happened. The leading priests and other leaders of the people are at the court of the high priest, Caiaphas, right now, talking about Jesus."

"I thought the people would riot after Jesus spoke against the Pharisees and scribes," Joseph said. "Everyone was shouting, one against another."

"Where could he be?" Mary said.

"He's probably lodging with one of his leper friends or a prostitute. Your son seems to prefer their company to that of his own family."

James's face reddened. "And if he did come here, would you welcome him, Abijah?"

"Not now! I'd sooner house a scorpion than him in my house. He's offended every Pharisee and Sadducee and priest in Jerusalem!"

"May the Lord open your eyes and ears to the truth." Mary covered her head with her prayer shawl and wept.

~~~~

Mary slept fitfully, dreaming of Jesus in the Temple. He was crying and raising his hands to heaven as men shouted in anger around him. She awakened, her heart pounding wildly. The room was dark. She rose and went to stand outside, wondering if it was only her imagination that made her think she heard angry voices in the distance.

All was silent.

Yet, the sense of oppression increased.

Where was her son? Surely, a mother sensed when something was terribly wrong. She was afraid. *Oh, Lord, why will you not speak to me as you did to Joseph?* She covered her face. Who was she to make demands upon God? She should have gone with Jesus the day he left Nazareth. She should have walked down that hill with him and never left his side. She should have left James and Joseph, Simon and Jude, and her daughters and their husbands in the hands of God, rather than trying to convince them Jesus was the long-awaited Messiah.

Oh, Lord, don't let it be too late. Help me find him.

Dressing quickly, she went out. She headed for the Temple, praying with every step that God would bring her alongside her son again. When she came up the Temple mount, a man ran by her, weeping loudly. She turned sharply, for she thought she recognized him. He was one of Jesus' disciples.

"Judas!" She called out, retracing her steps. "Judas! Where is my son?"

He fled into the darkness.

Mary found a man dozing against one of the huge pillars of the Temple. When she asked him if he knew where Jesus was, he yawned and said, "They took him last night from the Mount of Olives."

Her heart raced in fear. "Who took him?"

"They all went up after him: the leading priests, the other leaders, and a Roman cohort. They took him to Caiaphas and have been giving testimony against him all night. They took him to Pontius Pilate a little while ago."

"But why?"

"Because they hate him and want him executed." The man raised his head, his black eyes boring into her. "The Law requires that a blasphemer be stoned to death, doesn't it? And since we no longer have the authority to kill our own, we must plead Roman indulgence to do it."

Mary drew back from him. She had seen him before, but where? How long ago?

The man stood slowly, the movement reminding her of a snake uncoiling. "They will kill him, Mary."

Her body went cold. "No." She drew back farther. "No, they won't. He's God's Anointed One. He is the Messiah."

"He is the great I Am," the dark man mocked. "And he is going to die."

"Jesus' disciples will stand with him."

"His disciples?" The man threw back his head and laughed, the sound echoing in the Temple. He looked at her again with a feral grin. "They all deserted him. They've run like rabbits and gone underground into their warrens."

"I don't believe you." She shook her head, backing away from him. "I won't believe you!"

"Jesus stands alone. Go see for yourself. *Go and watch the work of my hands.*"

As she fled, she heard his laughter.

≈≈≈

A throng was gathered before the judgment seat of Rome. Mary saw the Pharisees clustered together like black crows near the front, talking among themselves. Pilate was sitting on the judgment seat, speaking with one of his officers. He waved his hand impatiently and the doors were opened. Mary drew in a sharp gasp when she saw her son and another man hauled forward. Jesus' face was battered and bruised, his mouth bleeding. He stood looking out at his people, his wrists chained together like a criminal. Sobbing, Mary tried to push her way through to him, but was shoved back. "Jesus!"

Pilate spoke loudly to the multitude, explaining that it was the Roman custom to show clemency to one prisoner of their choice during the festival season.

"Which one do you want me to release to you – Barabbas, or Jesus who is called the Messiah?" The guard nearest the governor leaned toward him in protest, for Barabbas was a notorious Zealot and enemy of Rome who had ambushed and slain Roman soldiers.

The crowd cried out, "Barabbas!"

"Jesus!" Mary cried out.

"Barabbas! Barabbas!" others shouted.

"Jesus! Jesus!"

An officer came out to Pilate and whispered in his ear. The governor frowned heavily and looked at Jesus.

The leading priests and other leaders turned to the crowd, moving among them. "Jesus is a blasphemer. Will you let him live? You know what the Law requires, what God demands."

"Barabbas!"

Pilate waved the officer away and stood, holding his hands out for silence. "Which of these two do you want me to release to you?"

"Barabbas!" They wanted violence and bloodshed. They wanted rebellion and hatred against Rome. *"Barabbas!"*

Pilate held out his hand toward Jesus. "But if I release Barabbas, what should I do with Jesus who is called the Messiah?"

"Crucify him!"

"Why? What crime has he committed?"

"Crucify him! Crucify him! Crucify him!" The multitude was turning into an angry mob, and Roman soldiers moved into position, waiting for Pilate's command to disperse them. But he didn't. He motioned for his slave, who carried a bowl of water to him. Then the Roman governor washed his hands, mocking the assembly of Jews who took such pains to remain clean. Drying his hands, he called out, "I am innocent of the blood of this man. The responsibility is yours!"

And Mary heard those around her cry out angrily, "We will take responsibility for his death – we and our children!"

"No! Don't do this!" Mary sobbed. She reached out toward Jesus as the Roman guards turned him roughly away.

≈≈≈

The angry crowd milled around, waiting to see the crucifixion, cheering when the doors were opened again and Jesus and two others were ushered out by Roman guards. Mary felt the blood drain from her face, and her chest tighten with anguish. A crown of thorns had been shoved down on his head, causing rivulets of blood to run down his face. His face was ashen with suffering, his back was bent over beneath the weight of the cross he dragged down the steps.

"Blasphemer!" People spit on him as he passed, their faces twisted and grotesque with hate. "Blasphemer!"

"Jesus!" Mary cried out, and saw her son tilt his head slightly. He looked straight at her, his eyes filled with compassion and sorrow. "Jesus," she sobbed and tried again to get closer to him, to reach out to him through the crowd. He passed by, whipped by the Roman guard when he stumbled and fell to his knee and struggled to rise again, and jeered by the mob eager to see him suffer and die.

"This can't be happening," Mary rasped. "This can't be happening … " She tried to keep pace with him, pushing her way through the throng that lined the street. She wanted her son to know she was there, that she loved him, that she would not turn away. "Jesus!" She cried out again and again, knowing he would hear her voice.

They took him outside the walls of Jerusalem to a place called Golgotha, near the main highway for all to see. The hill was in the shape of a human skull. Another man had shouldered Jesus' cross and was shoved aside after dropping it on the ground. A Roman guard gripped Jesus' shoulder and flung him to the ground. Another leaned down and offered him something to drink, but Jesus turned his face away. Two guards stripped off his garment and cast it aside. They took him by the arms and jerked him on the cross, lashing his arms tightly to the beams with leather straps.

One of the other two men who were being executed was screaming as a guard drove nails through his wrists. "I don't want to die!" The other cried. "I don't want to ... " He fought the guards, struggling violently and screaming as he was nailed to his cross.

Shaking, Mary moved through the crowd to the front, for those around her were less eager now to draw close. Her heart fluttered like a trapped bird as she saw a Roman guard raise a hammer in the air and bring it down. Jesus' body arched as he cried out, his feet drawing up. Sobbing, she fell to her knees. Three more times the guard hammered the nail through Jesus' palm, and each time, Mary's body jerked at the sound of her son's cries. Then the guard stepped over Jesus to secure his other hand while another hammered a spike through his feet.

Ropes and pulleys were used to raise the cross. Mary felt faint as she heard the hard thunk as it dropped into the hole. Pieces of wood were hammered in to wedge the cross into place and then the ropes yanked free. Every movement etched the agony deeper into her son's face.

And Mary would not take her eyes away from him. She clasped her hands. *Oh, Lord, you will come now and save him. You won't let him die. He's your Son. He's the Anointed One. He's our Messiah!*

A Roman guard leaned a ladder against Jesus' cross and climbed up to hang a sign that said "Jesus of Nazareth, the King of the Jews." Immediately, the leading priests began shouting angrily, "Take it down! He's not our king! He's a false prophet!"

"It hangs by order of Pontius Pilate," a Roman guard said, drawing his sword when several men started up the hill toward the cross. They backed down.

The great mass of people turned to walk away, heads down. But many remained to gloat. Some hurled abuse at Jesus, wagging their heads. "So! You can destroy the Temple and build it again in three days, can you? Well then, if you are the Son of God, save yourself and come down from the cross!"

"He saved others, but he can't save himself!" someone shouted mockingly.

"So he is the king of Israel, is he?" a priest called out. "Let him come down from the cross, and we will believe in him!" He shoved his hands into his priestly garb and stared, his face hard.

Mary shuddered at the laughter, her mother's anger so fierce she would have killed them herself if she had possessed the power. And then she looked into her son's eyes and felt the anger fall away, and confusion and sorrow fill her up to the brim as though she were a vial of tears that mourners wore around their necks.

Even one of the men crucified with Jesus cast insults.

Trembling in agony, Mary could not tear her eyes from her son. The crucified thieves were arguing with one another, and then one looked at Jesus, pleading with him. "Jesus, remember me when you come into your Kingdom."

Jesus looked at him and smiled. "I assure you, today you will be with me in paradise."

Mary wept silently, tears streaming hot down her cheeks. She wanted to cry out in anger against those who had done this to her son. *Oh, God, why? Why?*

The soldiers divided Jesus' garments among them, and hunkered down to cast lots for the tunic she had woven for her son.

A murmur of fear went through the crowd still gathered as darkness fell over the land.

"My God," Jesus cried out in a loud voice, "my God, why have you forsaken me?"

Mary covered her face, her body shaking with heart-wrenching sobs as her heart cried out the same question. *Why? Why?* All his life, Jesus had fought and triumphed over sin. She had seen him fight the battles and win. And now, during her people's most important celebration, her son's blood was being spilled like that of the Passover lamb.

"This man is calling for Elijah," a bystander said.

Someone ran up the hill with a sponge dripping with sour wine. He held it up on a reed so that Jesus could drink.

"Let's see whether Elijah will come and take him down!" someone sneered.

Dark clouds swirled angrily overhead and the wind came up. The sun was obscured.

"Mary," came a quiet, tentative voice. When she looked up, she saw John, the young son of Zebedee, standing nearby. "Mary," he said again and came close, putting his arm around her. As she buried her head in his shoulder, he whispered brokenly, "I'm sorry." He drew in a sobbing breath as she put her arms around him. She could not condemn him for running away when she had remained so long separated from her son.

John looked up at Jesus, tears streaming down his face, his chest heaving.

"Woman," Jesus said, looking at her, "he is your son." His gaze moved to John, his face softening even in his agony. "She is your mother."

Mary understood that she was being entrusted to John's care rather than that of her other sons and daughters. When John put his arm around her, she turned her face into his chest and wept harder.

"Father," Jesus said, and Mary looked up again, hoping to see the Lord himself come down to take Jesus from the cross. "Father, forgive these people, because they don't know what they are doing." She saw him heaving for breath, his body sinking lower. "It is finished!" he said, his chest rising and falling. "Father, I entrust my spirit into your hands!" Having said this, his breath came out in one last, long breath, and his body relaxed.

Mary stared in disbelief, her heart breaking, her mouth open in silent denial. "No. No."

John held her tightly.

The earth shook and people scattered. The Roman officer who was handling the executions looked up at Jesus. "Truly, this was the Son of God!"

"It's over, Mother," John said in a choked voice. "Come away from this place."

"No. I won't leave him."

"Then I will stay with you."

Soldiers came and broke the legs of the first man and then the second. Their screams were brief and then they gasped for breath, dying within minutes because they could no longer hold their bodies up enough to fill their lungs with air.

"This one is already dead."

"Better to make sure." The guard raised his spear and pierced Jesus' side. Blood and water spilled out. "He's dead." They hammered out the wedges and let the cross fall. As they yanked the nails from his feet and hands, Mary approached.

One of the guards straightened, the hammer in his hand. "What do you want?"

"My son ... my son ... "

Grimacing, the man stepped away, going to help take down another cross.

Mary fell down on her knees at Jesus' side and lifted his head into her lap. It began to rain, and she stroked the droplets over his face. Shifting, she sat and gathered her son closer, until the upper half of his body was in her lap, and she rocked him as she had as a child. "No," she whispered, kissing his brow. "God said you will save us from our sins ... " She gently pushed his hair back and kissed him again. She cupped his cheek and ran her hand down his arm and placed it on his chest, praying to feel a faint heartbeat. There was nothing. As she held him close, rocking and rocking, she felt the warmth of his body go out of him until he was cold.

And then she knew. Her son was dead.

Raising her head, she wailed in sorrow and then screamed out the despair of all humanity. The Messiah was dead, the world left in bondage.

All around Mary danced unseen beings, gloating and prancing in pride while their master laughed and laughed.

Didn't I tell you I would kill him? The earth is mine now, and all that is on it. I have won! Behold my power. Behold! I have won!

≈≈≈

Mary sat on the muddy hillside, carefully removed the crown of thorns, and held her son's head against her chest. The rain came down in sheets, drenching her. "Mary," John said, his voice gentle. "Joseph of Arimathea and Nicodemus are here."

"Who?" she said dully, looking up at two finely garbed men standing at a respectful distance. They looked like the wealthy men who were members of the Sanhedrin. Mary put her hand against Jesus' cold face as though to protect him from them.

John knelt down and looked into her face with compassion. "Joseph has been given permission by Pilate to take your son's body and bury him."

Bury him? Mary stroked Jesus' cold face. John put his hand over hers, and she looked up at him. His face was etched in grief. "Mother, it will be Sabbath soon. He needs a proper resting place." She looked away at the gray sky and at the small groups of people still standing around. The bodies of the two thieves had already been taken away. If she didn't give up her son now, nothing could be done for another day. "Joseph of Arimathea has offered his own tomb."

She looked down at Jesus. The rain had washed away the blood, leaving his face white as the marble in the Temple. Leaning down, she kissed his brow as she had when he was a baby sleeping. His hair smelled of perfume. "Take him," she whispered and spread her hands.

Nicodemus lifted him enough so that Joseph could wrap Jesus' body in a clean linen cloth. Mary sat in the mud, watching. John put his arms around her and lifted her. "Come, Mother," he said tenderly. "I'll take you home with me now."

"Where is the tomb?"

"In a garden not far from here. Joseph said it's hewn from the rock. It's a beautiful place with olive trees and a cistern. Jesus will rest in peace there."

Several women came to meet them, weeping and embracing Mary. She felt so numb, so bereft of any emotion. She didn't know what to say to them. As John led her away, she saw her sons standing together. They looked at her in shame and grief. She saw in their eyes that they expected her to reject them as they had rejected Jesus. "Oh," she said, the tears coming hard again. She went to them, weeping and embracing each one, kissing them.

"Come with us," John said to them, taking the place Jesus had assigned to him beside Mary. "I have a house in the city."

As they walked away together, Mary looked back in sorrow as two men she didn't know carried her son to a borrowed tomb.

※※※

Mary and her companions joined the disciples in an upper room. Most were too ashamed to look at Mary, for they had all run away and left Jesus. The women were not among them.

"Mary Magdalene and the other Mary are sitting near the tomb, waiting for the Sabbath to pass," someone said.

"Joseph of Arimathea and Nicodemus have already anointed Jesus' body with a hundred litras of myrrh and aloes and wrapped him in linen."

"We should all get out of the city."

"He's right. The Romans will be looking for us."

"Why would they bother looking for us?" Peter said, his face anguished. "We're no threat to anyone. It's finished. Jesus is dead." He thrust his face in his hands and wept.

"It's not over," Mary said quietly. How could it be over? God had told her Jesus would save his people, that Jesus was the Messiah. She believed him. So how could this be the end?

The men all looked at her in pity and then looked away.

"It's not over," she said again.

"Mother," John said gently, putting his arm around her.

She would not be silenced. "The angel of the Lord came to me when I was a virgin and said the Holy Spirit would come upon me. He said the power of the Most High would overshadow me. He said I would bear a holy offspring, a son. He said I was to name him Jesus because he would save his people."

They hung their heads.

"God said Jesus would save his people from their sins," she said, tears welling again. "*God said ...* "

They would not raise their eyes to hers. She knew they thought she was out of her mind with grief, clinging to hope when all seemed hopeless. But when God spoke, he always kept his word. "It can't be over." Her voice broke. "I refuse to believe it's over!" She gulped back a sob. "God ... promised ... " Covering her face, she wept.

The men were silent for a few minutes, and then began to talk among themselves again.

"I tell you, we should get out of Jerusalem."

"Yes, but how do we do it without being seen?"

"What if we are seen?" Peter said in bitter anguish. "What does it matter now? What does anything matter?"

Mary rose. She moved to the back of the upper room, lit a small lamp, and knelt down to pray to the God who had promised that salvation would come through her son, Jesus.

On the morning of the third day, they heard footsteps racing up the stairs. The men moved restlessly, casting frightened looks, not knowing what to do. The door burst open and Mary of Magdalene came in. "I have seen the Lord! He's alive!" She came excitedly into the center of the room, her face radiant as she laughed and cried with joy, turning and speaking so fast, her words tumbled one over another.

"We went to the tomb with burial spices, and the stone was rolled aside. When we went inside, Jesus wasn't there."

"Woman," Peter said, raising his hands to calm her.

"We went inside the tomb, and there were two men in dazzling robes. We were terrified! They said to us, 'Why are you looking in a tomb for someone who is alive? He isn't here! He has risen from the dead! Don't you remember what he told you back in Galilee, that the Son of Man must be betrayed into the hands of sinful men and be crucified, and that he would rise again the third day?' And we remembered." She spread her hands, turning around to look at them all. "You remember, too, don't you? You talked about it because you didn't understand."

Mary stood, her body tingling with the truth of the young woman's words. "He's risen."

"See what you've done," one of the men said to Mary Magdalene.

"He's alive, I tell you. I saw him!"

"Saw him? How?"

"I was weeping, and he spoke to me. He said, 'Why are you crying?' I thought he had taken the Lord away, and I asked him to tell me where he had put him so I could go and get him. Then he said, 'Mary!' I would have known his voice anywhere. And I looked up, and there he was. I clung to him." She clasped her hands against her chest. "I didn't want to let go, but he said to stop clinging to him because he had to ascend to his Father, our Lord and God."

"She's out of her mind with grief."

"Mary, you've let your imagination run wild. Just because you want Jesus to be alive, doesn't mean he is alive."

The Magdalene looked at them in frustration. "How can you not believe? Jesus told you this would happen."

The disciple, John was out the door, Peter on his heels.

"Let them go," another said dismally.

Mary Magdalene came to Mary, her eyes searching. "It's true. He said once that the Son of Man would have to be lifted up on a pole, as Moses lifted up the bronze snake on a pole in the wilderness."

Mary remembered what had happened in Moses' time: Because of the people's sin, the Lord sent poisonous snakes among them, and many of the people were bitten and died. But when the people confessed their sin and asked the Lord to save them, he did. God told Moses to make a replica of a poisonous snake and attach it to the top of a pole. Whenever those who were bitten looked at the bronze snake, they recovered!

Mary Magdalene took Mary's hands. "We were near the Sea of Galilee, and he said God loved the world so much, he was giving his only Son, so that everyone who believes in him will not perish, but have eternal life." Her fingers tightened. "None of us understood." Her gaze intensified. "Your son is alive, Mary. He is alive!"

"I believe you." If only she had been the one to see him for herself.

≈≈≈

Peter and John returned. "It's true," John said, his eyes aglow.

Dismissing what John said, the disciples looked to Peter for confirmation. "His body is gone."

They didn't know what to think, still afraid of what might happen to them. They feared death more than they feared God, shutting the doors and locking them because they were so certain the Council would send men to find and take them into custody for questioning.

They were all talking in low, frightened voices when a familiar voice spoke with a hint of good humor.

"Peace be with you."

Mary's head came up. Her son was standing among them. The men cried out in fear and fell on their faces. Mary's other sons stared in amazed terror and covered their heads. A sob caught in her throat as she stood. "Jesus." She rushed toward him, ready to embrace him as a mother. But when he looked at her, she was struck by the truth of who he was. *I Am Who I Am* stood before her. The sword of Truth pierced her soul, and she stopped. The son she had borne did not belong to her. Nor did he belong to Israel.

Long ago, the serpent Satan had enticed mankind to distrust and rebel against God, and then held all captive by the fear of death.

Mary looked up into the eyes of her son who was dead and was alive again.

Tears streaming down her cheeks, her heart humbled, she took Jesus' hands and kissed them as the words of the prophet Isaiah came to her, words Joseph had read aloud to her and their children so many times before: *"I would not forget you! I have written your name on my hand."* Now, she saw that Jesus was the Living Word. The full realization pierced her heart. Though she had carried him in her womb, he was God's Son. He had never been hers to command. Jesus was God's Son, God's gift of salvation to Israel. *"The Lord has laid on him the guilt and sins of us all."*

The awe of her first encounter with God came upon Mary again. Her soul exalted him. Her spirit rejoiced in Jesus, her Savior. All her life, she had struggled to find answers, to rise above her circumstances, to obey God and wait – not always patiently – for his plan to unfold, and now she was filled with awe at what God had done. She had mourned and was comforted with the promise of life eternal with him. She had hungered and thirsted for justice, and now beheld the one who would judge.

Mary fell to her knees before Jesus and bowed her head to the ground. "My Lord," she said in complete surrender. "My Lord and God."

eight

MARY lay upon her pallet, meditating upon the years since she had last seen Jesus. John sat nearby, praying. There were others present, just beyond the door of the small house she shared with him on the edge of Ephesus. She was troubled by their weeping.

"John?"

He rose and came close, taking her hand. "Yes, Mother."

"Why do they mourn?"

"Because they know your time with us is nearing an end."

She sighed. "They make too much of me."

"Because you are the mother of our Lord."

"Do you remember the forty days after the crucifixion? Jesus did not set me above the rest. He didn't give me an exalted place among his followers. Tell them."

"I have told them."

"Tell them again, John. We were all together, breaking bread with him while he told us about the kingdom of God. I served him and touched his hand and filled his cup with water." Her mind drifted. "Oh, I remember his smile. Do you remember his smile, John?"

John's eyes were moist. "Yes, Mother."

"That day when we stood on the Mount of Olives and we all saw him taken up into heaven, I thought my heart would break. I missed him the instant I saw him embraced in the clouds, and wondered how long it would be before I saw his face again. I hungered so much for one more look at him."

"We all did."

"Yes, and we stood staring up into the heavens, waiting and expecting him to come right back."

"Until the angels came." John closed his eyes, joining in her memories. "They said, 'Men of Galilee, why are you standing here staring at the sky? Jesus has been taken away from you into heaven. And someday, just as you saw him go, he will return!'"

Mary sighed. She had accompanied Jesus' followers as they walked the half mile back to Jerusalem. She and her sons had remained with them, meeting with the men continually for prayer, and waiting and waiting. ... She still waited. She and John had prayed together every day for Jesus to return, for Jesus to make them the instruments of faith they were intended to be. Each morning, she had risen from her pallet with the thought that today might be the day and she must be ready. But she knew Jesus would return in God's time and not because she asked it.

Still, Jesus was with them.

On the day of Pentecost, seven weeks after Jesus had risen from the grave, while all of his believers were gathered together, the Lord had poured out the Holy Spirit on them. She remembered that day, as clearly as if it were yesterday, for the Holy Spirit was still alive within her, just as he was in every believer. The joy of her salvation still filled her with exultation, just as it had that day when she had run outside with the others to spread the Good News throughout Jerusalem.

And then the persecution had come.

"They're all gone now, aren't they, John?" Tears filled her eyes as she remembered all of those who had died as Satan had sought to extinguish the message of salvation through Jesus Christ. She could almost see their faces. Young Stephen had been the first to die, stoned to death by Damascus Gate. Then others followed.

The apostles she knew and loved had scattered, taking with them the gospel message and spreading it like seeds across the world. And the seeds they planted had taken root, for there were believers in Syria, Macedonia, Greece, Rome.

Word had trickled back over the years of how the apostles had died. Some were mocked, their backs cut open with whips. Others were chained in dungeons. Some were sawed in half; others killed by the sword. Peter was crucified upside down near the obelisk in Rome; Paul was beheaded outside the walls of the city. Not one recanted his faith.

Among those martyred were her sons.

When she had heard of their deaths, she understood why Jesus had given her over to John's care. Jesus had known what was to come and made provisions for her even as he was dying on the cross. Her throat closed even now as she thought of it. Right from the beginning, Jesus had been pouring out his life for others.

John had brought her to Ephesus during the years of persecution, and she had lived under his care on the outskirts of Satan's city ever since, telling everyone who lived in the shadow of the Artemisian Temple about Jesus Christ who had died to save them. Paul had come to help the Ephesians, and then written to them as he traveled. His letter was still read at meetings.

Satan still waged battle against the truth, trying to cloud the minds of men. And so it would go on. Every day, the choice was the same: *Will God reign in my life, or will my desires win out? Will I make demands of Jesus and be distressed that he doesn't come back to us when I call?*

Waiting was the hardest thing to do. Mary had always struggled with waiting. But she was older now. She was eager now – not impetuous, not impatient. Each day was a refining fire. Each day brought the question, "Will you obey no matter the cost?"

"Today I say yes."

"Mother?"

"Today I say yes. And today, and today, and today, until there are no more todays left."

John squeezed her hand. "Each day has trouble of its own."

"And the Lord will carry us through it."

How was it God had chosen her, a simple peasant girl, to be his vessel? The privilege still rocked her. Jesus, born in darkness, was the Light of the World. He, the Bread of Life, had known hunger. The Living Water had known thirst. He had been misunderstood, sold for thirty pieces of silver, rejected by all, and crucified, and now he stood before the throne of God as the advocate of all those who believed in him.

She remembered how Jesus had prayed, unceasingly, in every circumstance – standing, sitting, lying down, and walking along the road. He had prayed, and now he listened to her prayers as well as to the prayers of all those who called on him. Unblemished by sin, he had given up his life as the atonement offering for all the sins of mankind, including hers. Defeating death, he had risen from the grave.

She had hoped her son would be victorious over Israel's oppressors. She had hoped he would reign as king. How small her dreams had been! How great and mighty was God's plan! Jesus was far beyond and above what man expected. *He is victorious! He is king above all kings! He is everlasting life, the holiness and righteousness of God. He is the Son of Man, Messiah, God in spirit and in truth.* And he had come to save not only Israel, but also the world.

Oh, Jesus, my sins are many, as you well know. I was so proud of you, so proud of the part I was given in bringing you into this world. I was so eager to see you reign on earth as king, with Joseph's sons at your side. ... And you knew, didn't you? I pressed you and prodded you to that end, didn't I? I didn't know that even I could be used by Satan to tempt you. Even I, the one chosen to be your mother, added to your burdens. I didn't understand you'd come to be the sacrifice. And I praise you for that. I praise and worship you for your tender mercy and compassion.

Oh, Lord God of my fathers, Abraham, Isaac, and Jacob, you were so kind to me. For how could I have lived with the knowledge that my precious baby was born to be nailed to a cross? I was in your presence for thirty years. I saw your beauty, experienced your love and mercy, witnessed your strength and righteousness, your perfection and holiness. I saw the living, breathing fulfillment of all your promises.

Lord, it was only during those last three years that I began to see what was to come. And still, I didn't understand. Through your death, you removed the barriers, and we can come before you and speak with you as Adam and Eve did in the Garden of Eden before sin came into the world. The fear of death no longer imprisons us.

She felt the change in her body. "I will be with him soon."

John leaned down. "I will miss you, Mother, but I will rejoice knowing you are with our Lord Jesus Christ."

Again, Mary heard the weeping just beyond the door. Deeply troubled by it, she looked into John's eyes. "More have come?"

He nodded.

Over the years, many had come to touch the edge of her garment. They thought because she was Jesus' mother, she had his power. Some had even bowed down before her, pleading with her to pray for them, because they felt unworthy to do so themselves. She was no more worthy than they were. Did they not see clearly? Did they not hear the message preached?

She had always corrected them firmly and with love. "Did Jesus die for you and rise from the grave so that you could come to *me* for help? Do not be fooled! Salvation is from *the Lord!* Jesus is Savior and Lord! Jesus loves you. He listens to your prayers. Trust in him."

She smiled sadly now. "Perhaps they will understand better when I go the way of all flesh." She felt the shifting inside her body, the loosening of the bonds of this earth. "When I die, John, bury me where no one will know. Don't let them make a shrine to honor me. It is by God's grace we are saved, by *his* power. Jesus died for them so that they would be free of sin and death. Remind them to love the Lord God above all others. It has always been that way from the beginning. Love the Lord your God with all your heart, all your mind, all your soul and strength, and love one another. Keep the gospel pure, my son. Keep it pure."

"I will, Mother," John said. He stroked her hand tenderly. "I will tell them the truth. Jesus is the Word, and the Word already existed in the beginning. He was with God, and he was God. He was in the beginning with God. He created everything there is. Nothing exists that he didn't make. Life itself was in him, and this life gives light to everyone. The light shines through the darkness, and the darkness can never extinguish it."

"Yes, my son. Tell them. Tell them ... to do what Jesus says."

seek and find

DEAR READER,

You have just read the story of Mary as perceived by one author. Is this the whole truth about the story? Jesus said to seek and you will find the answers you need for life. The best way to find the truth is to look for yourself!

This "Seek and Find" section is designed to help you discover the story of Mary as recorded in the Bible. It consists of six short studies that you can do on your own or with a small discussion group.

You may be surprised to learn that this ancient story will have applications for your life today. No matter where we live or in what century, God's Word is truth. It is as relevant today as it was yesterday. In it we find a future and a hope.

Peggy Lynch

CONSENT

SEEK GOD'S WORD FOR TRUTH

Read the following passage:

God sent the angel Gabriel to Nazareth, a village in Galilee, to a virgin named Mary. She was engaged to be married to a man named Joseph, a descendant of King David. Gabriel appeared to her and said, "Greetings, favored woman! The Lord is with you!"

Confused and disturbed, Mary tried to think what the angel could mean. "Don't be frightened, Mary," the angel told her, "for God has decided to bless you! You will become pregnant and have a son, and you are to name him Jesus. He will be very great and will be called the Son of the Most High. And the Lord God will give him the throne of his ancestor David. And he will reign over Israel forever; his Kingdom will never end!"

Mary asked the angel, "But how can I have a baby? I am a virgin."

The angel replied, "The Holy Spirit will come upon you, and the power of the Most High will overshadow you. So the baby born to you will be holy, and he will be called the Son of God."

Mary responded, "I am the Lord's servant, and I am willing to accept whatever he wants. May whatever you have said come true." And then the angel left.

— LUKE 1:26-35, 38 —

✛ From the above passage, what do we learn about Mary? (e.g., She was from Galilee.)

✛ According to Gabriel's greeting, what was God's attitude toward Mary?

✛ How did Mary respond to the angel's greeting?

✛ Gabriel reassured Mary and proceeded to explain his mission. List the things he revealed to Mary regarding herself. And what does he tell Mary about the child?

✛ Mary reminds the angel that she is a virgin and asks him how she can become pregnant. What additional information does Gabriel give her?

✦ How does Mary respond?

FIND GOD'S WAYS FOR YOU

According to the following passage from Scripture, God speaks to us today through his written Word.

> *All Scripture is inspired by God and is useful to teach us what is true and to make us realize what is wrong in our lives. It straightens us out and teaches us to do what is right. It is God's way of preparing us in every way, fully equipped for every good thing God wants us to do.*
>
> — 2 TIMOTHY 3:16-17 —

✦ How is God's Word useful to us?

✦ Mary was alone and quiet when God spoke to her. God speaks to us in small, quiet ways today, but are we available to hear? List the things that might distract us and keep us from hearing him.

✦ When you hear God's voice, how do you respond?

Read Jesus' words in the following passage from Scripture:

> *Anyone whose Father is God listens gladly to the words of God. Since you don't, it proves you aren't God's children.*
>
> — JOHN 8:47 —

✦ What reason does Jesus give for our not hearing God?

STOP AND PONDER

Read the following passage:

> *But people who aren't Christians can't understand these truths from God's Spirit. It all sounds foolish to them because only those who have the Spirit can understand what the Spirit means. We who have the Spirit understand these things, but others can't understand us at all. How could they? For, "Who can know what the Lord is thinking? Who can give him counsel?" But we can understand these things, for we have the mind of Christ.*
>
> — 1 CORINTHIANS 2:14-16 —

✝ Do you have the mind of Christ?

CELEBRATION

SEEK GOD'S WORD FOR TRUTH

Read the following passage:

At that time the Roman emperor, Augustus, decreed that a census should be taken throughout the Roman Empire. (This was the first census taken when Quirinius was governor of Syria.) All returned to their own towns to register for this census. And because Joseph was a descendant of King David, he had to go to Bethlehem in Judea, David's ancient home. He traveled there from the village of Nazareth in Galilee. He took with him Mary, his fiancée, who was obviously pregnant by this time.

And while they were there, the time came for her baby to be born. She gave birth to her first child, a son. She wrapped him snugly in strips of cloth and laid him in a manger, because there was no room for them in the village inn.

That night some shepherds were in the fields outside the village, guarding their flocks of sheep. Suddenly, an angel of the Lord appeared among them, and the radiance of the Lord's glory surrounded them. They were terribly frightened, but the angel reassured them. "Don't be afraid!" he said. "I bring you good news of great joy for everyone! The Savior — yes, the Messiah, the Lord — has been born tonight in Bethlehem, the city of David! And this is how you will recognize him: You will find a baby lying in a manger, wrapped snugly in strips of cloth!"

Suddenly, the angel was joined by a vast host of others — the armies of heaven — praising God:

"Glory to God in the highest heaven, and peace on earth to all whom God favors."

When the angels had returned to heaven, the shepherds said to each other, "Come on, let's go to Bethlehem! Let's see this wonderful thing that has happened, which the Lord has told us about."

They ran to the village and found Mary and Joseph. And there was the baby, lying in the manger. Then the shepherds told everyone what had happened and what the angel had said to them about this child. All who heard the shepherds' story were astonished, but Mary quietly treasured these things in her heart and thought about them often. The shepherds went back to their fields and flocks, glorifying and praising God for what the angels had told them, and because they had seen the child, just as the angel had said.

– LUKE 2:1-20 –

✛ Why were Mary and Joseph traveling to Bethlehem?

✛ When they were in Bethlehem, what happened to Mary? What details are given?

✛ Angels visited the shepherds. What sign was given to the shepherds regarding the event? What was their response?

✛ What was Mary's response to the shepherds' visit?

✛ List all the evidence of celebration from the above passage.

FIND GOD'S WAYS FOR YOU

✛ The best laid plans often go awry. How do you handle interrupted plans?

✛ Share a time when you had to "make do" with your circumstances.

Read the following verse:

You can make many plans, but the Lord's purpose will prevail.

– PROVERBS 19:21 –

✛ What do we learn from this verse?

✛ Mary found reasons to rejoice and events to treasure even when her circumstances were not what she would have chosen. What causes you to treasure things in your heart?

STOP AND PONDER

Read the following verses:

We can make our plans, but the Lord determines our steps.

— PROVERBS 16:9 —

How can we understand the road we travel? It is the Lord who directs our steps.

— PROVERBS 20:24 —

Your word is a lamp for my feet and a light for my path.

— PSALM 119:105 —

✛ Do you trip over — or treasure — interruptions?

COMPLIANCE

SEEK GOD'S WORD FOR TRUTH

Magi from the East came seeking the newborn baby. Following a star, they arrived in Bethlehem. Read the following passage about their arrival:

When they saw the star, they were filled with joy! They entered the house where the child and his mother, Mary, were, and they fell down before him and worshiped him. Then they opened their treasure chests and gave him gifts of gold, frankincense, and myrrh. But when it was time to leave, they went home another way, because God had warned them in a dream not to return to Herod.

After the wise men were gone, an angel of the Lord appeared to Joseph in a dream. "Get up and flee to Egypt with the child and his mother," the angel said. "Stay there until I tell you to return, because Herod is going to try to kill the child." That night Joseph left for Egypt with the child and Mary, his mother, and they stayed there until Herod's death.

When Herod died, an angel of the Lord appeared in a dream to Joseph in Egypt and told him, "Get up and take the child and his mother back to the land of Israel, because those who were trying to kill the child are dead." So Joseph returned immediately to Israel with Jesus and his mother.

— MATTHEW 2:10-15, 19-21 —

✛ When the magi arrive, what do they do?

✛ What gifts do they bring the child?

✛ After the magi leave, to whom does the angel appear? And by what means?

✛ What is the angel's message?

✛ What does Joseph do and when?

✛ Sometime later, the angel appears again. What event gave rise to this second appearance, and what was the message this time?

✛ How do Joseph and his wife, Mary, respond this time?

FIND GOD'S WAYS FOR YOU

✛ How do you handle the recognition and praise of people who are close to you?

✛ How do you respond to the praise of people you do not know well?

Read the following scripture passage:

Don't be selfish; don't live to make a good impression on others. Be humble, thinking of others as better than yourself. Don't think only about your own affairs, but be interested in others, too, and what they are doing.
— PHILIPPIANS 2:3-4 —

✛ According to the above verse, what should our attitude be?

✛ Mary willingly complied/obeyed when asked to be uprooted and moved. How do you handle major changes in your life?

STOP AND PONDER

Trust in the Lord with all your heart; do not depend on your own understanding. Seek his will in all you do, and he will direct your paths.
— PROVERBS 3:5-6 —

✛ Do you trust God and where he may be leading you?

CONCERN

SEEK GOD'S WORD FOR TRUTH

Read the following passage:

Every year Jesus' parents went to Jerusalem for the Passover festival. When Jesus was twelve years old, they attended the festival as usual. After the celebration was over, they started home to Nazareth, but Jesus stayed behind in Jerusalem. His parents didn't miss him at first, because they assumed he was with friends among the other travelers. But when he didn't show up that evening, they started to look for him among their relatives and friends. When they couldn't find him, they went back to Jerusalem to search for him there. Three days later they finally discovered him. He was in the Temple, sitting among the religious teachers, discussing deep questions with them. And all who heard him were amazed at his understanding and his answers.

His parents didn't know what to think. "Son!" his mother said to him. "Why have you done this to us? Your father and I have been frantic, searching for you everywhere."

"But why did you need to search?" he asked. "You should have known that I would be in my Father's house." But they didn't understand what he meant.

Then he returned to Nazareth with them and was obedient to them; and his mother stored all these things in her heart.

– LUKE 2:41-51 –

✛ What annual event took the family to Jerusalem?

✛ When did Mary and Joseph leave Jerusalem?

✛ What were they unaware of and why?

✛ Describe their search.

✛ Upon finding Jesus, what did Mary say to her son? And what did her son say to her?

✛ We are told that Mary and Joseph didn't understand what Jesus said to them. What is Mary's response to all that happened?

FIND GOD'S WAYS FOR YOU

✛ Describe a time when, as a child, you were not where you were supposed to be. How did you feel?

✛ How did your parents react?

✛ What was your response to their reaction?

Read the following passage:

God has said, "I will never fail you. I will never forsake you." That is why we can say with confidence, "The Lord is my helper, so I will not be afraid. What can mere mortals do to me?"

– Hebrews 13:5-6 –

✛ There are all kinds of fear. Children may fear their parents when they have been disobedient; parents fear for the safety of their children, etc. What confidence does a child of God have when facing frightening circumstances?

STOP AND PONDER

You will keep in perfect peace all who trust in you, whose thoughts are fixed on you! Trust in the Lord always, for the Lord God is the eternal Rock.

– Isaiah 26:3-4 –

✛ Where do you place your confidence?

CONFLICTS

SEEK GOD'S WORD FOR TRUTH

Read the following passage:

The next day Jesus' mother was a guest at a wedding celebration in the village of Cana in Galilee. Jesus and his disciples were also invited to the celebration. The wine supply ran out during the festivities, so Jesus' mother spoke to him about the problem. "They have no more wine," she told him.

"How does that concern you and me?" Jesus asked. "My time has not yet come."

But his mother told the servants, "Do whatever he tells you."

– JOHN 2:1-5 –

✝ According to this passage, what event was Mary attending? Who else was there?

✝ At the wedding, Mary noticed that the wine ran out. What did she do?

✝ How does Jesus answer her?

✝ How does Mary deal with her son's reply?

Read about another time:

Once when Jesus' mother and brothers came to see him, they couldn't get to him because of the crowds. Someone told Jesus, "Your mother and your brothers are outside, and they want to see you."

Jesus replied, "My mother and my brothers are all those who hear the message of God and obey it."

– LUKE 8:19-21 –

✝ What do we learn about Mary and Jesus' relationship from this passage?

✝ What appears to be happening to her relationship with her firstborn son?

FIND GOD'S WAYS FOR YOU

✝ Describe a time when you embarrassed yourself or a family member at a family event.

✝ What did it do to your relationship?

✝ How do you go about helping family members you think are on the edge of trouble?

Read the following passages:

Share each other's troubles and problems, and in this way obey the law of Christ. If you think you are too important to help someone in need, you are only fooling yourself. You are really a nobody.

Be sure to do what you should, for then you will enjoy the personal satisfaction of having done your work well, and you won't need to compare yourself to anyone else. For we are each responsible for our own conduct.

— GALATIANS 6:2-5 —

Stop judging others, and you will not be judged. For others will treat you as you treat them. Whatever measure you use in judging others, it will be used to measure how you are judged.

— MATTHEW 7:1-2 —

✢ What do we learn about relationships and responsibility in the above verses?

STOP AND PONDER

So be careful how you live, not as fools but as those who are wise. Make the most of every opportunity for doing good in these evil days. Don't act thoughtlessly, but try to understand what the Lord wants you to do.

And further, you will submit to one another out of reverence for Christ.

— EPHESIANS 5:15-17, 21 —

✢ Are you thoughtless or considerate in your relationships?

CONFESSION

SEEK GOD'S WORD FOR TRUTH

Read the following passage:

Standing near the cross were Jesus' mother, and his mother's sister, Mary (the wife of Clopas), and Mary Magdalene. When Jesus saw his mother standing there beside the disciple he loved, he said to her, "Woman, he is your son." And he said to this disciple, "She is your mother." And from then on this disciple took her into his home.

– JOHN 19:25-27 –

✢ According to this passage, where was Mary? Who was with her at the crucifixion? Who was missing?

✢ What does Jesus say to Mary?

✢ What provision does Jesus make for her?

After Jesus' death, resurrection, and ascension, his disciples gathered in Jerusalem. Read the following passage:

> *The apostles were at the Mount of Olives when this [the Ascension] happened, so they walked the half mile back to Jerusalem. Then they went to the upstairs room of the house where they were staying. Here is the list of those who were present: Peter, John, James, Andrew, Philip, Thomas, Bartholomew, Matthew, James (son of Alphaeus), Simon (the Zealot), and Judas (son of James). They all met together continually for prayer, along with Mary the mother of the Jesus, several other women, and the brothers of Jesus.*

– ACTS 1:12-14 –

✢ Where was Mary and what was she doing?

✢ Besides the disciples, who was with Mary this time?

Finally, Mary is remembered for her obedient servant's heart. In the Gospel of Luke, we find her song:

> *Oh, how I praise the Lord. How I rejoice in God my Savior!*
> *For he took notice of this lowly servant girl, and now generation after generation will call me blessed.*
> *For he, the Mighty One, is holy, and he has done great things for me.*
> *His mercy goes on from generation to generation, to all who fear him.*
> *His mighty arm does tremendous things! How he scatters the proud and haughty ones!*
> *He has taken princes from their thrones and exalted the lowly.*
> *He has satisfied the hungry with good things and sent the rich away with empty hands.*

And how he has helped his servant Israel! He has not forgotten his promise to be merciful.

For he promised our ancestors – Abraham and his children – to be merciful to them forever.

– LUKE 1:46-55 –

✛ List the names and attributes of God that you find in this confession of Mary's faith.

FIND GOD'S WAYS FOR YOU

Of all the Gospel writers, John knew Mary best, and yet he wrote the least about her. It is in his Gospel that we read Mary's last recorded words: "Do whatever he [Jesus] tells you." Since Mary said to do what Jesus tells us, let's look at what Jesus has to say in the following passages:

For God so loved the world that he gave his only Son, so that everyone who believes in him will not perish but have eternal life. God did not send his Son into the world to condemn it, but to save it.

There is no judgment awaiting those who trust him. But those who do not trust him have already been judged for not believing in the only Son of God.

– JOHN 3:16-18 –

✛ Contrast the choices that are before you.

✛ What does Jesus offer you?

"Don't be troubled. You trust God, now trust in me. There are many rooms in my Father's home, and I am going to prepare a place for you. If this were not so, I would tell you plainly. When everything is ready, I will come and get you, so that you will always be with me where I am. And you know where I am going and how to get there."

"No, we don't know, Lord," Thomas said. "We haven't any idea where you are going, so how can we know the way?"

Jesus told them, "I am the way, the truth, and the life. No one can come to the Father except through me. If you had known who I am, then you would have known who my Father is. From now on you know him and have seen him!"

– JOHN 14:1-7 –

✝ What are Jesus' instructions? What are his promises?

✝ Who *alone* saves us?

STOP AND PONDER

Read the following words of Jesus:

> *Look! Here I stand at the door and knock. If you hear me calling and open the door, I will come in, and we will share a meal as friends. I will invite everyone who is victorious to sit with me on my throne, just as I was victorious and sat with my Father on his throne. Anyone who is willing to hear should listen to the Spirit and understand what the Spirit is saying to the churches.*

— REVELATION 3:20-22 —

✝ Have you opened the door?

the genealogy of JESUS the CHRIST

THIS is a record of the ancestors of Jesus the Messiah, a descendant of King David and of Abraham:

Abraham was the father of Isaac.
Isaac was the father of Jacob.
Jacob was the father of Judah and his brothers.
Judah was the father of Perez and Zerah (their mother was **Tamar**).
Perez was the father of Hezron.
Hezron was the father of Ram.
Ram was the father of Amminadab.
Amminadab was the father of Nahshon.
Nahshon was the father of Salmon.
Salmon was the father of Boaz (his mother was **Rahab**).
Boaz was the father of Obed (his mother was **Ruth**).
Obed was the father of Jesse.
Jesse was the father of King David.
David was the father of Solomon (his mother was **Bathsheba**, the widow of Uriah).
Solomon was the father of Rehoboam.
Rehoboam was the father of Abijah.
Abijah was the father of Asaph.
Asaph was the father of Jehoshaphat.
Jehoshaphat was the father of Jehoram.
Jehoram was the father of Uzziah.
Uzziah was the father of Jotham.
Jotham was the father of Ahaz.
Ahaz was the father of Hezekiah.
Hezekiah was the father of Manasseh.
Manasseh was the father of Amos.
Amos was the father of Josiah.

Josiah was the father of Jehoiachin and his brothers (born at the time of the exile to Babylon).
After the Babylonian exile:
Jehoiachin was the father of Shealtiel.
Shealtiel was the father of Zerubbabel.
Zerubbabel was the father of Abiud.
Abiud was the father of Eliakim.
Eliakim was the father of Azor.
Azor was the father of Zadok.
Zadok was the father of Akim.
Akim was the father of Eliud.
Eliud was the father of Eleazar.
Eleazar was the father of Matthan.
Matthan was the father of Jacob.
Jacob was the father of Joseph, the husband of Mary.
Mary was the mother of Jesus, who is called the Messiah.

– Matthew 1:1-16 –

about the author

FRANCINE RIVERS has been writing for more than twenty years. From 1976 to 1985 she had a successful writing career in the general market and won numerous awards. After becoming a born-again Christian in 1986, Francine wrote *Redeeming Love* as her statement of faith.

Since then, Francine has published numerous books in the CBA market and has continued to win both industry acclaim and reader loyalty. Her novel *The Last Sin Eater* won the ECPA Gold Medallion, and three of her books have won the prestigious Romance Writers of America Rita Award.

Francine says she uses her writing to draw closer to the Lord, that through her work she might worship and praise Jesus for all he has done and is doing in her life.

books by francine rivers

The Last Sin Eater
The Atonement Child
Leota's Garden

A LINEAGE OF GRACE SERIES:

Unveiled
Unashamed
Unshaken
Unspoken
Unafraid

DATE DUE

JUL 0 1 2007		
MAR 0 8 2009		
NOV 2 9 2009		
JAN 0 1 2010		
MAY 3 0 2010		